BOUND TO THE BATTLE GOD

ANCHOR & ASPECT

RUBY DIXON

Map created by: Mr. Ruby Dixon

Cover created by: Kati Wilde

Interior Art: Alex Conkins

Edits: Aquila Editing

❀ Created with Vellum

I like to think that every creator stands on the backs of those that inspired her. This particular project was inspired by a few people that deserve mentioning.

For Kristen Ashley, who reminded me that I'm not the only one out there that still loves portal fantasy.

For Mariana Zapata, who reminded me that a slow burn can be utterly delicious.

For R. Lee Smith, who reminded me that a plot can be utterly wild, and if it's told with conviction, it can be amazing.

For Kati Wilde, who is confidante, cheerleader, girl-crush and quite possibly the world's nicest and most gifted person. You're amazing. Have I said that today?

For my husband, Mr. Ruby, who supports me, eats leftovers so I can write, made me this incredible map and encouraged me to swing for the fences again. <3

BOUND TO THE BATTLE GOD

When I went to my neighbor's apartment to investigate strange sounds, I never expected to fall through a portal into another world. Yet here I am, a stranger in an even stranger land...and I'm stranded. In this world, might makes right, men carry swords, and gods walk the earth. Within minutes of arriving, I'm enslaved.

Fun place.

How do I get home? GREAT question. Wish I had an answer.

The one person that might be able to help me is also the one person I want to throttle most. Aron, Lord of Storms, Butcher God of Battle, is my new companion. Or rather, I'm *his*. As Aron's anchor to the mortal realm, I'm the one that's supposed to be guiding him through his exile in the mortal world.

Ha. Joke's on him. I know nothing about this place.

But Aron and I have a common goal - get home. And we're bonded - anchor and god - with a bond unlike any other. So we travel together. We bicker. We bathe together. We fight our many, many enemies together. And sure, he's a god, but he's also an arrogant jerk. Brawny, smoking hot, irresistible jerk. I should want nothing to do with him. I certainly shouldn't want to do things to him.

Mortals and gods don't mix. We stick to the plan and ignore our attraction. Focused, with one goal in mind.

One task. One goal.

Focused.

I—oh heck, I'm going to end up kissing him again, aren't I?

CHAPTER 1

$\mathcal{I}$'m just sitting down with a pint of Häagen-Dazs to watch some reality TV when I hear a voice through the wall.

I frown, spoon halfway to my mouth, and turn off the television.

It's late. It's a week night. I have to be up early but I can't sleep, so I'm stuffing my face with ice cream. And for the neighbor in the next apartment to be shouting? That's just rude. I scowl at the wall for a moment longer, and when all is quiet, reach for the remote again.

A man laughs. Loud and strong, on the other side of the wall.

I take a bite of ice cream, listening like the nosy neighbor I am. The man keeps talking, his voice rich and smooth…and impossible to make out. He's loud, but I can't understand what he's saying. The walls muffle it. Or rather, it's like those Charlie Brown cartoons, where people talk but none of it makes sense.

I can't hear any other voices either, just his.

After a few moments of this, the man's sexy voice turns angry. Harsh. He's no longer laughing. He's arguing with someone—a silent someone.

Loudly.

I cringe when I hear a thump against the wall, like a fist is hitting it, and swallow my butter pecan quickly. I pull out my cell phone and record a few moments of the shouting, then decide to call the super.

Three rings later, the super picks up. "What?" His voice is impatient.

"Hi," I say cheerily. "It's Faith Gordon in 5D? Whoever you rented 6D out to is causing a disturbance. He keeps shouting at the top of his lungs and I'm pretty sure he just hit the wall."

The super groans. "Lady—"

I hate it when men call me "lady." It's never a good "lady," it's always a bad "lady."

"—there's no one in that apartment."

I stare at the wall next to my couch, where I distinctly heard a man yelling. "Yes there is."

"No. It's been empty since January. I have to fix it up before I can rent it again and that's lower on the list."

I knew my neighbor had moved out a few months ago but… "No one else has moved in?"

"No."

"Okay, thanks," I say, and hang up. I'm confused. I put my ear to the wall to listen again, but whatever—whoever—it was has stopped.

It's dreadfully quiet for a long moment, and then I hear the voice again. The angry man with the beautiful voice. He sounds frustrated. Cold. Ominous.

Frightening.

Creeped out, I get off the couch and peer through the peep hole into the hall. It's silent and empty. I take a deep breath, open my door, and approach the door down the hall from mine. 6D.

All is quiet.

I think for a moment, then race back into my apartment and

grab my keys. I head down to my car on the street despite the fact that I'm in pajamas, and lean against it, staring up at the windows of the building. There's my apartment, with the lights on and the half-dead fern on the stoop that I really need to water. To the right of it should be 6D.

The windows are black, the blinds down.

I head back to my apartment, confused. The moment I shut the door again, the voice starts up once more. Angry. Irritated. Superior. Argumentative.

A squatter, maybe? But who's he arguing with in the dark? I get up and head into the hall again, to the door. I knock.

It's silent.

I put my ear to the door.

Silence.

I carefully test the door knob. Locked.

Frowning, I go back inside my apartment and look at the window. We're four floors up, and the only window in the apartment is facing outside. There's not enough of a ledge out there for a bird, much less for someone to break in.

Even as I consider this, the voice on the other side of the wall starts again.

I grit my teeth, sit down on the sofa and pull my laptop onto my legs, firing up my browser. I google, "Symptoms of schizophrenia".

And then google, "I hear conversations no one else does".

And then google, "Am I being haunted?"

And finally search, "Sleep disorders causing waking dreams".

But none of it seems to match what I'm experiencing. I don't know what to do.

It's late, Faith, I remind myself. *Maybe he got pissed and shut the lights off and went to bed, and you're imagining things.*

I slap my laptop shut.

3

THE VOICE WAKES me up twice that night.

Both times, it's angry. Furious. Raging at something I can't hear or understand. The second time, just before dawn, it turns into a shout so loud and heartbroken that I clamp my pillow over my face and ears to muffle the sound of it.

It dies away and leaves a silence so profound it feels heavy.

What the hell is going on? I stare up at the ceiling and wonder what made my invisible "friend" so sad.

"It can't be that bad, buddy," I whisper to my empty room. "At least you're not hearing voices."

There's no response to my lame joke.

"FAITH, I'M WORRIED ABOUT YOU," Sherry tells me over lunch the next day. She clutches her egg salad sandwich tightly in her hands and gives me a dramatic look. "This isn't normal."

"I promise, I'm fine." I offer her a bright smile and wish she'd be quiet. She's a good friend, but god, she loves the drama.

Sherry shakes her head solemnly, and it's clear she doesn't buy it. "If everything's fine, why are you so distracted today?"

"Distracted? Me?" How does she know? I thought I'd been hiding it pretty well. I'm wearing my dressiest suit, I gave a customer service presentation a half hour ago that went over decently, and I'm having a good hair day. I thought I looked rather together. "How so?"

"Well for one, you're wearing black shoes with a navy suit."

Erk. Well, they already think I'm strange here at the office. No big deal. "That's not so weird—"

"And you're eating peanut butter and baloney on that sandwich." Her nostrils flare with horror.

I glance down at the sandwich I'm eating. Well, more like I'm "holding" it instead of eating. I haven't been hungry lately, and I seem to be going through the motions for most of the day. I just can't focus on anything but those odd voices.

Sherry's not wrong, though. A quick look at my sandwich shows me one half is peanut butter, and one half is baloney. Ick. I guess I got sidetracked when making my lunch this morning. Maybe the birds outside will eat it. I set it on my paper lunch sack and shrug. "I read online that it was a good combination."

"That's called 'trolling,' honey."

"Good one, huh? You want to try it?" I hold my sandwich out.

"Absolutely not." She doesn't share my amusement.

"Your loss," I tell her brightly and decide to show her that I know what I'm doing. I pick up my sandwich and take a huge bite out of it...and it's every bit as gross as I thought it would be. Oh god. It takes every muscle in my body to make my throat swallow the mess. I gulp my water to wash the taste out of my mouth.

Sherry gives me a stern look. "Are you sure you're okay? I worry about you."

"I'm fine. I promise. I just...heard something last night and it kept me up."

"Heard something? Like what?"

I get out my phone and pull up the video. "Listen to this. The apartment next to mine? It's empty, according to the super. But I heard this last night."

I hit "play" and...there's not a single sound. Other than the rustling of my clothing, it's all quiet.

She frowns at me again.

"I must have messed up the video," I say quickly, stopping it and picking up my sandwich again so she doesn't see how freaked out I am. I know I heard something. I know I did. "Maybe...maybe it was the guy in 4D. He does have a new dog."

She makes a noise of sympathy in her throat, as if that solves everything. "Talk to him—"

"And my coffee maker's broken," I add, because I need the lie to be convincing. Why not make it a dog pile of things? "And I was worried about the client retention report I was going to present today, which, spoiler, it turned out great."

Sherry doesn't care about my report. She's not here to climb the corporate ladder. She's here to socialize and bring home a paycheck for as little effort as possible. But I've spoken her language because she's wearing a look of horror on her face. "No coffee? I'd die!"

"Right?" At least now we're in safe territory. I've thwarted her concerns for the day by lamenting about caffeine. She gets up and turns on the break room coffee pot, determined to help me with my beverage troubles, and as she does, she launches into a story about her son Julian and how he broke her Keurig by shoving wooden blocks into the K-Cup tray. I smile and laugh at the appropriate pauses, but my mind is wandering back to that voice.

A voice that only I can hear. Why me?

FOR TWO DAYS, there's nothing. Not a peep, not a sound, not a sigh. Everything is completely silent, like it should be.

It weirds me out.

I pass by the apartment several times and knock, intending to be the busybody neighbor who introduces herself, but no one ever answers. I hang out on the street after dark with binoculars, waiting to see if a light goes on.

All is normal...which I'm pretty sure is bullshit.

I heard that guy. I heard him clear as day. So if someone's not living there, does that mean there are squatters in the building? Is it unsafe?

By the time Friday rolls around, I'm a sleep-deprived mess.

Between meetings, I rub my eyes at work and yawn, trying to stay focused.

"Still can't sleep?" Sherry leans over my cube and gives me a perky look that should be outlawed. "Or still haven't gotten a replacement for that coffee pot?"

"Just a bit of insomnia," I tell her. "Nothing big. And my coffee pot's being shipped. Should get here tomorrow." Man, I am getting so good at lying.

She waves a hand as if my troubles are too irritating for her to focus on. "Well, caffeinate up and go to lunch with me today. I have to run to the post office and then we can grab tacos."

Even though I don't feel like moving—much less walking anywhere—I have to admit it'd be nice to get out of the office for an hour. Plus, tacos. Beats what I ate last night, which was oh, nothing. I've been too distracted to go to the grocery store. "Tacos it is."

As we head out for lunch, Sherry tries to keep the conversation going for both of us to make up for my quiet. She talks in line at the post office, tells me all about her kid while we grab tacos from a street vendor, and I chug an energy drink. Sherry continues to yak about the horrors of finding a babysitter as we head back. We stop at a red light and wait to cross the street, tacos steaming up the paper bag I'm holding. I try to pay attention as Sherry goes on and on about her kid, I really do, but I'm so busy straining to hear the nonexistent voice in my head that I almost miss what I'm staring directly at.

There's a neon red palm blinking in the window across the street, with an eye in the center. TAROT. PSYCHIC READINGS.

Oh my god.

Of course.

This makes a ridiculous amount of sense. No one can give me a real answer, so maybe a supernatural answer is what I'm looking for.

I grab Sherry's arm. "How much time do we have before we need to be back?"

She checks her watch. "Half hour, really. Why?"

I shove my taco bag in a nearby garbage can, no longer hungry, and practically drag her across the street—in the wrong direction to get back to the office—when the light turns.

"W-what? What are we doing? Is there a bookstore I missed?" Her laughter dies when she realizes I'm charging for the psychic's doorstep. "Wait! Are you serious? Faith? You want to get your fortune told?" She looks at me as if I just told her I decided to join a nunnery. "Right now? On lunch hour? We haven't even eaten our tacos!"

"You can go back if you want," I tell her, eyeing the window. There are beaded curtains covering the tinted glass, and the red palm is the only sign on the door. I wonder if I've ever seen this place before. Is it new? Or has it always been here and I've never noticed it despite a hundred lunchtime walks with Sherry? "I won't be long," I tell her and open the door.

If I can't have a logical answer to what's happening, an illogical one will do. Maybe my problem isn't neurological or chemical but...mystical.

Okay, that sounds corny even to me, but I'm willing to roll with it if it gives me answers.

The shop itself is kind of disappointing. I was expecting mystical runes or lush velvet curtains hanging from the walls. Instead, the walls themselves are covered with bookshelves, and there's a glass counter along one side full of jewelry. The back wall has candles stacked in neat cubbyholes and some of them are set out on stands and lit, providing a thick, herbal smell to the shop. A woman comes from the back room as the door clangs with our entry.

"Hello! Welcome to my shop," she calls out. "How can I help you today?" She looks unimpressive as well—motherly and average, with a dumpy figure and curly, gray-peppered hair.

She's wearing leggings and a tunic, much like your average soccer mom would, with a dark scarf artfully tossed around the neck.

"I want to get my fortune told," I say, striding forward before Sherry can silence me. "I have questions."

She goes very still, and her gaze moves up and down over me for a long moment. Her eyes widen, just a little. "Who are you?"

I suck in a breath and step forward, forgetting all about Sherry. She sees something. I know she does. I'm in the right place. I'm so excited I can hardly breathe. "What do you see?"

The woman shakes her head slowly, never taking her eyes off of me. "You have a very...strong energy surrounding you. It's like nothing I've seen before." She moves to the back of her little store and pulls a tapestried curtain aside, gesturing. "I can give you a card reading. Give you some of the answers you seek."

Yes! Answers! I could cry, I'm so relieved. "How much?" I ask, getting out my wallet.

"Oh, come on," Sherry hisses at me, grabbing my arm. "This is crap, Faith. Of course she's going to say you have a strong aura. She wants you to spend money!"

It might be crap...but it might be answers. I shake my head at Sherry. "You can go back. I'll be there soon, I promise."

Sherry's lips tighten in a thin line and she crosses her arms over her chest, but she doesn't leave.

I give her a smile to reassure her, then follow the woman into the back room. Sherry follows at my heels, and the woman drops the curtain behind us. "Have a seat."

The room isn't much to look at. There are folding chairs—two on my side of the table, and one on hers. The table itself is covered in purple crushed velvet, and I bet if I peeked underneath the garish tablecloth, I'd see it's a folding table. Adorning the walls are a few posters on the walls of psychic-looking women and stars and planets and such. Crystals hang from

9

strings on the ceiling. I don't know what to make of this. It looks more like the cheap carnival fortune teller than the last room did.

But she sees something in me. On me. Whatever. And I'm so desperate for answers.

"A hundred dollars," she tells me, sitting across from me at the table. "Cash. No credit cards, no checks."

"This is crap," Sherry murmurs in a singsong voice as she sits down next to me.

Maybe it is. Maybe this woman's taken one look at my skirt and low heels, my white blouse and my blonde ponytail and decided that I have money to spend. I mean, she's completely wrong about that, but I guess I could see the mistake, seeing as how we're in the business district downtown. Lots of corporate business professionals around here.

Doesn't matter. I'm willing to blow some stupid cash if I can get answers. I pull five twenties out of my purse and hand them over.

She takes them from me, careful not to touch my fingers. Odd.

"Put your purse away," the fortune teller says to me as she picks up a small wooden box and sets it on the table in front of her. She pulls the lid off with both hands and reveals a deck of long-looking cards. Tarot cards. There's a spiderweb design over the back of each of them. "I'm not going to give you a typical reading. You need something different than mumbo-jumbo and a few platitudes, don't you?"

I nod, wide-eyed. It's like she's reading my mind. "How do you know?"

She wiggles her fingers in the air before pulling the cards out of the box and setting the stack on the table. "I see it around you. There's something that's different about you than your friend. Like I said, I've never seen it before. It's like an aura. No, not an aura." She frowns. "It's like you've walked through a spiderweb of some kind and you're covered in the residue." She wags a finger in my direction. "I've never seen that before, which tells me that there's a story behind it."

"Everyone has a story," Sherry says, her tone almost sulky. I think she doesn't like being called normal.

"Everyone does," the fortune teller agrees. "But not everyone has energy pulsing around them like your friend."

I feel a little quiver of anxiety at that. Sherry can have my weird spiderweb energy if it makes her feel special. I don't want it. I just want to sleep.

The woman gestures at the cards. "Take them and shuffle them as much as you feel is necessary."

I grip the cards and study them. They feel a little waxy but well-used, and the spiderweb on the back of each card seems to gleam as if shiny. I shuffle the cards lightly, flicking them a couple of times before cutting twice and then offering them back to her.

She taps a spot on the table, and I put the stack of cards there. "What's your first question?" she asks, watching me with intent eyes.

I think. I have so many but there's one that keeps rising to mind over and over again. "Who is it I heard? The strange man?"

The fortune teller nods slowly. I can see Sherry staring at me, but I ignore her. I have to, because if I feel silly, I'm going to get up and leave and I need to know what this woman sees. I keep my gaze on the fortune teller and watch as she carefully picks up the first card from the deck and sets it down on the table.

It's a dark haired man on a throne.

"The King of Pentacles," she says, looking thoughtful. "That's a strong, assertive man. One of power and ambition. He's someone that stops everyone in their tracks when they see him. He's..." She thinks for a moment. "He's like a force of nature. Takes over everything in his path."

11

I blink, staring at the card. It's a man. What she says matches the voice I keep hearing but...I still don't know who it is.

"Are you dating someone?" Sherry asks, amused. "And you didn't tell me about it? You hooker."

I shake my head. There's no one.

"Be silent," the fortune teller hisses at Sherry. "This is not about you."

My friend gasps and shrinks back.

Well, crap. I give Sherry an apologetic look and then turn back to the fortune teller. "I don't...I don't know this man. There's no guy in my life like this."

The woman tilts her head. "Are you asking who he is to you?" At my nod, she turns over another card. "The Lovers."

The card has two people standing apart, a man and a woman. They're both naked. I can pretty much guess what this is about. "You sure this is my fortune?"

"If he's not a lover, he will be soon," the psychic murmurs, ignoring my question. "The cards don't lie."

"But...how? I don't understand." It can't be someone at work, and I don't do much outside of work. Especially not lately. "Where am I going to meet this guy? I keep going to his apartment and there's no one there. There's never anyone there."

The fortune teller turns over another card. It's a woman, floating in midair, with a green wreath around her. "The World, reversed."

"What does that mean?"

She puts a finger to her chin, thinking. "When The World is right side up, it means that a journey of knowledge is coming to an end. The circle is being completed." She traces her finger around the wreath on the card. "But for you, the journey is just about to begin."

CHAPTER 2

*W*hen we get back to the office, Sherry doesn't speak to me for the rest of the day. She's either mad because the fortune teller was rude to her, or she thinks I'm crazy. I'll take her out for lunch tomorrow and apologize up and down. She'll forget all about it, other than teasing me at the next office happy hour. Now that I've had a few hours to stew on the reading, it does sound a bit like the usual "you're going to meet a man" schtick. As we left, Sherry filled my ears with how gullible I was to fall for it.

Maybe it was a silly thing to do. I don't care. I finally feel like I'm getting somewhere.

A man. Like a force of nature.

The lovers.

You're about to begin a journey.

Those thoughts repeat in my head over and over again as I shut down my computer at the end of the day and gather my things. More than that, though, I keep thinking of what she said about my...glow, or my aura, or whatever she called it. My spiderwebs.

You're about to begin a journey.

13

I wonder what that means. What damn journey? I've lived in the city all my life. I've worked at the bank for five of those years, and went to college here prior to that. I don't travel. There was never the money growing up, and there hasn't been a reason since my parents died while I was in college. There's no one to visit and no extra money for pleasure trips. I rarely date. I have friends, but I never hang onto them for long. They transfer to different departments, or move away, or get married and then we drift apart. I'm always more or less alone.

I'm boring.

So why me? Why is this happening?

I can't help but feel that the voice in the next apartment was reaching out to the wrong person. Maybe that's why he stopped talking to me. A psychic wrong number.

I don't know that someone as unexciting as Faith Gordon is destined to be the lover of a force of nature. I mean, my last boyfriend left me for an accountant. If that doesn't tell you everything about my life, nothing will.

Even so…I could use a little adventure. "Well, King of Pentacles," I dare the air around me. "If you've got something to show me, you can start that journey any freaking time now. I'm just saying. I get vacation time in two weeks."

The office is silent.

Maybe the King of Pentacles is more of a night shift sorta guy.

I WAKE up in the middle of the night, alert for no reason at all. My ears strain, trying to make out sound. There's only the distant rumble of thunder, an oncoming storm. I sit up and listen for voices, but there's nothing. So why am I awake?

Then, I hear it. There's a distant sound of drums. At first I think it's the storm brewing overhead, but it's got too even a beat, and when lightning clashes a short distance away, it sounds dissonant to the music. I get to my feet, wondering if it's someone playing a CD too loud.

But it sounds like it's coming from next door. The empty apartment.

Oh shit. It's him. It has to be.

I get out of bed, sliding to my feet, and tiptoe across the floor. I move toward the shared wall, the one that faces the so-called empty apartment. We're at the end of the hall, so there's no one on the other side of that particular wall except for it. I put a hand on the wall itself and then press my ear to it, listening.

Nothing.

Frustrated, I lean back and study the wall. Maybe it's not it. Thunder rumbles overhead, and the music's gone. Something about this feels wrong. All of it feels wrong. It's like...like I'm hearing something I shouldn't. Getting a glimpse of something that I have no permission to access.

The music starts again, and the hair stands up on the back of my neck. There's a low wail of a flute, and the drums begin their ceaseless beat once more.

This is not my imagination. My imagination can't even remember the lyrics to TV jingles, much less an entire song. I have to know what this is. Even if it's just someone messing with me, I'll be happier knowing than just wondering. I can't let the opportunity pass by again.

I pull on a pair of pajama pants to go with my pink pajama top, and a pair of slippers. I head to the front door of my apartment, and then pause, checking the clock. Four in the morning. Okay, that's a shitty hour, but it's still reasonably safe to assume I could be up, if I need the excuse. With that in mind, I open my door and head into the hallway.

It's a matter of steps to the neighbor's door. I head directly to it, suck in a steeling breath, and then knock.

There's still no response. I try knocking a third time, and when that elicits no response either, I get down on hands and knees and peer under the door, looking for light. I don't see anything.

The apartment's as vacant as it ever was. That doesn't make sense.

I frown at the door for a minute, then decide I have to know. I head back into my apartment and return with my credit card. I glance up and down the hall, hoping that no one's watching this. If someone is home and I'm breaking and entering, this could be really bad. But I have a hunch. If I'm right, there's no one home...and I'm just crazy.

Yippee.

I slip my credit card into the door and wedge it along the lock, trying to flick it open like they show in movies. Either luck is with me or it's easier than it looks—the door falls open and my credit card falls to my feet in two pieces.

Well, shit.

I'll worry about that later.

I stare into the darkness of the apartment.

Even from here, I can tell it's empty. I flick on the light switch by the door and look at nothing but dusty countertops and a discarded box half full of packing peanuts in one corner. No one lives here. No one has lived here since my neighbor left. "Hello?" I call out, just in case.

There's no answer. I didn't expect one. The floors here are tile, and my slippers are leaving prints in the dust. No one's been in or out of here in weeks or months.

"Well, what the fuck?" I mutter to myself. I shuffle to the wall that is adjacent to mine and press my ear to it. No music. I turn and look at the other wall, but it's nothing but windows and skewed mini blinds.

The music starts again. This time, the drums seem more

urgent, the pipes wailing more frantically. It's not any louder, but there's a real sense of...immediacy to it.

Like it's just in the next room.

I open every door in the apartment, peering into closets. They're all empty, but the music continues, always just the next room away. Eventually, there's nowhere else to look, and I groan, putting my hands to my forehead. "Either show me or leave me the hell alone, all right?"

God, I sound crazy even to my own ears. But this is just getting ridiculous. I can't sleep. It's interfering with my job. My friends think I'm crazy.

I'm not entirely sure that I'm *not* crazy. That all of this isn't just my brain deciding to go haywire and self-destruct, and it's picking some bagpipes and a catchy beat to do it to.

Frustrated, I lean against the kitchen counter. As I do, a light flicks on under the bedroom door.

Well, that's not creepy at *all*.

I look down at my feet. I've left trails in the dust on the floor. No one's been inside here for months.

The prickles on the back of my neck start again. I should turn around, maybe. Go back to my apartment, shut the door, go back to bed and forget I ever heard anything. I turn to the front door...

And pause.

And slowly turn back to the closed bedroom door.

I need to know what's going on. I need to know who the King of Pentacles is or why I have a "spiderweb" aura. Mostly I just need to know if I'm going crazy.

If this is a mistake, I suppose there's only one way to find out.

I open the door and step inside.

CHAPTER 3

*I*t's daylight.

I squint up at the blinding sun, surprised. There's not a cloud in the sky and the sun overhead beats down on me, hot and relentless and bright. How did it get to be daylight? Midday?

I wait for my eyes to adjust, wiping streaming tears from them as the too bright light makes my head pound. Slowly, I become aware of the world around me.

"Out of the way!" A man shoves past me, glaring.

"Sorry," I say automatically, moving aside...to where? I stare around me as the bright glare adjusts and now I can see.

I can see everything and...holy shit.

Toto, we are *not* in Kansas.

It's a marketplace of some kind. I think. Or a city? It's hard to tell. I see tall stone walls, at least fifteen feet high, and they cage me in on both sides. I must be standing in some sort of road, then, because underneath my slippers, it's dusty and dirty and there's not a patch of grass to be found. Nearby, an animal brays and I turn to see something in a harness that looks like a land-hippo, with a man leading its bridle. As I watch, he pulls a buff colored scarf over his bright red hair like a hood and glares at me.

Am I...on a movie set? But even as the idea crosses my mind, I know that can't be true. This is something bigger. Something vastly more different. I cross my arms over my chest, exceedingly aware that I'm in pink pajamas. I'm not wearing a bra and I feel a little conspicuous as I look at everyone around me, trying to absorb the picture.

Where the hell am I?

Why am I *here?*

I frown at my surroundings. The stone walls stretch out as far as the eye can see, and so do the dusty streets. I walk forward, dodging piles of animal poop in the middle of the streets, and people pass by, dressed in the same loose, flowing clothing that the man with the land-hippo was wearing. They all look at me as if I'm crazy, but no one stops to talk to me. A few women whisper as they see me.

Well that doesn't make me feel uncomfortable *at all.*

I pause, trying to figure out where I am and where I need to go. Can I turn around? I look behind me, but there's no hint of the room I was just in. There's no door, no nothing, just stone walls, people leading around land-hippos and the occasional shabby-looking booth propped up against the walls.

There's no obvious route home.

I pinch myself. Hard. Twice, just in case the first one didn't count. Nope, I'm awake. Awake and hating this. I look around one more time for a door or a portal of some kind that would have dumped me here, but there's nothing. It's entirely possible I'm having a stroke or I'm in a coma or something and my brain is firing up fantasy scenarios, because this definitely looks more like *Game of Thrones* than Chicago. I gaze at the land-hippos and try to match them up with known animals on Earth, but I come up with a blank. I don't think these are Earth creatures. And if that's the case, where am I and how did I end up on another planet? I hesitate, and when a woman with a large basket on her hip pauses to adjust her load, I approach her.

"Excuse me," I say brightly. "I seem to be lost."

She frowns at my mouth, as if my words sound weird. Her gaze slides down to my clothing. "What're you looking for? An inn?"

"An inn would be great. I don't suppose you can tell me where I am?"

Her uneasy look grows. "The slums?"

"No, I mean here." I gesture at the ground with both hands. "This city. Where is this?"

The woman's brows go up. "Aventine?"

Aventine. Okay, that's a start. I beam at her, trying not to panic. I've never heard of Aventine, but I'm admittedly not the best with geography. "And are we still on Earth?"

"Earth?" she echoes.

"The planet?" How has she not heard of Earth?

She makes a gesture over her chest – probably to ward off my crazy -and shakes her head, walking away. "Leave me alone."

Right. Just makin' friends wherever I go. I bite back a sigh of frustration. It's obvious I don't fit in here, which means that not only is this not Chicago, this is definitely not Earth. It's also hot as blazes, the air dry. Considering it was sweater weather back home, I've definitely changed locations. I glance back at the woman with the basket, but she's disappeared into the maze of crowded alleys.

All right then, I'm alone. Hot panic simmers in my chest. I can't be stranded here. I don't have my purse, or money, or even a fucking bra. I don't have shoes. I don't have the faintest idea of where the hell I am or how I got here. I want to press my hands to my forehead and cry. I want to collapse, but I know all of that won't do any good. So I take a deep, shuddering breath, straighten my shoulders, and try to figure out where I am. If I got dumped here, it stands to reason someone will know how to put me back. I just have to find that person.

Somewhat calmer, I put my hands on my hips and gaze around me, trying to figure out my next move. The music continues somewhere nearby, low and urgent, and I decide I might as well follow it. Seems about as good an idea as any other idea.

I head forward through the dusty streets of...wherever I am. One thing I've learned about people thanks to five years in a corporate environment is that if you look confident, people will assume you know what you're doing and where you're going. So I put confidence in my step and stroll forward like this is all part of my master plan.

Fake it until you make it and all that.

The stone walls snake around, and I follow them until they fork, splitting in opposite directions. One way seems more crowded than the other, so I pick the less crowded path.

Almost immediately, I regret it. It opens up into what looks like a big open area in the city, and here there are rows and rows of tents like something out of an old war movie. There are more land-hippos and more men. Armored men. To a one, they're all dressed in an overcoat of a dark red over armor. It makes them look alarmingly badass.

And they're all looking at me.

I get that uncomfortable prickle along my spine. Clearly, I'm not supposed to be here...wherever here is.

Clearly, this is very, very bad. I've stumbled out of a market-place in the slums and into a war encampment. I turn on my heel, moving back toward the walls I've just—stupidly—wandered out of.

A hand grabs my shoulder. "What have we got here?"

A man in armor gazes down at me. His face is craggy and rough, unshaven, and he stinks of sweat. He eyes me like I would a new flavor of cheesecake.

I try to feign a smile.

"You look like you're lost."

Boy he has no idea just how lost I am. I gesture back where I came. "Sorry. I didn't see the sign that said 'no girls allowed.' I'll be heading out now."

His hand just tightens on my shoulder and his eyes narrow at me. "Who's your overlord?"

"Pardon?" I try to slide out from under the grip of his gloved hand, but he yanks on my arm instead.

"Your overlord," he says, leering at the front of my pajamas. "If you're from Aventine, you'll have an overlord and a house symbol showing your allegiance. Wanna flash those for me?"

"Oooh, they're in my other pants," I say brightly. "But if you'll just let me go—"

He clamps down tighter on my shoulder. "We've got ourselves a runaway slave," he bellows. "Rodrick!"

A man starts running toward us. "Yes, Commander?"

"I'm not a slave," I protest, jerking at the man's grip. "Let me go!"

The commander backhands me and I go flying to the ground. "Rodrick" hauls me to my feet as I stare at the men in shock.

Someone just hit me. I touch my face in stunned surprise.

The commander just gives me an icy look, then focuses on Rodrick. "You know what we do to those who have no allegiance, don't you?"

"The slave pens, Commander?"

The man nods. "Make sure she brings a fair coin. She's got all her teeth."

I'M the unluckiest woman ever.

I push my face between the metal bars of the slave cage that's been my home for two days, trying to see the man that's just walked up. He gives me a look, and I try to smile prettily at the man in front of me, since I've learned that no one listens to a pissy slave. "Hi there. Are you from around here? Because I'm not and I really, really need to get out of here."

"Shut up, tart," the man says, barely glancing over at me.

Rude, I think, but I'm not surprised. No one in this place has even heard of the word "manners." I'm now two days into this new world, though, and I'm determined to find a way home. I'm long past hysterics, long past tears, and have ended up in the grim-resignation end of things. I'm here in this shithole, now I need to figure out how to get out. And getting out means getting out of this slave cage, first of all.

If that means being nicey-nice to this guy, I'll do it. So I flutter my lashes, give him a chirpy smile, and try again. "I'm from Earth. Chicago, actually. I know everyone thinks it's all crime ridden and cold, but it's actually pretty awesome. Great nightlife. Fantastic museums. I don't suppose you've heard of it?"

And I beam like I'm not in a slave pen on some Conan-esque planet, wearing manacles and what can only be described as a half of a skirt.

I'm going to get my way out of this place with the power of positive thinking, damn it.

The man just narrows his eyes at me. He glances over at the man in front of the slave pen and gestures at me. "This one's got a mouth on her."

"That can be fixed," the man says, counting coins in his hand and not looking up.

I swallow hard, thinking of the guy I saw have his tongue pulled out yesterday. Okay. New plan. "Did I say Earth? I meant… east. Totally meant east. Absolutely, one hundred percent from this land." I try to slide back behind the other slaves shackled in the pen. I only moved to the front because this guy looked clean and wealthy and maybe would be reasonably nice to a poor, down-on-her-luck woman that isn't supposed to be in a slave pen.

Or isn't supposed to be in this world at all.

No such luck, though. The man points a finger at me and looks over at the guy counting coins. "I'll take that one anyhow. Best looking of the lot."

The slave-master finishes counting his coins and grunts. "You'll want to collar her. She doesn't think she should be a slave."

They both share a chuckle at that, and someone puts a hand to my back and shoves me forward. With a yelp, I stagger to the front of the pen, and then I'm hauled out. I would say it's an improvement from the cramped, filthy pen I've been stuck in for the last two days, but given that I've just been sold as a slave?

"Improvement" is debatable.

So I smile at the soldier that bought me, determined to make a friend. If I can win him into friendship, maybe he can explain to me what I'm doing in this weird-ass world and how I get home. "Nice to meet you, sir. I'm Faith. I'd give you my hand to shake, but I'm a little tied up at the moment." I raise my shackled hands and put on my most winning smile.

The soldier stares at me. He smiles, then crooks a finger.

Even though it feels like a trap, I lean forward. "Yes?"

He grabs me by the neck, and then something rough and metal locks around my throat. A collar. I choke, raising my manacled hands to claw at the hair caught between my skin and the collar, since it feels as if it's all being pulled out. He slaps my hands away, then grabs them and loosens the manacles before snapping my lead chain to my collar. "Follow me, tart."

Coughing, I stumble after him when he tugs on my lead. "My name's not Tart. It's Faith. And I feel like we really need to talk—"

The man comes to an abrupt stop, and I slam into his front.

He gives me a shove backward, scowling. "I say I wanted you to lip off at me, Tart?"

"No—"

He glares again, and I go silent. I know when to take a hint. Fighting back frustration, I follow behind the jerk—my new owner—as he heads out of the slave pens and into the busy Aventine streets.

"Pleasure doing business with you again, Sinon," the slave-master calls.

His name is Sinon. I file that bit of information away, because knowledge is power, and right now I am absolutely on the low end of both knowledge and power. Words burn in my throat, because I desperately want to talk to this man. I need him to listen to me. I need him to realize I'm not from the filthy streets of Aventine, or anywhere else in this land. I'm not from here at all.

I'm from freaking Chicago.

I'm still not entirely sure how I got here. The kids from Narnia went through a wardrobe dresser and became kings. The chick from *Outlander* touched some stones and ended up with a hot kilted Scotsman.

Me, I knock on my neighbor's door because I hear voices shouting, and the next thing I know, I'm being shoved in a slave pen and referred to as "Tart."

Hollywood has definitely misled me.

The most frustrating thing of all is that no one will listen to me. I've told everyone I'm not a slave, that I'm not from here. What did I get?

First, I got backhanded.

Then I got shoved into a slave pen.

Now I've been sold and I'm following behind Sinon, the bitchiest soldier ever, all because I was trying to be a good neighbor.

"You keeping up, Tart?" Sinon growls as he pushes his way into the busy streets.

"Absolutely." I hop behind him as quickly as I can, considering I've got no shoes. Even though I don't like this guy—and "don't like" is being kind of mild—I know I can't be left alone on the streets of Aventine. I learned that lesson already. I don't have a "mark" that shows I'm from here, and everyone that doesn't gets enslaved because apparently Aventine is at war with someone.

Despite the flowery name, this place is a lot more like a barracks than any city I know of. The streets are nothing but trodden mud, there are soldiers crawling everywhere, and all around the city there's an enormous stone wall. It's like a fort. A scuzzy one.

And all of the soldiers that pass by in their regiments, that file out of the city on the regular, and that pour forth from every tavern—all male.

This is not a good place to be a slave girl.

Or a girl, period.

Sinon grunts as I trot up to his side like an obedient little waif. "That's better. Follow close. We're going to a special party and then I'm passing you over to your new owner." He gives me a thin-lipped smile that shows yellowing teeth and dark gums. "So behave and I won't bruise you up before then."

Whee. I don't know if I should be excited he's not going to be my permanent owner or if I should be scared. "Who's my new owner?"

He doesn't answer me. Just yanks on my chain again and leads me through the crowd of soldiers.

I study him as we walk. He's thick-looking, but that might be the layers of padded armor he's wearing. His head is shaven bald and the stubble there is a mixture of gray and black. He's sweaty and stinks to high heaven, and his nose has probably been broken more times than I can count. He's got a thick jaw so his shaved head actually looks more like a pear than a circle, and he's got questionable dental hygiene.

I really, really hope he's going to pass me off. If the outfit I've been given is any sort of clue, I haven't been sold so I can wash dishes and mend socks.

I really am gonna be a tart.

Since my pajamas were stolen, the only clothing I have now is the same as the other slave women I've seen. It's a long, unbleached skirt. That's it. No top, no bra, no nothing. Of course, I'm not about to go all bare-titty through soldier-town, so I hiked it up to my armpits and I'm wearing it like a minidress. Every soldier that passes by us stares as if I'm wearing something far more scandalous, and they leer.

So far? Not a fan of Aventine.

"This way, Tart," my new owner tells me and jerks on my chain again.

I put my hands to the neck cuff, trying to shield my abused skin from the next yank, and trot a little faster behind him. "Where are we going?"

He ignores me. In fact, he keeps ignoring me as we leave the mucky streets and head toward rickety, stinky docks that crawl with cats and fishermen. There are dozens of small boats moored here, and one flat-bottomed barge with a bright red linen top waits at the far end. We head there.

"Where you going?" the man standing in front of the boat asks Sinon.

I wait for Sinon to ignore him. Instead, he crosses his arms over his chest in a quasi-salute. "Heading to the temple. They're expecting me."

The sailor glances at me. "And her?"

"Tart's a gift."

I wave my fingers at him in greeting. Now's not the time to debate my name.

"Gift for who?"

"Ain't none of your business, is it?" Sinon's grumpy.

"It is if you bring uninvited trash to the temple tonight. Prelate'll have my head." The sailor crosses his arms and rocks back on his feet.

My owner snorts. "Who do you think she's a gift for, fool?"

Oh.

Okay, so I'm going to be for the prelate. I guess he likes... tarts. Lucky me.

The sailor smirks in my direction. "If I was placing odds, she'd be a cleaver bride."

"What's a cleaver bride?" I ask.

"Shut up, Tart," Sinon says, and when the sailor moves aside, he pulls me after him without answering.

We ride on the flat-bottomed boat, crammed next to a bunch of other people. Someone reaches out and pinches me, and I slap at hands, wishing medieval plagues on all these armor-wearing bastards. It's the longest boat ride ever, but eventually we pull up to the docks of the island...and the world is different.

This place is cool and clean and beautiful. I'm surprised. There are green manicured gardens and people in long red robes watering plants from what look like helmets. There are several marble buildings, all of them columned and lovely, and there's a scent of incense in the air. It's nothing like dirty, over-run, soldier-covered Aventine at all.

Clearly they take better care of their temples than their city.

We head to the front of the main building. Outside is a massive statue of a man, battleaxe raised. Immediately, Sinon drops to his knees and bows his head.

I wait behind him, fidgeting.

Sinon looks up and gives my chains a furious yank, sending me staggering forward. "You kneel before the gods, Tart! Lord Aron of the Cleaver, the Butcher God of Battle, deserves your respect."

"Okay, okay!" I drop to my knees. Sheesh.

Sinon continues to glare at me with his egg-shaped head, so I even go so far as to put my forehead to the ground. Sheesh.

I figure a little kneeling won't matter if I don't mean it—and I don't. I have no idea who Aron of the Cleaver is, after all. Clearly a god of some kind in this strange land. Maybe a war god, given that there's a lot of guys covered in armor around here.

My owner continues to sit in front of the statue, eyes closed, meditating. When this goes on for a while, I sit up and study my surroundings. The statue's made of marble, and the man behind the upraised battleaxe—Aron of the Cleaver—doesn't look friendly. Most of his face is hidden behind the axe itself, but his hair is long and straight, held back from his head by a braid at the crown, and his stern, unyielding face has a long, wicked scar that goes from above the left eye all the way down to the jaw.

Pretty sure he didn't get that from playing darts.

I continue to sit, watching my surroundings. More soldiers move past. Some pause to bow at the statue, some just pause, kiss their sword pommel and continue on. Definitely a war god. Maybe that's why they were watering plants with helmets.

Though if this is a war god's temple, why am I here? Why does their prelate want a tart? And what the hell is a cleaver bride? A nun of some kind?

Of course, I've been asking the same question for two days. Ten bucks says I'm not going to get an answer anytime soon.

I stare at the statue. If I'm in a new world, maybe the gods can send me home. "I'll be your best friend, Aron," I whisper. "Just get me back to Chicago."

Sinon gets up. He wipes his brow, sweating like a pig in his heavy armor. I move into place behind him. My neck is throbbing from how many times my chain has been yanked, and I'm tempted to pull a Princess Leia on this guy and grab my chain, loop it around his neck, and choke the life out of him.

We head into the temple itself, past columns shaped like

swords and statue after statue of the scarred, angry-looking god.

A pair of men in red robes wait by the portcullis. One raises a hand to us. "Halt."

My owner stops and effects an ornate bow. "Sword Sinon Dantali, here for the annual Anticipation." He straightens and then gestures at me. "I've brought an offering for the prelate."

"A blonde, I see," one of the men says with a smirk. "Original."

"The prelate knows what he likes," Sinon says.

"Truth. And it's not like the Butcher God will show his face tonight." The soldiers bark-laughs, and then one grabs my lead from Sinon. "Put her in with the other offerings."

CHAPTER 4

*I*n the antechamber, it's immediately obvious who the other "offerings" are.

The room is filled with women of every shape and size, all attractive. Some have huge breasts, some are waif thin. Some are older than me, and some look barely old enough to be in high school. They're all dressed in the long white loincloth and belt that I'm in.

They all have blonde hair.

The other slaves barely spare me a glance. Most gossip in low voices, oiling their skin and smoothing their hair. Some frolic near a fountain in the tiled courtyard, giggling. It's almost like I'm backstage at a beauty pageant, waiting for my turn to go on.

"Got any mascara?" I ask the girl nearest me.

"What?" She frowns in my direction and moves away.

"Never mind. It was a bad joke." I sigh to myself, looking for a friendly face in the room. "I guess I'm just talking for the sake of talking."

Another woman stares at me as she walks past.

The antechamber tiles of the floor are cool beneath my dirty feet as I walk around. There's a colonnade along each wall with more of the sword-shaped pillars, and I study the others. There must be at least thirty or forty blondes. Cleaver brides, I wonder?

Now if I just knew what those were...

A young girl sits by the wall, her legs tucked under her, tits out, her blonde curls pulled into an artful knot atop her head. She looks way too young to be here, but I'm guessing no one asked for ID at the slave pens. Still, she seems approachable, so I make a beeline toward her, smiling. *No pageant jokes this time, Faith,* I remind myself. *You're totally from this place, remember?*

When she casts a timid smile in my direction, I smile back and thump down on the ground to sit next to her. "Hi there! I'm Faith." I offer her my hand. "I'm new here."

Her brows draw together and she tilts her head charmingly. "An unusual name. Where are you from?"

"Oh, here and there." I wave a hand airily, because I know trying to explain that I'm from the US and from Earth will just be a mistake. "You?"

"Avalla. From Glistentide."

"Totally one of my favorite places," I lie, keeping my tone friendly. I sit down next to her and fold my legs under me in the same prim stance, my hands on my lap. "You're far from home, I think. How'd you end up here?"

"In Aventine?" She bites her lip and ducks her head, looking so shy and awkward it hurts me to think of her in the same situation I'm in. "My parents sold me to a traveling merchant. He was very kind but I did not enjoy his advances much. He was very old and I admit I had foolish dreams like any young maiden." She shrugs and her smile grows wider. "So he brought me here and then gave me as an offering to the temple, to be a cleaver bride. It is a great honor."

Avalla says the words, but her smile is a little forced, the look in her eyes a little too blank.

32

Yikes.

I lean in close. "Like I said, I'm new here. Is it *really* an honor or are we screwed? Be honest."

She looks startled at my words, and then her lip trembles. Her eyes become glassy with unshed tears and she blinks rapidly, wiping at the corners of her eyes with her fingers. "You will make me weep and then I will be blotchy."

Yeah, I'm pretty sure if this was an honor, she wouldn't be crying. Not crying like that, anyhow. That tells me everything I need to know. Cleaver bride is not a good thing to be. "Sorry."

"It's all right. I just want to look my best for when we meet the prelate at the choosing."

"Choosing?"

Avalla gives me a curious look. "The temple's choosing...for the Anticipation? You have not heard of such a thing?"

I shrug. "Really, *really* not from here."

"But surely your land has gods. It is the *Anticipation*." She says it as if there's a "duh" at the end.

"Well, I'm sure *anticipating* learning what it is," I joke.

She wrinkles her nose. "Your accent is strange," she agrees. "Are you from across the seas?"

"Something like that." I gesture with my hand, indicating she should continue. "Tell me more about this choosing? There are a lot of women here. Are we all being chosen?"

"Oh no. Just one. The others will become Cleaver Brides."

Just one. Not great odds, and I'm definitely not the hottest babe in the room. "So what happens to that one? The girl that's chosen?"

"She will be the servant to the prelate for the next year. He is the chosen priest of Aron of the Cleaver, and as such, she will serve all his needs until the next Anticipation day. After that, she is paid richly and can live a life of leisure having satisfied the gods."

All right, so it's clearly a religious thing. Sounds like a

personal slave for the local priest, and then freedom. Hard pass. I've had enough of slaving. "Life of leisure sounds great and all," I begin.

"Oh yes. It is a position of great honor." Avalla's pretty face is hopeful.

"And everyone else becomes Cleaver Brides? What is that, like a nun? Spend the rest of our lives serving the gods?" Maybe I can escape a nunnery.

"You…you don't know what a Cleaver Bride is?"

"No."

She pales and swallows hard. "Cleaver Brides are offerings to the god."

There's that word again. I'm starting to hate it as much as "tart." "Offerings?"

"Sacrifices." She swallows hard and tries to smile, but it has a glassy look to it. "It is a great honor."

Ok, that is *definitely* gonna be a problem.

CHAPTER 5

There's a huge knot in my throat and I clamp Avalla's hand in mine. I'm trying not to panic.

Sacrificed.

To a god.

Me and all these women in this room are going to die if we're not chosen to serve the prelate. I'm guessing we're not going to be "serving" like a waitress but more like serving in bed.

So it's either that or death. Shit is hitting the fan.

Choices, choices.

I look around the room, at the crowd of women. Their merriment seems to have a hard edge to it, and I realize some of the laughter is forced. In the corner, there's a girl weeping though she's doing her best to conceal it. Another one's staring at the fountain so intently I'd swear she wants to drown herself in it.

"We have to get out of here," I whisper to Avalla. "I need to get home."

Her eyes go wide. "We cannot. We would be shamed before the gods."

"I'll eat my stupid skirt if the gods actually know what's going on here." I squeeze her hand again. "And that's the only thing I have to wear. Come on. Do you want to die here?"

"No." Her voice is so small I can barely hear it.

"Then let's think. Do you know this temple? Is there a way out of here?"

She shakes her head, her movements jerky with fear. "My master brought me here last night. I am a stranger to this place, as you are." The look on her face becomes bleak. She looks ready to cry. "Do you think I will be a cleaver bride, then?"

"Of course not. You're awesome." I give her a faint smile and wipe her cheek when a tear slides down it. "It's going to be okay. We'll think of something. When's this ceremony?"

"Tonight. At sundown. The hour of storms."

That means nothing to me other than we don't have much time. An afternoon isn't going to be enough. But I squeeze her hand. "We'll figure something out."

I MIGHT HAVE OVERSTATED my abilities to figure something out.

There's no exit and the crowded room is heavily guarded. Best I can do? Try to help Avalla become slave numero uno, because she wants it so badly. She keeps talking about the prelate and how she'd love to serve him, so I want her to win.

Unfortunately for her, the only coaching I can come up with is to tell her to bite her lip and bat her lashes. I'm worse than a pageant coach. It's clear that there are a lot of experienced women in this room and some great beauties, so Avalla's got earnestness and that's about it.

I don't even have that. I'm all right looking, but I'm definitely no Helen of Troy. I think I passed her by the fountain. Spoiler—she's blonde.

Since I can't escape, I decide I'm going to go down fighting.

That means I need a weapon. I look around for one all day, and eventually find a chink of broken tile in a corner that has a hard edge and clutch it tightly in my hand. It's about the size of my finger, but it'll have to do.

I can always peck someone to death like the world's angriest blonde chicken.

Because I'm not going to smile all the way to my funeral pyre. I did not end up on some strange podunk *Game of Thrones* ripoff world just to be part of the Million Blonde Funeral March.

I am getting the fuck out of this place, one way or another.

AS THE SUN GOES DOWN, a familiar thrumming drumbeat begins. Goosebumps prick my bare arms and Avalla clutches my hand nervously. I grit my teeth, because it's the same drumbeat I heard back in the apartment. It's all tied to this somehow.

"You'll do great," I promise her as more guards file into the room. "Big smile. Fluttery lashes. Thrust your chest out. Smize."

It must be time. The women are lined up, and one of the guards swoops up and down the row, rearranging us by height and my grip tightens on Avalla's hand. She's shorter than me. I hate that we're going to get separated, because it was nice to have someone to talk to for a change. Someone that didn't call me "tart" or try to feel my tits.

I've felt so alone and friendless in this strange place. It was nice to have a buddy.

"You. This way," the guard says, indicating that Avalla should follow him. She looks at me nervously and I give her an encouraging two thumbs up.

She moves forward in the line, sandwiched between two very busty and older-looking women. Really, that's a win for her, because she's going to look youthful and nubile and all those great, creepy things that a sex slave is supposed to be. I'm sandwiched between two beauties, but I don't care because I don't plan on being "picked."

Of course, I haven't figured out plan B yet, but I'm hoping something will come to me.

The drum beats continue, and then the line of women marches forward, heads bent. I mimic them automatically, though I'm peeking around as we walk down the long, dark corridors. There's a scent of rain in the air, and I can hear thunder. It messes up the steady rhythm of the drums, which is more than a little jarring. There also seem to be even more people in this building than before. Not all of them are wearing the long red robes, but the number of soldiers seems to be greater, as does the number of civilians dressed in simple tunics. It's like everyone's turning out for a party.

I can just bet what the entertainment's going to be.

The line of blondes winds through the crowded corridor, and then we're led into a very large, smoky chamber. The drummers wait at the edges of the room, staring ahead, tapping out their rhythm.

The crowd is packed in here, and the humidity is making more than one sweat. There's a faint body-odor stink in the room, but no one's leaving. If anything, more people are crowding in. The entire room is wall to wall people except for the back wall, which is a massive feast table laden with foods of every kind. Up ahead at the front of the room, I catch a glimpse of a large stone throne up on a dais. It's empty, as if we're waiting for the guest of honor.

Behind the dais is a banner of sumptuous red cloth with the battleaxe symbol and a lightning bolt going through it. I scan the room, looking for my pear-headed owner. He's off talking to a few soldiers squeezed into a corner, but I notice he keeps looking in this direction. I want to make a break for it, but I'm being watched.

Suddenly, everything goes silent.

There's an ominous rumble of thunder, but the drums are quiet, the people are quiet, everything in the temple is quiet. A man strolls forward and the crowd—already packed to the gills—tries to part for him. People squeeze against one another to give him room to pass. He moves forward, heading to the row of blondes, and I get a good look at him.

He's not old. He's tanned and has a stern face that could be fifty or a hard thirty. He looks like he's in relatively good shape, and his head is completely shaven. Not my type, but maybe Avalla's. As he approaches, I notice his robes have a different sweep to them, and I realize his are crusted with gems and what looks like gold along the cuffs and hem. Fancy. Prelating must pay well.

The prelate moves in the mix of people, then raises his hands into the air.

Everyone drops to their knees, bowing their heads.

Well, shit. I clench my bit of broken tile tightly and kneel like all the others, bending my head. Instead of praying, though, I look for exits.

If I'm going to make a break for it, it needs to be soon.

"Rise," the prelate says. "Rise and let us celebrate the Lord of Storms, Aron of the Cleaver, butcher god of battle in his chosen hour, the hour of storms. Today is the day we celebrate the Anticipation."

Blah blah Anticipation. No one looks excited about anything except the food. There are looks of boredom on everyone's faces. I guess no one's "anticipating" all that much.

Ha.

The red-robed man raises his arms into the air again, like a preacher without a pulpit. "Every year upon this day, we celebrate in the hopes that the gods will send an Aspect, as it is told in the sacred scrolls. This temple is dedicated to Aron of the Cleaver, our Lord of Storms, the butcher of battle, but we welcome any of the twelve gods if they should honor us with their presence."

He turns and bows to the empty throne which remains, you guessed it, empty.

There's a bit of polite clapping. Everyone still looks bored.

The prelate turns back to the crowd once more. "In honor of this day and our Lord of Storms, we will feast in his name."

That makes people happy. A cheer goes up.

The prelate turns toward us. "One maiden will be chosen to serve me in the Lord of Storms's honor. The rest shall be given as Cleaver Brides."

No one responds. Someone makes an impatient noise. Another man rolls his eyes.

I'm thinking the Anticipation is a big let-down every year. I bet it's a lot like Christmas, when your parents promise that Santa Claus is on his way and then you find out he's not real. Maybe Aron of the Cleaver is about as real as Rudolph the Red-Nosed Reindeer and that's why no one seems to give a crap about this particular holiday except for the food.

"I shall choose the maiden to serve me," the prelate says, dragging my attention back to the center of the room. "Once I have picked the honored one, we will say the invocation and proceed to the feasting."

The prelate moves to the end of the row and begins to eyeball the blonde offerings. One by one, he looks them up and down, and I'm acutely aware that most women are half-naked. Everyone wears the same skirt, but I'm the only one with it hiked up to my tits. This is so incredibly *creepy*, especially when he reaches out to finger one girl's curly hair and brushes his fingers over the shoulder of the next, as if judging how smooth her skin is.

Ugh.

He continues down the row, and the room is quiet, the only sound the low murmur of the audience, as if they're making

BOUND TO THE BATTLE GOD

bets on who he'll pick. I notice that Sinon is staring at me from afar and I resist the urge to shoot him the finger. That won't do any good.

I mean, it'd *feel* good, but I'm in enough trouble as it is.

I'm toward the end of the line, so it doesn't take long for him to get to me. I slide my hands behind my back before he arrives, hiding the chunk of tile I'm holding. When he moves near, I catch a heavy whiff of herbs, as if he's bathing in this world's version of deodorant under those robes.

"Why do your ears have holes?"

I blink. That's a weird question. "My ears?"

He nods. "Your ears have holes. Why?"

Oh. "They're pierced? You wear jewelry in them."

The prelate wrinkles his nose. "Barbaric."

Is it? I didn't realize the people here didn't wear ear jewelry. What a strange thing to notice.

He flicks a hand at the front of my skirt-dress. "I should like to see your breasts. Disrobe."

So much for being chipper and accommodating. I clutch the front of my dress. "No thanks."

"What?"

"I mean...no?" I try to smile sweetly. "But 'no' in the nicest way, of course."

He recoils, aghast at my response. "You dare?"

"Well, they're very shy boobs." I promise. Something tells me I'm not getting picked.

The prelate flicks his gaze over me one more time. "Pleasant appearance...distasteful personality." And he moves on.

Sounds like my last annual review at work.

Even so, a knot forms in my throat. I don't want to be his little slave, but I don't want to die either. This is the medieval equivalent of "Tits or GTFO" isn't it? My fear gives way to anger.

Fuck this guy.

Fuck *all* these guys.

I'm going to go out fighting, I tell myself. This isn't the end. There has to be more to why I'm here than to just die in a pile of anonymous blondes.

I've been dragged from Earth, kicking and screaming. I have to be here for a reason. It can't be just to die because I won't flash some jerk my boobs.

There has to be a bigger purpose...doesn't there? My weird aura means something, doesn't it?

Unless everyone's just lied to me...which is beginning to look like it might be a thing.

The prelate continues to sweep down the line, talking to some of the girls and taking his sweet time making his decision. I hold my breath as he approaches Avalla, because I want this for her...if she wants it, of course. She looks up at the prelate with shining, hopeful eyes, practically trembling with awe at the sight of him. It'd be cute if circumstances weren't so dire...and he wasn't such a dick. I can see her slump with disappointment when he continues down the line.

Then, he finishes talking to the very last girl, the shortest one, and turns. He walks down the lineup of girls once more and pauses in front of Avalla. "Would you like to serve me, my dear?"

She drops to her knees and begins to kiss his hem. "It would be such an honor, prelate!"

"You may rise."

I do my best not to curl my lip because this is what she wanted, but man, you'd think the prelate was the god being served around here. Prick.

Avalla gets to her feet, and when the prelate indicates she should follow him, she glances over at me with excitement. I shoot her a thumbs up and give her an encouraging nod. One problem down at least.

Except now the rest of us are Cleaver Brides. I can already

hear someone quietly sobbing down the line. I'm not crying. I'm not giving up. I study the room, trying to figure out where we'll be executed. If enough of us rush the executioner all at once, some are bound to get away…

The prelate moves to the center of the room, and as he does, a chair is placed next to the empty throne on the dais. It's not nearly as big as the empty stone seat, but it's wrought with gold and looks expensive and throne-like just the same. The prelate sits down with a flourish, smoothing his robes. Avalla immediately sits at his feet on the stairs, looking starry-eyed.

He gestures at the throngs stuffed into the temple. "Eat! Eat in honor of Aron of the Cleaver." He waves at a servant and someone brings him a plate.

There's a rush toward the table of food, and then the room gets noisy and boisterous. Wine is passed around and the soldiers start to get hammered. I glance down the row of women and no one's offering us anything. They all continue to stand like statues, the guards in front of us as impassive as the others.

All right, I guess it's feast time for everyone except the "lucky" Cleaver Brides. That's fine. Every hour that they spend getting drunk and stupid on wine is another hour I get to form a plan to get out of here.

As time passes and people grow drunk with wine, the room gets rowdier. Another round of food is brought out, and I watch Avalla offering morsels to the prelate. She's doing her best not to look giddily happy and glances over at me from time to time, nervous.

More wine is brought out, and I fidget. The broken tile's cutting into my hand. "How long does this party go on?"

"Until dawn," the woman next to me says. "We wait for the hour of blood."

Dawn? So we're just going to sit here and watch everyone feast all night and wait to die? Man, these guys are dicks.

The drums stop their ominous beats and have been replaced by reedy flutes, and now drunken idiots dance and carouse in the center of the floor. Man, this really is like an office Christmas party. My nerves get more and more shot as the minutes tick past, and I start to worry that I'm not going to be able to get away. That I won't find a way out of this place.

That I really *was* brought to this strange world just to die.

I shoot to my feet. "I need to go to the bathroom."

"Bathroom?" One of the guards frowns at me.

"Is that not what it's called? Lavatory? Potty?" When he continues to stare at me blankly, I sigh. "I have to pee."

"The garderobe?"

"Sure?" I can't believe this hasn't come up in conversation yet and here I've been in medieval hell for a whole week almost. It doesn't matter, though. I keep my hand clenched around my bit of sharp tile. Maybe I won't need to use it after all. "I can escort myself. Just let me know the way."

The guards exchange looks.

"Sit back down," a different one says, scowling at me. "You don't need to go anywhere."

"My bladder is saying otherwise. You want me to pee all over the place? I'll do it," I threaten. "Won't that be a bit of a party ruiner?" I give them a defiant look.

The second guard sighs. "Fine. I'll take her."

The girl next to me stands up. "Wait. I have to go, as well."

"And me," says another.

"And me," adds a third. Two others raise their hands.

I bite back my frustration. My escape plan isn't exactly going to work if everyone has the same damn idea. They're ruining it for me.

"Sit down, all of you," the guard snarls. "You'll sit quietly and wait until the Hour of Blood, and if you do not, we'll cut your throat and toss your body into the river without so much as a blessing. Understand?"

44

Everyone sits. Even me. Jeez.

I watch the revelers with an increasing sense of disgust. As time passes, they go beyond drunk. Someone starts fondling a nearby woman and then suddenly there's a girl thrown down on a table with her skirts hiked up. I try not to stare, but from the noises she's making, she's having a *really* good time. I look over at Avalla, and she's migrated to the prelate's knee, her hand between his thighs as she whispers in his ear and pushes her breasts into his face.

Okay, maybe this is a bit more than your average Christmas party.

Maybe it's more like...New Year's? A really horny, horny New Year's, I amend as a naked man chases a naked woman through the crowd. If there's some sort of attention that's supposed to be paid to the whole reason for the holiday, these people have forgotten it long ago. No one pays attention to the throne on the dais, and I notice that the prelate sets his wine goblet on the arm of it, as if it's his own special armchair. Maybe it is. Fuck if I know. There's so much about this world that I just don't understand.

Namely why you'd have to kill thirty perfectly good blondes to celebrate a god no one gives a shit about.

Thunder crackles overhead.

The people in the room pause, and then laughter breaks out. "The Lord of Storms sends a greeting," calls one of the priests. I can't help but notice he's grabbing one of the local women, his wine spilled down the front of his robes. He's clumsy, turning and slapping people with the long end of his sword.

I really hope he's not the executioner.

The thought makes my stomach knot up and I feel like I'm going to be sick. I keep waiting for an opportunity to show itself but there isn't one. The guards standing near us are the only ones sober, and a runaway blonde slave girl would be too obvious in this crowd. I can't blend. I can't escape.

45

If there's a plan for me, a little hint right about now would be nice.

Thunder booms again, and the wind rises.

The torches flicker, almost going out. The heavy scent of ozone fills the sultry air, and I can hear rain starting outside. One of the terrified women next to me starts to cry. I pat her back awkwardly. "It's okay. I've got a plan."

Fake it until you make it and all that. I don't have a plan, but it feels better to pretend that I do.

The air feels heavier with the oncoming storm. The thunder booms again, and this time it's so loud that the entire building seems to shake. Wind whips through the temple, providing the first breeze I've felt in hours.

The torches die.

I jump to my feet as people cry out, startled. This is my chance. Time to escape.

"Someone re-light the torches," the prelate calls out in a lazy voice. People laugh, and I hear the sound of someone getting laid, all grunts and groaning and female giggles. Ew.

On tiptoe, I start to move through the crowd. Everyone's distracted. Time to make my escape. People are pressed against each other so tightly that it's impossible to push forward. I try to shove my way past a pair of men, but they just knock me backwards.

One of the torches is lit, and then the room floods with dim light.

Someone gasps. "He's here!"

There's a little scream, and then people start dropping to their knees all around me. I look around—and see that the big, empty throne at the front of the room is no longer empty.

A man sits there.

"Sit" seems like such a benign word for what's going on, though. His presence is so overwhelming that it feels like a stronger adjective should be used. Looms, maybe. Lords. Yeah.

The stranger's lording over all of us, equal parts arrogance and contempt emanating from him. He doesn't move a muscle, his arms calmly stretched on the throne as if he's been here the entire time. And as he gazes around the room, he's impossible to like. Fear, yes. Like, no. It's in every pore of his being that he hates what he sees in front of him.

I just wish he wasn't so darn beautiful to look at.

Fact is, he's gorgeous in the most intimidating sort of way. His shoulders are broad and muscular, his skin pale. There seem to be acres and acres of pale skin, and it takes me a moment to realize that he's totally naked. He wears it well, of course, his entire form so intimidating that it almost makes me feel like everyone else is just overdressed.

His hair is dark black and falls down his back and shoulders. It's unadorned, drawn back from his face at the crown. Instead of making him look feminine, it just highlights how blatantly masculine his features are. His jaw is sharp, his nose perfectly straight, and his eyes are narrow and bladelike...and mismatched in color.

The stranger also looks vaguely familiar to me, which is weird considering I'm a stranger in this land and I don't know anyone even remotely close to being as perfect as this guy...and then I realize there's a pale scar crossing over the left side of his face.

Oh my god. Like the statue.

No wonder everyone's dropping to their feet. I suddenly realize just what it means that he's dropped in mid-ceremony on Anticipation day. He's sitting in that throne because it was waiting for him.

This is Aron of the Cleaver.

I laugh. Aloud. "Ha!"

Christmas has come early, bitches.

CHAPTER 6

a god just arrived.

I find this far more exciting than everyone else does. I don't care that he's a god of battle or whatever. If he's a god, he can send me *home.*

I might have laughed out loud.

Aron's gaze turns to me and it's like ice.

I realize I'm the only one not on my knees bowing, and the moment our eyes make contact, I feel a shiver go through my body. There's power there, and even though I don't worship these gods, I drop to my knees because it feels like I have to.

The god—if that's what he is—continues to swing his gaze around the room, utterly silent. After a moment, he notices the prelate sitting in his chair next to his throne, and you can just tell that he does not approve.

The prelate turns sheet white and stumbles over Avalla in his haste to drop to his own knees. "Lord of Storms," the prelate says, and his trembling voice carries across the too-still room. "It is you. The Anticipation has been fulfilled at last."

I watch Aron of the Cleaver to see if he's going to say anything. He continues to study the room, his mismatched gaze burning with hostility. I shiver, wondering if he's a benevolent god. Something in me says *no*. There's an element in the way that he holds himself that suggests he's not a very nice god at all.

His gaze moves to the goblet on the end of one of the arms of his chair. It's the same golden, jewel-crusted goblet that the prelate put there earlier, too busy enjoying himself to pay attention. Very carefully, very slowly, Aron of the Cleaver flicks the goblet away and it clatters to the floor, spilling wine down the marble steps of his dais.

"Where am I?" His voice is lethal with dislike.

I'm shocked. This is the voice I heard back in the apartment. It's the gorgeous, smooth, deep voice that haunted me and drove me crazy. Except…

I didn't think the owner would be quite as intimidating as this guy. I'm just as terrified as everyone else. Was this what I was brought for? To watch this? To get killed with everyone else in this room once the war god arrived? I'm still confused, even if a piece or two slid into place.

The prelate practically quivers before the god. "This is Aventine, my lord. City dedicated to you."

"I know where Aventine is." His tone is scathing.

The prelate presses his forehead to the marble floors, and I can practically hear the man sweating. "We are honored to serve your Aspect. Just ask and—"

"It does not look as if you are honored to serve," Aron says caustically. "It looks like you are here for wine and wenching."

Well, he's got that one pegged. Wine and wenching seems to be the order of the day. Massive *burn*.

"No, no, my lord," the prelate says, sitting up on his knees. "You misunderstand—"

"Do I?"

The two words practically send frost through the room. I shiver as everything goes silent once more. Everyone's clearly terrified, including me.

For a moment, I feel bad for the prelate. It's clear that no one's ever expected one of the gods to actually show up. In a way, I can kind of understand. I'm not sure how Santa'd take it if he slid down my chimney and found me eating all the cookies laid out for him.

But then again, Santa's not real.

This Aron of the Cleaver clearly is, and he doesn't seem to be a benign sort of god. Much as I love seeing the prelate squirm, I wish I was anywhere but here.

"How can I serve?" the prelate asks, his voice turning obsequious. "Command it and it shall be done."

"How do you think you should serve?" Aron of the Cleaver's face is expressionless, but I still get a sense of distaste from him.

Trembling, the prelate picks up the goblet on the floor and offers it up to the god—

—Only to have it knocked from his hands again. "Do I look as if I wish your scraps?" Again, Aron doesn't raise his voice, but there's still an absolute sense of danger that follows those quiet words. This is not a man to be fucked with, that much is clear.

"Of course not, my lord." The prelate slowly gets to his feet and casts a frantic look around the room. "Servants! The finest wine for our honored Aspect! Cheese! Fruit! Meat! Fine robes! At once!"

The room bustles into activity. People scurry to do the prelate's bidding and others remain exactly as they were, on their knees. There's a palpable feeling of terror in the room and the girl next to me is trembling with fear.

And she wasn't trembling at the thought of her own death at dawn, so that kind of scares me.

Maybe these people should have worshipped a fluffier, kinder god. Someone with more hearts and cuddles than say, a god of war or storms.

"What else can we do for you, my lord?" The prelate bows

again, pressing his forehead to the floor. "Aventine is honored to serve."

I half-expect the god to give another venomous response. Instead, he raises a hand thoughtfully and stares at his palm. "This body is weak. Why?"

The prelate stammers for a moment, and when a serving girl moves timidly forward with a length of crimson material, he snatches it from her and then offers it to the god.

"I did not ask for this," Aron says, and he sounds pissy.

"Of course n-not, my Lord of Storms. I was simply anticipating your needs." The prelate bows his head and offers the clothing, and when it's not taken from his hands, he waits a moment longer and then slinks back, handing the robe to a quaking Avalla.

I guess a god doesn't like to be told to put pants on. It's kind of funny, in a surreal sort of way. Of course, knowing that makes me want to peek at his junk. The way he's seated, I can't see anything, but how often does a girl get to see god-dick? If he really is a god. I figure I can't be blamed for being curious, but I don't get up from my spot on the floor to peer.

Even I'm not that dumb.

"As for why you are weak, my Lord of Storms, m-might I offer a suggestion?" The prelate sounds more and more obsequious with every minute that passes. When the god flicks a hand indicating he should continue, the prelate goes on. "The sacred scrolls speak of this. As you know"—his voice begins to tremble again—"in the last Anticipation, the gods that were cast to the mortal world were forced to take an anchor."

Aron of the Cleaver nods slowly. "Anchor. I remember." He pauses and flexes his hand again, as if unused to it...or unused to wearing skin. After a moment, he looks up. "Who is to be my anchor? You?" His lip curls.

The prelate clearly misses Aron's distaste. "If it pleases my lord—"

"It does not."

It goes silent in the room once more. There's a faint smell of urine.

"Shall I choose someone, then?" Aron spits the words as if he is insulted that he has to even ask. "I grow impatient waiting for you to assign me my servant."

The prelate sits up. His bald head is covered in sweat and has a slick sheen in the torchlight. "The anchor must dedicate themselves freely, Lord of Storms."

The god sighs, as if he's the most put-upon person in the world. "Then let a volunteer approach."

The room is utterly quiet.

No one's stepping forward to serve the god. At first I don't blame them—he's kind of an asshole. But as the oppressive silence continues, I wonder how come no one's volunteering at all. Is it that bad a deal? No one's saying what an anchor is.

At all. And that worries me a little. It might just be another fancy word for "sacrifice."

As long seconds slide past and the god's face grows angrier, the storms overhead thunder and crash as if the entire sky is about to fall down on our heads. That's not helping the situation, I imagine. He's not going to get a servant if everyone's too terrified to speak.

"No one?" the god says, and I can practically feel the ice dripping from his voice.

I think of the certain death I have at sunrise. I don't want to die here.

I think of the drums, and the voices I heard back in my apartment. I've been brought here for a reason. Maybe this is it. Aron's terrifying, but I've worked for asshole bosses before.

And what's he going to do to me? Kill me? I'm supposed to die at sunrise anyhow. Maybe this absolute raging dick of a god is the King of Pentacles I'm supposed to meet. Maybe it's because he's the one that can send me home.

I shoot to my feet. "I'll do it."

CHAPTER 7

*T*he room sucks in a collective breath, and I wonder if I've made a mistake.

But I remain standing, unwilling to back down. I've made my choice. If I was brought to this crappy world for a reason, maybe it's right here, sitting in that throne and glaring at me.

The god looks me up and down. "You?"

Arrogant dick. "Me. I might not be a great servant, but it's freely given." I move forward, stepping over the cowering people. It feels a bit like I'm walking right to my death, but I tell myself that's just their fear getting to me. "That's your requirement, right?"

"You wish to serve me in all ways?" The tone of his voice is arrogant, his expression practically a sneer. He also makes it sound as if serving him is going to have layered implications, and I can just guess what some of those layers are by his tone.

'All ways' means *exactly* what I think it means.

I do my best to look unfazed and make a joke. "Does that mean butt stuff? Because I draw the line at butt stuff."

Aron snorts, and it's the first time he's shown any emotion other than disgust. His blade-sharp mismatched eyes narrow on me. I think for a moment that he's going to give me a nasty cutdown like he did the prelate.

Instead, he extends his hand, palm up. Waiting.

I swallow hard and wonder if I'm walking into a trap. There has to be a reason why no one else wanted to do this.

But I'm out of options, so I take a deep breath and walk forward, up the steps, and put my hand in his.

CRACK.

Lightning sizzles. It's like being electrocuted.

Power surges through my body and I'm dimly aware of my choking gasp before I'm flattened to the ground, collapsing at his feet. My jaw smacks against his ankle and I slide down the marble stairs a few steps.

No one comes over to help me.

It takes me a moment. My stunned conscious feels as if the world is collapsing in on itself and there's both pleasure and pain in this moment. It's like I'm being split and remade at a cosmic level, and then pushed back into human form again. Everything hurts.

Then everything refocuses, and the world becomes clear once more.

I don't realize the room is quiet until I hear a low, pleasant voice. Aron. "You are right. That is better."

I turn my head and look over and the god—I don't doubt that's what he is now—flexes his hand again. His color looks a little better than the paper-white shade his skin was before. It's like he's taken on some of my healthy glow.

Okay, maybe no one wanted to hitch their wagon to his because he's a vampire.

I try to get up, but my limbs feel like noodles. I roll onto my side, and then try to push myself up off the floor with my weak arms. Am I drooling? I might be drooling.

"I'm cool," I mutter. "No one help me get up. I've got it."

"Help her sit up," the god says coldly. "I don't like seeing my servant sprawled like that."

People rush over to my side, and arms grab me and haul me to my feet. I wobble unsteadily.

"Get her something to sit on," Aron of the Cleaver demands.

"Shall my throne work, my Lord of Storms—"

The god focuses his cold, angry gaze on the prelate and the man goes silent. "You should not have a throne at all, mortal. This is my temple, is it not?" When the man drops to his knees in supplication, the god looks over at me again. "Get her a cushion. She can sit at my feet."

It's on the tip of my tongue to gripe that he's far *too* kind, but really, a cushion sounds pretty good right now. I'm wiped out by whatever just happened. It's like my body is trying to recalibrate to something and not quite sure how. As I weave on my feet, a servant rushes forward with a fluffy, red pillow with decorative tassels that match the prelate's robes, and then a kind hand touches my arm and leads me over.

Then, I'm seated at the god's feet like I'm his toy. I don't know if this is a step up or not.

What on earth have I signed up for?

"You may continue celebrating my arrival," Aron says in his pompous, ice-cold voice.

Everyone's too afraid to disobey, so the revelry continues.

I kinda admit that I like seeing someone else jump to this dick's commands, because I'm thinking the prelate could stand being knocked down a peg or two and it probably doesn't happen often.

Rich, sumptuous platters of food are brought to the god by pretty female servants, their heads bowed, their naked breasts practically shoved onto the platters like the food's not the only thing up for offer. Another girl appears on the other side of him and offers him a wine goblet, which he takes. The smell of the food makes my mouth water and I realize suddenly that I'm ravenous. My stomach growls and I clutch at it, surprised at the ferocity of my body's response. I've been hungry before, but not like this.

This is new. This is *starving*. Ravenous.

Aron takes a bite out of something, and then discards it with a frown. He sips his wine, and then frowns at that, too.

My stomach growls. No one's offering me shit. All I do is watch Aron take a few small bites and then spit them out like they disgust him.

He notices my stare and turns that strange, mismatched gaze on to the nearest girl. "My anchor requires food as well. Serve her as you would me."

One of the serving girls breaks off and kneels in front of me, offering her tray (and boobies). There are fruits of all kinds, brightly colored vegetables cut into chunks, and dried meats and cheeses of various shapes and sizes. I'm so hungry I could eat all of it, and so I smile and take the entire tray from her.

I take a huge bite of the first thing I see, a slice of cheese. Then bread. Then a leg of meat. It's all *incredible*. I bite back a moan.

Aron gives me a curious look but says nothing.

I gulp down my wine and continue eating, even as I watch the room. I notice Aron doesn't do more than pick at the food, more interested in examining it and flicking it back down on the tray than eating, but I don't care. I cram it all into my mouth and wash it back with cup after cup of wine. I keep waiting to get drunk, but it keeps not happening. That's a shame—getting drunk would be really nice right about now.

I demolish everything in the platter. I wipe my greasy hands on a square of linen handed to me and then nurse another cup of wine while I watch the partygoers. Definitely more subdued and no one's having furtive party sex. I guess Aron's a boner killer. Everyone's too nervous at the sight of Aron of the

Cleaver, and I can't say I blame them. I'm not entirely sure what to think myself.

Seems like the longer I'm in this world, the more fucked up shit gets. I chug my wine and hold my cup out for more, wishing it would make me as sloshed as everyone else in this room. Sometimes it seems like Aron and I are the only ones sober...and that's depressing.

My wine cup is refilled and I drink again. As I do, I scan the room, watching everyone. The prelate has set his chair up across the room—on the floor this time—and I don't miss the fact that it's as far away from Aron as humanly possible. Can't say I blame the guy. Avalla still hovers near him, but uncertainty is in her eyes. Actually, I'm pretty sure uncertainty is in everyone's eyes. No one knows what to do now that the god is here in person. Something tells me they never expected him to actually show.

The soldiers still line the walls, but their expressions are equal parts wary and awe-filled. No one knows how to react. This has all the makings of a party that's about to be over soon.

The thought makes my stomach clench and I look back to the far end of the room, where the blondes are waiting for dawn. There's no reprieve for them, and I see a few trying desperately to be stoic while another has tears shining on her face. Dawn's getting closer and no one gives a crap about these poor women. I have to do something.

I glance up at the god on his throne. He stares ahead, his eyes narrowed, watching the people crowding his temple. I wonder what he finds so fascinating, because to me, they're not all that interesting to watch. He's not eating or drinking, either. He's not even trying. The cup he was offered a while back is still mostly empty and sits on the end of his armrest, and the platter of food being held by a quivering slave is untouched. Huh.

I should say something about the cleaver brides. I can't live with myself if I don't try to save them. I turn to Aron's throne and wait for him to notice me.

Of course, after a minute or two of staring, he continues to ignore me. So much for gods being omniscient. I clear my throat softly, and when that doesn't get me anywhere, I try again, a little louder.

Aron of the Cleaver turns to look over at me and scowls. "Are you sick?"

"Uh, no—"

"Choking?"

He really does make it hard to like him. "I was trying to get your attention."

"By irritating me?" He gestures out at the room of revelers. "Do you think I am not maddened enough by these fools? You have decided to join in?"

I choose to ignore that. "I need a favor."

He swivels back to me, a look on his face that's half amused, half irritated. "You are asking me for a favor? Are you not supposed to serve me?"

"I realize it's a little early in the game," I tell him breezily, deciding that confidence is the best tactic with this asshole. After all, groveling got the prelate nowhere. "But yes, I need something done and you're the only one that these dumbasses will listen to. So I'm asking—"

"Asking," he repeats flatly.

I sigh. "Okay, begging, if that's what you want to hear." I gesture at the cluster of blondes in the back of the room. "But they're going to sacrifice all those women at dawn in your name. As Cleaver Brides."

"And?"

"What do you mean, 'and'?" I stare at him. "You want that to happen?"

"I do not care if it happens or if it does not. Why should I? I am a god. They are mortals. Their life is as fleeting as a speck of dust." He slicks his thumb and forefinger together as if to indicate so. "Why should I bother myself with them?"

"Because they shouldn't have to die to honor you. It's barbaric and stupid. They could honor you in a completely different way."

"Such as how I've been honored on this night?" His mouth flattens.

"Look, I'll be the first to admit that these people are shit at being properly deferential to a guy of your status," I say, deciding to play to his vanity. When he grunts acknowledgment, I go on, "But that's no reason that these women have to die. They didn't have anything to do with it. They're just slaves bought up by some assholes and dragged here as offerings. It's not their fault."

He looks over at me. "You were one of them, yes?"

"I was. I was going to die at dawn."

"And instead, you have chosen to serve me."

"That's right." I don't tell him that I'm having regrets, or that fate might have brought us together. That's too corny even for me.

He watches the women with narrowed eyes. "Some of them are far more lovely and probably more servile than you. Are you telling me I can pick a different anchor?"

"It has to be freely given, remember? I'm the only one that stood up."

"Truth." His mouth twitches, and I can't tell if he's irritated or amused. Possibly both. After a moment of silent contemplation, he looks over at me again. "And why should I help them?"

"Because I'm asking real, real nicely?" I give him my brightest smile. "And we're a team?"

"We are not a 'team,'" Aron of the Cleaver says in that icy cold voice of his. "I am a god and you are my anchor to this world. There is no 'team' involved in any of that."

Sheesh. This guy could give lessons on dickery, he's so good at it. "Okay, then I'm begging you. Please save them. I can't stand the thought of them dying in the morning. I'll do whatever you want."

"But no 'butt stuff' as you call it." His tone is utterly imperious.

Is he teasing? I can't tell. "Other than that, whatever you want," I amend.

"You will do whatever I want anyhow."

"I'll do something extra special, then," I tell him desperately. If blowing an arrogant asshole means I'll save the life of two dozen terrified women, I'll get down on my hands and knees right now. "Just say it and I'll do it."

"You can be silent," he tells me.

Damn it. I open my mouth to protest his rudeness when he arches a brow in my direction. Fuck. Is this a test? I can't tell. Reading this guy is impossible. I close my mouth and slump on my stool, worried. I press my fingers to my mouth, anxious that I've not done enough. Should I have said something earlier? Bargained my "anchoring" to the god in exchange for all of our freedom? What if I've messed up and I have to watch all of them die? I can't take it. I squirm on my cushion, miserable.

I look over at Aron, wondering if I should speak up again. Before I can open my mouth to blurt out another plea, the god raises his hand. "Prelate." He flicks his fingers in that pompous way, indicating someone should trot over to do his bidding.

The prelate gets up from his chair and moves toward the god, his hands clasped in an attempt at piety. Something tells me he's probably feeling a lot less pious at the moment now that he's met Aron the Dickbag. He doesn't get down on his knees right away, and the god stares at him so hard that I can practically feel eyes boring into the prelate's skull.

The prelate clearly isn't used to not being in charge. He's practically bristling at Aron's pompousness and he stands in front of the god, waiting. It feels like a battle of wills, and all the while, the storm overhead crackles and gets more ominous. The pressure change in the air makes my head hurt, and I wince at the battle of wills.

Of course, the prelate is the one to bend first. He gets down on his knees and presses his forehead to the floor again before sitting up. "How may I serve you, Lord of Storms?" His voice is tight and it's clear he doesn't like being at the beck and call.

Aron tilts his head, then holds his wine goblet out to the side, in my direction. Oh. I guess I'm supposed to take it. I do, and as I touch it, a spark snaps at my fingers, conducted through the metal. I bite back a yelp and manage not to drop the cup, but just barely. The god rests his hands on the ends of his throne for a moment before getting to his feet, and then I'm "treated" to a bird's eye view of naked god butt.

CHAPTER 8

I have to admit, it's a pretty good butt.

I guess that's to be expected when you're a god. It's pale as the rest of him, but the globes are perfectly shaped and muscular. Not that I care, because it's attached to a holy pain in the ass. Literally. He puts his hands on his hips and surveys the room. "Who are those maidens in the back that are not allowed to celebrate?"

The prelate's gaze flicks to me and I get a chill down my spine. He knows I'm to blame for this. I lift my chin, unwilling to back down to him. I get a seat on the dais now, after all, and he doesn't. That makes me more important. He can suck it.

Granted, it's a seat at Aron's feet, but it's still a seat above his.

The prelate clears his throat delicately. "Those are offerings to the gods."

He makes it sound so benign that I can't help but speak up. "A bunch of people brought slaves to the temple. He picks the cream of the crop and then the rest are sacrificed at dawn," I pipe in.

Both men turn to glare at me. Sheesh.

Aron of the Cleaver turns back to the prelate, and the

thunder overhead rolls ominously. "Why are they sacrificed to the gods?"

"As an offering of our devotion, of course. It has been that way for many, many centuries, my lord."

Aron crosses his arms over his chest, all pale naked body and stormy anger. "Have the gods ever asked for such a thing?"

The prelate is silent.

"I asked you a question. Have you been commanded by me—or any other—to sacrifice innocents?"

"It is tradition," the prelate says faintly. "Slaves are given as Cleaver Brides every Anticipation—"

"I do not recall it being written in the sacred scrolls. Is it?" His voice is so casual and imperious at once, and I admit I'm hunching my shoulders every time he speaks, just because he sounds so darn mad—and the thunder crackles overhead constantly.

After a moment, the prelate licks his lips. "It is not, my Lord of Storms."

"Is any of this in the sacred scrolls?" Aron flicks his hand at the crowded, trashed temple full of drunk, stuffed partygoers. At that moment, a naked woman squeals and runs from a man in red temple robes. "This carousing?"

I can practically feel the cringe of the prelate. "It is not, my lord. But it is all tradition done in your honor—"

"Then stop," Aron snarls. He whips about and moves back to his chair, and I catch a glimpse of pale, hairless body and he's just as muscular in the chest as he is in the backside...and I notice that he's got large balls and an even bigger cock. Like, huge.

Okay, well, that answers that.

God-cock is apparently very impressive.

Aron flings himself back onto his throne and clamps his hands down on the arms. "This is my temple, is it not? Perhaps you should spend your time obeying my wishes?" His voice is practically a snarl.

The prelate drops his forehead to the floor again. "Of course, Lord of Storms."

The angry god flicks his gaze over to me. I notice one eye is brown and one is green, and I'm frozen underneath that unusual gaze. "What am I a god of, woman?"

Oh shit, is this a trick question? "Cleavers?"

Someone makes a terrified sound.

His eyes narrow.

Pin drop.

I smile brightly even though the air is so heavy and ominous it feels like I'm about to be throttled from afar. "I should probably point out that I'm not from here and so I don't know that answer."

"Battle," the prelate offers in a thin voice. "Battle and thunder."

"That was going to be my second guess," I add. "Don't see what that has to do with sacrificing maidens. You guys would probably be better off holding a duel or a fight or something."

The room gets quiet. The prelate stares at me with hot eyes as if he can't believe that I'm daring to speak. Well, tough luck. Speaking up got me a cushion on the dais, and if that's the only advantage I get, I'm going to use it. I suspect I'll be paying for my "privilege" soon enough.

I should have never brought up the butt stuff.

"My servant is correct," Aron says after a long moment. "You do me no honor with your sacrifice. If you wish to honor me with blood, do so on the field of battle. Release those maidens to go back to their families."

"They are slaves, my Lord—"

"Then keep them and feed them as you would any other temple slave."

"Of course, my Lord." He sounds like he's chewing glass.

One of the women in the back begins to sob loudly, and I can see the irritation spreading over Aron's face. He gestures at the woman, who's weeping as if she's just now realizing she's going to die, except she isn't. "Why does she cry?"

I have to admit I'm as mystified as he is.

The prelate straightens himself, as if finding his spine. "She is dishonoring her master if she is not sacrificed to honor the gods."

As I watch, Aron pinches the bridge of his nose, as if beat down by all of this. "How is it dishonorable if she is serving my temple at my wishes?"

The woman's crying eases and her sniffles turn to surprise, and then she stumbles forward, dropping to her knees a short distance away from Aron's throne. "I only wish to serve, Lord of Storms. However I can, I wish to be of service to the gods."

I actually feel sorry for Aron for a brief moment, because he looks so frustrated with the situation that his jaw clenches and I suspect he's moments away from rolling his eyes. "Serve my temple. And quit crying. The gods do not like tears," he snaps.

All the gods or just this one, I wonder?

The prelate bows and then the other women are dropping to their knees, weeping their thanks. Aron just looks even more annoyed and his hand curls into a fist against one of the arm rests.

He looks like he's about to change his mind, so I pipe up. "I bet all these new servants of the temple will start their work— their devotion," I correct, glancing over at Aron, "to the gods early in the morning. Someone should probably show them where they're sleeping so they can get some rest. It's late."

As in, get them out of here so Aron doesn't lose his shit.

I give the prelate a pointed look but he only glares at me like I'm the jerk for daring to speak up. One of the red-robed priests in the back seems to be smarter, though. He gathers up some of the weeping, prostrating women and begins to usher them down a back hall. The prelate bows to the god and backs away, returning to his chair, and some of the tension in Aron's jaw eases. The low hum of the room picks up again, conversations going once more.

I'm left alone, sitting at the feet of the crankiest, most beautiful man I've ever seen and he looks as if he's sucking lemons. What he did has made the hard knot in my chest ease a little, though. I touch his leg to get his attention and ignore the spark of electricity that shudders through me. "Thank you—"

"Do not thank me," he snaps, cutting me off. "If it did not suit my needs, I would not have spoken up. Do not mistake me for a kind, gentle god. I am not one."

Yeesh. I pull my hand back.

I go back to watching the room, though it seems a lot of people are clearing out now that it's getting closer to dawn. There's a lot of yawning and the food laid out on the tables has long since been demolished, and the smell of it is starting to turn. There are puddles on the marble flooring that tell of spilled wine and I delicately kick aside a crust of bread with my foot and try to hold back my own yawn. What happens now, I wonder. Even though I've stress-eaten through the entire platter, I'm still hungry, and the long day is catching up to me. Now that the spine-clenching fear of death is gone, I'm exhausted. I'm going to live for another day, and even if I have to deal with Aron and his shit, I'll take it.

Of course, it's been one long, never-ending shit storm ever since I got to this place. No wonder I'm tired. I watch as people glance uneasily in Aron's direction and sneak out however they can. No one knows what to do around the god. I can't blame them. He's not exactly shown himself to be a cuddly, kind-hearted sort.

Bet they're regretting this whole "Anticipation" thing now.

I glance up at Aron, but if he notices people are sliding away and leaving, he's not showing it. He continues to stare stonily ahead, watching the dwindling crowd, and his expression is the same unpleasant one it always is.

It strikes me that maybe he doesn't know what he's supposed to do now. If this is his first time being among people, maybe he doesn't know that at some point, people go to bed? They don't sit and glare at the crowd like they're insulting him with their presence? And if I'm his servant - his anchor - am I the one that has to break the news to him? Because for every person that slips away, there's another robed one waiting at the fringes of the room, faces a mixture of anticipation and exhaustion. I know how that feels.

I look around for the prelate, because maybe it's time to be mouthy and speak up about getting Aron a room for the night so everyone can get some sleep. Of course, that might mean I'll have to "serve" Aron in ways I'd prefer not to, but I'm so tired that I'm willing to just get it over with at this point.

The prelate's chair is empty, Avalla half-asleep and leaning against the side of it. Did he slip out, too? I scan the room, looking for the bald head in the red robes and find him in a shadowy corner. A chill skitters up my spine as I see that he's talking to a familiar, pear-headed soldier. My old owner. Sinon.

Both are looking in this direction and talking, and they're wearing unpleasant expressions. As I watch, Sinon fingers his sword pommel thoughtfully.

I have a bad feeling about that. The prelate looks just as unpleasant, and I suspect they're not happy with the god they got. Maybe they should have worshipped a nature god instead of a war one.

Their intense conversation continues, and they keep looking over at Aron. I know no one's a huge fan of the guy right now, but the way they're talking makes my skin prickle. I think we need to break that up, just in case. I glance up at Aron on his throne and notice that his eyes are a little glassy, his lids heavy. He looks tired.

Does he not know he doesn't have to stay in his throne all night?

Hesitantly, I touch his leg again. This time, I'm prepared for the shock that ripples down my hand as I graze his skin. "Should I ask the prelate to prepare a chamber for you?"

The god's gaze flicks down to me. "Why?"

"So you can sleep? Rest? Relax?"

"Sleep," he repeats, and I don't know if he's considering the suggestion or trying to figure out what it means. "Very well. Go and retrieve the prelate and tell him I wish for a chamber."

I get to my feet and dust off the bottom of my too-short minidress-slash-skirt. I have to admit I want to hear what they're saying. I cross the room and take my way winding through the crowd that remains.

I sidle up to the two men engaged in furious conversation in the corner of the room. They haven't noticed I'm approaching, and so I move ever so silently closer, trying to stealth in on their chat.

"It should be obvious which one he is," the prelate is murmuring. "The question is, what do we do about it?"

"What we have to," the soldier—my old owner—says. "If she can't be controlled, and he can't be swayed, Aventine might be better off..."

I accidentally kick a half-eaten piece of fruit that squelches against my foot as I move forward, and both men look over at me. Shit. I smile brightly, putting on my most vapid expression so they won't see the fear pounding in my heart. I don't understand most of their conversation, but I'm pretty sure it's not good news. "Hi. The god is ready to go to sleep for the night. Is there a room prepared for him?" And just because I can't help but be a little catty toward these two jerks, I add, "Something appropriate for his amazing godhood, of course."

Both men exchange a look. Neither one moves from their shadowy corner. "My rooms are the finest in this temple," the prelate says after a moment. "I can have them readied for him. And you? What do you require?"

They stare at me so hard that I feel like I'm on the spot. I get the sense that this question is loaded. "Like...sleep-wise? I'm pretty sure he wants me to sleep with him. In his room," I add because that might sound a little slutty. Truth be told, I thought I'd be getting into this gig and doing that sort of thing to save my hide, but so far Aron of the Cleaver has shown zero interest in my person. It's kind of a relief...if only he wasn't so insulting about it.

"Sleep-wise or anything else," the prelate says. "Do you require money? Wealth? Jewelry? Do you like pretty things?" He smiles creepily.

At first, I'm insulted. Is he asking if I like shiny objects because I'm a fucking girl? Then I realize there's a far more sinister aspect to this. I'm being bribed. At some point, because I'm now attached to that sparking, pale asshole of a god, I've become important. I can switch allegiances and go with these guys and whatever nefarious shit they have planned. I can help them take out Aron—because I have no doubt in my mind that this is the ultimate plan to take back control—and ask whatever I want in money or prizes. I can ask for all the slaves in the city to be freed. I can ask for anything and everything.

All I have to do is work with these two.

I consider it for a brief, shining moment. Aron hasn't won any love from me. Guy's an enormous dick and loves to make me feel small on a regular basis, and I've only known him for a few hours. I don't have anything in this world and these two are offering me safety and security...sort of.

But then I think of how Aron saved the lives of all the blonde slaves. Maybe there's something under that asshole exterior after all. I've been brought here for a reason, and Aron's that reason—I think. I can't betray him. Not when he saved me, too. He could have looked me up and down like the prelate did, sneered at me, and picked a different blonde. Instead, he tied himself to me and me to him.

I might be a lot of things, but I'm not a traitor. "I'm good, thanks."

Their expressions grow cold. Shuttered. The prelate nods. "So be it. I will have my slaves prepare the chambers for the Lord of Storms."

"Spiffy. I'll tell him." I keep the bright smile on my face though everything in me is screaming to run away. This feels... wrong. I can't quite shake the feeling that these two are going to try something, and I need to be aware of it.

Aron does, too.

CHAPTER 9

A short time later, Aron and I are led down the winding stone halls of the temple. They descend into the earth and I'm reminded of the pyramids back home, but we only go down a few floors, where the stones are cooler and overall the humid heat from above is nonexistent. The temperature change makes the place pleasant for all that it's endless carved stone and torchlit halls. At the end of one of the long hallways, double doors are opened and we're led into a sumptuous, enormous chamber. There are more torches along the walls, so the room is a little smoky, and straw is scattered over the stone floors, which seems like a fire hazard to me.

There's a large circular bed in the center of the room, ornate draperies hanging above it like a headboard. Anchored on one wall is a massive ornate axe, the symbol of Aron himself. The bed looks big enough for four people. This is a nice room...but I can't shake the feeling that we're not safe.

The prelate's nowhere around, though. There are serving girls, all dressed in the short linen skirt and nothing else, and they bow and simper and wait for Aron to address them.

He stands in the room and it's clear he doesn't know what to do next. Poor guy's pretty lost. I suspect this is all very new to him. I also think he wouldn't want them to see how he doesn't have basic knowledge of things like sleep or clothing. So I step forward and gesture at the serving girls. "You can all leave now."

They look surprised and hesitate. A few of them glance over at Aron, as if waiting to see if he contradicts me.

The god gives them his best imperious look. "Did you not hear my anchor?"

"Of course, my lord," one murmurs breathlessly and then they're all bent over, bowing and scuttling from the room like frightened crabs.

I wait patiently until they're gone, and then I shut the heavy wooden doors to the room behind us. After that, I move around the room, pulling up wall hangings and looking for secret passages. I find one behind an ornate tapestry in front of a statue, and push the statue back against the door there so no one can get in. And then I shove one of the heavy wooden chests against it, barricading us in. That done, I look over at Aron.

He stands in the middle of the room, watching me with a curious look on his face. Still naked. I realize a moment later I've more or less locked myself into a room with a naked man who can do anything he wants to me. God, I'm dumb. I hope he'll realize now is not the time to get freaky, though. "We need to talk."

"I thought we came to this room to sleep. Is that not what humans do?" Incredibly, he manages to sound as imperious in private as he does in public.

"You and I need to get some basic groundwork established so we can work together as a team—"

"We are still not a team," he snarls at me, and I can hear distant thunder rumble overhead.

"Fine, whatever," I exclaim. God, he's still pissypants even in private. What the hell? But that doesn't mean I can't work around this. I have to because I can't shake the feeling that the prelate is up to something bad. But I need to know more about Aron for starters so I know what I'm working with. "Can I ask you a few questions? I just want to know a bit more about this you and me thing." I gesture between the two of us. "I'm not used to being an anchor or whatever it is I'm called. I'm not entirely clear on what that means."

"You had to clear everyone out of this room so you could ask me what an anchor is?" He crosses his arms over his chest, stance arrogant as if he's not buck naked in front of me. It takes everything I have to maintain eye contact, because every time he moves, the jiggle of his hog is distracting.

"No, I cleared everyone out of the room to protect us. The less they know about you and me, the better. They're probably spying for the prelate."

He grunts. "I would be surprised if they are not."

"So let's pretend I'm new here. What does an anchor do? Something tells me it's more than just fetching your slippers."

The god's eyes narrow at me. "How can you not know?"

"Do you not know either?"

His mouth thins into a firm line and he's silent. "There are some things I seem to have forgotten."

"Well, shit." It's the blind leading the blind around here. I can't blame him, though. It sounds like there's a lot that's new to him and he wasn't the one that came up with the whole "anchor" thing. It's obvious that the prelate knows what's going on, but I'm also pretty damn sure he's the last person we want to admit a vulnerability to. "Okay, first things first, we need to find someone that will tell us what we need to know. Is there any place you can think of where they'd be loyal to you and open to telling the truth?"

His ice-pale eyes narrow and he looks furious. "Loyalty? This is my temple. Why would they not be loyal to me?"

I move closer to him because he's getting loud. "Look, just between you and me, the prelate? That expression on his face was not loyalty. You embarrassed him in front of his people. He doesn't know what to do with you, and I worry it's going to be something bad. He doesn't like you. I think he only obeyed you because it was in public."

"I am a god." His eyes blaze with anger.

"I thought you were mortal? Or an Aspect, right? That's what it is." I snap my fingers. "Do you have all your powers as an Aspect?"

His jaw clenches and he glares fire at me.

"*Any* of them?"

"Mortal," he says in a warning tone.

I raise my hands in the air, determined not to get frustrated. "I'm asking because I need to know what we're working with. You're a storm god, can you call down thunderstorms and shoot lightning at people? If you can, then all my worrying is for nothing." And really, I'd feel better knowing he's got massive loads of power and is just choosing restraint and pissy attitude to keep people in line.

Aron's jaw clenches, the scar on the left side of his face flexing. "I..." He shifts on his feet and then gives me his fiercest scowl. "I do not think I can."

My spirits plummet. I suspect he's just as wimpy as me in this form, with only a cool thunder soundtrack to make him seem impressive. "Can I ask why you were booted out of heaven?"

"The Aether," he corrects.

Apparently he knows that much. "Okay, the Aether. How come you were kicked out of it?"

His mouth flattens. "The High Father was not pleased with how I handled my duties. I am being punished." He says the words as if they taste badly.

"But there's a way to get back, right? If there's a way for you to get home, there's a way for me to get home, too." He doesn't answer me, and I wonder if he knows any of this. "Okay," I mutter to myself, twisting my hands as I think. "Okay, as long as we know our limits, we'll work with it. I gather you don't know much about sleeping, either. Or eating or drinking. Are you hungry? Thirsty?"

He shakes his head.

Well, that makes one of us. Despite the fact that I pigged out in the main hall, I could still eat. Probably stress related, I suspect. I ignore it for now. "Have you ever been mortal before—"

The look in his eyes flares like I've given him a grave insult. "I am not mortal. I am an Aspect."

"Okay." I clasp my hands together, because I'm being patient, I really am. "Narrow down for me the difference between an Aspect and a mortal."

Aron glares at me. "I owe you no explanation."

Probably because he doesn't know himself. "You're right, you don't. But it would really, really help me out if you told me, because I'm flying blind here."

He narrows his eyes. "I am a god. That has not changed. I am just…a god who has been stripped of his powers and forced to walk the mortal plane with you at my side." Again, he says it like he's spitting nails.

So flattering. "Is this your first time being an Aspect? The way they talked about it in the temple, this holiday's a recurring thing. The Anticipation. I assume it's happened before."

"It has happened before," he says slowly, gazing around the room. "But not to me."

Oh. "Think it's happened to anyone else at the same time? Right now? Should we try praying to the other gods and asking to get you home?"

The look he gives me is withering. "You think I am the only disobedient god?" He snorts with amusement.

All right. So Aron's a bad boy and all the other bad boys and girls have also been kicked from the heavens? Got it. "Can we find some other gods and have a chat with them?" He gives me a dirty look that's so irritated I go silent. Jeez, what did I say? "All right then, meeting up with other gods is out." Maybe they're the gods that booted him out of the heavens and that's why he doesn't want to find anyone else. "It's just us, then. We'll figure things out as we go."

Doesn't seem like Aron's going to get me home anytime soon if he doesn't know anything about what's going on. All right, then. This will just be a long haul. Fighting back disappointment, I consider our surroundings. The room's opulent, but I don't see anything we can use to defend ourselves if someone attacks, and that worries me. Even the food tray doesn't have a knife on it. I rub my brows, tired. It has been the longest of days. "So is it okay if I turn in?"

"Turn in?"

"For sleeping?"

"Ah, sleeping." Aron nods slowly. "This is where mortals lie in bed and close their eyes for long periods of time. I always wondered about that."

I'm starting to wonder if the transfer to being mortal—excuse me, an *Aspect*—scrambled his brains. "Yes. They sleep. The brain goes quiet and your body refreshes itself. Everyone has to do it."

"What if I do not want to?" The arrogance returns to his voice.

"It's sort of a requirement for humans, like breathing and eating and drinking." I pause, because he hasn't done the eating and drinking thing. "You sure you're not hungry?"

"I am certain." He looks around and then nudges one of the thick rugs on the floor with a bare, pale toe. "Do I sleep here?"

Dear god, he is helpless. "How about the bed, champ?" I even point at it, because I'm a nice person.

Aron grunts and then moves toward it. He places a hand on one corner and pushes on it, testing. How did this man know to sit in a throne but doesn't know how to use a bed? Maybe the gods have chairs but not beds, then. Wonder what else the gods don't have.

A sense of humor, I mentally tell myself as I watch Aron scowl at nothing in particular. He gingerly sits down on the bed and then lies back, and then frowns up at the ceiling. "How long does it take to refresh yourself?"

"Longer than two seconds," I say dryly. Impatient much? I consider the room and there are some nice rugs on the floor but not really any place for me to sleep. The bed that Aron's in is big enough for me, too, but I don't want him to get the wrong idea.

Floor it is.

I look for extra blankets and pillows. The only ones are on the bed and I think about asking Aron if he minds...then I realize he probably will. So I'm just not going to ask. I move to the opposite side of the bed and grab the least offensive pillow, but when I tug on a blanket, it nudges his shoulder and he opens his eyes and glares at me.

Fine then, no blanket. I grab my pillow and move to the floor, sinking onto the rug. It's made from some sort of furry animal and I really hope I'm not going to get fleas. I'm exhausted, too. There are a million things I should probably ask Aron about, but maybe it can wait until the morning. I yawn and curl up, holding the pillow against my cheek. Despite the fact that I'm sleeping on the floor, this might be the best sleep I get since I've landed in this hellish place. That'd be nice.

Of course, I don't have my eyes closed for longer than a moment before Aron speaks again. "Female. Female, wake up."

I open my eyes and glare at him. He's propped up on one elbow in the bed. "Two things," I say, lifting two fingers into the air (instead of just the one I want to shoot in his direction).

"One. My name is Faith. Not 'female.' Not 'slave.' Faith. If you don't call me by it, I won't answer. And two, it takes longer to sleep than thirty fucking seconds."

Aron just arches one of those pale brows at me. "If you will not answer to 'female,' then why did you answer me just now?"

I grab my pillow, glare at him, and turn my back. "Goodnight."

"Female—"

"We just talked about this!" I yell without turning around.

His chuckle sounds as dickish as he is. "Faith, then. I do not know how to sleep."

I roll onto my back and look over at him. "What do you mean you don't know?"

"Is there a trick to it? Because I close my eyes and nothing happens. Tell me how to sleep." He regards me from his reclining position on the bed, amidst the luxury of dozens of pillows and all of the blankets.

"Dude, you seriously have to give this time. You close your eyes and wait—"

"I did that—"

"For longer than a few minutes. Your body will eventually get tired and you'll go to sleep. I promise."

He grunts again, the sound pissy and impatient. If I wasn't so tired, I'd probably lecture him on the fact that he's still not wearing any clothing and lying around with your junk hanging out makes your company uncomfortable. No matter how appealingly sexy (despite his paleness and douchey attitude) said junk might be.

But I'm too tired to keep talking to Aron, so I point at him, make a gesture for him to turn around, and then go back to my bed.

That lasts for about five minutes. I'm just about to drift off when Aron speaks again. "This is not like I expected."

His voice is so quiet that it takes me a moment to struggle out of the clutches of sleep and back awake. "Mmm...what?" I rub at my eyes and sit up, because if I don't, I'm going to fall right back asleep again.

Aron gestures at the room. "All of this. You. I knew this would be punishment, but I had no idea..."

"Punishment for what?"

He says nothing.

"You can't just leave that out there," I tell him, annoyed. "What are you being punished for?"

"I do not need to tell you anything, human." His voice is as cold and dripping with arrogance as it ever was. His momentary vulnerability of a few moments ago is gone.

"We're gonna add 'human' to the list of words Faith won't answer to," I tell him, rubbing my eyes again. "'Slave,' 'servant,' 'tart,' and 'human.' Oh, and 'mortal.' That one always sounds particularly insulting out of your lips."

"It is meant to be insulting."

Yeah, I figured. I press my hand to my forehead and look over at Aron. He's lying in bed, staring up at the ceiling, and I realize I've still got all the torches lit. I'm too tired to blow them out—or whatever one does with torches. It's clear Aron's not going to let me sleep just yet, so I stifle my yawn and wait for him to continue. When he doesn't, I decide I'll do the asking for a bit. "Okay, so what's your end game here, Aron?"

"End game?" He looks over at me, his cheek brushing against the blankets on his bed, and for a moment, he looks so beautiful and masculine that it makes my heart ache. Was there ever a guy made so perfect? Sure, he's got the weird two-color eyes—one green and one brown—but I actually find it startlingly attractive. Then there's the perfect body, covered in scars, sure, but still utterly perfect. Even the scar on his face just adds to his sexiness.

Zero flaws in his appearance...but his personality is pretty shit, I remind myself. "Yup. End game. Like, you're a god and you're here on Earth—uh, the mortal plane. What's the plan? What do you need to do to get back home? Do you even want to get back home?" Maybe he chose to leave and I've got this all wrong.

He snorts. "I certainly do not wish to stay here."

"Okay, so you want to go home." I decide I'm going to ignore the insults or we won't get anywhere. "How do we do that?"

"You are my servant. My ears on this earth. My link to this world. Are you not supposed to be the one that knows?"

I sit up and scowl at him. "I'm pretty sure I'm your servant because no one else was beating down your door to volunteer and it was either you or dying, and I'm still not sure I chose correctly."

He snorts again.

"I'm not from here, in case you didn't notice. I'm from a place called Earth, thanks for asking. And it's nothing like this." I gesture at the room, then at him. "I'm just as clueless as you about a lot of stuff, but I know the basics. You know, eating, drinking, sleeping, basic human shit. So if you want to be completely on your own, just say so and I'll leave—"

"You cannot leave. You are bound to me."

"Then work with me, buddy." I want to throw something over at him on the bed but there's nothing but my pillow, and I need that. "I'm happy to help out, because I want to go home, too. We'll get you home and maybe we'll figure out how to get me home." Heck, I figure if anyone knows how to break the time-space continuum and send a girl back to Earth, it'd be a god. "So how do we get you home?"

There's a long pause. "I am not certain."

Well, at least we're getting somewhere other than just insults. "That's all right. You said this happened to other gods, too, right? Did they get back home?"

"Yes."

"So someone knows how to get you there. We just have to find that person."

Aron makes a noise that might be assent, might be annoyance. "I will speak to the prelate in the morning."

I bite my lip and think of the intense conversation the men were having in the shadows. How they tried to get me to "help" them. "Just between you and me, I don't think you should trust him. In fact, I think we should get out of here. Like, as soon as possible."

The god sits up in bed, his long, dark hair spilling around his shoulders. He narrows his eyes at me. "Why?"

"I overheard something." Quickly, I sketch out the details and then add, "I don't trust them not to pull something. I don't like it. They tried to turn me against you."

"A fool's task," he says condescendingly.

I arch an eyebrow. "We've really got to talk about your self-confidence. How do you know they wouldn't turn me?"

"Because they can't."

"Why can't they? For the right price, I think anyone can be bought."

The look he gives me is downright incredulous. "You are my anchor. My servant on this earth—"

I wave a hand as if brushing aside all that. "And I don't know if you've noticed, but you're not the most huggable and loveable of guys. But that's not what I'm talking about. I'm trying to tell you that if they approached me, it stands to reason that they approached other people and we need to be careful."

He stares at me for so long that I almost wonder if he's figured out how to sleep with his eyes open. Maybe we should have a conversation about blinking, too. But then he shakes his head slowly. "No. We will speak to the prelate. This is my temple. Aventine is a city dedicated to my name. It is my kingdom to rule over. I see no reason to leave."

I bite my lip again. Eesh. "See, it's that whole 'your kingdom' thing that the prelate is going to have a problem with. You came in and stole his thunder, no pun intended."

"What is a pun?"

"It'd take too long to explain. Stay with me." I shift on my seat, realizing I've been giving him a *Basic Instinct* flash for the last few minutes. Luckily it doesn't look like Aron is interested in that sort of thing at all. "You swooped in and now he's not top dog. He's not in charge, and he has to basically bow and scrape to you, and I get the impression he's not a bow and scraper. We need to get out of here before he tries something bad—"

"Bad," Aron restates, interrupting. It's a question, I'm pretty sure.

I plunge ahead. "We can maybe get some money and clothes on the sly in the morning. Get some food. We won't tell anyone what we're doing and tomorrow night, maybe we leave this place for somewhere more god-friendly. I'm not sure where that would be, but I bet we can ask around—"

"Silence, human." Aron's voice is almost as angry as his expression. The torches in the room flicker as if a gust of wind just shot through, even though the chamber's sealed. My skin prickles with a hint of alarm.

I'm silent. I might be mouthy, but I'm not stupid.

"We stay here. This is my temple. They would not think to do anything I do not tell them to," Aron tells me arrogantly. "I am a god. I am *their* god. Do you understand?"

I don't know whether to be irritated, frustrated, or full of pity for the guy. I can't shake the bad feeling I've got in my gut, and I keep thinking of the sneaky, evil looks that the prelate and my old owner were sharing. Those were not trustworthy men. But I'm helpless to make Aron listen to me. I'm a stranger here, and I've got nothing to my name except a skirt.

I shrug and lie back down on the blankets. "Can we at least get clothes in the morning?"

"We shall see." He's back to being completely imperious and irritating.

I bite back my groan of irritation and lie back down, punching my pillow and wishing it was Aron's handsome smug face. Arrogant prick.

I really hope for both our sakes that I'm wrong.

CHAPTER 10

I sleep so deeply that when I hear the banging, at first I think it's in my dreams. That the annoying, incessant drumming has invaded my sleep. But then thunder rumbles overhead so loudly that I feel the floor under me shake with the vibration, and I jerk awake, blinking my eyes.

Something pounds at the walls again, and the torches are flickering and sputtering on their last legs, the room dim. I look around and Aron is out of his bed, hands on his hips and staring at the statue and chest I put in front of one portion of the wall. As I watch, it shakes.

I gasp, jumping to my feet. That's the secret door. "Someone's trying to come in."

Aron gestures at the door, annoyed. "Then let them in."

"No," I breathe, rushing to his side. God, the man is still naked. What the hell is wrong with him? "Are you high? Think —why are they trying to beat the door down in the middle of the night? A secret door?"

He frowns, his perfect features creasing. It's clear he has no answer.

"Aron, this isn't good. Please, we need to reinforce the door.

Better yet, we need to get out of here." I tug on his arm, ignoring the shock that jolts through me at the touch and hoping that my frightened expression tells him how serious this is. My heart's hammering with fear and I don't think I've ever been so scared —not even when I landed in this strange place.

The doors shake again, and it sounds like they've got a battering ram of some kind. I suck in a breath and look to Aron. "What do we do?"

The god looks around the room and then his gaze lands on the gigantic, ornamental axe on the wall over the bed. It's mounted to a wood plaque that's just as fussy and ornamental as the axe itself, but that doesn't stop Aron. He climbs the bed with quick, agile grace and pulls the axe from the wall—kind of. More like he pulls the entire thing, plaque and all, down. He frowns as he holds the axe by the handle and shakes it, as if he can dislodge the wood from the axehead, and upon closer inspection, the entire thing seems fake. I don't even think the blades are sharp. When the secret door splinters, though, he just hefts the entire thing to his shoulder and goes to stand in the center of the room.

I wring my hands. "What should I do?"

He points to the far wall. "Stay out of my way."

"Right. I can do that." I race over to the far side of the room, dumping the uneaten food on the floor and clutching the tray to my chest as a shield. I hate that there's nothing useful weapon-wise in this room, but maybe that's deliberate. It's also a big stinking hint that the prelate's up to no good.

The door falls apart and two of the armored soldiers step in, swords in hand. Behind them are four more, and then a familiar face—the pear-shaped meathead of my old owner.

Sinon. That bastard.

"My Lord of Storms," he says, bringing his dagger to his brow and tapping it there in a strange sort of salute. "You are not yourself. Forgive me for what I am about to do."

I suck in a breath. I was right. This is an assassination. I thought this jerk was pious, but it seems that when he has to choose between the prelate and Aron, he's picking the prelate.

"I forgive nothing," Aron says in a cold voice, lifting the axe from his shoulder and swinging it slowly, testing the unbalanced heft of it. "That is another god entirely."

My owner nods. "Men," he says, lowering his dagger. "Get her."

Wait, what? *Get me?*

I let out a terrified squeak as the men try to rush past Aron and move to me. With a roar of outrage, Aron swings the axe—plaque and all—over his head as if it weighs nothing. It moves in a wide circle and then slams into one of the soldiers, knocking him into his buddy. Just like that, two men are down.

Of course, the other four are still coming for me. Frantic, I race across the room, heading for Aron's bed. One of the men tries to grab me and ends up snatching the end of my skirt, and then the fabric rips from my body, knocking me off balance. I slam into the bed, face first.

Somewhere above me, there's a furious roar. Weapons clang and the bed shakes. I roll onto my back, scooting backward even as Aron wades into the men attacking me, swinging the decorative axe like the world's biggest club. His eyes blaze with unholy light and thunder rages above like it's his own personal battle soundtrack. One man is flung aside with such force that he slams into the opposite wall, cracking the stone. Another flies over Aron's head and soars through the air, landing with a crunch. As another reaches for me, sword in hand, the gigantic decorative battleaxe swings over Aron's head and whirls through the air, then smashes into him, knocking him flat before he can reach me.

It's both poetic and brutal how quickly and efficiently Aron works his way through the men. I watch one go down and another pick himself up, flinging his weight at Aron with a cry.

The god smiles, baring his teeth, and it's almost like he's enjoying this little assassination attempt.

Something wrenches my head backward and hot pain shoots through my scalp. I scream, clutching at my hair, and find that someone else's hand is there. My owner. His face looms over mine and he brings the dagger closer to my throat.

In the space between one breath and the next, something big and shiny launches through the air. He's knocked backward and my hair feels as if it's ripping out of my scalp. I nearly black out at the intense pain, moaning. I cringe, waiting for the knife to cut my throat, but there's nothing.

After a moment, I sit up, clutching at my burning scalp. Aron stands, shoulders heaving, his pale skin gleaming with sweat. His hands are empty and covered in red spatters, and as I get to my feet, I see that the men on the floor are scattered and lying in pools of blood. I turn and see my old owner, the knife flung to the floor near his hand. His other still has a handful of my blonde hair in his fingers. There's a big sloppy mess where his face used to be, thanks to the gigantic axe that's even now sliding off of his front.

And Aron just smiles, happy for the first time since I've met him.

I feel sick. "Well," I manage faintly. "This is a bad time to say I told you so, but…I told you so."

"This makes no sense."

"No shit." I rub my head, wanting to cry with the pain of it, but crying won't do any good. Aron's not exactly the most sympathetic of audiences.

"This is my temple. These are my people. They worship *me*. Why would they try to kill me?" Aron's pale brows furrow and his scar seems that much darker against his skin. "Are they mad?"

"Or they know something we don't. Also, spoiler, it wasn't

you they came after. It was me." I jab a thumb into my chest. "So you want to tell me the reason behind that?"

He stares at me for a long moment and I expect one of his snippy comebacks. But then he just shakes his head. "I do not know. I understand none of this."

I press a trembling hand to my forehead and find it wet with blood. God. I just want to cry. Cry and then race to the nearest clinic where they can stitch me up and give me something to calm my nerves before I have a nervous breakdown. Someone sent a murder squad for me. Not the god I'm serving.

Me.

And he's no help in the slightest because he doesn't know anything. I can't blame him for that, but at the same time, I feel helpless in the face of everything that's happening. "Do you believe me when I say we can't stay here?" I ask him again. "Because someone's going to come looking for these men. And while you're a badass with that axe, if they send twice as many after us next time, you might not be able to stop them before they kill me."

I wait for him to say something shitty about how it doesn't matter if I die because he's the important one, but he only gazes at me thoughtfully and then nods. "Where should we go?"

"I don't know. I don't know anything about this place. I told you, I'm not from here."

"Then let us go to your land."

"I wish we could, believe me." I rub my bare arms, covered in goosebumps. "As for where we should go, we'll figure it out on the road. Maybe other temples aren't full of assholes. Maybe we can find a nice innkeeper or someone that has answers. I don't know. All I do know is that staying here is basically asking to be murdered in our sleep."

"I didn't sleep," Aron says absently. "I still couldn't."

"We'll add that to our growing list of problems," I tell him, trying to keep the crankiness out of my voice. I'm scared, tired, and hurting. Of course, that's been the norm ever since I arrived here, so it shouldn't freak me out as bad as it has. But someone just tried to murder me tonight. Me, not the god who showed up uninvited.

There's something about this whole "anchor" thing that no one's telling me, I suspect, and I don't trust the prelate or anyone else in this stupid temple to give us the right answers. For now, we have to leave and go somewhere where they might help us, and it's not here.

"Grab some shoes and some clothes, Aron," I tell the god as I kneel beside my old owner and begin to search his pockets. I find a pouch with a few coins in it attached to his belt and a holstered dagger, and grab them both. Then, I decide to take his belt because his seems way handier than mine. Actually, they all have better clothes than I do. I glance around at the dead bodies. It's awful to think of stripping the dead, but me in slave gear is going to draw attention to us, and it's freaking cold and has no pockets. I check the next body, but his tunic is covered in gore. There has to be one that isn't completely gross.

"What are you doing?" Aron asks, his tone imperious once more. "Robbing the dead?"

"No, I'm robbing the assholes that tried to murder us." I glance up at him even as I slide a few more coins into my pouch. "Or how far do you think we're going to get without money in this city? In any city?"

He frowns at me, crossing his arms over his chest. "I am a god. I have no need of coin."

"See, that's where you're wrong on both accounts," I tell him, and move to the next body. Success. This guy's neck looks like it was broken instead of blood everywhere. Yay. I grab one arm and then try to push him onto his stomach. "Help me with this."

Aron reaches over and helps me turn the guy. A moment later, I've got his long, red cloak freed and I'm working on dragging his tunic over his limp body.

"What do you mean, I am wrong?" Aron asks. "That I am not a god?"

"You know you are. I know you are. But to be honest, it's better for everyone if no one else thinks you are. I mean, what if these people have been 'Anticipating' your return so they can murder you and take your place? How do we know that's not the trick?"

He's silent.

I look up at him and there's a faint frown on Aron's face. I kind of feel like I just explained to someone that Santa isn't real, but we've got no other choice right now. "So what do we do?" Aron asks finally.

"We go incognito. Try to get some answers. And once we know what is going on, we figure out how to send you home, and send me home." I grab a scabbard and hold it out to Aron. "So we need weapons. And clothes. And shoes. And we need to hurry before someone else returns and sees that we've killed the welcoming party."

I expect Aron to protest, but he picks up a handful of the cloak and studies it thoughtfully. "Show me how to wear clothing, then."

A short time later, both Aron and I are both dressed in tunics stolen from the guards, belts with weapons, cloaks, and the strange, leather boots that lace up the side of the ankle. I've taken the allegiance tags from the guards and pocketed them. I'm holding onto the money, too, because I don't trust Aron to remember how important something like that is. I just wish I knew how much we had, but the coins here don't look like anything I can tie back to specific dollar amounts.

I'm pretty much the worst anchor he could have picked, ever. But we share a common goal at least—getting home.

It'll have to be enough for now.

"I do not like this," Aron tells me as we slip out of the secret passageway, clutching our weapons. He's got a sword and I'm holding a dagger in tight, sweaty fingers.

"Me either, buddy," I tell him. "Me either."

God, I really, really want to go home.

CHAPTER 11

*T*he moon is an unpleasant, bright red and huge in the sky over the night. I'm so tired that I don't want to do anything but crawl into the nearest bed and go to sleep, but I know we can't do that. I'm tempted to find a stable and a friendly horse that won't mind sharing his stall, but something tells me we'd be smart to get off this little island and out of Aventine entirely.

Aron doesn't say much—thank goodness—as we race out of the temple grounds and head for the docks. They're surprisingly not hard to find. Stragglers from the big festival are still along a wide, cobbled, torchlit path and so we follow them as they head to the ferry.

The ferryman's wearing soldier garb just like us and nods as we approach. It's too dark for him to see under our hoods, but I feel my heart pounding anyhow. He ushers us on and doesn't ask for money, and then it's that simple to get away from the temple itself. The ferry waits a few minutes for the last few stragglers, and then pushes off from the shore, the guards poling the flat boat across the moonlit waters.

I lean in close to Aron. "From this point on, your name is Grover."

Even though it's dark and he's hooded, I can still see a frown on his pale jaw. "That is a stupid name. Why?"

"Because no one's going to think a guy named Grover is a god," I whisper.

He grunts. "Do I not look godlike as it is?"

He does, but that can be explained away. "We'll just tell them you're a devotee. Just do your best not to touch anyone," I say, thinking of the electric shock that happens every time his hand brushes against my arm. "And keep your hood down. And actually, just stay quiet the entire time please."

That's probably best.

"Do not tell me what to do," he begins in an imperious tone.

I poke him in the chest to shut him up and jump at the spark that crackles between us. "Do you really want to go there right now, Grover?" I emphasize the fake name to remind him that we're undercover.

The god goes silent.

I turn to stare at the waters, trying to figure out our next move. Where's the best place to blend in this hellish medieval city? Where would one go to get information? I mean, it's clearly not a temple—

"What of you?" Aron leans so close to my hood that goosebumps prickle up and down my arms.

I look over at him in surprise, and our faces are mere inches away from each other. Another ripple of awareness flashes through me and I remember that I'm supposed to be his slave. Serve him in all ways. "What of me what?"

"What is your name? What are you called?"

Oh. I guess I should be insulted that he's never thought to ask until this point. Maybe I've got super-low expectations when it comes to Aron, because I'm kind of flattered he actually asked. "I told you before. My name is Faith."

"You told me before, but I did not care before." When I scowl at him, he arches that scarred brow at me. "Faith does not sound like a regular name. What is next? Door? Boat?"

"Okay, okay. Let's just focus on the task at hand, all right?" I tell him tightly, and turn back to glaring out at the water.

When the boat pulls up against the dock, people begin to peel away. We get off after them, Aron keeping close to me. I don't know where to go at this point, so I pick someone that's stumbling around and just follow him as he heads into the city itself. At night, it's a lot quieter. The narrow streets seem a little wider and less mucky, and you can't see how run-down some of the buildings are or how they all cluster together like they've fallen atop one another. Somewhere in the distance, a horse whinnies and another animal—a pig—snorts and grunts. I chew my lip, thinking.

"Where are we going?" Aron leans in and asks me, and I feel another shockwave go down my arm as he brushes against me. Overhead, thunder begins to rumble, a sign that Aron's mood is turning south. That's not good—he needs to keep that shit under wraps or he's for sure going to give us away.

As we turn down another narrow street, I hear the sound of laughter and someone shouting, and I see a distant wooden sign hanging over a building with light spilling out of it. As we get closer, I see the picture's one of a goblet. A few horses are tethered outside. Oh. An inn? That might be perfect. "We're going there," I tell him. Before he can say anything else, I point at the sky. "Might wanna get control of that or we're not going to be hiding for very long, if you catch my drift."

"As if I control that?" he states haughtily.

"Well it isn't me doing it, so you'd better fucking try," I snap at him. I know I'm being pissy, but I'm exhausted, scared, and I've had a chunk of my head ripped out tonight, all because of him. I'm tired of his shit.

He reels in surprise, and I realize he's probably never had

anyone talk back to him ever before. Well, there's a first time for everything, I suppose. I don't even regret it. I'm a little terrified that he'll pull out that sword and kill me, but then at least I'd get some rest.

The thunder stops, and we glare at each other for a moment. "That's better," I tell Aron.

His eyes narrow and he just stares at me. Slowly, he shakes his head. "You are not afraid of me at all, are you?"

I get goosebumps at that, wondering if this is the set-up for being eradicated by a god's temper. Being a pain in the ass has got me this far, however, so I lift my chin. "Should I be?"

"I don't know if I am amused or annoyed. I want to wring your neck and laugh at the same time. It is very curious."

"Well, you didn't ask for obedient volunteers, just volunteers," I say, and I jump when he barks a laugh. It's booming and almost as loud as the thunder. Still, I can't find it in me to tell him to quiet down. I like his laughter.

We could both use a laugh after the night we've had and I'd rather have a laughing storm god than a murdering one.

I pat his shoulder. "I'm sorry your prelate tried to kill you."

He grunts.

"Okay, we're going to go into the inn." I point at the sign. "I'll ask around and see what kind of answers I can get. You just... blend." I wave a hand at him.

He lowers his hood and arches a brow at me. "Blend?"

Right. He's about one skin tone away from being albino, has the same scar the god does, and strange bi-colored eyes. Oh, and he's unearthly handsome. "Hood up," I say brightly. "Sit in the back of the room and try not to talk to anyone. Keep a low profile."

"I should be the one asking questions while you blend. You look like all these other wenches."

Prince Charming, he's definitely not. I reach out and pull his hood back over his white-blond, flowing hair. "Something tells me that'd be a bad idea. Plus, I think we'll get further if someone's not tossing around words like 'wenches' and 'neck-wringing.' Just let me handle the talking, okay? Like you said, I look like everyone else. No one's going to notice another woman around here but everyone's going to notice you."

Aron grunts. "Let us go, then."

The door to the inn is made of more of the wrought metal, and light spills out in patterns onto the ground. We open the door and head inside, and immediately more music and the laughter of people surrounds us. Did I worry about thunder outside? I doubt these people can hear past their own voices. There's a cluster of small tables scattered around the packed room, and the place reeks of sour wine and sweat. Lovely.

Aron behaves, which is a relief. He ducks his head and moves to the back of the tavern, winding through the tables and heading for an empty one in the corner, by the fire. I watch him go and the crowd barely seems to notice him. He's just another man in soldier's clothing in a city full of the military. Works for me. I head to the bar and move to the counter, smiling at the woman behind it.

"Order something or move on," she tells me in a bored, tired voice. "Food's served here, drinks at a table. If you aren't buying, then head on back out—"

My stomach growls at the mention of food and I grab my pouch. "I'll have food and a drink, if that's all right."

That gets the waitress's attention. She pauses from swiping down the counter with a wet rag and looks over at me. Maybe it's something in my tone, but she looks suspicious. "Two crowns."

I pull my change out and start picking through it, looking for coins with crowns on them. I find two and offer them to her, but her lip curls. "You're not from here, are you?"

Right. I'm already fucking this up. I put the money on the bar and then pat the coins, and pull out the stolen tag that shows my Aventinian allegiance so I don't get sold into slavery again. I avoid her question and change tactics. "How about we do things this way. I'll give you any five coins you want, and you can give me some food and some answers about this place. Sound good?"

The girl leans over the bar and immediately grabs five of the smallest coins, dropping them into her bodice with a look at the man at the far end of the bar.

I slide the coins into my pouch again, mentally making a note that the tiny coins are the ones that are the biggest amounts. "Thank you."

A second later, I'm given a pottery bowl with veggies, shredded meat, and a hunk of bread. A goblet of the sour-smelling wine is set down next to it, and the waitress crosses her arms, looking at me expectantly. "What do you want to know?"

My mouth waters at the sight of the food and drink. It's impossible that I'm hungry again, because I ate like a pig a short time ago, but I could eat. I sop the bread in the juices from the meat and take a big mouthful. Heaven. "This is so good. Thank you."

Her impatient expression eases a little. "Long day, eh?"

Oh my god, she has no idea. "The longest." I take another bite and glance back at the corner, but Aron's just sitting, arms crossed and hunched over the table. So far so good. "So uh, if I need to leave the city tonight, what's the best way to do so?"

She picks up her bar rag again and shrugs. "You've got two options. Docks or south gate."

Ah. I consider this even as I shovel food into my mouth. We don't have a boat, and I don't know anything about sailing, so the docks are out. "So the south gate, then. That's the safest place to go?"

"Only place to go," she corrects. "All the other gates are

controlled by the army. South gate's the only way in or out of Aventine."

I nod thoughtfully and take a gulp of wine. It's strong enough to make a shiver go through me, but I drink it anyhow. "What's there?"

"Past the Dirtlands, you mean?"

Dirtlands. Interesting. That explains the fine grit that seems to catch the wind constantly. "Yeah, past the Dirtlands."

The woman eyes me skeptically for a moment and then swipes at the bar. "Not much out there but a few temples and outposts. It's a long, long road to Katharn."

She assumes I know where Katharn is. Or what it is. But a long, deserted road with only a few temples and outposts sounds better than staying here. It's a start, and I can work with that. "So tell me more about—"

There's a crash at the back of the room at the same time thunder crackles overhead. My head shoots with sudden pain. Oh shit. That'd be Aron. I grab my coin bag, shove my last bite of food into my mouth longingly, and then race to the back of the inn, where Aron has a man by the collar and pinned to a wall.

I can't leave the guy alone for five minutes.

"Hey Grover," I hiss as I move to his side, crossing the crowded room that's now completely focused on him. "Can we not?" His hood is slipping off of his head and I hitch it back over him before it falls back and exposes his pale skin and jet black hair.

He turns and glares at me. "This mewling mortal wanted my table—"

"This nice man," I correct, peeling Aron's fingers from the shocked man's clothing. I ignore the sparks that touching him sends through me. Maybe if I ignore it, this other guy will too, since he's bound to feel it as well. "Can have this table since we're leaving."

"We are?" Aron frowns at me, and it's visible even through the depths of his hood. "We just got here."

"We got what we needed," I tell him and pull him away from the man. The "mortal" staggers, staring at us with more than a little fear. I brush my finger over my lips, indicating silence, and shake my head. "Let's get out of here and no one gets hurt."

Aron makes a huffy sound but allows me to drag him out, and the thunder gets quiet once more as we emerge into the night. "These people have no respect—" he begins.

"That guy was probably drunk," I interrupt. "And again, we're working on keeping a low profile. We just need to let that go and move on." At Aron's indignant sound, I'm guessing that "moving on" and "letting shit go" aren't high on the priority list for a god of battle and storms. I might be over my head here. "I found out where we need to go next," I tell him to distract him. "The next big city is called Katharn and it's down the path once we get out of here."

I don't point out that it sounds way, way down the path. It's all going to be the same to a god, I suspect.

"Katharn. Yes. I know this name."

I look over at him, surprised. "You do?"

He nods even as we head through the dark, twisting alleys of the nighttime city. "Indeed. That is a city claimed by no gods, but if one is there, I will force their priests to welcome me."

"Forcing priests to welcome him" sounds a bit like we're going to end up in the same situation we are right now—on the run for our lives. But maybe he's right. Maybe someone else is having a better experience with this whole "Anticipation" thing, because it sounds like a bunch of gods were dropped out of the heavens. "Great. So we just need to head in that direction. The girl at the tavern said there's a couple of small temples along the way. We can avoid them if we need to and just do our best to hide out."

Aron says nothing. I'm not sure if he agrees with my plan,

but he's not offering one of his own, so that's as close to agreement as I suspect we're going to get. We hurry through the muddy streets, and the air feels heavy with humidity, as if warning me that Aron's just barely keeping his shit together.

I guess I can't blame him. We're sneaking out of the city like a couple of thieves and I suspect he expected to be greeted with naked dancing girls and riches since he was a god. He was, but not the way he wanted. Instead, he got me—a salty Earth woman who has no time for his bullshit, and a midnight run out of Dodge. Definitely not what he expected.

I don't know the layout of the city, but I keep us heading toward the long city wall that encircles the place. I vaguely remember this gate from days ago, and when I see the large, guarded portcullis, I breathe a sigh of relief. Almost there.

It looks the same as it did when I first saw it, the walls tall and made of smooth river stone mortared together. The portcullis is another iron gate, this one big enough to let two elephants through, side by side. Two guards stand on each side of the gate. Four people. Not a problem.

"That's the south gate," I tell Aron unnecessarily. "That's the way out of the city. From there, it leads through the Dirtlands and toward Katharn." I mean, I don't have a map, but I'm guessing that's how it'll go. If it doesn't, we'll pivot and figure something out from there. Any place that's not "here" works for me.

Aron pauses and we both stop. I realize I'm still clinging to his arm and I let go, and for some reason, I feel a sense of loss. Maybe because those tiny electric shocks aren't rippling through me any longer. He fingers the sword at his belt. "It's guarded."

"That's easily handled," I tell him, sounding more confident than I feel. "We'll bribe them to let us out. I've seen it done before." In the movies, but hey. He doesn't need to know that. I pause and dig through my coin pouch, pulling out a few of the smaller, more valuable coins and clutching them tight. Pretty sure that bribing the guards might just bankrupt us, but we're low on options and can't stick around to see what happens by day. We need to be out of this city before the prelate realizes that Aron's escaped, because something tells me that if he finds out that the god is gone, he's going to do his best to make Aron disappear entirely.

And I have a sneaking suspicion that my fate is now tied to his in all kinds of bad, bad ways.

As we get closer to the gate, I can see even in the dark that the two men guarding each side are armed. I would really prefer to just deal with one easily bribed guard, but if this is what I have to deal with, so be it. I'm just ready to leave Aventine and all its issues behind.

Time to be brave and get shit done.

CHAPTER 12

*W*e get closer to the gate and I can see that despite the massive portcullis that blocks the way out, there's a smaller wrought-iron door that only needs to be opened by one person. I guess that's for bottlenecking travel, but either way, it's encouraging. Opening one small door is an easier bribe than opening the whole massive gate. I turn to Aron and his hood is almost back from his face, his skin and strange eyes practically glowing white in the moonlight.

Yeah, he's going to stand out like a sore thumb. I move closer to him and tug his hood back over his too-handsome features, hiding them. "Keep this shit hidden."

"You act as if my face is a problem. I am handsome enough to suit any."

"Handsomeness isn't the issue, and wow, arrogant much?" I pull it down just a little further, because I can see the edge of his scar when he turns his face, and it's a dead giveaway. "You're pale as hell and you stand out in a crowd. Until we get on the road, you need to pretend like you're a leper and keep that shit under wraps."

"A what?"

"A leper. You guys don't have lepers? You have every other stupid medieval thing I can think of." Actually, I'm not sure if this culture—Aventinian? Aventini?—is more Roman than Medieval. For every castle-like building, there are dudes in linen kilts and sandals. I guess it doesn't matter. We're leaving. "Diseased dudes. Whatever."

He recoils. "You want them to think I'm diseased? That I am Kalos?"

The outrage in his tone would probably make my hair straighten if I was afraid of him. I still am, but I'm more afraid of what the prelate is up to. I can deal with one cranky god who's also pretty damn helpless. I can't deal with an entire city full of assassins.

"No, I just don't want them to realize you're you," I tell him impatiently. "Can we just get on with this? Keep your hood down and let me do the talking."

"Fine," Aron snarls, and he doesn't sound pleased. Too bad for him.

I eye the guards at the gate. They're staring at us now, probably because we've stopped in the road in the middle of the night and stand out like a sore thumb. Not a great start to our "secret" escape. I start to pull down my hood and then decide that no, that looks a bit too much like we're up to no good. We need to look like we want to do a different kind of no good. So I turn toward Aron and wrap my arms around his neck.

Or I try to. He's easily a foot taller than me and not cuddly in the slightest. I lean in even as he stiffens, his eyes flashing.

"Now is not the time for fucking, servant—"

"I know," I hiss at him, and cock one foot in the air like we're getting all cozy and romantic. At least, I hope it looks like that from a distance. From a very far distance, it hopefully won't look like I'm gritting my teeth because I want to beat his head in. "Just follow my lead and pretend you're my lover—"

He snorts. "You should be my lover, not the other way around. No one's going to believe—"

I slap a hand over his mouth before I decide to abandon his ass. "Stop right there," I say sweetly. "We're tricking them, all right? Follow my lead and pretend that you want to have sex with me, all right?"

He grunts.

"Thank you," I tell him, relieved we're finally getting somewhere. I release his neck and then try to put my hand in his.

He just slaps one of his big paws on my ass and gives it a hard squeeze that sends a ripple of electricity through me. I give him a shocked look, and there's a weird charge in the air that makes me shiver. He looks thoughtful, and my pussy clenches somewhere deep inside.

Okay, that was weird.

Gritting my teeth again, I slide closer to him and loop my arm around his waist. "Follow my lead," I murmur one last time before heading forward.

For once in his stubborn life, Aron doesn't protest. He keeps squeezing my butt cheek and slows his steps to match my paces, and we approach the guards.

No one moves as we approach, but they start to give me speculative looks the moment we get close enough for them to see my face.

"You lost, tart?" one asks.

I'm really getting tired of the word "tart." "Nope! Just taking my lover out of the city for some privacy." I wink at him and then pat my coin purse. "What'll it take to convince you to open that door?"

"Door ain't for sale," the man says flatly.

"Oh, I don't know about that," another says. "Don't be so hasty." He moves closer and eyes me in a way that makes my skin crawl. "I'm sure we can come to some sort of agreement."

"I'm sure we can," I say brightly, pretending to misunderstand. I pull my coin purse off of my belt and open it, shaking a few coins into my palm. "How about—"

"How about your cunt instead of your coin?" the man says, giving Aron's cloaked figure a dismissive look before he reaches out and grabs my tit.

It happens so fast that I can't do more than squawk in outrage, and the coins go tumbling from my hands onto the muddy ground. Thunder rumbles overhead and suddenly Aron's hand isn't on my waist anymore.

It's on the guy's throat, and the man's hauled into the air, his legs thrashing.

"That's mine," Aron growls low. "I didn't say you could touch it."

The other guards rush forward, and then things are a total blur. I watch in horror as Aron casually tosses aside the man he's holding and wades forward, unarmed, as the others unsheathe their swords.

I back up in fear, because I have no weapon and no way to protect myself. Not that I'd be able to against a bunch of armed men.

Aron seems to have no problems with that. He flings himself forward, and as one man points his sword at the god, he casually bats it aside as if it's nothing and then grabs the man's wrist. There's a crunch of bone and then the sword falls uselessly to the ground as the guard screams. The Lord of Storms moves almost gracefully as he grabs the men, crushing windpipes, snapping arms, and batting aside swords as if they're nothing. It doesn't matter that they're armed and he's not—it's clear there's no contest here.

He grabs the last guard by his neck and I expect him to fling him like the others, but he just flicks his wrist and there's another crunch of bone and the man falls to the ground, limp.

Dead.

Aron turns to me, breathing hard, and his eyes are alight

with some sort of peculiar glee. His pale skin gleams with a hint of sweat and he grins, pleased with himself. "Gate's clear. Let's go."

I make a wordless sound of protest in my throat.

"What?" he asks, frowning as if I'm the problem here. Me. Meanwhile, I just watched a man relentlessly slaughter a bunch of men that stood in his way. Unreal.

"Are you going to do this all the damn time?" I ask, rubbing my arms against the sudden chill that's swept over me.

It's clear Aron doesn't like being questioned. "Do what?"

"This?" I gesture angrily at the dead men strewn in front of the gate. "I mean, hello, this is not what civilized people fucking do!"

"It is what the Lord of Storms and god of battle does."

"But still!"

He adjusts his cloak, pulling the hood back over his head. "Are you going to tell me that you had it under control? Because I seem to recall this one"—and he kicks one of the dead bodies —"grabbing you."

I swallow hard, because my boob still hurts where he squeezed it. That doesn't give Aron the right to just slaughter a bunch of people though. "I also remember you stating that I'm your property."

His eyes gleam with that unholy light again, and his grin widens, showing his teeth. It's not a friendly grin, or even a pleasant one. "That is because you are. You are my anchor in this world. You are mine to do with as I please."

I shiver at the deadly confidence in his voice and the meaning behind his words. I hug my clothes tighter to my body. "Well, if you grab my tit, I'm going to be pissed."

"There is no time for that right now. Let us open this gate and be gone, as you have demanded for hours." He turns away and stalks toward the portcullis.

I swallow the emotion bubbling in my throat. Part of me

wants to turn away and tell him to fuck off. That we're done and I'll find my own way in this strange place. But then I watch him study the portcullis and then fumble at the gate, as if he can't figure out how it opens.

Just like he can't figure out how to sleep.

I sigh. If I leave him alone, I'm sure he's going to die. It might not be from a fight, but it might be from starvation just because he's that clueless. I signed up for this no matter what and he did save my life…and the other women.

I probably need this guy to get home. He's a god, right? It stands to reason that if he gets back to his world, he can get me back to mine.

I sigh again. Damn it. "I hate this," I mutter to the dead people around me, and then spot a key ring at the belt of one of the guards. I grab it—and a money pouch one has at his belt— and then head to Aron's side. "Just please don't keep murdering people, all right?"

"They stood in our way. You said yourself we do not have time to lose. Now, are you going to keep sobbing over the corpses of men who would have fucked you to open a door, or are you going to come with me?"

I hate this man sometimes, I really do. I really hate it when he's right. I head forward with the keys. "How long exactly am I stuck being your servant? Asking for a friend."

"No, you are not." He smacks the door, frustrated. "How does this open?"

I facepalm. Oh, this man. I don't know what I'm going to do with him.

CHAPTER 13

$\mathcal{W}$e head out of the city and into a wasteland.

I blink the dirt out of my eyes and pull my hood tighter around my face, even though it's dark outside and there's no one out here to see us. But there's dirt constantly flying in the air and it slinks around our boots like a fine layer of sand peppering everything. There are no trees out here in the open, and even though it's dark, I can't make out any grasses or foliage. I can barely make out the cobblestones of the road because they're so covered with grit. Everywhere I look, as far as the eye can see, there's nothing but naked hill after hill.

It makes me nervous.

"What is this place?"

"Outside the mortals' city," Aron says, his tone implying that the answer is obvious. "The prosperous Aventine, devoted to the God of Storms." The sarcasm is rich in his voice.

"I know that. It's just…was there a fire recently?" I know the question's as stupid as the last one. They called this the Dirt-lands, didn't they? Clearly this is dirt. A whole hell of a lot of it. "There's nothing out here. How do they make a city out in the middle of nowhere? Shouldn't there be farms or something? Pastures?"

Roads?

Freaking trees? Something? This empty wasteland is hard for me to fathom.

I'm used to cities and buildings crowding every bit of space they can. Cars and roads and sidewalks and landscaping. This place hasn't felt truly alien to me until now. Maybe some part of my head thought I was just in a weird sort of amusement park and that at some point, someone would peel the curtains back and real life would be on the other side.

Looking at my surroundings, though, I realize that's a dream. However I got here, I've been dropped into a world that's very different from my own. For the first time, I lose hope that I'm going to get home.

I might be stuck here.

Forever.

I tighten my grip on the cloak around my shoulders. Fuck that. I refuse to let this place defeat me. It's only been days but I've already survived slavery, an execution, and an assassination attempt. If I can survive all that this place throws at me, I will find my way home.

Aron grunts. "Aventine is on the edge of the ocean, so I imagine they do fishing and trading. Do you truly care or are you yapping just to yap?"

I clench my jaw and walk.

The dirtlands are eerie. The moon is high and bigger than the moon back home, dominating the night sky and so close that I can make out the pockmarks and craters on the surface without a telescope, which is a little eerie. I can't help but feel like the moon's going to crash into the world if it gets any closer. Then again, Aron doesn't seem all that concerned so that must be normal.

Then *again*, Aron doesn't know how to work a door.

I shiver as we move farther and farther away from the walls of Aventine. I know it's wisest to get away—especially after Aron did his "killing six guards" thing, but I can't help but be creeped out and worried about the direction we're heading.

A city named Katharn is this way, I remind myself. The barmaid had no reason to lie to me. There's a city in this direction. We just have to keep going through this awful nothingness —the Dirtlands—until we get there. "Hopefully this isn't a long walk," I say aloud, because it's reassuring to hear my voice. "If this was like a desert, then I don't think the city would get a lot of travelers, and they did. At least, I think that's how it would work, though I'm not entirely sure that we shouldn't turn around and get more food and water—"

"I know this place," Aron says, his voice ringing out over the gently sloping hills of dirt.

"You what?" I turn and stop when I realize Aron has stopped, too. I glance uneasily at the walls of the city. We've been walking for what feels like a half hour, but we're still far too close. Someone on horseback—or hippoback, or whatever those animals are—could easily catch up to us.

"I know this place," he states again and lifts his hands. Faint sparks glimmer at his fingertips and the air feels charged with electricity. I can feel my hair standing on end as if I'm being shocked, and above us, the skies crackle with thunder.

I gasp at the sight. He's lit up like a firecracker. "How did you do that?"

Aron ignores me. He lifts his hands toward his face, studying them with a frown furrowing his brow. As he does, I realize that the sparking light coming from his hands is being...sucked away. Like there's a gigantic invisible vacuum and it's pulling all of the energy out of him. He clenches his jaw as if concentrating, and the light coming from his hands grows stronger. It makes my head hurt to look at it, and I wince, squinting at the light.

The auras that surround his fingertips elongate and bleed away toward the distant horizon. He turns, his back to me, and I move to watch as he does the same thing in the opposite direction. Again, the magic bleeds away from his hands in the exact same direction as before.

Something's sucking away his lightning, and it's something over the hills.

"This is a dead place," he tells me after a moment, and his fingers go out like snuffed candles. He drops his hands and looks around us thoughtfully. "There is no magic or life in these lands. It is being pulled towards Citadel."

"First of all, this is fucked up. Second of all, you could have done the lightning thing with your hands all this time and you break necks instead? What the fuck, man?" I give him an incredulous stare.

He grins at me, and it feels like more of a showing of teeth than a friendly gesture. "I like to break necks. Especially the necks of those that anger me." He stares down at his hands. "And the lightning is...difficult. I do not think I am supposed to be doing it."

I shake my head slowly, amazed. This man has no idea of what it means to be a person. Not yet. He makes my head hurt. "So your lightning is...what, being drained?"

"Everything is. The spark of life, my essence, everything. If we were to stay in these lands long enough, it would bleed our lives from us." He points in the distance. "It is all being sucked away to Citadel, the bastion of Tadekha, goddess of magic. Her devotees pull the force of every living thing for many leagues to power her temple. The High Father is not pleased by it, but he does not stop her." He looks thoughtful. "Or so I thought. Perhaps she is part of the reason we have all been cast out."

"Mmm. Lucky me." I shiver in my long cloak and brush my fingers over my skin as I get another faceful of wind-blown dirt. "You think she's there in her citadel like you showed up here?"

"It is possible. I feel a great magic there, but it might be that I feel her followers draining everything." Aron studies the distant horizon, frowning at it. "If she is there, I do not know if we should venture in that direction." He flicks a glance over at me. "She is not a goddess that is friendly to me. Aventine and Citadel have long been uneasy with each other."

Lovely. "So if she's being punished, she'll be there, sucking up all the energy in the world like her own personal black hole. But if she's not, do you think they would help us? Maybe give us some horses to get to Katharn?"

He shrugs. "Does it matter how fast we get to our next destination? Are you late for something?"

"Well, no—"

"Then we walk on. I have no wish to visit Tadekha or her sniveling worshipers."

I clench my jaw. "Fine. We'll keep going, then."

So we walk.

And we walk.

And walk. It feels like we're walking endlessly toward a horizon that never changes shape no matter how long we walk. My feet hurt and the gigantic moon moves through the sky, disappearing behind the distant mountains on the horizon, and still we walk.

Occasionally I glance backward to see if I can see the city walls, but they disappeared hours ago, which makes me feel better.

Slightly.

As the sun rises, the skies bleed gold and pink, and I have to admit, I have a new appreciation for this day. This is the Hour of Blood. Dawn. Sunrise. I was supposed to be executed along with dozens of other blondes just because we had the bad luck to be slaves. A knot forms in my throat but I ignore it, just like I ignore the ache in my feet. Aron's not slowing down, so I don't either.

By the time the sun is up, though, I'm ravenous and so thirsty that my mouth feels like a desert. I'm also starting to resent the fact that Aron doesn't seem to be stopping for anything. He doesn't look tired, and his walk is just as brisk as ever. Me, I'm dragging. I'm sleepy, hungry, and exhausted. I also have to use the bathroom, but I haven't seen one or even a bush to hide behind. There is literally nothing in the Dirtlands and I'm not about to pop a squat in front of my good buddy Aron.

I force my aching legs to move faster and stride up to his side. I've been walking a few steps behind him all this time because I simply can't keep up with his effortless speed, but it makes conversation difficult. "Hi," I say breathlessly. "Can we talk for a sec?"

He glances over at me dismissively. "You are talking. Speak."

God, this guy really is a dick. I hate that I let him grab my ass. "What's the game plan? We don't know how long it's going to take to get to Katharn, so like, when are we stopping to eat and rest?"

He scowls at me as if I've said something highly obnoxious. "You are tired?"

"You aren't?" When he shakes his head, I sigh with frustration. "Well, here's the thing. I'm mortal, right? Mortals need to rest and pee and eat and all that good stuff and you might not, but I sure do."

That makes him pause in the middle of the dusty, dirty road. "Rest and pee and eat?"

"Not all at once of course—"

He tilts his head. "Should I be doing these things since I am now mortal?"

Tricky question, and I have no answer for him. "I don't

know? Do you feel the need to, uh, relieve your bladder?" This is such a weird conversation to have with a god.

Aron thinks for a moment. "No?"

"Then maybe gods don't use the bathroom. Look, I don't know. All I know is that I need to do these things." I press the heel of my hand to my forehead, and I'm not surprised to find that I'm trembling with exhaustion. "So please, can we take a break for a few?"

He considers this. His hands go to his hips and he studies the wide open fields around us, then the road. Then he gazes back behind us, as if he can still see the walls of Aventine. After a moment, he glances over at me again, his expression sour. "Am I going to have to carry you, Faith? Is this what you are going for?"

My jaw drops. "You arrogant prick. No! I would like five fucking minutes to rest my feet. Can we do that?" I drop to the ground and sit on the dusty cobblestones, glaring at him. "The very last thing I want from you is a free ride."

Aron snorts, as if he doesn't quite believe that, and I want to punch his smug face. What a huge dick.

I ignore him, because truth is, it feels so damn good to sit down and rest. I'm thirsty and my feet hurt like there's no tomorrow. I'm starving, too, but we didn't bring food supplies. I wonder how far away Katharn is. I'm starting to worry that leaving the city was a mistake, but we couldn't really stay there, either. I don't know what to do. I look around at our barren surroundings. Somehow I thought journeying outside the walls would be okay. That there'd be a nice road and some trees for shade. That there'd be countryside and farmland or something. Maybe a stream to drink from.

This place is just empty. There's absolutely nothing. It's a little creepy and definitely makes me feel defeated just gazing out at it. "I need to stop for a bit," I tell him. I'm suddenly exhausted from everything we've been through over the last few

days. It feels as if it's all crashing in on me and I don't think I
could get up if I tried.

As I sit and try to catch my breath, Aron paces. When it's
been all of two minutes, he gives me a cross look. "Well?"

"Well what? I'm still resting."

He lets out an impatient breath. "For how much longer?"

I stare at him, irritated and a little aghast that he wants to get
moving again already. "I don't know—an hour? Two? Does it
matter?"

"We should get going. You were so eager to leave and now
you will just stop? This is not a safe place. We are not safe here."
The god gestures angrily at the mounds and mounds of dirt that
make up the landscape. "Every moment we spend in this place,
we are in danger."

"For a guy that doesn't even know what a bathroom is, you
sure are certain of that," I mutter.

Aron scowls at me. "I wish to go, Faith."

As if that solves it. "Yeah, well, I wish I had better company.
We don't always get what we want."

He looks incredulous, as if he can't quite believe I'm not
jumping to my feet to do his bidding. "Faith," he says impatiently.

"Aron," I reply in just as testy a voice.

"Get up. We are leaving."

"You know what, Aron? People prefer it if you're nice to
them. I hear you get a lot more done. You should try it."

"Nice?" His lip curls as if the very thought is repugnant.
"Why must I be 'nice'? I am a god—"

"*Were* a god," I point out. "You were, and now you're an
Aspect."

He narrows his mismatched eyes at me and then strides over
to where I lie in the dirt. The hairs on the back of my neck
prickle, but I don't get up. I wait to see what he's going to do.
Aron moves to my side and touches my cheek with the backs of

his fingers, a gentle caress. The brush of his skin against mine makes a spark jump through us, pleasurable and sharp.

I stare up at him in surprise, fascinated at that gentle touch. My non-existent panties are totally in trouble right now, because just that small touch is making me crazy.

"Faith," he murmurs, voice gentle as he strokes my cheek.

It takes everything I have not to lean into his caress like a kitten. I close my eyes and sigh. "Mmm?"

"Get your ass up," he says in that same gentle tone. "Because I am fucking leaving."

I open my eyes and scowl up at him. "Bye."

His nostrils flare. "I was nice! Get up!"

"Bye," I say again and stretch my legs on the cobblestones. It's not comfortable, but it infuriates Aron, and so it's worth it.

We glare at each other for a long moment, waiting for the other to break. I'm determined not to, though, and I feel a triumphant surge when he turns his back and stomps away. Score one for the mortal. Of course, when he continues to storm away, I start to feel uneasy. "Where are you going?"

"I told you. I am leaving. It is not safe here." He doesn't turn around. "If you are wise, you'll leave, too."

That warning's a little unnerving, but I don't like the fact that he's telling me what to do. I've had enough of that already, and the stubborn part of me just wants to ignore him even more. He's trying to scare me into trotting after him, and it's not going to work. "See you around, then. Good luck finding another shmuck to be your anchor."

He doesn't stop.

Fine, then.

I feel uneasy as he leaves. I watch his back retreat for quite a while, because the ground is so level. I wonder for a moment if I should go after him, and then I decide that no, I'm not. It's only our magic bond—one that I never should have volunteered for —that's making me have second thoughts. And I've been alone up until this point, haven't I? I might be better off without Aron at my side. So I watch him go until he's no more than a distant speck on the horizon.

That's that. Fuck that guy.

The sun gets high in the sky. It starts to get warm. Really warm. Time to get moving, then. I get to my feet, which ache the moment I put weight on them, and start to head down the cobbled road in the same direction as Aron. For a moment, I feel foolish. We're traveling in the same direction anyhow, but like petulant children, we're not going to be together. It's so silly.

Of course, he started it.

Of course, that sounds even more childish.

My head throbs and my entire body hurts. I realize it's not going to get any better the longer I stay in one place, so I head after him on the road for a bit. Strangely enough, I start to feel better the moment I begin traveling again. I do wonder if it has something to do with our bond.

Before I can contemplate that thought for too long, I hear a low, rhythmic pounding. I press a hand to my breast, but it's not my heart. As it grows louder, I glance up at the skies. Is this Aron's doing? Some weird thunder god bullcrap to intimidate me? But the skies are clear and light blue with the early morning. I notice in the distance that there are clouds of dirt. That's odd. Either it's really windy...or something's moving.

Unease worms through my belly.

A moment later, I see shapes slowly lumbering into view. A moment after that, I realize they're not so lumbering after all. They're actually going pretty fast for the land-hippos, and there are riders atop them. Their movements match the steady drumming I hear, and I frown at the sight. My first instinct is to hide, but there's nowhere to go. I glance ahead down the road, but Aron's not in sight any longer. Maybe I can beat them. They look as if they're coming up from one side of the Dirtlands, so I haul my tired body to my feet and limp into a half run, moving as fast as I can. Fear makes me move faster than I thought possible.

It's still not fast enough. The thundering of hooves gets louder and louder as they grow closer and closer, and I start racing full out, my breath panicked and rasping. The land-hippos are almost upon me now, but I can't stop, mindless fear pushing me forward. Even if I get run over, I'll have at least died trying.

Hands grab me around the waist and haul me into the air.

I scream as I'm pulled against an armored stranger, flailing my fists and kicking against him. He laughs as if my attacks are nothing. "What have we here?" His hippo slows, the thunderous clod of its feet quieting.

"Fuck you," I tell him, trying to hit once more.

The man grabs my arms and pins them at my side and grins down at me. "A runaway slave, I think. Unless they're letting pretty women into the Aventine militia now?" He eyes my stolen military tunic. "How good are you with swords, love?"

Well that's a dirty question if I ever heard one. I scowl at him, struggling against his grip. "I'm not a runaway, and let me go! Put me down right now or you'll be sorry."

"Is that so?" Another rider comes up next to him, and I notice that all of the hippo riders—four of them—have paused to watch me attack their friend. I don't stop squirming or struggling, because I'll never give up. Giving up means that they win, and I'm tired of the bad guys winning. "She's a pretty face. We can take her to the slave pits in Aventine and sell her for a fair coin, I think."

"More than a fair coin," the one holding me says. "Look at these fine tits."

"Hey, remember me?" I say snarkily, jerking my shoulders. "I'm my own person and you can't sell me." I don't point out that someone did just that a few days ago, because they don't need those details. "And besides, I'm already claimed by the big guy."

"Big guy?"

"You know, Lord of Storms? Aron? Kinda cranky? Has a scar? Arrogant as fuck?"

They laugh at me. "By a god?" One sneers in my face. "Do you think me a fool?" He gives me a jiggle. "These tits are nice but they're not *that* nice."

"Clearly you missed the memo," I tell them, twisting. Jesus, how is this guy managing to hold onto me like this? I swear his arms are like a steel trap, because no matter what I do, I can't get free. Of course, I'm tired from walking all night, so maybe I just don't have any strength left, but I'm frustrated nevertheless. "Aron returned and he picked a servant and it's me. So you need to let me go unless you want a lightning bolt up your butt."

Hey, it sounded good in my head at least.

The men just laugh again. "Storytelling—a good trait in a pretty slave, but I imagine her mouth will be put to other uses."

"Ew," I tell him, revolted.

"Wrap her in your cloak and let's go before someone shows up to reclaim her," the rider closest to my captor says. He reaches over and grabs the tasseled reins from his buddy, who wraps me in his dark green cape. Dick.

"I swear, I belong to Aron," I tell them. "You have to believe me. I'm his anchor."

"If that's so, where is your god?" One arches an eyebrow at me, amused.

"Er, around." Shit.

He snorts and it's clear no one believes me.

And then, despite my protests, they continue to set off across the hills of the Dirtlands. They ignore the cobbled path and go cross country, and I realize they're taking me in the opposite direction I was heading with Aron. To the Citadel, like the one said. The goddess's Citadel, though I don't remember her name, just that Aron wasn't a fan of her.

I still struggle, but my movements grow more fatigued with every beat of the land-hippo's hooves. I'm tired and all of my energy is gone, but I can't give up. I can't be sold into slavery again. I just can't. Is that all this land does is freaking enslave people? Why am I here if I'm just going to be sold from person to person? Frustrated, I glare up at my captor, but he just grins down at me as if I'm the most adorable little runaway slave he's ever seen, no doubt mentally counting money in his head. I hate this guy.

At least he didn't call me "tart."

I blow out a breath and relax for a moment to regroup. I'll need energy to run away, I tell myself. I'm not giving up. I'm conserving my strength and I'll slide off the land-hippo when we stop. Somehow. Then I can wiggle free and run away. Sure, it sounds good in my head. More than anything, it doesn't sound like giving up, and that's the only thing I've got right now.

Aron's nowhere to be seen, but of course he's not. We're crossing hill after hill of dirt, the hippos plodding over them with fierce determination, and Aron stuck to the road. As I stare out, I realize there's something big and dark floating in the air in the distance. It's the Citadel, and it looks like a gleaming castle in the sky.

I gasp at the sight of it. When they said it was a citadel, I thought it'd be a fortress of stone, similar to Aventine's thick walls. This is a glorious, delicate castle that gleams in the sunlight with a thousand colors and floats above the ground like it's on a cloud.

"How…" I begin, but a wave of pain hits me and I black out.

CHAPTER 14

I'm lost in agony.

It rolls over me with surge after surge, unending and growing fiercer by the minute. The pain is so strong that it makes me black out, only to surface again with new pain and succumb once more. I have no concept of where I am or what day it is. I don't know how long I'm being tortured out of nowhere. I just know that it keeps going and going and going. It's needles in my scalp and knives in my gut and a million things all at once. It rocks through me so hard that I vomit all over myself and I'm pretty sure I lose bladder control. How can I not? My entire body feels like it's clenched into someone's throbbing fist or I'm being turned inside out.

I scream. A lot. I keep screaming, and when I run out of voice, nothing but raspy gurgling escapes my throat. It still hurts.

It feels like it's hurting forever.

Vague flashes of thought appear through the haze of agony. Of the soldiers talking in low, concerned voices only to disappear. Of being dumped into a bed of straw, a door slammed behind me. Of being left in the dark. I sink into the violence of my body turning against me, and time slides away.

FOG. My head throbs.

Someone kicks my leg and I turn over in the cot. Everything aches and throbs. Clearly I'm dying. I open my mouth to scream, but my throat feels like fire itself.

A hand touches my ankle and for a moment, everything washes away. Cool relief moves through me and I open my eyes to see the face of a woman with long, dark hair and silver jewelry. She studies me with a little tilt of her head and then gets to her feet.

Immediately, the pain crashes over me again. I moan, pushing my face into the straw as if that will somehow stop the agony.

"She has been screaming like this since you arrived?" The voice is cool. Sweet. Perfect. Just the sound of it makes me ache all over, makes me want something intangible and out of reach. It's the woman.

"Yes, my lady Tadekha. The soldiers said that she mentioned Aron of the Cleaver and that she was his anchor. Of course they thought she was lying..." The voice trails off.

The woman gives a sweet, musical chuckle. "Indeed. She is his anchor, true enough. The pain she suffers can mean nothing else. A lesser mortal would have died by now under such agonies."

"Then she did not lie." His voice is full of astonishment.

"Why would anyone lie about being the anchor to that one?" She makes a soft sound of disgust in her throat. "I cannot imagine who would volunteer to serve him with their life, not even this unfortunate creature."

I want to protest, to speak up, but my brain feels like an egg being fried. I press a fist against my brow to try and stave off the worst of the pain, but it doesn't work. Panting, I manage to spit out, "Who...you?"

The voices ignore me. "Which Aspect do you think it is?" one says.

"Who knows. It could be any."

I try to open my eyes and look at the speakers, but the dim light in the cell fills me with new, fresh pain. This is like the worst hangover and migraine rolled together and I just want it to end.

"Do you think he'll come for her?"

"Without a doubt," the woman says. "We should be ready for him to arrive soon. If she's in pain, he will be, too."

There's a swish of robes.

"Treat her better. Get her out of this filthy hole. I will not have Aron claiming I mistreated his mortal anchor. Gods have long memories."

"As you wish, my lady Tadekha."

Hands reach for me, and the moment they touch my skin, it sends a sizzle of pain through my body. I fall into blackness once more, screaming.

Always screaming.

IT TAKES a while for me to realize I'm no longer in pain. I remain with my eyes closed, lying down. I don't make any sudden movements in case one of those migraine-from-hell things trigger again. I don't know what caused it before, but I never want that to happen again. My memories of the last few days are vague and my throat hurts like the dickens.

I vaguely remember a visitor. A woman. My thoughts are muddy beyond that, though. A woman, having a conversation about me, and then sliding back into the migraine-of-death.

"My lady, are you awake?"

I frown to myself, wondering who is in the room with me. And...are they talking to me? I've been "tart" and "slave" ever since I got here. I've never been anyone's lady so far. I squeeze one eye open, testing.

No pain. Huh.

The room I'm in is pale white and beautiful. Cool sunlight filters through delicate glittering glass windows that take up an entire wall. I'm no longer resting on hay but on soft woven blankets, and there's a pillow under my head. I still feel grimy and achy with exhaustion, but my circumstances have changed. Slowly, I sit up and look around. "Where am I?"

There's a sound of pouring water, and I flinch automatically, expecting a shockwave of pain at the sound. There is none. Whatever happened to me seems to be gone as mysteriously as it arrived.

"You are in Lady Tadekha's Citadel," a woman answers, and her voice sounds like it's behind a nearby screen. I glance around the room, frowning to myself. It's all pale curtains and pale screens and white everywhere. Not an antiseptic white like a doctor's office, but something a little purer and sweeter. Soft fluffy cloud white.

"Someone brought me here," I say, swinging my legs over the edge of the bed (also white) and onto the marble floors (white as well). "They snatched me from the road I was on and dragged me here against my will. I'm a prisoner."

The woman makes a soft, absent-minded noise of dismay as if she's sympathizing but doesn't really give a shit. The faint scent of flowers touches the air. "Would you like a bath?"

Gee, thanks for listening to my concerns.

I feel for my belt with my money pouch and my knife, but they're gone. The only thing I'm wearing is my filthy borrowed guard tunic, and it's stinky from days of my sickness. Even if I'm weirded out by this place, I really, really would like a bath. "I think so."

"Come over here then, child. We'll prepare you for your master."

My master?

I test my balance but there's no pain when I get to my feet. It's so strange. I keep expecting everything to hurt but it's like all the pain just decided to up and vanish without reason. I pad forward on the cold floors and move toward the woman's voice, behind the white screen.

Standing there over a deep marble basin for a bath is an angel. I gasp at the sight of her. Holy shit. She really does look like an angel. Her hair is so silvery blonde it looks white. Her skin is milk pale and crystalline wings sprout from her back. She wears a white dress that cascades down to the ground in soft ripples.

My jaw drops at the sight of her. "Am I dead?"

Her mouth quirks. "No, my lady. You are not."

"Who are you, then?"

She inclines her head. "I am one of Lady Tadekha's priestesses. All of us here at the Citadel serve her. Come. Would you like to bathe?" She gestures at the bath. "The water is warm and you have time to wash your hair before dinner tonight."

"Dinner?" I echo dumbly. I'm having dinner with someone?

"Yes. You have been summoned by Lady Tadekha. I suspect your master must be here."

"Master?" I echo again, equally dumbly.

"Lord Aron of the Cleaver. You said you were his anchor, correct?" The angel looks perturbed at my ignorance. "I am told you shouted it quite repeatedly to everyone while you were…ill" She clears her throat delicately.

Ill? She makes it sound like I'm making things up—or that I wasn't really hurting. "I don't remember."

She makes another sympathetic noise and then gestures at the tub. "Come. You must be clean for your master."

"Can we quit calling him that? We're more of a partnership than a master-slave sort of thing. I'm not down for that sort of vibe." I tiptoe toward the bath, and god, it smells good. Steam rises from it and a delicate floral scent touches my nostrils. It smells so much better than I do at the moment.

"And you are not in any pain?"

"Er, no?"

She nods knowingly. "Then your master must have arrived to retrieve you."

"Still not my master, and I'm pretty sure he's not here?"

The angel smiles. "I am sure it is not my job to speak of such things."

The woman reaches for my clothing and I let her help me undress, since I'm not really sure how many options I have here. I'm fascinated by the way her prismatic wings ripple and sway as she moves around the room. They really do look as if they're attached to her body and not just some sort of ornament she's wearing. It's so pretty. "So what did you say your name was again?" I ask, stepping into the tub.

"I need no name as long as I serve my lady. I am but an extension of her."

Well isn't that just great. "So I guess your goddess is not big on free will, huh?" I sit down in the perfumed water and do my best not to moan with pleasure, because it's so hot and wonderful and I'm so very grimy. I close my eyes in bliss. "I'm Faith."

"Mm." A wet hand towel is slapped against my arm and then the nameless woman starts to scrub me with rough, abrasive strokes that defy her gentle appearance. Ow. I squeeze an eye open and see that she's got a frown on her pretty face. I guess I hurt her feelings.

"I'm sorry," I offer. "I'm not from around here and I don't

know the customs. And it's been a rough few days. I wasn't trying to be rude."

Her gaze flicks to me and her scrubbing turns gentle. She smooths the cloth up and down my arm as if I've never washed myself before. I want to protest that I can do it myself, but it feels rather nice. I settle into the tub and let her wash me.

"It's all right," the angel says softly. "You aren't familiar with our customs. Do you know anything about Lady Tadekha at all?" When I shake my head, she continues, her hand smoothing water up and down my arm. "Those of us that serve the goddess live here in the Citadel all our lives. We choose her glory over our own. It is a great honor to wear her wings and serve at her side."

"It sounds like it," I say, trying to appease her as she has me lean forward so she can wash my back. I wonder if I should take the washcloth from her but I'm afraid of offending again. Still, it's strange to be washed by another woman when I'm fully capable of doing it myself. Her touch has changed to delicate and tender, and the cloth moves over my skin like a caress. "So…did you say your goddess was here?"

The woman's face turns radiant with excitement. "Our lady arrived on the day of Anticipation. I have been chosen to be first among those that serve her needs…other than her anchor, of course." For a moment, she looks jealous.

"Can I call you 'First' then? It beats 'hey you.'" At her nod, I continue. "So your goddess is here and er, my god is too. Is this a common sort of thing? All the gods showing up at once?"

"It is the Anticipation," First says as if that explains everything. Her hands glide over my buttocks. "I do not know about any other Aspects, though. As I said, we do not leave the Citadel. We remain here to focus our lives in prayer. Our needs are supplemented by caravans of tithes from Aventine."

Didn't Aron say that Aventine was getting ready to go to war with Citadel? Maybe I misheard.

Overall, being one of Tadekha's servants sounds way better than being Aron's anchor. You get angel wings, beautiful gowns, perfumed baths, and get to live here. Meanwhile, I'd been dragged through the gutters of Aventine, almost beheaded and nearly had to whore myself. I have to wonder though...have others been pulled into this world like I have? Or am I the only one out of place?

I decide not to ask. I suspect it's information I need to keep to myself.

She dips the cloth in the scented water again and then begins to wash my breasts in teasing, delicate strokes. I gasp, shocked at the intrusive touch—and how my body responds to it. I should *not* be turned on. I barely even like this woman. I snatch the cloth from her hands. "I got it, thanks."

First gives me a questioning look, then sits back on her knees and watches me bathe.

I scrub my skin, hard. Time to get this bath over with quickly. "So...do you know Aron?"

"I have only been privileged to meet my Lady."

I snort. "Oh, meeting Aron isn't a privilege. It's more like a test of your patience."

First gasps, her hand flying to her mouth.

Ah, crap. I've offended her again. I just shake my head and continue scrubbing. I'm giving up on being polite and unobtrusive. "Trust me, when you meet him, you'll see exactly what I mean."

CHAPTER 15

$\mathcal{I}$ finish my bath with awkward bits of conversation with First, but it's clear she doesn't know what to make of me. That's fine, since I'm not entirely sure what to make of her. She brings me a dress made of a white gauzy material that looks innocent and virginal when First pulls it out, but when I put it on you can see every body part through the fabric.

Every. Body. Part. Nips, snatch, you name it, everyone can see it. I glance over at First, plucking at the material to pull it away from my private parts. "Bra? Panties?"

"What?" she asks, and when she approaches with a comb, I see that her dress is the same as mine. She's just so pale everywhere that I never noticed until now.

Well, damn it. I'm not leaving the room wearing this. I already feel weird enough after that bath. I look around the pale white chamber only to see that my stolen soldier's uniform has disappeared. "Can I have my clothes back? I think I'd be more comfortable in them."

"Oh no, it wouldn't be appropriate for you to have an audience with the goddess in such wear." First looks offended at the thought. "My lady loves beauty in all things, and you must be garbed in accordance to your status."

"Ah," I say, as if I understand. I don't, though. "What exactly is my status?"

"You are an anchor to a god. You serve him before all others." She sniffs haughtily. "And he would not want you looking like an underfed waif."

I don't know if she's right or not, but sometimes it's easier not to argue. What do these people have against a nice sweater and jeans? It's like covering up boobs is grossly offensive to them.

Weirdos.

Since I've lost the battle in regard to my clothing, I let First fix my hair. She plaits it into an intricate, five-stranded braid that coils around the top of my head like a crown, and then gently fixes a few sparkling flowers into the plait. She rubs a sweet-smelling gloss onto my lips and my cheeks and then gives me a kiss right on the lips. "You look worthy of the greatest of gods' attentions."

That was...weird. "Too bad for me that all I got stuck with is Aron, eh?"

First gives me an unhappy look. "You shouldn't say such things. They are gods."

I probably shouldn't, but it's clear First gets along a lot better with her goddess than I do with Aron. "I know. I just run my mouth. Aron can be...frustrating."

"He is a god," she murmurs with a small shake of her head. "He deserves our patience and understanding."

Yep, she has definitely not met the man. "You're right of course," I manage to puke out, and even put a smile on my face.

"Come. My lady will be waiting," First says, and with a flutter of her wings and a wave of her hand, she sweeps out of the room. I'm supposed to follow her, obviously. Except...no one gave me any shoes and I still feel naked in this dress.

I adjust the gauzy layers of my dress, patting them over my boobs and thighs. Here goes nothing. With a deep sigh, I follow her out of the room.

First walks ahead of me, her steps brisk despite her flowing gown, and I trot behind her, doing my best to keep up. It's difficult, because all I want to do is stop and stare. This place is amazing. I gape as we walk through crystalline hall after crystalline hall. It's like a fairy-tale palace made entirely of shining quartz. The floor is patterned crystal and shines like a diamond, but it's smooth and cool under my feet. We walk down one hall and I see a massive, icicle-like staircase that curves and descends into the depths of the citadel. I peer over the railing and it looks like there are layers and layers to the citadel itself, all made of the same sparkling materials. It's fascinating and the place practically hums with an internal vibe that makes my hair prickle. It feels almost electric, but I doubt anything here actually runs off of power, so it must be magic. We pass by a large window and below, I can see the Dirtlands with white roads snaking through them. We're extremely high up, and when I comment on that to First, all I get is a haughty sniff in return, as if that should be obvious.

I try to remember everything Aron said to me about this place, but all I remember is magic. Magic magic magic, and that it pulls all of the life out of the surrounding lands. I wonder how First feels about that, but I bet she doesn't care. As long as it's what her goddess wants, she's cool with it. Seems kind of fucked up to me, though, if they're killing Aventine and the surrounding area just so they can have a floating place to live.

The citadel itself is a paradise, though. Other women pass by us, speaking in low voices, hands clasped in their wispy robes. They all have the pale, metallic hair, milky skin, and glittering wings that First does. Someone's singing off in the distance, and this entire place feels like a cross between a dorm and a church. Which is a weird intersection, but no one asked me, I suppose.

We descend the icicle-dripping staircase, and I'm glad I'm barefoot, because the steps themselves are rather slippery with the crystal surfaces. First walks down, wings bobbing, but others fly past us, and it makes me wonder why there's a staircase if everyone has wings. Finally, we get to the bottom and First takes me down another hallway. Then she pauses in front of double doors and turns to me.

"Do we need to wait to enter?" I whisper, because this place feels like somewhere you would whisper.

The look she gives me is patient, and she licks her finger and smooths a stray hair back from my brow, then takes the gathers of my dress and adjusts them out with a few tugs. So much for hiding the nips. When she's satisfied with my appearance, she turns and opens the double doors, then sweeps inside. "Follow me. My lady is waiting."

I follow. What else can I do?

The room itself is arching and vaulted, and it reminds me of a massive gazebo. Thin, fluting crystalline columns support the arching, glittering ceiling and the floor itself is a dull, polished patterned quartz that doesn't reflect the light. There are people gathered along the edges of the room, like an audience before a performer, and I notice idly that they seem to be both the crystal angels of the Citadel and normal people. First pushes through the crowd, sweeping past them as if she's got someplace important to be, and I trot after her as she heads to the front of the room.

There, on a dais, sits a lovely woman. It must be the goddess. The first thing I notice is that she's tiny. The throne itself is another crystal monstrosity with a fan of spikes arching along the back, but she seems dwarfed by it, her bare feet resting on a crystal step as if she won't quite reach the floor otherwise. She's not a child, though. Far from it. The goddess herself is dressed in a barely-there string of sparkling beads that seem to emphasize her bare breasts instead of hiding them. She wears another strand of beads around her waist and wispy, gauzy skirts that flow around her calves like a rippling waterfall. Her skin is a lovely copper, her eyes a piercing pale gray, and her hair is bound up in a sweep of pearls and knotted high atop her head, then cascades over her shoulder in a jet-black waterfall.

She's easily the most beautiful and most intimidating thing I've ever seen.

First's demeanor changes the moment we're in front of the goddess. Her steps grow more rushed, and then she sinks to her knees at the bottom of the dais, prostrating herself in front of the goddess. "My lady," she says, and it practically sounds like a moan of pleasure.

I'm not sure how to respond. Do I do the same? After a moment's hesitation, I get down on my knees and lean forward, putting my head to the cool floor.

"Arise," the goddess calls out. "I would see you for myself."

I don't know if I'm supposed to call out a greeting or if that'd be too familiar, so I stand there like a lump and let her look at me. Her gaze flicks over my face and hair, down my breasts— which are outlined in the gown—and farther down my figure. I feel oddly flushed at her scrutiny. It's strange, because she's remote and just a little bit terrifying, so I'm not entirely sure why I'm blushing.

"Not much better cleaned up," the goddess says, studying me. "What is your name, mortal?"

"Faith."

Her brows draw together. "Is that a joke? Do you mock me?"

Why does everyone have a problem with my name? "It's common where I'm from. Faith Hill, Faith Evans, uh, Faith No More…" And now I'm officially out of famous Faiths. Not that she's going to know who any of those people are.

"Mmm." The frown goes away but she continues to study me, and I feel a bit like a bug trapped under a glass. I do my best not to squirm when she indicates I should turn. I don't know why her opinion matters, but I feel like I want her to be pleased with how I look. I do a circle and then wait before her once more. Is she...going to dismiss me? The thought is disappointing. I have so many questions. After a long moment, Tadekha speaks. "Are you in pain?"

"Me? No. Should I be?"

She gestures with one elegant hand, and the movement is oddly hypnotic. "You tell me."

I force myself to quit staring at that hand and meet her gaze. "Whatever migraine hit me, it's gone now. Maybe it's because of the um, Citadel." I don't have an answer, but that seems as good a guess as any. All I know is that the debilitating, terrible waves of pain have vanished as quickly as they arrived and I'm so damn relieved.

She laughs, the sound utterly musical and enchanting. "I'm trying to decide if this is a game with you or if you are truly this ignorant."

The goddess is so beautiful that it's hard to be offended despite her words. "Unfortunately, I'm going to have to put money on 'ignorant.' I'm not exactly from around here." I'm puzzled by her amusement. "Care to explain?"

Her eyes flare at my question, but she crosses her legs—slowly and sensually—and then leans in. "You are an anchor, are you not?"

"That's what I volunteered for, yeah."

"Do you know what that entails? It is clear you do not." She laughs again. "Oh, this is delightful. I suspect poor Aron is as ignorant as you are. An anchor is supposed to guide their Aspect through the Anticipation, and Aron has you? He might has well have no one. How very delicious."

I frown at her tone, because I don't like the way she's talking about Aron, oddly enough. Sure, he's a jackass, but he's not exactly here to defend himself. "Aron's a...good guy." I kind of choke on the words, and she only laughs harder, the sound tinkling off the crystalline walls. "Not the most patient of men and a little bloodthirsty, but I think he has a good heart. Somewhere."

Tadekha purses her pink lips and another laugh shakes her shoulders. "Such praise."

"He's nice," I say, and it feels like a lie but I say it anyhow. "You should meet him. I'm sure you'd get along great."

Her eyes widen and the delighted smile curves even wider. "Oh, my sweet child. This is too much. You have no idea, do you?"

No idea about what? I don't ask it out loud, because I'm getting the distinct feeling that the goddess is making fun of me, and it hurts my feelings. Which is stupid, because I shouldn't be surprised that she's kind of a jerk, but for some reason, she's so appealing that I want to like her.

Tadekha flicks a hand in the air, indicating to someone nearby. I see a flash of rings and hear the tinkle of bracelets as she moves. Off to one side, one of the angels rushes forward with a tray full of fruits and sweets, and a diamond-looking decanter.

Just glancing at it makes me hungry. And thirsty. I'm always hungry and thirsty lately it seems.

The angel kneels at the goddess's side instead of setting down the tray and holds it aloft, as if her only job in life is to be a table for this woman. As I stand in front, waiting, Tadekha reaches over and plucks something that looks like a chocolate bonbon out of the bowl and my mouth fills with saliva. God, that looks so good. I watch as she takes the world's tiniest bite and licks her lips. "Shall I share a few secrets with you, Faithful?"

"Faith. And yes, please." I'm trying not to stare at the food. Or her lips. She really is perfect looking. It's amazing.

"There are things you should know about being an anchor. First and foremost..." She licks her lips and both myself and the angel stare at her adoringly. "When you are separated from the god you are anchored to, it is very, very painful. You see, you are his anchor here in the mortal world and should remain at his side at all times. That is how the bond is designed. He cares for you, and you anchor him. If you do separate, you are punished." Tadekha bites her lip and gives me a winning smile, spreading her hands. "What do you think of that?"

I think it sounds like bullshit, but I can't quite be angry. Not when she's smiling at me like that. "But I'm not hurting anymore."

"Precisely." Her smile widens. "That means your Aron has arrived and is here."

Son of a bitch, First was right.

CHAPTER 16

*a*t Tadekha's words, a large man comes out of the audience surrounding the goddess. Dark, long hair. Pale face. Bright red scar down one eye. Mismatched eyes. Forbidding scowl on his handsome features. He's still dressed in the uniform of the Aventinian soldiers, the red and gray kilted tunic and gladiator sandals. His cloak is dusty and his hair slightly disheveled, but other than that, he looks just as I left him.

Well hell. Aron *is* here. When First was talking, I thought she was just making conversation.

I get to my feet as he strides to my side. "Aron! What—" My words cut off as he shoves me behind him and steps forward, blocking me from the goddess's sights.

"Tadekha," he says in a flat voice.

"I was wondering when you'd introduce yourself," she purrs. "Hello, dear friend."

"We are not friends," Aron says tightly.

Well it's nice to see that some things haven't changed. Aron's the same guy he ever was. I touch his arm to get his attention, and that little spark ripples through me. "How did you know where to find me?" He turns and glares at me so fiercely that I take a step back. "Sorry I asked."

"Do not move from where you are," he commands me, pointing at the floor. Like I'm a bad dog or something.

Before I can smart off about that, Tadekha chuckles and the warm, lovely sound rolls through the room. "Come, come Aron. Do not be so upset. I mean no harm to you or your anchor. In fact, I have one of my own." She reaches out to stroke a hand over the hair of the girl holding the tray and a blissful look crosses the angel's face. Tadekha smiles absently at her, chucks her under the chin, and then returns to petting her head. "I think it's marvelous that we get to spend time together. After all, we are both exiled, are we not? Perhaps we can pool our resources. Work together."

"Us?" He laughs as if the idea is insulting. "You know that is a bad idea."

The goddess waves a hand absently. "If I was not a fan of bad ideas, I would not be here."

Aron grunts as if this makes sense to him.

She wags a finger at a few of the angels fluttering on the sidelines, and then three of them rush forward, a gilded chair in their hands. They float up to the dais with their tinkling wind-chime wings and place the seat near Tadekha's throne, arranging it just so before bowing to the goddess and floating back to rejoin the crowd.

Tadekha gestures at the empty seat, indicating that Aron should join her. "At least enjoy my hospitality since you are already here." When he remains perfectly still, she picks up another bonbon and nibbles on it, raising an eyebrow.

My stomach growls.

Aron sighs heavily as if this all bugs the crap out of him. He turns to me and flicks his gaze over my gown, eyes resting on my nearly naked breasts for a long moment. "Come."

And he heads for the throne designated for him.

RUBY DIXON

I scurry after him, gathering my skirts as I walk. There's no seat for me, not that I expected one. I glance over at Tadekha's chair and she's seated regally upon her throne, caressing the cheek of the girl kneeling at her feet and clutching the tray as if it's an honor to serve the goddess. Heck, for her, maybe it is.

Then again, she wasn't stuck with Aron.

Then again, maybe Aron expects me to be all kissy-kissy to him and is pouting that I'm not. Of course, even as the idea crosses my mind, I dismiss it. Aron's a lot of things, but he's not a crybaby. And really, he's handsome. If he hit on me, I...

My mouth goes dry as I think about Aron. Kissing Aron. Touching Aron. Aron's big body thrusting into me as I rake my nails down his back...

I'm shocked at my thoughts.

Of course, the moment I do, I can feel myself blushing. I wait for Aron to sit in his throne, and he immediately gestures that I should sit next to him, but on the floor. Yeah, I expected that. The chair he's sitting in isn't much in the way of legs, though, and there's no place for me to rest my back or get comfortable. After a few moments of shifting in my skirts, I tentatively lean against his leg. That pleasant little electric ripple moves through me again.

"Lovely. Shall we eat and drink, then?" Tadekha seems pleased.

"I do not need to eat."

"Ah, but it's such fun. You should try it. I've no doubt your anchor is famished. Is that not right, little Faithful?"

I open my mouth to speak.

"Do not address her," Aron growls, and I can see his hand clench on one arm of the throne. "She is mine."

Jeez. So possessive. I should be irritated, but instead, a warm flush rushes through my body. I nudge his leg with my shoulder, but I'm kinda pleased. You'd think the guy hadn't abandoned me on the road with the way he's acting. Maybe it's my endorphins

140

rushing back after days of being tortured with pain, but I'm feeling pretty good right now. I'm happy Aron's here, because he's familiar. He's my rock in all this madness, oddly enough. And in his weird way, he's acting like he's happy to see me, too.

Tadekha gestures, and a winged servant arrives with a small tray of food and a cup for me. I'm starving and thirsty, but I hesitate. Maybe Aron wants me to hold off for some reason I can't imagine. I glance up at him and he makes a dismissive gesture with his hand, indicating I can have it if I want it.

I want it. I'm starving. I take the tray from the angel and balance it on my knees, then plow into the food. God, it's so good. Every bite is like heaven.

Dancers come out onto the floor and musicians move forward with their instruments. They set up and begin to play. The dancers leap about in their skimpy outfits and tinkling, delicate music fills the room.

Okay, this is nice. Food, music, entertainment. Tadekha knows how to live. Aron could take some notes from her.

I keep eating. Even if I wanted to stop, I'm not sure I could. I don't know what any of this stuff is, but it's all shaped into intricate designs and tastes amazing. I do my best not to stuff my face like a wild woman, but I eat and drink without stopping, licking my fingers when all of the delicious treats are gone. Someone moves forward and takes my tray, then offers me a napkin. As I wipe my fingers with the floaty, see-through napkin given to me by one of the angels, I notice that neither Aron nor Tadekha are talking to each other. The room is very quiet, and it's like they're waiting for something...or testing each other out. It's odd but Aron's also made it very clear he's not friends with Tadekha.

He must be here because of me.

That makes me feel absurdly warm and pleased, like he's gone out of his way for me. I curl a hand around his stiff, naked calf and give him a squeeze. "Everything okay?" I whisper.

He glances down at me and gives me a brief nod, but he's not as much of a douche as he normally is. In a way, that's sweet. I think he's trying to be nice. I stroke my hand up and down his bare leg absently and then turn to watch the room. I didn't pay much attention to the dancers while I was eating, but I'm looking now and...well, they're rather sensual. Their movements are not "dancing" so much as "writhing" and their clothing sways around almost naked limbs. I feel a bit like I'm at a high-end strip club, and when one dancer grabs another and begins to slowly undress her, I change that from strip club to orgy.

It's weird, because I'm not offended by the sight of the two angels making out. Instead, it makes me hot and flushed with my own arousal. That's...odd. I clutch at Aron's leg, watching as one woman bears the other to the ground, their mouths locked together, hands on each other, in front of the entire room. Are all of the dances here like this? Or are we just being treated to a special show that no one feels like stopping?

And why is it turning me on? I stroke my hand up and down Aron's leg, unable to help myself. I have to touch him, have to feel that crackle of energy that comes between us. I can't tear my eyes off of the women as they continue writhing and the music flares faster and louder. I lean against Aron's knee, and I know I'm clinging to him. I can't seem to stop myself. I'm in a lust-filled fog and when he reaches down and puts a hand on my shoulder, grazing his thumb over my bare skin, it sends a shockwave of pleasure through my body. My pussy squeezes on nothing, and I'm growing hot and wet between my thighs.

The lusty music comes to a crescendo and the dancers fall flat, their song ended. The room breaks into applause and I feel breathless and needy. I turn to peer over at the goddess...and gasp at what I see. The goddess's anchor—the beautiful angelic-looking woman—kneels before the goddess as she sits on the edge of her throne. Tadekha's legs are splayed open and her hand is on the silvery head of the woman before her. The anchor has her head buried in the goddess's lap, and when Tadekha closes her eyes and her lips part, I realize that she's being pleasured.

A goddess is getting head right in front of everyone and doesn't give a damn.

A moan escapes my throat and I can't stop staring. I know my mouth hangs open in surprise and I should look away, but I can't. I'm too fascinated by the bob of the angel's head as she licks her mistress, the way her bare toes are curled and her wings shudder as if she's getting intense pleasure out of this, too. Tadekha keeps one hand on the girl's head and gestures for new musicians, and they stroll out to the center of the floor as if nothing is happening.

As if this is an everyday sort of thing.

Maybe it is. Maybe this is how an anchor serves their god. Maybe this is why Aron is so impatient with me, because I haven't touched him. I'm touching him now, though, and as I watch Tadekha get pleasured by the mouth of her servant, it makes me want to do more. The weird hum in my body and the arousal I'm feeling heightens. I want to do something. I look up at Aron, who's gazing straight ahead as if he's deliberately avoiding looking over at Tadekha. Me, personally, I can't stop staring. The goddess is beautiful, and even more so when she parts her lips and moans loudly enough to be heard over the music. It makes my belly tighten, and I lean in and brush my mouth against Aron's skin. The belted Aventinian tunic only goes to mid-thigh, and I could push it up and put my mouth on him like the other girl is doing to her goddess.

The mental image of that makes me suck in a deep breath. I haven't thought of Aron in a sexual way until now, but in this moment, I can't stop thinking about the hard planes of his features, the firm line of his mouth, the scar that makes him look rugged despite the elegant stamp of his cheekbones. I think of his pale skin and mismatched eyes which should make him look creepy and instead makes him look dangerous and other-worldly.

I press my mouth to the side of his leg again, and then lick him. Just a little.

Aron doesn't move, doesn't react. I want more, though. I want to please him like the angel's pleasing Tadekha. The goddess is making little cries that still slide through the hum of music, and I want to do the same to Aron. I want to see his face contort with pleasure. I want to blow his ever-loving immortal mind with everything my mortal mouth can do. So I get on my knees and turn until I've got my hands on both of his thighs and I'm facing him. I slide my hands up underneath the hem of his tunic and reach over to cup his length.

Jesus, the guy's packing. I gasp with pure delight at the discovery. He's definitely not like regular men in this sense. I don't think I've ever handled a cock this big. I circle my fingers around him and can't close my grip. This enormous dick would feel amazing if he fucked me. He's long and hard and my mouth waters as I gaze up at him, full of yearning.

He gives me a slow shake of his head, his pale eyes blazing as his gaze meets mine. No.

"Let me put my mouth on you," I tell him desperately, the music and Tadekha's cries adding to my urgency. I lean in and rub my face against one of his thighs shamelessly. I lick the skin and moan when I feel another little shockwave curl through me. "Please, Aron."

"I do not think this is like you," he says as he nudges me to my feet. He gazes up at me, his expression unreadable. "You are being affected by Tadekha."

"Tadekha does nothing for me," I purr at him. "It's all this big hog underneath your kilt."

He groans when I reach for him again and stops me before I touch him. "You do not want to do that, Faith. This isn't you."

"I know, right?" I say breathlessly. "I'm being such a dirty slut." And I am so damn horny at the moment I can't stand it. I can feel my nipples brush against the front of my filmy dress and I want to strip it off. Heck, that seems like a good idea. Aron won't let me touch him and suck his cock, but maybe if I'm all naked and quivering on his lap he'll give in and give me what I need.

Or maybe he'll just impale me on his thick shaft in front of everyone and fuck me without getting up from his chair. I close my eyes in ecstasy at the thought.

Aron lets out a breath that almost sounds like a sigh. "This is ridiculous. Come here, Faith." He takes my hand and tugs me forward, and then I'm in his lap. I try to straddle him, but he shakes his head and slides my thighs together until I'm sitting sideways on him. I curl my arms around his neck and make out with his ear.

"Why won't you let me touch you?" I moan, so full of need that it almost hurts.

He tilts his head toward mine and whispers in my ear. "We will talk about this in the morning, but you're going to be very upset."

"Not if you let me pleasure you," I tell him, panting my need. I look over at Tadekha and she's writhing in place, the angel's head working furiously between her thighs. The music plays on and everyone in the room doesn't seem to notice—and I realize they're all making out, too. I can't blame them.

I'm turned on like *crazy*.

Aron sighs heavily, but his hand goes between my thighs. "You aren't going to like that I do this." But he touches me and I realize just how wet and needy I am. I've never been so aroused in my life.

I moan and bury my face against his neck as he touches me between my thighs. "You don't know how to sleep...but you know how to do this?" I pant, shocked at the feeling of his fingers sliding through my folds. Oh lord save me, but it feels so good. I rub up against him, biting back a whimper.

He rumbles with low laughter. "You think the gods do not fuck?"

Ooh, I never thought about that. I gasp as he strokes his fingers against my pussy, because I'm so wet I'm practically dripping, and the intrusive slide of his touch makes me want to come out of my skin it feels so good. I should tell him to stop, to take his hands out from under my skirts because we're in public and I'm not keen on the idea of putting on a show. But then he finds my clit and I forget everything. He strokes the hood with expert fingers, in just the right way that makes me wild, and it doesn't take long before I'm bucking up against his hand and biting at his neck, frantic to come.

Aron grabs my neck, his big hand practically pinning me as his other works my pussy. I lift my head and our eyes meet—and that's enough for me to come and come hard. The orgasm explodes through me, leaving me gasping and breathless and without a hint of shame at what we've just done.

"I'm sorry," I pant, collapsing against his shoulder as he moves his hand out from under my filmy skirts. "That's not like me."

"I know," he says quietly, and leaves it at that.

I try to touch him once more, sliding my hand to his cock, because I'm still feeling aroused, but he pushes my hand away and focuses on the dancers. Nearby, Tadekha gives a throaty little laugh, and when I look over, the angel is lifting her flushed face from between the goddess's thighs, a look of rapture on her expression.

And that just sets me on fire all over again. I turn back to Aron and rub up against his chest, letting my nipples scrape against him. "God, you're sexy. God, I'm *so* horny."

With a small sigh, Aron slides his hand between my thighs once more and gets to work even as the music starts up again.

CHAPTER 17

*D*aylight streams into my room, so bright it hurts my eyes. I squint as I wake up, disoriented. I'm in bed, the covers tangled around my legs. My hair's still pulled into that tight braid, and my filmy, see-through dress has bunched up around my hips. I squint, opening up one eye and gazing around me. It still looks like I'm in one of the crystal chambers, but I roll on my back and rub my head, trying to remember what's happened. I ache between my thighs, and when I slide a hand there, I'm wet as if I've spent all night feverishly masturbating. I feel a little wrung out...

And hungry. My stomach growls loudly in the quiet morning air.

There's a nearby grunt. It's Aron, and he's near a window, gazing out onto the horizon, hands clasped behind his back. He is in new clothing—not nearly as wispy or ridiculous as my own —but his hair is a disheveled mess. He doesn't look at me as he speaks. "Back to yourself again or do you need my hand once more?"

I freeze.

Vague memories of last night slide through my head. The

goddess. Aron's return. The goddess getting pleasured right in front of everyone. Me rubbing myself all over Aron's leg until he dragged me into his lap and diddled me.

Oh god. He made me come several times. Not just once. Like, a *lot*. And I just kept writhing like some sort of freak who wanted more and more. A low sound of humiliation rises in my throat. "Aron...I..." I pull the blankets up to my chest, feeling shy and awful all at once. I'm utterly beyond mortified. I took our friendship—if you can call it that—to a weird, *weird* place. Even more humiliating, I can remember reaching for his cock repeatedly, only for him to pull my hands away. "I am so sorry. I don't know what came over me—"

"You were not yourself," he says in a succinct tone. "I am well aware of this, Faith. The blame lies with Tadekha and Tadekha alone."

"You think she spiked my food?" My jaw hangs open in surprise. I didn't consider it, but looking back, the evening was rather lust-fueled...and only on my part. Aron didn't seem to be affected.

"Spiked?"

"Drugged it. Made me want, uh, sex. Like, a lot."

"Ah. No, that was not it." He glances over at me, gaze flicking over my body where I'm clutching the blanket to me like modesty is a bell I can un-ring after he had his hand between my thighs last night for oh, hours and hours. "Tadekha is an Aspect. It is clear to me now which kind."

"I don't understand." I knew she was an Aspect like him, but I'm not sure how that's supposed to have some extra sort of meaning. "There are different kinds of Aspects?"

He grunts. "This is information that an anchor would have if..." He trails off. "It does not matter. This is not the time or place to discuss things."

Annoyance flashes through me. "Really? Because I'd sure fucking like to know why I acted like a ho if it was something she did. You weren't the one grinding on someone in public all night."

"You think I wasn't affected?" His eyes narrow as he glances over at me and then turns his attention back to the window.

That confession comes as a bit of a surprise. Aron always acts like he's above everything, but I remember putting my hands under his tunic last night and finding a very large and very erect cock. Okay, yeah, I guess he was affected too. Maybe that's why he's so pissy.

"I'm not sure I want to be here anymore after last night," I tell him, squeezing my thighs tightly together. God, they're still wet and sore. I'm so embarrassed at how many times I came last night. Five? Six? Eight? *Twelve?* Aron's probably got freaking hand cramps this morning. Just the thought makes me moan with fresh humiliation.

I huddle under the blankets, wishing the ground would swallow me up.

I'd really, really like to go home now, please.

"We are not staying here," Aron says firmly. "I am surprised that Tadekha has let us live, which tells me that she has plans for our use, and we will not like them."

"Enemies, right?"

"Long enemies," he says with a nod. "I have disagreed with her abuse of power when it comes to the citadel, because it has stripped the land and bankrupted Aventine. My city. We have fought over it many times."

Right. I'm sure that went well. "But we're alive—"

"And if we intend to stay that way, we will be leaving, just as soon as I figure out how." And he gazes thoughtfully out the window once more. "Tadekha will not want us to go. She is in her element here. She has control over everything. And she will be having us watched."

A shiver crawls up my spine. The goddess had seemed so pretty and delicate. I can't imagine her being as ruthless as he's making her sound...but he knows her. He knows what she's capable of. And if Aron misbehaved and got dumped here in the mortal world, Tadekha must have, too. "So what do we do?"

He gives me a sharp glance. "If I had a plan, we would already be executing it."

I make a face at him. "I missed you, too."

"That much is obvious."

Oooh, is that a crack at how I grabbed at him? "That wasn't me, dammit. That was whatever Tadekha did." I fling one of the pillows in his direction.

The pillow smacks him and he gives me an incredulous look, as if he's shocked I somehow dared to throw something at him. "You should mind yourself."

"Or what? You'll tickle me between the thighs again?"

Aron scowls and turns back to the window, silent.

I sigh. We're supposed to be a team and here we are, picking at each other. "Look, I'm sorry, all right? I'm just embarrassed about what happened last night. I can't believe I did that."

"It wasn't you," Aron says gruffly.

I guess that's about as much of an apology as I'm going to get from him. "At any rate, I'm glad you're here. How did you know to find me?"

He leans forward, studying something out the window. "The pain. It began once you left and grew less when I headed in a certain direction. I figured it must have had something to do with our attachment, and so I followed it." Aron snorts and gives a little shake of his head. "I didn't know you were foolish enough to head straight for the Citadel despite my warnings, though."

"I didn't. Some guys riding these big animals came through and snatched me up. They carried me off and that was when the pain started. I passed out, and when I woke up, I was in Tadekha's citadel dungeons. I think whoever grabbed me figured out something was wrong and brought me here."

Aron grunts.

I gather the blankets closer to my body. "So this pain thing, that's part of the bond?"

"I suppose."

"Well, I wish someone would have pointed that out before I signed up." Of course, since my choice was death, I'd probably still have done it, but I'm feeling petty and abused at the moment.

He casts me an impatient look. "I am as in the dark as you are. We need answers, but I do not trust any that Tadekha will give us."

I nod slowly. He's not wrong about that. I don't trust her, not after last night's quasi-orgy. Heck, I'm still blushing thinking about that. "I'm ready to get out of here when you are."

"Have you looked in the hall? There are at least a dozen guards just outside our room."

"Well, you can take them down, can't you? You went through those guys at the city gates like they were nothing."

"It is not my safety I am concerned about," Aron says, turning to face me. "But yours. Tadekha knows we are bonded. You think she will not have them go after you? I can take out any number of guards, but before they get to you?"

Right. Because for some reason I'm the target. "Why does everyone keep trying to kill me instead of you?"

"That is the question. And I don't want to know what happens to me if you die." He clenches his jaw. "An anchor is supposed to guide but we are both lacking knowledge. And I cannot ask Tadekha or her minions, because they will realize how truly clueless we are."

"Well I don't want me to die either!"

"Then we figure out another way out. And in the meantime, you do not leave my sight. I do not need to chase you all over the countryside once more. You are my anchor. Anchor yourself to me."

I glare at him. God, I would feel so much better about our pairing if he wasn't such a jerk. "Fine," I mutter, and leave it at that.

Hours pass in our chambers. Aron's in no mood to chit-chat, gazing out the window with impatience stamped all over his features. I nap for a bit in the bed, and when servants arrive with food, I scarf mine down. Aron doesn't eat, so after a short hesitation, I eat his, too. I notice that everything on the tray is finger-foods and no cutlery is provided. Nothing that we could use as a weapon. After that, I give myself a furtive sponge bath behind a screen and then dress in another wispy gown. No shoes are provided, and it just reminds me that Aron thinks Tadekha means to keep us prisoner. I think he's right.

On a whim, I take the food tray and carry it to the entrance of our apartments, then open the door. I put the tray down outside and glance around. Sure enough, guards line the walls, and they all turn to look at me as I peek out. I quickly duck back in, feeling a little sick to my stomach.

We need a plan.

CHAPTER 18

*A*ron continues to gaze distantly out the open window. I want to ask him what we're going to do, but I remember how pissy he was earlier. I suspect that if he knew, we'd already be doing it. Well, shit. I begin to pace, and when that doesn't help, I start to go through the room itself, looking for ideas. There's a chamber for toiletries, complete with water basins and pitchers, and a table of soaps, perfumes, and other things I don't recognize but might be cosmetics. I open every cabinet and find soft, fluffy towels, more soaps, and a variety of hair combs. Gee. I guess Tadekha figures the combs can't be weapons. I take a few of them anyhow, because fuck her, I'll figure something out.

I move to the main chambers of the apartments. The rooms we're in today are bigger than the one I was in yesterday—probably because Aron's with me now. The ceiling is high and arched, with triangular glass windows near the top of the ceiling to let light in. Everything sparkles, and the furniture is artsy and delicate and utterly useless. I have no doubt that it'd all shatter into a million tiny pieces unusable for weaponry, or she wouldn't have left them. I still grab one of the chairs and try to break it against the wall anyhow, just because I'm stubborn like that.

Of course it doesn't break. I turn to Aron and gesture at the feather-light chair in my arms. "Can you break this? Maybe we can make weapons out of it."

He grunts and moves to my side. With one swing, Aron's able to shatter it against the wall, and then we're surrounded by nothing but tiny glass shards, none large enough to use as a knife. Figures. Tadekha's thought of pretty much everything, damn it.

"Shall I break anything else for your tantrum?" Aron inquires, and I resist the urge to shoot him the bird.

"Let me think," I tell him, pacing the room—and now avoiding the area with glass shards. I've got nothing but a boatload of towels and a bed and...I turn and stare out the window that Aron's been so fascinated with. Oh. In the movies, someone would make a rope ladder and climb their way out of captivity.

I race forward, pushing past Aron's big body to stare out the window. Immediately, I get dizzy at how high up we are. Jesus. "How high up do you think we are? One hundred feet? Two?"

"Feet?" He frowns at me. "You measure your feet?"

He really is a teeth-grittingly infuriating man. I snap my fingers in front of his face. "Focus, big guy. What's the unit of measurement in this crazy world? Feet? Meters? Leagues? Lengths? What?"

"How should I know? I am a god, not some fool tradesman."

I groan. "You really are impossible sometimes." I lean over the window and stare down at the ground below. It's more of the desolate waste of the Dirtlands, nothing but rock and dirt and more dirt. I notice that the Citadel is floating...no, drifting like a cloud. In the distance, there's a rocky outcropping that looks a little higher than the rest of the surroundings. All right, then. That's what we aim for, provided I'm not out of my everloving mind in thinking we might be able to reach this with a rope ladder. I look around the room, then push past Aron, racing toward the bathroom once more.

"What are you doing?" he demands.

I ignore him, grabbing one of the cakes of soap and returning to the window. I lean over, gazing below, and then carefully drop the soap, trying to count the seconds it takes for it to hit the ground below.

One.

Two.

Three.

Four.

Five.

Six.

The soap disappears into a puff of dirt far below.

Okay, six. So that's…what, sixty feet? Six hundred? I don't know enough about physics to make my experiment work. All I know is that we're up high and we need a way down, and this is it. I take a deep breath, wondering if this is going to kill us. Then I think about how Tadekha turned last night into an orgy. Yeah, fuck that bitch. I'm not staying here. I glance down again. Two hundred feet is a good estimate, I decide. Surely between all the towels and blankets I can make enough rope to cover that length. I slap the windowsill as if to put an exclamation point on my plan and turn away. "Time to get to work."

"What do you mean?" Aron follows behind me as I head to the bathroom and grab armfuls of fluffy towels, hauling them out to the bed. "What are you doing?"

"I'm making a rope ladder so we can climb down."

He snorts with derision.

"Oh, I'm sorry, did you have a better plan?" I haul the linens onto the bed and then go back for the second armload. I wish there were more, but my second armload is pretty paltry. That's all right, though. I'll make it work. I can rip the towels into strips. Same with the bed linens. It doesn't have to be the best-looking rope. It just has to be long enough and sturdy enough to hold my weight.

He crosses his arms and watches me as I sit down on the bed with piles and piles of towels. I grab the first one and begin to rip it in half. Or, I try to. Fabric doesn't tear as easily as I expect, and I struggle with it for a painfully humiliating moment before giving up and using my damn teeth. That works, and I'm able to rip it in half and then tie the two together. "This is your plan," he states, as if I've lost my mind. "A rope."

"Yup."

"You do realize we are quite high up?"

"You said we weren't going to fight the guys in the hallway, right? Because they'd go after me to get to you? So yes, this is my plan. I'm not staying here for Orgy 2.0 and I'm sure not staying to see what other fun ideas she has for us. You said she's your enemy. That's enough for me. We need to get out of here, and this is the only way out. So yes, this is what I'm doing."

He grunts and crosses his arms, watching me as I work. "What do you know of this land?"

"So far? I know it sucks and everyone thinks I'm a tart and all the gods wandering around are assholes, including you. That's all I need to know." I take my frustrations out on the fabric in my hands. Man, it feels really freaking good to rip it into strips. I imagine it as Aron's unhelpful face.

Riiiiiip. Oh yeah. That's the ticket.

"I know that Aventine is a city that worships me," he says, his voice cutting and blunt.

"I remember that part," I tell him. "I also remember the part where they tried to kill your ass."

"Nevertheless, they pray to me. And in their prayers, they ask for certain things. Lately, they have asked for glory as they mount their attack on the Citadel. It has stripped their lands and bankrupted their people, and so they are mounting an offense against it. They plan on destroying it and everyone inside. And they ask their god for glory as they do so."

I pause. "When is this happening?"

"Soon. Very soon."

"Today soon?"

He shrugs.

Yeah, okay. Not helpful. I go back to making my rope.

I tear sheet after towel after sheet after towel. When my hands start to ache from tearing, I switch to knotting, and my rope grows by leaps and bounds. It's utterly quiet in the room except for the sound of me working, and my occasional glance over at Aron shows that he hasn't moved from his watchful spot at the window.

Yeah, I guess it'd be too much to ask for him to help his poor lil ol' anchor with, you know, the freaking escape plan.

That's all right, though. A girl wants to get out of here, she'll just do it herself, I reason. If he doesn't like it, he can just stay.

Then I remember that we're stuck together, and my jaw clenches. I'm not going to worry about Aron right now. I'm going to focus on getting out of here.

After a good hour or two of this, I'm starting to run low on strips, my rope covering the bed itself. At his spot at the window, Aron grunts. "They're here. Come and see."

I glance over at him. His mismatched eyes gleam with excitement as he leans out the window to get a better look at something. "See what?"

The smile on his face is brutal. "Aventine and its troops. And they've brought trebuchets."

Trebuchets? I don't know what those are, but a vague memory brings a mental image of catapults. Yeah, that isn't good. I scan the surrounding area. To me, it looks the same as it always does, nothing but dirt and hills and more dirt. It's brown on brown and ugly as sin. The clouds roll through the blue sky, and it looks like a beautiful day. I don't see anything, and I'm just about to say so when something in the distance gleams like metal. I squint, and sure enough, one of the clouds hangs lower than all the others. It's dust kicked up from horses, I realize...or land-hippos. He's right. Someone is coming.

And if it's an army of men from the city that just tried to assassinate Aron...

I grab his arm, wincing at the angry buzz his skin gives me. "We've got to get out of here before they arrive."

"I have been saying such a thing," he tells me, with a slight roll of his eyes. "You think Tadekha and her people are equipped to fight an army? They will just play music at them and blow kisses and this pretty, floating city of hers will topple at the first lob of the trebuchet."

"All the more reason to go," I tell him, racing back to the bed. I snag one end of the rope and then race back toward the window. "Help me find something to tie this to."

Aron sighs heavily, but he takes one end and we search the room. Eventually, we figure out that tying it to one leg of a long shimmering chaise and then wedging it crossways against the enormous flat, cushion-like bed provides the best anchor we've got. It makes me nervous, but there's no time to spare, and nothing budges when we tug on it, so it'll have to do. I tuck a few of the combs and soaps into the front of my filmy dress, since we have no money or weapons—again—and I'm hoping maybe we can barter once we get away from here. I'm not going to think about the fact that I have no shoes and my dress is see-through. One problem at a time, and I've got Aron with me. He's like a weapon all on his own.

For a brief, shining moment, I wonder if we should take our chances with the guards in the halls. I hesitate, staring at the ornate double doors. There were at least a dozen guards waiting out there, sure. But I can try and hide in the room, let Aron handle things, and come out when it's safe. But I don't trust Tadekha to not have something up her sleeve. For all I know, they could lob a grenade into the room the moment Aron shows his face at the door, and then I'm toast. Even if we do take the guards down, what then? We're still trapped here with Aventine about to attack.

Rope ladder it is.

I turn back toward the window...and Aron is already climbing out the damn thing. "Hey!" I sputter. "Wait for me, asshole!"

"Then hurry up," he says impatiently, already out the window and moving down the rope. "You take far too long to get moving. Or is that the plan? Be recaptured by the Aventinians?"

"Wow, just when I think you've hit the height of arrogance, you prove me wrong yet again," I tell him, heading to the window myself. "So kudos for that."

"Less talking and more climbing," he tells me, and then his head disappears over the side.

"It's my damn rope," I declare, but it's pointless trying to reason with Aron. He's a god and he's got the ego to boot, and I shouldn't be surprised. With an irritated sigh, I grab onto the sheet-rope and turn to climb out the window.

CHAPTER 19

They make this shit look so easy in the movies, but in reality, it's a nightmare. My arms are weak and strain under my own weight. Aron below me makes the rope shift back and forth, and the high breeze makes it almost like trying to climb down a pendulum. We're so high up it's terrifying, and I'm actually glad I don't have shoes on, because my toes cling to each knot. It's only the knots themselves that keep me from falling to my death, because I can rest my hands on each one. If I had to rely on my arm strength, I'd be dead already.

Still, I don't make fast enough time for Aron. He paces ahead of me quickly, shimmying down the rope as if he's done this a hundred times. Me, I've never realized just how out of shape I am until I have to use my arms for climbing down. I know we have to hurry. I'm trying.

I refuse to look down at the ground, because if I notice just how high up we are, I might freak the fuck out. I've never been afraid of heights that I know of, but I don't want today to be the day I acquire that fear. I just hope no one from above figures out what we're doing and cuts our rope—

Oh god, why did I just *think* that?

I force myself to move faster, to keep going. Because this is not safe, and no matter how scary it is, I have to get to the ground, and fast. Whimpering, sobbing, I keep moving down, foot by painful foot. My hands feel raw from how tightly I've gripped the rope, and each knot burns against my skin. Doesn't matter.

Just keep moving down.

Just keep moving down.

Something grabs my ankle. I let out a terrified scream, nearly losing my grip. Only sheer terror of falling to my death keeps me from letting go.

"Calm yourself," Aron shouts up at me.

I look down, and sure enough, it's his hand on my ankle. "Don't fucking *do* that," I hiss at him. "You almost made me fall!"

He lets go of my ankle and then gestures at the open expanse below us. "There is no more rope. There is nowhere else to go."

"What?" Horrified, I try to peer around him. I don't see any more rope dangling below him, and so I study the ground. Or I try to. It's still a huge drop away. Thirty feet, maybe. Fifty? Does it matter? I can't do that and survive. "Oh my god. We've got to go back." A sob forms in my throat. I'm not sure I can go back. I press my face against the straining rope knots. This is an utter nightmare.

"We cannot go back," Aron calls up to me. "Look at the troops. They are almost upon us. If they see our rope, they will fling their trebuchet at us, thinking we are with Tadekha and her minions."

I force myself to lift my head and scan the horizon. It's not hard to do, because with Aron and I both at the bottom of the damn thing, we're swinging and swaying in the breeze like a true pendulum, and the rope just keeps twisting and spinning us around. It eventually spins in the direction of the soldiers, and sure enough, what was a faint *maybe* sort of line before is much,

much closer. I can now see lines of troops and big wooden machines that must be the trebuchets.

I hate that he's right. I hate that we have to get out of here, and fast. But there's nowhere to go. Frantically, I look around. "Is there an outcropping nearby? Have we drifted close enough—"

"No time." Aron grabs my ankle again. "Slide down farther and hold onto me."

"What? NO!" Is he insane? He's insane.

"Do as I say," he barks up at me, and I resist the urge to kick his face. His hand tightens on my ankle and then he's pulling on me, the asshole. "Move farther down—"

"What the fuck are you doing?!"

"Let go, Faith—"

"No!" The rope twists, swaying, and Aron tugs harder on my ankle. Oh fuck, now he's climbing up the rope, and his big body is covering mine. "Stop it," I cry out, wanting to slap at him, but I don't have a free hand to do so. "Fuck off! We can't—"

"Let go," he says again, and his voice is in my ear, the heat and electricity of his big body against my back.

I don't let go.

I don't have to, because in the next moment, the rope snaps somewhere above and all the tension disappears from my hands, and then we're falling, and falling...

I smack into the ground with enough force that the air slams out of my lungs. Everything hurts and throbs with pain, and I lie completely still for a moment, stunned.

It takes me a moment to realize that I'm not dead.

It takes a longer moment to realize that I didn't land, belly-down, onto the dirt. I landed on top of Aron.

Gasping, fighting off the blackness that creeps at the edges of my vision, I struggle to sit up. I'm having trouble focusing and the world is a messy blur. My head throbs and there's still no air in my stupid lungs and I can't breathe and that's terrifying enough on its own—

And then I'm able to take a shallow breath. Then another. I cough, desperate and relieved. The blackness fades away and I'm able to focus on my surroundings despite the throb in my head. I realize after a moment that I'm still straddling Aron, my legs thrown over his, my butt resting in the cradle of his hips.

I landed on top of him and it nearly killed me. I don't know how it *didn't* kill me, and yet I'm still here. Even so...that must mean Aron's dead. I stare down in horror at the man underneath me, his eyes closed, his dark hair spread out around him like a halo in the dust. That dusky red scar that bisects one half of his face stands out like a bloodstain.

He opens his mismatched eyes and scowls at me.

"Oh my god," I choke out. "You're alive."

"Why would I not be?"

"Because we shouldn't be?" I glance up, looking for the dangling end of the rope. It's swaying in the wind, high above us, barely visible in the shadows of the Citadel. Oh god. "How did we survive that?"

"I believe I am still immortal, despite being trapped on this plane. You are the mortal part of this pairing. As long as I protect you, I suspect I am safe."

That makes a lot of horrifying sense. It explains why I'm eating and why he's not. Why I'm sleeping and why he's not. Why everyone would attack me and not him. "I have no idea how that makes me feel," I whisper.

"Me either." And Aron frowns to himself, as if displeased with this realization.

As he does, it comes to my attention that I'm still straddling him. My hands are splayed across his chest. Our bodies are posed not as if we've just taken a tumble but as if we're in bed together and I've decided to be on top. I can feel my cheeks grow heated at the thought, and Aron's eyes narrow as he gazes at me, and I wonder if he's thinking the same thing.

Then I remember last night's humiliating dinner in the audience chamber with Tadekha, when I rubbed myself all over Aron like a cat in heat and he petted me between my thighs like it was some sort of obligation. Ugh. I fling myself off of him, rolling to the ground.

I flop down on my back, staring up at the sky. The rope swings back and forth high above, taunting me. The Citadel itself is beautiful in the sunlight, glittering like a translucent many-tiered wedding cake floating in the deep blue sky. It's the prettiest thing I've ever seen…too bad it's filled with assholes. Or just one big asshole. I think of lovely, dainty Tadekha and the smug smile on her face. I think of the adoring shimmering-winged angel women she surrounds herself with. I think of last night, when Tadekha's anchor eagerly planted her face between the goddess's thighs and muff-dived as if her life depended on it.

Next to me, Aron staggers to his feet and dusts off his plain red tunic. His hands slap at the fabric and it sends a wave of dust into my face, causing me to choke and cough again. "It is time to go," Aron tells me.

I don't want to get up just yet. In fact, it would be great if I didn't have to move again, ever. "Everything hurts," I tell him. "Let's give ourselves a few minutes, okay?" The thought of hauling myself to my feet and walking these endless dirt plains seems like a terrible idea. Damn it all, maybe we should have taken our chances with the guards, tried to shanghai the Citadel from Tadekha's grasp.

"Get up," Aron says bluntly. "There is no time to waste."

Isn't there? The Citadel is peacefully drifting overhead, and while there are no birds chirping, it's still rather serene. I want to stay here just long enough to have a nap and let my throbbing, aching body recover.

As I stare up at the floating crystal city, something small and dark flies through the air toward it. For a brief moment, I think it's a bowling ball, and that makes me pause, because why would a bowling ball be flying through the air—

A crashing sound like a thousand glasses breaking interrupts the silence. Overhead, I watch as one delicate tower collapses on itself and a rain of crystal chunks fall from the sky overhead toward the ground.

Toward me, stretched out on the ground.

I gasp, but before I can do anything, Aron's covering me with his body, and there's a tinkle like windchimes all around us as the crystals rain to the dirt.

"What was that?" I manage to choke out, covering my mouth with one gauzy sleeve. The air's filled with dust and crystal fragments.

"Trebuchet," he tells me, voice abrupt. His expression is that pissy, impatient look he always wears, and I know what he's thinking—he just had to save my ass again. "It is time to go."

"Let's go," I tell him faintly. I don't want to be underneath the Citadel as it's attacked. That might be the worst place possible— death from above and death from the troops that approach closer and closer.

Perhaps escape wasn't such a good plan after all.

CHAPTER 20

We walk across the dusty, crumbly hills of the Dirtlands. Or at least, Aron walks. I sort of stagger behind him, my entire body throbbing with pain. If he's hurting from his fall, he doesn't show it in the slightest. His form is as straight as ever, his clothing unblemished by what we've gone through. Meanwhile, my filmy dress is torn in several places, and the hem is covered in dirt. I'm sweaty and the fabric sticks to me in unpleasant places. Elegant, I'm not.

How I look doesn't matter, though. All that matters is getting away from the Citadel because it is most definitely under attack. Every so often, there's a sound like a crash of windchimes, and when I turn back to look, smoke pours up from one of the graceful, spindly towers of the floating city. I think of all the people there with horror, because where are they supposed to go? Sure, Tadekha's ladies have wings, but they didn't strike me as particularly warlike. I don't see anyone flying around the Citadel itself, so I'm guessing they're not much in the way of defenses. I think of the soldiers in the hall—they didn't have wings. Seems like an oversight to me. I stare up, shielding my eyes against the sunlight, wondering if they're all doomed.

A hand grabs mine and I yelp, even as a shock jolts up my arm.

"This is no time to stare," Aron tells me. "We are still too close."

"Sorry," I tell him, and grab a handful of my long, flowing skirts with my free hand, because he's not letting go of my other. I'm forced to trot behind him, no easy feat considering I have no shoes and the ground beneath our feet is crumbling and loose dirt, but we manage.

We continue like this for what feels like hours, Aron half dragging, half hauling me along behind him, and me stumbling after him. Without shade, the day gets hot, and there's no food or drink to be found. I want to cry at how overheated I am, but there's no point—it's not like there's a lemonade stand anywhere. I just need to suck it up and keep going. It's towards sunset that there's a terrible, roaring sound and the ground trembles beneath our feet. I tear my hand out of Aron's ruthless grasp and come to a halt, gasping and staring at the ground. "What...the fuck...was that? An earthquake?"

He frowns at me, probably for stopping, and then gazes over my shoulder, off into the horizon. "Tadekha's Citadel," he says after a moment. "It's gone."

Gone?

I whip around, staring at the area we've left behind. I don't see the Citadel itself anywhere on the horizon, which is shocking in itself. There's just a dark smear of smoke. "Where is it?"

"Gone," he repeats, clearly impatient. "Does 'gone' mean something else in the mortal tongue? It has been destroyed."

"Don't be a dick," I retort, putting a hand to my brow as if that'll help visibility. To be honest, visibility isn't the problem. Even from the distance of a few hours' walk, I can see the red line of the Aventine troops, splashing like blood against the dirt.

I can see the smoke pouring from the skies, and ahead of them...glitter on the ground.

Oh no. So much glitter. The Citadel's nothing but a bajillion broken shards. "Oh my god. What about all the people inside?" I turn and look at Aron in horror. "What about Tadekha?"

"Dead," he says flatly. "Her own fault."

I give him a shocked look. "How is this her fault?"

"She knows perfectly well what the Citadel was doing to the land. She did not care. Aventine has taken it back. Maybe someday something will grow here again." He shrugs. "Now the battle begins. I imagine it will not be much of one."

"If there's anyone fucking left!"

"If there is, they will capture any survivors and sacrifice them in my name as thanks for their victory. Or they will make them slaves." He shrugs.

"What? Is that why you don't give a shit?" I'm horrified. "It doesn't matter that all those people just died horribly because hey, fuck it, I'll get a few good prayers out of this?" I spread my arms wide. "Are you fucking serious, Aron?"

"I am a god of battle. Not sacrifices. I do not ask for such things, nor do I approve them. They do this of their own accord." He shrugs those big shoulders. "As for Tadekha, she has been warned many times over the years." He looks thoughtful. "I wonder what happens to your Aspect if you die. Has she already returned to the Aether?"

"Jealous much?" I say sarcastically.

"No," he replies. "Tadekha—if she lives—will be tortured for quite some time. It is not one to be envious of."

"This is not making me feel better, Aron!"

He gives me a stern look. "You feel sorry for her? When she would rather enslave her faithful into sexual play instead of protecting them? She cares nothing for their fates, because she is immortal. She cares nothing for this land." He spreads his arms wide, and I gaze around at the ruined, dirt-filled place that should be crops and trees and birds and is just awful nothing-ness. "She does not care about anything but herself, so do not feel sorry for her. She doesn't deserve it."

I can't disagree with him after hearing that, and I wonder if it makes me a bad person. I'm unhappy about the fates of the others—First, the goddess's anchor, and all of the other young, happy, devoted faces I saw there. So many people.

But Aron's right. They threw their lot in with her. If everyone knew this was going to happen...someone should have done something.

When he extends his hand out again, I swipe at my eyes (didn't even realize I'm crying) and take it once more, letting him lead me away.

When the sun goes down, Aron takes pity on my constant staggering and stumbling. There's a large boulder on one side of the road, and he leads us to it. "I suppose we must take shelter for the night. It's clear to me that despite the danger, you can't go on much further."

I'm not even mad about his arrogant words. I'm just too relieved that we're going to actually stop. My body throbs with pain like it's one big bruise, and my feet are blistered from walking barefoot all day. I haven't complained, though. At least I'm alive. I keep thinking of First and her beautiful, crystal wings—and the fact that she's probably been crushed under a hundred tons of falling Citadel. That puts things in perspective. No matter how big of a dick Aron is, he wants to keep us both safe and alive. He protected me when we fell, and I won't forget that. It had to hurt a lot.

Aron releases my hand when we reach the boulder, and I collapse gratefully at the base of it. I lie down, not even caring that the cobbled road is covered with a fine layer of grit and dirt. All that matters is that we've stopped. I close my eyes, wallowing in my pain for long moments.

I'm alive and that's all that matters.

"Thank you for stopping," I whisper through parched lips.

Aron only grunts acknowledgment of my words. There's no snideness, no pissy commentary. I open my eyes a slit and glance over at him. He's not sitting. He's staring off into the distance, his hands on his hips, his tunic plastered to his back. He must be sweaty. I find that strangely odd, because Aron seems unaffected by the elements. Even in the heat of the day, he was cool and unbothered while I panted and huffed and choked on mouthfuls of dust.

He glances down the road, in the direction we're heading, and for a terrifying moment, I think he's going to demand that I should get up, and we should keep going. But he doesn't. He merely looks thoughtful and I relax.

When I lay my head back down on the dirt, I realize that his back is glittering.

I frown, slowly sitting up, and as I do, the crystals flash and catch the fading light. "Aron, your back."

He glances over his shoulder at me. "What of it?"

"You've got crystals embedded in your skin." I get to my feet and hobble to his side. Sure enough, his tunic is sticking to him not because of sweat, but because it's pinned against his flesh by crystal shards. I think back and remember how the crystals rained down on top of us with the first trebuchet hit to the Citadel...and then I remember Aron landed on his back, with me on top of him. Oh dear. Guilt hits me. "Are you okay?"

"I am standing and whole. Of course I am fine." He scowls at me as if it's a stupid question to even ask.

I do notice he doesn't say his back is fine, though. I'm starting to read between the lines the longer I get to know Aron. He's full of bluster—piss and vinegar, as my mother would say—

but he's not heartless. He just doesn't understand a lot of this world. I know how that feels.

"Come sit down by the boulder and I'll pick them out for you," I tell him, reaching out and taking his hand. There's a skittering shock as I touch him, but he doesn't protest and lets me lead him forward. I go back to my spot by the rocks at the edge of the path, sit down, and cross my aching legs, then pat the spot in front of me. "Here."

He sits, his back toward me. As he does, I realize again just how massively big this guy is. His shoulders spread wide, thick with muscle, and I think he's more than twice the size of me. I'm not exactly dainty, either. I'm a nice, solid, average girl, but Aron's sheer size makes me seem like a delicate Disney princess to his Conan the Barbarian. Of course, he is a god of battle. I don't expect him to be built like a scholar, but it's still good to know this guy's on my side.

Concentrate, dummy, I tell myself as he shifts, his shoulders bunching. I'm doing a crappy job of helping him by just staring at his back (no matter how appealing a wide set of shoulders is, they're still attached to him). I reach out and pluck the largest chunk of crystal shard from his back and set it down carefully on one of the cobblestones. It's the size of a needle and I feel terrible that I didn't notice it before. In my defense, though, he's run me to the point of exhaustion.

That's about the only defense I have, because now that I'm looking, he's got dozens of these terrible things pinning his tunic to his skin. As I stare, a spot of blood blooms where I've pulled the first shard. Great.

He remains silent as I get to work, plucking shards and unpinning fabric bit by excruciating bit. If it hurts, he doesn't indicate it. In fact, he barely moves. Me, I'm wincing with every tug, imagining just how painful it must be and how much he's hurt all day and I didn't pay attention. The blood dotting the back of his tunic isn't helping me feel better, either. As I pull out one particularly big chunk, I set it on top of the pile and decide to say something. "Aron?"

"Mm?"

"Thank you for saving me back there. I'm pretty sure I would have died if I'd landed flat on the ground."

"You would have," he agrees.

I frown absently at his back as I tug another piece out. My fingertips are bleeding and raw, because this crystal makes no friends, but that doesn't matter. "I'm grateful."

"You should be."

I bite back my irritation. This is just Aron. This is who he is. A big, arrogant douche. "Anyhow, thank you for saving my life."

He is silent for a long moment. Then he glances over his shoulder back at me. "Do not imagine yourself important. I need you. I save you because I am saving myself."

Dick. "Gee, thanks."

"Would you rather I coddle you with lies?"

"I would rather you be nice about it. I'm thanking you and you're kind of being an ass about it."

He merely snorts. "If I was being an ass, I would demand you show me your gratitude on your knees, as Tadekha would demand of her anchor. Instead, I am letting you rest and tend to me." He spreads his arms. "Am I not the most benevolent of gods?"

"No, you most definitely are not," I mutter under my breath as I pluck another crystal.

CHAPTER 21

*T*he next day, I'm so hungry and thirsty I'm delirious. It takes everything I have to move one foot in front of the other, and even that I'm doing badly. Aron has to haul me along by one arm, dragging me beside him all morning. The sun gets high in the sky and then it's too much to do even that. I'm panting and not sweating despite the heat, which I know is a bad thing. I need water and shade and rest...and there just isn't any.

Eventually, Aron realizes that I'm not being lazy as much as being "collapse" and hauls me into his arms. He carries me as he walks down the road. "You are not allowed to die, Faith," he tells me sternly.

I give him a weak thumbs up. "I'll keep that in mind."

He frowns down at me. "Put your arms around my neck. You are sliding out of my grip."

"I really don't want to," I begin, but he gives me a hard jiggle and I have no choice but to do so. I'm burning up and touching him just makes everything hotter and more miserable. Sunstroke, I bet. There's no shade and I'd give anything for a drink. "You might have to get yourself a new anchor," I tell him woozily, the world tilting. I'm so tired.

"I will not." He gives me another hard jostle. "Wake up."

"Asshole. Let me sleep through this misery." He shakes me again, until my teeth are clenched with frustration and I have to knot my fingers against his collar to keep my grip there. "I hate you."

"You think I care? You are here to serve me, and yet here I am, carrying you because you are too lazy to walk." His words are dickish as fuck, but he says them in a quiet, calm manner, as if he doesn't truly mean them.

I don't know what to make of that. Or of him at all. Damn arrogant prick. I wish I'd been found by the god of cupcakes or kittens instead of the arrogant god of battle. And storms.

Wait.

"Aron," I gasp, clutching at him. Blackness fades in and out of my vision, and I'm so overheated it feels like I'm going to die. "Can you make it rain?"

"You wish a storm? Why?"

"I need a drink," I whimper at him. I know I'm whining, but I don't care. "Please. I'll do anything."

He sighs and holds me close against his chest. "I forget how fragile you mortals are." For a moment, I think his voice sounds curiously gentle, but that has to be the heatstroke talking. But then thunder crashes overhead and clouds roll in. The terrible sun that feels as if it's baking me like a potato disappears, and a moment later, a downpour drenches the skies.

The temperature changes immediately, so quickly that it sends a sharp pain through my head. I gasp as cold, wet rain pounds my skin and soaks me, washing away dirt and heat and all the terrible things of the day. Even so, it's wet and refreshing and I don't care how much it makes my head hurt. I moan and tilt my face back, catching the rain in my mouth.

"Better, little mortal?"

"Thank you," I gasp, and then drink more. I cup my hands to drink as much as I can, and then collapse back against his chest, exhausted.

THE DOWNSIDE of rain is that after it fades away, the air is humid and sticky once more. My wispy gauze dress is soaked, and I suck on the moisture there for another drink later, and then fall back against Aron's shoulder, unconscious. I want to tell him that I'm not normally such a wimp. That I can usually handle myself and I'm a decent hiker, but I don't have the energy.

This is what it feels like to be dying, I think. Strange how it came on that fast. Shouldn't it take a few days for me to die of thirst? But I feel like I'm at my end as it is, and Aron seems to think so, too.

"Not much farther," he tells me as I fade in and out of consciousness.

I'm pretty sure he's lying to me. That's all right. It's a nice lie.

Distantly, I hear the sound of thunder, and I feel more rain patter against my skin, but I'm too far gone in sleep to pay much attention. I want to wake up and thank him, but it feels like a huge effort, a mountain that I'm sitting at the base of, and it's much too far to climb.

"Not much longer, my friend," Aron says, his voice a whisper against my hair.

Aw. He thinks we're friends now. It's a nice thing to hear right before I die. I struggle awake despite the mountain of effort and manage to open my eyes. The storm clouds roll overhead, highlighting Aron's unearthly beauty.

"Look," he tells me. "Shelter."

It takes everything I have to turn my head, but when I do, I see...grass, like a green carpet. In the distance, there are small bushes and neat rows of what looks like a tended field. Off atop a distant cliff there's a tiny building with a plume of smoke rising from the chimney.

Huh. We've reached the edge of the Dirtlands.

I must have drowsed off, because the next thing I know, I open my eyes and the house is right in front of us. Come to think of it, it looks less like a house and more like an old timey church, complete with long stone walls and straw roof. I don't care, though. As long as they have food and water, I'll sleep on a church floor.

Aron, being Aron, goes up to the heavy wooden door of the church and kicks it. "Open up," he calls out in that imperious voice of his. I want to tell him that's not exactly how you ask for a place to stay for the night, but I'm too tired. I just rest my head on his shoulder and try not to think about how dry my throat is. He looks down at me with alarm and gives me a rough jostle. "You are not allowed to die."

"Sure," I tell him faintly, even as the door opens.

It's a man, dressed in gray robes, his white hair parted down the middle and hanging in two long braids on either side of his face. Even though I'm struggling to stay conscious, there's no mistaking how pale the weathered face gets as he sees Aron. He immediately drops to his knees and bows his head. "My Lord of Storms. It is an honor."

"Good," Aron says curtly, pushing inside. "My anchor is dying. She needs help."

"Whatever I have is yours," the man stammers. "Is she injured?"

"Hungry," Aron says.

"Thirsty," I manage to croak out. I am hungry, but my throat hurts so much that I think I might die in the next minute if I don't get a drink.

"Of course. Just a moment." He scurries off, disappearing behind a shelf and I hear a clatter of pots and pans.

Aron glances around and gives a haughty sniff at our surroundings. "I suppose this will do for a day."

Like we're flooded with choices.

I fight my heavy eyelids and peer around, too. It's not a church after all, but a library. Books of all shapes and sizes line the walls, shelves groaning with the weight of them. There are books in stacks in the middle of the room, along the walls, and covering every surface imaginable. It's not dusty, just cluttered. The place is dark inside, lit only by a few small lanterns, and off to one side there's a large table with parchment, ink, and a book open in front of it. Whoever this guy is, it looks like he's the one writing the books.

Aron heads deeper into the place, moving past shelves and knocking over stacks of books as he goes. I bite back a protest, because it seems wrong to bother this solitary man...but on the other hand, I feel so awful that I'm not sure I care. At the back of the building, past another massive stack of books that topples as he moves through, there's a small cot, the bed neatly made. Aron lays me down on it even as the monk—because he has to be a monk—scurries in with a pitcher of water and a bit of bread and cheese.

"This is all you have?" Aron scowls as the monk moves to my side and scoops a simple clay cup into the pitcher, then offers it to me.

"I apologize, Lord, but I live simply," the monk says. He's not disturbed by Aron's words, his serene expression unruffled.

I take the cup from his hands, sucking the water down greedily. It's the best thing I've ever had, and it's gone far too soon. I drink it all and hold the cup out for more.

"You should drink it slowly," the monk begins, only to be interrupted by Aron again.

"Give her all that she wants," he snaps, crossing his arms over his chest. "I cannot have her dying."

The monk sighs, dips another cup, and gives it to me. I hesitate, because Aron seems to be in a real mood, but I'm so thirsty I can't pass up the water. I gulp it down, and a third cup when he hands it to me. He offers me bread, but I skip it—too dry—in favor of the cheese, and gnaw on it for a moment. The taste is sharp and overwhelming, but I eat it anyhow.

Aron's just watching me carefully, not eating or drinking. He has to be hungry and thirsty, too. When the monk gives me another cup of water, I nod at Aron. "You should drink something," I tell him around a mouthful of cheese. I don't miss the way the monk's eyebrows go down, as if surprised by my offer. Maybe he expects me to be as big a dick as Aron is.

"Unnecessary," the god says, watching me closely. "You drink it."

My stomach's starting to cramp and I feel a sweat breaking out on my forehead. I put down the cheese and lift the cup to my lips. I don't feel so good. I want to drink, and I want to throw up, too. "Um," I say, and then my mouth floods with saliva. Oh. Oh no.

With a kind expression, the monk holds up the nearly empty pitcher, offering it to me. I snatch it from his hands and manage to tuck it under my chin just before I vomit up all the water I just drank.

Off to the side, Aron makes a sound of disgust. "Mortals."

The monk pats my knee as I puke a second round. "I thought that might happen if you drank too much. I will bring you something to clean off with, my dear, and some tea to settle your stomach."

I watch in surprise as he beams a serene smile at Aron and then heads off to what must be his kitchen once more.

Aron lifts his chin at me. "Stay there. Rest until you feel better."

No one has to tell me twice. I set down the pitcher, lie back on the blankets, and allow myself to pass the fuck out.

I WAKE up the next morning with a big hand stroking my hair, my face smushed against a hard chest, and my arm (and leg) flung over someone.

Er.

I look up groggily and it's Aron. I'm not surprised, but I am a little bewildered.

"Your hair needs a washing," is all he says.

"I'm sure I would have put it higher on the priority scale if I would have known you were going to climb into bed with me," I mutter, struggling to sit upright.

He snorts. "No, you wouldn't have."

"You're right, I wouldn't have." I scrub a hand over my face and sit on the edge of the cot, a little unnerved that he's pressed up against me. "Why are you in bed with me?"

"It's clear to me that you get into trouble wherever you go, so I'm keeping a close eye on you. You're not leaving my sight again."

"Great," I say without enthusiasm. I squint at him because even as he gets out of the bed, his muscles are rippling and his hair perfect and yet he looks...off. Tired. "Did you sleep?"

"I need no sleep."

"Really? Because you look tired to me."

He gives me another imperious look. "I did not ask you."

All righty then. I yawn and push my hair off my head. He's not wrong. After the dump to the ground when we fled the Citadel, my hair's caked in all kinds of filth and sweat. I've probably still got crystals tangled into it. Still...he was petting it. As if he liked it, or me. For someone that professes to find me annoying, he let me sleep sprawled on top of him all night, all without sleeping on his own.

Aron puts his hands on his hips and frowns at his surroundings. "Where is the mortal that lives here?" He cups a hand to his mouth, all imperious god once again. "Mortal! We have need of you."

I cringe. "Aron, don't. That's rude. I'm sure we can find our way around..." I let my words trail off because the monk comes scurrying in, his long robes flapping around his legs, his weird braids bouncing on his shoulders. He's got a big tray of food—fruit, cheese, nuts, more bread—and a pitcher.

"Good morning," he says, beaming at us. "I've brought food for your anchor, Lord of Storms. Do you require anything from me?" He sets the tray down on a nearby stack of books and plucks a cup from the tray, filling it and then offering it to me. "Drink slowly this time, my dear. Your body needs time to recover."

I take the cup and sip it, even though I feel much better. Vaguely, I remember waking up in the middle of the night to have someone give me sips of water. I remember pale hands and a soothing voice offering encouragement, but when I look at the monk, his hands are brown and weathered. Hmmm.

"I need nothing," Aron says in a clipped voice. "Make sure my mortal gets her fill of food and drink and then she needs a bath." He stalks out from the shelves and his feet thud heavily against the creaking wooden floors. "I am going to scout the area to determine how safe it is. When I return, we will need clothing. Both of us."

"I have extra robes," the monk says in a cheery voice. "They are yours for the taking, as are my savings."

I cringe at that even as I sip the delicious, cold water. This guy sure is ready to give everything to Aron at a moment's notice. I worry we're going to ruin the poor guy's life just by dropping in and he's been so darn nice. I mean, we dropped in on Tadekha in a sense and look where she is now—at the bottom of a pile of rubble.

"Eat, eat," the monk tells me as he pushes a bread bowl into my hands. It's full of fruit wedges and nuts and cheese and all kinds of delicious things and I immediately tuck into it.

"Thank you," I tell him between mouthfuls as he putters around. Oh my god, I've never tasted anything better. I stuff my gob for a few minutes, and then I remember how awful it was to puke yesterday and force myself to slow down. I take small nibbles of food and wash them down with water as he bustles about in the room, straightening piles of books and putting things away while flicking excited glances in my direction. "What's your name?" I ask after a few minutes of this. "I'm Faith."

"You're what?" He turns and looks at me, eyes wide.

"Is that not a common name around here? It's pretty common where I'm from." I sound defensive even to my own ears. "It doesn't mean anything. It's just Faith."

"Fascinating," he tells me with a delighted smile. "And such a perfect name for an anchor to our esteemed Lord of Storms."

"I dunno," I say as I eat the world's biggest wedge of cheese and love every moment of it. "I'm pretty sure he thinks my name is 'mortal.'"

The monk just giggles at that. "You will have to forgive him. He is a god, after all, and not used to this plane or the ways of mortal people."

"Oh, I've been with the guy for a few days. Trust me when I say there's a lot of forgiving going on." I take another drink. "It's either that or murder him in his sleep."

The monk's eyes go wide as saucers. After a moment, he lets out another little giggle. "That is a joke, yes?"

"Yep."

He straightens a stack of big books across from the cot and then sits down on them like it's a stool, watching me with a fascinated expression. "My name is Omos. I am a humble monk who serves Magra, goddess of plenty." He nods at us. "And now, it is an honor to serve you and Lord Aron, Faith. Whatever I have is yours."

"Hi, Omos. I have to admit I'm not from around here, so I'm a bit lost." I give him a faint smile. "It's nice to finally see a friendly face."

Compassion moves across the monk's features and he gives a heavy sigh, then nods. "It is a hard road you have chosen, to be an anchor."

"So you *have* met Aron," I joke. When he doesn't smile, I'm a little worried. He just looks troubled. "Can I admit something? I don't know what I signed up for. In fact, I don't know anything about any of this. It was either sign up to be Aron's anchor or die as a human sacrifice. I thought I'd take my chances with Aron, but the longer we're together, the more questions I have."

"Of course. I spoke with Lord Aron while you slept. I will do my best to help you both prepare for your journey."

"Can you tell me how I get home?'

"I can try." His lined face crinkles in a smile. "Where are you from? The coast? Glistentide?"

"Chicago?"

Omos's frown deepens and he gets to his feet. "I do not recognize the name." He moves to one of the shelves, his hand fluttering over it as I take another drink of water and eat. A moment later, he pulls out a rolled up parchment and spreads it on one end of the bed, and I realize it's a map. "Shago...Shago..."

I swallow hard and put a hand to my lips, murmuring around a mouthful of food. "You're not going to find it on that map. When I say I'm not from here, I mean I'm really, really not from here." I hesitate, watching his face. "I'm from another world entirely. I don't know how I got sucked here, but I went through a door in my world when I heard drums and I woke up on this side in a strange place." Omos watches me quietly, his eyes wide, and my heart sinks a little. "I know you don't believe me, or think I'm crazy—"

"No, not crazy, not at all." Omos jumps to his feet and races away, and I start to wonder if I'm the crazy one. He comes back

BOUND TO THE BATTLE GOD

a moment later with a heavy, thick book covered in red and gold, and sits down atop another stack of books. He pages through it, frowning to himself. "It's here somewhere."

"What is?"

He looks up at me. "Why, the tale of Queen Natasha. She came from another world and conquered the Fair Plains back before it became the kingdom of Yshrem. She ruled for thirty years...twenty? No, I'm pretty sure it's thirty." He frowns absently and flips through the book. "Maybe twenty-three..."

I put down the bit of fruit in my hand. "Natasha...she was from Earth?"

"Where?" He looks up at me, peering.

"Earth? That's where I'm from."

"I thought you said you were from Shago."

"No, no, I'm from the city of Chicago. State of Illinois. Country of the United States. Planet Earth."

"Oh. Goodness." He beams at me. "You'll have to tell me all that again later so I can record it. How very fascinating. This world is Aos, if you do not know. I have never heard of Earth." He picks up the book and flips through it again. As for Natasha, it's not stated where she's from, just that she came from a place beyond all lands. She said it was another world, but there are varying theories on such things. From what I hear, she was a very good queen. Very learned. There are a few books about her, I think, but I don't have any in this library." He looks wistful. "They're probably all forgotten in some Yshremi library." He closes the book and smiles at me. "My point is that while it is unusual, it is not the first time I have heard of such a thing."

"That's amazing." I'm actually ready to cry I'm so relieved. Someone else has heard of my situation. "I thought I'd be stuck here forever. Do the books say if there's a way to get home?"

Omos blinks at me. "Go home? But you are Aron's anchor. You can't leave. Not until he ascends once more."

Obviously there's a piece of information or three that we're missing between us. "Ascends. Back to Heaven or wherever he's from?"

"The Aether, that's correct."

"Can you tell me more about this? Like why a god's been booted out of Heaven? And what we have to do to get him back there?"

"Oh goodness, yes. Of course." Omos clutches the book to his chest, looking rapturous. "This is the Anticipation. It's finally upon us once more. It's a time when the twelve minor gods must account for their sins to the High Father."

"So...this has happened before?"

"Twice before in recorded history, and it was foretold that it would come once more. We have always celebrated the Anticipation every year, but I don't think anyone truly expected it to happen now. These are troubling times."

For a man that lives in troubling times, he looks really darn pleased. "But you're not surprised. At least, you don't seem so."

"Me? No. I saw the moon fade like the prophecies foretold three days prior to the Anticipation and knew it'd be upon us."

"Prophecies?" When he gets to his feet, no doubt to look for another book, I grab his arm. "Wait. I don't care about the prophecies. Just keep telling me more about the Anticipation." If he goes to hunt for another book, I'm going to be here all damn day long and I'm finally getting answers. I don't want to be interrupted by anything at all. "What's this about accounting for sins? And there are twelve gods roaming the earth right now?"

He settles back down on his seat. "Well, no, not exactly. If this is going how the prophecies have told, then I imagine there are forty-four Aspects wandering about our lands."

Wait, forty-four? "I thought you said there were twelve gods? Aron—"

"Is an *Aspect*," Omos tells me, and gets to his feet again. "I have the perfect book to show you. I'll be right back."

I sigh and let him go, taking another large bite of food. Might as well eat. This could be a while.

CHAPTER 22

I eat as I hear Omos puttering around in his books. He's humming to himself, and it's clear that even though he lives alone here, his books are all the company he needs. It's kind of sweet. An "Aha" comes from the far end of the building, and then the monk returns to my side a few moments later with another beautifully bound, oversized book. He sets it down on the bed and flips through it.

"The last time the gods were outcast in an Anticipation, there were forty-four Aspects cast down from the heavens. The High Father is pure and just, of course. He is immortal and eternal. The other gods are eternal but not immortal, since they were born of human parents."

"They were?" I'm surprised to hear that. Nothing about Aron seems all that...normal.

"Oh yes." He straightens and studies his shelves. "I have another book—"

"Let's just focus on this one," I tell him, patting the one on the bed with me. "So the forty-four are from humans...?"

"Twelve gods," Omos corrects. "Twelve born of humankind and lifted up to rule over them. Aron of the Cleaver is the god of battle and lord of thunder, but I'm sure you knew that." He carefully flips through pages and then smooths the book out, turning it toward me as he opens up to a two-page spread. "Here are the others."

There's a gorgeous diagram illustrated across the two pages, full of symbols and figures and swooping, swirling lettering that looks like it took a hundred years to draw. Unfortunately for me, it's all written in a language I don't read. "I can't make out any of this. I don't read your language, Omos. I'm sorry."

"Ah, of course." He angles the book a little toward him and taps at one picture. "This is Aron of the Cleaver."

I look closer and nod, because I see it now. Dark hair. Bright red scar down side of face and an eyepatch. The guy in the picture is holding an axe flat across his chest like a shield, and I haven't seen my Aron do that, but maybe it's because he doesn't have one yet. "Eyepatch, huh?"

"His greatest legend is how he lost an eye to a dragon."

"I see." Kinda looks like he found it again. Maybe gods regenerate that sort of thing.

"This is my goddess, Magra. She is the bringer of plenty." He taps a figure across the page, of a beautiful woman dressed in long, loose green robes with arms full of wheat.

Off to one side, I see another woman, this one holding a swirl of magic. Her hair is long and dark and her eyes are practically flashing as her robes fly about her. "Tadekha?" I ask.

"Goddess of magic," he agrees.

"I met her," I murmur, wrinkling my nose. More like horndog of magic.

Omos makes a sound of surprise in his throat. "You did? How was she?"

"Er...unpleasant. Let's keep going. So all of these gods are different...things?" I gesture at the book. It reminds me a bit of the ancient mythologies I studied back in grade school, the Greek and Roman gods with crazy stories told about them.

187

"Yes. This is Gental, god of family, and Kassam, Lord of the Wild." He points at a drawing of a man brandishing antlers. "Rhagos, Lord of the Dead. Anali, goddess of—"

I pat the book, interrupting him again or else I'm going to be subjected to the entire pantheon and their history. "That's great, but let's get on to the part about how there are forty-four people here in the mortal realm – on Aos - instead of twelve. How does that happen?"

"Like I said," he gently rebukes me, turning a page. "The twelve are eternal but not immortal. They are flawed, and sometimes those flaws become too great. The world shifts off balance and the gods no longer have the best interests of the world at heart. They grow greedy and selfish and lost in their own petty squabbles. That is when the High Father takes action. He casts them out and splits them into Aspects to teach them a lesson."

All right, now we're getting somewhere. There's that Aspect word again. "And Aspects are…"

"Incarnations of their flaws." Omos flips through the book again, flicking page after page. "There are four divine virtues and four divine flaws. Because the High Father wants to extinguish the flaws from his gods, he casts them out and fragments them into four copies of themselves. Each copy represents the flaw they are working to purge from their system."

It's weird to think of Aron as a fragment of a god. "What are the four flaws?"

"Lies, Hedonism, Arrogance, and Apathy."

Oh. I think of Aron. "And each Aspect personifies one of these particular flaws?" At his nod, my mouth twists a little. "I can guess which one Aron is."

Omos chuckles and gives his head a little shake. "It's easy to see that he's Arrogance. Even when he wants to be kind, he doesn't know how to be. That's why you must be patient with him."

That explains why Omos isn't ruffled by Aron's constant demands. I think of all the times I've wanted a kind word from Aron and got a douche comment. No, not douchey, really. Just incredibly arrogant.

Because that's who he is.

It feels like so many things are clicking into place. I think of Tadekha and how Aron wanted nothing to do with her. I think of her with her angel servant between her thighs. That would be hedonism. Maybe that's why I rubbed myself all over Aron like a dick addict. God. I can feel myself blushing. "This makes sense," is all I say to Omos. "But your math is off. Twelve gods and four Aspects per god means forty-eight gods, doesn't it?"

"Normally, yes. But the Spidae—the three fates —are never counted when the Aether is purged. Even the High Father must leave some things alone." He smiles. "The other eleven gods are not subject to the same rules."

It sounds like a damn mess to me. "But this Anticipation thing—it's happened before?"

He nods. "Oh yes. At least twice in recorded history. The four Aspects of each god are scattered across the lands, never too close to one another."

Ah. It's happened twice before just like this, right. Still, this all seems kind of a strange thing to do. "Okay, but why split them and cast them out? So the copies can all learn life lessons and shake hands and learn how to be better people or something? This is all very After School Special and all, but it seems a bit convoluted if you ask me. I mean, if they're dicks, tell them not to be dicks."

I mean, I've met Tadekha and she was a huge dick. A big, manipulative dick. Aron's a dick too, but in an entirely different way. I nibble on a piece of cheese as I wait, studying him.

Omos blinks at me as if I've said something puzzling. "What?"

"You know, agree to be better people? Meet up with each other, shake hands and walk away?"

"Shake hands? No, no. He's casting them out, my dear. He doesn't want them back. There are four Aspects and if Aron wants to return to the heavens, one Aspect must destroy the other three."

I stare at him in shock. "What?"

"In order to live, Aron must kill the other three Arons."

CHAPTER 23

I wiggle a finger in my ear and then shake my head. "I'm not sure I heard you correctly."

"You did," Omos says with a sigh. "One Aspect must kill the others. Once that is accomplished, the other is free to return to the heavens at the High Father's side, where his dominant flaw will be tempered by the disposal of the other three."

I can't believe what I'm hearing. This is the most ridiculous, crazy thing. "So they split Aron into four pieces just so he can murder the other three?"

"It is a cleansing of the soul for a god." Omos inclines his head. "I can research and find which of the Aspects defeated the others on the last Anticipation, if you like."

I'm not sure I want to know. What if this Aron—my Aron—gets defeated every time? "But how...Aron fell from the sky when we left the Citadel. A long way, and I fell on top of him but he wasn't hurt. I'm not sure he can die."

"He is eternal," Omos agrees. "He does not age, does not get sick, and cannot be killed by normal means."

"Then how is it that one Aspect is going to kill the others?"

Omos gives me a gentle look that makes my stomach churn.

Oh no. Well, that explains why everyone keeps trying to kill me. "I'm the target," I say flatly. "Not Aron. He doesn't have to kill the other Aspects, he has to kill their anchors."

Omos's voice is gentle. "An Aspect is vulnerable only through his anchor. He—or she—is the tie that binds him to mortality. She must eat for him, sleep for him, and perform all mortal functions on his behalf since he cannot. He gets his strength through her. And if she is destroyed..." He lets his words trail off.

"No more Aron," I say faintly. I set my food down, no longer hungry at all. In fact, I feel dangerously close to vomiting. No wonder no one else wanted to volunteer to be Aron's anchor. The odds are three out of four that I'm going to die horribly at the hands of Aron. Not Arrogant Aron, but one of the other flaws.

Fuck me, this is such a mess.

"Aron said he didn't know. Was that a lie?" I look at Omos, trying to understand all of this. "He doesn't remember about anchors, but he knew to protect me from others."

Omos nods thoughtfully. He notices that I'm no longer eating and picks up the tray. "It's likely that his mind has shielded parts from him...or it has been so long that he truly doesn't remember. Or perhaps the Aspect of Apathy won out last time and he just didn't care." Omos bustles away with the tray. "Whatever it is, I don't think he was lying to you. There are parts that he truly doesn't remember, whether planned by the High Father or not. Let me put this tray away and we'll see about getting you some shoes and fresh clothes."

He heads off and I just stare blankly at his retreating back. I've just been told that the gods—bunches of them, it seems—are going to try and off me. Shoes are a lot further down on the list of things I want. I'd rather have a grenade. Or like, an automatic rifle.

Or a do-over. Yeah, I think I'd like a do-over.

Omos chatters from the kitchen, talking about how he has clothes that the occasional traveler leaves with him, but I'm not listening. I'm too absorbed in what I've just learned. I'm going to die. I want to cry, but I don't know that I have tears left inside me. There's a numbness that's spreading in my gut as I try to get used to the idea of death.

No, wait. That's hunger. I just ate and I'm already hungry again. Fuck.

She must eat for him, sleep for him, and perform all mortal functions on his behalf—that was what Omos said. No wonder I'm hungry all the time. No wonder I need water constantly. No wonder Aron doesn't know how to sleep. He can't. I have to do it for him.

Someone re-enters the room and I look up. It's not Omos, but Aron. He's got a scowl on his face and his red tunic is covered with grime and dust and old blood. He looks pissy as hell and searches the room with his gaze, obviously looking for Omos.

I burst into tears at the sight of him. Guess I have tears in me after all.

Aron sighs. "Why are you crying, Faith?"

"B-because I just l-learned what a fucking anchor is," I tell him, sobbing. "And I'm going to d-die." I bury my face in my hands and weep, feeling helpless and full of despair.

He sighs heavily again. A second later, the cot creaks and shifts as he sits down next to me. I'm surprised to feel a big arm go around my shoulders. Aron's...hugging me. Comforting me. I look over at him in tearful astonishment.

"I know you are afraid, but I have a plan."

"A plan?" I wail. "How can you have a plan when you don't know what's going on?"

He frowns at me. "I remember more as time passes. And the monk has shared information with me." He nods at Omos, who is hovering in the doorway nearby, a bundle of clothing in his arms. "Leave us, mortal. I would have a word with my anchor."

"Of course, Lord of Storms," Omos says in that gentle voice of his. He disappears and I hear a clatter of pots in the kitchen, probably deliberately loud.

Aron strokes my hair and then gives me a focused look. "You will stop this weeping, Faith. I do not like it."

"I don't like being told I'm going to die," I say indignantly to him.

"And I have told you I have a plan. You are not going to die because I am going to defeat the others."

For some reason, that just makes me cry harder. Of course he'd think that. He's Arrogance personified. I shake my head, fresh sobs piling up in my throat.

He pulls me against his chest and hugs me, stroking my shoulder. "Trust me. I will not let anything happen to you. You are not leaving my sight. Am I not the best fighter anyone has ever seen? If anyone can protect you, it is me."

I lean against him, letting him comfort me. "Why are you being so nice?"

"Omos says I am Arrogance. That does not mean I am heartless." He squeezes my shoulder and leans close, whispering in my ear. "You have my word that I will let nothing happen to you."

I know it's because it'll nuke him, too, but it's still nice to hear.

CHAPTER 24

*T*hat day, we spend with Omos in his little church and make plans on what to do. Aron consults maps, trying to determine where his other "selves" would be so he can go murder their anchors. I don't like to think about that, but I suppose it's good to have a plan instead of waiting for someone to come find us.

Omos scuttles back and forth between his books and his kitchen, packing supplies for us. Even though he doesn't have much, he's determined to give all of it away, and I'm touched by his willingness to give us everything he's got.

Me, I get a crash course on Aosian money so I don't hand over our life savings, and I'm currently trying to memorize what I can of the gods in this world so I won't be so completely and utterly unaware.

"You can't stay here long," he tells us. "As much as I am thoroughly enjoying this, it wouldn't be prudent." And it is clear to me that he is enjoying all of this, oddly enough. His eyes gleam with excitement, and I suspect if the guy enjoyed this any more, he might burst into giggles. It's bizarre to realize that he's thriving on our misfortune, but he doesn't mean it in a cruel way.

I think he's lonely and bored and loves the thrill of excitement that our visit has brought. Of course he does. He's not the one in danger.

The moment I think that, I feel guilty. Omos has been the most helpful person we've run into so far. We'd truly be lost without him. He's even emptying out his little coin purse to give us money so we won't be in danger of starving on the streets. He probably doesn't have many visitors here in his sea of books. This is probably the most thrilling thing that's happened to him, ever.

"When we leave, why don't you come with us?" I suggest to Omos, ignoring the indignant look that Aron shoots my way as he pages through one of the monk's jillions of rolls of maps. "We can travel slow, and we can go looking for your goddess. I bet you'd want to say hello to her."

"Oh, all the stars, bless you for thinking of me, my dear." Omos just shakes his head at me and wraps cheese in a cloth, stuffing it in a bag. "You don't need this old man slowing you down."

"He is right," Aron says, unrolling another map. "He would be a burden."

I ignore Aron, because, well, he's Aron. "Yes, but you could meet your goddess. I wouldn't take that away from you. This is your one chance. I mean, how many Anticipations will there be in your lifetime?"

"Oh, no more, I sincerely hope," Omos says good-naturedly. "It is a time of great upheaval. It means there are problems to be found everywhere and the world will be a very dangerous place for some time. And..." He pauses and then gives me a gentle smile. "I do not wish to meet my goddess."

"You don't?"

"As she is? No." He runs a weathered hand down one of his braids. "I do not know which of the four flaws would be the least problematic to meet." His face colors, and I can guess which flaw he's thinking of.

Aron snorts. "It would take more than a bit of hedonism to make Magra interesting."

"Nevertheless, I would prefer to meet her when she is whole, and she is herself. I will meet her when I cross over from this life and journey to her arms." Omos gives us a peaceful, sweet smile. "I am content to wait."

"Makes sense," I tell him, and flip another page I haven't read. I'm supposed to be studying a text on the Aosian gods, but my eyes are crossing with all the information they're trying to stuff into me. "Do you want to send a message with us, then? In case we run into her?"

"Oh." A look of pure longing crosses the monk's weathered face. His hands flutter over his braids. "Could I?"

"Dude, of course. I don't think we should leave until morning, anyhow. Take your time. Write her something heartfelt."

His eyes shimmer with emotion and he grabs his candle. He raises a finger as if to say something, then shakes his head and shuffles off. I can hear paper rustling at one of the back desks and I suspect that by morning, we'll have a small book of our own to give to Magra...provided we even find her.

Aron just shakes his head at me, his mouth pulled into a frown of distaste.

I stick my tongue out at him and go back to my book. I don't care what he thinks. Just because he's arrogance personified doesn't mean I have to be rude.

"We should leave this day," Aron tells me in a low voice, so low that Omos won't overhear. "Overnight. Travel in darkness."

"Yeah, sounds like fun," I tell him absently and study another page. This chapter's about Aron and I admit, I pause a little longer than I probably should to snoop. "Except he's being awesome to us and carrying a letter is the least we can do."

Aron stalks away from his maps and moves to my side. No, correction, he moves to come loom over me. "And if we stay behind, it gives assassins that much more of a chance to find us if we remain in one place."

Assassins? Damn. I hesitate. "Won't they just as easily find us in the dark, then?"

He grunts and rolls his eyes at me. "Are you done learning?"

"Done" learning. This man, I swear. "No. In fact, it'll probably take me all night to finish cramming." I carefully flip the page back so he doesn't see that I was reading about him. I don't want to seem like a creeper. "So it's a good thing we're staying. Besides, I'm hungry anyhow."

"You should eat," he agrees, moving to the supplies that Omos just packed and pulling out a small wheel of cheese. "Here."

"Er, okay." I take the cheese but don't chow down on it. Not yet. Feels strange to gnaw on something the size of a plate anyhow. "In all seriousness, let's think about your other selves for a second. You know you the best, right? So let's consider how your other Aspects are going to react. How they'll strategize. And then we can determine the best way to go forward."

Aron stares at me for a long moment and then grunts approval. "A good idea."

I feel like I was just awarded a trophy.

He merely gazes at me, watching, and I can't tell if he's trying to figure me out or waiting for me to talk. My skin prickles with awareness at his stare and I rub my arm absently. "So? Let's think about this. We know the three Aspects that are left because you're, ah…"

How do you delicately tell a guy that he's arrogance personified?

"Arrogance." A thin smile curves his mouth. "You can say it. You think I am unaware? There is no hiding what an Aspect is, no more than Tadekha could hide her nature."

I blush at the mention of Tadekha, thinking of how I rubbed up against Aron like a kitten in the middle of her audience chamber. A really, really horny kitten. "Oh, I remember." I toss my hair and avert my gaze, staring at the cheese wheel to try and collect my scattered thoughts, because now I'm remembering how he touched me...and how very detached he was. Gah. "So okay, let's think about the slutty Aspect, then."

"Hedonism," he corrects. "Gorging oneself on all the pleasures that the mortal world has to offer."

Splitting hairs, but okay. "So the biggest things are food, drink, and sex."

"And battle."

I frown at that. "Why battle?"

"Because I am a god of battle and war. The spilling of blood pleases me." His smile is rather chilling. "Another Aspect of me would seek out pleasure—any of them. Preferably all of them at once."

I try to picture what it would be like if I'd met that Aron instead of this one and for some reason, my stupid brain goes back to when I slid my hands under his kilt and caressed his dick. Something deep inside me clenches pleasurably, and I can feel my cheeks heating. When I meet Aron's gaze, he's studying me and I wonder if he's thinking the same thing.

I clear my throat and gesture at the map in front of him. "You're the expert on this world. You tell me where you think you'd head."

He glances down, his dark hair spilling over one hard, muscled shoulder. All that pale skin and long hair should make him look gothy. He's anything but. There's a powerful air about him that makes one sit up and notice, and he's so muscular and imposing that there's no way anyone would think he's old. Ageless, sure. Withered? Never. Not with those cheekbones and piercing eyes. His colorlessness just seems menacing instead of ageing, and the scar on his face stands out that much more.

Aron's gaze flicks to me, and our eyes meet. For a moment, I feel flushed again, but then his eyes narrow at me and I realize he must have said something and I'm just sitting here, creeping on him. "Well?" he demands.

"Sorry, you were saying?" Sometimes I really hate myself for being such a perv.

"I was saying it does not matter where we think an Aspect will go. It depends on where they arrive during the Anticipation. After all, I arrived in Aventine, and it was supposed to be a city loyal to me." His lips thin with distaste. "We might as well point at a spot on the map and head there. It's as good a guess as any."

"Okay, well if you were hedonism and you wanted to head someplace specific, where would you head?"

He thinks for a moment. "Mephis, I suppose. They are fond of nose-spices there."

Drugs. "It's as good a guess as any other," I admit, because I don't have any ideas of my own. I don't know this place like he does. "And it's somewhere to start, I suppose. Is Mephis far from here?"

"Is Mephis far?" He snorts. "Is Mephis *far*? What a foolish question. Are you *human*?"

"Wow, are you a huge asshole?" I retort. "I was just asking."

"Everything will be far. Every place we travel will be grueling. Do you think the High Father sent me here so I could trot gamely between two neighboring cities and then return to him with my tail tucked between my legs, lesson learned in a day?" He straightens and crosses his arms over his broad chest, the look on his face downright scathing. "The High Father means to break me to his will. He plans to remake me and to teach me lesson after lesson until I come crawling to him, begging for forgiveness. So yes, it will be a long journey. It will be terrible. It will be dangerous. My other Aspects of self will be doing their best to purge my existence from this world to ensure their own survival. So no, it will not be a pleasant little voyage."

I gape at him for a moment as he bends down to study the map once more. "Wow, I think I really, truly hate you."

Aron shrugs. "I do not imagine I came to the mortal plane to make friends. It is no concern of mine what you think."

Yeah, he made that pretty clear from the start. For a moment, I glare hatefully at his shoulders, wondering how one person can be so damn unpleasant when a moment ago, I was blushing at the thought of him. I'm the idiot here. He's just being who he is—Arrogance. It doesn't mean I have to like him.

I really, really want to go home. For a brief, despairing flash, I think about packing up my things and abandoning him. Better yet, sending him on his way to Mephis or wherever the fuck he wants to go and staying behind with Omos and his cheese and his goats and his books.

Except...I can't. I remember the wracking pain when Aron and I were separated. I'm stuck with him.

And everyone's going to try to kill me because of it.

I lie down on the bed, too depressed to even consider what the next few weeks—or hell, months! years!—of my life will be like. I pull the blankets over my head and roll over to face the wall.

"What are you doing?" Aron snaps, rustling the map. "We are discussing strategy. Stop this foolishness."

"Go fuck yourself," I tell him and ignore him. If he wants to be an asshole, I can be one, too.

I ignore Aron for the rest of the day, no matter his attempts to get my attention. After a while, he gets surly and leaves to go prepare for our journey. From my half-assed listening, he chided Omos that the monk had no weapons at his house, and has spent most of the afternoon creating his own. He's whittled wood, broken pottery, and used the shards to craft some deadly-looking objects. Omos has fluttered around the little library itself, sometimes scratching notes into one of his books, sometimes packing up more food.

I ate. And slept. And ate some more. No one seems to think I can help out. I'm not talking to Aron and Omos just shoos me away when I try to help, so I keep busy with making clothes for myself and washing what I do have. Omos donated one of his gray robes, but it hangs on me like a potato sack and chafes against my skin, so I've done my best to modify it and make it less bulky. I ripped up the seams under the arms and took out a large chunk of fabric, then knotted the sides so they fit tighter. I tore off the hem of the robe and made myself a long wrap-around skirt that's easier to walk in. The remnants of my filmy dress from the Citadel have been scrapped and torn to pieces and now serve as a belt and scarf to keep the worst of the sand and dirt out of my hair.

I made a bra band out of it, too, because everyone seems to think a girl should jiggle but me. Screw that. They might not believe in bras in this world, but I can stage a one-woman revolution if it means I can run unhindered. I work on shoes, too. Omos gave me a pair of sandals that were far too big for my feet and seem to be nothing but straps attached to a wedge of thick hide. I do my best to work those down and resize them, too, because I suspect I'm going to be doing a lot of walking in the near future.

I'm still mad at Aron, of course. I carry that irritation with me throughout the day, though it fades as Omos makes a warm vegetable stew for dinner and adds fresh-baked bread. Aron's just being his usual dick self. He is the way he is because the High Father is working on purging the dickishness out of him. It could have been worse, I suppose.

I could have ended up with the lust Aspect of his personality.

I ignore the way certain parts of me tingle at that thought. I also ignore the fact that my mind goes back to the log he was packing under his kilt and the way I rubbed up against him and how good he felt.

Ignore, ignore, ignore.

CHAPTER 25

*a*s I eat my third bowl of dinner, Omos fusses over both myself and Aron, who is poring over maps as if they'll give him answers. I still have a million questions that need answering, but Omos carefully steers the conversation to neutral territory. I suspect he doesn't want to piss off a god...or he and Aron had a conversation this afternoon about keeping things from me. Either way, it doesn't take long to realize I'm not going to get what I need tonight.

I crawl into bed and pull the covers over me, achy and tired. I still hurt from our last journey and the thought of starting another in the morning makes me want to despair, but I like breathing. If we stay in one place too long, someone's going to come after us with murder on his mind. There's no choice but to leave.

I'm just about to drift off to sleep when the narrow cot shakes and an enormous body thumps down next to me, pushing me over to the side. What the fuck? I look over, yanking my blankets back as I realize it's Aron, coming to lie down next to me. "What the hell are you doing?" I hiss at him, trying to keep my voice down.

"Getting into bed with you."

"I realize that! Why? You don't freaking sleep, remember?"

"I didn't say I was going to sleep," he tells me, cranky. "But you need to sleep, and this way I can keep an eye on you."

Aron ignores the outraged noises I make and gets under the blankets with me. After a moment, he steals one of the pillows and shifts his big body, trying to get comfortable. I grit my teeth, enduring his constant bouncing of the bed.

"Hm," he says after a moment.

I fight the urge to roll my eyes. "What?"

"This is rather comfortable. I see now why mortals are so lazy."

Boy, he really is something else. He puts his hands behind his head and I shove back at the elbow jabbing me in the back of the neck. "One of us has to sleep, you know."

"So sleep."

"You could get on the floor."

He snorts. "I am a god. I do not sleep on floors."

"Fine. Then I will." I grab the blankets and start to get up, only to be dragged back down into the bed by Aron. I make an outraged sound as I fall backward, flailing into the cot.

"You will stay right here," he says again. "If someone comes to assassinate me in the night, I can at least cover your body with mine and shield it."

I don't know if I'm touched or alarmed.

I lie stiffly in bed, wondering if this is some sort of colossal joke. "You are seriously not going to stay here."

"I seriously am."

I sigh and close my eyes, shoving the blankets up to my chin even though it's stuffy in the house. "Fine. Let me sleep, then."

He grunts acknowledgment, and I settle in. If I can't ditch him, I can at least try to ignore him, and I'm tired. I'm always tired. Now that I know I'm sleeping for two (so to speak) it explains a lot. Kinda sucks, too, but so has almost everything

205

about being in this world. I've just about drifted off when Aron taps my shoulder.

I bite back a groan. "What?"

"How is it that you were enslaved by the Order of the Axe?"

I have to think for a moment, then realize that the "Order of the Axe" must be his priesthood. "I wasn't. They bought me from the guy that initially enslaved me. They dumped me into a room with a bunch of other women and were going to sacrifice us in your name, remember?"

"Mmm. None of them stepped forward. I recall this."

"Yeah, they were all smart enough to realize that they were getting saddled permanently with you." I yawn. "I'm the fool that didn't know. Can I go to sleep now?"

"I am not stopping you."

"You're talking," I tell him and close my eyes again. "You have to be silent for me to sleep." When he has no response to that, I say, "Well?"

"You said I had to be silent. I am being silent. Which is it?"

This is worse than arguing with a three year old. "Good night," I emphasize and close my eyes again.

"How long were you a slave for?"

I stare at the wall and grit my teeth. It's clear that I'm not going to get any sleep while Aron's around. Correction: while Aron is bored. "Like three days, max."

Aron grunts. "I thought it was longer."

I frown to myself. I shouldn't ask. I shouldn't. It's just going to make him keep talking. And yet... "Why did you think that? Did I have a 'slavey' look to me?"

"No. You glared at everyone in the room as if they were a problem. I admit, I appreciated that."

Some of the irritation I have with Aron fades away. "I was pretty pissed at being enslaved. Where I come from, that shit was abolished a long time ago."

"And where do you come from?"

"Oh no, don't change the subject. You still haven't told me why I looked slavey."

He sighs heavily, and his breath brushes against my hair. "Are all mortal women this difficult?"

"Yes. Now answer."

Aron snorts. "Because you had a very appealing body. If I was enslaving females, I would not want ugly ones. I would pick ones like you."

"I have no idea if that's a compliment or not. I'm going to go ahead and take it as one," I tell him with a yawn. "Can I please go to sleep now?"

"Go. Sleep. This is an idiotic conversation anyhow."

I roll my eyes and then settle in again. As I do, I can't help but think about the fact that he said I had a good body. He didn't say I was beautiful, of course. Arrogant Aron would never go out on a limb like that—but he liked my body...a body that's currently pressed against his in the bed.

I shouldn't even think about that.

Or the fact that I pretty much had my hands all over his dick at Tadekha's Citadel. And that I begged for it. A lot.

Like, a *lot*.

Of course, Aron hasn't brought it up again, so I won't either. It's just a shameful bit of history that I pray won't repeat itself again.

Even as I ponder this, he nudges me in the back. "You did not say where you are from."

"No, I didn't." After the first few rounds of getting the snot beat out of me every time I brought it up, I stopped saying anything at all. Even I'd find it a little hard to believe if a stranger came up to me and said they weren't from my world. It's not something that comes up in casual conversation.

"Where is it, then?" He nudges me again, this time so hard I nearly roll off the damn cot.

"You finally decided to ask?"

"I still don't care," he says arrogantly. "But you are...somewhat interesting."

Wow. I bite back a sigh of irritation. "I told you before. I'm not from this world. My world is Earth. I don't know how I got here. I kept hearing voices in an empty apartment next door, and when I went to go check it out, I got sucked into this world. Some jackass grabbed me the moment I showed up in Aventine and the next thing I knew, I was a slave girl."

I don't bring up the fortune teller. The King of Pentacles card.

The Lovers card.

God help me, I forgot all about the Lovers card.

All Aron says is, "Mmm."

"What's that 'mmm' mean? That you don't believe me?"

"Why would I not believe you? You are speaking to a god. I know what is possible and what is not."

That makes me turn over. I sit up on my elbows and look down at him. That's right. He *is* a god. It's evident in his perfect form and coloring, and the way he seems to be just so much *more* than everyone else he encounters. "You don't think I'm lying?"

He tilts his head and raises one shoulder in a half-shrug. "When I was cast out, I imagine the boundaries between worlds grew thin so I—and my fellow gods—could come through. It stands to reason that you were pulled in through the same circumstance."

That's the most logical explanation for why I'm here, and I feel a little bit like crying and laughing both. I'm not special. I'm not a chosen one. I'm a doofus that wandered through the wrong place at the right time. It makes sense and yet...I'm disappointed because if it's just random happenstance as to why I'm here, there's no grand game plan for how I get back, either. And that's damn depressing. But it's an answer, and I finally have one. "Thanks, Aron."

"For what?"

"For believing me. No one has until now."

"I am a god," he says, as if that explains everything. Heck, maybe it does. He pats my shoulder. "Go to sleep. You keep talking and we will be leaving early in the morning."

As if I'm the Chatty Cathy. I bite back a snotty retort, because it won't do any good. "Going to sleep now."

"Good." His arm goes around my waist and he pulls me tight against him. I'm surprised when a moment later, he sniffs my hair. A hot flush moves over my body as I remember the night in Tadekha's citadel and how I crawled all over the man as if my life depended on getting his knob. He'd made me come, but every time I reached for him, he pushed me away.

But...he'd been hard as a rock. I distinctly remember how hard he was, how erect every time I touched him. I think of the Lovers card again, and heat floods through me. If he touched me right now? I'd be wet. The realization is shameful.

He sniffs my hair again, and I wonder if he's hard right now. Is he overcome with lust for me?

"You smell bad," Aron says. "When was the last time you bathed?"

Man, fuck this guy.

⚔

MORNING ARRIVES FAR TOO EARLY, and then Omos is there, handing us our packs and is all smiles of excitement. "It is a good day for traveling," he tells me as he helps me put on my pack. "The weather is fair and lovely and there's a nice breeze. The gods are smiling down on you."

I want to retort that the gods are ill-tempered brats and that's why they're on the mortal plane, but I don't. Omos is just too nice. My pack is heavy with food supplies, extra blankets, a change of clothing, and anything else he could think to give us.

209

I'm utterly touched by his kindness. As I look around his little monastery, a fat goat rambles past, heading for the crops, and he immediately chases it down, pushing it back toward the field. I smile at the sight, because this is such a peaceful existence.

Then, I glance over at Aron. There's nothing peaceful about the guy at all. Even standing still, he screams authority and arrogance...and impatience. His big arms are crossed over his chest and his long hair has been pulled back into a tail at his nape. The scars on his face are vivid against the sunlight and his strangely colored eyes look like slits as he watches me. I get the impression he's impatient and ready to be off, but I'm not ready to leave yet.

I like it here with Omos. For the first time in what feels like forever, I feel safe. Like the world's not falling apart around my ears. And for a moment, the realization that I have to leave this safety is too much. I'm overwhelmed.

A gentle hand pats my back. "It'll be all right, my dear."

"I don't want to leave," I whisper to him, even as I fuss with the straps on my pack.

"I know. But you have a greater fate ahead of you than that of this poor monk." He smiles at me, so peaceful and fatherly that I fling my arms around his neck and hug him close. He pats my back and then whispers in my ear, "Be careful, lest Aron decide I'm stealing you away from him."

"Aron can go fuck himself," I murmur into his ear, but when I pull away, Aron's glowering at us both. He looks...jealous. It's not in a sexual way, of course. Not with Aron. It's more of a someone-else-is-playing-with-his-toys way. I ignore him, still mad about last night.

Omos just chuckles and pulls something from his belt. "He is who he is, Faith. Remember that. Do not expect him to be more or less."

"Yeah, yeah." I'm still sad that I have to trade sweet, gentle Omos for Aron and his Big Dick Energy. Even now that energy is practically blazing with impatience, and he casts another look at the road, as if he were hoping we were already on it. His pack is twice the size of mine, but he's a bigger dude, and strapped to it are what look like a half-dozen homemade spears. On his lower arms, he's got crude leather bracers and has knives strapped there, as well. He's been busy while I slept and talked with Omos.

He looks like he's going to war, and that gives me a chill.

I turn to look at Omos again, and he sees the panic on my face. "It will be all right," he tells me in a gentle voice. "You are here for a reason, Faith. Remember that."

"Yeah, to be a target," I mutter, but I hope he's right to a certain extent. I don't think I'm a chosen one or anything, but maybe the fact that my wagon's hitched to Aron's means something.

Omos shakes his head and presses a pouch into my hand. "This is all the coin I have. It will do you more good than me."

"Oh, Omos, we can't take this." I feel so guilty, because it's clear that he's stripping his kitchen to feed us, and now he's giving us all his money?

"You can and you must. You have a hard road ahead of you, and if a little coin makes it easier, then it is the least I can do." He hesitates and then pulls out a scroll from within his robes and holds it toward me. "This is my letter to my goddess."

"I hope we find her."

"I hope you do not," he says in that same gentle voice. "I would rather you find your way home instead."

My eyes fill with tears. "Me too."

CHAPTER 26

ONE WEEK LATER

I eye the piles of land-hippo poop littering the road and sidestep, only to end up in mud anyhow. "Man, these roads are terrible."

"That means we are close to Katharn," Aron tells me. "Very close. It will get worse."

"Let's pause for a moment so I can switch to my boots, then," I tell him, and sit down on a grassy spot off the edge of the road.

Aron sighs heavily with irritation, but he follows me and waits nearby. I'm getting used to his surly personality, though, and his bitching and moaning no longer sets me off. It is what it is—just part of his "arrogance" personality. And, well, he's a god. Or part of one. I kind of expect him to be a dick to "mortals." In a way, I kind of appreciate his griping, because it makes me remember that someone else hates being here as much as I do. It's funny, because this is his world, but he doesn't seem to appreciate any of it. I can understand my dislike of it given that it's so very different and crude compared to my modern world.

Just like right now, I'm covered in mud and sweat and grime from a week straight of traveling, and Aron looks as fresh as a daisy. The traveling doesn't bother him, even though my feet blistered up and swelled like balloons. I glance over at his sandal-clad feet and he doesn't even look as if he steps in mud. I can't seem to keep out of it. He's just as cool and handsome as he was the day he first showed up...and that could be a problem.

He doesn't blend.

Our surroundings are muddy road and cottages that trail toward a distant walled city. Katharn, which we've been heading steadily toward for a week. The scenery has changed slightly from the Dirtlands in that there are trees and fields and pasture animals. We've passed a few outlying farms here and there, but this entire area is pretty quiet and settled...and poor. The few people we've seen working in fields as we walked looked tired and worn and hungry, shoulders hunched from long hours of labor. They stared at Aron, his strong, proud body, and then at me, and I felt acutely vulnerable.

No one tried anything, of course, but they were farmers. Now, we're approaching the city and I'm trying to imagine all the horrible things that might be waiting for us. Thieves and cutthroats for sure. Worse, if there's another god Aspect nearby. I work on fastening my boots, which are too tight and uncomfortable compared to the sandals, but seem smarter if we're heading into the city itself. "Do you know much about this place?" I ask, trying to think of the best way to phrase what I want to say next.

"Katharn?" Aron grunts. "Only that it exists. It is claimed by no god as a stronghold."

"No? How come?" I wiggle my feet in the boots, trying to stretch the leather.

"Look around you. Do you think the sight of this would

make anyone proud?" He sweeps an arm through the air at the distant buildings. "This is a poor place. A place for pickpockets and mercenaries. There are no grand temples or manicured gardens, no noble houses or anything of the like. It is the armpit of the mid-lands, necessary but foul."

I stand again and tuck my sandals into my bag. "Thought you didn't know much about this place."

"Do not try my patience, mortal."

I just roll my eyes at him. "Oh, I'm not just trying. I'm succeeding."

He makes an irritated sound that I ignore. We're fond of pricking at each other, he and I. Or at least, I'm fond of pricking at him, since I'm stuck at his side and he can't do anything about it. In a way, it's the most fun I've had all week, knowing I'm driving him crazy. I sling my pack back over my shoulder and move closer to him. "So what's the plan?"

Aron narrows his eyes at me. "I thought we had discussed this already. We enter the city, get supplies and weapons, and listen for news of other god Aspects. Katharn is the hub of the mid-lands and we can find our way to other countries if we must. Adassia is to the east, Yshrem to the north-east, and—"

I raise a hand before he lists off the litany of small countries once more. He's told me this a bunch of times this week already. Off to one side, I notice a distant man in a field that's staring at us—probably because we've been paused on the side of the road for too long. I grab Aron's arm and move him under the nearest tree so we can have a little privacy. "I know that part of the plan. That wasn't what I meant, big guy. I'm talking what is the plan for this?" And I gesture at him, drawing a little circle in the air and indicating his proud, handsome face. "You don't exactly look like one of the locals."

He crosses his arms over his chest again, bracers practically bristling with weaponry. "Why should I?"

"Let's talk about low profiles and what a good idea it is to not be noticed," I tell him brightly. "In fact, let's think about this. Let's say you've heard that the gods are walking the mortal plane again. Let's say one of the gods put a bounty on the head of a rival, because why not?" When Aron frowns, I continue. "And then let's say you and I saunter in. I might look like another dirty woman fresh off the road but you, my friend...you do not blend. From your eyes to the scar to the way you hold yourself, you're not exactly a low-key individual."

Aron scowls down at me. "You do not look like a camp follower."

Is that a compliment? "Why, thank you, Aron. I think."

He grunts. "You merely sell yourself short. For a mortal, you are passably attractive."

"You are positively killing me with flattery here." I can't help but smile, though. Lately I've started trying to determine how Aron's words would sound if he wasn't "poisoned" with arrogance, and I bet that would be something nice after all. "You're not so bad yourself. But let's stay focused. You don't look mortal, either. You're big and beefy and you practically radiate otherworldliness. If they did a police lineup, you'd stick out like a sore thumb." I gesture at his face. "The coloring doesn't help. The scars sure don't help. You might as well wear an axe atop your head and scream to everyone that you're Aron of the Cleaver and you've come to steal their wives and eat their children."

Aron's hard mouth twitches with a hint of amusement. "I want no one's wives. I have a hard enough time with you at my side."

I just laugh, because that is something so very Aron, and I'm getting used to him.

He rubs his jaw, studying me. "So you tell me I am too handsome to mingle with these people."

"Well, you are a god." Suddenly it feels like the conversation is turning, and I'm getting flustered. "But I, ah, meant the scars and the coloring."

"Of course." He doesn't sound like he believes me though. "I cannot change the scars, I am afraid. I won them in battle against the dragon One-Tooth who took my left eye before I found another."

Okay, that's weird and I'm not going to ask, because I'm not sure I want to know more about dragons. We've got enough problems in this world. "Maybe we start with a cloak and see how these things progress."

Aron grunts and pulls the hood over his head, hiding his jet-black hair. It's in a messy braid and most of it has fallen out of said braid, and I realize that he might not know how to braid it himself. How do the gods function if they can't do simple things like this, I wonder? Or is it just a matter of waving a hand and being perfect? Either way, it reminds me how shockingly vulnerable Aron is. If I wasn't with him, he'd probably just wander into town, demanding people give him informa-tion...and he'd end up murdered right away.

Or wait, I'd end up murdered and Aron would die because of it. Neither one sounds good. I frown to myself as I reach up and pull his hood on a little deeper, completely hiding his features. "Keep this on at all times."

He tilts his head back and gazes down at me. "How am I supposed to see anything?"

"You're not. You're supposed to hide and let me handle things." I pat his chest, and then wonder why I keep touching him. Dammit, Faith. "Just in case, though, I should give you some of the money. In case we get split up."

"If we get split up, we have bigger problems than money," he says, and catches my hand when I pull it away. "I am going to be watching you closely. If you feel threatened or worried, simply invoke my name and I will slaughter all close to you."

I stare at him, eyes wide. I shouldn't be flattered by that. I shouldn't. But it sounds protective and in a bloodthirsty way, kind of sweet. A weird thought comes to mind: Is this the way a god of battle flirts? Surely not. But all I say is "okay."

Aron pulls one of the makeshift blades—a shiv, really—off his leather bracer and offers it to me. "Put this in your boot and do not be afraid to use it."

"How bad is this city?" I ask him, but do as he says.

"How bad is any big city? Better to arm you in case someone decides you should be a slave again."

Okay, he has a really great point. "Let's just go before I freak out and decide we should keep going to the next city."

"All outlying cities lead to this one. Katharn is a necessary evil."

Lucky us. "We stick to the plan, then. Get in, listen for rumors, find what we need, and head out from there." When he nods, I take a steeling breath. "All right. Let's do this."

Showtime, Faith.

CHAPTER 27

We walk for maybe another hour before we get into Katharn proper. The scattered streets grow increasingly dense as we move forward, and then lift up, surprisingly enough. They change from rutted, muddy roads to paved bridges and cobbled, wide roads, and I see why soon enough—Katharn has a big river running right through the middle of town. Of course, just because the streets are better doesn't mean that the buildings themselves are. The small, crowded houses look to be made of clapboard wood and push against each other like dominos just waiting for the right strike to topple. They crowd all the way along each street right to the massive sewer tunnels and up to the water's edge, where the stink of people turns into the stink of dead fish and people. The water itself is a brown, toxic-looking sludge that looks foul and smells worse, and I'm reminded of a history lesson from high school that said the river Thames in London was once so filthy with waste that you could walk on it. I couldn't picture it at the time, but seeing just how nasty these docks and the river itself is, I believe it. The massive sewer system that runs underneath the crowded streets of Katharn dumps right into the water, and as we move along the wharf, between the small boats lining the edges of the docks I can see waterfalls from where the pipes empty out.

There are people everywhere, too. They crowd around us, pushing their way through the streets as if they own them. There are fewer horses—land-hippos, whatever—here, simply because there's no room. There are tons of rats, though, and long-eared cats that chase after them.

And there's filth everywhere. It's piled up in the streets, against buildings, and everyone looks so damn dirty.

I'm really not liking the look of the place, but I didn't expect it to be so nasty. The little farms we passed were crude, and Omos's library was small but clean. Aventine was dusty but orderly. Heck, Tadekha had a glittering crystal palace floating in the air, so I know these people can be clean.

It's clear that Katharn just chooses not to be.

I study the piles of buildings, all falling onto each other, and move a little closer to Aron as I do. He's quiet, but the hood is pulled over his head so far that it's not exactly conducive to conversation. Still, I wish he'd say something. I feel better just hearing his voice, even if he is making sourpuss comments. A man with a dead chicken hanging from his hand leers at me as he walks a little too closely and I move closer to Aron. "So, uh, what's an inn look like in this dump?"

"You ask me as if I stay here often."

Good ol' Aron. "It's your damn world, not mine."

"This is not my city. Were it my choice, we would never set foot here." He pulls the hood down lower.

Well, that makes two of us. I avoid chicken man and walk a little faster, and I'm relieved to see that Aron stays close to my side. We turn down a side street and find a marketplace, and before we can leave, Aron drags me over to a small tent where someone's selling knives. Aron points at one, so I buy it. Then he points at another, and another, and a short time later, we're light on money and loaded with weapons. I want to gripe that we need to save our money for better things, but then Aron will just gripe back at me, and he's at least staying quiet.

And if we need the weapons? We'll be glad to have them. So I shut up about it.

After that, I flag down a woman who's got an enormous basket of laundry on her hip and ask her where the closest inn is. Her answer is friendly enough, but there's a hard glint in her eyes as she looks us over and that makes me think I should hold our money a little closer. She instructs me to look for a building a few streets over with a red roof, and I hold my belongings tightly to my chest, worried I'm going to get knifed in the back, as we walk there.

But we make it, and I'm so damn relieved to see the red tiled roof of the inn itself. The sun is going down and I didn't want to be out on the mean streets of Katharn after dark. The inn doesn't look so bad, I decide. The building's a big two-story that only sags a little. The windows have shutters and little pots of herbs outside each one. There's boisterous laughter and light pouring out from inside, and it smells like hot food. My stomach growls despite myself, because it's been days since I've had a hot meal and I'd really, really love a bowl of stew. I head to the door and then pause, glancing over at Aron. "We ready to do this?"

"Going inside?" He peers out from under the hood with a scathing expression. "Did you plan on standing out here all night?"

I bite back my snotty retort—*arrogance, arrogance, arrogance, he can't help himself*—and push the inn door open, heading inside.

The inside of the inn is about what I expected. The ceiling is low, the floor is old, creaky wood, and it's smoky and poorly lit.

One side of the wall is nearly taken up with a massive fireplace, and there's a pot of something bubbling over it that smells fucking delicious. My mouth waters and I don't even care that there's a roaring fire going and it's about ten degrees warmer inside than it is outside. I'll sweat a little if I can get a bowl of food. I glance around, and while there are several long tables, they're crammed full of people. I can't help but notice that they all seem to be men, and they're staring at me.

I pull my cloak a little tighter around my clothes, even though it's warm. I feel naked despite the layers of clothing. Naked and unsafe. Maybe this was a bad call. There's a real rapey vibe to this place. Goody.

Aron nudges my shoulder, and I glance over at him. He's still got the hood pulled down heavily over his face, which is good. He's waiting on me, though. Right. I look around for someone that might be in charge, and when I see the bar off over by the enormous fireplace, I head there.

A big bearded man stands behind the bar, and he's the first person that doesn't leer at me in this building, so I like him already. He nods at me. "Travelers?"

"Yes. We're looking for a room." I give him my brightest, most businesslike smile.

"Three drabs a night," he tells me. Omos walked me through how money works here, and so I know what coin that is.

I feel around in my money pouch furtively and then toss the coins down on the counter. "One night."

"One room, then?"

I grit my teeth. "Yup."

This time the man smirks and takes the coins. "Room two's open tonight. Bowl of stew and tankard of ale included with the room. More than that and it'll cost you."

"Thank you," I say politely, and then glance around the dirty, poorly lit room. "Sit anywhere?"

"Anywhere ya want. Inside, outside, all the same to me." He pockets the money and turns away.

All right, I'm guessing this doesn't work like most restaurants back home. Fine then. I glance at Aron and gesture over at the fire. "Let's get some food and find a seat." I move forward without checking to see if he follows me, and by the fire, there's a stack of earthenware bowls. I manage to ladle my own stew without burning myself and grab one of the big wooden spoons tossed in a shallow basket. Not very clean, but I'm starting to think nothing in this town is. "You grab a bowl, too," I tell Aron, and then I survey the tavern area for two empty seats.

There's room at the end of one of the longest tables, but there's also a very gross-looking man I'd have to cuddle up next to, and the thought makes my stomach curdle. His dark hair is greasy, his face is several days unshaven, and he's missing half his teeth. He keeps looking over at me and rubbing his crotch, and I swallow hard.

Well, shit. If the goal is to spend the evening gathering information and listening to rumors, I guess I'm going to have to sit next to someone. I move forward with my bowl—

only to have Aron push in front of me. He takes his food and slaps it down on the table and sits next to the filthy creep, then has a seat. He gestures at the open spot on the far side of him—at the end of the table, where no one will sit next to me.

In that moment, I could cheerfully kiss Aron.

I happily slide into the empty spot and clean my spoon on the hem of my tunic. As I do, I notice it's quiet, but when I start to eat, the conversation picks up again. A woman swings by and drops two mugs in front of Aron and me, and a quick taste reveals that it's a watery-tasting beer of some kind. Ugh. I drink it anyhow, because I'm thirsty as hell. The stew is a little greasy but otherwise heavenly, and I devour mine with gusto. I sneak a glance over at Aron, and he's sitting, hood still over his face, idly dragging the spoon through his food.

"Where you from?"

I look up at the old man across the table from me. Bearded, scarred, but mostly clean. Seems fairly harmless, I hope. "Me?" When he nods, I think quickly. "Aventine."

He nods over at Aron. "You too?"

"Oh, my master doesn't speak," I say quickly, putting my hand on Aron's arm before he can talk. "He's mute."

The stranger looks at us suspiciously, but when Aron doesn't speak up, he grunts and returns to his food. "Long journey to Aventine."

"Definitely wasn't fun," I agree.

"It true what they say? 'Bout the Citadel?"

I pause. "What about it?"

"Destroyed?" His eyes are piercing.

I blink and feign ignorance even as Aron kicks me under the table. I kick him back. "I wouldn't know. Haven't been there… so. Where are you from?"

"Here," he says, and belches. "Better to be leaving this place than arriving, if you ask me."

That sounds ominous. "Oh? Why?"

"Riots. Thieves. A plague of dead babies. Haunted fields. Take your pick," says another man farther down the table who can't stop staring at my clothed boobs. He's a bit pervy, but he glances over at Aron and makes his gaze more respectful.

That all sounds terrible. "Why is it so crazy?" I ask, and reach for Aron's bowl of stew. He pushes it toward me and I trade him bowls, handing over my empty one.

The men look at me like I'm crazy. "How long have you been traveling?"

"A while," I say vaguely.

"Haven't you heard? It's the Anticipation. Rumor has it that the gods are appearing."

I make my eyes go wide. "You don't say."

The bearded man nods sagely, as if he's been at the center of things. Next to him, the other man speaks up. "Has to be truth. Why else would the Citadel fall to ruin? Goddess Tadekha must have struck it down with vengeance."

Aron snorts deep in his hood. I kick him and shove my spoon into my mouth so I'm not tempted to make a reply.

CHAPTER 28

*T*urns out that we don't need to speak. Now that the topic of the gods has come up, the whole table's on fire with gossip. They all speculate about Tadekha's Citadel though none have actually ever seen it. They speculate if one of the other gods killed her and eventually it's decided that Kalos, God of Darkness, destroyed her because she turned down his advances many, many eons ago and he's apparently always held a grudge. Aron's totally silent so I have no idea if this is fact or not.

"There's another god on the coast, you know," someone at the far end of the table speaks up.

"Vor?" Another asks.

"No, different. Said he won't give his name but I know someone that saw him. My wife's sister was traveling back from Yshrem and saw him. Said he was as handsome as could be, took her breath fair away at the sight of him. Beautiful eyes, she said."

My skin prickles with awareness and I strain to hear the conversation. Aron's beautiful. Aron has striking eyes. It could be one of his Aspects that we're supposed to kill.

"Did she approach him?" Another person asks.

"No, he wouldn't speak to anyone. Had a female companion with him as anchor, but that was it. He wouldn't talk to anyone else. Didn't mingle. She said she wanted to talk to him and get a blessing, but she was afraid."

I nudge Aron's foot with mine, hoping he's listening. "Was he scarred up?" I ask. "Like, say, Aron of the Cleaver?"

This time, Aron kicks me hard.

The man turns to me, his lip curled. "Are ye daft? I said he was handsome. Aron's as hoary and grizzled as the lot of us, mark my word." He straightens and thumps his fist below his breast in the sign I've come to realize is one for Aron's followers. "The Lord of Storms won't be prancing around the countryside with a woman. He'll surround himself with the strongest of warriors and challenge them to fight him every day."

"My bad," I say quickly. "Maybe it was someone else."

"Probably Gental of the Family," the man speculates. "Though what he's doing in Yshrem is a mystery. Those book-loving weaklings are Riekki's followers to a one." He shrugs. "Even if they have a Cyclopae king now."

I eat some more of my stew, hoping the conversation continues on this line. I want to hear more about this beautiful god on the coast with a woman. After all, *I'm* with Aron, so they're wrong about a god like Aron not being with a chick.

And I personally think he's beautiful. A dick, sure, but downright gorgeous.

"It's the end of days," one greasy man laments.

Next to me, Aron snorts again.

Everyone at the table goes quiet. They're all watching us with far too much interest, and I figure it's now a good time to leave. "Think I'll see if this inn has baths. I bet my master would like one," I say brightly, a little louder than I should. "Thanks for the company, boys."

A big hand clamps down on my shoulder and I yelp, turning to see a pair of men behind me. My eyes go wide as the one with his hand on my shoulder grins down at me. He's at least six feet tall and massive, with a dirty beard and stumps of rotten teeth. "How much for your master to let us borrow you for a night?"

I try to shrug the guy's hand off as Aron gets to his feet. "I'm sure he'd say I'm not for sale—"

"Why don't you let him decide that, tart?"

Fuckin' tart. I'm really starting to hate that word.

Aron moves to my side and pats my back, as if to indicate all is well. He's still wearing the heavy cloak over his face, but I worry it's going to fall off if he beats the shit out of this guy for touching me, and then our cover will be blown.

"Master," I begin, but before I can say more, Aron puts his hand out, palm up.

The disgusting man grins at his buddy and then reaches into his pocket, pulls out a few coins, and places them in Aron's hand—

—or tries to. The moment his hand makes contact with Aron's, quick as a snake, the god's pale hand grips the other man's and twists it viciously. There's a crunch of bone that everyone in the inn can hear, and the stranger drops to his knees, screaming.

It gets deathly quiet in the inn, and no one moves.

Aron studies the coins in his hand, then flings them to the ground. Then, he puts a hand firmly on my shoulder and squeezes. The possessive gesture isn't lost on anyone, even me. He's branding me as his property without so much as a word.

The stranger's friend hastily backs away, abandoning his buddy to roll around in pain on the straw-covered floor of the inn. I glance around and everyone in the inn is staring at us, even the barkeep.

"Well," I say brightly, as if this is a normal sort of thing.

"Where can a girl get her master a bath around here?" And I kick the guy that's down, just to show that I'm not afraid.

The room I share with Aron is small and grungy. We're given a greasy-smelling candle to serve as light, a pitcher of water to wash up, and a pile of blankets. The mattress itself looks like lumpy straw but it's not the ground, which makes it better than where I've slept for the last week. The room itself is about half the size of my bedroom at home, but there's a massive shuttered window that's open to let in a breeze. It'd be nice if Katharn itself didn't smell like a sewer and the view is that of the roof next door, which is so close I can practically touch it.

I'm still getting used to this world and how different it is from my own. I'm grateful to have this room, thanks to Omos's generosity with his funds, but I can't help but compare it to hotel rooms I've slept in back in my reality. Beggars can't be choosers, though, and when the innkeeper shows up with a small wooden tub and a few more pitchers of warmed water, I decide that I like this place after all. I pay him for the bath, then shut the door behind us and lower the heavy wooden bar over the door to "lock" it. I turn to Aron to ask if he wants first dibs on the bath—

—but as I turn around, I realize he's already undressing. Of course arrogant Aron would think he gets to go first. I should have expected that. I'm...not even mad, though? Because he tosses aside his cape and his tunic immediately and then I'm staring at a massive expanse of pale, perfect chest that looks as if it's carved from marble. It makes me feel curiously breathless, and I resist the urge to gawk. Funny how that after a week of travel, Aron still looks as glorious as ever and I'm like, entirely made of dirt.

Of course, then Aron unbelts his pants and shoves them down, kicking them across the floor, and my mouth goes dry. He's completely hairless and as perfectly sculpted on top as he is on bottom. I remember touching him—vaguely, so vaguely—but seeing him naked again makes me get all flustered. His cock is thick and long and brushes against his thigh, and his muscles flex with his movements. He's huge. Definitely a show-er not a grow-er. I watch as he moves toward the tub in a few powerful strides and with a flex of his too-perfect butt, seats himself in the tiny tub.

Damn. I blink repeatedly, trying to focus my thoughts while the slow-motion reel in my head plays back his casual stride to the tub. Over and over and over again.

Aron settles into the tub, shifting his big body and splashing the water everywhere. He splashes a handful over his skin, rubbing it and completely ignoring me. After a moment, he looks over his shoulder at me. "Well?"

"Well what?" I snap out of my dick-fueled trance.

"Aren't you going to wash me?"

Wash him? Is he serious? As I gape at his back, he casts another impatient look over his shoulder, his arms resting on the edges of the wooden tub and I realize that yes, he is serious indeed. I get that I'm his servant—of a sort—but this is the first time he's demanded I actually serve him.

Maybe he doesn't know how to wash himself, my brain chimes in.

Maybe he wants you to touch him, my other body parts chime in.

I feel a hot flutter in my belly. Even if it's innocent, it gives me a chance to touch him again, and I hate myself for wanting to do it...but I do.

So I shrug my dirty cloak off and pull one of the two pitchers of water near me as I sit behind his tub. I'm so close to him that I can see the beads of water on his shoulders. I swallow hard and wet a cloth, then lightly swipe it over his shoulders. "So...what did you think of all that downstairs?"

He grunts, which isn't much of an answer. "I think they were more interested in how to get between your thighs than what's going on in the land."

I drag the cloth over his shoulders and then rub the cake of soap over his skin, since I need to make it look like I'm actually washing him and not just drooling over his physique. "I thought they had some interesting things to say. I mean, some of it was garbage but that thing about another god being to the east?"

"Mm. It's not enough to go on. It could be Gental, like they said." He gives his head a shake, his hair playing over my hands. "I have no wish to travel for weeks only to say hello to Gental."

I mentally count back through the laundry list of gods that Omos made me memorize. "Gental is…the sea?"

"Family. Home. Hearth."

Ah. "Yeah, I guess he's not one of your closest buddies."

"We have nothing in common." He leans forward so I can dip lower with the washcloth. And of course, now I'm noticing how much his hips taper, and how there's two dimples at the base of his spine where his glorious bubble of a butt rises. Damn it, Aron. I wonder if he's going to want me to wash his front, and I squeeze my thighs together tightly because my body likes that idea more than it should. "It's a lead, though."

"We need more leads before we go in pursuit of one. Travel is not cheap. We'll need mounts. Guides. Supplies. Yshrem is inland and it will be a long journey."

"My favorite," I say dryly, and then run my hand over his soapy shoulders. Shit. Why did I just do *that*? I make sure to use the washcloth for the next swipe, because I'm an idiot who can't stop thinking about touching this guy. It's just because he's so damn pretty. It's certainly not his winning personality, that's for sure. "Okay, so tomorrow we wander around the city a bit more? Maybe find another inn to snoop around in?"

"It is as good a plan as any."

I continue to swipe the cloth over his shoulders and back, doing my best not to pay attention to just how well built he is.

He's a god. Of course he's going to be well built. If I were a god, I'd make sure I had a kick-ass body too. No sense being a total slob. Still…he's a god of battle and thunder. Did he have to be so damn sexy? I bite back a stab of irritation and make my movements more brisk. There is no sense in being attracted to this guy. None.

Zero.

CHAPTER 29

*H*e flexes, rolling his shoulders as if working the muscles out, and the breath catches in my throat, because...damn. That one sensual movement just made my brain fry. Aron tilts his head back and forth, working his neck muscles, and then shakes his head, his long, dark mane flapping right in my face.

That kills the attraction a little, I admit. "I hope you know you're going to do your own front," I tell him defensively.

"Am I?" He sounds amused, and I can feel my cheeks heating. "It wasn't too long ago you couldn't keep your hands off my cock."

Grr. He would have to bring that up. I throw the towel into the bathwater. "Fuck you, I'm done for now."

Aron only laughs and takes the cloth up, washing himself with oddly awkward movements. "You are too easily offended."

"Maybe I'm the one wanting a bath considering you've been telling me for days how bad I smell."

"You can have the water soon enough...unless you'd like to climb in here with me?" He looks over his shoulder at me, and it's less of a sexy invite and more of a challenge.

BOUND TO THE BATTLE GOD

I think.

Either way, no. "One, there's no room, and two, the only thing I want to do with you and that water is hold your head under until you twitch."

He throws his head back and roars with laughter. Nothing like a little murder humor to amuse a god, I guess. It's hard to stay mad at him when he's laughing, though, and I move to the edge of the bed and sit there, picking through the bedding we've been given. It's scratchy and full of small holes, but seems to be clean enough.

"So we're staying here for a few more days? I kind of hate this place," I say.

"It is not my favorite, either," he admits, rubbing the soap along one corded arm. "Dirty hovels built atop the ruins of a once-glorious civilization."

"Oh? So Katharn was not always Katharn?" I guess Rome went through several iterations itself. It shouldn't be surprising to me.

"No. Long ago it was part of a grand empire. This place was once called Suuol and it was one of many great cities ruled by the Mephisians. The Mephisians were fierce warriors who took over all of this land by might. This land and every-thing surrounding the sea was dotted with temples in my name and that of Kassam, Lord of the Wild. They conquered people after people, and a great many wars were fought in my name." He leans his head back, contemplative. "I miss those days."

"What happened to them? Why'd they end?"

He shrugs. "All empires get too large and crumble from within. When the last Anticipation happened, the magnificent kingdom was splintered and lords fought each other over petty land squabbles." He looks thoughtful. "That was the last I saw of Kassam, as well."

"Kassam? The other god?" I can feel my eyebrows rise high.

"You mean not everyone returns from this little trek you guys are doing?"

"Not always, no. I assumed that he had not finished whatever lesson he was intended to learn." Aron shrugs and gets to his feet, water sluicing off his pale body into the tub. "He always was hard-headed."

"I don't know anyone like that," I say dryly and offer him one of the towels from the pile of linens.

He turns to me and grins, wrapping it around his hips and then stepping out. "He will turn up eventually, Faith. When it is his time, he will return to the heavens."

"Mmm. You done with the tub?" My skin's starting to itch just thinking about how dirty I am. When he nods, I get to my feet and start stripping off my layers. I'm past the point of caring if he sees me naked, or if the water's warm, or even if it's clean. I just want to wash my damn hair and get half of the grime out of it. I'd be real happy with half. When I'm naked, I plop into the water and then reach over and add the rest of the water from the pitcher into the tub. It's all lukewarm, but it's the first genuine relaxing bath I've had since I got to this hellish land, and I plan on enjoying every bit of it. I sink down into the tiny tub, my knees practically at my tits, and sigh, closing my eyes.

"Do you have to do that?"

I don't even open my eyes. "Do what?"

"Make those noises."

I crack open one eye and glance at him. He's got a perturbed look on his face, as if he can't quite figure me out. I'm about to ask just what noises he's referring to when his gaze flicks to my breasts. Oh.

A wild thought occurs to me—did he watch me while I undressed like I watched him? I ignore the funny squiggle of heat in my belly and sink down lower into the tub, because the last thing I need is to get hot and heavy with someone like Aron.

The incident at the Citadel already made things awkward. I don't need them being even more so. "Just leave me alone and let me wash, all right?"

He grunts a response, and then I hear the jingle of his bracers as he puts them on again. Probably for the best.

I make my bath as quick as possible, scrubbing myself hard and giving my hair a quick rinse. I'm a little horrified at all the dirt rising in the water, but that can't be helped. At least it's now in the water and not on me. Once I'm done bathing, I step out of the tub and grab Aron's wet towel, noticing that he dressed while I bathed.

I dress, too, in my one change of clothing. It's an old gray tunic of Omos's that goes past my knees. I think it's meant to have trousers of some sort under it, but mine are dirty. I just wear it as a dress anyhow. It's not like it's sexy.

Of course, I don't think sexy matters to anyone in this land. They'd rape me if I was covered in dog poop, I think. I shudder at the thought and stuff my dirty clothes into my bag, and glance over at Aron. He's busy polishing his weapons and strapping them onto his forearms, as if we're going to be going somewhere in the next few hours. I guess being comfortable doesn't matter if you don't sleep, though. I examine my shoes. I have a pair of leather sandals that seem to be more straps than protection, and a pair of old boots that are a little too big but protect my feet. I'm wondering which ones I should wear tomorrow for more snooping around the city when there's a heavy thump at the wooden door to our room.

Aron and I both look at each other.

I slip my boots on, unlaced, and then get to my feet as someone jiggles the door. It has to be either a drunk, or a person making a mistake. I open my mouth to call out only to find a hand over my lips. Aron.

"Quiet," he murmurs into my ear. "That's not the innkeeper."

His hand slides away from my mouth and it's on the tip of

my tongue to ask him how he knows, when someone screams below. Not a small scream, a long, brutal scream — that cuts off abruptly in midstream.

Oh fuck.

More screaming starts, and the door to the room thumps again, the handle jiggling as if someone's desperate to get inside. "He's in there," shouts a voice. "Burn the place down if you have to, but get him!"

Aron and I exchange a look.

Immediately we separate and grab our things. The screaming downstairs gets louder, except it's not just one voice, it's a dozen of them. The door's not shaking anymore, but when I look over, I see a wisp of black smoke.

Aron grabs my arm, hauling me against him. "Time to go."

Even as he touches me, I can feel the weapons covering his arms and his belt practically clanks from the knives hidden there. "Should we stay and fight? I mean, you are a god of battle."

"And I know when a war cannot be won." He glances around the room, his gaze lighting on the enormous window shutters. "We both know it's not me that's in danger."

Oh fuck, that's right. Another scream pierces through the night and I feel sick. "What do we do?"

Aron points at the window. "Out to the roof."

I get a flashback of when we fell from the Citadel and groan. Is that what this is going to involve? Falling out of building after building while people try to murder us? This place sucks.

CHAPTER 30

The door shakes again, and I race for the window, because I like living. We fling open the shutters once more and look out on the roof. It's piecey and falling apart, with unsafe-looking patches, but it's also really close to the next roof. In the distance, I can see a cluster of torches and hear the shouts of angry voices.

How did they know it was us? We were so careful. Part of me hopes they're just thugs trying to rob an easy mark, but I know in my gut it's more than that. Whatever's going on in this world, these people are scared and trying to do something about it.

If that means running Aron out of town—or worse—they'll do it.

"Come on," Aron says, and grabs my arm. Before I can hesitate, he's moving out onto the steep roof. I have no choice but to follow.

"My boots aren't done up," I protest as we move forward.

"You can do them up later, or take them off, but we're leaving now." He releases my hand, hops the two-foot gap to the next roof, and a few tiles slide as he lands with a heavy thump.

He turns and extends his hand to me, impatiently flicking his wrist and indicating I need to follow.

I hesitate, then kick off my flopping boots. When I jump, I wince, expecting my feet to hurt—but he catches me mid-air and gently lowers me to the roof. Oh.

"Next roof," he murmurs, pointing at the nearest building a short distance away.

"Where are we going?" I whisper, sliding my hand into his instinctively.

"Away from here. We'll figure out the rest as we go."

Seven roofs later, and we're almost down the street. We jump down to a lower building and then Aron jumps down again, landing on a stack of moldy, filthy hay that hasn't been yellow in years. He hops back up to his feet again and then gestures that I should follow. Biting back the cuss words rising in my throat, I jump down onto the hay, too.

It feels like landing on scratchy concrete. I huff, choking on the air that whooshes out of my lungs, and get to my feet. Aron snags my bag from the pile next to me and then half-drags me forward. "Keep moving, Faith."

"Need...time..." I wheeze.

"You don't have time," he warns, glancing down the street.

"Don't...be...dick..."

"Hey! Hey you!" someone shouts. "There they are!"

With a growl, Aron hauls me to my feet, and I find I can run a little after all. We go down a narrow, filthy alley, my toes squelching in mud—at least I hope it's mud. At the end of the alley, we turn and go down a side street that leads to another side street...only to run into two men with torches waiting for us. Their eyes widen in surprise to see us race right for them, and one opens his mouth to call to his friends.

Aron grabs him by the throat, quick as a whip, and slams him into the wall. There's a horrible, wet crack, and the torch drops to the ground, sputtering out in a puddle. A second later,

Aron tosses him aside and slams his fist into the other man's face, and he collapses to the ground.

It all took less than a breath.

Aron turns back to me, not even breathing hard. "Come on. It's clear we're not safe in the main part of the city. Let's head toward the river."

When he puts his hand out, I take it. I'm still shocked by the quick, effortless violence of his actions, but I have to remind myself that those men want to kill us. I pull my cloak over my face and Aron does the same, and we hide in the shadows, moving from alley to street and watching out for others. There are people everywhere in the streets tonight — not just men but women and children, fear and anger on their faces.

You'd think Aron was the boogeyman instead of a god. But maybe because he's a god of battle, people are afraid. I think of the two men he brutally attacked and can't blame them for being afraid.

We get to the river's edge and go down the creaky wooden stairs towards the docks. At the docks, though, there are just as many people as there were out in the streets. These are almost all exclusively men and I feel even more unsafe here. Despite our hoods, they eye us with way too much interest, and they seem to be more focused on me than on Aron.

I trot a little closer to my companion as he pushes his way through the waterfront docks. "I don't want to be here, Aron. This is worse."

"What do you suggest, then?"

"I don't know! Something! Anything! Someplace we can hide and sneak our way out of the city."

He thinks for a moment and then steers me down the docks, past crates and shanty buildings and along the edges of the cliffs. I look up at the stairs that lead back to the city, but it doesn't look like we're heading in that direction. I can't figure out where we're going until he pulls me next to a huge, smelly sewer grate and then looks around furtively. There are a few people watching us on the docks, but it's more of an idle curiosity than anything else. The mob clearly hasn't come this far yet. Aron drags me behind a few crates and then we crouch low in the shadows.

"When they stop looking in our direction," he murmurs, "I'll pull the grate up and you get inside."

What? "Oh no, no," I protest, but he puts a hand over my mouth and shakes his head, indicating silence. As I watch, a sailor comes up to the grate, pulls out his dick, and pees a hot, heavy stream into the sewer itself.

Oh, god. This is nasty. I don't even have shoes. My stomach clenches as the man shakes off his member and then wanders away. I glare at Aron as if to say *really* and he only nods, his gaze on the others down near a small boat.

I eye the sewers with trepidation. The grate itself must be about twelve feet high and just as wide, which makes me wonder just how much poop is coming through this city. The sewer itself looks to be made of stone bricks or mortar, and the walls are scummy with sludge. There's an iron grate over the front to keep people from wandering in, and I'm pretty sure I hear rats. I shudder even as Aron gets to his feet and grabs one side of the grate, pulling it away from its moorings so I can slip through.

Distantly, I can hear the men on the docks laughing as someone speaks in a language I don't know. They sound distracted, which is good. Hopefully they've forgotten we're here.

Aron manages to create a wedge large enough for me to slip inside, and nods at it, indicating I should go through.

I hesitate. I really, really don't want to be girly and prudish while our lives are at stake but...barefoot and sewage and rats...? Can't there be another way? Something that won't involve a raging case of conjunctivitis?

As I hesitate, there's a low shout at the other end of the docks. That spurs me into action. With an irritated curse, I push forward, squeezing into the sewer. As I do, cold mud—please let it be mud—squelches between my toes and I slip, nearly losing my balance. Choking on the stink, I put a hand on the curved wall to steady myself and it's equally slimy.

"Pick up your cloak," Aron says, already at my side. I barely have time to haul it up against my side before he grabs my hand and hauls me forward. I half skid, half run after him. His footing is far surer than mine, and he doesn't even seem to notice that we're splashing through the sludge as we head into the darkness.

"Where are we going?" I hiss at him, a little terrified as the scarce light from dockside torches recedes and we plunge into darkness.

"Away from our pursuers. That's all that matters."

"Do you know where this heads?" I ask, skidding along a little and clutching at his arm.

"These are a remnant from the ruins of Old Suuol. They network all along underneath Katharn."

"These tunnels are huge," I admit, and see a circular patch of light up ahead. I look up, and as I do, more water splashes down, narrowly missing me. I bite back a squeal of disgust as I realize it's coming from the street above. These tunnels are pure worked stone, and I'm shocked to think that people are walking right above us. Those filthy streets above? That means all that filth came after the fact. That under a foot of land-hippo poop and people sludge and dirt there's a paved street.

God, Katharn is so damn gross. I am ready to leave this city as of yesterday.

Aron squeezes my hand. "Silent, if you can," he murmurs. "We don't know how much sound will carry down here."

He's right, but I can probably guess. Even those quiet words ring with a hollowness, echoing in the oversized tunnel. There are more distant rings of light up ahead, and I don't know if I'm glad to see them or frustrated. Glad because there's at least some light in this awful darkness, and frustrated because it means we're so close to the street above that it feels like we could be caught at any moment. All they have to do is look down.

I cling to Aron's hand as we walk. Eventually, the sewage gets deeper and we're no longer splashing through the muck but wading in knee-deep water. The stone under my feet is cold, the water too, and before long, I'm shivering and my toes feel like ice. The noise from the streets above grows quieter, and we're either moving away from the busiest parts of the city or its getting late and they're heading off to bed. My teeth start to chatter and I bite down on the edge of my hood to quiet them, trying not to think about how much sewage I might be covered in. All the poop in the world doesn't matter if my clacking teeth give us away. So I clamp down, keep quiet, and walk.

Aron doesn't seem to get tired, so I try to do my best to keep up with him. When the tunnels fork, he picks path after path, as if he knows where he's going. For the most part, the tunnels don't seem to be a bad path to take, for all that they're filled with sewage. It's private, mostly level, and it seems to be going somewhere.

In a way, it's also beautiful. Because as moonlight from the double moons pours in from the grates above, it illuminates just how precise and gorgeous the ancient stonework is. Every now and then I see something that looks like a sigil carved into the rock, and it makes me wonder about the civilization that vanished, leaving nothing but dirty, scrubby Katharn behind.

But damn, why did they need such a big freaking sewer system?

We walk until my feet start to slow, and Aron has to hook me by the elbow and pull me along beside him. I'm trying to keep up, but I'm not used to this sort of thing and my cloak and clothing are sodden with the wet sludge that seems to get higher with every step. Eventually, Aron pauses to let me catch my breath, his mouth a firm line of displeasure.

"I'm sorry," I wheeze, adjusting the bag on my back that's digging into my shoulders. "I'm trying."

"I know. It isn't enough, though." He takes the pack from my shoulder and slings it over his. After another glance around, he points at a grate in the distance. "That looks like the last one for a bit. We'll climb out there."

"Is it safe?" I can't help but ask.

"None of this is safe," he tells me, voice cutting. "But we can't stay here all night."

"Why not? We're already covered in poop."

"Because this is a sewer and the water's rising." Aron looks at me like I'm stupid. "The tide's coming in. Unless you want to drown in someone else's shit, we have to get out of here."

"It is?" I look down and sure enough, I guess the water (if you can call it that) is higher than it was before. I thought it was because the tunnel was just, getting deeper in this part, but it's past my knees and soaking the hem of my tunic. "I didn't realize."

"How is it I'm the immortal and you're the one that has no clue how a city works?"

I slap his arm, irritated. "Don't you start that shit with me. You want to know how it works where I live? We go into a tiny little room, sit on a toilet, take a dump, and then jiggle a handle and the magic poo gods take it all away. Whoosh. That's it. That's the extent of my knowledge. Once a month I pay the water bill and that's all I do. So if your stupid city doesn't work the way my stupid city did, don't blame me."

I glare at him, waiting for his answer.

He just watches me. His mouth twitches, just a little. Finally, he says, slowly, "Magic poo gods?"

I throw my hands up in the air. "You're impossible and I hate you. If we're leaving, let's just go."

"Should we say a prayer to the magic poo gods first?" When I shoot him the bird, he snorts with amusement. "Here I thought you didn't believe in any gods."

"There's just one where I come from, and he doesn't put up with any lesser god bullshit like this place, thank you." I stomp ahead, splashing through the horrible, sludgy water so I can get away from my equally horrible companion.

Aron's laughter rumbles through the sewer pipe, and I ignore him, pushing forward. I'm so tired and the night has been so long. To think I just took a bath and now I'm covered in crap and mud once more. It's like this entire world is conspiring against me. Heck, maybe it is. Maybe I've been cursed since I stepped through that portal. Given that I'm stuck with the infuriating Aron, I believe it. One minute I think he might be okay, and the next I want to choke him.

CHAPTER 31

I finally get to the grate he pointed out and sure enough, it's the last one for a while. The tunnels disappear into an alarming, deep darkness, and I'm glad we're getting out of here. It's quiet up above, so if someone's waiting for us, they're being really stealthy about it. I don't hear a mob, though, and that's a good thing.

I don't see a ladder, either. This worries me, especially when Aron pulls a rope out of his bag and makes a loop at the end of it.

"What's that for?" I have to ask.

He looks at me with smug arrogance. "To get out, of course. Unless you have a better idea."

"Ladder?"

"Did you find one?"

"Well, no—"

"Then we climb out."

I stare at the rope as he manages to hook it on a decorative flourish on the edge of the grate and then wraps the rope around one big hand. "I'm not sure I can do that," I tell him tiredly. I want to cry with how exhausted and dirty I am. We're supposed to be resting in an inn right now, not running for our lives through a sewer. I just want a nap and another bath and maybe a day where someone's not trying to kill me.

Aron puts a hand under my chin, tilting my head up until I look at him. "I won't leave you behind, Faith."

For some reason, that makes me feel better. I nod, trying to maintain a stiff upper lip, because I know that's what he'd want. When he smiles at me, it's stupid, but I almost feel like I won his approval.

Not that I want it, or need it.

But it's nice to have it anyhow.

I remain standing in the middle of the sewer while Aron shimmies up the rope, all the way to the top of the grate. He hooks his hands into the metal of the grate itself, then presses his face against the bars. He spots something through them, because as I watch, he takes the length of rope and works it around something up top, his arms straining, and then when he's done, he curls one hand around the rope again, drops a few inches and hangs by the strength of one arm as he uses the other to push the heavy metal grate to the side. Then, he climbs up.

It'd be an impossible feat for any normal human, but of course Aron isn't normal. Or human.

He tosses the length of rope back down to me and I catch it. Aron leans over and peers down at me. "You won't be able to climb."

I shake my head. "I'll try."

"No, Faith. I don't want you to hurt yourself. There's a loop at the bottom I made. Slip your foot through that and I'll pull you up."

Thank god. I step into it and wrap the rope around my hands to anchor myself, and then Aron's pulling me out of the sewer and into the moonlight. When I get close to the top, he takes my arm and hauls me onto the grass and I lie there for a moment, panting with relief.

At least, I do until I look up and see that he's anchored his rope to what looks like a creepy white statue. Huh. It looks like something you'd see in a graveyard. Of course, when I take a look around, I realize that that's exactly where we are. "We're in a cemetery?"

"At least it's quiet," Aron says. "No mob here."

He's got a point. I stare around me in the darkness, still shocked at what I'm seeing. Headstones and monuments dot the grassy yard we're in, and distant trees rustle their leaves against an iron fence. For such a big city, Katharn has a very crowded graveyard, and I get to my feet, shaking my clothes off. "How is it that there's a grave over the sewer?"

Aron looks at me as if I'm crazy, then points at the cobbled gutter I appear to be standing in. "No one's buried there. They're buried in the grass."

I study the graveyard itself. He's right. The graveyard itself is about the size of a football field, all told. There's the gutter that cuts through the middle of the graveyard and ends right in front of a fountain. The gutter itself is angled and sloped so the water runs away from the hillsides and over the grass itself, there are headstones. Not dotted and delicately arranged like in the graveyards I'm used to, but lined up in tight rows with nowhere to step except on someone's final resting place. It's clear that space optimization is the name of the game here, and there's not an inch to be wasted in Katharn's graveyard. Even the trees aren't wild growing. They're in enormous earthen pots set at the four corners of the courtyard, and at the center of the courtyard, there's a fountain with another statue of an enormous robed man with big shoulders and a cowl hiding his featureless face. He's got a sword made of bones in one hand, a skull in the other, and the crown atop his cowl looks as if it, too, is made entirely of fingerbones. At the base of the fountain's lip, there are dozens of old candles, half melted and all unlit. This has to be a representation of another god, though the name escapes me. All I know is that he's a scary-looking motherfucker. I turn to Aron and point at the statue.

"Rhagos, Lord of the Dead," he says, and then gestures at the cobbled gutter and the stepping stones raised up inside it. "If you're done fawning over his visage, I'd like to get going before someone realizes we're here."

"God, you're such a cranky bitch," I snap at him, moving to his side. I nearly trip over one of the stepping stones, and kick it, my mood foul. "And why are these stones raised up in the gutter? A person could fall and hurt themselves."

"It's so you can cross when the gutter is full." He narrows his eyes at me. "I worry about your cities. It sounds like they're a mess. No sewers, no gutters, no cemeteries." The god shakes his head. "I'm picturing a bunch of helpless fools sitting atop a mound of trash and calling that home."

I grind my teeth. "My home is very nice, thank you very much."

He only snorts in disbelief. "If it's so nice, then why are you here?"

The throbbing vein in my forehead threatens to explode. "Oh my god. I don't WANT to be here, Aron! I'm trapped here! You—" I break off in shock when he glances over his shoulder and there's a hint of a smirk on his firm mouth. He's joking. "Oh, you are such a dick."

"A dick that wants to leave this place behind for fairer cities, yes."

On that, we're agreed. When he puts his hand out for me, I take it again and move to his side. My sodden cloak squelches and slaps against my legs when I move, but I can't abandon it. At this hour, it's growing chilly, and my breath is starting to frost over. At least his hand is warm, and I instinctively move closer. "It's really quiet. No one's here in the graveyard even at night?"

Aron shrugs. "The prayer candles are dark. I guess no one

bothers when they know Rhagos is not in his deathly kingdom to hear them."

I look around, half expecting to see mobs of people with torches in the distance, but things are quiet. Off at the front of the gates, I see what looks like a lantern, but no one's coming to check us out. Why guard a graveyard? Are they having trouble with looting? I'm afraid to ask Aron because he might make another salty comment about where I come from and make me feel stupid. Still, I can't help but wonder. "It's odd that no one's checking out this part of town. They were all over the place every other street we turned down."

He grunts. "We might have lost them."

"But there are guards at the gate and they're not even bothering to look for us," I point out. There's something about this I find creepy and wrong. Either we lost them, or people are deliberately avoiding this area.

I wait for Aron to make another shitty comment, but he's only thoughtful. He gives me the grunt that tells me he's considering what I said, but doesn't stop moving. He tugs me forward and I wince at the fact that we're walking over people's graves. Other than staying in the gutter, there's just not many other places to walk. "Where are we going?"

"Away from the city." He points at the far side of the graveyard. Past a few more decorative trees and the endless lines of tombstones, I can see a break up ahead that looks a bit like a road in the moonlight. "That leads out. We'll follow it for a bit and regroup."

"All right."

We move silently through the graveyard, the only sound the cold, wet slap of clothing against our bodies. The farther we get from the fountain and the center of the graveyard itself, the more...run down things look. The graves go from stone to wood, and they look even tighter together than before, which I didn't think was possible. Even here, the poor get screwed. I bite back my whimpers when we cross over fresh dirt, because I know it's just superstition, but it creeps me out.

Of course, then we come to the mass grave, and then I'm *really* freaked out. How is this okay with anyone? I stare in horror at the cloth-wrapped bodies carelessly tossed atop one another, as if they're discarded dolls instead of people. "What is this, Aron?" I grab his arm and make him stop. "I don't understand."

He gazes out at the enormous pile of dead in the trench, and the curt comment I keep waiting for doesn't come. "There must be plague."

"Plague?" I have to bite back the shriek rising in my throat.

"Either that or the poor have no money to bury themselves and so this happens." Aron gestures at the pit of corpses. "I think I prefer the thought of plague."

"Well, I don't," I hiss back at him, trotting at his side when he starts to walk away. "Aron, what do we do if there's plague? Like...black plague? From rats? Are there more plagues than that one?"

"I would not know. I am not the god of plagues."

Right. Health and sickness is someone else's forte. "So is this happening because that particular god is nearby? His Aspect?"

He pauses and gives me a hard look. "You keep asking these things as if I have the answers."

"That's because I'm scared."

Aron turns toward me and to my surprise, he tucks my hand into his, giving it a comforting squeeze and slowing his steps so I can walk at his side. "Do not fear. I am with you. I will keep you safe."

I study his face and some of my panic subsides. If I'm safe with anyone in this crazy world, I guess it's with him.

Well...unless one of his Aspects shows up and tries to murder me. But overall, it's nice to hear him be understanding and not a dick. "Thanks, Aron. You're all right sometimes."

Before he can say something douchey, I add, "But only some-times. Don't let it go to your head."

He snorts. "Are you going to chatter all night or can we leave this place?"

"I would very, very much like to leave," I tell him, and I can't hide my eagerness. "I'm not a fan of Katharn, or its crazy-sized sewers or its bloodthirsty mobs. I would rather be anywhere but here, in fact."

"You and I both." He thinks for a moment as we walk. "Well, almost anywhere."

"What's worse than here?" I can't get past the fact that my cloak is covered in filth and slapping against my legs, or that if I breathe deep enough, I can probably smell the dead piled up nearby.

"Tadekha's Citadel."

I'm silent at that. Tadekha was very strange, true. She fed me and clothed me—and okay, made me sex crazed—but I'm surprised to hear him say that. I don't know what to think. Was me touching him (and him touching me) so awful that he prefers this? Why are my feelings hurt at the thought? You'd think I was rubbing him off with a damn cactus instead of my very eager hands.

Arrogant jerk.

How much does it suck that I still think about that night? Like, a lot?

All the time?

Obviously I'm the only one who even gives it much thought at all. But I force a laugh to my throat. "Yeah. That was the worst, wasn't it?"

"You nearly died and ended our journey very abruptly."

"You were the one that wanted us to leave quickly! How was I supposed to know the rope was too short?"

"I was *referring* to the fact that we were both suffering from the parting sickness, but come to think of it, you nearly died twice." His tone is utterly sour.

Before I can make a protest to that accusation, there's a low, creaking groan that rolls through the cemetery. Aron pauses, his hand going to my breast as he pulls out one of his blades. I want to point out that he's grabbing dangerously close to tit-meat, but the look on his face is anything but playful.

There's danger here. I scoot behind him, my heart pounding as the nighttime cemetery is silent around us except for the blowing wind that teases at my hair.

The creaking sound happens again, followed by a scratching. It's weird. The sound seems out of place here, and I squint into the darkness, trying to figure it out. "What is that?"

"Hsst," Aron tells me with a sharp look, indicating I should be silent.

I bite back my irritation, because the sound happens again, followed by another round of scratching. Then more scratching.

Then it sounds like the entire graveyard is full of scratching.

My stomach clenches uneasily. I move closer to Aron. I want to ask what it is. Rats? Lots and lots of rats? An army of insects?

Near my feet, one of the graves shivers, the earth moving. I yelp and stumble backward, and as I do, I turn and see another mound moving, the loose dirt piled atop it rolling away so something can break free.

Oh.

My.

God.

That sound of scratching? Of groaning? It's people trying to get out of their coffins.

Dead people.

I think of the mass grave, completely uncovered, a moment before I hear a low, gurgling moan coming from that direction.

"Aron," I manage to choke out, wrapping my hand in his cloak. "I would really like to leave now."

CHAPTER 32

*I*nstead of making a dick comment, Aron nods tightly
and sheaths his blade.

Wait, that wasn't what I suggested. I want him to protect me,
damn it. He's the one that knows how to sword fight and I don't
even have a thing to use as a weapon—

In the next moment, he grabs me by the hips and flings me
over his shoulder like I'm a sack of potatoes. I don't protest. I
grab double handfuls of his cloak to anchor myself and choke
out a "Run!" as Aron sprints down the path, my stomach slam-
ming into his shoulder with every movement.

All that matters is escaping this place, which seems to go
from bad to worse with every moment that passes. Aron sprints
out a large double gate, and I hear a man bark out a warning.
Aron doesn't even stop, and when the man races alongside him,
he casually reaches out, crushes the man's windpipe, and then
keeps sprinting.

Well, then.

Aron races out of the graveyard and into the dark hills. The
lights of Katharn dim with every bobbing step and the trees

RUBY DIXON

grow thicker on the edges of the road, the hills seeming taller and more shadowy. My stomach begins to protest, bile creeping up my throat, but I fight it back. I can't be sick right now. I'm still thinking about those awful, scratching sounds and the groaning. The mass grave that was open to the world. I can't stop shuddering, my skin crawling at the thought of the dead rising.

Eventually, Aron slows, and he's barely breathing hard. He pulls me off his shoulder and sets me on the ground. "I think we're a safe distance away unless there's a few dead along the side of the road." He glances around, his features creased with annoyance, as if it's irritating him to run away from the undead.

Me, I can't stop shaking. I sink to the ground and press a hand to my forehead. "I need a moment."

"Why? You weren't running." But he parks himself on the ground next to me and puts a hand on my nape. "Sick?" At my nod, he rubs the back of my neck, trying to comfort me.

Even though he can be frustrating, I know he's trying, in his way. Plus, his hand feels really good. I close my eyes, willing my stomach to settle, and concentrate on his nearness. "Thanks, Aron."

"That was not something I expected to encounter this night," he admits, and I guess that's the closest he'll come to saying "whoops, I made a mistake."

"Is it normal for the dead to rise? Here in this world?" I shudder, rubbing my arms. I want to hug my knees close to my chest, but my lower body is filthy.

"No. It is not a good thing. Not a good thing at all."

"King of the understatement," I mutter to myself. "No shit it's not good."

"It means that all of the gods have been exiled," Aron says thoughtfully. "Not just some, but all. I wonder at the reasoning behind this."

"You were all very naughty children?"

He grunts. "It seems foolish to make humankind suffer because we are disobedient."

I stare at him in shock. That is not a very Aron thing to say. "Maybe he was sick of your shit and cleaned house. And I don't know if you've noticed, but no one cares what mortals think. I mean, hello, you're not exactly the most understanding guy yourself."

"Mm." He frowns, thinking. "I do not think we should go to the coast after all. I think we should visit the Spidae."

"The Spidae?" I furrow my brow, trying to think where I've heard that before. "Wait, aren't those the fates?"

"The three lords of fate, yes." He nods, looking a little worried, even as his hand remains possessively on my neck. "We will go to their tower and look for answers there."

"Wait, they live here?" I look at him in surprise. "Like...there?" I gesture at Katharn, horrified. If I were a god, I wouldn't want to go anywhere near a place like that.

"No, they have a tower at the far ends of the land, past the Ashen Sea." He gets to his feet, brushing off his clothes. "That is where we are going."

"Um?" I look up at him in surprise. "So we're not going after your Aspects? We're not going to take out the other 'yous'? I thought that was the whole plan."

"Plans change." He offers me a hand, and I take it, letting him help me to my feet. "If all of the gods have been exiled, this world is not safe to explore at a leisurely pace. Best we visit the Spidae and get answers quickly. Besides, they owe me a favor."

I swallow hard. "So...we're going to go visit the fates. Do you think they could send me home? I thought we were going to get you back to the heavens so I could go back to my world and everyone could be happy."

Aron gives me a sharp look. "You think about yourself?"

"Well, yeah. I don't belong here, so my goal is to get home. I thought that was your goal, too."

He scoffs. "I should think it is far more important for me to get home than for you. I am the one that is a god. Let us focus on me first."

I just roll my eyes.

CHAPTER 33

e start moving again, and head through the dark hills, avoiding the thickest parts of the trees and underbrush. There's a wide path along this way, but we avoid it for obvious reasons, opting instead to go cross-country. I climb rocky slopes and avoid bushes the best I can in the darkness, but I eventually start to stumble and I'm relieved when we run across a small, bubbling stream that cuts through the woods and Aron suggests we stop here.

I move to the bank and wash my face, doing my best not to think about e. coli or giardia or any other parasite that might be in a wilderness stream. It can't be worse than what I was wading through back in the sewers, after all. Once my face is clean, I realize just how nasty the rest of my clothing is, and immediately start stripping layers off so I can wash them. I wade into the water to my hips and begin to scrub. My cloak, my leggings, and the hem of my long tunic are all encrusted in filth, and they're going to be clean before I put them on again, damn it.

"Once you're done with those, wash mine," Aron says.

I look up and he's stripping his clothes off, getting absolutely naked in front of me. He's all pale glory and scars, and I swallow hard, averting my eyes. I am not going to creep on him. Not at all. I'm certainly not going to think about that evening at Tadekha's citadel when I was all over him and his hands were between my thighs. No siree. "How about you get in here and wash them yourself?"

"You are my servant, remember?"

"Answer's still no. You need me alive, remember? We're equals as far as I'm concerned."

He gives an arrogant little huff of a laugh that I choose to ignore. When he tosses his clothes down at me, I immediately wad them up and toss them back at him, which makes Aron laugh. "I like your spirit, little mortal."

"Good, because you're gonna be seeing a lot of it," I mutter, and climb, shivering, out of the water. It's getting colder by the hour and my clothes aren't much in the way of warmth. "Can we build a fire?"

"And draw attention to ourselves? Should we just go lie in the road, spread eagle, and wait for them to step upon us—"

"A simple 'no' would suffice," I tell him, interrupting. "You don't have to be such a dick every time I say something, you know." But I know that's who he is. He's arrogance incarnate. I just have to remind myself of that. "Enjoy washing your own clothes," I say pointedly, and huddle on the banks.

He just smirks at me as if I'm a constant source of amusement and wades into the water, groin-high. Of course, that calls a lot of attention to his godly equipment, and I pointedly avoid looking in that direction as he half-heartedly swipes at his clothing in the water. "Fear not, Faith. The sun will be up soon enough and I will keep you warm until then."

"Goody."

Aron continues on. "We will journey to the next town and get a map and mounts for the next leg of our trip. I imagine that the Spidae's tower will not be anywhere near the mortal lands, so we must prepare for a long journey." He doesn't sound upset.

If anything, he sounds pleased, like this is a road trip and he's having a blast.

I'm glad one of us is having such a good time. Me, I just want to collapse and cry like a child. It seems that every time I turn around, someone's trying to kill us—or just me—and this entire world feels like one big death trap. I want my quiet apartment back home. I want my boring desk job and my boring reruns on television. Did I think my life was humdrum and monotonous? Clearly I was insane. I have a new appreciation for "safe" and "boring" and "quiet." I'd like any and all of those things.

I should have never visited that fortune teller.

King of Pentacles—a man like a force of nature? Try a god of storms.

A journey about to begin? Fucking understatement of the year.

Lovers? I shiver at the thought. I'm not sure if I hate it or want it so badly I ache.

I give myself a little shake and force myself to concentrate on what Aron's saying. "A road trip needs lots of preparation, Aron."

"I know. This is why we need mounts and supplies. Pay attention, Faith."

"With what money? Unless Omos taught me wrong about your money, we have enough for an inn room or two but nothing big like that." I pull the tiny purse of coins off my belt and open it, counting the strange coins.

"We will steal woales if we need to."

"Woales?"

"The large creatures everyone rides upon?"

"The land-hippos? Okay." I didn't realize they had a name. Of course they do. "You sure we can't just buy one?"

"You said yourself we have no money. We steal everything." Aron thinks for a moment. "Supplies as well. Weapons, too. Might as well get everything we can."

"Are you serious? We're going to thieve our way to visit your buddies in their tower? Don't you think that's against the rules that the big guy set for you? You're supposed to be improving as a person, not turning to a life of crime." I get up and hang my sodden cloak from the nearest branch in the dark.

"Bah. The High Father wishes to purge my flaws, and thievery is not one of them. I am the god of storms and battle. If I cannot get what I need, I suppose I could always threaten to wash away their homes in a violent deluge. Or I can demand that they go to the field of battle with me and fight for woales." He rubs his chin thoughtfully.

"You know what? All of that sounds awful. Let's just go with stealing. Jesus. I never thought that would be the least evil of our choices." I shake my head, hanging the rest of my clothing to dry and then digging through my woefully small bag for something fresh to wear. My cold ass is hanging out and I need something warm to cover me.

Plus, I'm feeling weird being naked around Aron after the bathing. I'm pretty sure he's impassive to human things like lust —well, except for his other Aspect that is nothing but lust—but me, I'm having a hard time figuring out where I stand with him.

"You sound upset, Faith." He wades back to the shore and offers me his wet clothes, as if I should hang them. When I don't take them, he tosses them over my wet clothes on the same branch, as if the problem is solved, and I have to bite back a curse of irritation. "It is a good plan."

"For you, maybe. What about the people you're stealing from?"

He snorts. "If they are anything like Katharn's fools, I should be glad to rid them of their belongings. They need to be taught a lesson or two. What kind of treacherous idiots try to kill a god?"

Apparently a lot of them, since that seems to be the agenda for oh, half the people we meet lately. "If they're like the Katharn people, I won't feel bad about stealing from them," I admit. "But what if they're more like Omos? What if they're moms and dads with kids to feed and we show up and demand their money and horses?"

Aron gives me an incredulous look. "You think I would cripple those that already suffer? What kind of man do you take me for, Faith?"

"An arrogant one?" I shove my arms through the sleeves of my new tunic.

"Arrogance is not selfishness or cruelty," he says, and pulls a tunic out of his pack and then offers it to me. "Wear this. You're still shivering."

I'm surprised—and touched—by his offer. "What about you?"

He shrugs. "I do not feel the cold nearly as much as you do. And we can huddle together for warmth if I do start to feel it. Are you going to sleep now?"

It almost sounds like he wants me to go to sleep. Is it because he's tired of talking? Or because he wants to hold me? I flush at the thought, discarding it from my mind. Probably not that. "Is it safe?"

"Safe enough, and you need to be well-rested for the morrow's journey." He sits, leaning against the trunk of a tree, one arm resting on a thick root as if it's a throne, and I can almost ignore the fact that he's bare-assed in the dirt. He still looks regal and imposing, and when he flicks a hand toward me, indicating I should join him, I do.

I delicately spread his tunic over his lap so I won't snuggle against his naked cock and balls, and then slide against him. "Thanks," I murmur. "Wake me up if we're in danger." I don't think I'm all that tired, but my eyelids grow heavy as he puts his arm around my shoulders.

I don't fall asleep right away, though. There's a rock under my butt, and Aron's shoulder is hard with muscle. Plus, he's started to play with my hair, which is...distracting. I think about our earlier baths. I think about that night in Tadekha's citadel, too. Man, I really need something new to think about, because creeping on Aron is not going to end anywhere good. He's already shown he's very uninterested.

I yawn.

"Go to sleep," he tells me.

"I'm trying. Quit talking to me."

"I will once you go to sleep."

I poke him in the side and shift against him, doing my best to get comfortable. It's almost too quiet around us, and I didn't realize how noisy the town was until we got out here. It feels unnervingly silent, and every time something in the distance makes a sound—a branch snapping, an animal moving through the bushes—I tense up.

"Why are you afraid?"

"Well, let me think. We were chased out of town by both an angry torch-wielding mob and a graveyard full of undead. Gosh, I can't imagine what there is to be frightened of."

He pokes my face, an Aron attempt at being playful. "You are here with Aron of the Cleaver. Nothing shall harm you."

"Mmm. How come you're Aron of the Cleaver and I have yet to really see you wield an axe? Or wear an eyepatch?"

"Should I announce my presence to everyone, then? Demand that they come and try their luck killing my anchor?"

"Good point." I settle back down against him. "Will we be safe at the Spidae tower?"

"No."

"You could sugar-coat it for me, just a little."

He continues to toy with my hair. "Why? I will never lie to you. That is another Aspect's job."

Har de har. I shift against him again, not entirely sure where to put my hand. I want to rest it on his chest or his thigh, but that seems a little too intimate. "So why isn't it safe? Is the countryside full of people waiting to kill us, then?"

"Not at all. It is the wildlands." Aron grows thoughtful. "No mortals live there. The mountains are full of foul creatures and ruins of places long overtaken by them. None dare to cross into those lands, so that is why the Spidae are there. They are safe from all those save the most foolhardy of pilgrims."

I shiver, thinking of "foul creatures." I can only imagine. "So what you're saying is that we shouldn't go there, either."

"It is the place we will get the answers we seek."

"Yay."

He grunts agreement and pulls me closer to him, tucking fabric over my exposed skin as if to keep me warmer. "It will not be an easy journey. Go to sleep."

I close my eyes obediently. "What do you do while I'm asleep?"

"I think."

"What about?"

"Many, many things."

I poke him again, yawning. "Such as?"

Aron sighs. "How I am going to leave this mortal realm behind. How I will be free of our tether. Where my other Aspects are and how I can best ambush them to ensure victory, because it is clear you will not be much of a fighter."

"Wow, I'm so glad I asked." I should learn at some point to stop while I'm ahead.

"I mostly think about the other Aspects, though. They will be thinking of ways to defeat me, so I must be ready. Your life depends on mine." And he plays with my hair again.

That soothes some of the irritation I'm feeling. I notice that he mentions me, and for all his arrogance, that's sweet, in an Aron sort of way. I know he's trying. I know it's against his nature to think of anyone but himself, and I should be more patient with him, but I'm only human, and man, Aron can be a real pain in the ass. But I move a little closer to him, because he's warm and because I'm feeling a little more affectionate toward the man. "You need to teach me how to fight," I tell him between yawns.

"I did not take you as my anchor because you were a fighter." He sounds amused, as if the thought of me with a sword is extremely funny.

I poke him in the side again. "You act like you had a bunch of options. If I recall, I was the only volunteer and your brain was still foggy from being booted out of heaven." I put my hands over my eyes and assume a deep voice, mocking him. "Oh look, I'm Aron and I don't know how to sleep like humans."

He pinches my side and I bite back a squeal, but I can feel the laughter rumbling through his chest. "You are full of fire to me, I see."

"Well, sure. You can't do squat about my sassy attitude," I tell him sleepily, and this time when I put my hands down, I do put one on his chest. Why not. "You're stuck with me."

Aron grunts.

"I'm serious, though," I tell him. "I should know the basics of how to fight. Nothing fancy. Just enough to protect myself. This world's way more dangerous than mine. And if you were on Earth, I'd show you how to drive a car and use a debit card. You should do the same for me."

"I will think on it."

I pat his stomach. "Don't strain yourself."

His laughter rolls through the trees and I go to sleep, smiling.

CHAPTER 34

*S*omething hard nudges me awake, and I groan, rolling over only to get a mouthful of leaves. Sputtering, I sit up, wincing at sore muscles and wiping detritus from my cheek. We're still in the forest, and somehow I managed to fall asleep and crash for several hours. Judging from the pale light wafting through the trees, it's incredibly early. I grab a handful of Aron's tunic and press it under my cheek as a pillow, lying back down.

The hard thing nudges me again. I turn over and glare. Aron stands over me, his boot nudging my backside. I swear, this man. "What the hell is your problem, Aron?"

"You wanted to learn how to fight. I have decided to show you." He flicks his wrist, making an entreating gesture. "Get up."

"Right now?"

"Was there a time you had more in mind? When we are surrounded by another mob? Perhaps when the dead finish crawling out of their graves and arrive?" He pulls a sword from its sheath and admires the blade, running his thumb along a sharp edge.

"God, you are such an ass," I mutter as I manage to get to my feet. I'm covered in dirt and leaves from my sleep under the trees, and I ache all over. Last night, I wasn't keen on the thought of stealing horses but today? Today I am all for it if it means I don't have to walk any longer. "Fine. I'm up. Show me how to use weapons."

His lip curls as if I've said the dumbest thing imaginable. "You cannot learn it all in one day."

Like I'm stupid. I put my hands on my hips, my irritated pose nullified by the leaf that chooses that moment to flop from my hair onto my forehead. "I know that. Just show me what you can today."

"First, show me your hands." He flips the sword casually in one hand and then stabs it into the dirt, then approaches me.

I stick both hands out, palms up, and wait for the next round of insults. This is Aron, after all.

He takes one of my hands in his and lifts it closer to his eyes, studying it. His thumb skates over my palm, sending ticklish sensations all through me. I want to jerk away, but I don't. I just go very still. "What are you looking for?"

"Callus. You have none." His mouth quirks in a half-smile as he meets my gaze. "I don't know why it surprises me."

"My world's really, really different. No one works with their hands if they don't have to. We have desk jobs. Like…clerks and scribes and stuff." It's a huge generalization, and I don't want to get into an argument about farmers and laborers, who really do still work with their hands. Even they wouldn't have the callus built up that he does, I think. Even now, where his hand brushes against mine, I can feel the hard pads of his hand where he's used to gripping weapons. Instead of feeling disgusting, though, I'm oddly aroused by how weathered his grip is.

And that makes me look around suspiciously, just in case Tadekha's waiting in the trees. But she's not, and Aron only gives me a curious stare. "Something wrong?"

"Nope." I slip my hand out of his. "So do I get to use your sword?"

He shakes his head, and I notice that despite an evening of roughing it under a tree, Aron looks as glorious as ever, his smooth black hair pulled back in a loose tail. His clothes aren't even wrinkled, the bastard. "No sword for you. Your wrists are far too delicate. We'll start with daggers."

We try his knives, and it soon becomes apparent to both of us that you require skill and aim, neither of which I have when it comes to weapons. I can't throw them and hit a target. I have to be in extra close to use one to stab, and even then, Aron isn't happy with my technique. He picks through the daggers—I don't know how he acquired so many of the damn things, but I swear he has a half-dozen of them—and finds none that he thinks are fitting for me. "You are terrible with all of these."

"Wow, thanks for the vote of confidence."

"Do you want lies or the truth?"

I sigh heavily, because we both know I want the truth. I need to be able to defend myself, and compliments won't get me anywhere if they aren't sincere. "So what do we do? The sword is out. The daggers are out. Unless you're carrying a can of mace somewhere under your cloak, I'm screwed."

"A mace would be difficult for you. They are very heavy."

"Not what I meant, but good to know."

Aron scratches his chin thoughtfully. "A bow, perhaps?"

"Because my aim's so good with knives you want to give me a bow and arrows?" I retort, defeated. I sit on the ground, sweating, exhausted, and angry at myself for not being a master with weapons. Who knew that defending yourself was going to be so challenging? I expect to be unskilled, but I'm fumbling so much that I even cut my fingers trying to fix my grip on one of the knives. I swipe at the sweat on my forehead, feeling rather pitiful. "I need a weapon for idiots."

RUBY DIXON

He snaps his fingers. "Of course."

I look up, indignant. What does he mean, of course? But Aron's heading into the trees, preoccupied, and he returns a few minutes later with a big branch. "A staff?"

He studies it. "It might be too short to be a staff, but we can make it work." He lops a twiggy offshoot off of it, then holds it out to me. "Come, give it a try."

I get to my feet, and even though my arms are aching and I want to whine, I give it a shot anyhow. It was my idea to learn weapons, after all. I can't bitch and moan that I suck at them, not when he's taking the time to teach me. So I heft it in my hands. The wood isn't all that smooth and tears at my palms, but the weight isn't bad. It comes up to mid-breast for me, and there's a knobby, ugly knot at one end. "Okay, it's a staff. How do I do this? Where do I grip it?"

Aron looks at me like I'm stupid. "You hit people with it."

"Duh. I mean, I just walk around with a giant club? And people are okay with that?" Then again, he's wandering around bristling with weapons, but I feel like a girl wandering the countryside with a giant stick kind of screams obvious.

He gives it a thoughtful look. "We can decorate it. Throw some charms or fripperies on the end so it looks like an affectation instead of a weapon. And then when they dismiss you for a soft female, you hit them with it." He taps the knot at the end. "Especially with this part."

"So...I clock people with it like a bat?" I heft it in my arms and hold it at one end. It's a bit too long to be a bat, so I adjust my grip and give it a careful half-swing. It pulls at my wrists, but I think it's doable. "I can knock a home run with this, I think. I played softball when I was a teenager."

"You'll break your wrists holding it like that," Aron warns.

"Then make me wrist supports, Mr. Weapons Expert."

"Do I look like an armorer?"

I drop the staff again, toying with the heft of it. "You look

268

like someone that wants to be hit in the head with a bat if we're asking me," I mutter.

He throws his head back and laughs. "You're very violent for one so soft, Faith. I like that."

His words make me flustered. I'm not sure if it's a compliment or not, since I just offered to knock him in the head, but he's a god of battle. Maybe that shit turns him on. "You're a very strange man, you know that?"

"Your first mistake is thinking I am a man," Aron tells me, and his eyes gleam with amusement, little sparks flicking in them and making me think of lightning.

Of course, seeing that makes me shiver, just a little. He's a god. Just because we joke around and he gets muddy like I do, it doesn't mean we're the same. Sometimes I forget. I'm so used to the electric charge when we touch I barely notice it anymore. I didn't notice it when I bathed him.

Good god, why am I always thinking of him naked? "I have far too many problems right now," I tell myself under my breath. "And all of them are named Aron." I shoot him a look, but he's still got that speculative, eyes-flashing-lightning expression on his face and I avert my gaze. "We should get going," I say loudly. "Just in case someone's coming after us."

"Indeed." He sounds thoughtful, but he doesn't move.

"I'll practice with my bat later," I tell him, and deliberately avoid eye contact, even when he moves closer to me. I focus on the branch itself, pretending to pick at a particularly knotty spot as he stands next to me, his gaze still fixed on my face...or my body. I wonder what he's thinking.

I wonder if he's going to touch me.

Goosebumps prickle up and down my arms as I remember that night in Tadekha's citadel. The way I crawled all over his lap like a cock-hungry ho, begging for his dick. Is he thinking about that? Is me handling a weapon turning him on? I wait for him to say something, do something, and I keep prickling with awareness. I know he's watching me.

My stomach growls, the sound overloud in the early morning quiet.

Aron turns and walks away. "You have a few minutes to eat before we leave. I suggest you do so because I do not plan on stopping again."

CHAPTER 35

*A*ron's wrong of course. We do end up stopping again, though not for several hours.

The weather turns to a misty rain, which makes our clothing stick to our skin and everything damp. There's a muddy, rutted road that cuts through the countryside, but we avoid it. Walking on it would probably be easier than creeping through the trees and bushes, which is what we're currently doing since Katharn is still on the distant horizon, but every so often someone rides past on a horse, or in a wagon, and I don't complain about hiking next to a road.

Even if Aron's pretty clueless about some things, he's right when it comes to keeping us safe.

Just when I've about hit my limit of walking for the day, a small farm comes into view on the horizon. It's no more than a square cottage in the midst of an enormous plowed field, but Aron points to it. "That is where we're going."

"Sounds good." I'm not so sure about his master plan of "steal horses and supplies" considering the place looks pretty bare to me, but he's the one in charge, and I'm too tired to argue.

We pick our way through the barren fields, and I can't help but notice that they've got the saddest-looking crops known to mankind. The ground here seems to be mostly rock and the plants are choked with mud and sludge and look wilted. My feet sink into the carefully tilled rows, messing up their symmetry and making me stagger behind Aron a good distance. Him, you'd think his feet were made of air. He doesn't notice the mud, and even the rain doesn't seem to be soaking him quite like it is me.

I hear him sigh heavily as he pauses. I catch up to him, about to retort that if he wants me to keep pace with him he needs to walk at a human speed, when I realize he's not even looking in my direction. He's looking ahead at the farmhouse, and so I stop at his side and gaze, too.

At first, I'm not entirely sure what we're supposed to be looking at. It's all foreign to me. The walls look like stone spackled with mud, and the roof is thatched hay. In the distance there's a second shack that might be a stable of some kind, with a fat land-hippo chewing hay nearby, his legs encased in mud. Then I see them.

There's a man and woman at the front of the cottage, their heads bent as they kneel in one of the puddles. They're both incredibly thin and dirty, their clothes faded and poor. The woman clutches a swaddled baby to her breast and her belly is huge with another kid on the way. The man has both fists over his heart in Aron's symbol, as if he's holding an invisible axe to his chest.

Oh.

"Look," I tell Aron brightly. "Superfans."

He gives me a dark look and doesn't move forward. Even as we stand there, the rain seems to pour down harder. They ignore the rain, but I can see the woman trembling as water drips down over her, and the baby starts to cry.

I glance at Aron. He looks highly annoyed, as if this has

ruined all his plans. "Why aren't we approaching?" I whisper, leaning in.

He leans back toward me, not taking his eyes off of the couple. "They know who I am."

"Well, you don't exactly blend," I point out. Even now, my hair's streaming water into my eyes but Aron looks only lightly misted upon, and just as overwhelmingly sexy as ever. At least, he's sexy until he opens his mouth. "And they don't look all that dangerous."

"They will tell others we have stopped by."

"So tell them not to," I whisper. "You're a god. It's clear that they're scared of you." The baby wails louder, but still Aron doesn't move, just scowling in their direction.

"Please, my Lord of Storms," the farmer calls out. "We are your faithful. Bless us."

The hollow-eyed woman gives us a terrified look, clutching her baby tighter, and then leans forward, as if ready to prostrate herself in the mud but prevented by her big belly.

Oh boy. "Come on," I tell Aron, grabbing him by the hand and ignoring the pleasurable little jolt of touch. "He's coming," I say to the couple. "Blessings for everybody around in exchange for dinner and someplace dry."

"Faith," Aron warns me.

I glare at him, even as I drag him forward. "New plan. Instead of stealing, why not let your adoring worshipers gift you with things? Or at least give us shelter and get out of the rain?"

"They could be dangerous."

"They're starving," I point out to him, gesturing at the swampy field. "Look at this. They're farmers. You think they're rolling in dough with this crop here? I realize you're arrogance personified, but they have a small baby and it's getting wet."

He glances over at the couple, who quiver in fear at his

baleful look. "Very well. But if this is a trap, I shall be very displeased with you, Faith."

"Fine. I will accept full blame if this turns out to be a sham," I tell him. "Can we go inside now?"

"Please come in," the man calls out, kneeling and putting his head to the mud despite the driving rain. "Let us honor you and your consort, Lord of Storms."

I already like them. "Consort" is way better than "tart." I give Aron another encouraging smile and he nods, squeezing my hand in acknowledgment as we head inside.

The woman casts me a grateful look as she struggles to her feet, dripping mud and rain, her baby wailing. Both she and her husband wait at the door, their eyes wide. I gesture that they should enter. "After you, please."

"We cannot walk before a god," the woman whispers, juggling her crying baby as she tries to make Aron's symbol over her chest.

"You're not. You're just preparing the way for his comfort," I reassure them, trying to make it sound as if they're doing us a favor.

They look to Aron, and he gives a terse nod. "My consort and I would sit at your fire."

"Of course, my Lord of Storms. Whatever you need." They're super nervous, these two. Poor things look ready to fling themselves to the ground again, then think twice when Aron crosses his arms and heads into the cottage itself.

I start to follow, but Aron puts a hand in front of me, indicating he should go first. He pulls out his sword, and I remember that everyone wants to kill us. Right. Better that the immortal guy goes in first. I wait as they all disappear inside for a long moment, rain splatting all over me, and then Aron finally appears in the doorway and nods, giving the all-clear.

Thank goodness.

I step inside, and it's humid and smoky but there's no more rain, so I'll take it.

The interior of the cottage is clean, if dark. The floors are dirt, but there's a stone hearth along one wall that dominates the room and it has a cauldron of something that smells delicious bubbling over it. A wooden table sits across from the hearth, and herbs and dried roots hang in strings from the rafters. Off to one side, I can see a bed, and a second tiny room that has been set up for the baby, complete with cradle. There are barrels of goods and farm implements stacked in one corner, and everywhere there is clutter, but it seems cozy.

"Your home is lovely," I offer, sliding the hood of my sodden cloak off my head. It just feels good to get out of the rain.

Aron looks at me like I'm crazy, and the two farmers just duck their heads, still clearly frightened.

"We require supplies," Aron tells them imperiously. "Food and drink for travel. A mount. And my consort needs a bath."

"Dude, are you going to tell everyone we meet that I need a bath? You're going to give me a complex." I make a face at his back.

"I will until you stop smelling."

"I don't smell," I tell him, lifting my sleeve to my nose and inhaling. "I...oh god, okay, I still smell like sewer." Bile rises in my throat and I choke, waving a hand in the air. "Never mind."

Aron moves into the house and takes the best chair, the one by the fire that's probably for the pregnant woman. He sits on the edge of the seat and glares imperiously at the two terrified farmers who still stand in place. "Well? Will you be able to help us? Or do you work against me?"

"Never, Lord of Storms." The man drops to his knees and presses his forehead to the floor. "Please. We will give you whatever you need. Just...we ask for a blessing."

That's not the first time they've asked for a blessing, and I wonder what they're talking about. Aron ignores them, looking satisfied, and relaxes in the chair. "Get my consort her bath."

The woman jiggles her baby, casting me a worried look. "Of course. My soaps are poor," she begins.

"Hey, if you have soap, you're a step ahead of me." I try to seem as friendly as possible to make up for Aron. "And we totally appreciate it, even if it doesn't seem like it."

The man nods, racing outside and back into the rain. A moment later, he appears with a tub, and drops it in front of the fire.

Oh shit, am I supposed to bathe in front of everyone? I cast a worried look at Aron, but he's got his dagger out and is sharpening it by the fire. I'm not sure if that's him "relaxing" or if it's a subtle threat, but it's obvious he sees nothing wrong with this scenario. "I hate to be a pain, but can I bathe somewhere private?"

"My husband will not look upon your beauty," the woman says shyly, then tugs the cauldron off the fire with surprising strength and puts an empty pot on the hook.

Aron snorts, not looking up from his daggers.

I move to Aron's side and put my hand over his face, covering his mouth. "I'm a shy, delicate flower," I tell her with a wink. "And I'd rather some privacy if it's all the same to you. Ignore this man."

She gives us a startled look but nods.

Aron just calmly removes my hand from his mouth, as if women manhandle him every day, and then goes back to his dagger. "Do you have a sharpening stone I can use?"

"Of course," the man says, then hesitates. "Should I get water first or the stone?"

"I can get the water," I offer, "If you show me where it is." Heck, this poor woman's got a baby to juggle and her husband looks ready to fall over with exhaustion.

They give me horrified looks, as if the thought of me tending to myself is abhorrent. Aron just rolls his eyes.

"We will tend to you," the woman says. "Please, take your rest."

I feel guilty about that, given that she's very heavily pregnant and they're both underfed. But they look terrified at the thought of displeasing Aron, and he's clearly not going to make any effort, so I look around for a seat. There's a stool, but I want to leave that for her, so I move to Aron's side and plop in his lap. "Hope you don't mind if your smelly consort takes a load off, then."

His hands go to my waist and he leans in to murmur to me, "As long as I do not breathe deep, I am fine."

"Prince Charming," I tell him. "You're going to make me swoon with your flowery words."

Aron just chuckles low, pats my hip, and then we watch as the poor farm couple scurries to make Aron welcome.

CHAPTER 36

*I*t should feel good to have someone waiting on us after days and days of being run out of every place we go to by a frightened mob of god-killers, but I can't relax. I just feel sorry for these two, because it's clear that they're very poor and very tired. They're also very worried, if the looks the wife casts in our direction are any indication. I don't blame them for being worried. They don't look like they have much, and Aron wants to take what they do have to make our journey easier, and somehow that feels wrong to me. We'd totally screw them if we took their food and their one horse. Well, land-hippo. They do have a donkey, though, and I picture Aron on a donkey and immediately get the giggles.

"Your bath is ready, my lady," the woman eventually says and sinks to her knees, averting her gaze. She gestures at the baby's small room, hidden by a thin burlap drape. "Shall I attend to you?"

I'm about to say that it won't be necessary, but Aron pinches my hip and I guess I'm getting attended. Yay. Maybe I'm supposed to butter them up and find out what we can take, or just get information, or something. Whatever it is, I smile brightly. "That would be awesome, thanks."

We pull the curtain closed and I undress, then slip into the tub of water. As Aron and I sat by the fire, the husband and wife worked to heat water and bring more in to fill the small tub, and as a result, I have a very small sit bath with tepid water. I don't complain, though, because I know they worked extra hard just to get this much done. "I appreciate you both opening your house to us."

"We are faithful to the Lord of Storms," she says quietly, taking my clothing. "I will have my husband rinse your clothing with fresh water." She takes them with delicate fingers, and they must smell worse than I thought.

"We got trapped in the sewers," I tell her, desperate to explain. "I don't normally smell like that."

Her smile is soft. "I suspected not."

She leaves and I soap up the rag provided, scrubbing at my skin. On the other side of the curtain, I can hear the woman murmuring to her husband, while Aron *scrape scrape scrapes* and sharpens his many weapons. I wash, even though the soap cake is as hard as damn rock, but it smells like flowers and clean herbs.

After a few moments, the woman returns, juggling her baby over to her other hip. "Shall I wash your back for you, my lady?"

"What? Oh, no." I can feel myself blushing, comparing this to my last bath. "I can do myself, thanks. You've got plenty on your hands already." When she remains, hovering, I try to make this seem normal. "So what's your name?"

"Me?" The woman looks surprised and then blushes, the color standing out on her thin, pale cheeks. "I am Vian. This is Anora." She shifts the baby in her arms.

"I'm Faith," I tell her, and I'm not surprised at the puzzled look on her face. I guess "Faith" isn't a name around here. "Thank you for opening your home to us."

"Of course," Vian says, and that hint of confusion returns to her voice, as if she's surprised anyone would dare not to.

"I know Aron can be a bit much at times."

"He is the Lord of Storms," she acknowledges. "He is allowed to be whatever he likes." The look on her face is troubled. She glances at the curtain, and then edges closer to me, taking the cloth from my hands and washing my back even though I told her I didn't need it. I don't protest, just hug my knees to my chest and lean forward. "You're...not afraid of him?" Vian's voice is a low whisper as she moves the rag over my skin.

Afraid of Aron? Oddly enough, I've been afraid of everything in this world but him. It's been an awful week—oh god, has it only been a week?—but the one constant is that Aron is at my side. In that sense, I do have a buddy experiencing all this hell with me. So no, I've never been afraid of him, ever. But I think of that torch-wielding mob and Vian's fear and I wonder if it's smarter to foster that intimidation of Aron instead of friendliness. People that aren't afraid try to kill him. If the farmer and his wife view Aron as vulnerable, they could easily cut my throat to be rid of him.

Disturbed by that fact, I snatch the rag out of her hands and pretend to scrub my knees. "It's in our best interests to be together in all ways," I tell her, hoping that makes us sound like a unified front despite my earlier ribbing. "He commands and I serve." Yeah, that sounds appropriately humble, even if it chokes me to think he might possibly overhear that.

The answer seems to appease Vian, but she leans in closer, whispering in my ear. "Do you need deathwort?"

"Deathwort?" I echo, curious.

"For preventing pregnancy?"

Oh my lord. I look at Vian, her earnest face and pregnant belly, the child on her hip who's still probably nursing. I know she's being thoughtful and kind, but...just...oh my word. "I'm not with Aron like that."

Her brows furrow. "But he has chosen a female anchor. You are his consort."

"Well, yeah, but..." I don't finish the statement. What am I going to say? He's not trying to get his rocks off? Should he be? Is that what all the others do with their anchors? I think of Tadekha and her angelic servant, who knelt between her thighs and used her mouth with obvious enthusiasm. What do I say that won't make things worse? I decide to just leave it at that. "I'm good."

She pats my wet shoulder. "If you need more, I will leave some under the pillow tonight. I have heard the gods can be demanding."

Aron's demanding all right, but just about the only thing he hasn't demanded from me is sex. Which...come to think of it, might be odd. Is he supposed to? Did I get the only celibate Aspect out there? Or am I not Aron's type and he took me only because he had to?

Why is the thought of that offensive? Because I threw myself at him and he ignored me? I bite back my scowl and wash myself, trying not to think about how many times Aron has told me that I stink. I mean, I do stink. But lots of the people here stink.

That doesn't mean I'm unattractive. He told me that he liked the way I looked...once.

I don't know why I care. I don't plan on staying around this place. I'm with Aron because he wants to go home, and so do I. It's a mutual interest thing. He needs a way back to his heavens, or wherever he went, and I need a way back to my world. Both of us get what we want—hopefully—if we manage to restore him.

That's all that this is.

Sexual attraction has nothing to do with anything. Aron's attractive to me because he's a god. Doesn't mean that he finds mortals attractive at all.

I try not to be irritated at that thought and finish my bath quickly, then let Vian pour a cold bucket of water over my hair to rinse it. "Your hospitality has been amazing," I tell her as I wrap up in the clean, worn blanket she offers me. "I'll be sure to tell Aron all about how kind you are."

For the first time, her eyes light up with hope. I can practically see her entire body tremble. "And he will bless us?"

"I'll ask."

The answer seems unsatisfying to her, but she nods and manages a smile, and I'm left wondering what response she was looking for.

$\mathcal{V}$ ian and her husband Cathis feed us and let us dry off by their fire that night. It's a quiet meal because both of them are too afraid of Aron to talk much, and I'm too busy stuffing my mouth. They seem unsurprised by my appetite, as I'm the only one that takes four bowls of stew, but during bowl number four, I realize that I might be eating them out of house and home and that curbs my appetite. I finish my portion and give them a bright smile. "We'll pay you for your hospitality."

"No we won't. They are honored to serve," Aron says arrogantly.

I kick him under the table and continue smiling. "Yes, but they have babies to feed. It's enough that they've offered." I don't pull out the coin purse just yet, though. I remember the greedy eyes back at the tavern, and I wonder suddenly if the mob came after us because we flashed too much money, not because Aron was a god. I'm so naïve. "It's so nice of you to welcome us," I say again.

"Of course." Vian gets up and clears the table. "I have

prepared your bedding. We will sleep in the stable tonight to give you and your consort privacy, my Lord of Storms."

"Oh, but that's not necessary," I begin, but this time Aron kicks *me* under the table. I look at Vian and Cathis and it occurs to me that despite the muck and damp (and the sad, pitiful state of the stable) they might feel safer out there. "But thank you," I amend. "My lord and I are most grateful."

Aron pats my thigh, as if pleased by my chirpy response.

I just kick him under the table again, because it's fun, and he snorts with amusement. Sometimes I think he has fun being challenged, too.

The baby starts to get fussy, and then Cathis and Vian retreat to their stable, leaving us alone in their small cottage. I feel guilty, because I think of how pregnant Vian is and of the muddy, sloppy rain that's still going outside. It can't be a comfortable night for them, but they also looked as if they wanted nothing more than to get away from us. I guess there's no winning this particular battle.

My clothes are fresh and warm after baking by the fire for a few hours, but I'm reluctant to change into them to sleep. I'm still wearing Vian's shift dress, which is made of a papery, thin material that itches. I can't wear it to bed, either. I consider for a moment, and then pull on one of my backup tunics as a night-gown. No panties, though.

I'd give a kingdom for panties right about now. No one on this planet seems to wear them.

Yawning, I crawl into bed as Aron sharpens his knives, and I'm just about to drift off to sleep when the lumpy hay mattress sinks in on one side, and then a big body crawls into bed next to me.

"For real?" I groan as Aron promptly shoves his way onto the narrow mattress and proceeds to take up most of the bed. "You don't even have to sleep."

"You know this is how I protect you best."

"What's going to attack me while I sleep?" I ask, yawning.

"A wizard could send poisonous snakes to rise up from the floor, creep into bed and kill you."

Jesus. I'm awake now. I roll onto my back and stare up at the ceiling as Aron shifts next to me, trying to get comfortable. "So undead, snakes from the floor, gods wandering the earth... anything else I should know about in this world of yours so I can never sleep again? Dragons? Killer mermen?"

"Don't be foolish. Mermen are long dead."

"You didn't say dragons were."

"Do not go looking for dragons, then," he says, and I don't know if he's joking or not.

"I'm not a big fan of this whole place, just so you know."

"Neither am I. Which is why we are doing our best to return to our respective homes." He thumps in and then pushes an elbow against my side. "Turn over. It is more comfortable when I cup my body against yours."

"You mean when we spoon?" I obediently turn onto my side, hugging the pillow to my head. Aron molds his body against mine and slings his arm over my hips, and I hate that he's right; it does feel way more comfortable like this. I fight back another yawn, because I'm tired. All the food I have to shove into my mouth makes a girl sleepy. At least I'm not gaining weight, even though I'm pretty sure I'm eating triple what I normally do. "So what's the plan for tomorrow?"

"Get the lay of the land from the farmer. He will know where all these roads lead to and the safest way to head. Take a mount, get supplies, and be on our way. We cannot stay here for long like we did with Omos. They are not nearly remote enough."

"I figured." I think of Omos, that kind, sweet man who opened his home and offered everything to us. His letter to his goddess is still in my pack, and I wonder if he worries over it. I hope he's doing well. He's the only person on this planet I'd wish good things for. Well, no, I guess that's not true. I want to help Vian and her poor, worried husband.

And I guess Aron is okay, too.

I think for a moment of the two farmers. "Are we really going to take their supplies?"

"You would rather starve?"

"Well, no, but I would feel really, really guilty if we stole all their stuff and left. They have a little baby. One on the way, too."

"Your heart is too soft, Faith." Aron pats my shoulder. "We will leave them coins if that will ease your fears."

Oh. We do have some money. "That's a great idea. Thanks, Aron."

"They will do us no good where we are going, unless you are fond of chewing on coins instead of food."

I should have guessed that Aron wouldn't be totally selfless. Still, he's thinking of others at least, even if it's only to shut me up. "I'll talk with Vian in the morning and see how much it would cost them to replace the supplies we take." The farmer's wife will probably try not to take the money, but I can push it on her. She has mouths to feed. Of course, thinking of Vian makes me also think about our conversation we had earlier.

I put my hand under the pillow, feeling around, and sure enough, there's a tiny pouch. Deathwort. For preventing pregnancy, she'd said. Good lord.

"You realize they think we're sleeping together?" I point out to Aron.

"We are sleeping together."

"No, not like that. I mean *sleeeeeeping* together. Like, doing the dirty."

"Do your people have no words for fucking?"

Gah. When he says it so bluntly, it's a little embarrassing and shocking. "No, we do. We have lots of words for it."

"Good. I was starting to wonder."

He sounds completely unconcerned, and I frown into the

darkness, my fingers around the little pouch of herbs. "We should tell them that we're not." I pause, and then continue. "Fucking, you know."

"Why?"

"Because we're not? I didn't agree to fucking! Just to being your servant."

He laughs, and the sound is low and arrogant. In the next moment, he leans in and I feel his breath against my neck. "I remember your terms. No 'butt stuff.'"

"That's right." A shiver races through me at the feel of his mouth so close to my skin.

"I could have you in this moment if I wanted you."

"Bullshit you could." My heart trips in my chest. I'm not afraid. I'm...excited.

"You think if I did not caress you and tell you sweet things, that you would not put your arms around my neck and beg me to take you?" His hand strokes down my arm, sending goosebumps through my body. "You think a god could not give you more pleasure than any mortal could?"

"I think..." And boy, is it hard to think when he's being sexy and flirty. "I think that you would struggle with the whole 'tell me sweet things' part."

Delighted laughter booms from his chest. "Perhaps that is so." He continues chuckling. "That is why I like you so much, Faith. You are not afraid to speak your mind."

Is that so? Because I have to admit (even if only to myself) that I was hoping the dare would go a little further than that. But I just squeeze my thighs tight together and close my eyes. "Go to sleep, Aron."

"I do not sleep," he tells me, amused.

I don't either. Not for a long time.

CHAPTER 38

*V*ian and her husband return in the morning and she immediately gets busy with cooking breakfast. My stomach's growling, so I admit that I hover a shameful amount near her as she cooks. The rain's still pouring down outside, which means it's going to be another miserable day of travel.

Even worse, things are oddly tense in the tiny kitchen. I glance over at Aron as he glares at poor Cathis, who has his hat in his hands.

"What do you mean, you cannot draw me a map?" Aron demands. "You live in this land. You should know better than anyone how it is laid out."

"I...have no schooling, my Lord of Storms." The farmer looks ashamed, his shoulders hunched. "This was my father's farm before me. I have always lived here. I have not traveled."

Aron flings up his hands and casts me an exasperated look.

"Maybe you can tell us where the roads near here lead?" I ask, trying to be helpful before Vian's baby starts crying from all the noise Aron's making. "And we can take notes?"

"Do I look like a scribe?" Aron snaps.

"I can write it," I tell them, moving toward the table where the charcoal stick and animal skin are located. I sit down, "But the only language I write is English."

"Yeeng-lesh?" Vian echoes.

I smile tightly. "Foreign tongue. Let's just…" Aron squeezes my shoulder, reminding me that we're on a mission. "Let's just focus. We're trying to go north, right, Aron?"

"To the Ashen Sea," he agrees.

"Is that north?" I ask Cathis, and when he gives a reluctant nod, I start to write on the skin. *North to Ashen Sea.*

"You do not want to go there," the farmer says, twisting his cap. "There is nothing but death in that direction."

"I am Aron of the Cleaver," my traveling companion says oh-so-confidently. "And I do as I please."

Cathis gives me another uneasy look and I just smile, nodding encouragingly. He hesitates, then continues. "Go north on the road for a week, through the mountains. The last city you find will be Novoro, the Nest of the Cliffs. Once you pass through its gates, there is nothing but wild, ravaged lands. The Ashen Deep is on to the north and the Red Glacier to the east."

I write quickly. *North. 1 week. Mountains to Novoro. Pass through gates. Red glacier = wrong way.*

"What is this Red Glacier?" Aron asks. "It is not in my memories."

"Maybe you forgot it?" I ask. He did, after all, forget sleeping (which I'm never going to let him live down).

"No. This is new."

Cathis gives a small shake of his head and then freezes, as if realizing he's disagreeing with Aron. His face pales and he drops his gaze to his hands, where he's constantly twisting his hat.

"Well, I'm sure it's not a problem. So we avoid this Red Glacier thing and then what?" I prompt the farmer. "Just keep going north? How many days to the Ashen Sea?"

He shrugs. "Possibly. The Ashen Sea is the edge of the world.

No one goes there. I only know of it from my father's fathers. I do not know of anyone that has gone there in recent times."

Hmm. "Well, we can ask for more directions in..." I study my scribbly handwriting that's already smearing thanks to the charcoal. "Novoro."

Vian coughs, and when I turn to look at her, she's focused on her baby.

"Is Novoro a bad place?" I ask.

Cathis looks as if he'll faint. "No."

"Then why do you cower, man?" Aron demands.

"Their customs are very different than ours." Vian says, and her cheeks are red. "Two men share one wife. Sometimes three."

"Well that sounds like hell," I say drily.

Aron snorts, thunder rumbling overhead.

"They are a good people," Vian continues, her voice soft. "Just...different."

"All righty, we'll keep open minds, then." I smile brightly at her. "Which brings us to the topic of supplies. We're going to need some for our journey."

"Of course we will provide you with whatever you need," Vian says, casting a look at her husband. "We live to serve the Lord of Storms."

"We need a mount," Aron says. "And food supplies. And clothing for my consort." And then the bastard plays with a lock of my hair, as if to prove to everyone that I'm servicing his arrogant ass.

I wish his leg was under the table so I could kick him.

"I have but a donkey and a woale," Cathis says. "You are welcome to either. Or both."

"Let me see both and I will choose." Aron releases my hair and then the two men head outside.

I'm alone with Vian, who's very carefully stirring the cauldron over the fire, the scent of porridge in the air. "We really appreciate this," I tell her, because she's awfully quiet.

"Of course."

"Is it going to put you out?"

She bites her lip. "All we ask for is a blessing."

That's not the first time she's brought that up, but I'm not entirely sure what she means. "We'll pay for whatever we take, of course. Just tell me how much money you need."

Vian turns, startled, and her baby begins to cry. "It isn't necessary—"

"Sure it is," I say, and get to my feet. I wipe my charcoal-smeared hands on my tunic and then reach out and take the baby from her. The little one immediately grabs a fistful of my hair and begins to tug. Vian hesitates, then turns back to stirring the food. "We're imposing on you guys. The least we can do is help monetarily."

She pauses, and then turns back to me. "Money will help, but it will mean nothing if the rain doesn't stop. That's why we need Aron's blessing so much."

I blink. Then, the light goes on in my head. He's the Lord of Storms and their fields are one big mud puddle. "Oh my god. The rain. I'm an idiot. Of course we can ask him to stop it."

"Do you think he will?"

"Positive," I tell her firmly. "If he can do anything about it, I know he will. He's kind of a dick but at heart, he's a good guy. Once we tell him how it's wrecking your fields, he'll take care of it...and we'll still pay you, because it's the right thing to do."

Vian bursts into tears.

That makes me feel even worse. "Please don't cry."

"It's just..." She swipes at her face, her nose running. "The farm is everything and if we don't have enough to sell, we all starve. I will give him my woale if he asks for it. I will give him my body if he asks for it. By all the gods, I will give my firstborn child if he promises to feed it, because very soon I will not be able to." Her eyes are blazing with frustration.

"I'm sure that's not necessary," I stammer, shocked at her

words. "He's the god of storms, right? It thunders every time he gets in a bad mood, so I'm sure it's easy for him to stop the rain. We can just ask him." How many times have I paid zero attention to the weather around Aron just because I'm used to the rain and mud now? I could have asked him to stop a million times and I didn't, because I was too focused on how awkward I've felt around him. "I'll make sure he stops it right now."

I get to my feet, because her weeping is making me really uncomfortable and I want to escape. It would be so much easier if she was greedy and just wanted a handful of coins. Her sorrow tells me just how deep her struggle is and how worried she is. I look at the baby in her arms and imagine how stressful it must be for her to think about food and if they have enough to feed themselves.

"I do not wish to be a bother," she begins.

I wave her off. "I'll be the bother." I go to the door and sure enough, it's still raining. Fat drops splash from the roof like a waterfall. This needs to stop now. I see my cloak hanging from a peg next to the door and pull it on over my clothes, then storm out into the mud. Aron is by the stables, an annoyed, impatient look on his face as Vian's husband saddles his woale—the land-hippo creature—and babbles prayers. I'd laugh at how annoyed Aron looks at any other time, but right now I just feel guilt. I can only imagine how frightened and worried Cathis is, hoping to please Aron (who, let's face it, will never be pleased with him).

"Hey, Aron," I call out, my boots squelching in the mud. "Can we talk for a few?"

He flicks a hand at me, indicating I should go to him.

"Privately?" I call out, stopping in the middle of the soaking field as Cathis looks up, his face white and pinched.

Aron turns his irritated gaze to me, but I smile brightly because I know it's all hot air as far as I'm concerned. "You are standing in the rain."

"No shit. Now come stand with me." I cross my arms, tightening my cloak around my body, and wait.

The god points at Cathis. "Finish saddling my beast. My consort and I are leaving soon." He moves to my side and blasts me with a scowl. "What do you need, Faith? I'm trying to prepare us for the road."

"So, I don't know if you've noticed," I point out as he moves to my side. "But it's wet."

"This is why you wished to talk?" Aron puts his hands on his hips. "Truly?"

"I'm also standing calf-deep in mud that should be a field. A farmer kind of needs his fields, you know? To grow crops?" When he crosses his arms and waits, I continue. "All right, I'm clearly going to have to connect the dots for you. These people that are so nicely helping us out? They're starving because their fields are one big sludgy mud puddle. And I'm traveling with the god of rain. You put two and two together."

"Lord of Storms," he corrects me.

"Rain, storms, whatever—"

"Not whatever. Storms are battles in the aether. He taps his chest. "That is why they are my domain."

"Where I come from, they're clouds of condensation that eventually make water, but I don't want to argue. Aron, if you can do something about this, please. Just dry up the storms over their farmland so they won't lose their entire crop. It's the right thing to do." I give him a pleading look.

He shrugs. "Very well, if it will get you to cease this begging."

"It totally will."

Aron grunts, and an expression of concentration crosses his face. He frowns in my direction. "I forgot how difficult it is to do anything on the mortal plane."

"Try harder," I encourage. "I can feel the change in the air." It's making my head hurt, so I know it's working.

He nods and extends his hands, as if that will help him focus.

His fingers curl as if he's gripping the air between them, and pain spikes behind my brows. Aron's face grows flushed with concentration and his body tenses. My head throbs and the thick feeling in the air clears.

The rain spattering on my cloak slows, and then stops. I pull my hood back, squinting up at the gray skies. "Holy shit. You did it."

"I am a god, you know." He gives the skies a pleased look.

"Yeah, you never let me forget that part." I reach out and touch his arm, giving him a squeeze and enjoying the little spark that flies between us at the contact. "But thank you."

Aron glances down at my hand where it rests on his forearm.

"Sorry." I pull back.

He gives me a speculative look. "I did not say I disliked it."

That response gives me all kinds of confusing feels. "Oh."

Aron frowns and then moves forward, brushing his fingers over my upper lip. "Your nose is bleeding."

"It is?" I touch my face and sure enough, the wetness there isn't just rain, it's blood. "It must have been the change in the weather." I put my sleeve to my nose to try and blot the bleeding. "I'm going to go tell Vian the good news. How long do you think you can get it to stop raining?"

Aron watches me closely, eyes narrowed, as if he's not thinking about rain at all. After a long, tense moment, he says, "Perhaps a week. After that I would need to return to this area. I do not have the control I do in the heavens."

"A week's a good start. I appreciate it. It's the right thing to do."

"You make it sound as if I'm doing it for you," Aron says, amused. He studies my face for a moment longer and then releases me.

"Well, aren't you?" I retort back. "Doing this for me? Unless you were planning on doing it before I said anything out of the goodness of your own heart?"

"No," he admits with a chuckle. "It did not occur to me."

"That's why I'm here," I tell him sassily, turning back toward the cottage.

"So you can be my heart?" he asks as I start to walk away.

My own heart skips a beat. I smile as I hold my sleeve to my nose and head for the cottage. Even before I make it to the door, the heavy, oppressive moisture in the air feels as if it's drying and in the distance, sunlight pours onto the trees as if the clouds are breaking up overhead.

Vian meets me at the door, her eyes wide with surprise. "He did it? Truly?"

I nod. "He says it will last about a week, after that he'd need to come back. I hope that's all right."

She sags against the doorframe. "I can't believe it. You must have a great influence on him."

"Me? Nah. I mean, he's a good guy, but he needs a bit of steering now and then. I don't think it occurs to him to think like a mortal." I put an arm around her waist to support her. "Why don't you come sit down inside?"

"I can't believe he did it," she whispers, stunned. Vian lets me lead her to the table and sits down, her expression blank. Eventually she looks over at me, her expression wary. "It's not a trick?"

I like Vian, but her reaction is making me feel defensive for Aron. "He really isn't that bad—"

She grabs my hand. "Swear to me he's not lying. Swear to me that he's made it stop. That we haven't offended him and this is but a trick—"

"Why would he lie?" I pull my hand from hers. "Aron can be a dick at times, but he's never downright cruel. I've never known him to go back on his word and we've been around each other pretty much twenty-four-seven since the Anticipation.

When he says he'll do something, he'll do it. Changing the weather was easy for him."

"Easy," she whispers, stunned. She looks at me again and shakes her head slowly. "You have more of an influence on him than you think."

"Why's that?" I mean, it's flattering to think that, but I don't know that she's right.

She hesitates, worry on her face, then bites her lip. "We didn't want to say anything...but you two have been so kind..."

"What is it?" I demand. "Tell me."

"Aron," Vian says slowly. "He's been here before. A few days ago. And he brought the rain with him."

Her words confuse me for a moment. Aron here? But he just got here last night with me...

Oh. Another one of his Aspects.

CHAPTER 39

*a*nger flares in my mind, and frustration. She wasn't going to say anything? I jump to my feet—and then stop, looking at her terrified face. Sympathy replaces any anger. She doesn't know him like I do, and it's clear she's scared she's going to lose her family, her farm, or worse.

I put my hand over hers. "I'm going to get Aron—my Aron—and bring him in and then I want you guys to tell us everything, all right?"

She gives a quick, jerky nod.

Furious, I jump up to get my Aron.

A short time later, Vian sits down at the table in front of the fire, her husband's hand on her shoulder. Both of them look ready to faint at the slightest indication of rage from Aron. To my traveling companion's credit, he's calm. It's as if he expected this sort of thing. Me, I still feel slightly betrayed that we stayed here overnight and were friendly and they're just *now* deciding to tell us about the other Aspect that's looking to kill both of us.

I remind myself that Vian is mortal and poor and pregnant and worried and possibly starving. We're the enemy in her eyes, and she's making a great concession by telling us. It's clear from her husband's tight mouth that he didn't want to say a thing at all. Him, I can't like. For all of his obedience and terrified kneeling to Aron, he was ready to not say a peep about the other guy that came through a few days ago.

I kind of hate him for that.

Vian gives me another worried look. "Travelers stop by our farm all the time," she tells me. "At first we didn't think anything of it. They wore cloaks and they brought more rain with them. It's the rainy season anyhow, but there's been more and more ever since the Anticipation, and our crops have suffered. These particular travelers were a large band, maybe ten men, all armed. There was a wizard with them." She purses her lips. "And a man in a cloak. They asked to stay at our farm and for us to feed them, but times have been hard, and we didn't realize..." She trails off, then gives her hands a nervous twist. "We told them it would cost a drab a day if they planned to stay. That's when their leader took off his cloak and we realized..." Her mouth trembles and her eyes fill with tears.

"That it was Aron," I say, voice flat.

"Yes. With two eyes and no axe, of course, but it was impossible to mistake him." She stares down at her hands in her lap. "Once we realized our error and that we had been blessed by the god's presence, we gave them whatever they wanted, of course. We let them clean out our stores and take two of our woale. We had three, you know. It's just that...the only reason they left the one behind was because it was limping." She won't look me in the eye. "They stayed with us overnight and the god never spoke to us. Not directly. Until it was time to leave. Then he came up to us and said that we had been good hosts and he would reward us suitably. We thought he meant coin, compensation for what he and his men were taking. Instead, they beat Cathis and rode away, and he left the rain behind. It has been pouring ever since. It will not stop. Not ever." She picks at a string on her tunic. "I guess we were not good hosts after all."

298

Aron and I exchange a look.

"Lies," Aron says.

"Unless he's trying to make us think that, and he's actually something else." I eye Vian and her husband. "Uh, so while they were here, did they have sex?"

She frowns at my question, confused. "Do you mean the god and his devotees? He had a concubine that he shared with the wizard, but that was it."

Sharing? That dirty bird. I'm guessing the wizard is his anchor, like I am to this Aron. "I mean like...you guys. Did you feel overcome with the need to have sex?"

"My wife is very heavy with our child," Cathis tells me, outraged. "I would not dream of touching her while she is carrying."

I don't bother to tell him that I've heard that's not a problem, but I also don't care about him, secret-keeper that he is. Fuck him. "No orgies amongst his soldiers?" When they give me baffled looks, I sigh. "Okay, maybe it wasn't hedonism then."

"It is lies," Aron says again. "And he is heading to the tower as well."

"How do you know for sure?"

"Because I am him and he is me." He crosses his arms over his chest. "We are heading there ourselves, are we not?"

He has a point. But if we're drawing parallels... "So you're telling me that you'd share a hooker with your wizard, too?"

"Why does that matter?" He frowns at me as if I've lost my mind.

Oh, sure, it might not matter to him, but it sure as fuck matters to me. "No reason. Just that we're tied together until one or both of us dies, that's all. I need to know if I need to make room in the damn bed." And I cross my arms over my chest.

Aron's mouth twitches. "Are you jealous?"

"What? No! Don't be ridiculous."

"You are the one being ridiculous. And I am a god. If I wanted to fuck all of them, is it not my right?" He looks down his nose at me, so very arrogant.

"No," I say flatly.

"They would not refuse me." He looks over at Cathis. "If I asked you to give me your wife right now, would you?"

Vian hunches her shoulders. Cathis bows his head and puts his fist over his chest. "We live to serve, Lord of Storms."

Ew. "Don't be gross, Aron."

"I am a god," he tells me, as if I don't know this. "If I ask anything of a mortal, they will give it to me." He shrugs. "If I am in a mood for a fuck, I will take whoever and whatever I want."

"You arrogant sack of shit," I tell him, jumping to my feet. I ignore Vian's gasp. "I don't care if you're the sun god or the god of dirty brown assholes, but my life is tied to yours now. You need to have respect for me and my choices too! You..." My words die in my throat because his mouth is twitching with amusement, and his shoulders shake as if he's fighting back laughter.

Aron finds this all funny.

I smack him on his chest with my hand. "You are an arrogant *asshole*."

"The god of dirty brown ones, apparently," he agrees, laughter rumbling out of him. He grabs my hand before I can smack at his chest again, and holds my wrist, giving me a teasing look. "Speak the truth, Faith. Are you mad over the things that I have said just now? Or are you mad because you imagine me taking other lovers when you have staked your claim on me?"

"Oh bullshit," I say boldly. "I have staked no claim at all. You can sleep with whoever you want."

He arches an eyebrow as if he doesn't believe my words. Funny, I don't know if I believe them either. Sometimes I think all it would take is a word and I'd be on Aron like white on rice. Other times I want to cheerfully strangle him.

Right now is one of the latter times.

Aron leans in, my hand still trapped in his grip. Little sparks shiver through my skin at his touch, reminding me that he's not mortal—as if I'd ever forget. "I remember what you have sacrificed, Faith," he murmurs, expression intent. "And the only one allowed in your bed is me."

With that, he releases my hand and leaves me wondering exactly what the heck he meant just now.

He turns back toward Vian and Cathis. "We will take the woale you have offered us, and any food supplies you can share. The rain will not return. I am not the Aspect of Lies, so this is truth I tell you. And we will pay you for any supplies you give us. Is there anything else you would share with us that can help? Remember that it is not just my life in danger on this journey, but hers." And he gestures at me.

Vian's wide eyes go to me, and then she shakes her head. "There is nothing."

I have to believe her. Even if there was more information to be shaken out of her, it might take days to get her to admit it, and we don't have that. Aron's made it clear we need to get to the tower, and pronto. His urgency drives mine, because if a god is worried about something...well, we all need to worry.

But I look at Vian's thin face, her arms (and belly) filled with children, and I think she has enough on her plate.

WHEN WE LEAVE THE FARM, the sun is shining hot overhead, the air dry and rain-free. The roads are drying, thanks to the heat, and our woale—or land-hippo, as I like to think of him —plods along a rutted path, contentedly going about the speed of a bicycle with two flat tires. Our bags are saddled, and Aron and I sit atop the thing's wide back on a blanket that passes as a saddle. I sit behind him, clinging to his waist, because it feels as if any moment I'm going to slide off the thing's side. Aron lightly holds the reins and he sits atop the thing as if he's ridden woales all his life. Maybe he has. Maybe this is what gods do for fun.

The thing makes a gronking noise, shits all over the road behind us, and then pauses to eat some grass on the side of the road. Aron mutters a curse, tugs on the reins, and our woale reluctantly starts walking again.

"Remind me why we're taking this thing instead of walking?" I ask him, shifting carefully. My backside is hurting from the thing's spine and it's been less than an hour since we left. It's going to be a long day in the saddle—so to speak. "I imagine we could crawl faster than this thing's going."

Aron just snorts.

"I'm serious. I bet if I look behind us I'll see the farm still."

"It's not about speed, Faith. A well-trained woale will continue along a road all day and all night without stopping. They don't need to sleep or rest for days on end. They're useful for their stamina."

"Goody. So you're telling me we get to somehow ride on this thing through the night?"

"If we must. If we find someplace suitable, we'll stop and rest for a while." He doesn't sound bothered either way.

Must be nice. I hold onto his leather belt and grit my teeth as the thing lumbers along, swaying. I want to rest my cheek against Aron's back, but I don't want him to read more into my body language than he should. Resting against him would also mean pushing my boobs against him, and I'm still mulling some of his comments from the last few days.

Especially the one about how he could have me anytime he wanted. I think it's more arrogant bullshit, but he's also becoming increasingly touchy-feely and it makes me both breathless and confused. My thoughts start to migrate in a sexy direction and I carefully steer them back to the present, watching as Aron pulls one of the waterskins from the saddlebag in front of him and takes a sip, then offers it to me.

"Thanks," I say, surprised at his thoughtfulness. I take a sip—warm, yummy—and hand it back. "Cathis and Vian were sure grateful for the money, weren't they?"

"Of course they were. They should be grateful they kept their heads. The fact that we rewarded them for withholding information probably seems like it's too good to be true." His tone is sour.

I poke him gently in the side. "We didn't pay them for withholding information. We paid them for giving us supplies and letting us take the world's slowest mount."

Aron chuckles. "I have been on slower, if it makes you feel better."

"When?" I demand to know.

He shrugs. "I do not recall. Only that I know it is truth. Perhaps in the last Anticipation?"

I keep forgetting that this has all happened before. "Do you remember much about it?"

"Some. The memories are fragmented, I suspect because when all Aspects reunite, the individual is lost."

"Mmm." That's strange to think about—that the man I'm holding onto might not exist once this is done. I wonder if it bothers him to think about that, or if he's accepted it as fact. "So who won last time?"

"Won?"

"Yeah. Which Aspect won out? Hedonism? Lies? Arrogance? Laziness?"

He thinks for a long moment, considering. "Hedonism, I think. I know it was not arrogance."

For some reason that makes me sad. It's hard to think that it's all the same person, just split into four different ways.

That this isn't the real Aron, just some piece of him. I'm growing fond of the guy, all said, and I don't like the thought of him disappearing, or dying, or whatever happens when this is over. Not that it'll matter to me, of course, since I'll be home.

But I still think about it. "But it wasn't lies that won last time, either?"

I guess I'm pretty transparent, because Aron casts a look over his shoulder at me. "If you are worried about confronting him, speak your mind, Faith."

"Well, seeing as how we haven't exactly been killing it on our own, yeah, I'm worried."

"Killing it?"

"Doing well? Thriving?"

He snorts, turning back to the road. "I think we are doing quite well. We have supplies and weapons. I have an anchor. You have a full belly and no plague. I see nothing wrong with our position."

Plague? He just casually throws *plague* out there? I bite back my horror and decide to point out the bigger problems first. "Vian and Cathis said that the other Aspect had mercenaries with him. Like ten. And a wizard. A motherfucking wizard. Aron, what do we do against those things?"

"We make sure that we remain aware of them and plan accordingly."

"How do you freaking plan against a wizard? You need to help me on that part because where I come from, the only wizards are racist assholes and can't actually do magic." I poke his side again, and I'm surprised when he shudders. Aron's... ticklish? What the heck? Why do I find that so ridiculous and yet delightful? "Maybe you should have hooked up with a wizard."

"Did you see any wizards volunteering upon my arrival?"

Good point. "I'm sorry you're stuck with me."

He grunts. "You have not been a bad companion, Faith. Do not vex yourself on that front. You have been adequate."

"You're killing me with all that praise," I murmur, but I am pleased, weirdly enough. That's a compliment, considering where it's coming from. "Still, what do we do against a wizard?"

"That depends."

"On...?"

"On whether or not he is a true wizard or a pretender. True wizards are rare. Pretenders are far more common." His tone is dismissive and clearly unworried.

Obviously I get to be the worrier of our party. "Let's assume he is real. Just for giggles. What do we do then?"

"Try to stand behind him." He chuckles at his own joke.

"Helpful" is obviously not in Aron's repertoire. I frown at his back. "Wizard aside, they said the other Aron has troops. Like ten or twelve of them. Should we get mercenaries or soldiers for our protection? We're only a day or two away from Katharn. Much as I'd hate to go back, I'd hate being dead a lot more."

Aron shakes his head, idly flicking the woale's reins as if it's a lovely afternoon jaunt and not a ride into danger. "You worry too much, Faith. And before you prattle at me about how one of us needs to be concerned, remind yourself how many men I took down that first night we were attacked, and I was far more confused and disoriented then."

My open mouth snaps shut. He's got a point. He took down a half-dozen men in the blink of an eye and without a weapon. "I'm sorry to doubt you. This is all really new for me."

"Troops are a distraction only, nothing more."

I nod to myself, thinking. "You did say he was lies. Unless..." A new, disturbing thought occurs to me. "They said he had a consort with him. You don't suppose he's hedonism and just trying to throw us off?"

I'm not ready to confront any other Arons, but on my list, hedonism is dead last. I don't want to think about what that'll mean for us, because it makes me get all flushed and awkward and things are already awkward enough.

"No, he will be lies. Hedonism will be far more obvious. A consort does not mean anything. My cock works as well as any other mortal's."

Oh, I remember. My cheeks feel hot with just how much I remember. I change the subject quickly. "You think they'll be setting a trap for us?"

He chuckles and glances back at me over his shoulder. "Undoubtedly."

"Then we should practice weapons more, Aron." I tap a hand on his arm. "Maybe we should stop early for the night and get some sparring in. Some swords, some staves, all the good stuff so I can be prepared."

Aron just shakes his head, watching the road in front of him, and flicks the reins. If anything, the woale speeds up. Slightly. Like a gently caffeinated snail instead of just a regular snail. "Faith. You are trying to stall, are you not?"

I mock-snort. "Me? Not wanting to rush into danger and certain death? Psh. Can't imagine why a girl would stall."

"I will keep you safe. Do you doubt me?"

"Dude, you're arrogance. Of course you're going to say that." I ignore his bark of laughter that peals down the dirt road. "It's just that...you're a badass fighter. He's you, so he's going to be a badass, plus he's got a wizard, plus he's got mercenaries. All you have is me." Just thinking about it makes my hands tighten on his belt. At what point do I trust him and at what point is his arrogance going to get us killed? I don't have the answer, and that worries me. "All I'm saying is that we should practice some fighting when we stop, so I can help with the combat."

"Faith. We could stop and practice for two years and it would not be enough." His voice is surprisingly gentle, for Aron. "If Lies is meant to conquer Arrogance, then there is nothing I can do."

The thought makes me sick. I'm not ready to die. I'm not ready for him to die. "I refuse to lie down and give up, Aron. Not without doing as much as I possibly can to stop it from happening."

"No one is saying we are going to give up," he tells me. "But perhaps our time would be better spent trying to think of a trap for them, since they will inevitably be setting one for us."

"Fair enough." It doesn't make me feel much better, though. Aron's life is tied to mine, and mine to his. If the other Aron decided that he needed a posse to protect himself...why aren't we doing the same?

CHAPTER 40

*F*or two days, we ride the slowest mount known to mankind. Like Aron said, the thing doesn't need to take breaks. It can keep plodding endlessly, and it does. It plods over hills and down the muddy path. It plods through fork after fork of road, and the farmlands turn to scrubby trees and distant gray mountains begin to loom on the horizon.

My ass can't take the endless riding, though. It doesn't seem to bother Aron in the slightest—not much does—but my mortal butt cheeks are sore by twilight on the first day. That's when I learn how people sleep on a woale—we pause to sling two hammocks against the woale's fat, rounded sides. It goes from one end of the saddle to the other, and for the first time, I see why the woale saddle has two pommels in front, and two in back (that have been digging into my ass for the last bajillion hours). The hammocks are slung from one side to the other and then, like the world's ungainliest saddlebags, Aron helps me slip into one side and he gets into the other to balance me out.

At first, I don't think I'll be able to sleep, especially not with my head bouncing so close to the woale's hindquarters, but the next thing I know, it's dawn, my ass is one big aching bruise, and my stomach's growling. While the sun is up, we ride on the woale's saddle. When the sun goes down, we sleep in the saddle slings, and the time—and miles—creep past agonizingly slowly.

I'm mentally gearing up for another crappy night in the swing on day three when Aron abruptly halts the woale, and we grind to a halt.

I yawn at him. "Bathroom break again? I don't really have to go."

"No." He's all tension as he slides off the creature's back, his body alert as he gazes off into the distance. "I saw campfire smoke."

All of my sleepy exhaustion instantly vanishes, replaced by fear. "Where?" I whisper, sliding off the side of the woale and landing (okay, tumbling) on the ground next to him.

Aron catches me before I can fall on my ass and helps me to my feet. "Look to the tree line," he tells me, pointing.

Heart hammering, I scan the trees. Sure enough, there's a thin plume of smoke on the horizon that would be impossible to notice unless I was looking for it. He must have been watching the skies constantly, ever alert, and I feel like a bad companion.

"Is it them?" I ask, clinging to his arm in terror. We've been talking about this for days but it's too soon in my eyes. I don't want to run into them. I don't want to fight. I sure don't want to lose.

I feel like I'm on the verge of a nervous breakdown.

"One way to find out," Aron says, and then moves to the woale. I think—stupidly—for a moment that he's going to get out a telescope or something, but he hands me the reins. "Wait here."

I let out a terrified squeak as he slings his sword and scabbard over his shoulder and then heads into the woods. "Wait," I hiss, afraid to speak too loud.

He doesn't wait, of course. This is Aron. I'm left holding the reins of the woale, who doesn't bother to lift his head from his feedbag. The damn beast could care less if death is imminent. Me, I care. I half drag, half lead the thing toward the side of the road and crouch in the bushes, breathing hard. It doesn't matter that we haven't passed anyone all day and the road has gotten steadily more deserted the closer we get to the mountains. I'm terrified of the men waiting to kill us. I've never had someone want to murder me before I met Aron, and now it seems everyone wants to kill us.

I should have never taken his hand that first day we met.

I frown to myself. No, that's not fair. If I hadn't taken his hand, what would have happened to Aron that first night? He wouldn't have lasted an hour with one of those milquetoast cowering girls, and no one else was volunteering to be his anchor. And me? I would have been sacrificed on his altar the next morning.

Remembering that calms me. Aron's kept me safe so far. I need to trust him. I do. So I hunker down in the bushes, clutch the reins, and wait for him to return.

Time passes.

The forest grows dark. Insects chirp, the woale craps on the road, and birds rustle the leaves. There's nothing out of the ordinary in this night so far, and my frayed nerves ease a bit. My entire body flares with pain for a brief moment, signaling just how far Aron's gone, but it fades almost as quickly as it arrives, and that tells me he's coming back.

I hear his footsteps before I see him, which tells me that he wants to let me know he's arriving. Aron's too careful to clomp through the forest. I get to my feet just as his dark hair catches a beam of moonlight and gleams. He looks strong and resolute, his mouth in a thin line of displeasure, his mismatched eyes intense.

I don't need to be a psychic to understand that expression. "It's them, isn't it?"

He moves to my side and gives me a quick nod. "They're camping a short distance away. I counted twelve heads, including the concubine and wizard. There are four tents, one for me, and one for the rest of them. I wasn't able to tell if the wizard was a true one or not, but they do have several mercenaries that are heavily armed. We'll have to be careful."

"What do we do?" I ask him, worried. "Can we avoid them? Hide? Wait for them to keep going north and follow farther behind? What?"

"We're going to confront them," he tells me.

"I was afraid you'd say that."

"Faith." Aron's voice is calm as he puts a hand on my shoulder. The woale grunts and poops again, ruining an otherwise grim moment, but Aron's focus is entirely on me. "This would have to happen at some point. I cannot avoid a confrontation forever. I must find him and defeat him."

I know. I know he's got to do this, but I'm not ready. But I grit my teeth and force myself to nod, because at least right now, they don't know where we are. We've got the upper hand and we need to use it. "I'm just nervous. All right, then. What's the plan?"

He turns and gestures at the forest. "I circled their camp to see the best defensive spot, but there's nothing we can use to our advantage but the trees themselves. So, you're going to climb one of them close to camp, and throw rocks into the bushes. His mercenaries will come looking to see what's causing the noise, and when they do, I'll take them out one by one until they're a more manageable group."

I gape at him. "That's your plan? Throw rocks while sitting in a tree?"

"Did you have a better one?"

"No," I sputter. "But—"

"But nothing. A simple plan is sometimes the most effective. If you are in the trees, you will be safer than on the ground. I did not see any bows and arrows, just swords. If they are climbing a tree, they will not be able to use their swords."

"I thought you said you could handle mercenaries," I remind him faintly. "You said they weren't a problem, remember?"

"And they are not a problem," Aron says calmly. "But I also do not want to risk you. As you have pointed out many times, you are not a fighter. I do not want you anywhere near battle where you might be taken unawares."

I sigh. "All right. Tree. Rocks. It's a good thing I played soft-ball as a teenager."

"Soft...ball?"

"A game with clubs and tossing balls. Forget it." I wave a hand in the air. "I'll manage. Let's get some rocks."

"And mud," he agrees.

"Why mud?"

He touches my cheek, sending a shiver (and a spark) through my body. "This pale skin and hair of yours will stand out, even in the dark, if someone is looking for you. The mud will provide more camouflage."

"This is sounding better by the minute," I mutter, but I move to the woale, empty one of the satchels, and start looking for rocks. Even as I do, I keep thinking about that touch, how he caressed my cheek.

It was almost like he wanted to touch me.

CHAPTER 41

a short time later, our woale is tied to a tree a fair distance from the road, grazing. My bag is filled with small rocks and hangs heavily over my shoulder, and clacks so loudly that I have to press it against my chest to keep the stones from banging against one another.

I'm also covered in mud from head to toe, and because it's chilly, I'm wearing the darkest cloak I own. I look like a mess, but I do blend in the shadows at least.

We head carefully through the woods, moving slowly, Aron lifting me carefully over craggy spots of terrain where the uneven ground falls away in a rocky crevice or two. It seems to take forever, but then I can smell the campfire on the breeze and hear the lower murmur of voices.

We've arrived.

"This tree is good," Aron murmurs, pointing at a tall, leafy bastard nearby. I see the branches don't start until about five feet up, maybe more, which means I'm going to need a boost.

I suck in a breath and then nod. I want to complain and whine, but that won't do any good. I'm just scared, but Aron promises he'll make sure I'm safe, and I have to believe that he's right and it's not just arrogance talking. I pull the heavy bag of stones off my shoulder and then set it carefully on the ground. "You'll have to pass that up to me."

He nods, and then cups my filthy cheeks as I look up at him. "Stay safe, Faith. I need you."

I gaze up at him, at his beautiful, godlike face and stern features. Coming from any other man, I would think that's practically a declaration of love, but Aron's impossible to read. I just nod and move toward the tree.

Aron grabs me by my waist and lifts me overhead as if I weigh nothing, and I manage to flail enough to grab the limb with my feet and heave myself up. Once I'm settled, he hands me the bag carefully, and I loop it over my shoulder, then begin to climb. I move higher and higher, trying not to look down because I'm too high up to fall safely. I mean, sure, I fell from a large height when we were escaping Tadekha's floating citadel, but I also landed on Aron. If I crunch to the ground here and break something, the wizard—and Liar Aron—are just going to put me down like a crippled racehorse.

I shake that image out of my head, then climb a bit higher. Once I'm safely hidden amongst the leaves, I peer down and look for Aron. He nods up at me and then gestures off into the distance, indicating where he'll be hiding.

I give him a thumbs up and then pull out my first rock, studying the small camp. It's visible given how high up I am, and I can see everyone.

Aron's right, the fire is small. Beyond the cluster of tents, I see men in armor with sword belts, standing around and talking. There's one guy in robes and a short, black beard who looks like every cliché of a wizard ever.

I peer into the shadows, pulling a rock into my hand even as I do. I have to admit, I'm less interested in the soldiers and more interested in seeing the other version of Aron. Is he going to look the same? Will I automatically know it's the wrong one? I scan the soldiers' faces and as one laughs and takes a pull from a small metal flask, I realize they are completely relaxed and have no idea we're here. Good. Silently, I encourage the one to keep drinking. A drunk guard will be easier for us to take down. I rub my fingers on the edge of the rock in my hand, trying to decide the best moment to throw.

Something rustles in the bushes below my tree. I freeze, my free hand clutching my bag of stones against my belly so they don't clack against one another. A guard? Have I been discovered?

To my surprise, a woman emerges. She's got long, curling ropes of dark hair that swing to the middle of her back, and even though it's night and slightly chilly, she's wearing a filmy dress that clings to her curves as she walks and sets off her dusky skin. And Jesus, she's got some serious curves. Her tits are enormous, each one pendulous and sways with her steps, and her waist is tiny, corseted by a girdle that seems little more than a belt. Her hips are rounded and I'm acutely envious of her figure. This must be the concubine. Damn. This group doesn't play around, because she is utterly gorgeous.

Behind her is a cloaked figure, and I hold my breath as she peeks over her shoulder, the look utterly flirtatious. She glances around, then moves to a tree close to my own, as if picking a spot that's in the perfect line of sight. "Here?"

"Not here," comes the voice, and I stiffen, a reaction shivering through my body. I recognize that voice. It's Aron. Bad Aron. Liar Aron.

The concubine gives a throaty little laugh, tosses her hair, and puts her hands on the bark of the tree, even though he just told her not to. She leans forward and bends at the waist, sticking her butt out with a wiggle.

I suck in a breath when the man accompanying her grabs the edge of her skirt, pushes it up, and exposes her equally perfect ass. He moves behind her, and then she surges forward with a low cry.

Holy shit. He's doing her right in front of me. I clutch the rock, both fascinated and horrified all at once. My jaw drops, and as I stare in shock, he begins to thrust in fast, hard pumps, the force of his movements making her bounce forward. He's angled so I can't see his face, but I can definitely see him driving into her. I watch as he fucks her, wondering if I should throw the rock now, or wait until they're done. He's drilling her so hard that it can't take long...can it?

Her cries get louder and louder, as if he's killing her vagina, and he steadies a hand on her shoulder, holding her so he can pound into her that much harder. I squeeze my thighs tightly together because it's affecting me. I'm fascinated by his brusque, efficient movements, and part of me wishes he was naked so I could watch his back flex as he moves over her. The hood of his cloak falls back, and then I see the dark hair and strange eyes that mark him as Aron.

That changes everything. I'm watching Aron—my Aron— have sex with a gorgeous woman and...it's weird. I know it's not really him, but at the same time, I feel jealous. This Aron doesn't know me, but for some reason, it bothers me that he's fucking someone else. My Aron's never laid a finger on me...

Well, that's not true. My brain helpfully fires up several reminders of that night in Tadekha's citadel, where he fingered me as I crawled all over him.

Doesn't make me feel better.

Another figure crashes through the underbrush, and I clutch my rock tighter. Bad-Aron doesn't stop in his relentless fucking of the busty concubine, who's squealing as if she's dying. Even if I threw a rock right now, I doubt anyone would notice, so I guess it's just as well I wait and watch. I swallow hard as a second man approaches, dressed in a dark cloak and long robes. He's young, which surprises me, his beard nothing but scruffy wisps. He arranges long robes around his body as they snag on the greenery and gives the busy twosome an irritated look as he approaches.

Aron doesn't pause in the slightest. "Louder," he tells the female, and she quiets down. Weird. Maybe he likes disobedience.

The wizard—because it has to be the wizard—moves to stand next to Aron, watching them with glittering eyes. "I want to go next," he says. "Before you take her again." His gaze is locked onto the shuddering woman, who's clawing at the bark of the tree and panting. Her tits heave with every thrust Bad-Aron pumps into her, and it's clear she's loving what she's getting. Even the people back by the fire—the mercenaries—are glancing over. She's quieter, but not quiet enough.

Aron ignores the wizard.

"Let me have a turn," the wizard tries again. "You'll have her all night. We've shared her before."

Aron pauses, his movements stopping. He's still buried deep inside her, and he turns to look at the wizard. The woman moans and squirms back against him, clearly not happy with the pause. The wizard cringes back from Aron's look, retreating a step.

"Of course you can go next," Bad-Aron says, and his voice is so familiar that it sends shivers down my spine. "I love the taste of your cum on her lips."

The concubine giggles.

The wizard flushes, his mouth thinning into an angry line, and stalks back to the camp. Aron watches him go, then grunts, and turns back to the concubine. He puts his hand on her shoulder once more, and then grinds into her.

"Oooh," she moans.

"Louder," he snaps, and she goes quiet again as he starts to fuck her once more.

I'm a little confused. Everything they do is in direct contradiction to what he says. I watch him continue to drive into her against the tree, and her cries are muffled against her arm. It takes a moment, but then it dawns on me.

He's the Aron of lies.

Mine is arrogance, so everything he does and everything he says comes from a place of arrogance. This one clearly can't tell the truth, and so everyone's interpreting what he tells them. Oh. Suddenly it makes sense.

With a grunt, Bad-Aron stiffens, and I watch, almost hoping I could see his O-face. I guess it's good that I can't. It still feels surreal to think of Aron screwing another woman...and doing an amazing job of it. I'm still feeling that weird surge of jealousy, and I hate that. The god pats the woman's flank as he pulls away and she straightens, lowering her skirt. "Let the wizard touch you next," he tells her. "I'm done with you for tonight. You know how fond I am of sharing."

Her face is flushed and she gives a little wobbly curtsy, panting. "I won't let anyone touch me but you, my lord of storms."

He grunts, pleased, and then adjusts his clothes and heads back to the encampment. A moment later, she follows, straightening her gorgeous hair. I watch them go, shell-shocked, and then remember the rock in my hand. Right. My Aron's going to think I've fallen asleep.

Or maybe he was watching that, too. I wonder for a moment if he found her pretty. Of course he would. It's still Aron, right? So he would have the same taste in women. I hate that.

With vicious force, I fling a rock into the bushes and imagine nailing Aron's head with it.

CHAPTER 42

The underbrush crunches, the leaves shaking, and one of the guards pauses, flask almost to his lips, and glances into the woods. He turns back to the camp, counts heads, and then says something low that I can't quite make out. After he puts his flask away, he pulls out his sword and heads into the brush, disappearing.

Nothing happens.

I watch, waiting, and all is quiet. The guard doesn't emerge, no one goes to check on him, and there's no signal from Aron that he's taken care of the problem, either. I have to wait and hope that things went according to plan. I give it a few moments, and then I chuck another rock in the same direction.

This time, his buddy is the one that pauses. "Gracel?" He takes a few steps into the woods. "Anything?"

When there's no answer, he pulls out his sword, too, and then disappears into the shadows. Two of the other guards are paying attention now, frowns on their faces, and I wonder how many are going to fall for this before Aron's plan goes awry.

Apparently the answer is two. I throw a third rock after enough time has hopefully passed, and the Bad-Aron by the fire begins to look wary. He frowns deeply and I hear thunder rumbling overhead. He points at three of the guards, and they nod and head into the woods while three more pull their swords and gather close to Aron.

The wizard sidles closer to Bad-Aron, his face pinched with an expression like irritation. "What is it, my Lord of Storms?"

"It is not one of my Aspects, I think. I cannot feel it in the air." The god crosses his arms and looks so much like my Aron that my heart stutters. His gaze swings through the trees, and for a brief moment, I think he sees me. But then he keeps scanning, and I breathe again. "Look for his anchor," Bad Aron demands. "I do not sense him near. There is not power close by."

The concubine shivers and runs to hide in a tent.

We're in trouble now.

I don't know what to do. The guards are scattering through the woods, but there's still far too many of them. As I watch, Bad-Aron finds a sword, and the wizard moves toward the fire, pulling a pouch from his belt. He stands near it and closes his eyes, reaching for what looks like a purple dust and begins to sprinkle it in the fire.

He begins to chant, and a strange smoke begins to curl up from the fire. If he was a fake wizard, he wouldn't bother. This must be the real thing, and I suspect that spell isn't going to be anything good. He keeps murmuring words, his hand waving over the fire, and the smoke begins to move in a pattern that looks completely unnatural.

Full of panic, I do the only thing I can think of—I throw one of my rocks at him.

I peg the guy right square in the middle of the forehead. The wizard grunts and hesitates, and for a moment I think he's going to come for me. Instead, he falls onto his back and lies still.

I've knocked him out.

Hot diggity. I didn't know my aim was that good. I bite back a laugh of pure delight, because I need to stay silent. As I watch, Bad-Aron moves to the side of his fallen wizard, touches the bloody mark square in the middle of his forehead, and then glances up into the trees, looking directly at me.

A new kind of panic hits me, and I squeeze my eyes shut so he doesn't see me. The darkness will hide me, I tell myself. There's nothing to worry about.

"I know you're there," he says in a low, deadly voice I recognize. "You can either come down now and let me take a look at you, or I won't make your death spectacularly unpleasant."

My throat goes dry. I swallow hard, thinking. Will it even do any good to pretend I'm not up here? I clear my throat and then manage, "If it's all the same to you, I'd rather stay where I am. I love the view and all."

Bad-Aron rises to his full height. "I am not the Lord of Storms. I can't destroy that tree with a single bolt of lightning," he says, voice utterly calm. "Think hard on how you would like to die."

I clutch the bag of rocks to my chest, terrified. I don't want to die at all, and yet it seems like I can't avoid my life being put in jeopardy no matter what I do. Freaking arrogant Aron and his arrogant, stupid plan. Rocks in trees, for Pete's sake. I pause, stalling the inevitable. "You won't hurt me if I come down?"

"I promise."

I slide down a few branches, skittery with panic. *Think, Faith, think.* The wizard must be still breathing, or else Bad-Aron would be dead. The woods are silent—too silent—and I worry that my Aron has been taken out or incapacitated. It's up to me to kill the wizard, which is going to be downright tricky given that I've got nothing but a bag of rocks and he's got a god standing over him.

Maybe I can distract this Aron long enough that I can...do something. What, I don't know. *Something.* I move down another branch or two, and then I remember just before I hit the lowest branch—did he say he would hurt me or wouldn't hurt me? "Wait—"

Bad-Aron stalks over to my tree, lightning fast, and jerks on the edge of my cloak. I tumble from the tree, flopping onto my back. Pain shoots through my ribs, and I groan, clutching at them.

He looms over me where I lie on the ground, tilting his head as if I'm some weird sort of science experiment. Then, he goes down to one knee and grabs me by the throat. Not hard, just pinning me. His thumb moves against my jaw, forcing my head to turn as he studies my features. "Not what I would have picked."

"Bitch please," I manage, coughing. "I'm amazing."

Bad-Aron's brows go up and a smile curls his hard mouth. "I fail to see the appeal now. It is good we meet under such circumstances. I imagine you make the most unpleasant companion." His voice is whispery soft, and my body responds despite the situation. I can feel my nipples prick, and his eyes regard me with such familiarity that I feel a sudden, stupid urge to kiss him. Or to let him kiss me. But all he does is gaze down at me, and then his thumb brushes a few flakes of mud off my chin. "You…"

When he doesn't continue, I lift my chin. "I what?"

But he doesn't say anything. He doesn't move at all. As I watch, he slowly fades out like an undeveloped picture, and then the hand on my throat is gone. The entire man is just… gone. I gasp, sitting up, and as I do, I see Aron. My Aron.

He kneels beside the body of the wizard, a dagger jutting from the man's throat.

"Oh," I murmur weakly, putting a hand to my forehead. "Thank god. Aron, I almost screwed that up really badly."

"I noticed." Aron gets to his feet and gazes down at the wizard, his thoughts consuming him.

I manage to stagger to my feet, dusting leaves off of my

body. "No, no," I wheeze. "Don't worry about me. I'm cool. I fall from trees all the time. I've got this. No need to help me up." When he doesn't respond to my griping, I frown to myself. "Aron? Are you okay? Where are the mercenaries?"

"Some are dead. Some alive.." He nudges the wizard's body with one boot, then looks at me. He flicks his hand, indicating I should move to his side.

I limp over to him, wincing at the pain that shoots up my ankle. "If they're alive, where are they?"

Aron gazes down at me. "Faith. I am telling you the truth. Do you understand?"

"Uh, okay? Why would I doubt you?" I rub my hip absently. "I think I landed on a rock, by the way. Never thought I'd wish the woale was here to carry my ass back to the road, but here we are."

"I am telling you the truth," he repeats.

I frown at him, confused. "I heard you the first time."

"You're not listening to me." He touches my chin, and for a moment I'm reminded of Bad-Aron gazing down at me like he wanted to kiss me. "I'm glad you climbed down the tree. It was a smart thing to do. I'm not mad about it at all. Understand?" He crosses his arms over his chest and glares at me. "Next time we plan things, I don't want you to listen to me."

I squint at him. "Are you...are you lying to me?"

"No."

For a moment, I have a gut-wrenching burst of fear—that the wrong Aron lived. Except...I saw him fade out. I saw him disappear right before my eyes. The wizard's dead and I'm alive. I look down at the dead guy just to be sure, then back to Aron. My Aron. He blinks, waiting.

"I...are you lies and arrogance *both* now?"

He exhales deeply, as if relieved. "Not at all. That's not how this works."

Oh, fuck me.

CHAPTER 43

*T*he remaining mercenaries immediately surrender to Aron the moment they realize their leader is dead, replaced by...the same guy. They prostrate themselves on the ground, but not before kissing the pommels of their swords and offering them to him. The concubine emerges from her tent with a swish of her hips and does the same, raising her too-perfect ass into the air.

Aron watches all of this from the center of the encampment, one foot still on the wizard's dead body. Eventually, he looks over at me. "Well?"

"Well what?" I look up from the bags I'm searching for weapons. I see some coin, but it's mostly supplies.

"Do you want them to live or die?"

I stare at Aron in horror. "You're making me pick?"

"No. If it were me, I would let them go, but I'm asking you since you have a hard heart." His tone is curiously playful despite his words, and he crosses his arms over his chest, watching me and waiting.

I swallow hard, deciphering that. Fuck. He *is* making me pick. He wouldn't let them go, but he thinks I'm soft. Okay. I gaze down at the men (and woman) bowing before Aron. "Um. I'm not used to having people's lives in my hands."

Aron just shrugs and gestures at them again.

I study the mercenaries. They wear piecemeal armor, which makes it impossible to tell how young or old they are, but they remain with their faces down in the dirt, waiting. The woman next to them trembles, her arms outstretched, and I feel a surge of pity. I know I need to be ruthless. I know these people would have killed us without a second thought, but I'm not from this world. I'm not like that.

I look down at the dead wizard under Aron's boot and shudder.

Aron grunts. "I suspect I do not know your answer."

"I suspect you do," I say, feeling faint.

"Do not sit up, all of you," Aron says, voice blunt. "I would not like to see your faces."

They all immediately sit up, and I blanch to see that all four of the men are young. Two of them have beards, but all of them could be college kids if they were in my world. There's fear on their faces, but they're resolute, as well.

Aron thinks for a moment, and then flicks a hand at me, suggesting I go to his side. I immediately jump to my feet and race over, feeling their eyes on me. Aron leans in, his breath tickling the dried mud on my ear. "I can say this properly. Tell them that I will be lenient if they betray me."

I mull that, then nod. He's giving me a lot of power, letting me speak on his behalf, and I suspect that's as deliberate as anything else Aron does. I clear my throat and take a step forward, deliberately kicking the wizard. Just because. "All right, listen up, people. This is a new Aron, and we do things differently." I clasp my hands together, pitying the flickers of hope I see in their eyes. "If you can't follow him a hundred percent, we're going to leave your ass behind at the first city we come to. Aron's in charge, and I'm Aron's anchor. That means you listen to me as much as you listen to him, and if I say jump, you say how high. Understand?" I point at each one of them, feeling a bit like a schoolteacher speaking to naughty children.

One man clears his throat and puts his hands to his chest, holding an imaginary weapon in Aron's gesture. "We followed the Lord of Storms because we are believers, lady. That has not changed. We still follow the Lord of Storms."

To a one, the men put their hands on their chests, bow their heads, and echo his gestures.

I'm a little surprised—and pleased. "You're not mercenaries?"

"No. We chose to serve our Lord of Storms," the first one says. He's beardless and can't be more than twenty. "There is no greater honor than serving at my god's side." The others nod.

"Oh. Okay. We'd better be able to trust you, then." I turn to the woman. "What about you?"

Her smile is sweet and guileless. "My lord Aron bought me to serve him and his wizard. I am a bed slave from the esteemed houses of Rastana. I serve my master in all ways he requires." And then she licks her lips and lowers her eyes. I could swear I see her arch her back slightly, thrusting her tits out further.

I fight back the stab of irritation I feel at her presence. There's no need for me to be bitchy. I know in my heart she's just trying to ensure her survival. I think briefly of Avalla, back in Aventine, and how she couldn't think any further than serving the most powerful master she could find. It's not her fault this is what she's used to. "Okay, cool. Since you're not a mercenary, if you touch a weapon, we're leaving your ass behind, too." I point at all of them again. "Serve Aron well and you can live. If you try to betray him, he'll gut you so fast you won't see it coming."

I turn to look at Aron, to see if I covered everything.

"Faith speaks lies," is all Aron says.

"That means truth," I interrupt.

"We know, my lady," the first soldier says. He ducks his head. "We have learned to interpret my lord's words."

"Then interpret this," Aron continues. He crosses his arms over his chest and kicks the wizard's fallen body. "Faith is not my anchor. You will get near her. You will speak to her. If you touch one hair on her head or so much as breathe incorrectly in her direction, I will be lenient. I am not a god." His expression is dark and baleful, and as I watch, lightning crackles in his gaze, and I shiver. "If you harm her or betray me, I will *not* torture you in this world and the next. A god's vengeance is not eternal. Understand?"

They all go pale. The woman drops her forehead to the ground again, shivering.

"I think they get it," I whisper to Aron. A threat shouldn't sound so very flattering, but I can't help but be pleased that he's speaking so highly of me to them. It's kinda sexy. Heck, it's more than kinda sexy. I'm totally aroused at the authority in his voice and how sternly he's glaring at all of them. Never has a bitch-out session been so damn hot...and it's coming from Aron.

Has any man ever elevated me so highly? Hell, I've been called Tart more often than I've been called my name in this world. I know this is a big deal and I'm appreciative of it. I touch Aron's arm. "Thank you."

He puts a hand on my shoulder, and I like that more than all the hugs in the world. We're united, together.

CHAPTER 44

The men all swear fealty to Aron, and one by one, we learn a little about them. There's Markos from Aventine, who comes from a sailing family. Solat, who hails from Katharn and has the most beautiful, fine black curls. Kerren, who has darker skin and comes from Mephis, and Vitar, who is a farmer's son and also comes from Katharn. They've been with the Aron of Lies for about two weeks now, and served him faithfully. They have three woale with them and took turns walking as Aron rode with the concubine and the wizard. The men ask to have an evening to bury their fallen dead, and while Aron doesn't look as if he wants to do so, he turns to me and I nod. I want an evening off, too.

So I sit by the fire and clean my face and arms of mud while the men dig in the forest and Aron hovers, watching them. The concubine sits with me, and I learn her name, too—Yulenna. When I ask where she's from, she just smiles and shrugs. "My last master was in Rastana. A slave claims no home."

"You don't have to be a slave any longer," I tell her. I was a slave and I hated it. "I'm sure Aron will free you. Heck, you're free now."

She frowns, as if this makes her unhappy. "It is a great honor to serve one of the Aspects. Being his slave will be one of my life's true joys."

"Aron doesn't need slaves."

"You see to his pleasure, then?"

Well this conversation just escalated to eleven. "That's a bit personal and I don't have to tell you."

Yulenna just smiles sweetly and plays with her long black hair. "I can help with that if you're tired of servicing him. I'm good in bed and I know what Aron likes."

"You mean you knew what the Aron of Lies liked. This is a different Aron."

"They are all Aspects of the same god," Yulenna points out, and for a shining moment, I want to punch her in her pretty mouth, even though I know she's right.

"It's not the same, and you won't touch him unless he asks for it. No volunteering, either."

"But, my lady, I just want to please him." She clasps her hands in front of her chest, eyes beseeching. "I'm a bed slave. How do I earn my keep if I don't please him?"

"You could try cooking?" I gesture at the camp fire. "Or like I said, we could set you free. We can give you money and you can go to the nearest town and start over."

Her eyes fill with tears. "If I go to Katharn with no papers and no male guardian, I will be captured by the first slaver who sees me and sold on the cheap. Please, do not do this. I have served my Lord of Storms faithfully." She drops to her knees and prostrates herself, weeping.

Well, shit. "Yulenna, get up. Please." I hate that her words make sense. I hate that when she sits up, she still looks beautiful and perfect, her eyes shining with big tears that just make her prettier. I know that she's not wrong—she would be enslaved again. That's what happened to me back in Aventine. I can't condemn her to a crappy fate just because I'm feeling jealous and territorial. "I'll ask Aron if he wants a bed slave."

The words stick in my throat.

She beams at me, her face full of relief. "I can service both of you if needed. Just tell me what is required and I'll do it."

"Er, no, I'm good, thanks." I hastily move away from her before she can start offering to demonstrate. I've gone from hating Yulenna to feeling sorry for her in a matter of moments. I remember how terrifying it was to be enslaved, how objectified I felt. How can I dislike someone else for just trying to survive in this world in the only way she knows how? I move away from the fire, drawing my cloak closer, and follow the sound of digging into the woods.

Before I can take more than a few steps into the trees, Aron is there before me, glowering. "Where are you going?"

"Oh. I was coming to talk to you."

He scowls at me. "I told you not to stay by the fire."

It takes a moment for me to process that. "Right. Well, I was just coming straight for you—"

"Faith." Aron takes me by the arm, sending tingles up and down my body. If anything, the electric shocks seem to be stronger than before. Maybe they're doubling up because he's two Arons now. "I do not want you by the fire where I can watch over you. I trust these men. They have proven themselves."

Ah. He's worried we might still be betrayed. Of course he is. Haven't we been betrayed by everyone in this land so far? "I'm sorry, Aron. I just needed to talk to you. I'll stay by the fire...but do you want a bed slave?" I rush the words out before he can scowl at me again.

Aron cocks his head, amusement on his handsome, arrogant face. "You are volunteering?"

"What? No!" I can feel a hot blush on my face. "You wish!"

"Do I?"

I...can't tell if that's a lie or not. He's still casting that slow smile in my direction, the one that makes my belly flutter, and I don't know what to think. "Yulenna," I manage to say. "She wants to stay on as your bed slave."

"And what do you think?"

Okay, now his questions are getting on my nerves. "I think you're in charge of your own damn dick. You tell me."

He studies me for a long moment. "Because I have defeated Lies...it means that I am him. The thought of having her in my bed is appealing."

I open my mouth to snap at him for being a pig—when I realize that I'm supposed to read the opposite from his words. Right. It's still taking me some getting used to. I can't help but preen a little. "So you don't want her in your bed? She's going to be disappointed."

"And I care?" He arches one arrogant eyebrow at me.

"Hey, you know what? That's kind of neat—if you ask a rhetorical question, we can get around the lies thing." I give him a little poke in the chest with my finger. "Remember that, because talking to you now is confusing."

"Is it?" His grin is practically flirty, and my pulse hammers in my throat. "Again, should I care if you're confused since you are here to serve me?"

Good ol' arrogance, rearing his head again. I give his chest a little pat. "I'm going to ignore that. So what's the plan now?"

Aron studies my face, and then glances down at the hand I have on his chest. I leave it there, just to be obstinate, and I get the distinct impression that he expected that and it amuses him. He puts his hand over mine a moment later, and then I'm trapped against him, little shockwaves of lightning skittering through my skin. "Nothing has changed, has it?"

"Everything has changed," I whisper. "You're different now."

"I am," he tells me.

Oh sure, he can pretend nothing is different, but I'm having to interpret every word he says now. "I'm just glad you won," I admit. "I don't like to think of ending up like the wizard." I shudder, still picturing him as the last time I saw him, his slender, robed body tossed atop the pile of fallen soldiers. "Promise me you'll win against the next two, also."

"I can promise nothing, Faith," he says in a low voice, and his thumb brushes over my trapped hand. "You think I would let harm come to you?"

I smile faintly at him. "I have to admit this puts a kink in our plans. Soldiers and a bed slave?" When he snorts, I shake my head. "I don't feel safer. You'd think with extra people around, it would feel like we're less vulnerable. And yet..." Now I've seen what happens when a god's anchor is killed. I watched Liar Aron fade out before my eyes.

Fade into *nothing*.

I'm not sure which image disturbs me more—that the wizard was slain to get rid of Liar Aron, or that Liar Aron could just vanish into nothing. I think of that happening to my Aron and impulsively, I move forward and give him a hug, pressing my cheek to his leather-armor-covered chest.

He strokes my hair, and for a change, Aron is quiet. There are no lies coming from his mouth, no arrogant bullshit. He just smooths my hair and holds me close, and I tremble against him, full of worry.

"You think I would let anything happen to you, my Faith?" he murmurs again, and I feel warm and relaxed at those words.

"I just worry I won't be enough to help you," I whisper.

"You aren't." And he strokes my hair again.

CHAPTER 45

$\mathcal{W}$e camp in Liar Aron's camp that night, since it's already set up and the hour's late. The woales are tethered to a nearby tree and fed, and Yulenna chit-chats non-stop by the fire, as if determined to talk out her distress over the changing situation. I let her talk, murmuring agreements when she needs a response, but mostly I'm not listening. I'm tired and distracted.

This could have ended badly. I could have died. I can still feel Bad Aron's hand on my neck as he gazed down at me. I nearly fucked it up for both of us, and I can't stop thinking about how Bad Aron just...faded away.

And now my Aron is both of them.

I don't know what to make of that. I know that he's supposed to be here in the mortal realm to purge all the bad stuff from his system, so why is he now unable to speak the truth? What happens to him once all four are put back together like the fantasy version of Voltron? Does my Aron disappear forever, lost inside the god himself? That makes me sad.

Another thought occurs to me—what happens when we find the Hedonism Aron? I eye Yulenna as she warms her hands by the fire. I hate that my thoughts went there. I hate that I keep seeing Aron flipping her skirt up and the noises she made as he pounded into her. It doesn't matter that it wasn't *my* Aron, because it's my Aron now, and I might murder him in his sleep if he touches her.

Or...just cry a lot. One or the other.

Eventually, the soldiers come back from burying their comrades, their expressions sober. They keep their distance from me, silent as they wash up and head to their tents to sleep. Aron points me to the big tent, where old Aron slept, and I can't fight my yawns back any longer. I head inside, and I feel a stab of relief when Aron follows me in. He's still going to sleep with me.

Yulenna follows us, too. Her expression is timid when she sees my surprise. "I slept at my Lord of Storms's feet while he relaxed, in case he should need me through the long night. Should I not?"

I look at Aron.

"This is not Faith's tent now," he declares. "She does not make the rules here." And he puts a big hand on my shoulder.

I bite my lip, wondering how much to push, and then decide that fuck it, I'm pushing. "Aron won't need your services anymore. You can sleep in the wizard's tent."

With an uncertain look, Yulenna nods and sees herself out.

The tent's definitely better living than Aron and I have experienced so far...well, except for maybe Tadekha's citadel. Lush tapestries hang on the walls, and thick blankets are tossed atop a plush pad of a mattress. There's a freaking mattress out here in the woods, and I practically squeal at the sight of it. It's atop a woven reed mat to keep the dirt off it, but there's no mistaking the thickness of it, and I kneel beside it to touch, just because I'm so shocked. A real mattress. With pillows, even. They're pretty, decorative pillows for the most part, but still pillows. Nearby, coals rest in a hammered brazier in the center of the room and there's a scent like incense. Off to one side is a flat-topped trunk with a cushioned seat for a lid. "Holy crap, he's living in style in here," I breathe, scarcely able to believe it. I pick up one pillow and am surprised to feel that the embroidered unicorns on the front are as soft as velvet.

Aron just grunts, and he sounds irritated. "All of this is necessary for travel."

"I don't care if it's necessary or not, it's awesome." I run a hand over my face and arms, feeling for any last flakes of mud, and then touch the bed again. "Can we use it? Even if it belongs to the bad guys?"

"It is not yours now," Aron tells me. " If we plan on making good time to the Spidae's tower, we are not leaving all of this behind."

His emphasis tells me the truth of the matter, and I sigh. All this bedding was too good to be true after all. I know he's right. But tonight, these luxury accommodations are mine. "Is it safe to sleep, do you think?" I ask him, lowering my voice to a bare whisper. "Or should we stay on alert?"

"What is there to guard against?" he whispers back, a mocking edge in his tone. "Do they not serve Aron of the Cleaver? Am I not the only one here?"

"Point taken," I agree, and give him a little pinch just because he's back to being his normal ass self. "If it's safe, then I'm undressing and sleeping now."

"You should not," he agrees, putting a big hand on my shoulder. "We will not be rising early in the morning. You do not need your sleep."

I pull off one boot with a nodded yawn, then the other. All the adrenaline is leaving my body and I feel like a sleepy mess. I haul my dirty tunic off my head before I realize I'm almost naked in front of Aron. Oh well, it's not like he hasn't seen goods like mine before. I smack my lips and adjust the leather band I'm wearing around my tits so they don't bounce, and then crawl into bed in nothing but leggings and a bra-band. "Tonight, I get to sleep in luxury at least. Come here, my pretty," I tell a pillow, and tuck it under my face. Oh man, this is heaven. "I'm going to be sad to leave you all behind tomorrow. Shhh, don't cry." I stroke a pillow. "I will remember you in my dreams."

Aron snorts.

"Oh, what's that?" I tell the pillow, still pretending to have a conversation. "Aron's a dick? I know, right? I'm not sure why he's so against you either, considering this is his tent. Well, not his tent, but Bad Aron's tent. It's okay, though." I pet the pillow one more time and fight a yawn. "If you love something, set it free and all that. You'll be free in the morning, pillow. Just right after I'm done with you."

I tuck the blankets under my chin and a moment later, Aron stabs me in the side with a finger.

"Ow. What?" I roll over and look at him. He's squatting next to the bed, one arm resting casually on his knee.

Aron just smirks at me. "You think this is my tent? Why would I have a bed? I do not sleep, remember?"

My tired brain processes that for a moment, and then I remember that he doesn't lie when he's asking questions. Then, I sit upright, shocked. Shit. He's right. I look around the tent, and notice the feminine touches I didn't see before. A shawl draped over the seat. Fringe on the pillows. Freaking embroidery. Dudes don't care about that shit. I bet if I open the pretty trunk, the clothes in there will be dresses just like the filmy one Yulenna's wearing. "This is her tent, isn't it?"

"You think I would cuddle with the wizard?" Aron asks mockingly.

I give him a wry look. "Good point. I didn't realize this was hers, though." I touch the unicorn pillow thoughtfully. "Should we bring her back in here?"

"Yes," Aron says flatly.

"Okay, okay, don't get touchy. I'm trying to be polite."

"Why should you be polite to the conquered?" he asks, and reaches out to brush a stray lock of hair off my shoulder. I get goosebumps at that small touch, and not just because of the shockwaves.

"Right," I say, distracted. I'm trying to think about Yulenna, but Aron's nearness is kind of pulling me in a million directions. Not that he's all *that* near, of course. I'm sitting up in bed and he's next to me but not standing. We're still close enough for... well, a lot of things. My brain reminds me of Aron flipping up Yulenna's skirt, and then I'm back to reality. I know the nice thing to do would be to invite her back in here, but...I'm still seeing the vision of his dick pushing into her whenever I close my eyes.

She can sleep in the wizard's tent tonight.

I lie down again, gazing up at Aron. "What do we do with her? I suggested freeing her and you'd think I was talking about execution."

He grunts. "Give her to the soldiers?"

I blanch. "Aron, no. She's a person. She just makes poor choices. Or maybe she didn't have choices. Either way, she doesn't have to service anyone if she doesn't want to. Let her figure out that she doesn't have to earn a living on her back and maybe she'll choose a different way."

Aron just arches an eyebrow at me, clearly disagreeing.

Sheesh. I reach out to swat at him. "Be nice. I didn't want to be a slave handed off to men. Why would I wish that on someone else?" Even if she thinks she should be servicing Aron right about now?

"And the soldiers? Any plans for them?" Aron murmurs, his voice taking on a more intimate tone. "Assuming they will not prove themselves, that is."

Ugh. I'm not sure I like the idea of riding around with a posse. It's very different from how Aron and I have been traveling so far, and it feels very...conspicuous. It might be safer, but

I just don't know. I feel like everything's going to change. Then again, everything already has. Aron can't speak without spouting lies, and when I close my eyes, I can't stop seeing Bad Aron bent over Yulenna. Bad Aron grabbing Yulenna's hips. Yulenna squealing as he drives into her. "We'll see," I tell him. "We're stuck with them for now, I guess. If we can't get along, we can always dump them at the closest city if they slow us down."

"Novoro," he agrees, and then reaches down to pull the blankets up to my chin again. "You must not sleep, Faith. I won't watch over you."

I smile up at him. "You won't, huh?" I tease, unable to resist, and my heart flutters just a little when his mouth curves in a hint of a smile. If nothing else, I like that I can make him smile. Lord knows we have little enough to smile about lately, what with being hunted down and chased out of every place we stop. Maybe we're safer with a posse after all...provided they don't betray us.

The thought makes my soul ache. Is there no one Aron can trust to not screw him over but me? Poor Aron. How are the gods supposed to learn anything on this little test the High Father sent them on? They're too busy being attacked by the power hungry.

Unless the only thing they're supposed to learn is humility. Then, I'd say this is working fantastic.

But it makes me worry for Aron all the more. I lie back down and turn on my side, but when I close my eyes, this time, I don't see Aron and Yulenna humping. I see the other Aron, his hand on my throat, close enough to kiss...and just fading away into nothing.

There's a one in four chance—now one in three—that my Aron's going to have the same fate. The thought makes me sick. I reach over and grab Aron's hand, pulling him forward. "Lie down in bed with me," I tell him. "I know you won't sleep, but I'll feel safer with you close."

For a moment, I expect biting sarcasm or even a flurry of lies. Instead, Aron just lies down next to me, sliding under the blankets. I don't mind that he's got his boots on or that he's fully dressed, because he puts his arm around my waist and tucks me close against him, and that familiar electric shock jolts through me and then settles away. I breathe in his scent and feel his warmth, and some of the worry relaxes.

But only some. I put my hand over his at my waist, holding him closer. "Promise me everything will be all right," I whisper. "That we've got this handled."

"I promise," Aron murmurs.

Yeah, that was kind of what I figured.

THE NEXT MORNING, there's a thick, honey-laced porridge simmering over the fire, and I watch the others eat, stomach rumbling, until I'm sure that it's not poisoned and this isn't a trap. Then, I help myself to a bowl. And then another. And a third, because their supplies are far better than the ones we have.

The soldiers watch me scarf down the food quietly, and when I make myself a fourth bowl, the one called Markos has a look of disbelief on his face. "You can eat all that?" He glances at Aron, unsure, but when he's not struck by lightning for talking to me, he turns back to me again. "Where does it go?"

I decide I like Markos. I shake my spoon at him. "You sweet talker, you. And dude, I'm an anchor. We're eating for two." With my spoon, I wave it at Aron, who stands nearby, watching us eat with a hint of impatience. "I have to fuel up."

"You eat more than any soldier I have ever seen," Vitar whispers into his bowl as he eats. "We will not have enough supplies if this keeps up."

I just keep eating. "Oh please," I say between bites. "You act like this is shocking. Didn't the wizard eat a lot?"

"Yes, but he was a wizard."

"Well, I'm a girl. I'm allowed to eat." And I take another heaping mouthful just to prove that I can.

Vitar looks uneasy, but Markos grins and takes a bite almost as big as mine, as if to prove that he can. Big goof. We eat in companionable silence, and a few moments later Yulenna comes out of her tent, wearing leggings and boots for a day of travel. Her hair is pulled back into a fashionable knot and she looks less like a slave and more like a fine lady about to go on a journey. I glance down at my belted tunic—one of Omos's old ones —and remember that I didn't brush my hair this morning after I rolled out of bed.

Markos prepares a bowl of porridge for Yulenna and offers her a spoon, and she smiles sweetly at him and sits down next to me. "So much food," she murmurs, and then takes a dainty bite.

I make a face into my bowl, and I can hear Vitar muffle a laugh.

Breakfast is eventually over, though, and the tents are packed up, the woales loaded with gear we've opted to take. There's a small mountain of it left in the bushes, and I look mournfully at the bedding I slept in last night. Goodbye, mattress. Goodbye, pillows. Goodbye, delicious night's sleep. Even though I understand it—we need speed if we want to stay ahead of anyone else that might be following us—I'm still a little bummed at the thought of sleeping on woale-back again.

I'm never going to complain about taking the bus again when I get home, I decide. Never, ever again. Woale-back is ten times worse and twenty times slower.

When the camp is nothing but a firepit, Kerren kicks dirt over it until it, too, is no more. Then, one by one, the men drop to their knees and put their fists over their hearts in Aron's symbol.

"We are ready to serve, my lord," Markos declares. "Tell us what you desire."

"Faith and I are not going to Novoro," Aron says in that imperious voice of his. "That is our next stop."

I watch the others closely, because the moment he mentions Novoro, one shifts, and the other grimaces. Another just stares at the ground.

"Novoro?" Markos asks hesitantly. "I...you truly wish to go there, my Lord of Storms?" He swallows hard and ducks his head. "Not that I question your ways—"

"Novoro," Aron repeats in a firm voice.

"Where were you guys planning on heading with the old Aron?" I ask, curious. "Isn't Novoro the only place up in the mountain pass?"

One nods. "My lord Aron told us he wished to go into the mountains and establish a hideout so he could have defensive ground."

I glance over at my Aron. He just shakes his head, and I speak up again. "I think he lied to you guys. We're going to Novoro, and I bet he was, too."

"But why Novoro?" Vitar blurts, looking confused. "They do not open the gates of their fortress to anyone."

"They will open for me," Aron declares.

He's right. They'll probably welcome him with open arms... even if it's only to betray him later. But hey, one problem at a time. "Yeah, I'm pretty sure getting in won't be our problem. Novoro's the destination."

"It is the end of the world." Markos's expression is solemn.

"Not quite the end," I add in. "We're going somewhere after that."

"There's nothing past it," Vitar says, curious.

"I require your services." Aron speaks again, his tone grave.

341

He doesn't clarify where we're going, just that we're going. "If you choose not to follow, I will be angry."

Markos clenches his hands over his chest, the expression on his face full of intensity. "We are here to serve you in this life and the next, my Lord of Storms. There is no greater honor. Forgive us for questioning you."

Aron grunts, but it's not a mean grunt, just an acknowledgement.

"We're the ones that are new here," I tell them. "If you have questions, ask them. I don't think we can ever have too much information. Aron wants to hear your feedback. Isn't that right, Aron?"

"No," says Aron. "Faith is wrong."

I beam at him, and I'm glad to see the men visibly relax. Communication's important, especially if these guys know something we don't.

"After we go to these places," Solat asks, sitting back on his heels. "Will you remain at the Tower? Do you have the same plan? To create a stronghold and defend yourself?"

All of the men watch Aron closely. I notice Yulenna is silent, her expression one of worry. I can't blame her. We're going to the edges of the world apparently, to extremely dangerous places and she's a bed slave who isn't wanted by her owner. She's probably wondering what her place is in all this and what will happen to her. I make a mental note to befriend her and reassure her that she's safe...and if she doesn't want to stay, I want her to feel comfortable with leaving.

Aron shakes his head. "Waiting like that is waiting for death, is it not?"

It's the right thing to say. The men's eyes light up with enthusiasm. "Shall we hunt them down, my lord? Raise an army in your name?" Solat asks.

"Perhaps not." Aron rubs his chin thoughtfully, and he seems to like the idea. "Perhaps on to Yshrem?"

Yulenna makes a face.

"What?" I ask, narrowing in on that. "What's bad about Yshrem?" Jesus, do these people hate everywhere? No one wants to go to Novoro, or Yshrem, and Katharn and Aventine were crap. Where is it that's safe and relaxing to go to?

She flinches, pulling her cloak close about her shoulders when everyone stares at her. "It is just..." She wrinkles her nose. "A kingdom of scholars and wizards. Adassia is much nicer."

"Adassia is conquered by the Cyclopae," Markos corrects. "As is Yshrem. And the Cyclopae are devotees of my lord Aron."

Cyclops? Freaking cyclops? I've heard everything now...but I'm not surprised. I mean, if there are zombies and angels and gods walking the earth, why wouldn't there be cyclops?

"My lord Aron, may I ask what is in Novoro and beyond that you seek?" Kerren—the quiet one amongst the soldiers—speaks up and asks.

"Yes, you may ask," he says, and turns his back to them. Aron stalks toward me and then puts his hand on my chin. "Say everything to them," he murmurs. "We keep no secrets."

Right. As in, shut your mouth, Faith. "Will do, big guy."

He studies my face thoughtfully, and his thumb moves against my skin, just inches from my lips. Before I can wonder if he's going to touch me more, or kiss me, he releases me and turns away, his cloak swirling. "Let us not be on our way."

The men scramble to their feet, full of enthusiasm. All of them except Kerren, of course, whose face is flushed with embarrassment at being ignored. The others clap him on the back as if to sympathize, but then everyone is mounting up on the woales and Aron looks impatient at me, waiting for me to join him on our land-hippo.

"I'm coming," I mutter, my butt already hurting at the thought of another day (or a week) in the damn saddle.

CHAPTER 46

*O*ddly enough, I enjoy the company of the soldiers and Yulenna as we travel.

The dynamic's weird at first—no one is sure whether or not to talk around Aron or even me, and so it's awkward and quiet when we're around. I get tired of that and by the time we hit the road on the second day, I start nagging the men (and Yulenna) to tell me about where they came from, how they got to be soldiers, and anything else I can think of. When Aron doesn't smack them down for daring to talk to me, they ease up a little and soon the conversation is flowing.

For all that the men are battle-hardened and have been soldiers since about the age of sixteen, they feel so young. They laugh and make merry, playing pranks on each other as they ride their woales and teasing about wenches they left behind in other cities. Kerren—the quiet one—has a sweetheart back in his hometown, whereas Solat is the ladies' man. Yulenna even joins in the teasing, chatting with the men and laughing with them.

Me, I feel a bit like a team mom. Maybe it's because I don't know jack about this world other than what I've overheard or what Omos taught me. Maybe it's because they all look at Aron guiltily when they're a little too loud or boisterous. Aron, for his part, doesn't really take part in the conversations. He occasionally snorts with amusement at overhearing something, which tells me that he is paying attention, but he's quiet.

And he's extremely, extremely protective of me. He hovers near me and frowns if anyone moves too close. He makes sure I never lift anything heavy. He keeps a possessive hand at my waist at almost all times. He insists I get the best tent and largest portions of food first. And if one of the men laughs a little too hard at one of my jokes, Aron gives them the stink-eye.

It's kinda cute but it also makes everyone just a little afraid of him.

He also completely, utterly ignores Yulenna.

Yulenna, for her part, has tried really, really hard to get into Aron's good graces. She tries to flatter him with conversation, makes herself available at all times, tosses her hair so much that she looks like a high-spirited horse, and constantly goes up to him, trying to figure out what he wants or needs. It's obvious that she'd feel more certain of her place if he would just fuck her, but he completely and totally ignores her.

"You're going to give Yulenna a complex," I whisper to Aron one night as we're under the blankets in my tent. "She really, really wants to please you, preferably on her knees."

He just snorts. "I have interest in her," he lies. And then he holds me close, his hand on my waist. "Go to sleep."

Aron always sleeps in my bed. Between that and the fact that he ignores Yulenna, it's clear that they all think we're fucking. One morning I get out of the tent, my hair a tangled mess of snarls, and catch the men smirking as if sharing a secret joke. I guess it makes sense that they think we're together like that. Heck, I have days where I wonder why we're *not* together like that. I let them go on believing it, too, because what am I going to say? That Aron isn't interested in sex? It's clear from Yulenna's hurt confusion that he is. That he likes sex a *lot*.

But Aron's never put the moves on me. He's never even really come close, and other than that night at Tadekha's citadel, you'd think we're brother and sister...which makes me feel all sour and irritated inside. I start to study Yulenna, trying to determine what she has that attracts Aron that I don't.

Not that I want to attract Aron, of course.

But if I did...

I watch as Yulenna rides next to Solat. She's laughing and giggling at his flirting, and her loose breasts sway under the thin fabric of her dress. Her hair is in a sexy, loose braid over one shoulder and she looks clean and pretty. I glance down at my own tunic. It's got a stain from breakfast on it, it's faded and old and belonged to a man. My hair's pulled into a wild topknot just because I don't have the mental fortitude to touch it while it's dirty, and my tits are tightly bound under the leather band.

I am most definitely not bringing the sexy to travel.

I wonder if that's a mistake, though. I wonder if I should be trying to seduce Aron so he'll help me get home once he gets home? I don't know what to think.

The weather stays nice for most of the next week, even if the environment continues to change. The thick, tall forests thin out and the roads get progressively rockier. It gets colder with every day that passes, as if we're climbing in altitude, and in the mornings, my breath puffs visibly in the air. I wake up with my body plastered to Aron's for warmth, but if it bothers him, he doesn't say a thing. As we ride, the flat lands turn into hills, and then the hills turn into massive, craggy mountains that loom overhead.

We're getting close to Novoro.

"You're mine, Faith," Aron murmurs, his breath hot against my shoulder. He peels my dress back, exposing my skin. *"We've fought this long enough, don't you think?"*

"I'm not fighting anything," I protest, moaning. *"I've wanted you since day one."*

"Show me how much you want me," he says, and he hikes my skirts up, his face disappearing between my thighs. *"Let me taste it—"*

"Faith."

I jerk awake, disoriented—and a little pissed off—that I've been woken up from such a vivid dream. Someone just had to wake me up *now*? Before it got to the good part? *"What?"*

Aron's hard face gazes down at me. "You were talking in your sleep."

"Was I? No I wasn't." I tug the blankets higher, wishing I'd slept in more than just my breast band and leggings. I swear I can still feel his breath on my thigh. "Don't be ridiculous."

But Aron isn't paying much attention to me. He's gazing off, a thoughtful expression on his face. After a moment, he seems to remember that I'm there, and raises his chin in my direction. "Ask me a question."

"Was I really talking in my sleep?"

"Yes." He grunts. "I am not lying to you."

"Are you sure?" When he gives me an irritated look, I shrug. "Let's test it again, just to be sure, because I'm positive I wasn't talking in my sleep." Because if I was, oh god, I hope I wasn't begging him to touch me in filthy, filthy ways. "Is my hair blonde?"

"Yes."

"Are you arrogant?"

"Yes." He grins at me, all boyish pleasure. "See?"

"You're right. What changed?" I stifle a yawn.

"He no longer influences me." Aron shrugs. "I am back to just me."

I can't say I'm displeased. As I get dressed for the day's travel, though, part of me grows uneasy. If it's that simple to just wipe an Aron out of existence...what happens to the Aron I'm with when this is over?

CHAPTER 47

*T*he first sight of Novoro takes my breath away.

First there's nothing there—just more endless mountains and craggy, snow-covered peaks. Then, we round a corner and suddenly there's a massive citadel tucked high amidst the cliffs. It blends in so well it's impossible to see from afar, and if there wasn't a well-traveled road leading up here, I'd think I was imagining things. The massive fortress looks as if its hewn straight from the rock itself, and it lofts high, hundreds of windows carved into the side of the mountains. The longer I look, the more windows and fortress come into view, until all I can see before us is just one big stone anthill of humans. It's fascinating to see, and I wonder how many people live here. Two thousand? Ten thousand? How deep into the mountain does this go? Two massive doors that look as if they're made of steel bar the entrance, and each one is easily three stories high and wide enough to fit two lanes of traffic.

They're also shut tight. Of course they are. Dozens of tiny plumes of smoke tell me that someone's home, though—not everything can be hidden away.

RUBY DIXON

Markos sidles forward on his woale, moving to the side of the land-hippo I share with Aron. He gazes up at the massive gates that dwarf our small party. His expression is downright indignant, as if he's been insulted. "They do not welcome us, my great Lord of Storms. Shall I let them know of your presence?"

I wrinkle my nose, inwardly wincing. Do we really have to announce anything?

But this is Aron, Lord of Arrogance. I can practically feel him stiffen with indignation. "Demand that they let us in."

"At once, my lord." Markos gives a firm nod and then spurs his woale into action. The thing gives a deep belly squeal and then trundles forward, grunting, and Markos approaches the gates.

The hair prickles on the back of my neck and I'm tense as I watch him move forward. He looks impossibly tiny as he walks up to them. Woales aren't tiny creatures, and yet Markos and his mount look like toys in front of those huge gates. I hear him shout for entrance, but his voice gets lost in the cavernous canyon, as if soaked up by the rock itself.

We wait.

The gates don't open. Eventually, someone leans out a lower window and shouts something back, gesturing at us while we wait. Markos puts a hand to his mouth and calls back, and then...they sit there and bicker for what must be a good five minutes.

"Well, everyone does say Novoroans are weird," I mutter to Aron. "Novorese? Novorians? Novoroni? What do we call them?"

"We call them fools for not welcoming our lord," Solat says, his hippo restless.

I just roll my eyes. If there was a suck-up in the group, it'd be Solat.

Something moves in one of the windows, and then another.

Nothing big, just a small shift of movement, but both Kerren and Vitar immediately push forward, drawing shields and blocking in front of us. The tiny movement gleams again, and then something points at Markos.

Arrows.

Oh fuck. I stare, shocked—it didn't occur to me that we'd be turned away at the gates. "Is there another way through these mountains?" I breathe, my voice low.

"Climbing," Solat says. "But woale are not sure-footed except on flat lands. We would have to lead them and travel over foot ourselves...and it would be dangerous for us, as well."

"No. We are not doing that." Aron taps a hand on my hip. "Get down, Faith."

I automatically slide off the side of the woale, all too happy to take a leg-stretch or three. Yulenna slides off of Kerren's mount and lands beside me, rubbing her butt. "Are we turning around? What are we doing?" I ask, curious.

Aron points at Kerren. "Wait here with them. The others, come with me." And he rides forward, his woale doing that grunting little trot like Markos's mount. I didn't even know woale could move that fast. It's almost a horse-gallop, complete with fat bouncing sides and the jangle of supplies as all three men ride forward.

"What the fuck are they doing?" I hiss, shocked. I clutch at the neck of my cloak, horrified as Aron boldly takes off his cloak and casts it to the ground, revealing his dark hair and noble features. Solat and Vitar ride next to him, but they're not close enough to protect him with those shields. "He's going to get fucking killed!"

"My lady," Kerren says gently, looking at me. "He is not the target."

Oh.

Oh, right. It's *me* that's the target. I rub my arms, suddenly glad that he left me behind. "It's still not safe for him to ride forward like that," I tell Kerren and Yulenna. "I don't like it."

"He goes to show them that he is who he claims," Yulenna says in a reasonable voice, watching Aron ride forward. "Then they will bow to him and give him the welcome he deserves."

"Mmmhmm." They weren't with my Aron in Aventine, when someone tried to assassinate us. Or Katharn. Or at the Citadel. Or...man, we really get attacked a lot. That sucks. Maybe it's a good thing we now have bodyguards. I frown to myself at the thought and I wonder if the other Aron got constantly betrayed all the time or if we're just the lucky ones.

We watch, and I hold my breath as Aron approaches the fortress, his long hair waving like a flag. He makes a wonderful target, and I cringe inwardly when Markos and the others move to his side. I'm torn between watching Kerren for reactions and watching Aron, because I have a feeling Kerren's going to know something's wrong before I do. As I wait, I see a small door—inset in the much, much larger ones—open below and someone comes out to talk to Aron and the men. They all stand there, distant dots, and I wish I could hear their conversation.

The newcomer drops to his knees before Aron's woale and stacks his fists over his heart. I release the breath I didn't even realize I was holding. There's a great shout, and as I watch, the people in the windows retreat. The man gets up from his knees, and then there's a massive groan as the gates slowly shudder open.

"Looks like we are welcomed," Yulenna says.

Kerren glances over at her. "Give Faith your cloak and switch mounts with her."

She nods. "At once."

I want to protest, but I'm ashamed to say that I don't. He's setting up Yulenna as the target, just in case we're going to be betrayed again. It's smart, but I can't help but feel guilty as Yulenna comes to my side and envelops me in her cloak, even as

Kerren raises his shield and steers his woale in front of us to hide what we're doing. "I'm sorry," I whisper to her as she fastens it around my neck.

"Do not be. I know I am expendable." Her smile is bittersweet. "At least this way, I can be of service." She tugs the hood over my head and then pulls my cloak around her shoulders, pulling my hood over her long, curling hair.

"Well, I hope it's all not necessary."

Kerren dismounts, his armor jangling. "We all hope it is not," he says easily, and then offers his hand to Yulenna. "Let us get my lord's anchor mounted once more. I think you should walk, Faith, so you seem like the servant."

"I can do that." For once, I'm glad that Yulenna's the one in the flowing dress and I'm the one in a stained tunic. It adds to the feeling that she's the important one and I'm not.

Kerren grabs the reins of the woale, and Yulenna adjusts her clothes, delicately smoothing out the cloak. She holds onto the pommel, and then we move forward to greet Markos, Solat, Vitar and Aron at the gates where they wait for us.

The walk across the rocky field feels as if it takes forever, and a thousand eyes seem to be staring at us, even if the windows remain dark and empty. The gates continue to groan their way open and I watch them with fascination. I bet the Statue of Liberty could stroll through them and not have to duck her head, they're so tall. As we move forward toward the gates, armed soldiers arrive, flanking a man in a swirling black cloak lined with white. They pause.

Then, to a one they kneel before Aron and bow their heads, waiting to be addressed.

Aron doesn't speak to them right away, though. He watches us as we approach, his eyes narrowed. His gaze lingers on me for a moment, flicks to Yulenna, and then he turns to look at the rest of our men. No one's saying a thing or even looking at me, which means we're all on the same page.

"Rise," Aron says finally.

The man on the cloak gets up, and the others flanking him follow suit. He's a tall man with a grim face, a thick black mustache and salt and pepper gray hair. His eyes are alight with excitement, though, and he reaches out to Aron. "It is the greatest of honors for Novoro to host a holy Aspect, my Lord of Storms. You are well loved here. I am Secuban, lord of this stronghold and all that dwell within. Let us host you and your servants."

Aron ignores the outstretched hand. "We require private quarters."

"You shall have mine," Lord Secuban says immediately, and doesn't look upset that his handshake was ignored. If anything, he just looks thrilled to see Aron, and the glee on his face makes him look like a freaking fanboy. "You bless all of Novoro with your presence here. We shall celebrate the honor of your company—"

"Later." Aron gives an impatient flick of his cloak. "I wish to go to my chambers and bathe, and my anchor will have needs as well. My soldiers and my concubine"—and this time he gestures at me—"will also need to be quartered close. Our mounts must be taken care of as well."

"Anything," Lord Secuban says fervently. "Anything and everything you desire will be yours."

Aron grunts approval. "Good. Show us in, then."

The lord of Novoro moves to Aron's side and speaks to him in a low voice, giving him a tour as we head inside. Stable boys rush forward to take the reins of our woales, and then Yulenna slips to the ground next to me, pulling her cloak tight.

I'm fascinated by Novoro. This place, more than anything else, looks like something out of a *Game of Thrones* set. The entire place is one big fortress, and inside I expected to see hundreds of little houses tucked behind the walls, but it opens up into a muddy courtyard and then lifts high up into row after row of windows. Everyone lives in the castle carved right out of the rock. Everything's gray, too, and people lean from stone windows and peek out of turrets and watch us. They wear heavy fur-lined cloaks in dark colors, and soldiers are all over the place. Someone leads away our woales, and Solat follows them to get our gear. Aron is led forward by the lord of the place, who talks a mile a minute, eager to share his home and its splendors. People bow as they pass, cloaks flopping onto the wintry cobblestones, and we follow a short distance behind. There's awe and pleasure on the faces of these people—which is a relief. I don't think they'll be betraying Aron, and I start to feel a little better about things.

To my surprise, Yulenna grabs my hand and pulls me close. "Stay with me," she says tightly, and her steps grow faster, as if she wishes to somehow catch up with Aron and the Novoro lord. I speed up, too, wondering what's crawled up her butt. I glance out at the crowd...and then I see it.

They watch Aron with awe and affection all right, but the look they cast in Yulenna's direction—and mine—is a little more...creepy. I catch the eyes of someone in an ornate cloak and the look he gives me is downright lascivious. Another man licks his lips as we walk past, and it doesn't take more than a few more steps before I'm clinging to Yulenna's hand, too. Bunch of creeps. Maybe they don't get out much and so any new woman that walks in gets leered at.

"Aron will protect us," I tell Yulenna. "Don't worry about that."

"He will protect his anchor," she says tightly.

Right. Me and not her. I just squeeze her hand reassuringly, because I'm not going to let these people creep on her.

More and more people arrive, and as the crowd fills out, I'm relieved to see women and children in the crowd, too. They all gaze at us with awe, and I see more than one make Aron's gesture and bow their heads in piety. Even though Aron's a war god, he's well known enough that even the moms and grandmas are fisting his gesture.

At the far end of the courtyard is a massive set of steps flanked with torches, and the lord leads Aron in, so we follow. Once inside, I blink at the low light. The smell of torch-smoke increases, and then as my eyes adjust, I can make out the hall itself. A large chair sits atop a stair-stepped dais at the far end of the room, by a massive fireplace. My skin prickles at the sight of it. Nothing good ever happens in rooms with a dais, I'm learning. They had a dais in Aventine—and tried to murder us. They had a dais in Tadekha's Citadel—and a rampaging army arrived. "Third time's a charm," I tell myself, though my stomach gets sour when I hear the scrape of chains and two slave women peek out from behind the throne. They have cloaks to keep them warm in the drafty keep...but it looks like they're not wearing anything underneath.

Great. This place falls a few more notches in my estimation. Less and less of a fan of Novoro.

Aron gives the throne room a curt look.

"Please, my lord, sit and make yourself at home. Everything I have, I share with you." Lord Secuban's eyes gleam and his gaze flicks to Yulenna, and he licks his lips. "In Novoro, to share brings great honor."

"My mortals are tired and wish to rest," Aron says in that same imperious voice I've grown to know. "I want private quarters for myself and my anchor."

"Of course, of course." Lord Secuban looks nervous, and if he had a hat, he'd wring it like a cartoon sycophant. "Forgive me for not anticipating your needs. This is the first time Novoro has been honored by the gods. Everything you need, it shall be provided. We will give you a place to rest and time to yourself, and tonight, a great feast will be shared. We hope that you will stay for a few days and bless us."

I relax a little. Everyone just wants a blessing from the gods.

I get that. Maybe this place isn't as creepy as I thought it was. They're just the Aos version of backwoods hicks. They don't get out much, they don't see new people, and they don't know how to act. I pat Yulenna's hand.

Nothing at all to worry about.

CHAPTER 48

*a*ron leaves us behind immediately.

"I wish to speak with their priests and scribes, to see if they've received any prophecies," he tells Yulenna as I stand next to her. "I will not be far. Send one of the men if you need anything." He flicks a glance at me and then is gone.

Well, he must feel safe, I think sourly. Never mind that he's arrogance and could be putting all of us in danger. I'll keep those thoughts to myself for now, though, especially since Yulenna is posing as me. With Markos, Vitar and Kerren surrounding us, we're shown to quarters by a serving girl who bows and scrapes and giggles with excitement. The men are shown a room down a great hall, the quarters of Novoro's greatest knight. When they're told they will be staying there for as long as needed, they nod, and then continue to follow Yulenna and me. We're led forward down the same hall, to double doors that are carved with gorgeous symbols of the mountains, and when the doors are flung open, the chamber itself is pure opulence. Heavy drapes hang from the stone walls, and a window is open, showing thick, wavy glass to keep out the cold and revealing a gorgeous view of the mountains. A woman sits near them, and gets to her feet when we arrive.

"My ladies," she says, sinking to the floor in a deep bow and Aron's gesture. "I am told you are Aron's property. This will be your home while you honor Novoro with your presence."

I glance behind us as the doors close, leaving Yulenna and me alone with the woman and the servant girl. Markos and the others are stationed just outside, but I can't shake my unease. Maybe it's because I'm so far away from Aron that I feel a faint tingle humming through my body. This is the first time in a while that he's left my side and I'm not a fan of it. Not one bit.

"Thank you," Yulenna says in her most arch, haughty voice. "This is Faith, Aron's concubine." She gestures at me and then sweeps her cloak off. "We will be staying in this room together, so my lord Aron will not be inconvenienced."

"Of course, the woman says, bowing her head again. "I am Lady Gerline, Lord Secuban's wife and mistress of Novoro. What we have is yours. We will be honored to share with the gods and hope they will share with us in return."

"I'm sure that is for Aron to decide," Yulenna says sweetly.

"You must be tired," Lady Gerline says. "And dirty. Let me have my women draw hot baths for you both and get you fresh clothes."

"Oh," I blurt out. "Our clothes are with the woales—"

"No, honored guest," Lady Gerline continues, putting up her hands. "In Novoro, we share everything with our guests and hope they will honor us in the same fashion. You will wear my finest gowns this night. I imagine they are much warmer than anything you have." And she beams at us, as if the thought of two strangers in her clothes is all she's ever wanted. "You will want to be fresh and pretty for my lord Aron and the feast, will you not? To show him honor?"

Boy, they sure like tossing around the "honor" word. Maybe these people have a cleanliness thing. Yulenna just nods and then Lady Gerline sweeps away, her clothes dusting the cold stone floors. "I will return shortly with my ladies."

"We'll be here," I joke. It could be worse.

The moment they leave, Yulenna turns to me and clutches my hands tightly. "Faith, please don't make me go to the feast."

I'm surprised at her question, but I didn't miss the way the men leered at us as we came in. There's real fear on her pretty face, and coming from someone who's a concubine, I can't imagine that she would get skittish over nothing. "Of course not," I tell her. "You're the anchor of the Lord of Storms as far as they know. You can do what you want."

She shakes her head, her grip on my hands tightening. "They will want me at his side. Or he might give up the lie and tell everyone I am a useless concubine." Her eyes brim with tears. "I am afraid. I do not have the protection of the god's claim on my body like I did before. Please, Faith."

My old friend guilt returns, and I give her hand a reassuring squeeze. "As far as they know, I'm the concubine. If they want Aron to have company, I'll go volunteer to sit at his side and look pretty." I don't point out that I'm secretly glad, because I don't like the thought of Yulenna having to fawn all over Aron at dinner while I sit somewhere nearby. I don't want her to touch him, and I'm startled at my own possessiveness. "Besides, if you hide out up here, they'll probably just think that Aron's protecting his anchor from any that would hurt her."

Her expression brightens, and one perfect tear slips down her perfect cheek. "Do you truly think so?"

"I do. Don't stress, okay? Let's just enjoy a bath and try not to worry too much."

Unfortunately for me, I think about Tadekha's citadel, and how that turned out. I had a bath there after I arrived and then shit went to hell.

I think of how I fondled Aron.

And I think about my dream of Aron earlier today.

Man, that fortune teller was straight up wrong when she said the King of Pentacles was gonna be my lover. I keep offering and he keeps on not taking.

IT'S SO FUCKING nice to get clean I almost forget to be worried. Like in Katharn, there's an old system of pipes running through the Novoro keep, and while the bathroom quarters are shared and not what I'm used to, they're a hell of a lot better than washing in two inches of tepid water in a tub like I did in Katharn. The "bath" is a pool room with hot water and waiting serving girls who wash us with sponges and floral soaps. Yulenna lets them wash her, and since she's the one "in charge" I don't bitch about it, even though I'm creeped out by strangers running wet sponges over my skin.

The hot water helps, though, as does the cleansing wash they put in my hair. When they comb it out for me, it feels clean for the first time in weeks, and I don't even mind that they smooth scented lotion into my skin and rub a gentle, textured stone over my legs that makes the hair disappear as if sanded away. The bath at Novoro gets an A plus as far as I'm concerned.

It gets a little weird when Lady Gerline returns with clothes for us, though.

"Yours are being washed and tended to," she explains with bow after scraping bow. "It is custom for honored guests of Novoro to share, however, and I have brought two of my favorite feast gowns. It would bring great honor to our hall if you would wear them."

Her smile is guileless and sweet, and she looks as if she'd love nothing more than for us to wear her clothes. Weird people. I let her and her servants help me dress, and they help Yulenna at the same time. When I'm "clothed" though, I have concerns. It's a soft, lovely gown, sure. It's the same dark navy shade that is favored by the Novoro people and is thick and warm, with a pretty white fur trim on the hem.

The neckline is open to my waist, though.

So's the slit in the skirt.

I clear my throat gently, a silent question on my lips as I play with the (one, small) tie at the waist that holds it together. "Are we missing a piece?"

"Feast wear is very formal," Lady Gerline says, with a downright devastated look on her face. "Do you not like the dress?"

"It's very nice," I reassure her, and I'm relieved when her expression turns into a smile again. Jesus, you'd think I'd kicked a kitten the way she looked so upset. Someone comes forward with a thick, wide belt, and I relax. Obviously we're not done dressing. Thank goodness.

I lift my arms and remain still as servants cinch my waist in the ornately tooled black leather belt, and my fingers brush over Aron's symbol. They didn't know he was coming, so all the axes etched into this leather means they truly do worship him. It's a good sign. With the belt on, my dress doesn't gape open nearly as far, but the slightest breeze will expose everything in a completely scandalous matter. I tug and fuss at the fur hems, but stop when I see that another woman sweeps down the hall in a gown just like mine. All right, then. When in Rome and all that.

"Let me fix your hair for you," a servant says, and I'm ushered to a padded stool in front of a copper mirror. "Does your lord prefer your hair up or down?"

It's on the tip of my tongue to tell her that he doesn't get a say, but then I remember I'm supposed to be the concubine. "Let's go with up."

"And you, my lady anchor?" Lady Gerline asks Yulenna politely as another waiting woman combs out Yulenna's thick tresses.

"I'll be staying in my chambers this night," she says in an

imperious voice, making it sound as if she's the lady of the castle and not Gerline. "You can have my food sent up here."

Lady Gerline looks shocked. "Oh...but my Lord of Storms must have a companion for the feast. It is tradition." She wrings her hands, distressed.

"The concubine can go," Yulenna says with a flick of her hand and then yawns. "I am weary."

"That's right," I say brightly before Lady Gerline can protest. "Aron's asked for me tonight." And I give her an exaggerated wink.

A look of relief crosses her face. "Very good."

Yulenna retires to the sleeping chambers and I'm left alone with Lady Gerline and the serving maid. Lady Gerline's nervous as she gets ready for the dinner herself, fluttering about as if she's a schoolgirl meeting her first crush. It's strange to see. At least I'm not the only one wearing skimpy clothing. She asks if we have clothes to share with her—it seems that I wear her clothes and she wears mine, which is a weird custom, but I'm learning there's a lot of weird in this land. Most of mine are tunics and men's clothing, which aren't appropriate for a concubine, so I give her one of Yulenna's gowns and hope she doesn't ask too many questions. (I also hope Yulenna doesn't notice.) Lady Gerline seems satisfied when she puts on the gown and it's completely see-through. She fusses with her hair, then applies a pigment to her nipples so they stand out under the gown's sheer fabric.

I avert my eyes and do my best not to stare. When in Rome, I remind myself. When in Rome. I adjust the deep vee of my gown, and I'm glad it covers as much as it does. Sure, one wrong move and I'm going to be tits out, but the girls are covered at least. The slit in the dress is a little worrisome—instead of going up one leg, it goes straight up the middle, following the part of my thighs, and goes practically to my waist. It's like they gave me an overcoat and forgot to give me the garment that goes underneath.

Other than the breezy clothes, so far these people have been nice and welcoming. Just because I had a bad experience at Tadekha's citadel doesn't mean this place is going to turn into an orgy. Maybe the men like eye candy while they eat.

The serving woman pulls my hair into a tight knot atop my head and shows me a series of pots that contain makeup. It's not the usual foundation-highlighter-powder-blush-etc. routine that I'm used to. There's a pot of color for lips (or, ahem, nipples), several pots of darker powders that must be eye shadows, and a carved stick that applies the darker stuff to lashes. I use it all sparingly, because I don't want to look like a clown, but I also don't want to insult my hostesses. When I've got the barest hints of color on my face, I get beaming looks of approval from the women, and then we sit and wait for dinner.

Lady Gerline shifts and adjusts her clothing over and over again, clearly nervous. It's not a bad nervous, though, but one of excitement. She keeps looking at the door with a smile and giggles to herself now and then.

"Newlywed?" I ask, smiling.

She just tilts her head and gives me a curious look. "Lord Secuban and I have been wedded since I was twelve."

Well. A lover, then. My smile turns over-bright and I hope fervently dinner starts soon.

Eventually, a manservant comes to retrieve us and Lady Gerline is all giggles once more, smoothing her borrowed dress and fussing with her hair. Admittedly, she looks great. She's about my age if not a few years older, with thick dark hair. She's got fantastic tits that are outlined to magnificence in the sheer dress. A purple girdle cinches her waist to a ridiculous, exaggerated amount and she looks impressive even to my unknowledgeable eyes. Whoever she's meeting at dinner is sure to be pleased.

The manservant gestures that we should follow him, and I give my gown one last tug and then hold the bodice closed with one hand and the skirts closed with the other as I follow Lady Gerline to the hallway. I'm not surprised that Kerren falls into step behind me, with Markos and Vitar staying behind to guard Yulenna. Poor Kerren—his cheeks are bright red and his gaze is stiffly ahead, as if boobies will turn him to stone if he so much as looks in our busty, busty direction. We head down a long flight of stone stairs and then down another hall. I can hear a low murmur of voices as we approach the banquet, and a nervous flutter starts in my stomach.

I wonder what Aron'll think of my dress. It's been a while since I looked pretty and the last time...

Damn it. Someday I'm going to stop thinking of Tadekha's citadel. Someday.

CHAPTER 49

*T*he doors to the banquet hall are opened and I'm surprised to see that everyone jumps to their feet, gazing in our direction. Everyone except Aron, of course. He remains seated in his throne on the dais, his cool eyes watching everything. Lord Secuban rises, and if I thought Lady Gerline was excited, her husband looks as if he's about to lose control with eagerness. He looks at his wife proudly, and then his gaze moves to me with approval before he turns to Aron and puts his hand over his heart. He's brimming with enthusiasm and as I look around the room, it's full of men who seem just as eager.

Wow, these people must really love a feast.

My stomach growls, reminding me that I, too, love a feast, and some of my nervousness slides away. I ease a hand from the bodice of my dress, and when no boobs come flying out, I let it go so I can walk properly. I notice Aron is watching me, and my shoulders straighten a little. I can feel the heat of his gaze—his and a hundred other men in the room—as I walk next to Lady Gerline. She takes my hand in hers and leads me toward the dais, where Lord Secuban and Aron are waiting for us, and as we swan through the room, delicious smells hit.

There are roasted meats and something cheesy cooking, and I smell fruit and something sweet. My mouth waters, and I decide tonight is going to be amazing. If these people throw half as good of a feast as they do a welcome, we're in for a treat.

The closer we get to the dais, the more Lady Gerline begins to tremble. Her hand is sweaty in mine, and when I look over at her, she's blinking rapidly, a fine sheen of perspiration on her face. Wow, she really is nervous, though she's still smiling with pleasure and it seems genuine. Even so, I start to get a sense of unease. I glance around the room, looking at the people gathered. I don't see weapons anywhere, or armor…but there's definitely a lot of men in the room and they're all staring at us as if we're the buffet.

Granted, we do have boobs for miles, so that might be it, but it's still unsettling. I'm not sure what to think, and I don't blame Yulenna for not wanting to come down. Aron will protect me, but it's hard to say if he'll do the same for her.

She bows, and so I do too, though mine is more of a curtsy so my dress doesn't spill open. When we straighten, she looks at her husband with bright, shining eyes, and then to me. All right. I turn to Aron, smile, and take a step forward.

Lord Secuban frowns, putting a hand out. "Did my wife not speak to you of our customs?"

I turn to look at Lady Gerline, who has an equally puzzled look on her face. "She said you guys share everything?" This seems like a weird place to talk about clothing, but maybe I'm supposed to thank them for the swap? "The clothes are nice. Thank you."

He smiles, and then it turns into full-fledged laughter. He glances over at Aron, amused. "Your concubine has amazing wit."

"She does," Aron says. That's all he says, his expression impossible to read. He hasn't moved from the throne, and he looks for a moment as remote and ominous as the first night I met him. A little shiver creeps up my spine.

"It is tradition in Novoro to honor guests by sharing all that we have with them," Lord Secuban agrees, inclining his head slightly. "We will give you and your party all that you ask for. New clothes, fresh food, weapons, anything you need, it shall be yours. We only ask that you share your blessings in return."

Aron's eyes narrow, his gaze focused on Novoro's lord.

I'm still not following his meaning. "I...okay?" I gesture at Aron. "Should I not sit with him at dinner, then?" I keep my voice to a low whisper so I don't embarrass anyone. "I'm not sure what you're getting at."

"We share our bounty with the gods, and we hope that the gods share their bounties with us," Lady Gerline whispers, her words pointed. She licks her lips, smooths her hands down the front of her dress—Yulenna's dress—and then sinks to her knees in front of Aron, putting her forehead to the floor. "It will be the greatest honor for Novoro to share with you, Lord Aron."

Er.

I blink. I'm starting to get an idea of what they mean by sharing, and surely...surely I'm wrong. I look at Aron, and his eyes are tight, his mouth a thin line of disapproval as Lady Gerline lifts her head and then crawls over to his leg and touches it with her hand, practically fawning over him.

Lord Secuban waits, watching me.

They...have to be joking.

Share me? I look around the room with horror, at the lascivious, leering faces of the men in the hall. Their gross, leering stares suddenly make sense, and I clutch at the deep neck of the gown. No fucking way. Secuban thinks he gets me...does everyone else, too? Is that why're they're all piled in to the feast hall so eagerly? It's not for the food?

Yulenna was right to hide upstairs. I should have, too. No

wonder Lady Gerline freaked out and insisted one of us had to come down. One of us had to be the sacrificial lamb. Fuck.

Lord Secuban moves forward and reaches out to take my arm.

Before I can jerk away, Aron's cold voice cuts through the room. "If you touch her, it will be the last thing you do."

A hush falls through the room. Thunder crackles overhead and my ears pop with the force of the sudden storm. A headache stabs between my eyes, too. Lady Gerline cowers at Aron's feet, but she doesn't move away. No one moves at all.

Lord Secuban recovers first. He bows to Aron, his expression one of confusion. "My lord, I thought you brought your concubine as a gift to share with those of us in Novoro. It is tradition—"

"I do not give a fuck what your tradition is. That one belongs to me." Aron points at me, and the air practically crackles. I'm gleeful at his defiant claim.

"But—"

Aron turns his wrathful gaze on Lord Secuban. "Did you not hear me?" He leans forward, his hands clenching the arms of the throne, and there's so much electrical energy building that my hair is starting to float around my head. Oh Jesus. I've never seen Aron this angry.

And it's all because they want to share me. I'm a little stunned, because in the past, Aron's made it clear that mortals are expendable and not on the same level as he is.

Lord and Lady Novoro drop to their knees. "Tradition—" Lord Secuban begins.

I swear, the man does not know when to shut up. I step forward, moving to Aron's side. There's a little pillow at his feet where I guess a good slave girl is supposed to sit, but fuck that. I slip into Aron's lap, and I'm relieved when he lets me and then puts a possessive hand on my hip. "Aron is the Lord of Storms,"

I tell them. "He does what he wants. If he doesn't feel like sharing, he doesn't feel like sharing. End of story."

"I do not feel like sharing," Aron says, biting out each word furiously. "I would rather raze this place to the ground and salt the earth." His hand tightens on my hip and he pulls me closer, until I'm practically astride his big lap.

Woo, all righty then. "Let's not salt anything," I say, keeping my tone conciliatory. "I'm sure they didn't mean to offend. It's just a difference in customs."

Lord Secuban sits up, rocking back on his heels. His face is pale, grave with the realization of his insult. "Simply bless us, my Lord of Storms, and we will be your army."

"I need no army," Aron tells him arrogantly. "I need nothing from any of you. If I left now and burned this place to the ground, it would change nothing."

Gerline quivers, her forehead still to the floor. Lord Secuban's mouth works, opening and then shutting silently. I look around the room and see everyone is silent, from the knights to the serving women. Off in a corner, I see Secuban's slave women curled up in the laps of other lords, and one of the maids stands between two men, frozen, their hands on her. The plates on the long tables are only one for every two people, same with the goblets. It's clear that sharing is part of the culture here.

It's also clear that Aron hate, hate, *hates* the idea. I can tell by the change of the pressure in the air, the hallmark of one of Aron's temperamental storms. My head throbs in response to the sudden onset of weather, too.

I see Markos and Vitar out of the corner of my eye. Their faces are tense, their hands at their sword belts, ready to act. Aron might be fine if he fights his way out of here, and me too—but what about our people? What about Yulenna, who's cowering upstairs?

"Aron," I murmur quietly, and put a hand on his chest. I lean in and whisper in his ear, his nearness threatening to distract me. "I don't think they meant to offend you. Let's bring it down a notch, okay? No one's going to touch me but you. I promise."

His eyes blaze at me for a long, silent moment, and I feel as trapped under his outrage as the others do. I don't dare breathe, my hand still on his chest. When he continues to remain silent, the air practically crackling around us, I rub my thumb against the fabric of his new tunic, just over his heart, and arch an eyebrow at him.

The terrible tension in him seems to ease a bit. His hand relaxes on my waist, and Aron gives a curt nod.

"Why don't we just enjoy the celebration of your arrival?" I ask, sliding my hand up and down his chest like a good, flirty concubine would. It's not a hardship.

Aron's hard dual-colored gaze rests on me, and he nods, slowly. "If you like."

Why not. We're already here and I worry that if we leave now, we'll make everyone angry enough to hunt us down. I've had enough of that. If I have to spend an awkward evening at a feast, I'd rather do that. "I would like," I tell him, smiling. "I'm sure Markos and the others would, too."

He leans in closer, his voice low. "You know I care nothing for them."

For some reason, I get goosebumps. Maybe it's the way he says it—as if it's a caress and not a statement of an arrogant god. Whatever it is, it makes me shiver. I keep smiling and turn towards the lord and lady, who are watching us. "No one touches anything of Aron's, and we'll stay."

"Of course," Lord Secuban says, dipping low to touch his forehead to the floor again. "Of course, my lord. Whatever you desire, it shall be. We are simply honored to host you."

Aron grunts.

I pat his chest again and glance over at the lord. "Eat and

celebrate," I tell him with an encouraging smile, trying to smooth things over.

Lady Gerline lifts her head, her body trembling. She looks at the pillow at Aron's feet, then at me, and I can practically see the wheels turning in her head. No wonder she's been giggling like a schoolgirl and so nervous about the feast. If sharing is the big custom here, she probably thought I'd be boinking her husband and all his buddies, and she'd get to fuck Aron.

For some reason, that makes me feel incredibly possessive. I tighten my hand on his shirt and slide a little closer to him, as if I can lay claim on the man. Her gaze meets mine and she watches me for a moment, then composes herself and sits down on the pillow at her husband's feet. Her expression is tight, as if she's miserable and doing her best not to show it. I feel a little guilty knowing that her evening was ruined and she's probably been shamed in front of her people...but only a little.

Fuck all this sharing crap.

"Do you need a chair?" Aron asks, his hand sliding to my bare hip. My legs are tossed over his thighs, and I realize belatedly that my skirt has fallen open, exposing most of my calves and thighs to everyone in the room. "Say the word and I will have them get you one."

I think for a moment and then pretend to adjust Aron's collar. He's wearing a new tunic, this one of a pale, cream-colored weave with deep red knotwork on the edges. "Can I stay here? With you?"

He nods and then glares at the lord of Novoro over my shoulder as the man takes his seat.

"I am sorry, my Lord of Storms," Secuban stammers, because the man clearly does not know when to shut up. "It is just...you are the god of battle. I thought blood would be the only thing you thirst for—"

Before he can finish, Aron puts a hand on the nape of my

neck and pulls me in. His mouth crashes against mine and the spark slams between us, sending a shockwave through my body.

I'm stunned. This is the first time Aron's kissed me, really kissed me. At first I think it's just more pretending, him trying to convince the others that I'm really his concubine. But then his tongue slides between my parted lips, teasing me, and hot need such as I've never felt before comes crashing through me. Aron is...a really good kisser. I mean, he's a god, so of course he should be, but I'm still taken by surprise. His arrogance bleeds through the caress of his mouth on mine, and what starts out as simply a press of lips becomes a conquest. Within moments, he's slicking his mouth over mine, as if he's hungry and I'm the only thing he wants. Over and over, he kisses me so deeply until I'm lost to everything around us. My body is humming with need and when he pulls his mouth from mine, not only do I lose the taste of him but I lose that delicious electric tingle between us.

I whimper a protest.

"Faith," Aron murmurs, cupping my jaw. He studies me, my swollen lips and heaving chest, and plants a hand firmly over one of my breasts, cupping it and teasing the hard nipple with his thumb. As he does, he casts a defiant look over at Lord Secuban. "Do not tell me what a god hungers for, mortal. You know nothing at all."

I cling to Aron, doing my best not to squirm on his lap. It seems that Lord Secuban isn't the only one that knows nothing at all, because I'm totally stunned at the kiss, and at the possessive hand that still teases my nipple, driving me mad with aching hunger. If he just wanted to show them I was his slave girl, his concubine, all he had to do was smack my ass and tell me to sit on the floor, and I'd have done it.

That was not a pretend kiss.

That was not a pretend anything.

CHAPTER 50

reathless, I do my best not to stare at him as people settle into their seats and music begins. The feast starts around us, women carrying dishes to the table and pouring wine. Someone discreetly sets a small table next to Aron's throne and sets two cups of wine out. Minutes pass, and Aron simply watches the crowd, not saying a thing. I have no idea what's going through the god's head, but there's very little going through mine. I'm too stuck on the memory of his mouth on mine, the feel of his tongue as he conquered my mouth.

The hand on my breast that still teases my nipple through my clothing, as if I'm just his plaything.

"A plate, my lord? My lady?" a girl asks, stepping forward, her eyes shining and eager to please.

My stomach growls, and I look at the feast table. It's practically dripping with delicious things and the people here seem to have forgotten all about Aron and their leader and are settling in to feast. I'm hungry, and I nod at her.

"I should eat," I murmur to Aron, and try to stand up.

He immediately pulls me back down into his lap, my butt pressing back against him. His hand slips into the deep vee of my dress and then he's teasing my nipple with callused fingers against my bare skin, and I nearly orgasm. "You're staying here," he murmurs, and nips at my ear.

Oh fuck. I squeeze my eyes shut, wondering if it's rude to climax in front of strangers. A chilling thought hits me, and I lean back against him, resting my head on his shoulder so I can lean in and whisper. "Aron, is there another Aspect nearby? Hedonism?"

That would explain all of this.

He gives my nipple a light, teasing pinch, and I bite back another whimper. "No," he murmurs, low enough for just me to hear, and he says nothing more.

But he doesn't take his hands off me either.

Oh god, I don't know what to think. I'm practically writhing in his lap by the time the girl returns with food, so aroused I can hardly stand it. In Tadekha's citadel, he touched me because I was affected by her nearness, and he was, too. If there's no hedonism Aspect nearby, what's behind this? A sudden image of Bad Aron fucking Yulenna against the tree flashes through my mind.

Gods have needs just like anyone else. And as I shift my weight on his lap, I can feel the hard, erect length of him pressing against my backside.

He's not immune to all of this. Not by a long shot. I want to turn around and look at him, to ask him what he's feeling, but the music swells and then the serving girl sets a plate of food down, and my mouth floods with saliva.

I'm starving.

I reach up and touch Aron's jaw. "I'm going to eat now," I murmur to him. "And unless you find it sexy for me to get distracted and dribble food all over myself because you keep playing with my nipples, you'll let go of me."

He throws his head back and laughs, and the music players miss a note. The conversation swells after a moment, and Aron gives my breast one last proprietary squeeze before releasing it. "You stay here," he tells me, keeping an arm locked around my waist. As if he's just now remembering where we're at, he glances over at Lord Secuban as I pick up my wine goblet. "How big is Novoro's army?" he asks, tone mild.

The lord of the keep wastes no time in announcing numbers. I don't pay any attention to what he's saying, because it's already clear to me that Aron has no interest in having these people be his army. He's just toying with the guy while I'm occupied. I take a couple of bites of food...and moan. Holy fuck, these people can make some amazing dishes. Everything has a wealth of delicate spices that make even the most basic vegetables incredible. I take a bite out of everything and nibble on some buttery, fresh-baked bread. It's all delicious, and I lick my fingers as I eat while Aron talks to Lord Secuban. Lady Gerline sits on the pillow at her husband's feet, but she's not eating. She looks rather defeated, her shoulders slumped. And when she looks over at me, I can see the jealousy in her eyes.

Tough titty.

I feel another possessive stab at the thought of another woman touching Aron. I don't like the idea at all. She can sit on her pillow and pout, I decide as I eat another mouthful of bread. I watch the rest of the room as I pack away the food, ignoring the astonished looks that the serving girls give me as I clear my plate and another is put before me. They'll figure out soon enough that my appetite isn't human. Until then, they can just keep bringing the food. I chew on a bit of chicken—at least, it tastes like chicken—and glance down the hall. The enormous tables are full of people sitting shoulder to shoulder on the long benches, and the conversation's turned boisterous now that Aron's relaxed. Serving girls flit between men, all wearing the practically open dress like the one I've borrowed. They seem to enjoy the clothing, though. As I watch, one brunette deliberately leans over far to fill someone's wine, and as she does, her breasts are exposed by the deep vee of the gown. One of the men reaches forward and fondles her breast as if it's part of the meal, and I stiffen.

The girl just laughs, grabs him by his hair and gives him a fierce kiss, and then moves down the row to fill someone else's cup.

Well, they did say these people were weird.

Music starts, and a new course of delicious things is brought out. I try a few of the sweets and then give up, holding my overflowing belly.

"Sated?" Aron asks, his arm moving around my waist and pulling me back when a servant clears my plate.

I shiver, because he didn't ask if I was full. He asked if I was *sated* and that feels like it has a billion different meanings, all of them filthy. "I'm good for now." I put my hand over his and lean back against him, relaxing and listening to the music as Lord Secuban discusses defenses of his keep and how much more defensible it is than the Citadel, which rumor has told him has fallen to Aventine's army. I notice Aron doesn't confirm anything, so I don't speak up, either. Let him wonder.

Plates are cleared away and I watch the servants work. No one's getting up from the tables, and as I scan the room, I see the men are getting handsier and handsier with the girls, tugging on their clothing as they pass by and grabbing at boobs and butts. One girl mock-spills into someone's lap and then she's all flustered giggles as the man buries his face in her practically exposed breasts. I'm a little scandalized when their seat neighbor joins in, kissing the girl and slipping a hand under her skirt.

It occurs to me that no one's looking at this as unnatural. It also occurs to me that there aren't any children at this party.

Sure enough, the man stands up, pushing the girl forward on the now-cleared table. He leans over her and starts pumping while everyone else around cheers and calls out encouragement.

The girl just laughs and reaches for the man sitting across the table, as if one guy isn't enough. I watch in horrified fascination as the man blasts into her quickly and shudders a scant minute later. His buddy taps him on the shoulder and then the guy offers her to his friend, and number two takes his turn on the girl.

I really hope that's not rape.

I don't think it is, though. The women spill back into the room, full of smiles and head for the men. The tables turn into a sea of arms and entwined limbs, and more than one person is piled on in each group.

"Enjoying the view?" Aron asks, stroking my side. His fingers brush against my breast and I feel that hot shudder of need rip through me.

I just shake my head. "Goddamn it, Aron, does every party have to be a fucking orgy?"

Laughter rumbles through him. "I take it mortals in your world celebrate differently?"

"Uh, yeah, we usually just like beer." I shake my head. "This is just fucked up."

"Why?" he asks, and tips a finger under my chin to make me meet his gaze. "They are happy. They celebrate my arrival and hope for a blessing."

"Oh, so you're cool with this as long as they don't touch your toys?" I retort. "Is that how we play?"

He arches an eyebrow at me in the same annoying way I normally do to him. "If they wish to fuck Markos or Yulenna, I do not care. They can fuck all of my soldiers at once for all I care. They are just not allowed to touch you."

And just like that, my irritation vanishes, quickly replaced by hot lust. I remember his hand on my breast from earlier, the way he held on as if I belonged to him.

As if I were his personal property.

"But you're allowed to touch me?" I ask, my voice a mere whispered tease.

He just gives me that lazy, confident smile that tells me everything I need to know. One hand strokes over my belly, and for a moment, I don't care that we're in a room full of people. I want him to push his hand under the opening in my skirt and touch me until I come.

Aron doesn't, though. He just slides his hand to my breast, holding me and branding me as his possession, and turns to Lord Secuban. "You have won my approval for now. My party will be here for a few days before moving on. I expect supplies and for my servants to be treated with the utmost respect."

"Of course!" Lord Secuban's practically gushing with delight.

"My men will need new armor and weapons, and my women will need clothing."

"You shall be given everything and anything you need, my great Lord of Storms," Secuban declares, and there's such shining excitement on his face that I can't hate the guy or his weird people. He snaps his fingers and one of his chained slaves —the naked ones—comes forward and he pulls her into his lap, as if he can truly party now that Aron's pleased.

I just shake my head and drink more wine. I think if there's another party like this one, I might pull a Yulenna and stay upstairs, too. Then I frown, remembering how they were going to give Aron some lap candy.

Nah, maybe not. I need to come down and stake my claim, much as I'm not a fan of public orgies. I glance around. Yup, they're all still fucking. At least the women look like they're having a great time and don't mind being railed by several guys at once. I guess if it's normal for you to expect that, it doesn't seem so weird.

Still weird to me, though.

I look for Markos, Solat and Vitar—they're at the table closest to the door, and the expression on Markos's face looks like he's sucking on a lemon as a female gyrates in the lap of a man nearby. Solat has a girl in his arms, his face buried in her cleavage. Guess he's right at home. Vitar's tossing back wine and trying not to look as uncomfortable as he clearly feels.

I wonder if this world has such a thing as hazard pay, because these guys clearly deserve it. Well, not Solat. He's having too good a time.

But then Aron absently moves his hand over my breast in a casual caress and I'm lit up with need all over again. I squirm in his lap, the hot bar of his erection pressing against my backside. "You're doing that on purpose," I tell him, accusing.

I just get another lazy, heated smile, as if he loves torturing me like this.

I kind of love it, too. I know I shouldn't, but…when in Rome and all that.

CHAPTER 51

By the time the party winds down, I've drunk several jugs of wine, probably eaten an entire cake all on my own, and I'm so aroused and horny that I can barely walk back to the quarters I'm supposed to share with Yulenna. Aron keeps an arm firmly around my shoulders as we head up the stairs, flanked by Markos and the others. Lady Gerline cast a few longing looks in Aron's direction, but I'm pleased that he completely and utterly ignored her. As far as he's concerned, she doesn't exist.

We head up to Yulenna's chamber, the one the anchor's supposed to be sharing with Aron. There are a few guards in the hall, but Aron glares at all of them until they make a hasty exit, and then it's only Kerren at the door.

Aron glances at the four men, his arm still locked possessively around my shoulders. "This chamber is going to be mine and Faith's alone. No one is to enter without my express permission. You can wake us at dawn. No earlier."

Markos's face turns bright red again and he gives Aron a crisp salute. "Of course, my lord. No one will disturb you or your anch…ah, female."

Solat and Vitar try to hide their grins, while Kerren manages to keep a straight face. It's obvious what's going through their heads, though. They saw Aron groping me all night. Now they're all going to think we're fucking.

Wait, *are* we fucking? I'm flustered at the thought, but even so, my nipples are hard and my body pulses with awareness of Aron's big frame and the crackling energy that surges through his body to mine. His casually possessive touches all night have me totally primed and ready, and I admit that if I had panties, they would have slid off my legs hours ago, too soaked to stay on.

Aron nods at them, and then heads down the hall with me. Before we can even get to the door, Yulenna is there, covered in my cloak, her satchel in her arms. She gives us a little bow and then scurries down the hall to where Kerren and the others are waiting. She must have heard…or she guessed. Either way, some of my guilt disappears at the thought of kicking her out of her room. Clearly she's been expecting it all along.

That means it's just me and Aron and a great big bed.

We enter Lady Gerline's private chambers—now our chambers for as long as we're visiting. There's a warm fire in the hearth, and a covered dish on a table next to an ewer of wine. I ignore all of it, though, flustered and heated with need. Is Aron going to touch me? Kiss me again? Or is he waiting for me to make the first move? I look over at him, but he heads toward the bed, undoing his sword belt and pulling off his new clothing.

I lick my dry lips, my pulse pounding. "Do you want me to get naked, too?" My voice is breathless with arousal.

"No." The bastard gives me an inscrutable look.

That…isn't what I expected to hear. "No?"

He shakes his head. "I will not be touching you again this night. It would be a mistake."

I stiffen in outrage. "So what was that out there? Just a show? Was your dick hard just for show, too?"

Aron just glares at me, as if I'm bringing up stuff he'd rather not talk about right now. Well, I don't give a fuck what he wants. I'm hurt that he's all over me all night—I can still feel the heat of his hand under my dress—and then the moment the door closes, he goes cold again. For a moment, I think about all the people downstairs, still fucking and swapping partners like it's no big deal. They're having a grand time. I consider telling Aron I'm going to go down there and join them, but it's the last thing I want.

I thought before tonight that I wanted to be left alone. Now I know that's not the truth—I want Aron to touch me. I want him to give in to this crazy attraction that we've been fighting. I'm ready for it. I'm ready for more of his touch. I've wanted him for what seems like forever. I don't care that he's a god, or that he's arrogance personified. He's Aron and my traveling companion, friend, and protector. I want the guy.

Powerfully.

"Fine," I tell him when he says nothing. I move to the bed and toss aside the wide belt that cinches my dress closed. It gapes open and I undo the one small tie holding it together, and then shuck it, too. I'm completely naked in front of him, and while we've bathed in front of each other several times, it feels different tonight. Tonight, my breasts are tight with need, my nipples aching from his caresses. Tonight, my pussy's flooded with wetness, and he's going to ignore all of that.

And it's killing me.

His hard gaze sweeps over my body, and he arches an eyebrow at my nudity, as if quietly asking if this is some sort of ploy. It's not, though. It's more like a "fuck you."

I shake my head and get into bed, pulling the covers up to my chin and turning my back to him.

"You wear no nightclothes," he points out, and the bed sinks with his weight behind me.

"Yeah, well, they didn't give me any," I tell him. "So just keep your hands to yourself while I sleep if it bugs you." Normally he puts his hands on my waist and holds me against him as I sleep, and I'm desperately hoping he'll do it anyhow. If he's so immune to everything my nudity shouldn't matter, should it?

"You're angry," he says, and I can't tell if it's a statement or a question.

I thump the pillow and stare at the wall, even though his presence is looming behind me, larger than life. There's a knot in my throat that I can't quite shake, and I swallow a few times before I give up and speak anyhow. "You didn't have to kiss me like it meant something," I whisper.

"No one said it did not mean anything."

I turn around and sit up to look at him. The blankets fall to my waist, and I'm rather viciously pleased to see that his gaze flicks to my naked breasts before going back to my face. His arms are crossed over his massive chest, and the expression on his face is hard and unyielding as ever.

But that's not the only part of him that's hard. Even through the skirted part of his tunic, his cock bulges against his clothing, making it obvious that he's affected.

Good. I want him to be affected. I want him to be as aching with need as I am.

"Faith," Aron says, and his voice is softer and gentler than I've ever heard it. "You are my anchor. I must protect you from everything if I am to ensure that we both return to our proper places. I cannot become distracted."

My nipples feel like they get even harder at his tone, and I arch my back just a little, letting him get a good look at what he's missing out on. "And you think I'm distracting?"

"A mortal liaison would be distracting."

I don't like how vague he's trying to make that. I slip a hand to my breast, thumbing my finger over my nipple and sure enough, his gaze flicks there again and his mouth tightens. "But am *I* distracting?"

"You always distract me, Faith." The air practically crackles around us and shivers with intensity, like it did downstairs. If anything, his gaze is more intense than ever before.

"Good," I tell him, and lie back down, tugging the covers back up. "I'm glad both of us are going to bed with blue balls."

He chuckles, and the sound is low and delicious and oh, it makes me wet all over again. "I do not know what that means, but I can guess."

"It's unfair," I tell him, and slide my hand between my thighs, a wicked idea occurring to me. "I guess I'll just touch myself to ease the problem—"

"If you do, I will tie your hands to the bedposts," he warns.

I raise my hand out from under the blanket and give him the finger, instead. "You suck."

Aron just laughs again. "Go to sleep, Faith."

Oh sure, like I'm just supposed to turn things on and off like a switch. I fight back my irritation and close my eyes, trying to ignore the throbbing heat between my thighs and the nearness of the man I want so badly. The man that won't touch me, despite the endless sexual tension building between us.

At least it explains why he had such a hard-on at Tadekha's citadel and never touched me. Mortal liaisons are *distracting*.

He doesn't know the half of it. If he thinks I've been distracting so far, he hasn't seen anything yet. I vow to be the most frustrating, distracting, cock-tease of a mortal that this world has ever seen. Aron has needs like any other man. I'm going to break him down, make him realize he's torturing himself over nothing.

And when he snaps, it's going to be glorious.

CHAPTER 52

*P*roject Tease begins the next morning.

When I wake up, Aron is distant, already distracted with his plans for the day. He glances over me to assess my mood. "Are you angry about last night?" he asks as he dresses.

"Me? Nah." I yawn. "You're the one in charge. I'm just the lowly mortal."

That makes him pause. One eyebrow goes up. "You are the mortal, but I also know you, Faith."

I wave a hand, indicating he should leave. "We'll talk about it some other time. Go do your thing."

Aron studies me for a moment and then puts his belt on, heavily decorated with daggers and the like. "I want you and the other girl to keep up the pretense."

"Yulenna?"

He shrugs. "Whatever her name is."

All right, I shouldn't be such a gleeful bitch that he can't remember her name...but I am. "She's the anchor and I'm the concubine. Got it."

"Stay in these apartments until I return."

"Did we say 'concubine' or did we say 'prisoner'?" I ask lightly.

He just gives a shake of his head. "I knew you were still angry. Faith, do not test me on this. As you saw last night, these people have very set customs. I will be extremely cross if I find you gone and in some other mortal fool's bed all because you did not listen to me."

Well, that would make me pretty cross, too. "Is he a hot fool?" I ask, though, and my toes curl when Aron looks over at me with a vicious frown. "Don't worry. I won't go anywhere. I might be pissy but I'm not an idiot. I have no desire to be shared with half the fucking city like they think I should be. Your concubine is going to take a nap." I fluff my pillow and turn away, forcing another yawn. "And tell them to send up breakfast. Lots of it."

I wait to see if he's going to say anything else, but Aron is quiet. After a long, tense moment, he leaves the room and the door shuts behind him.

I roll onto my back and glare up at the ceiling. So Aron doesn't want to play with his toys...but he doesn't want anyone else to play with them either. I'm not going to let him sit me on some shelf, though, and only acknowledge me when he needs to show off in front of others. We're a team. That won't change if we sleep together. I run a hand down my front, palming my naked breast and thinking of his hand last night. Hot shivers move through me and I remember the heat in his gaze, the way the air crackled so ferociously as if we were about to be struck by lightning where we stood.

God, that thrill of danger should not have been as sexy as it was. But it's arousing because it went with Aron's heated looks, Aron's possessive touches, Aron's big hands all over my body as he declared in front of the world that I was his. That I was his alone.

Project Tease is definitely a go, I decide.

I jump up from bed and throw on a robe that's hanging from a hook. It's of a soft weave and not all that modest, so I'm guessing Lady Gerline dresses like a castle ho on the regular. Maybe women are just showpieces to these men after all. Great. All the more reason to stay in the apartments like Aron suggested. I might be angry at him, but like I said, I'm not stupid. I know this world isn't safe like my own, and I don't know that I'd be all that safe dressed like this in *my* world, either.

But if I'm not leaving the apartments, anything goes.

So I wrap the robe tightly around me, hiding all my girl bits despite the wispy fabric, and move to the door. I crack it open a hair and I'm not entirely surprised to see Solat and Kerren out there. I peer out and clear my throat to get their attention.

Both turn. Kerren gives a bow but Solat only grins knowingly.

"No bowing," I whisper. "I'm the concubine, remember?"

Kerren blushes. "Of course." He straightens, looking like an overgrown schoolboy in leather armor. "What can we get for you?"

"Where's Aron?"

"Lord Secuban was waiting for him. They are touring the keep."

"Showing off," Solat adds lazily. "Probably still trying to convince Lord Aron that he should be his army."

"Ugh. Aron doesn't want an army." I don't point out that he barely wants them around. "Did he send up breakfast?"

"It will be here shortly," Kerren says, and almost bows again but stops himself. "Can we get you anything else?"

"Yulenna," I say. "And some servants that are good with hair and makeup. Aron doesn't want me going out so I'm going to have a spa day."

"A what day?"

"Never mind. Basically I'm going to do my hair and take hot baths and other girly shit. Are you guys on guard duty all day?"

"We are proud to serve," Kerren says stiffly, even as Solat stifles a yawn. They both look tired.

"Where's Markos?"

"With my Lord Aron."

"And Vitar?"

"He is guarding Yulenna's apartments—"

"Cool, let's condense things then. You guys look tired. Bring her here and you three trade off watching the door. One of you can come in and nap in between shifts. There's an extra cot in here," I tell them, pointing off to the side. I'm guessing that's for bed guests of all kinds. Yeesh, Novoro, turn it down a notch.

They hesitate, glancing at each other.

"You'll all three still be guarding, right? We'll be safer than ever if we're together. And if Aron gives you any shit, you were following my orders."

That convinces them. Kerren heads down the hall to go retrieve Vitar and Yulenna, and Solat gives me a flirty grin. "You're good to us, lady."

"Faith. And I have a soft heart, what can I say?"

"Invitingly soft," he says, his smile growing wider.

I put a hand up. "I'm going to stop you there, Solat, because we both know Aron would neuter you in a heartbeat if he heard you were flirting with me. I'm sure you want to keep your balls."

Even though it's difficult to tell in the shadowy corridor, I'm pretty sure he pales. "An excellent reminder, thank you."

I give him a little nod and smile. "Save it for Yulenna if you want to flirt with anyone." Even if I was interested, his mouth was on as many women as he could possibly manhandle last night, and that's just gross.

Plus...he's not Aron.

The lord of storms might be ruining me for all men in the future.

◇

IT'S the laziest day I've spent since I arrived in this world. I don't leave the rooms, and staff bring up delicate sweet treats and fine wines for us to feast on. I eat my weight in candied fruits as servants massage my limbs and rub scented oils into my skin. My hair is washed, trimmed, braided, and perfumed. It sounds amazing, but there have been so many awful days since I arrived in this land that I can't even relax for this. I keep one eye on the door and watch every new person that comes in suspiciously. I keep a small dagger (meant to cut food) under my thigh at every moment, just in case someone decides to murder me. Yulenna relaxes and enjoys every last moment as if it's her due, though. She bosses around the servants and picks through the clothing brought for her as if she's lived this sort of life for all her years.

And she flirts. Lord, how she flirts. She flirts with Solat. She flirts with the male servants that empty out the bathwater. She flirts with anything that enters the room and has a penis. I just watch her with amusement, wondering if she's trying to secure her future or she just genuinely likes men that much. It's clear she's in her element, though.

Not me. I feel like a fish out of water as I always do, constantly out of place and not sure what to do with myself. Oddly enough, I wish Aron was here to talk to. He'd say some snippy, arrogant shit that would remind me that even when he's a dick, he's still kind of fun to be around. We'd share a smile over something. More than anything, he'd understand if I complained about feeling out of place.

He knows what that feels like, after all.

"Did you bring in the concubine's new dresses?" Yulenna asks in an imperious voice when the servants bring another round of food. I shove a nut-covered pastry into my mouth, licking my fingers as she turns and gives the servants an angry look. "Haven't we asked for our clothes? Repeatedly? She needs them so she can be ready to greet our lord of storms when he returns to our chambers this evening."

"I'm sorry, revered anchor," a female maidservant stammers to Yulenna. "We were told to bring the clothes, but then you asked for more food and—"

"And now the food is here, and we still need the clothes." She looks down her nose at the woman. "Go and retrieve them."

"Right away, revered anchor." The servant drops into a quick bobbing curtsy and then races out the door.

"Laying it on a little thick, aren't we?" I murmur to Yulenna, who just gives me an impish grin. "I mean, she's got a point. I did ask for more food. Whatever these little nutty things are, they're fucking amazing." They're shaped like stars and taste like heaven and I might have already eaten an entire tray. Or two.

Definitely two.

Yulenna just tosses her hair. "Oh, if we don't order them about, it messes up the pecking order. The more demanding that we are, the more it cements our power. We act like they're here to serve our every need and it reminds them who's in charge."

That's an odd way of looking at things, but it makes sense. I've been nice and polite to the soldiers, and while Markos and Kerren are kind and courteous to both me and Yulenna, Vitar smirks a lot and Solat flirts far too much for his own good. Maybe if I'd been firmer with them and established that we weren't supposed to be buddies, things would be smoother. As it is, I inwardly grimace every time Solat stares at me a little too long.

It's just a matter of time before Aron catches him and removes his head with his bare hands.

Of course, I'm a sick woman because that thought gives me a stupid little thrill that Aron would act jealous over something like that. Not that I want Solat to lose his head...but I like the thought of Aron being possessive over me.

Yulenna's smarter than she lets on, though. I eye her with new appreciation as the servants return and she gives them impatient looks and acts displeased. They all scramble to do her bidding and fill the room with their apologies, until her frown lifts and she gives them a tiny incline of her head, indicating they're back in her good graces.

She's got this shit down pat. For a moment, I feel a twinge of remorse. Would Aron do better with someone like Yulenna at his side? Someone who knows how to play the game and who knows this world and its customs? Probably.

Instead, he has me. I don't know anything, I can't fight for shit, and I'm bad at pretending that I do.

I suck as an anchor.

"There. I think these are acceptable. Try one on, Faith." She moves to the long chest of gowns and pulls the first one off of a stack.

I wipe my fingers, take one last sip of my wine, and then get up to join her. "Did you say these were new?"

"Yes. I figured I'd ask and see what we could get away with." She gives me sly look. "The men only think about armor and weapons, but you and I both know that sometimes our only weapon is the way we look."

I hate that she says that, because I hate that I have to agree with her. It's become quite clear to me that the rules in this world don't always apply like they do back home. Women are most definitely not equal here. Not *anywhere* here. That's been a hard lesson to learn. I hate that I'm about to play up the only weapon I have because I want Aron to notice me. "Which gown's the sluttiest?"

Her eyes gleam with approval and she puts the one in her hands back on its hook and pulls out another. "This one, I wager. Look at the material. It's as thin as cobwebs."

It *is* rather pretty and shimmery. The pale fabric reminds me of opals, with different colors swirling through the fabric as it moves. I touch it and it feels buttery soft against my fingers. "That is pretty," I admit. "Think it's my size or yours?" She's got a bigger bust and a tinier waist than me.

Yulenna just laughs. "It'll fit. Disrobe and I'll show you."

Sure enough, it does fit. I mean, how can it not? Once I get naked and she drapes it over my head, I see why she laughed. The word "gown" is a very loose term. There are two embroidered frog-clasps on each shoulder, and the rest of the gown falls to my feet in a shimmering, sheer fall of fabric that slithers over my skin. And it's sexy. The fabric is sexy. The sheerness of it is sexy. Even the way it hugs my shoulders as if barely managing to stay on is sexy. The material itself clings and slinks against my body as if it's a second skin, outlining everything and leaving nothing to the imagination.

"Want to rouge your nipples and cunt?" Yulenna asks. "So they stand out under the fabric?"

"Um, no, I'm good." I resist the instinctive urge to put my hands over my privates as she studies me. Stand out? Everything's already standing out. My nipples are standing at attention, sticking out against the dress and completely outlined. The now-trimmed strip of bush I'm sporting is utterly visible. I don't think I could stand out more if I tried.

"Yes, I suppose he likes how natural you are. I can see it holds a certain appeal to him." She studies me. "Lick your lips."

"What?"

"Lick your lips. Wet them. Make them glisten." She arches an eyebrow. "That's what this is about, right? Seducing Aron into your bed?"

CHAPTER 53

I can feel myself blushing. "Maybe I just wanted to feel pretty."

"Uh huh," she says, unconvinced. Her expression turns gentle, sisterly. "Look, I know what it's like. You think I haven't been sold to a dozen masters before? You're only as safe as your master's favor extends. I understand the need to secure yourself. And I want to help you, because if he's happy with you, we're all safe."

I don't know what to say to that. "Thank you?"

Yulenna just smiles. "This is the best moment of your life. You have the favor of the gods. Use it. Enjoy it. Get everything you can out of it."

She thinks this is the best moment in my life? Seriously? I open my mouth to protest, because the world I came from is so much better than this one, when a servant rushes through the door. "The lord of storms is coming," she says, breathless. The other servants in the room scramble to get out, and Vitar rises from the cot with a yawn, moving toward the door to take his post.

Yulenna studies me for a moment, then puts a hand to the

back of my neck and pulls me against her in a kiss. Her mouth works against mine, her lips shockingly soft, and then she bites my lower lip and slicks her tongue over it before releasing me.

I just gape at her.

"There," she says, pleased. "Now you look like you're ready to fuck. He'll like that." She winks at me, gathers her skirts, and follows the other servants out of the room.

I stand there, alone, my mouth throbbing from her kiss. I can't believe she just kissed me. How weird. Her mouth was a startling contrast to Aron's, too. I think I like his better, though. I touch my lips, wondering if I look as distracted as I feel. It takes me a moment to shake myself out of it, and then I move back to the reclining couch just as Aron enters. I pick up my goblet of wine and hold it as I try to look sexy.

He storms into the room, tossing off his cloak and throwing it down on the bed. "Idiots," he mutters under his breath. "An entire keep full of fools."

"Hi there," I say, and manage to take a tiny sip of wine. "How was your day, dear?"

Aron pauses in his tirade, mid-removal of his sword belt, and looks over at me. He's wearing one of the long, fur-lined tunics that these people favor and it covers him practically from head to toe. His big thighs are encased in fur-lined leggings and he looks like a mountain man, ready to take on the snowy peaks surrounding Novoro. Kind of hilarious, given that I'm dressed in something that would bring zero warmth. I guess the ladies of Novoro don't leave home much.

He slowly approaches me, his gaze locked on my body. My nipples prick under the fabric and I carefully set down the goblet of wine again and rest my arm on my hips. I'm half reclined on the couch and pillows, propped up on my side so I can show off my body. And he's looking, all right. He's looking real, real hard.

"New dress?" he finally says.

I smooth the fabric over my thigh. "Thought I'd wear something pretty since I'm going to be sitting around here until we leave." Remembering Yulenna's advice, I lick my kiss-swollen lips.

His gaze flicks there and lingers for a moment, then drops back to my nearly bared body. He's seen me naked before, but this is different. Things are slowly changing between us, and we're both utterly aware of it. "Is this because of our conversation last night?"

"Maybe I just wanted to enjoy a nice day of pampering?" I keep my voice light.

Aron snorts and strips off his tunic, holding it out to me. "You can be pampered in something like this just as easily."

I ignore it. "So you *don't* like my dress?" I slide a hand up to my breast, almost touching my nipple, and love that his eyes follow me. The air's getting heavy, and I can practically feel it crackling with the force of his internal "storm." For some reason, I find that sexy as hell.

"You will not wear this?"

"Nope."

He shrugs and turns toward the door, pulling out his knife.

"Wait, where are you going?"

"To remove the men's eyes so they don't look upon you."

I yelp and scramble for the tunic he tossed to the floor. "Aron, don't you fucking dare!" I snag the tunic and hold it to my chest. "Just wait, okay?"

He turns around slowly as I hurry over to him in bare feet, his expression impossible to read. "If you will not cover your body, I'll make sure they can't see it."

"I'm getting dressed, you son of a bitch," I mutter, pulling the tunic over my head. When I slide it onto my shoulders, it hangs over me like an oversized sleeping bag. "Heaven forbid a girl want to look sexy," I mutter, and then to my astonishment, his lips twitch.

That asshole. He's teasing!

I reach out and smack his arm. "You jerk! You scared the shit out of me!"

"Did I?" His smile grows wider. "That wasn't your goal, then? To entice me in a jealous rage to blind the others?"

"No, you ass." I give his arm another little swat. "Maybe I just wanted you to enjoy looking at me. Dick."

He grabs my free swinging braid and wraps it around his hand, dragging me forward. It tugs gently on my hair, but he knows his strength and he's utterly careful. "Faith, I always enjoy looking at you. It does not matter if you're covered in mud and wearing a monk's clothing, or wearing nothing but suds from your bath. I always enjoy looking." His voice is a silky, low caress that makes heat pool between my thighs. "Which is why I don't like the thought of others doing so."

"You being a jealous dick should not turn me on," I tell him, breathless. I'm fascinated by the nearness of his hard mouth, the way he's pulled me so close that I can feel the heat and electricity coming off of him in waves.

"I'm not jealous."

"Then you weren't going to cut out Markos's eyes?"

"He doesn't look at you. Now Solat and Vitar..."

"No," I say, smacking his bare chest lightly again. I want to put my hands all over that chest, but he's made it clear where I stand with him. Still...this is flirting, isn't it? And it's making my heart race with excitement even though he says we can't be anything. "No eyeball removal."

"Their cocks, then."

"No."

"Then you'll wear my tunic and stop showing off what's mine?" He arches that arrogant brow at me.

I sputter. "Yours?"

He pulls me closer to him, until our mouths are almost

touching. "Aren't you mine, Faith? We're connected in every single way."

"Not every way," I point out, and touch a finger to the abline just above his belly button. I'm shocked at how quickly we're progressing. It's like the Novoran party broke something open between us. Before it was just sniping and a bit of casual flirting. Now? Now it seems to be a lot more. I trail my fingers up the muscled ridges of his belly.

His eyes flare with possessive heat and electricity crackles between us.

"Faith."

I love the way he says my name. "Yes?"

"You are not going to dinner tonight."

That...wasn't what I expected to hear him say. "Huh?"

Aron's gaze moves over me in a heated caress. "I don't want them looking at you. Thinking about having you. I want you up here and safe and mine alone."

For some reason, that makes me feel...good. I don't want to go down, either. "But you'll still come to bed with me?"

He nods.

"And you won't let them put some lady-candy on your lap just because you're the lord of storms?" And I reach up and twine my fingers in his long, silky hair, holding him against me like he holds me against him.

"They will not dare, precisely because I am the lord of storms." But he's smiling.

"Good." He doesn't release my hair, so I don't release his. Aron's mouth is so close, I could close the distance and kiss him...but I won't. So I just ask, "How much longer are we staying?"

"A day, maybe two. Ravens have been sent out to retrieve information. We'll wait for their return, and then leave."

Makes sense. "Are we taking any of their troops with us?" I

think of how eager Lord Novoro was to volunteer his people, and how insulted he was when Aron didn't take him up on it.

Aron snorts. "Absolutely not. Bad enough that we have these other fools."

"Be nice." I grin. "I like those fools."

"I don't, because we're not alone."

How can I be mad about that?

CHAPTER 54

e end up staying in Novoro for a few more days to rest up our woales and to rebuild our supplies. The Novorans are totally fine with this. They want to continually celebrate Aron's presence in their midst, so another banquet is thrown.

This time, Aron won't let me leave his rooms. He makes Yulenna stay with me, and the three soldiers keep guard at our door. I'm not sad about it, because the last party was not *exactly* what I'd expected. In fact, I'm exceedingly nervous as Aron goes down to the party alone because I imagine all kinds of women throwing themselves at his godlike feet, but when he comes back up several hours later, he's irritated and bored because all the Novorans want to do to "honor" him is have sex with each other and feast.

I'm a terrible person, because I'm secretly pleased at how disgusted he is at their idea of a good time. It just means he won't be tempted. Not that we're together...but in my mind, he belongs to me and the thought of him touching another woman makes me want to scratch her eyes out.

And then scratch his eyes out too, just for good measure.

After that evening, though, the Novorans wise up to the fact that Aron isn't on board with their way of partying, and the celebrations change into a several-days-long fighting tournament. Again, not something I can really participate in, and Aron gets weird whenever someone looks at me, so I stay inside. I can see the fighting in the courtyard below and Aron is in the mix with the Novorans, clearly enjoying himself.

He always wins, too. I'm pretty sure they let him win—who wants to be the one to beat a god?—but he enjoys himself nevertheless and so we stay at Novoro for longer.

This means Yulenna and I spend a lot of time together. We work on sewing, since it's what Yulenna does in her spare time. She sews embroidery onto the delicate edges of her gowns, and I sew pockets into my traveling tunics, because pockets are awesome. As we sew, we talk, and I learn that I like Yulenna quite a bit. She's smarter than she lets on and knows a lot about this world that I don't, so I try to pry information out of her without giving away how little I actually know. I think she suspects that I'm not from anywhere around here, but she's smart enough to not ask.

Since we're spending so much time in our room together, Markos, Solat, Kerren and Vitar spend a lot of time with us, too. They watch us in shifts, one man at Aron's side at all times, two at our door, and one resting, so someone is always on guard.

I get to know them pretty well, too, and after a while it's like spending time with old friends. Solat ends up being the life of the party, sitting with us, flirting with Yulenna and then telling all kinds of stories of things he'd seen in Novoro or tales of his time before he served Aron, when he was a mercenary for a fat lord in Glistentide that had more money than sense. Most of his stories are completely hilarious, involve him being caught with his pants down, and having to run for his life on to the next job. We end up looking forward to Solat's arrival every day, just to hear more of his ridiculous tales.

This particular day starts out like any other. Aron heads off to enjoy the tournament, which means Yulenna and I are sewing. Solat stops by to see how we're doing and before long, he's invited himself to sit down and eat with us, telling another story of how he met a "murderous" concubine who was arrested for assassinating an emperor, even as Solat hid inside her trunk, naked, and quivered like a chicken while holding his balls.

The image of him sniveling in hiding while holding his junk? I admit, it's pretty funny, and I'm giggling madly when the door opens.

Aron storms in, sweaty and dirty from the tournaments. He sees us laughing, and Solat's feet are kicked up on one of the decorative tables. I'm the first one to see Aron come through the door, and my laughter dies in my throat at the furious look on his face.

Solat has his back to him. He gives me a disarming wink. "You needn't worry about my balls, Faith. I assure you they're all in one place."

"Not for long," Aron growls behind him.

The color drains from Solat's face. He jumps to his feet, back stiffening. "My lord."

Aron immediately moves in front of my chair, as if he's blocking me from Solat's sight. "Are you flirting with Faith?" His hands flex, and I realize he's inches away from pulling his sword. "Is this what goes on in my chambers when I am away?"

Oh shit.

Solat goes pale. "My lord...no. I would never...she is yours!"

Yulenna is instantly still, her gaze averted. She says nothing, but her sewing is frozen mid-stitch. Markos and Vitar watch from the doorway, worry etched in their faces, and I realize just how dangerous this is. We've all been joking around and having a good time, getting to know each other and acting like friends.

Because we're mortals. It's what mortals do.

But Aron is a god, and I'm his anchor. He doesn't understand

402

human friendship, any more than he understands sleep, and he would just as easily kill Solat as breathe.

I get to my feet, because I realize that I can't have friends—at least not male ones—because Aron's jealous. It's a human emotion and he doesn't know how to handle that shit.

He's not human. I can't assume he's going to act like one.

"Time out," I say cheerfully, and head to Aron's side. I can practically see the flop-sweat on Solat's brow as he tries not to shake. He knows he's fucked up somehow, just by being too friendly. In a way, I can't even blame him. Judging from his stories, Solat has always made his way by being charming and ingratiating until he got chased off.

He doesn't realize that Aron won't chase him off—he'll just cut his head off without a thought.

"What is time out?" Aron asks, frowning at me. He plants his feet when I grab his arm, ignoring the electric shock between us.

I tug again, unwilling to be ignored, and he relents, letting me drag him away. I need to get him out of the room so he doesn't kill Solat for breathing the wrong way—and then killing the others for being upset that he killed Solat. I can see it turning into an awful domino effect. It's weird, too, because I feel protective of our small group. Even though I haven't known them for long, I feel so much older and wiser than they are, strangely enough. Being around Aron gives me a different perspective, and while they're just looking at this as an adventure serving a god, my *everything* hangs in the balance.

This could be my life *and* my Afterlife, because what happens to me if I die while I'm here and tied to Aron?

The moment I shut the door behind us and we're alone, I forget all about Afterlives and my world, because it's clear that Aron's furious. He pulls away from me with a jerk and his hands are clenched as he paces the bedroom.

"What's crawled up your ass?" I demand. My temper's flaring, too. "Why are you being such a dick?"

"He was flirting with you," Aron says, gesturing indignantly. "Laughing *with* you! And you were laughing *back*!"

"I was having a good time! Why is that a crime?"

He stalks toward me, his eyes so intense I can practically see the lightning crackling off of him. "You think I don't know what you're doing?" His voice is low and smooth, even if the words are deadly.

I arch a brow, determined to look cool and collected. What is he talking about? "What is it that you think I'm doing? I'm curious."

His eyes glare lightning into mine. "You are trying to make me jealous."

My jaw drops. "Are you serious? With Solat?" I laugh at that. "Yeah, no. He's not my type."

Aron goes very still. "Which one is your type, then?"

I swallow hard, because that feels like a loaded question. Not for me, but for whoever I answer. If I tell him I find Markos sweet and gallant and that he's got great hair, is Aron going to go out there and kill him? Or that Kerren's blushes are adorable?

Is he going to murder his way through half the country if I enjoy myself around other people? I don't know how to deal with a jealous god, and I swallow hard as I'm reminded that Aron isn't the god of puppies and warm hugs. He's a god of battle. It's in his nature to pick a fight.

And because he's a god, he's going to win, every time.

"I'm not going to answer that," I say slowly, determined to defuse the situation. "But no, I am not trying to make you jealous. You've already said we can't be anything, even if I wanted to be."

He moves closer.

I instinctively lean back against the door, as if it'll save me from his advancement. Aron's inches away, and he's so intense I can feel energy crackling between us.

He stops inches in front of me, looming. There's an intense look on his face and I should be terrified, but I'm not. I'm utterly turned on. "You are not trying to make me wild with hunger for you, then?" he murmurs, a deadly calm in his voice, as if he's inches away from his control snapping. "You're not trying to make me give in and touch you?"

I lick my suddenly dry lips. "I mean, I wouldn't say no if you absolutely insisted—"

Aron looks down at my dress, which is in the Novoran style. It's low cut with only an artful corset to keep the drapery in place. With a breath, he could have his hand in the front of my gown.

And we're both extremely aware of it.

"You mortals," Aron murmurs, leaning in so close that I can feel his breath fan against my face. "You are so bad at saying what you want. I think you do want me to touch you. You just won't admit it."

He's right. I don't want to admit how much I need him to touch me right now. Saying "yes, please touch me" would give him all kinds of power over me. He'd hold it over my head. He'd remind me of it constantly. He's so arrogant that I don't want him to have one over me.

But god, I want him to touch me.

"Admit it, Faith."

"I admit nothing." My voice has a wobble in it.

"Not even the truth?" The tip of Aron's nose brushes against mine, and he's so close I can see each thick, dark eyelash that frames his intense gaze. "You won't ask? Not even to receive the pleasure you know I can give you?"

That makes me quiver all over. Oh Jesus, he is way too good at this game.

Aron leans in closer, and his lips are practically against mine as he speaks. I feel them move, forming the words he says, soft and slow. "Shall I touch you?"

I whimper, unable to fight it any longer. "God, yes."

One big hand pushes through the slit in my skirts, and then his callused fingers are stroking over my pussy. I'm soaking wet, my thighs damp with my arousal, and I can feel my need coating his hand. I want to close my eyes so I don't see the expression of triumph on his face as he puts a hand against the wall. It's like he's bracing himself so I can ride his hand, and fuck me if that isn't the hottest thing I've ever pictured, ever.

He says nothing, though, simply dragging his fingers through my wet folds and stroking back and forth. He's not hitting anything in particular, just coating his hand with my arousal and teasing me. Then, he looks me in the eyes. "Tell me who this belongs to, Faith."

"You." I breathe the word, unable to hold back.

"Tell me who it is that's touching you," Aron says casually, grazing a finger over my clit before stroking deeper. "Tell me who's got their fingers deep in this soaked cunt. Tell me who's spreading you wide." And he does just that with his fingers, thrusting deep into my core before pulling out and dragging his spread fingers across my folds, pulling them apart.

"You know it's you, you son of a bitch," I grit out, my hands fisted, my breath panting. I desperately want to cling to him… and I don't want to give him the satisfaction. I feel weak, trembling, unmoored. Fragile. And I suspect this is all part of his game. He wants me to break down and hold onto him for support. He wants me to beg him to fuck me.

And I don't want to give him the satisfaction.

"Are you going to come for me, Faith?" His hot eyes blaze into mine.

I choke at his bold words. "N-no."

"Yes, you are," he says firmly.

"Fucking make me."

Oh god, *please* make me.

He slaps my pussy, shocking me. It's not that it hurts—just hard enough to sting—but it's the shock of the contact and the spark that flies between us that somehow turns me on even more than before. "You know I own this," Aron tells me. "It's mine as surely as your life is mine. Mine to claim, day or night, anytime I want."

I moan.

He gazes down at me. "Your nipples are hard, Faith. They're just begging for my mouth, aren't they?"

Oh fuck, they are. I can feel how tight they are, how aching. When I look down, my nipples are clearly outlined against the fabric of my dress. I can also see Aron's hand as he moves back and forth, stroking my pussy, his wet fingers sliding between my folds.

And I whimper again.

"No other man will ever touch this, will he, Faith?" Aron leans in, his lips grazing over mine again in another one of those almost-kisses. "No other man will come near this. Not because he knows I'll murder him, but because it's going to be clear to anyone that looks at you that this belongs to me and only me. That this pussy has been so thoroughly pleasured that I've ruined it for any other cock, any other hand. It comes for me and only for me."

He sinks a finger deep inside me, even as his thumb strokes my clit.

"Mine and mine alone," he growls.

I detonate. It's impossible, but I come so hard that I cry out, my hands fisted in the front of his tunic as he continues to rub my clit with his thumb, working his finger inside me as if determined to wring every last bit of pleasure from me. I'm panting like a bull ready to charge. And I'm coming so hard that I see stars. I sag against the wall, my legs weak, and Aron's arm loops around my back, holding me up. His hand leaves my pussy and then I'm vaguely aware of him stroking my hair, holding me gently against his chest as I struggle to come back to earth from that universe-destroying orgasm.

Soon enough, each touch of Aron's hand in my hair becomes too much. The sparks he sends through me are too much to my overstimulated body, and I slowly slide out of his grasp, aware that his hand—and my body—smells of sex.

"Satisfied now?" he asks, and he sounds so damn smug.

"Mm." I look at him, and there's still heat blazing in his eyes. Still raging with need, with heat. I'm the only one that came, I realize. And I can take back a little bit of power—and okay, have some fun—if I make him come now, too. I reach for his belt, sliding my hand between his legs to cup his enormous, hard length. Oh god yeah, he's hard as hell, straining against his pants as if they can barely contain him.

Just as swiftly, Aron takes my wrist in his grip and pulls my hand away. "No."

That makes me pause. "What do you mean, no?"

His eyes gleam. "Touching me wasn't part of the deal, Faith. I'll pleasure you if you insist on being a brat, though. And I'll look forward to it." The look he gives me is positively predatory.

Somehow, I feel like I just lost even more ground in this battle of wills between us. I lift my chin. "There's no deal, Aron. There was never a deal—"

"You flirt with the others, I remind you that you are mine. That is the deal."

"I'm not sure I like this deal—"

"You act like you have a choice," he tells me in that arrogant voice of his, and then pushes back out of the room.

Just like that, the conversation is done. And just like that, I can't decide if I want to run after Aron and kiss him, or choke him.

CHAPTER 55

*A*ron doesn't come back into the room, so I guess we're done. I fight back a blush—and irritation—as I move to a side table and give myself a quick bath to try to get rid of the sex smell. I adjust my clothing, fix my belt, and pace around the room until I'm sure my nipples won't be taking out anyone's eyes.

When I feel mostly like myself again, I emerge from the room.

Immediately, it feels like a mistake. Solat is by the door and does his best to pretend that I'm not here. Markos avoids eye contact, and Kerren's face is tomato red. Vitar keeps clearing his throat. Only Yulenna seems calm, sewing in her seat, a tiny smile on her lips. I...guess we were louder than I thought. Oh man. I wonder if they heard Aron dirty talking to me? If they heard him slap my pussy and tell me that it belongs to him?

Awkward.

I take my seat next to Yulenna and pick up my sewing, but I can't concentrate. I'm still all messed up from Aron's claiming of me—because that's what it was. I'm not sure how I'll ever look Kerren or the others in the eye again.

"Give them time," Yulenna murmurs, picking out a stitch.

It's like she read my thoughts. "What?" I feign ignorance. "Time for what?"

"They have considered you one of them," she says easily. "Another soldier in Aron's army, of a sorts. Now they realize that you serve him in an entirely different way."

My cheeks get hot. I'm not sure if I'm offended at her "serving him" comments or if I'm baffled that it took Markos, Vitar, Kerren and Solat this long to figure out that Aron and I have a rather...tumultuous relationship. "And you? How do you feel about this?"

She shrugs, biting her thread off. "He's a god. He takes what he wants, women included."

And suddenly I'm no longer feeling secure in my position. I no longer feel like Aron's Faith, because I remember his other aspect—the Aron of lies—slept with Yulenna. A lot.

"You don't have to worry," Yulenna says, and it's like she's reading my mind. "He's never looked twice at me. For all that they're Aspects of the same god, there are parts of them that are very, very different. This Aron sees no one but you."

"Because I'm his anchor," I agree, and the thought doesn't sit easily with me.

"Mmm. Is that all it is?" Yulenna arches a brow at me.

I have no answers. I stare at her for a moment longer, and then pick up my sewing. At least if my hands are busy I can pretend to be focused.

Right now, though, I can't think of anything but Aron and his hands. Aron slapping my pussy and saying that it belongs to him. The heat in his eyes.

The hard length of his cock under his clothing...and the way he pushed me away.

WE STAY in Novoro for two more days after that, and during that time, I see very little of Aron. At first I think he's avoiding me, but as Vitar and the others cycle through their guard duties, I realize that they're spending time with Aron and the Novorese suppliers. I hear talk of mounts and blankets, tents and weapons. Food supplies. We're preparing to leave, and I'm relieved.

Relieved, and a little frustrated.

After our torrid moment in my chamber, Aron's only returned when I'm sleeping, and left before I woke each time. The only reason I know this is the vague realization as I sleep that someone's next to me, and the indention of a large body in the blankets next to me when I wake. I know part of it is because he wants to "resist" me. It doesn't mean my feelings aren't hurt, though. Or that I don't miss him.

Because I miss Aron terribly. Even though he's arrogant and a jerk and impossible, he's my friend and my protector. He's the only person I completely trust to have my back, and the only person I feel I can be completely open with.

He's mine as much as I'm his, and I miss him.

I'm tired of being in this place, too. They've been monopolizing Aron and because he doesn't want me around them, I've been confined to these rooms. Granted, they're nice rooms, but I miss his company. So I'm more than ready to leave Novoro once and for all.

Servants arrive with warm cloaks and tailors fit me for new, warm traveling clothing to go over the mountains. They confirm what I already know—the tournament is over and Aron has made it clear that it's time for him to move on. After that, it's a whirlwind of fittings and packings, and feasts for Aron as they celebrate him. Again.

No wonder he wants to move on. He can't get shit done around here because they want to party constantly.

On the morning of the third day after my cataclysmic

rendezvous with Aron, he returns to my rooms just as Yulenna and I are waking up and eating breakfast. He sweeps in, covered in a long, black cloak trimmed with white fur, a sword at his waist and studded armor on his chest. His long hair is pulled back into a tail, emphasizing the hard lines of his face and he looks so good I could eat him with a spoon.

His gaze immediately sweeps past Yulenna as if she's a gnat and focuses on me. "Faith."

"Hi," I say around a piece of toast. "Are we leaving now?"

Aron nods. "Dress warmly. There is a storm coming." He eyes me again, and then adds, "Can you be ready to leave once you finish eating?"

"Yup." I get to my feet, licking my fingers. "I'll have them pack up my breakfast. Come on, Yulenna." I grab a new piece of toast and shove it in my mouth to eat while I dress. I'm glad— I'm more than ready to go.

"My lord of Storms," a familiar voice calls from the hallway. "I have heard rumor that you are leaving our keep? Surely not now, with a snowstorm on the horizon?"

Irritation flashes across Aron's features, and his jaw clenches. I recognize Lord Secuban's voice an instant before he comes into my rooms. I get the impression Aron is equally tired of Lord Secuban, because I can see his face practically shutting down as the man moves to his side.

"Did I invite you into my concubine's private chambers?" Aron asks coldly, not looking over at Lord Secuban.

Both Yulenna and I freeze at Aron's dangerous tone of voice.

"I apologize for the intrusion," Secuban says, not moving from his spot at Aron's side. He totally does not realize how in danger he is. I've seen Aron kill men in an eyeblink for less. "But I must speak to you. Stay in Novoro longer, my great lord. We will give you everything you need to ensure that you win your battle against the other Aspects."

Aron's nostrils flare. "Not necessary."

"We have the strongest army in the mountains, my lord. No one can take this keep, and we are the sole path to the northern wastes. Here, you can defend for months. Years, if you must. And we will be your army."

"I am not interested in taking a defensive stance," Aron tells him with a dismissive look. "It is better to take the battle to my enemies than to wait for them to approach."

Secuban nods slowly. "I understand. Such are your teachings. But, my lord, if you will not stay, allow me to send my army with you to protect you and your anchor. It would be the greatest of honors for Novoro."

Aron gives a dismissive snort. "I need no army. I am a god."

Secuban looks worried. "I have heard rumors that other gods are building armies, my lord. In Adassia—"

"I am a god," Aron states again, his tone brooking no argument.

Secuban bows deep. "Of course. Forgive me if I overstepped." But he looks concerned, and I realize he knows more than he's letting on. If others are forming armies, shouldn't we do that, too?

I bite my lip and study Aron. As much as I don't want to travel with an army, I also don't want to die. But the look on Aron's face tells me that no army is coming with us, regardless.

And I'm reminded that in addition to being a god, Aron is the personification of arrogance. I hope it's not arrogance that makes him want to set off without extra men.

Really, really not a fan of dying, after all.

CHAPTER 56

a short time later, we set off on our woales, heavily laden with supplies. Yulenna rides behind Solat, and I ride with Aron. It's bitterly cold and despite the layers of clothing I'm wearing, I'm shivering within minutes. Snow falls in a relentless blanket as we head out the north gate of Novoro and onto the rocky mountain path. Ahead of us stretches a trail that leads into the mountains, and I can see far ahead…and there's nothing to see. There's only more mountains, more snow, and more forbidding landscape.

It makes me wonder if we should have stayed in Novoro after all.

But Aron takes a deep breath as the imposing Novoro citadel disappears, and he relaxes. I can't help but laugh, and I poke him in the side. "Glad to be gone?"

He glares at me from over his shoulder. "You have no idea how much that lord simpers and natters on, desperate to win approval."

"Oh, I can guess." Aron hasn't had a moment's peace since we arrived at Novoro. "Are you sure you won't miss the titty buffet?"

"Titty...buffet?"

"Yeah, the all-you-can-eat, all-the-pussy-you-can-stand parties he put on every night?"

Aron snorts with amusement. "As if that would please me. A 'titty buffet' as you call it is unnecessary."

"Because you don't eat?"

"Because no tits hold my interest save yours."

And just because I like hearing that, I press them against his back.

✕

THE SNOW GROWS THICKER as the hours pass and the day steadily colder. No amount of layers keeps me warm and I'm shivering as I hold onto Aron. The woales seem utterly unaffected by the change in weather, plodding onward and chewing feed from ice-crusted feed bags. I look over at the other mortals in our group and see they're all suffering as much as me. Yulenna's teeth chatter constantly and her face is buried against Solat's cloak. The other men have their heads down, shoulders hunched as they lean into the wind and try to endure it.

"Can we stop for the night?" I ask Aron when the sun goes down under the horizon. "I know a woale can go all night, but my ass quit about two hours ago. I need a fire and to get out of this wind before my nose freezes off my face."

He looks over his shoulder at me in irritation, but his expression softens as he gazes on my face. I must look really bad because he nods. "We'll set up camp here."

"Here?" I ask, surprised. I look around and we're still in the mountains, on the muddy, nasty path that winds between the rocks. It doesn't look like any place I'd want to walk, much less spend the night. "In the middle of the road?"

"We're not going to be out of the mountains tonight," Aron

says, tugging on the reins of our woale. "This is as good a place as any."

"But it's the middle of the road," I protest. I guess I envisioned a nice copse of trees, a nearby creek, something more camp-like than just parking our asses here. We're not even on an even slope.

"You heard Novoro's lord," Markos calls out. "They are the only ones with access to the northern wastes. They will not let anyone through to threaten my lord Aron."

He's got a point. And I do want to stop.

"Don't be so fussy, Faith," Aron murmurs. "Would you rather go back to Novoro and endure another titty feast?"

"It's buffet, and good point."

Aron helps me down, and then I huddle with Yulenna while the three soldiers make two tents—one for me and Aron, and one for the rest of them to huddle in. I know Yulenna won't say a thing, but I don't like the thought of her sleeping with the guys. I pull Yulenna close. "You're sleeping with us tonight, all right?"

"I would be honored to service you both," she says, smiling at me.

Erk. "In a purely non-sexual way. I just want you to sleep somewhere where you don't have to worry about being groped."

"Markos would never," Yulenna protests immediately.

Interesting that she mentions Markos out of all four. "And Kerren would never, either. But Vitar and Solat might not care."

She laughs and nods. "I thank you, Faith. You've been good to me." And she huddles up against me again.

I feel like a jerk as I share warmth with her. She's been nothing but nice to me and I was terribly, horribly jealous of her when we first met. I'm learning a lot about myself and maybe Aron's not the only one that had a touch of arrogance that needed to be eradicated. I hug her close, determined to be a better friend.

Vitar builds a fire in the center of the road, and then small folding stools are produced for me and Aron. Aron—who hasn't lifted a finger—immediately sits and pulls me into his lap. I don't even protest. It's too cold, and he's far too warm. I wrap my cloak around both of us and snuggle close. His big hand closes over my inner thigh, and for a moment, my girl-parts get excited, thinking they're about to get more attention. But all he does is hold me, one hand splayed over my lower back.

And really, it's kind of nice to just cuddle.

Yulenna stands near the fire until Markos grabs the stool and indicates she should sit. She does gratefully, putting her hands out toward the flame for warmth. Kerren puts a pouch of water over the fire to boil, adding vegetables and hunks of dried meat as he goes. I notice Solat avoids Aron (and me), and he's unusually quiet. Poor Solat.

Vitar crouches near the fire, putting his hands out. "Never thought the edge of the world would be so cold."

"You thought it would be warm?" Kerren asks, surprised.

"No, of course not. Just...not quite like this. My balls are about to shrivel into coins." He glances over at me. "Apologies."

I just shrug. I like hearing the conversations, because it lets me glean more about this place that I've landed. Aron's not much help since he's as much a stranger here as I am. "So this is the edge of the world? Really?"

"Of course not. Mortals are fools," Aron murmurs into my ear.

"It is not," Markos says, nudging Vitar as he crouches next to him. "We're simply far north. That's all."

"Edge of the world," Vitar says again. "And we're heading to the edge of time, where the spiders dwell. Just like the stories say."

Solat snorts.

"It's true," Vitar protests. "When you were a boy, didn't your mam tell you stories about the gods of time that lived in a tower made of webs and rode spiders? Who could kill with a jerk of a thread? And how if you step on a spider, you have to apologize to the Spidae so they don't remove you from the weave?"

"Children's stories," Markos protests.

Vitar tilts his head. "You mean like the Anticipation?"

No one answers him.

Vitar turns to Aron. "Is it true, my lord? You would have the answers."

"To which question?" Aron's hand smooths up and down my back under my cloak, and I'm two seconds away from purring with pleasure. It should not be this delicious to be cradled in a man's lap, damn it.

"Is it the edge of the world, truly?" Kerren asks, his eyes wide. "Will we fall off the edge?"

"No edge," Aron says, his focus on my face and not theirs. "But the Spidae do exist. That's where we are headed even now."

"I knew it," Vitar crows, launching to his feet. He stabs a finger at Markos. "I knew they weren't just tales!"

"You're pleased that we're to meet spider gods?" Markos gives him an incredulous look, batting away Vitar's finger.

"They really are spider gods?" I ask Aron, surprised. I remember Omos's scrolls, but only vaguely, and I remember something about a triad of fates, but not that they rode spiders. I'm pretty sure I would have remembered something as creepy as that.

"They are not spiders. Just like I am not made of lightning and thunder is not my displeasure." His mouth curls with derision.

I say nothing to that. Does Aron not realize it thunders every time he gets pissy? It's the easiest way for me to tell his mood. He's so oblivious sometimes. Still, I'm glad they're not spider gods, because I'm really not a fan of insects. "So we're visiting them. Are they expecting us?"

"Does it matter? They will know where my other Aspects

are. I intend to find out what they know. Gain the advantage over my foes." His fingers slide lower, stroking over my backside, even as the fingers on my thigh move slightly, grazing my skin in the most ticklish way. "We will find where my other Aspects hide and take our fight to them."

"Without an army," I point out.

"How quietly do you think we can move with an army?" Aron asks, amused. "And as the god of battle, I know which warriors I want to go into battle with, and it is not the Novorese."

That elicits a chuckle from the other men. Okay, maybe Novoro isn't known for its soldiers. He's got a point. Still, a shit army beats zero army, doesn't it?

"The Cyclopae," Markos says. "They would make a worthy army."

Aron nods. "That they would."

"And already dedicated to you," Vitar adds. "I've heard they remove one eye in your name when they reach adulthood."

"More tales," Kerren begins.

"It's true," Solat interrupts, speaking for the first time. "I rode with a Cyclopae barbarian for a time. They remove their left eye to honor Aron's fight with the great dragon One-Tooth, and to prove that they only need one eye to best any man."

"Well, that's fucked up," I announce.

Aron arches an eyebrow at me, the scarred one. "You do not approve?"

I lean in. "Can I just point something out to you, almighty lord of storms? Because I'm seeing two eyeballs in that face of yours. Your Cyclopae are gonna be mighty disappointed to realize they plucked out their eyes on your behalf and you didn't do the same."

He throws back his head and laughs, utterly pleased at my retort. His hand slides higher on my thigh, and he's smiling as he looks over at the men. "One of you tell her."

RUBY DIXON

Kerren clears his throat. "Faith, have you not heard the story?"

"She has never asked," Aron says, utterly amused.

Oh. He's right, and I feel silly. Maybe I should have asked. All of his statues and his worshipers talk of a one-eyed Aron, but the man I'm with has two eyes. Aron's smirking with pleasure like I've missed something obvious all along. "Am I going to hate this story?"

"Bah. It is a glorious story," Aron says. "You will love it."

"Thanks, Arrogance," I tease, but I like his hand on my thigh. I want to shift my weight so that hand can slide a bit higher up. It's so hard to try and stay still. "Okay, let's hear it, then."

Kerren pauses, then begins. "It happened many, many years ago, back when Old Suuol ruled the mid-lands." When Aron nods, he continues, gaining confidence. "The great Lord of Storms was at war with Kalos, god of darkness, who had claimed the kingdom of Sollist for himself and enslaved their people. Old Suuol fought a glorious war against Sollist and the armies of darkness, but they were no match for Kalos and his ghouls. Aron led battle after battle, but the people of Suuol begged him to end the war. He went to the god Kalos and demanded that he free Sollist, but the dark god said he would end the war if given an ancient magical sword called Bright-blade, which was once carried by the finest of heroes in the land.

"It seemed simple enough, but what Aron did not know was that the sword was hidden deep in the mountains, in the lair of Old One-Tooth, the most ancient of dragons."

"Oops," I say, and take Aron's hand in mine. "And the dragon...temporarily blinded him? What?"

"No, I defeated him," Aron says proudly, taking over the story. "Slew him with a single blow of my mighty axe. But then Rhagos interfered."

420

"Rhagos?" I echo, then mentally go through the list of gods in my head. "God of…the Dead?"

"And Kalos's brother," Kerren adds. "He brought the dragon back to life and it attacked Aron once more."

"Damned hard to kill something that won't stay dead," Aron says, all grumpiness. "That was when I lost my eye."

I stare at his handsome mien, at the scars that crisscross the left side of his face, over the bright green eye. "How…"

"It is a lesser known legend, because Rhagos does not like for it to be told." Aron grins fiercely. "After I delivered the sword to Kalos, I went to the underworld and took one of Rhagos's eyes in repayment for the one I lost."

I stare at Aron in horror. Is this why he's got two different colored eyes?

"You did not know this?" He rubs his thumb over the back of my hand.

Wordlessly, I shake my head. For some reason, I don't find the story funny or clever. It makes me ache for him. How hard it's been for him. No wonder he doesn't trust the other gods. Not after the loss of an eye…and stealing someone else's. Yikes. "If other gods have treated you like this, how can you expect the Spidae to help you, Aron?"

He holds my thigh tightly, as if to reassure me. "Not all of the gods are enemies. Many would not dare to cross me."

I think of Tadekha, and how she coyly suggested an alliance with Aron and he shot her down. He didn't trust her in the slightest. "But you trust these gods? The Spidae?"

"They do not take sides." He shrugs. "They will give me the answers I seek."

"And that's great, but what if your other Aspects have the same idea?"

Aron's mouth forms a hard, hard smile. "Then we are all in the same place at one time."

I push his hand off my thigh, because I'm suddenly no longer feeling very cuddly. "I really hope that's just the arrogance talk-ing, because I really, really don't want to die, Aron."

To my surprise, his eyes practically blaze with emotion. He hauls me against him, tighter than before, and the look on his face is fervent. "No one will touch you, Faith. I will never let you come to harm."

I gaze up at him. "You can't promise that. You have two other Aspects out to take you down. You can't promise I'll be safe, Aron. Not if I'm the target."

His jaw clenches. I think for a moment that he's going to argue with me, but instead, he jerks to his feet. Before I can protest, he's carrying me away from the others and into our tent. Inside, it's just as frosty, but a bed has been made for me on a linen tarp to protect from the mud, and it's here that Aron sets me down gently. Aron kneels so we're both on the ground, and then he cups my face, forcing me to look up at him.

"Faith," he murmurs. "I know you're worried. I know you feel isolated and alone. But I will never, ever let anything happen to you."

"Because I'm tied to you," I joke, nervous.

"Because you are mine," he corrects. His fingers skate lightly along my cheeks. "My companion. My woman. My anchor. My Faith. I will protect your life with my own."

"Aron." I press my hands over his because I feel like he's not grasping just how out of place I truly am. "My life is your own. It's been tied to you since the moment I put my hand in yours. If I die, I don't know what happens to me. You go back to your heaven, your Citadel of Storms, and I go...where? I don't even know if my afterlife exists in this world. If you die, you're just one step closer to your ultimate goal, but I'm destroyed utterly."

He shakes his head. "Faith, you don't understand. I will cease to exist if I die. All of who this Aspect is," he gestures at his chest, "will be removed from who I am."

"But you'll still exist. Aron will still exist."

"I won't be the same. *He* won't be the same. He won't know what it means to make the rain stop for a starving farmer and his wife. He won't know what it's like to race away from a crumbling citadel and have glass picked out of his back. He won't know what it's like to hold you close."

My breath catches in my throat.

He caresses my face. "I told you once that you're my heart, Faith, and I mean it. You've shown me a different way of looking at things, and not just because you like to argue." His hard mouth curls into a hint of a smile. "I learn from you. I learn to think about how my presence affects others. I think of how I can be a better god to my faithful. Every day that I am here on the mortal plane with you changes me, Faith. I don't want to lose that. I don't want to lose you." He smiles. "That's why I'm going to win."

For some reason, I'm equally terrified that Aron will die. I thought he was eternal...but liar Aron got wiped out, and I know he's different from this Aron.

My Aron could die.

"Well," I say after a moment. I clear my throat. "I guess we'll just have to fucking beat their asses into the ground."

He laughs, pleased. "Now you sound like me."

I'm pretty sure I don't, but I'll take the compliment anyhow.

I CAN'T SLEEP that night. It's not the cold. It's that every time I close my eyes, I see Aron dying. Aron turning into a wisp of sparks, Aron fading out like a bad polaroid. I saw it happen to his rival right in front of me. Liar Aron had his hands on me, was looking me in the eye...

And then he was just gone.

Ceased to exist.

I'm terrified of that happening to my Aron. Of course I'm

worried about my own safety. That's a given. But it's a fear I've lived with for so long that I'm comfortable with it. It's not new. It's not fresh. My own safety is old news; Aron's is increasingly worrying me.

If we don't succeed, we're both screwed.

Aron's arm tightens around my waist. "Go to sleep, Faith. You need your rest."

I do need my rest, because I'm his anchor. I'm his mortal tie to this plane. I have to keep myself healthy for the both of us. Even so... "I'm scared, Aron."

He strokes my arm, comforting me. "If you were not, I would say you were a fool."

Huh. No over-the-top declaration there. No arrogant posturing. Somehow, it makes me feel better. When I'm at his side, I feel safe. Like everything's going to be okay even if we're looking certain doom in the eye.

He makes me think maybe we do have a shot at this. We just have to be smart.

CHAPTER 57

hree days in the mountains feels painfully long. It's three days of cold camping, three days in the saddle, three days of damp clothing and relentless wind. My lips feel chapped. My ass feels chapped. My everything feels chapped. If there's one thing I've learned in this world, it's that I am not an outdoorsy type.

I regret ever complaining, though, because the moment the landscape changes, I realize I'd rather stay in the mountains.

It's late afternoon on the third day of travel when I catch a glimpse of a distant plain. It disappears from sight as we go around a bend, and then returns again a short time later. It's a dismal gray plain, and utterly flat as far as the eye can see.

And rising up behind it, in the distance, is a slim, pale needle.

"Is that it?" I ask, pointing. "Is that the tower?"

Aron grunts. "I have never approached it over land, but I suppose yes, that is it."

There's something eerily familiar about it, the flatness that stretches for what must be miles. The stillness. "Is it like the Dirtlands?" I say, thinking of Tadekha's Citadel and how it pulled all the life from the land surrounding it. "Everything's dead?"

"This is a lake," Aron corrects.

"But other than that, it's the same, isn't it?" I recognize just how...dead everything is.

Aron grunts. "It is. Mortal things cannot live where gods dwell."

Which makes me worry about my future, since I'm tied to Aron. One problem at a time, Faith, I remind myself.

The path eventually descends out of the mountains, and as we get closer, I can see that it is, in fact, a massive lake. It's completely and utterly flat, as gray as a storm cloud, and starts almost immediately where this side of the mountains ends. Across the incredible distance, on a small island, is the delicate tower itself, stabbing high into the sky.

Our woales pause on the shore, twitching and uneasy. Markos, Vitar, and the others watch Aron carefully, waiting. They look just as uneasy as the land-hippos.

Aron says nothing. He simply gazes out at the gray, dead waters.

So I poke him. "What now, o leader?"

He grunts, gesturing at the water. "We cross it."

"Like...swimming? It's too damn cold."

Aron makes a sound of pure arrogance. "Of course not. We make a raft of some kind. Surely there are materials somewhere."

"I see no trees, my lord," Kerren ventures. "What shall we build a raft from?"

"There will be something," Aron says bluntly. "We simply have to find it."

And because there's no arguing with a god, the men dismount and start to head down the shore. It's clear they're uneasy. I'm uneasy, too. Everything feels unnatural here. Awful. Even the water that laps on the shore seems to have an off sound to it. I'm sure as hell not going to drink it or get into it if I don't have to.

Aron dismounts and then helps me down. Nearby, Yulenna holds the reins of her woale, watching us. The god gives me a hard kiss on the mouth, surprising me, and then storms down the shore.

"Wait," I call out. "Where are you going?"

He turns around and looks at me. "To find the materials for a boat, of course." And then continues to walk on.

I stare at his retreating back, surprised. Aron is...helping?

"Is he supposed to do that?" Yulenna asks, her voice hushed. She sounds just as baffled as me.

"I have no idea."

She turns and looks over at me, a speculative look on her face. "He's different around you, you know."

"Aron?" I'm surprised to hear her say that. Surprised...and strangely happy. Flattered. Because if he's different around me, it means he was very different from Liar Aron, and I don't like to think of them as the same man. "Different how?"

Yulenna shrugs. "I don't know. Less remote. More...human if that makes sense."

In a way, it does. I bite back my smile and gesture at the retreating backs of the men. "I guess if they're all heading off, we're safe here." Aron would never leave if I was in the slightest bit of danger. He's incredibly protective of me.

"I can't imagine anything can live out here. Can't you feel it?" Yulenna shivers. "It feels like this part of the world is a dead branch on a tree."

That's a pretty apt description. It does feel like that...like a dead area that needs to be pruned away and instead just lingers on. No, it feels creepier than that. It's like a dead arm that's rotting and infecting the rest of the body. I shudder.

I pat the woale's nose and put his feed-bag on him since he seems anxious. The woales always seem to calm down on a full stomach. Hell, maybe I should try that theory myself. I'm getting nervous just looking around at this place, at the ominous tower in the distance, the equally ominous gray lake that seems to have no end to it.

"I guess we should have a look around," I say to Yulenna. "I'll feel better doing something instead of just sitting here."

Yulenna hesitates. I notice she shies away from the water itself, and her face is pale.

"What?" I ask. "What is it?"

"I was talking to Vitar," she murmurs.

Oh boy. Fucking Vitar. The man says nothing for weeks and then the moment we cross the mountains, he's the herald of doom and gloom. "What now?"

"He says there are legends of guardians." She bites her lip.

"What kind of guardians?"

"Not good ones." When I give her an impatient gesture, she hesitates and then moves closer to me. "Guardians in the lake that prevent those that are unworthy from crossing."

"Like...sea monsters?"

She shrugs. "Vitar says no one has ever returned to tell of it."

I consider this, staring out at the water. If anything was full of sea monsters, I don't know if this cesspool would be it. "Monsters have to eat, right?" I gesture at the gray, still waters. "What could a monster that lived here possibly eat?"

"Travelers," Yulenna says immediately.

She's not helping. "No, really. We're the only ones that have come this way for a while, according to the Novoro keep. So what would it survive on?"

"What if it's magic? What if it doesn't need to eat anything other than intruders?"

I put my hands on my hips. "Then it won't eat us, because Aron's a god. If the gods in that tower are the fates, they know why he's coming here. Right? So they won't send their guardians out to eat him."

428

I hope.

Yulenna looks like she wants to argue, but her face goes chalk white. She stares at something over my shoulder, frozen.

Ugh. I close my eyes, not wanting to look, but I force myself to turn around. There, floating in the water, heading towards us in a gentle drift, is a raft. It moves towards us with barely a ripple, and the hair on the back of my neck prickles, because there's no breeze, no tide, no nothing that could be propelling it.

"Is that what I think it is?" I whisper to Yulenna.

"It's a raft."

I know it's a raft. Of course it's a raft. It also looks like no raft I've ever seen before. It's flat, sure, and it floats atop the water, but it's round instead of square, and it's made entirely of some white, ropy material I don't recognize. It continues to drift in our direction and then stops just before where I stand.

Creepy invitation or coincidence?

Aron jogs over to where we stand, his gaze on the raft. "I see we are expected."

I point at the raft. "You expected this?"

"Of course." He arches a brow at me. "They knew I was coming."

More arrogance. I shake my head, crossing my arms over my chest. "Is this safe?"

"Is anything?" Aron gives me an impatient look.

Someday I'll learn to stop asking him questions.

We tether the woales together, tying the lead to an outcropping of rock. Once they're set with their food bags, they calm down and ignore us, content to eat. The men arm themselves and carry light packs—all except Aron, who watches them with a lofty expression on his face.

Vitar steps onto the raft first. It dips into the water around his feet, but doesn't flood, and reminds me of a blanket somehow floating atop the surface. How is that going to hold us? All of us? But I look at Aron and he nods. Vitar holds his hand out to Yulenna, who quickly joins him, looking down in wonder. "It is like stepping atop a cloud," she calls out to me.

"Goody. I can't wait." I watch as the other soldiers step on, Kerren and Markos holding tent poles for some reason.

Then it's my turn, and Solat—the last one on the raft—holds his hand out to me. Aron growls, and I see Solat blanch.

I slap Aron's arm. "Stop it already. He's the one closest to the edge. Everyone knows I belong to you." I take Solat's hand and step onto the "raft." It's like Yulenna said—it feels spongy but solid. A cloud on the water.

Aron is the last one on and he pulls me close the moment he steps away from the shore. Then, we're all on the raft, standing around and looking at each other. Slowly, it begins to inch toward the far end of the lake, where the distant pale tower is now ringed by a low hanging cloud.

Vitar sticks his pole in the water and grunts. "It's not deep." He pushes against the pole and we surge forward. Markos does the same, and then we're moving at a decent rate as they push us forward, stroke by stroke. I notice the poles sinking deeper into the water the farther we move out, but so far, they're still able to hit the bottom.

We're close to halfway when something ripples under the raft.

Markos frowns at his pole, stabbing a little harder toward the bottom. "I thought I felt something."

"In the legends, there is always a test before speaking to the gods," Vitar tells us solemnly. "Perhaps we are about to be tested."

Aron blows out an impatient breath. "You are speaking to me, aren't you? I am a god. Nothing here is being tested but my patience."

"Oooh, burn," I whisper.

The others look worried. I notice that Kerren and Solat

exchange looks from behind us, and I worry. Are they right? Is this a test?

Vitar pushes his pole deep into the water, silent, then shakes his head. "I don't mean to be rude, my lord of storms, but you were exiled. They live here. That is different. They could have guardians—"

His pole gives a jerk, and there's just enough time to see the surprised look on Vitar's face before it surges forward and sucks him into the water.

The raft ripples in response.

Yulenna screams.

CHAPTER 58

"*V*itar!" Solat yells, even as he surges forward. Then, Kerren and Markos pull their swords, Markos's pole slipping into the water.

I lean over and reach for it, because we need oars. I do it without thinking, and just as I grab the end of the pole, I see something pale and snakelike slither under the raft. It pushes up against the center of the raft, and the entire thing capsizes underneath us.

A moment later, I hit the water, and it shocks the breath out of me with how cold it is. It feels wrong, too, thick and heavy, and I claw at my surroundings, trying to find the surface. I'm utterly terrified, my mind full of anacondas and crocodiles and whatever else this world can cook up that will eat us. I can't breathe, either. I can't find the surface, and I swivel helplessly in the murky depths, looking for light.

There's a bright spot below me, and I realize I'm flipped upside down. I turn over in the water, then surge toward the light. I hit the surface and cough, gasping and choking as I suck in lungfuls of air. Confused, disoriented, I squint, wiping water from my eyes. My traveling robes are heavy and with water soaking them, I'm dangerously close to being pulled under again. It's cold as hell, and my teeth chatter.

I don't see anyone, though.

"F-Faith?"

Behind me, I hear Yulenna's voice. Oh. I turn around and there she is, clinging to the side of the capsized raft. I swim toward her, even as I hear Markos yell something and Solat responds. I move to the raft and hold onto it. "Where is everyone?"

She shivers and just huddles against the raft, not answering.

I look around, and Kerren is thrashing in the water. For a split second, I think he's drowning, and I start to move toward him, but then I realize he's stripping off his armor as quickly as he can. Markos's shoulders are bare as he stabs at the water with his sword, and Solat dives under with a flash of bare leg.

"Has anyone seen Vitar?" Markos calls out.

"Where's Aron?" I ask a split second later, realizing I don't see him anywhere. "Aron? Are you here?"

I count heads in the water. Yulenna. Solat. Markos. Kerren. No Vitar.

No Aron.

"Aron!" I bellow out again, terrified. He can't die. We're tied together, I remind myself. I'm his anchor. He's stuck in this world with me. "*ARON!*"

"Get the women on the boat," Markos calls out, swimming toward us. "Hurry, before it surfaces again."

"What is it? Where's Aron?" I cry, even as they crawl onto the floppy raft and haul Yulenna up. Kerren reaches for me and I splash at his hand. "I'm not leaving without Aron!"

Another person grabs at me—Solat—and I'm hauled onto the raft. "He's here somewhere," Solat says. "I promise this, and he'll be mad if you die on him."

"Vitar?" Yulenna asks in a pitiful voice.

"Gone." Markos sounds hollow. "Just…gone."

She sobs, and I crawl to the edge of the raft, staring into the water. Aron doesn't need to sleep, so maybe he doesn't need to breathe, either. Maybe he's just waiting under the water for us to notice him—

Something white flashes under the boat again and I feel it ripple underneath the flimsy raft.

"Oh shit—"

The raft capsizes again, and back into the water we go.

My mouth and nose fill with water. Coughing, choking, I claw to get to the surface again, but something snags my heavy skirts and tugs me back under. I sail through the water, dragged along by my hem, and I realize dimly even as I claw for the surface that I'm being pulled away from the others.

I'm going to drown. First Vitar, now me.

Then Aron.

Something flashes all around us, and a jolt rockets through my body. The charge rushes through me, like prickling heat, and then it's gone, leaving nothing behind but an intense, throbbing headache.

Everything goes still.

Something brushes against my legs, but I realize it's floating past me, toward the surface.

My lungs burn and I swim forward, desperate for air. Darkness swims at the edges of my vision, but then I make it to the surface and gasp, sucking in deep breaths.

The air above strangely feels as heavy as the water below.

"He's losing his mind," Solat screams, and he sounds very far away.

Who? I want to ask. Who's losing his mind?

Something crackles again, even as pain lances through my head. Lightning streaks across the surface of the water, and thunder crashes overhead, so loud and fierce that it feels like it's right on me.

I know who's losing his mind. I'm filled with relief even as I'm filled with fear.

Aron. My Aron.

A floating object bumps up against me and then bobs against the surface. It's a tentacle of some kind, pale and unearthly and made of the same material as our boat. All along the surface of the water, other dead, limp tentacles are gently bobbing to the top, motionless and still.

Lightning crashes overhead again and I fight back a moan. It feels like my brain is being squeezed dry, and I nearly black out with the pain. Red and black dots swarm through my vision, and I struggle to stay conscious, desperate to focus. Something hot runs from my nose and ears. I swipe it away in irritation. Aron.

Where's Aron?

Hands grab me, fishing me from the water even as the sharp pain racks through me again. What's happening? Have I been bitten? Electrocuted?

"She's bleeding," I dimly hear Solat say, and someone swabs at my face. "Where's she wounded?"

"It's him," Yulenna cries. "He's going to kill us all."

I struggle to sit up, because I know she's talking about Aron. My red, hazy vision won't focus, but I can barely make out a dark form drifting over the water a short distance away. Not in the water, but floating above it. Wind whips my hair, ice cold, and more thunder rumbles. I watch in shock as Aron—because it has to be Aron floating out there—extends his hands and lightning curls around his palms.

Then, he blasts at the water again. Thunder shakes the boat and the air grows heavy with the force of the lightning.

And this time, I can't breathe. I'm like a sponge being squeezed of every bit of life. It's the water in my lungs, I think. The water and the cold. That's why I'm so weak. Why there's so much pain. Why it's so hard to focus.

435

"He's pushing the boat forward," someone cries. "Toward the shore!"

I want to smile with relief. Of course Aron's rescuing us. He won't let me die.

But the moment lightning crackles again, my vision goes red —then black—and then I crash with the thunder. My head feels as if it's splintering. Something tears inside me.

The world goes utterly dark as pain sweeps me away.

Maybe Aron didn't save me after all.

CHAPTER 59

I fade in and out of consciousness. I'm vaguely aware that I'm not quite dead. Not yet.

There's far too much pain for that. Everything hurts. I whimper, because I want it to go away, to stop hurting me, but it just keeps pounding at my head, determined to split it open. This isn't a migraine. This is every nerve ending staging a revolt, and the pain is so intense I want to die just to have it end.

Someone touches my back, lifting me up. I can't see—everything's hazy.

"Drink this," a low voice murmurs. Markos. A moment later, I taste hot broth against my lips. I manage a swallow before my stomach churns and I want to die. Even the small act of drinking that makes my body hurt so bad it feels like a mistake. I sag, sinking back into unconsciousness.

"You have to drink, Faith," Markos says, shaking me lightly. "We have to get something in you. It's been days—"

"No," a stern, familiar voice snarls. "You do not get to die."

A second later, rough hands grab me. It shoots horrible pain through my body, followed by the familiar crackle of sparks that tells me that it's Aron, and somehow the pain lessens. I'm tucked against a broad chest, my cheek resting against his shoulder, and he strokes my hair.

"You will not die on me, Faith," he says again, the tone imperious. "I will not allow it."

"S'not the plan," I manage, though it really does sound like a good idea right now. I just want to stop hurting. I'm so tired and there's so much pain. I just want to sleep.

"This is my fault," Aron says again, stroking my hair so hard it feels as if he's going to pull it from the roots.

I want to wince, but that requires too much effort. Aron's heart pounds under my ear, strong and powerful, and I sigh, because I feel better against him, weirdly enough. I still hurt like nothing I've ever felt before, but somehow it's tolerable because he's holding me. "W...what happened?" I manage to ask. "Boat..."

"I do not know how to swim," Aron admits in that same imperious tone I've come to recognize and love. "So I waited at the bottom, watching. And then I saw it attack you. And it made me...angry."

I've seen Aron lose his temper before, I realize vaguely. Each time, it brought on a flash of his powers—and a headache for me. "You drained me," I realize. I'm his anchor and he's not supposed to use his powers. Somehow he tapped into them and nearly killed me doing so. "I'm your battery and you drained me."

He holds me close, squeezing me so tight that everything aches. His mouth presses to my brow and his voice is low, so low that I'm pretty sure only I can hear it. "It was my mistake, Faith. I didn't realize I was hurting you until it was too late. I'm sorry." He strokes my hair again, then lays me gently back down in the bed.

I want to protest. I want him to keep holding me, because it feels better, but my mind is disoriented. I'm just...so...tired. So I lie back and close my eyes.

Aron's hand brushes against mine once more, sending that familiar spark through me, and I hold onto his fingers, stopping him before he leaves.

"Did we make it?" I croak out. "All of us?"

"Almost all," Aron says. "One of the soldiers is gone."

He doesn't know his name. "Vitar," I murmur. It's important that we remember.

"Yes." His thumb brushes over my fingers, caressing them. "Rest, Faith. We'll talk more when you feel better."

"Did...did they help you?" I ask him. "The fates?"

"Rest now," he says once more, and then lets go of my hand.

As if a cord has been cut, I fall unconscious again.

CHAPTER 60

J don't know how long I'm out of it, I only know that when I wake up, I'm fucking *starving*. I've never been so hungry in my life. Ugh. I would straight up murder someone for a cheeseburger right about now. My stomach growls as I open my eyes and blink at my surroundings.

"Faith?" A low voice murmurs.

I turn my head, and I'm relieved that it's tiring to do so, but it doesn't feel like so much effort that I want to just go back to sleep. I look over at Solat. His jaw is covered in a scruffy almost-beard that wasn't there before and there are rings under his eyes. At my side in the bed, Yulenna sleeps, curled up in a blanket.

"I'm so damn hungry," I whisper.

Solat grins, his mouth crooked, and reaches over to a nearby table. It's full of dried meat and a couple pieces of fruit, next to a waterskin. I'm guessing that's his meal, but he takes the plate and offers it to me. "Do you want broth?"

"Nope." I grab at one piece of fruit and eat it, bitter rind and all. Then I grab another, and another, and I'm shoveling food into my starving mouth, washing it down with his waterskin.

I've never been so ravenous, and I know it's because of the bond. I have to eat twice as much as a normal person to fuel my body now that I'm tied to Aron, and I'm guessing I've been unable to eat for a long, long time.

"You might want to slow down. You'll make yourself sick," he cautions.

I might—I've been sick before, but this time it's different. Somehow, I know the food will stay down. My body is craving this and it's different than when it was in the desert. Right now there's a bottomless pit inside me that needs to be filled. Even as I polish off the last bit of meat, I'm still starving. I still need more. It's like a drop in the bucket. I drink the last of water from his skin and lick the top. "I need some more."

"You…do?" He looks shocked. "You just ate all my rations for the day."

He doesn't get it. None of them do except Aron.

Aron.

My mind flutters with vague memories of him. Of Aron's nearness even when I was sick. Of him being in my bed and holding me against his chest, rocking me. Taking care of me. Brushing my hair back and caressing my face. Speaking in a low voice of endless things I don't remember, just that he was speaking, as if he knew I needed something to focus on to bring me back. That he needed to be with me.

My heart squeezes with affection, but he's not anywhere to be seen. "Where's Aron?"

Yulenna sighs and turns over in bed, oblivious.

Solat watches her closely for a bit too long, and then looks over at me. "Last I saw him, he was arguing with one of the spider gods."

I swallow hard. "Spider gods, huh?"

"One of the three Spidae, Lords of Fate." His mouth flattens and he doesn't look thrilled. "We are at their mercy here in the tower."

I'm not afraid. Aron wouldn't put me in danger. I just need to know what's going on. What he's found out from the Spidae. What happened back there on the lake. I get to my feet and nearly collapse again. My legs feel as unsteady as a newborn foal.

Solat is immediately at my side, holding me up. "You're supposed to stay in bed, Faith. I'm to watch over both of you, protect you with my life."

"Protect me from what?"

"Anything. Everything."

"I thought we were safe here?"

"I do not think there is a safe place anywhere in this world," Solat says, the words so solemn and ominous I'm surprised they came from him. He's the lighthearted one.

For the first time, I look around at my surroundings. "Are these bad guys?" I ask hesitantly. Because this doesn't look like the home of the "good guys." It's a stronghold of sorts, but not like any I've ever been in before. Aventine was dirt and soldiers and crowded, clustered buildings. Katharn was hovels on top of hovels atop the bones of what had once been a magnificent city. Novoro was an opulent keep in the mountains, with rock and stone everywhere.

This is...almost blank. It's like there's no personality in these walls. They're stone, but such a smooth, unnatural pattern of bland gray that for a moment I think I'm looking at an optical illusion and not stonework. The walls are perfectly symmetrical, without a window to be seen, and the bed Yulenna and I slept on is the only furniture, other than the camp stool parked next to the bed.

Even the bed itself is unnatural. It doesn't look like a normal mattress, but a large, puffy cocoon of...something. Like a cloud of cotton that's been draped with our familiar blankets. The cotton reminds me of the boat, actually, but I'm not sure why.

I take a step forward, working on regaining my balance, and

this one's easier than the last. I'm wearing one of my Novoran nightgowns, with a furry hem and a long, wrap-around length. I hold it tight against me so I don't flash Solat. I've been asleep long enough that my hair is dry, my clothes are dry, and my nails are longer. Jesus. No wonder I'm stiff.

Several more steps forward, and I make it to the wall. I place my hand there, only to draw back in surprise.

The walls are coated with spiderwebs.

This close up, I can see there's a fine layer of webbing covering the stones. I look up and they stretch to the webby ceiling, and along the floor. I glance over at the bed again and wonder if it's made entirely of webbing, too. And the raft…

I shudder.

"Faith," Solat says, moving to my side. "Please return to bed."

"I'll be fine." I shrug off his arm before he can help me. "Aron would be hovering if I was in danger, wouldn't he? We're safe here."

Solat gazes at me with solemn eyes. "He'll kill me if I let you leave."

I shake my head. "No, he won't. We'll tell him I didn't give you a choice. That I insisted on finding a bathroom and then a kitchen." Neither of which is entirely a lie.

Solat doesn't look as if he believes me.

"I won't let him kill you," I reassure him. "We need all of the guards we have." Especially now that Vitar's gone. I swallow hard. Poor Vitar. He wasn't my favorite, but he didn't deserve to die being eaten by a giant worm in a lake.

The lake.

I think of Aron, the way he floated above the water, seething with rage. He didn't look like my Aron then. He looked like a very angry god…and he almost killed me. I need to talk to him. I don't remember much about the last few days that I lost to healing up from whatever he did that flattened me, but I know he's got to be upset and stressed. I want to reassure him that I'm okay. That I'm more resilient than he gives me credit for.

I part the cobweb draped over the doorway and peek out into the hall. It's empty, and so I step out, ignoring Solat's protest. The need to find Aron is throbbing through me, almost as overwhelming as my hunger. He's a craving, and I wonder if it's a natural one or more of our strange bond. It doesn't matter either way.

I move down one hall and then another. There are no stairs, just a gradual elevation as the hall twists along the edge of the tower. Occasionally, I'll pass by a cobweb-covered parapet that leads outside, but I don't go out there. There's nothing inviting about it, and all it shows me is that we're very, very high up. I pass a few doors, but when I try the handle, they're locked, so I keep going, hoping for something new. All I see are more cobwebs, in some places so thick that they look like clumps or bubbles.

No spiders, at least.

Not yet, my brain helpfully reassures me.

I go endlessly up the empty hall as it winds up the length of the tower, and just when I'm about to turn around and find Solat, I hear something. Humming. Not like an electrical hum, but the faint strum of a million harp-strings played a great distance away. Curious, I pick up the pace, and up ahead, past two more twists of the hall as it winds around the great length of the tower, I see an archway. There are no doors, just more of the thick cobwebs that hang over the place like curtains. But behind them, there's a faint golden glow, and the melody of all those strings.

So I part the "curtains" and go inside.

The room itself is much bigger than it seemed in the narrow hallway. The ceiling slopes up so high that it's hidden in shadow, and the room's walls are completely rounded, as if we're in the center of the tower itself. Here, the spiderwebs are so thick that I can't see the stonework, and it feels a bit like I've walked into a cocoon. The music starts again, the notes not a melody but still somehow beautiful, and I realize that the center of the room is a gigantic, glowing spiderweb made of millions of strands. Unlike the walls, these glow and hum with life, and they don't seem to be connected to anything at all. It's like the web is anchored on nothing but thin air. The strands themselves stretch into the darkness and descend down into the musical tangle at the center of the room.

I'm drawn to it despite myself, fascinated at the hum, at the gentle glow. As I move closer, I can see the individual threads. There are thousands—no, millions—of them here, all inter-weaving and crisscrossing without a distinct pattern. Each thread looks slightly different from the others, with this one darker and smudged, while another glows with brilliant light. Fascinated, I reach out to touch one of the brightest strands.

"Do not do that," a cool voice echoes in the room.

Goosebumps prickle up and down my back and I straighten, quickly turning around. As I do, I see a man standing in the doorway behind me. The spiderwebs along the wall shiver and something twitches, and I get the impression that I just missed seeing the world's biggest spider. Gross.

"I'm sorry, I thought I was alone."

"I know." He stares at me, but even as he does, I get the impression he's not seeing me, which is strange. It's like he's only turning toward me out of courtesy.

There's no denying he's beautiful, though. The man wears a long, colorless robe that flows to the ground and pools at his feet. The sleeves are long and his hair is equally as pale and long. The face that stares out at me has bright, unnaturally silvery eyes, but his face is as gorgeous as a model's, right down to the pouty mouth.

I turn away from the musical web, unsure if I should extend a hand or what. "I'm Faith—"

"Yes. I'm aware." He blinks slowly, as if unaccustomed to it. "Are you looking for your strand?"

My strand? What's he talking about? I can't tell if he's accusing me or trying to be friendly—he's so emotionless it's hard to decide. "I actually was looking for something to eat." I smile at him. "You must be the Spidae."

I mean, there's really no one else he can be, and I feel stupid the moment I say it aloud.

"I am one of three, yes." He blinks slowly again.

"Pleased to meet you," I say, and decide to extend my hand anyhow, taking a few steps forward.

"Are you?"

Er. I pause. How do I answer that? Do I tell him I actually find him creepy and unnerving? Do I point out that I'm Aron's anchor? That Aron and I share secrets? Or do I run the fuck out of the room and hide like a little girl?

Choices, choices.

The Spidae—one of three, as he liked to point out—blinks in my direction again. "If you are hungry, I can retrieve you something."

That's an odd way of phrasing it. I debate my answer for a half second, but my fiercely growling stomach makes that choice for me. "Food would be great."

He closes his eyes.

I grimace, because did I just pick wrong? "You know, I'd really just like to see Aron—"

"He is busy dictating his wants to another of my Aspects and will be busy for a time." The Spidae opens his eerie silver eyes again. The wall behind him ripples, and this time, I see it. A spider, as big as a pony and as pale as the gossamer strands it steps on, descends from the wall. It moves to the Spidae's feet and then drops a bubble of webbing on the floor.

Oh ew. Now I see what he meant by "retrieve." Just like that, my hunger dies.

The spider scuttles back into the web, gliding up the wall and disappearing back into the shadowy ceiling, and I fight the urge to scrub at my skin. Instead, I watch as the pale god standing before me bends down and picks up the cocoon, then holds it out to me.

Well, shit. I guess that's mine now. "Yummy," I manage, and take it from him. Whatever it is in my arms is the size of a football, about as heavy, and doesn't move when I hold it. Thank fuck. "I should probably get going."

"Leaving?"

I'm not sure how to answer that. "Possibly yes? I don't want to be a bother."

For a second, his mouth ghosts up into a hint of a smile. "After I took the time to keep Aron occupied so we could speak privately?"

Well that's completely unnerving. "You...did?"

"Are you not curious about how you got here from your world?"

My mouth hangs open. I'm shocked. Of all the things I thought we were coming here for, that wasn't on the list. But it's a piece of information I'm desperate to have. "How did you know I'm not from here?" I clutch the webbed football to my chest. "Did Aron tell you?"

He gestures at the singing web, his weird, unfixed gaze on me. "I know everything. He did not tell me. He would not share a secret that would compromise you."

For some reason, I take that as a compliment. It just reminds me that Aron's surprisingly decent when he wants to be. "So you know how to send me back to Earth?" I mean, if he knows everything, he'll surely know that. "You know how I got here, and how I get back, right?"

The Spidae gestures at the web again, his movements elegant. "Come. Let me show you something."

As he glides forward, I follow after him, careful not to step

447

on his flowing robes. He approaches the web, and as he does, the singing increases, as if welcoming him. He moves so close that it's almost as if the strands are flowing around him, pulling him into their web. They're alive around him, whereas when I came closer, they were just strings. Just shiny threads. With him here, though, they're a symphony of light and color and sound.

It's the most beautiful thing I've ever seen.

He reaches out and gestures at one section of the web, swiping his hand to the side as if swiping right on the biggest dating site ever. That casual flick sends the strands fluttering away, and then he pulls at open air. One shining, bright golden strand fills with light, and I step forward to get a better look at it, fascinated.

"This is Aron," the Spidae says. He holds the thread delicately, and as I lean in, I can see where dozens of other threads cling to it, crossing over back and forth at various spots. The Spidae gestures again. "The other threads are where he meets with other mortals, where he intersects in their lives. Humanity is a web, crossing back and forth over one another, interweaving. No thread stands alone. Do you understand?"

I follow the beautiful thread of Aron's, gazing up to see how high it goes, and I'm not entirely surprised to see that it extends far beyond the rest of the web, stretching high into the shadows. "Why does it go so much farther up?"

"Because he is anchored to the High Father's realm. The Aether. Once he is torn from the mortal tangle and the Anticipation is complete, he will no longer be connected here." The Spidae points at the web, and near his finger, I can see where the shining golden strand splits into three different threads. "He is still anchored there, to the cosmos above." He gestures up, and when I glance overhead at the shadows, I see nothing but darkness, and it's easy to imagine the thread leading all the way up to the heavens. "Each thread must follow its path to completion."

I lean in, gazing at the split in the threads and the messy

snarl of what looks like nothing but tangles. Paths crossing, he said. Lives interweaving with one another. Despite my worries, it's fascinating. I follow Aron's thread and notice the loose string dangling on one end, cut free from its moorings. I point at it and look over at my companion. "Liar Aron?"

He nods.

It creeps me out to see that loose thread sitting there, dead. It's what we had to do, of course, but I still don't like to see it. Farther up, I see another loose strand made of shining gold, and I wonder if it's Tadekha. Hedonism Tadekha. I follow that thread as far as I can, but I can only see two connections left.

I return to Aron's thread, gazing at it closely. "Where am I? If I'm Aron's anchor, shouldn't I be in the weave here somewhere?"

The Spidae smiles, and I can't decide if it's a creepy gesture or a fascinating one. "You catch on quickly, my dear. Allow me to show you."

He doesn't point at the front of the web, as I expect him to do. Instead, he takes a few steps to the side, moving away from the main tangle of the threads. Curious, I follow him as he moves behind it and from there, I can see a few strands stretching across from an entirely separate web.

Holy shit. There are two webs.

CHAPTER 61

*T*wo webs.

I gape, unable to stop staring as I look at the threads that crisscross between the two webs. They're maybe a foot apart, the two webs, but each tangle seems completely separate save for a few rogue threads. There aren't many—maybe a dozen? Maybe fewer? Each of the rogue strings are pulled taut between the two webs, and when the Spidae gestures at "my" thread, it gleams with an unnatural light and I can see where I'm connected to Aron in the other web. My thread is twined around his, as if they're lovers. It's very clear mine cannot be separated from his.

Fascinated, I set my football "pod" down on the ground and step forward to study the webs closer.

"He's not actually tied to this web at all," the Spidae murmurs. "You are what anchors him here. When your connection is severed, so is his."

I follow my "connection" back to my own web, staring nose-height with my thread. The web for Earth—because it has to be Earth—isn't lit up with as many colored threads as the other. There's a deeper, darker tangle, as if billions of people are all caught up in the mix together. Makes sense. I want to ask where our gods are, which religion is right, what happens after we die, why my web is next to Aron's if it's two different worlds, but I zoom in on something else entirely. "Is...my thread breaking?"

I stare at my connection to the Earth web. It looks...really fragile. Frayed. Like the thing could snap at any moment.

"Your tether to your world is tenuous at best," he agrees.

"What does that mean?"

"It means if you leave now, I can weave you back into the web of your world." He gestures at the strand, completely taut between the two webs. He points where I'm intertwined with Aron's thread. "If I cut here, your thread is loose and can be worked back into your world's weave."

I gasp. I can go *home*? All of this bullshit can be over and I can go back to my normal life? Back to a world with cars and phones and cheeseburgers and medicine? Where no one's trying to kill me on a regular basis? My heart skips with joy for a brief moment—very, very brief. "You can snap your fingers and send me back?"

The Spidae inclines his head. "The veil between worlds was thin when Aron and the Aspects came through. I wove them into this web, and others were caught in the confusion. You were not the only one to cross over between worlds." He gestures at the handful of threads crisscrossing between the two tangles. "Nor are you the only one that has found your way to the side of an Aspect. Even now, others from your world serve the gods."

Nifty. I don't care about them. I care about me. I still can't help but feel that he's giving me all this information as a test of some kind...like he's dissecting my brain to try and read my thoughts. It feels like a trap, like if I say the wrong thing, I'm going to fuck myself over.

Or fuck Aron over.

Belatedly, I remember that Aron and Tadekha didn't get

along. I never asked if Aron and the Spidae got along. Shit. "Let's just play a few scenarios out," I say mildly, trying not to stare at my stretched-tight-about-to-snap thread. "What happens if I go back? To Earth?"

"I cut you free from this world." His eyes seem more silver than ever.

I straighten, frowning. "I thought if I died, Aron died too? That I'm what's anchoring him to the mortal plane?"

The Spidae nods again. "I cut you free...and we are down to two Aspects of the God of Storms, not three."

My mouth goes dry. My heart hurts and all hope ends right in this moment. If I die—if my thread is snapped from this world's weave—my Aron goes up in smoke. "He said that the Aron that's left after all this...that he won't be the same. The Aron I know won't exist any longer."

I look over at the Spidae, waiting for an answer.

He simply stares back.

Fuck.

Fuck fuck *fuck*.

If I go home, I screw over Aron. My Aron. I take him out of the running. I look at my thread again. At that fraying connection to Earth. "What...happens if I stay here?" I whisper. "For good?"

He gestures at the Earth-web. "Your connection here will snap soon. You will then only be connected to this world. To Aos."

Fuuuuuck. "So I'm stuck here even after he ascends again? Assuming we win?"

He blinks. "Are you?"

I grit my teeth. It's clear he's playing with me. I'm not dumb. There's something he's not telling me. Scratch that, there's a *lot* he's not telling me. Instead, I pace closer to the thread tangle, forcing myself to really, really look at it. What am I missing? What am I not seeing that he expects me to see? I lean in and stare hard at the thread tangle of myself and Aron. We're woven into the web all right, but something about it still strikes me as odd. I want to touch my thread and pull on it, to see where it's anchored, but I don't dare. What if I end up lopping my own head off? "I'm missing something big here, aren't I?"

"Are you?"

I make an exasperated noise. "You realize this is the most annoying game ever?"

He laughs, the sound hollow and rusty, as if he doesn't do it often.

"You said you wanted to talk to me. To give me answers. Here I am." I spread my arms wide. "Waiting for answers still."

The Spidae tilts his head. "You are not asking the questions. You are waiting for me to pose them myself."

"I thought it was pretty obvious." I cross my arms over my chest. "Let's say Aron wins and wipes out the other two Arons. That leaves just him as the big winner, right?" When he inclines his head, I continue. "So, then he's still in this web, yes?"

"Yes." His eyes begin to gleam again.

"So he's stuck on the mortal plane until...the High Father snaps his fingers and calls him back?"

The Spidae simply arches an eyebrow at me.

Yeah, I'm guessing that doesn't happen. I turn and stare at the threads again. Okay, something has to happen for Aron's thread to be severed—

Oh my god. I whirl around. "Aron has to die?"

He inclines his head again in an elegant nod. "Now you understand."

"But I thought the point of this was for Aron to learn a lesson? To beat the other Arons out of existence so he can return the big damn winner?"

"That is what he has been told, yes. He will learn no lesson if he has nothing to strive for."

I stare at the Spidae, feeling hollow. It's like a punch in the gut. Aron's doomed. None of this matters...because we're all going toward the same end anyhow. "So the Aron I know will cease to exist?"

"No." He crosses his arms over his chest and glides toward the web. "The strand that survives the longest becomes the dominant thread. His memories will remain, but all the ills—lies, hedonism, arrogance, and apathy—will be purged from him. He will return to the Aether to take up his mantle and continue on, serving as he should...until we repeat the cycle all over again."

"All over again?" I echo, the words a sick whisper in my throat. "This isn't the first time it's happened, then?"

"All gods become corrupted eventually," he agrees, reaching a long-fingered hand out and running his fingertips lightly through the web, as if petting it. "Too much power warps the one that holds it. An immortal loses the sense of who he is without a mortal anchor to tie him to reality. It happens to the best of gods, no matter the intentions. Even the kindest will turn their faces inward, dazzled by their own reflections." He pulls one gleaming string, fingers it thoughtfully, then returns it to its spot. "Which is why the High Father purges them every millennium."

I blow out a breath.

There's no saving Aron.

Maybe you are my heart, Faith.

I'm too shocked to even hurt. This is all just a big game to someone up above, so Aron and the others can learn lessons and be better gods or something. It's awful. "So...Aron has to die. Does he know this?"

"Do you think he would be fighting so hard if he did? He thinks winning will save you."

And that makes the ache spread. Oh god. "But there's no winning, is there? I have to die in order for him to win."

The Spidae nods again.

"So you're asking me to pick between my life and his. If I go home, I'm okay. If I stay here, I die. It's just a question of when."

"Is that what I'm asking from you?" He studies me intently.

I fling my hands in the air and stalk away, frustrated. As I do, my nightgown sweeps the floor and I notice little bits of what look like fuzz or dust cling to my hem and stick to my feet. I lift one foot...and pluck a short string from it. Horrified, I look over at the Spidae. "What is this?"

He tilts his head in that weird way of his. "The god of family is not in the heavens. He is in the mortal realm."

I throw the string away from me as if burned. "That's a *fucking* baby?"

"Is it?"

"Oh my god, I hate you." I press my fists to my forehead, because it's throbbing again. "It's a dead person, then?"

"The god of the dead is also split and wandering this realm."

My temper explodes. "Well who the fuck thought this was a good idea?"

"It is not a good idea," the Spidae admits, and for the first time, his voice is sad. "But those that become corrupted must remember who they serve. What better way to remind a god of what a mortal endures than to make him walk in their footsteps? Sleep in their beds? Eat their food?"

Except Aron doesn't sleep, and he doesn't eat. I do it all for him. I'm about to point this out when the Spidae reaches into the web, plucks out a strand, and flicks it to the floor.

"Why did you do that?" I ask.

He just blinks at me.

All right, I'm not entirely sure he's sane. I pace back and forth in the room, trying to digest all of this.

Aron has to die, but he can only die after the other two Arons die.

I have to die, period.

I feel like collapsing. I want to put my hands to my head as if

455

I can squeeze out the things I just learned. I want to go back to being ignorant, because it hurt so much less. A sob rises in my throat but never makes it past the knot that feels lodged there.

If I go home, I live, but Aron's zapped out of existence. He won't learn his lessons. He won't be the Aron that goes "home" to the Aether. He'll be part of the god that was "purged" and either Hedonism or Apathy will remain.

I feel dead inside. Defeated.

Resigned.

Even though I'm terrified, I won't abandon Aron. I can't. He's kept me safe all this time—

He thinks winning will save you.

The knot in my throat grows harder. He's not doing this entirely for himself, then? He's doing it for me, too? *Oh, Aron, you big arrogant lug. If you were here right now, I'd kiss the shit out of you.*

I look over at the Spidae, who stares at the web in front of him, obviously seeing things that I don't. His eyes have that strange, unfocused look, and every so often, he reaches up as if to adjust something, only to stop himself again.

Wait, he's a god, isn't he? If so, where's his anchor? Maybe he's crazier than I thought. Didn't Aron say an anchor was the only way for the gods to learn? To relate to mortals?

Maybe the Spidae is wrong—maybe we do survive if we win and he's just fucking with me.

I look over at him again with a narrowed gaze.

The Spidae's watching me out of the corner of his eyes. Mmmhmm. That fucker thinks he's smarter than me. Even though he's thrown a few bombshells, I still think there's more to learn.

CHAPTER 62

I cross my arms over my chest and saunter toward
him. "So buddy, where's your anchor?"

The question clearly takes him by surprise. I can practically
see a "malfunction" sign flashing in that creepy mind of his. "My
anchor?"

"Doesn't everyone have an anchor? You said yourself that
was one of the rules."

"Yes. An anchor." His gaze grows distant as he studies the
web. "I suppose an anchor is necessary to make one connect
with the mortal realm. I fully admit I am not entirely in charge
of my own faculties. The web can become…distracting." He
caresses the strands again, like a lover. "An anchor must be
offered freely, anyhow, and who would come here?"

He's got a point. Even so…something doesn't add up. "If you
don't have an anchor, how do you stay on the mortal plane?"

The Spidae looks over at me, a cunning smile on his face.
"How do you know that is where we are?"

"Because I'm standing right here? Pretty mortal, last time I
checked."

His smile widens, and he glides toward the second web, the

Earth web. "As I have said before, the veil between worlds is thin in places. I can exist here without an anchor, but I cannot leave this tower, ever."

"What happens if you do?"

"Why does that matter?"

I shrug. "Just curious. Do you and your brothers die?"

"Brothers?"

Now I'm confused. "Am I misremembering my crash course in the gods of this world? I thought there were three fates, past, present and future?"

"Yes."

"But...you're not brothers?"

"Is Aron brothers with his Aspects?"

Huh. I didn't think of it that way. "So you're an Aspect."

"Did I say that?"

I huff out a breath. "Jesus, you're frustrating."

"I said I would give you answers," he tells me, moving toward my direction once more. "I did not say how many answers, or to what."

Right. Answers. "You haven't given me any answers. You realize that, right?"

"Haven't I? You can go home, or you can stay here. Aron dies either way, it is just a matter of when. The choice is yours."

I clench my fists. "You know that's no choice."

"Is it not?" He arches an elegant brow at me. "This particular Aspect has a one in three chance of ascending back to the Aether in the correct order...provided he does not murder you first."

"*Murder* me?" Now this guy's just making me angry. "Aron would never hurt me—"

"Not willingly, no. Have you forgotten how you arrived here, lovely Faith?"

And that shuts me up, because he's right. I have totally forgotten. Aron drew on his power to kill the damn lake snake, and in doing so, he nearly destroyed me. He wasn't trying to, he just lost his temper and pulled on our bond too much.

"He is a war god," the Spidae says again, his voice cool. "He cares for you, but he would not be the first or last god to destroy his anchor by accident."

I think of Aron and how tenderly he held me as I fuzzed in and out of consciousness. The nosebleed I had at the farm when he made the rain stop. The crashing headache and the feeling of being sucked dry as he floated above the boat, wielding magic in a show of power I'd never seen before. Aron wouldn't hurt me willingly.

But he still hurt me.

I could still go home to Earth. Abandon him here and forget he ever existed. He'll still live on in a certain way. Just...not that Aron. He'll wear the same face but he won't be the same man.

I hug my arms close to my chest, feeling very small and alone. "I don't know what to do."

"That I do not have an answer for, I am afraid." For the first time, the Spidae sounds sympathetic.

"Which one are you? Past, present or future?" I look over at him, an idea occurring to me. "Can't we go ask future for the answer?"

The Spidae's mouth turns up in a smile. "He is busy with Aron, because I wished to speak to you."

You mean you wished to fill my head with questions and doubts, I mentally retort, but keep the words to myself. The Spidae is pretending to be benevolent, but I haven't forgotten for a moment that he's a god. An unbalanced one with no anchor, no less. All of this could be a ploy to manipulate me into doing something that he wants me to do. "Do I have to decide if I'm staying here or going home? Right now?"

"You have time," he says, inclining his head. "Aron will acquiesce to your request."

"Request?" I frown in his direction. "What request?"

459

"Your request to stay for a while longer. To relax here." He gestures at the tower. "You are tired and want time before you must confront his next Aspect. I have seen it in the web."

"I thought you said future was busy with Aron?"

He only smiles mysteriously.

"You suck."

"But I am never wrong." The Spidae nods at me and gestures at the open portal that leads to the long, winding hall. "You will find Aron at the base of the stairs, in the large chamber there."

I can't thank him for that tidbit. I feel…hollow. Like I've been dragged over a wringer for the last half hour. He's given me hope and destroyed it all over again. There's nothing to be thankful for about that. I want to cry. I want to give up.

I want Aron to put his arms around me and stroke my hair until all the pain goes away, but even that won't make me forget. I have to choose between myself or Aron. There can't be an "us" ever. We won't be allowed even the tiniest bit of happiness. Fate's going to fuck us over.

Even so, it feels weird to just turn and leave silently. It feels like a retreat. I hesitate, then take a step toward the door. "Later."

"If he asks," the Spidae begins, and I bite back a snarl of irritation. Of course he has to have the last word. Of course. The Spidae continues, oblivious to my mood. "Tell Aron he needs to go to Yshrem and meet the army there."

"What?" I cast him an irritated look.

"That is where Aron will meet his destiny," the Spidae says, then adds, "This particular Aspect of the Lord of Storms."

My mouth is suddenly dry as a bone. Him meeting his destiny sounds…dire. Add in "army" and I'm terrified. "Is he going to make it through that battle?"

The Spidae just stares at me.

Right. I'm sorry I asked. I shake my head and turn away again.

"You forgot this."

When I turn around, he's right behind me, and I jump in surprise. The Spidae holds out the football-sized pod and gives me a wintry smile. When I take it, he moves away again.

"Think on what I have said," he calls as I leave the room. "Think on the choices you make…because they are all yours to make, Faith."

CHAPTER 63

Once I'm in the hall, I rush down the slope at breakneck speed. I just want to get away.

Away from all of this.

Away from everything I've been told in the last few minutes.

The Spidae and his non-answers have wrecked me. Fucking destroyed me. I stumble over my skirts, skidding to my knees, and the sticky webs that cover everything stop me from tumbling all the way to the bottom of the tower. I skid a few feet and then collapse against the wall, crying like a baby. I curl up, hugging my knees to my chest and sobbing.

Everything is so fucked right now.

I can screw over Aron and hate myself for the rest of my life if I return to Earth. It's a selfish choice, and even if I wanted to make it, I wouldn't. I want to save Aron, but I have to think of everyone. Poor Vitar is dead. What about Yulenna, Markos, Solat and Kerren? Will they die if I choose to stay? Am I picking their deaths for them, too?

And Aron—my Aron—has to ascend for things to be "fixed." That means I have to die.

I don't want to die. A fresh sob escapes me, and I grind my

fists against my eyes. Why have I fought so hard for the last month to go home, to help Aron win, only to find out that none of it matters? If I go home, I destroy Aron.

It doesn't feel fair.

I cry and cry, feeling sorry for myself. For being the one that's responsible for Aron's death. For being the one that has to make a choice, and for the fact that there are no good choices at all. There's no right answer in any of this, only more heartbreak.

If I'd known that taking Aron's hand that day would have led to this, would I have done it? I think for a moment, then let out a bitter laugh, shaking my head. Like I had any other choice? I was going to be executed—a cleaver bride sacrificed in the god's name. Beyond that, though...I can't regret volunteering to be with Aron. I think of him with another anchor, holding her close, laughing with her...

And I'm hit with an ugly gut-wrench of pure, seething jealousy.

I'm shocked at how violent my thoughts get. Just imagining Aron with someone else makes me want to claw his—and her—eyes out. Fuck that. He's mine.

Somewhere along the way, I've come to care for the arrogant jerk.

I love him. Not that I want to admit that to myself, but isn't that why I'm not going to return to Earth? Why I'm going to let that connection thread snap and take with it my hopes of living past all this? Because I can't abandon Aron.

Because I love him.

I am such an idiot.

Shaking my head, I bury it in my hands again, marveling at how stupid I must be to fall for a guy that's been nothing but an arrogant prick since I met him. A guy that holds me tightly and strokes my hair, who touches me and makes me come because he wants me to think of him and only him. Who got jealous when he thought Solat was flirting with me. Who won't let anyone touch me because he wants to be the one touching me. I wipe away my tears, sniffing.

Yeah, Aron's a jerk and a half, but I still love him. His arrogance is the perfect foil for my salt. He doesn't care that I'm a potty mouth, that I'm surly in the morning, or that I have a soft heart underneath all my vinegar. He likes all of that about me.

Thunder crashes outside, and I lift my head, surprised. Uh oh. That's not a good sign.

I get to my feet, rubbing my temples. So far, no brain-shattering migraine, which means this is just a show of temper and not an actual drawing on his powers. Even so, I need to find Aron and talk to him, calm him down.

I head down the ramp, mindful of what the Spidae said. Bottom of the tower. He's there. I head in that direction, picking up my football and my skirts so they don't drag on the floor. I can still see the discarded strands everywhere at the Spidae's feet and fight back a shudder. I can't imagine those were anything good.

Another blast of rage echoes through the tower, and I wince as the parapet I pass by lights up with lightning. The sky outside is fading to twilight, the evening sun bleeding red across the horizon. I need to find Aron before it's dark because I don't see a single torch, and I don't want to think of what's waiting in the shadows. I clutch my football to my chest, suddenly a little afraid of this tower and its denizens. I know I saw a giant spider in the room with the Spidae. I don't want to know what he eats.

I mean, the answer could be "travelers" like Yulenna suggested. Then all my choices will be made for me. I bite back the hysterical laugh bubbling in my throat and walk a little faster.

I pass by a new pair of rooms, where I see Markos and Kerren lying on pallets on the ground. They get to their feet at the sight of me, Kerren pulling out his sword. I shake my head, indicating that they should stay, and continue on. The next room has Solat and Yulenna, but they're completely unaware of me, judging by the way Solat looks like he's trying to suck Yulenna's face off. Okay then. I don't say anything to them, just continue on as more thunder rumbles.

Aron's the one that matters. I have to get to him.

Every crack of lightning, every peal of thunder hurts my heart. Not in a physical sense, but in an emotional sense. I know Aron's hurting. He's upset, and I want to help him.

He thinks he can save you.

Has my big arrogant jerk fallen for me, too? My heart hammers at the thought, and it makes me speed up.

I can hear Aron before I see him. The boom of his voice carries through the hall, shaking the cobwebs as I approach.

"You have to let me see her! She is *mine!*"

"I do not have to do anything," the Spidae says, the voice cold and utterly familiar. It sounds just like the man I left upstairs… but this is future, isn't it? Unless the one I talked to was future. Unless they don't have divisions like that at all. Unless he was just fucking with me the whole time.

Entirely possible, given that he's a god of fate. Or an Aspect of one.

Thunder crashes again, and I inwardly wince, imagining Aron's fury. My head is still okay, and when I put a finger under my nose, it's still dry. No nosebleed. This is all just flash.

"You don't understand," Aron's voice carries as I hesitate outside the doorway. "I hurt her. I have to let her know I didn't mean to. I have to make it up to her. She's mine to protect. My responsibility."

"Why should I let you see her at all?" the Spidae asks.

Thunder crashes so loudly that I jump. *"Because she's mine,"* Aron roars, fury making the small hairs on the back of my neck stand up. The air is charged with lightning.

"And look at how you break your things."

The thunder dies away.

I'm surprised to hear this—that Aron's anger is over me. That he's demanding to see me. Wasn't the whole purpose of coming here to find out where Aron's other Aspects are? Wasn't that the whole goal?

"Tell me what you need from me," Aron says, his voice deadly calm. "I know you have her hidden away somewhere in this tower. Tell me what you need to return her to me."

"Well, you can ensure me that you will not harm her after we've gone to the trouble of saving her."

"You know I would *never*—" More thunder, but it dies just as quickly. "I need her back, my old friend. I need you to return her to me."

"Mmm." There's a long pause, and I wonder if I should enter the room. Just before I decide to step forward, the Spidae speaks again. "What if I told you that you could have another anchor? Surely the raven-haired wench would suit your needs."

I stiffen, horrified. That fucking bastard. Is the Spidae trying to replace me? I'm convinced now more than ever that the fates —the spider gods—are toying with us, holding information over our heads and using it to confuse.

"I want no other anchor. I need no one but Faith. She is mine."

"Any anchor will belong to you, Aron—"

"Faith is *MINE*."

I wait to hear more thunder, but instead, all I hear is a faint, eerie chuckle. The Spidae laughs. "Have you fallen in love with a human, Aron? After all this time? How many Anticipations have you gone through and never given your heart? Such a thing has never occurred before. You know no good can come of a mortal pairing with a god."

Silence.

My heart pounds in my chest, and the only sound is that of my quick breaths.

"What if I told you," the Spidae says, "That to ascend to your place in the Aether you must destroy her?"

I hold my breath. Is that their game? Turn us against one another and see which one of us breaks first? But if so...the Spidae has to know I'm listening. He has to know I'm here. He knows what I chose.

"Impossible," Aron says after a moment.

"Is it?"

"You spin lies to confuse me."

Fuck yeah. You tell 'em, baby. I silently fist-pump, wishing I'd had the balls to go back and give the Spidae hell for throwing so much misery on me.

"Fate is a tangled web," the Spidae agrees, amusement in his voice.

"Just let me know she is safe," Aron says, and there is such weariness in his tone. "Nothing else matters but her."

"She is safe. I do not keep her from you to play games."

There's a long, slow exhale of breath.

Aron was...holding his breath? He was that worried about me? Does he not realize that I was just upstairs chatting with the other Aspect?

I clutch the football to my chest. He really does care for me. He might even love me, in his Aron-ish way.

"You know you cannot take her with you, Aron," the Spidae says, and his tone is surprisingly gentle.

"I am an Aspect and she is my anchor. That is all that matters."

I can practically hear the scowl in his voice.

The Spidae laughs once more. "Yes, well, your anchor awaits you, my lord of storms."

CHAPTER 64

*B*efore I can step inside the room, Aron's rushing out. He nearly bowls me over, and I stagger backward, about to lose my balance.

Aron doesn't let me, though. He grabs me and crushes me against him, his big arms wrapping around me. "Faith!" A moment later, he claims my mouth in a hard, brief kiss, and then runs his hands all over my body. "How...do you hurt? Are you well?"

I'm shocked at how out of sorts he is. He looks as if he's just seen a ghost. I was just upstairs, though. "I'm fine. A little tired and hungry, but...why are you so freaked out?"

To my surprise, he drags me against his chest again and holds me close, his expression fierce. "You've been gone for days. I thought—I thought they'd sent you back to your world."

Days? Huh? I pull free of Aron's grip—not the easiest task—so I can look him in the eye. "What do you mean, I've been gone for days? I was sleeping upstairs next to Yulenna. I went looking for you and ran into one of the Spidae and we had a brief conversation. That's all. I don't think I've even been awake an hour..."

My words trail off because he's shaking his head, his expression furious. Thunder rumbles outside. "You've been gone for days. They manipulate time, move it back and forth to suit their needs. It's been days since Solat saw you leave the room. I nearly killed him thinking he had lost you, and then I knew the Spidae were just manipulating us to see how we would react." Aron's gaze roams possessively over me again, his hands moving over my body. "They did this purely to toy with us."

"They're dicks."

"Huge dicks," he agrees.

"Massive, massive dicks." I reach up and touch his face, loving the electric shock between us. "I'm fine, truly. All I did was talk to one of the Spidae."

He grabs my hand and presses a fervent kiss to my palm. "I thought I'd lost you," he murmurs against my skin. "That they'd convinced you to leave me behind."

"They tried," I admit.

Aron's jaw clenches. "I will murder all of them—"

I shake my head, putting my other hand on his chest. "It's not important. They were talking to both of us, trying to get responses from us. You know how a cat toys with its prey? That's what it felt like. They were prodding us to see how we'd react. I'm thinking they need to get a new hobby."

A hard, barking laugh erupts from him and he drags me close again, pressing me against his chest.

Oh. My heart squeezes for Aron. I know he likes to pretend he doesn't have feelings underneath all the arrogance, but he keeps hugging me and holding me so tight that I know he's upset. The constant thunder tells me that much. I've never seen him this messed up.

And I know I can never leave him, not to save my own skin. "I'm at your side until the end." I reach up and caress his strong jaw, letting my fingers trail over his gorgeous face, the scar that

469

carves down the left side. "You're mine and I'm yours, remember? You tell me that every time I turn around."

I expect him to laugh, because his mouth turns up in a hint of a smile. Instead, he lowers his head, and then his mouth is on mine.

We're kissing. We're really, really kissing for the first time since that fateful banquet in Novoro. This is different, though. Then, he was staking his claim on me in front of everyone. Here, it's just us and it's far more intimate. He cups my chin, tilting my face up to his, and then his tongue slicks into my mouth and he's claiming it like he's claimed my pussy with so many touches. Funny how he's given me orgasms repeatedly and yet we've kissed so rarely.

Everything feels different today. It's not the push-pull game between us. It's not the endless dance of teasing him and having him tease me back.

The time for teasing is over.

Aron's hungry mouth claims mine with a fierce stroke of his tongue, and hot waves of pleasure rush through me. The spark moves between us like it always does, but it feels like it's just driving the pleasure of his kiss even higher. I love the press of his mouth on mine, the way he claims my mouth as if it's always belonged to him, the feel of his big body looming over me. For a moment, I want to forget everything and just revel in Aron's touch.

With a groan, he hauls me up against him, his hands on my ass as he lifts me. I wrap my legs around his hips, my arms around his neck, and I don't lift my mouth from the kiss. It's too wonderful a kiss to ever let it go. In this moment, I'd cheerfully let him consume me if he'd only keep stroking his tongue over mine.

"I can't lose you," he breathes against my lips. His mouth nips at mine, unable to let up for a moment. "I can't."

"I'm here, Aron," I manage. It's hard to speak between kisses, but I'm not complaining. His mouth feels too good—too right—against mine.

I moan when my back bumps into the spiderwebbed walls, and then I'm crushed between the stonework and Aron's heavy body. His tongue thrusts deep again, claiming my mouth, and the stroke of it makes my hips arch with need.

"You're mine," he says, even as he rucks my skirts up, shoving them up my hips.

I gasp at the feel of his hands on my bare ass, my nails digging into the shoulders of his tunic. I'm not wearing panties, and in a moment, everyone's going to be able to see all of my lady business. "Aron," I manage between intense kisses. "We're in the hall—"

"No one would dare interrupt us," he growls, and smothers my protest in another heated, drugging kiss. I moan against his lips, even as he tears at his belt, his hand moving underneath my thighs. "Tell me you don't want this right now, Faith, and I'll stop."

Stop now? When I'm moments away from riding that glorious body of his that I've lusted after for weeks now? If he says no one's going to bother us, then I don't care. "Fuck no. Never stop." I lean in and bite at his jaw, then lick the red mark I leave there. I tangle one hand in his long hair, twisting my fingers into it. I need him to feel my urgency, to feel how badly I've needed him. Hasn't he always been the one that's held me at arm's length? Does he think I'm going to let him get away now?

Aron growls, clearly a fan of the biting. A moment later, both of his hands are on the undersides of my thighs and he spreads them wide. That's the only warning I get before he pushes me back against the wall once more and slicks his length through the folds of my pussy, wetting it with my arousal.

I gasp at the feel of him against my most sensitive parts, and he looks me right in the eye when he drives his length along my folds once more, the thick, fat head of his cock rubbing against my clit as he does. "I'm going to take you hard against this wall, Faith. You feel my cock? You feel how big it is? How hard it is for you?"

Oh god, do I ever. I whimper, nodding.

"I'm going to claim all of you," he says, moving one hand to caress my jaw, and he drags his thumb over my lips. "If you don't want that, tell me now. Tell me to stop before it's too late."

Is he trying to get out of this? Fuck that. I bite down on the thumb that's teasing my lips, letting him know I want it hard and I want it rough.

The groan that shudders out of him is unholy. Thunder rumbles overhead again, and then his mouth is on mine, hot and fierce and so, so good. Our teeth clash as we kiss, and it's frantic and deep and wild and—

And then he shoves that big, hulking length of him into me and I gasp, shocked.

Knowing that Aron's got a big, godlike cock is very different than having it thrust into me. It's been a long time since I've had sex—a really, really long time—and everything feels tight and stuffed to the brim. "Oh fuck," I exhale, my body shocked at the sensation. My legs are quivering around his hips, and I'm not sure if I want him to stop or do that again. "Aron—"

He reaches between us, pressing me back against the wall and pushing that enormous cock deeper into me. One hand cups my breast through my nightgown, teasing my nipple, and I gasp, my inner walls clenching around him. I feel like I'm impaled on his length, but god help me, I'm starting to love it. Everything's rippling and tightening, and when he flicks my nipple with his thumb, I feel it deep in my core, and I choke on another moan.

"My anchor," he murmurs. "My mortal. You know you're

mine, don't you?" And he thrusts deeper into me, impossibly. He's claiming all of me, driving me down on his length. "You know that this cunt belongs to me. That these legs are going to clench around no hips but mine."

I twist my hand in his hair. "You have to promise me the same."

He laughs, and I feel the movements all through my body, but especially in my pussy. "How demanding of you, my anchor." The words are full of affection. "You think I would touch another when I can touch you? No mortal has interested me in millennia. They are nothing to me. And then you come along, and..." He thrusts deep into me, and I cling to his neck, whimpering. "You have bewitched me. You have made me want things I have not wanted in a very long time."

"Good," I manage, rocking my hips against the massive length of his cock. "Good. I don't want you to want anyone but me."

Aron laughs again, and then he pumps into me once more. Not as hard, but when his hips begin to rock in a steady rhythm, it sends all kinds of new sensations through me. I don't know if this is better or worse—killing me fast with each hard, rough stroke, or killing me with small, quick pumps.

All I know is that it all feels amazing.

"You're mine," he whispers as I cling to him and try to set pace with his rhythm. He moves so fast that all I can do is hang on to him while he fucks me. As he moves, his hands go back to my hips and then he's drawing me down with rough strokes even as he spears into me, making each thrust as hard and fierce as he can.

And oh god, it's so good that it doesn't take long for that tingle to spiral through my belly. He's not even rubbing my clit and I feel as if I'm going to come. "Aron," I pant. "Fuck, Aron, I need—"

RUBY DIXON

"I know," he murmurs, and then, impossibly, shifts the angle of his thrusts.

I cry out as it rubs something inside me, something white hot and so good that my legs jerk like a puppet's, and then I'm coming, everything clenching and growing tight as he fucks the hell out of me. He growls low in his throat again, and his thrusts change, becoming hard and rough, and thunder crashes overhead as he comes, burying his face against my throat as I gasp for breath.

We rest against the wall, panting and breathless, until I'm vaguely aware that the insides of my thighs are sticky with come, both his and mine, and I've thrown my head back so often that half of my hair feels stuck to the spiderwebs on the wall. Aron lazily kisses my neck, pressing his lips to my pulse. I'm not ready to move yet.

My stomach growls.

Aron chuckles. "Hungry?"

"Always," I admit.

He leans in and kisses me again, this time softer, gentler, and then he eases his cock out of me, leaving me feeling as hollow as one of those chocolate Easter bunnies. I wonder if anyone would notice if I walked bow-legged back up to our rooms? Probably.

Aron sets me down gently on the ground and my knees wobble, and I have to lean on him for support. This time, he frowns. "You are weak?"

"Aron," I say, exasperated. "You just fucked the shit out of me. Of course I'm weak in the knees."

He studies me, as if to reassure himself, and then the look he gives me is definitely post-coital smugness. "I was excellent, wasn't I? Not rusty at all."

I roll my eyes. "I'm not giving you a trophy, if that's what you're aiming for. Don't think I've forgotten that your other

Aspect slept with Yulenna. You're not as unskilled as you pretend."

Aron grunts at that and helps me adjust my skirts. "I thought about it for a while, because she holds no interest for me and I tried to understand my other Aspect. Why he would do that."

"What was the reason, then?"

"The wizard must have wanted her. I—that Aron—would have taken her just to prove he could."

"Well that sounds dickish."

"I never said I was a nice man, Faith. Or that I was a just god. I am a god of battle." He caresses my cheek, gazing at me thoughtfully. "And of storms. That means I have a temper. I rush into decisions. But I will never touch another human, not when I have you. So you need not worry over such things."

"Oh, I'm not worried." And I'm not. Aron could have had Yulenna a hundred times over. It doesn't matter that she's upstairs messing around with Solat. She's made it quite clear that she's here for Aron's pleasure and no one else's. As for Aron? He's pretty much looked at her like he's looked at the others - as people to be tolerated, not enjoyed. Strangely enough, I'm not threatened. I smile fondly as he carefully pulls my hair free from the spiderwebs on the wall, because even now he's taking care of me.

"What made you change your mind?" I have to ask. "You said it was a bad idea for us to get together."

"It is." He frees the last bit of my hair and then puts an arm around my waist. "It's a mistake for any warlord to focus on anything but the battle at hand. You are a distraction I don't need, but I am already lost." His gaze moves over me possessively. "When I thought the Spidae had sent you home, I realized how much I need you with me if we are going to win."

My heart gives a painful little squeeze, because I know there's no winning this. Not the way he thinks. "I want you to be the last Aspect standing."

"With you at my side." Aron grins at me.

I try to smile back, though it feels forced. "Can we eat now? I'm starving."

He pulls me against his side, holding me close against him as he walks. Hell, he's half-carrying me, but I don't mind. I like leaning against him as we head back up the winding ramp. "There is food back in the bedchamber. We'll send the others packing and then I will feed you so you're not weak the next time I take you."

His hot look promises a very toe-curling taking indeed, and my stomach flutters. Even though I ache in all the right ways, I totally want to do that again. I'm still wet with his seed from a few minutes ago, and I can feel it slicking my pussy and inner thighs when I walk.

I think of the bed upstairs, where I'd slept next to Yulenna. Yeah, they'll definitely have to find somewhere else to sleep. "Maybe there's another room the others can set up in."

He grunts. "No need. We'll be leaving once I get answers from the Spidae. Tomorrow, hopefully."

"Tomorrow?" I echo, and I'm suddenly exhausted. I don't want to leave tomorrow. Suddenly, I don't want to leave, ever. I want to stay right here, in this creepy, spider-infested tower, because it means I'm here with Aron and the outside world is a billion years away…or at least over the other side of the mountains. Here, we can be left alone.

No wonder the Spidae said I'd request time to relax. Right now, that's what I want more than anything. I stop walking and turn to Aron. "The Spidae told me where we need to go." I don't want to withhold the information from him, because that seems wrong. "I know where we need to go, but Aron, can't we stay here for a while? Rest? Relax? Enjoy ourselves for a few weeks?"

"Here?" He arches an eyebrow, surprised, and those mismatched eyes study me. "Are you that tired?"

"Yes. No. I mean, if I have to, I can keep up. I'm just so tired of racing from one place to another." I sigh and lean forward, and he pulls me against him so I can cuddle against his chest. "It seems like ever since I met you, we've been running from someone or to someone. Can't we just relax and take a break for a few weeks? Do you have a deadline? Is there a time you have to be back by?"

I can feel the laughter rumble up in his chest. "A deadline? No. There are some gods who never returned from the last Anticipation. Kassam, the lord of the wild is still missing. And Tadekha remained here in the mortal realm in her Citadel. You met her."

Oh, I can't forget good ol' Tadekha. "I remember. So this doesn't have to be done soon?" I look up at him. "I don't care that this tower is weird. I just want to relax and wake up knowing I don't have to do anything that day except spend time with you. That sounds like paradise."

"You have an odd idea of paradise," he murmurs, and strokes my hair. "Very well. If you want to stay for a while, we will stay."

"Thank you."

My stomach growls again, interrupting whatever he was going to say next. Aron chuckles, and presses a hand to my stomach. "We had better feed my anchor before she fades away."

"God, yes, I'm starving."

"You have eaten nothing since you awoke?" His tone becomes angry.

"Actually, I cleaned out Solat's lunch. And dinner," I admit. "And then I went looking for more. The Spidae gave me a pod but..." I glance around, because I must have dropped it at some point. Probably when Aron crashed into me from the other room.

He shakes his head. "You probably don't want to see what was inside it."

No, I probably don't.

477

"Come," Aron says. "We will speak to the others and I will have you fed."

"You make me sound like one of the mounts," I mutter. Have me fed, indeed.

"If you mean to imply that you will get ridden, then yes," Aron says slyly, and I blush for what feels like the first time in ages.

CHAPTER 65

"We're staying here for a while?" Yulenna echoes, her nose wrinkling slightly as she toys with a bit of meat in her bowl. She's only picking at her food, which makes me absolutely crazy, because I would totally throw down right about now.

Actually, I am throwing down right about now. Ever since we returned to the others, I've been eating. Well, no, first we ushered everyone out of the room so I could quickly clean up with a sponge bath. Once all traces of Aron's release were washed away, I swiped a fresh cloth over my face and arms, and changed into one of my Novoran gowns.

Then I started eating. I haven't stopped eating since. The stew bubbling in the fireplace (who knew there was a fireplace? Not me). Hard bread from Novoro. Fruit. Dried meat. Grain cakes. More meat. More fruit. Another helping of stew. I wash it all down with cup after cup of Novoran wine. It seems that while I was recovering-slash-sleeping, the woales and all our supplies were mysteriously retrieved and brought to this side of the lake. That means I don't have to eat whatever is in the spiderweb-wrapped pods, and for some reason, I'm weirdly thankful for that. So I eat, and eat, while the others pick at their food and listen to Aron's plans.

"Faith needs to rest. She is tired and I don't want to risk my anchor."

I can feel the gaze of the others on me, but I don't care. I tear off another hunk of bread. "What? We stayed in Novoro for a few days. Why can't we stay here for a few weeks?"

"Weeks?" Kerren asks, clearly shocked.

"Why is everyone freaking out?"

"This place is not natural," Yulenna whispers. "We don't belong here."

"I know that. But the Spidae said we can stay for a while, so that means we're safe here. I'm sure there's another room you guys can set up and—"

"Two rooms," Aron says. "Yulenna is not sleeping with Faith any longer."

"I'm not?" Yulenna echoes, blinking her big eyes. "Did I do something wrong?"

A piece of bread lodges in my suddenly dry throat and I cough. Why didn't I think of this before? Aron and I slept together with Yulenna in the room before, but we weren't really sleeping together. He was just holding me. Of course she's going to wonder why things have changed.

"Faith will be sleeping with me," Aron says firmly, and I blush bright red again. I chug more wine, trying to be cool about things, but everyone stares in my direction. Porn music plays in my head.

"Yeah, we're doing it," I admit. Best to get it out in the open. "If you've got a problem with that, tough titty."

Solat laughs. No one else does.

"You are Aron of the Cleaver, Lord of Storms. We serve you in all ways." Markos bows stiffly. "I will make sure quarters are available for both Yulenna and your remaining men."

I flinch at that. Is that a jab about Vitar's death? I haven't forgotten it. I don't think I'll ever forget it. I take another gulp of wine, sad that the mood is so tense. I watch quietly as the others gather their things and leave the room, and then I'm alone at the small table near the fire, the fluttering web curtains falling over the doorway and giving Aron and me privacy.

"They're not happy," I murmur as I set down my cup.

"*They* do not make the decisions. I do." Aron paces slowly, his hands clasped behind his back. "If you want to stay here for longer, we shall."

"Do you think it's a bad idea?"

"No. It will give me time to think, to plan for when I meet my next Aspect. I tried to think ahead in Novoro, but that foolish Lord Secuban would not stop nattering for a moment." He gives an irritated shake of his head. "At least here it is quiet."

"Are we safe?" I finally ask. There are a few pieces of fruit left, and I idly pick one up, toying with it and deciding if I want to eat it. I might save it for later, but I could definitely eat it. I flip the round, orange-red fruit in my hands, back and forth. "Here, I mean? There's spiders and the Spidae, and that thing in the lake—"

"—all guardians controlled by the Spidae. If they do not mind us staying, then we are quite safe. If they wanted us to go, we would know it." He glances over at me. "You must intrigue them."

"Me? I thought they were helping you."

He snorts. "You have seen their method of helping."

Ugh, he's right. Hiding me away for two days just to see how Aron would react. Dicks. I can't imagine what they're thinking, other than they just like to toy with us. "They did tell me where we're supposed to go," I offer. "You'll never guess."

"Yshrem?"

I point at him, taking another sip of my wine. "That's it." The fruit in my hands smells heavenly, and I'm still a little hungry. I put down my wine cup and sniff the skin, enjoying the tease. I mean, I'm totally going to eat this, but I'll give it a little foreplay first. "Yshrem. He said you would meet your destiny there."

Aron nods thoughtfully. "The Cyclopae are warriors dedicated to me, and they conquered Yshrem years ago. I believe their king rules from there now, so it does not surprise me that I will meet my other Aspects on the field of battle before Castle Yshrem's gates."

Field of battle? I don't like the sound of that. "Is it safe to go there?"

"Do you mean, will the people of Yshrem try to kill me as my own priests did back in Aventine?" His lip curls with the memory. "There is only one way to find out, but the Cyclopae king is an honorable warrior."

"Whereas the prelate was a corrupt asshole looking out for himself. I gotcha." I nod and nibble on the skin of my fruit. It's so juicy that a droplet dribbles onto my hand, and I absently lick it up.

Aron watches me, his gaze intent on my actions. For some reason, I immediately think of sex. The way he's watching me tells me it's not about the fruit. Not anymore.

Flustered at his intense scrutiny, I try to keep the conversation going. "So you don't mind staying here until we head out to Yshrem then?"

"Staying in bed with you for a few weeks? It does not seem like such a chore." He slowly gets to his feet, and his gaze is devouring me.

I feel all fluttery and weak. Does he really want to spend the next few weeks in bed? "You know, for a guy that didn't want to touch me for the longest time, you're pretty gung-ho now."

"I told you." He stalks toward me, like a predator chasing prey. "I am already lost."

I watch him, fascinated and breathless. "What are you doing?"

"I find that I need to eat as well," Aron murmurs.

Confused, I automatically hold out the fruit in my hand. Sure, I've taken a bite out of it, but it's really the only thing left to eat. I've cleaned out everything else.

"That's not what I hunger for, Faith." And he slides to his knees before my chair, his hands moving to my hips.

I whimper.

With slow, methodical movements, Aron opens the slit of my Novoran wraparound gown and exposes my pussy. He stares down at it for a moment, and I squirm in response. Did I think the way he looked at me before was intense? It's nothing compared to how he's looking at me now.

His hands grip my hips and he tugs me forward, ever so slightly. When I remain completely still, he glances up at me, at the uneaten fruit in my hands. "Don't let me interrupt you. My anchor needs to eat and keep up her strength."

Oh.

It feels like the world is in slow motion as I put the fruit to my lips and lick away a bead of juice. Even as I do, Aron leans forward, his face moving between my trembling thighs.

And he licks me.

I can't stop the moan that pours from my throat. This is the first time he's put his mouth on me, there, and the spark that ripples between us feels like foreplay. I lean back in the chair, panting, as his tongue moves over my folds, dragging over my most sensitive spots, before he sucks lightly on my clit, drawing it into his mouth.

I'm whimpering with full-blown lust and need even as I raise the fruit to my lips and take another small bite. My mouth fills with juice as he works my clit, and it's the most erotic and insanely filthy thing I've ever done.

He strokes a finger deep into my core, and I sink my teeth into the red fruit as he does. Instead of thrusting into me, using his finger like he would his cock, he doesn't move. I'm confused, and in the next moment, I feel it.

Oh fuck. He's tickling something deep inside me and *oh fuck*, it's the most amazing thing I've ever felt. My hips surge off the chair and I cry out, the fruit forgotten. It slides out of my grip and slaps wetly on the floor as my hands go to his head. Impatiently, he lifts one of my clamping thighs and pushes it over the arm of the chair, making sure that I remain spread wide for his pleasure.

Because even though this is turning me inside out with ecstasy, I know this is for his pleasure, too. He rubs my G-spot as his mouth moves over my clit, and I'm babbling his name and clutching at his long hair even as he makes me come so hard that it feels like the thunder crashing outside is in my veins. He continues to lick and suck at my clit, finger working inside me as my hips buck with the force of my orgasm. Aron's determined to wring out every bit of pleasure from me, and it feels like he makes it go on forever, beyond the point of comfort, but he won't pull away, no matter how many times I tug on his hair or pant his name.

Aron finally listens for my pleas for him to stop, that I can't possibly come any longer, and lifts his head to give me the most arrogant, most Aron smile ever. "I liked that."

Oh god. I'm totally going to melt into a puddle at the sight of that smile. "Yeah," I manage breathlessly. "That was pretty good."

He arches that scarred eyebrow. "Only pretty good?"

He starts to lower his head again and I squeak, grabbing his hair before he can go down on me again. "W-wait! Wait. I need to catch my breath."

I love the rumble of his laughter. He merely kisses the inside of my thigh, slides my legs together, and gets to his feet. He takes my hand and pulls me to my feet, then tugs me into his arms and kisses me so hard that I'm left dazed. The taste of my orgasm is all over his mouth, and I find it strangely erotic to taste myself on his tongue. I cling to him as his mouth lazily explores mine, lost in the play of our lips.

Aron caresses my head, his fingers in my hair, and then nips lightly at my mouth. "Shall we climb into bed?"

Bed? I nod, dazed. I'm tired, but more than that, I want him to hold me. Bed sounds like a very good idea right about now.

He slips an arm behind my thighs and lifts me into his arms and carries me to the bed like a bride on our wedding night. In a way, I guess this kind of feels like one. I feel as if Aron and I are starting a new life together. Instead of just anchor and Aspect, we're man and woman, together.

I won't think about the future. Not right now. Not until we leave this tower. It can wait. It can all wait.

Aron's gaze is locked on me as he gently pulls the buckles free of my wide belt and then slowly removes my long gown. When I'm naked on the bed, he straightens and begins to undress. I always forget just how powerful Aron's body is. There's not an inch of fat on him, and he's all corded muscle and obliques. His six-pack ripples down his abdomen, and he's no longer as pale as he was when I met him, as if he's gained color —and life—simply by being in this world. Scars cover practically every inch of his skin, though, and I forget just how many he has until he undresses and shows me again. The long-healed gashes show red and sometimes white against his skin, some smaller and rougher, others large and long and deadly. The one on his face that crisscrosses over his green eye is the one I'm most familiar with, and I look up at him, worried. So many scars. So many brutal battles. Seeing him like this can get a little overwhelming, and every mark of a blade on him is a reminder that we might not win.

"You're frowning. Do you not like my scars?" Aron asks, and there's amusement in his voice as he stands over the edge of the bed, looming in that arrogant way of his. Of course he's arrogant. He's a god, but more than that, he's fucking amazing and he knows it. I no longer see his arrogance as irritation, more just a quirk of who he is. And I love all of him. "Do you want to know the stories behind each wound? All of them have a tale behind them."

I shake my head and raise a hand to him. "I just want to hold you, actually. Can we do that?"

"I can withhold no request from you," he says, and climbs into bed next to me. We're naked together, flesh pressed to flesh for the first time, and this feels way more intimate than anything we've ever done before.

Tentatively, I put my hand on his stomach. We're facing each other, inches apart, and his hand goes possessively to my hip, as if he has to touch me at all times. "This is the first time I'm getting to touch you, do you realize that?"

"You've grabbed me before. I distinctly remember several times in which I had to pry your eager hands off of my cock."

I laugh, because I remember that, too. "So are you going to push my hands away again today?" And I slide one down to his dick, just to test that theory.

"Never again," he says solemnly. "I am yours to claim, just as you are mine."

I am totally going to test that theory. I sit up in bed, gazing down at him as he rolls onto his back and tucks a hand behind his head, the most casual of men. As if we've done this a dozen times already. Truth is, I'm itching to touch him. I remember each furtive touch I gave him in the past and how he pulled me away. The realization that he won't do that again is a heady one.

And the man is stinking beautiful. It doesn't matter that his body is covered in scars. There's no part of him that isn't perfection. I trace a finger down one long, jagged red mark that crosses his belly and arches over to his hip. His pectorals are hard and flat, his shoulders broad, his hips narrow.

His dick is just as enormous as I remember from those furtive touches and our time earlier in the hall. I knew he was well equipped. I mean, no god is going to have a teeny weenie. And when we made love a short time ago? He was so big that it felt life-changing. Looking at him now, I see that it wasn't just my imagination. His cock is long and thick, the head prominent. Veins trace up and down his shaft, leading down to a lightly-furred ball sac that can only be described as thick. Every inch of him is thick and meaty and my mouth waters at the sight. I think of all the times that he made me lose control, and I want to do the same to him.

Out in the hall? That was the first time I ever saw Aron lose his shit. When he pushed me against the wall and fucked me as if he would die if he wasn't inside me in the next moment. That was heady stuff, and I want to see it happen again. I want him to lose his mind with pleasure.

Which means figuring out what he likes.

Which means I get to play with his cock. I smile, feeling a bit like a cat that licked the cream, and lean over him. He's a god, and so he's probably done everything a million times before. I don't want to think about that, so I'm going to focus on enjoying him myself. On pleasing me with his body, because that's all I have to offer in this equation—me.

So I lean over him and let my long hair tease his thighs, tilting my head to the side as I study him. I make sure not to block his view, because I suspect he wants to watch. His gaze is on me, and I can feel his body tensing ever so slightly. It makes me feel powerful.

I'm the first mortal he's wanted in forever. Me. That gives me all kinds of power over this strong, sexy god. He might be the lord of storms, but I'm the one he lost control with. I'm the one he was so desperate to fuck that he pushed me against a wall and plowed into me where anyone could see.

Smiling, I slowly wrap my hand around his cock, testing his girth. He's so thick that my fingers don't meet, and I shiver a little at the memory of how he'd felt deep inside me. I lazily squeeze the base of him, liking the intake of breath that he makes, and then release him so I can glide one finger along a vein, tracing it to the prominent head of his cock, where it disappears underneath the edge of the crown.

He growls, all impatience, and as I watch, a bead of pre-cum appears on the head of his cock, swiftly followed by another.

"What does a god taste like?" I murmur, moving forward so I'm leaning over his cock, my hair falling around my shoulders.

"See for yourself," he rasps, and the look in his eyes is intense. How did I ever think this man wasn't affected by me? I know at some point I'm going to tease and he's going to break, and then he's going to fuck me hard again, just because he won't be able to help himself.

My thighs squeeze with excitement at the thought, and that hollow ache in my belly returns. I want that. I want to make him break with lust. I love that thought.

I lean in and use the tip of my tongue to lap up each salty drop, cleaning his cock. He tastes good, but I'm probably biased and it has nothing to do with him being a god and god-cum somehow being tastier. I just love everything about Aron—even his arrogance. "It's just all right," I tease.

He scowls. "My seed tastes better than any other seed and you know it. Taste me again." And his hand goes to my hair, as if he'll guide me down.

I shrug, leaning in to the game, and give his cock-head another swipe with my tongue. "Not bad."

Aron's breath hisses out. "Woman—"

"I'm just saying, I've had better."

"No, you haven't." He gives me another one of those smug grins, then pushes my head down again. "You must not have tasted it right. Take more of it into your mouth."

I feign ignorance. "You think I should?"

"Absolutely."

An erotic thrill charges through me as he gently tugs my head downward. It makes me feel sexy, and I'm squirming with need, wiggling my hips as I lean down and grip his cock again, then take him into my mouth. He's so big that he stretches my lips, and it's hard to tongue him properly. I glide him as deep as I can, and then ease him back once more, giving the head a lick.

"Well?" He's breathing harder.

"I need to taste again, just to be sure," I murmur, then pull him into my mouth again, working the base of his cock with my hand. I keep my mouth wet, coating his big cock with my saliva, and take him a little deeper this time, and then deeper still when I work his shaft back into my mouth, gliding him along my tongue. I take him so deep that he hits the back of my throat and then I rise up, biting back the choked sound that threatens to erupt. And I look up at him.

His eyes are slits of pleasure, the hand in my hair loose, and there's such a blatantly erotic look to him that I'm breathless with need.

"Do you know how beautiful you are when you do that?" he murmurs.

"You're just saying that so I'll go down on you again."

"You'll do it anyhow," Aron says, his fingers gliding to stroke my chin. "Because you get aroused from pleasuring me."

He's right, the arrogant jerk. Right now my pussy is totally wet and sensitive, aching with need. I love touching him, his hot skin, his big cock, and I love that he's turned on, too. Just knowing I can do this to him makes me crazy with need. I just smile and take him deep again, working him with my mouth, with my tongue, with everything I can because I want to see him lose control.

The low groan he lets out makes my pussy clench. I redouble my efforts, licking the length of his cock from base to tip, teasing his sac, doing everything I can to make him snap. I've barely taken the head of his cock into my mouth again when he rocks his hips lightly, thrusting, fucking my mouth. He shuttles his cock in and out, using my face as he breathes my name. I love it, and with my free hand, I slip my fingers between my thighs so I can touch myself. I'm so aroused I can't wait for more. I need to come just as badly as he does.

"No," he grits out, and then gives my hair a tug, just enough to make me lift my head off his cock. "That's mine."

"What's yours?" I pant, breathless.

"That pussy." His eyes flare with heat.

"I need more." I squirm, rubbing my fingers through my soaking folds. "Is that so bad? Touching you gets me worked up—"

"You'll wait," he says, all arrogance.

I groan at his words, because as dickish as it is, it also makes me hot. Is this going to be a contest between us then? Because I can play that game, too. I pretend to acquiesce, moving my hand back to the bed, and take his cock with my other hand. I lean in, letting my breath fan over the wet head and hovering over it, teasing him.

"Faith," he breathes, his gaze utterly fascinated as he watches me. "Take me into your mouth again."

I look over at him and give him a sultry little smile. "You'll wait."

Laughter barks out of him, and in the next moment, he's got us reversed. Suddenly I'm on my back and he's the one over me. His hair slides over his shoulder and he grins down at me, full of lust and amusement. "You're the only mortal who thinks she can go toe to toe with a god, aren't you?"

I suck in an eager breath as his hands go to my body, jerking my thighs apart and sliding them around his hips. "Maybe I just like giving you a taste of your own medicine."

"Or maybe you just like it when I take you hard and rough," he murmurs, then leans in and claims my mouth with a punishing, possessive kiss. That's the only warning I get before he thrusts into me, taking me just as hard and rough as he promised.

And oh god, it's *so* good.

My hands go to his head, cradling him as he kisses me, sinking into the sensation as he pumps into me again and again, claiming me as his. I don't care that his movements are a little rough, or that every stroke feels as if he's pounding deep inside me. It means I can let loose, too. I grab his shoulders and dig my nails into his skin, and I arch when he thrusts. When he kisses me, I bite down on his lip, and that only makes him wilder. The bed shakes, pushing against the wall with a shivering noise like hay rustling, and it's barely audible over the thunder crashing outside.

When I come, my entire body clenches and I cry out, shocked at how intense everything feels. Aron covers my breast with his hand, sending another shockwave through my body, and keeps taking me, wringing another orgasm through his hard, rocking thrusts. By the time he comes, I'm whimpering with the aftermath of the intense climax, and I clutch his sweaty body against mine as he collapses atop me.

I feel so at peace. So...happy.

I think of Yshrem, where Aron will "meet his destiny" and I squeeze my eyes shut. I don't want to think about that today. I'll just think about the man sprawled atop me, who feels so good I never want him to move.

"Tell me you love me," I whisper, stroking his hair back from his face as he sits up.

Aron frowns, gazing down at me. He touches my cheek, caressing my face, and then shakes his head. "I am a god, Faith. We do not love."

Strangely enough, that response doesn't bother me, because I'm pretty sure he's wrong. "You'd miss me if I died, though, wouldn't you?"

His brows draw together, and thunder snaps overhead. "Why would you die?"

"I'm just saying—"

Aron shakes his head slowly. "You are not allowed to die,

Faith. Do you understand me?" His jaw is clenched, and there's a wild look in his eyes I haven't seen before. "I forbid it."

I nod, and when he leans in to kiss me again, I fight back a smile. Yeah, dude's totally in love with me.

He just won't admit it to himself.

CHAPTER 66

*W*e don't leave the bed for three days.

Well, that's not entirely true. I get up to pee, to eat, to drink, but other than that? I spend every moment with Aron. Kissing Aron. Touching Aron. Aron touching me. It's a magical time, really. I think of it a bit like a honeymoon, where we've finally joined at a higher level and now we're just enjoying each other and learning more as we go. I learn that Aron likes for his hair to be brushed, and that it arouses him. I learn that he gets aroused by watching me eat, because I enjoy it so thoroughly. I learn that Aron gets aroused by the soft sounds I make when I sleep, because he wakes me up and fucks me hard, then lets me go back to sleep.

Really, I learn that pretty much everything turns Aron on.

I've never been the object of intense fascination of a god before. He doesn't eat, doesn't sleep, and focuses all his energy entirely on me. In the three days we don't leave bed, I orgasm more times than I think I have in my entire life. The scent of sex feels permanently etched into my skin, and like a wanton slut, I only crave more. How can I not? The guy knows how to work a

RUBY DIXON

clit, he knows where a G-spot is, he's got a massive cock and undying stamina.

Of course I'm eager to jump into the sack with him every time.

After a few days of this, though, I wrinkle my nose at my own smell. "I don't suppose this tower has a bath, does it? Because I sure could use one."

Aron lifts his head from where he's kissing down my belly. "You want to bathe? I can bathe you." His eyes gleam. "It would be my pleasure."

I snort. "In a tub? Because I haven't seen a tub here."

"This was a human tower once," Aron says. "It might have a tub."

"It was?" I'm shocked. This place is so creepy and surreal that I can't imagine anyone living here...then again, haven't we been hanging out here for days? Weeks? So maybe I need to rethink my idea of 'creepy'.

Sure enough, Aron asks Markos and Solat, and they've seen a washroom a few floors down. A short time later, we're in the washroom together and the massive marble tub has been filled with steaming hot water, thanks to Yulenna. I relax against Aron's broad chest as he cradles me in his arms.

"Now this is the life," I murmur, trying not to look too hard at the clusters of cocoons in the spiderwebby corner directly across from us.

"It does not take much to please you," Aron says with amusement, and twines his fingers with mine under the water. "A tub full of water, at least five climaxes a day, and all the food you can stuff into your mouth."

"When you put it that way, you make me sound terribly demanding," I say, smiling as I close my eyes and rest against him.

"Being an anchor is demanding work," he murmurs, lips brushing against my hair.

494

"Work." I snort. "There's a lot of things being an anchor involves, but I don't know if I'd call any of them 'work.' The biggest task I have is putting up with the bullshit you spew on a regular—"

My words choke off as he cups my pussy and slicks a finger between my folds, rubbing my clit. "Watch what you say, sweet Faith. You don't want me to punish you, do you?"

Oh lord. Aron's definitely got a dominance streak and it comes out when he's feeling frisky. Now I'm getting even more turned on. "Right here? In the bath?"

"You can bathe first," he reassures me, and gives my pussy a pat as if telling it to be patient. "Are you hungry?"

"Is this a full-service bath? I *am* spoiled." I slide deeper into the water, which means my hair is sticking to his chest, and his rock-hard thighs are beneath my arms. "But no, I can wait for now."

Aron runs his fingers through my wet hair, then begins to soap it with a bar we borrowed from Yulenna. "Is this much like the baths in your world? On Ert?"

"Earth," I correct. "And yes and no. We have running water, where you turn a spout and the water comes out of the pipe hot." Yulenna filled basins and heated water to make this happen. "And on Earth I'd have shampoo and body wash and conditioner for my hair and all kinds of good-smelling bath products. And bubbles."

"But no war god to soap your body for you," Aron says, and drags a handful of water over my breast.

Nope, he's got a point there. I arch against his hand, smiling when he begins to tease my nipple into a hard point. For a guy that didn't want to get involved, he's been nothing but touchy feely ever since, not that I mind. "I'd trade bubble baths for you, every day."

"Is there anything you miss?" He releases my breast and smooths soapy water over my shoulder. Is he washing me, then?

Or just caressing? I sit up again, so he can do as he likes, and one big hand smooths up my back.

I moan at his touch, because it feels so good. "Hamburgers," I murmur, hugging my knees and resting my cheek against them. "Big, fat, sloppy hamburgers. With cheese and extra pickles, mayo and mustard, tomatoes, lettuce, and a sesame seed bun. Bacon, too. Oh yeah, totally dripping with bacon." And now I'm hungry.

Aron chuckles, rubbing the washcloth up and down my back. "It's always food with you."

"Hell yeah, it is. I'm always hungry. That's your fault." I smile.

His fingers dance up my spine, then the washcloth brushes at the cleft of my ass. "Because I keep you in my bed and use you until you are begging for relief? Because I make you come at least twice before I slake my own needs? Because I am not satisfied until your cunt clenches tight around my cock and pulls me deep?"

I suck in a breath at his words. "Well, there is that, but I meant I'm always hungry because I'm your anchor. I have to eat for both of us." In fact, I could eat right now, but I'm too lazy to get out of the water, because it's warm and a flirty, thoughtful Aron is irresistible as he washes me.

I love the sound of his lazy chuckle. It fills me with warmth even as he glides the cloth over my back. "Do you miss your world, then?"

I knew this question would come up eventually. If anything, I'm surprised he hasn't asked sooner. I'm also a little surprised I haven't thought about it more myself. Earth hasn't been on my mind much in the last few days. My thoughts have been completely and utterly about Aron. "Do I miss Earth? I don't know. I mean, I miss hamburgers and strawberry milkshakes and cars—remind me to tell you about cars sometime. But it's more like that was the world I was familiar with. I knew Earth. I knew how to get around on Earth. I knew what I was doing, and I knew what my choices entailed. I feel out of my depth here, and some of the stuff Aos doesn't have scares me a little. Like, say, health care. Do you guys follow the whole "slap a leech on it" method for sick people? Because I really can't approve of that. And I shudder to think of what passes for a gynecologist in this world."

Aron chuckles again. "Is that...a yes?"

"It's an 'I don't know.' It's an 'it's complicated.' I'm sure as time passes, there will be a lot of things I miss. But right now? Right here, I can't think of anything." I'm too lazy, too happy, too content to be in this bathtub with him, cradled between big thighs as he washes my back. "Is that a bad answer?"

"It's an honest one," he says, and then I feel him touch my shoulder, and he presses a kiss to it a moment later. "You can return to your world, you know."

My heart gives a funny little flip. "Gee, can I? Because I'm your anchor and last I heard, those sorts of bonds were set in stone."

"They are for most, but the Spidae are different. If anyone can sever the bond between a god and his mortal anchor, it would be them."

This sounds perilously close to what the Spidae told me when I was alone with them...when they were trying to manipulate Aron and me both by separating us and questioning us. Why is this coming up now? I turn and give him a worried look. "Have you been talking to the Spidae, Aron? Did they tell you I need to go?"

He arches a brow at me, surprised at my vehement reaction. "No. I have not spoken to them. I have been at your side, remember?"

Right. He hasn't left me alone in days. My speeding heart slows down a bit. "Good. I just...I don't trust them."

"No one does." He gestures at his scarred chest. "Lean back so I can continue washing you."

I start to, and then hesitate, biting my lip. "I don't want to leave you, Aron. Not to go home. I'm with you until the end, until the day you leave me."

His expression grows solemn, and he stares at my shoulders, carefully lifting my wet hair from my skin and easing it over one side. "Part of me wants this to be over, because I am power-less on this plane. I chafe at the idea that the High Father feels the need to 'remake' me because I was so broken before. But part of me...part of me wants this to go on forever. Just me and you, always." And he reaches up and cups my face. "I do not know what happens after I win, Faith. I wish I did. I wish that was still in my memories, but I can see nothing of what happens once this is over."

My heart aches. I know what happens. If the Spidae weren't lying to me, it's not good. None of this is good.

"But I am a god," he continues, voice low but firm. "I am the lord of storms and god of battle. I will bring you to my side and keep you with me, always. You are mortal and unimportant to the rest of the world." He squeezes the cloth over my shoulder, sending sudsy water down my skin. "But not to me. To me, you are everything."

Everything but winning, I want to say, but I bite back the words. I don't want to ruin this good thing we have here. I don't want to ruin the perfect few moments we have together. I'm going to enjoy every single one of them.

"It will mean staying in my world," Aron says as I settle in against his chest. He dips the cloth in the water and runs it over my breasts, giving my nipples extra-special attention so they stand up. "Would you stay here with me?"

"Always," I tell him, and I mean it.

CHAPTER 67

a week passes. Maybe more. I lose track of days. All I know is that I'm happy. Sure, we're in a creepy tower, and the Spidae lurk around every corner, and we're out of our traveling supply of food so we're now eating whatever we find in the pods the Spidae have scattered around the keep.

But every morning, I wake up in Aron's arms. Every night, I go to sleep in Aron's embrace. Every day, we spend together—making love, talking, or laughing.

And that's worth everything. I don't care if a million days pass by. If they're all like that, then sign me up.

It's easy to forget the world outside of this tower. It's so easy to forget that out there, in this strange world, dozens of Aspects are roaming the world, looking to put an end to anyone that has the same face. It's easy to forget that our lives were—and still are—in danger. Here, we're safe from the world because no one wants to cross the mountains and that awful lake. I'm still not entirely sure how our woales got on this side of the lake with our supplies. Every time I ask, Aron just laughs and says "not easily."

Whatever it is, it doesn't matter. If this is what happiness looks like, I'll grab it with both hands.

One morning, though, I wake up to the sound of swords clashing. To male laughter. Aron isn't in bed with me, and I frown to myself as I get up and pull on a robe. There's no window in our room, but I know the sounds are coming from outside. I pad into the hall, where there's a large, spiderweb-covered balcony and find Yulenna there. She nibbles on fruit, a pod half-opened in her arms.

"Hi Faith," she says cheerily as I move to her side. "You hungry?" She offers me some fruit.

It seems that the pods are a bit more benign than I'd originally thought. The ones that we've split open have had a variety of food items—from vegetables to fruit—and though some had a bird or fish in them, it was alive. It's like the spiders bring back food for the Spidae...who don't eat.

It's all very odd.

At any rate, the food has served us well enough, and I don't feel weird about taking a handful of the small, purple cherry-like fruits and popping a few into my mouth. Down below, the men are sparring. Aron has a long sword in his hand and he's got one arm tied behind his back, and he's blindfolded. He's fighting both Kerren and Markos and winning handily, it looks like. Each time one of them jabs, he's there to parry it instinctively. As I watch, Solat creeps forward, half-hidden behind a large shield, readying to strike at Aron's side. Before he can even get close, Aron whirls, knocks the shield free, and then spins around to block Kerren's next attack.

They all laugh, and I hear the words "I yield" float up as Markos grins.

Aron's smiling, too. His face is lit up with pure, unadulterated joy, and sometimes I forget that he's a battle god. He loves a fight. As I watch, Kerren approaches Aron and helps him remove his bindings. Aron slips off the blindfold and immediately looks up at the balcony to me.

He grins, utterly pleased.

I wave back at him, then lean over to Yulenna. "What's this?"

"The men were bored so they started sparring. Aron must have heard it and joined them. They've been at it for hours." Yulenna picks up another piece of fruit and eats it daintily. "They want to be ready for war."

War? My good mood sours. Aron says something with the guys below and point at weapons, discussing. As I watch, Aron talks with Kerren, showing him a sword move and how to block. It's clear Aron's in his element.

I don't want him thinking about war or battles.

"He is a god of war, though," an eerie voice says behind me.

Yulenna gasps and steps closer to me. I grit my teeth, turning to look at the Spidae who stands in the background. He waits in the hall, watching us out on the balcony. The phrase "waiting like a spider in its web" springs to mind but I bite it back. "Don't you have threads you could be pulling right now?"

The smile that curves his mouth is unfairly pretty. "I do. But I sensed your mood. There is no need to be angry over things you cannot change, Faithful."

Faithful. That was what Tadekha called me. It irritates me to hear it, but I know why he's doing it. He's showing me just how much he knows. Yulenna cowers behind me and I glare at him. "I haven't forgotten who Aron is, all right? I just want him to enjoy his time here. We're supposed to be taking a break from all this shit."

"He cannot 'take a break' from who he is. You must accept all of him or none."

Is that a warning? Angry, bitter words threaten to spill forth but I bite them back. There's a sympathetic note in his voice that makes me pause. I don't know if he's trying to be nice or to mess with me. I never know. I clutch my robe tighter to my front. "Is it so wrong to be unhappy at the sight of him sparring? I don't want to lose him. I don't even want to think about it."

"You will lose him no matter what you do," he intones. "The question is, what are you willing to risk for him?"

Is this an offering? A way out? "Everything," I breathe, taking a step forward despite Yulenna's frightened grip. "I'll do anything—give everything—if you can save Aron."

He merely smiles and turns away.

Shocked, I watch him leave. So that wasn't him offering to help me? That was just more fortune cookie bullshit. I clench my teeth, utterly annoyed.

"Who was that?" Yulenna asks, awed. "Was that one of the spider gods?"

"The Spidae. And yes. I don't know which one, but I think they're all the same. They're assholes and manipulators, and completely, batshit crazy." I turn back to the narrow strip of beach, where the men are sparring again. "Let's just forget we saw them, okay? I don't want to ruin this day."

Funny thing, though, the day already feels like it's ruined.

IT FEELS a bit like I'm pouting. I know Yulenna thinks I am, but I really don't begrudge Aron his time with the others. If they were fishing or wrestling, I don't think I'd care. It's the sword in his hand, the battle strategies that he teaches them with every breath he takes…those are what scare me.

You can take the boy out of the battle, but you can't take the battle out of the boy. Aron is and will always be a soldier, a warrior, a warlord. He's going to want to leave this place behind soon enough to go and meet his destiny in Yshrem, a place I've never heard of but already hate.

I feel like I'm losing him. That's why I hate Aron's sparring practice. That's why I hate the swordplay.

It's too soon. I don't want to lose him just yet. Or ever.

But definitely not this soon.

The men pause for a while to take a break. Kerren groans loudly, and the others flop down on the pale shoreline and I know the reality of it—they're exhausted. No one can keep up with Aron. He's immortal and has had millennia to hone his battle tactics. They've tried every way they can to slow him down, from tying him to Kerren's back while blindfolded to binding his fingers together, and he still won. Each and every time, he wins. He smiles that arrogant, heartbreakingly gorgeous smile of his, and then glances up to see if I'm watching him.

But when they take a break? He comes to see me.

Aron arrives, sweaty and covered in sand, and pulls me into his arms. "My body craves another kind of battle right now," he murmurs, sliding a hand under my dress. "Luckily I have the fairest anchor in six kingdoms to please me..." His words trail off and he frowns. "What's wrong?"

I feign ignorance. "Wrong? Nothing's wrong."

"You look upset."

"I'm totally not upset," I lie. I don't want to explain to him why I really am upset. That I'm terrified of losing him. That not only will I lose the man I love, but I'll lose my life and whatever afterlife I had planned.

His eyebrows furrow and he puts a finger under my chin, tipping my face up so he can study it. "We were simply sparring —you know I would not get hurt. I cannot get hurt."

"I know."

Aron frowns at me for a moment longer, and then realiza-tion flickers over his face. "Ahhh. You are jealous of the time I've spent with the men. That's it, isn't it?"

It's the most absurd and arrogant thing and a laugh bubbles up inside me, because it's so typically Aron to say that. "No!"

"Yes," he agrees, grinning. "Do not worry, my lovely Faith.

You have my undivided attention, I promise you. Shall I spend all night in your bed so you can have your way with me?" He leans in and nips at my mouth.

I don't know if I want to laugh or cry. "Have my way with you, you say?"

His eyes gleam. "You can tie me down and we can pretend I'm your anchor and you're the fierce goddess who must lick my cock for endless hours to sate herself."

I snort. "This sounds suspiciously like a male fantasy."

"Of course it is. But you'd still enjoy it." His hands fasten on my ass and he holds me close, twirling me slightly on the balcony and grinning. I can't help but smile back at him, and my heart is aching.

I want this moment—this silly, ridiculous moment—to last forever.

But I have a terrible feeling it's all about to come to an end.

CHAPTER 68

*N*othing comes to an end for weeks, though. We pass another two glorious, lazy weeks in the Spidae's keep, and the men spar on the beach every day while Yulenna and I chitchat about nothing in particular. Aron is true to his word, though—when he's not sparring and speaking of moves and discussing battle plans for troops he doesn't have—Aron's with me. He's as thoughtful and kind a lover as he is brutal and magnificent.

I'm head over heels in love with the big guy. I've never been so happy. Those two weeks pass in an instant.

One morning I wake up, though, and I immediately know something's wrong. Aron's not in bed with me, and at first I think he's out sparring with the men. It's awfully quiet, though, so they must be talking strategy or discussing plans. I get dressed, slip on a pair of shoes, and head to the balcony so I can watch.

But Aron's on the balcony, much to my surprise.

"Oh, hey, you're up here? No practice today?" I move forward and slide my hand into the crook of his arm, pressing a kiss to his bicep.

"Not today."

There's something in his tone that seems…off. He doesn't look at me, doesn't give me one of those heart-melting smiles, doesn't even act like his normal arrogant self. He just puts his hands on the balcony ramparts and stares out at the wide, gray lake.

"Aron?" I ask again, starting to get worried. For the first time, I notice that his long hair is slightly disheveled, as if he hasn't brushed it or run his fingers through it after getting out of bed. His clothing looks like what he wore yesterday, wrinkled and the laces undone. I notice he's got no shoes on his feet.

This isn't like him at all.

"I'm fine, Faith. Go back to bed."

I playfully run my fingers up his arm. "Only if you come back to bed with me."

He shakes his head. "I'm not in the mood."

Not in the mood? Not in the fucking *mood*? I'm hurt, but it quickly passes. This isn't Aron. Something's wrong. Something's different about him and it's worrying me. Aron has been in the mood ever since we first made love. Sometimes I wake up to him pushing between my thighs because he doesn't want to wait until morning for me to wake up—and I love that. I wake up to him kissing me or going down on me because he loves my taste. The man loves sex.

How can he *not* be in the mood? He's always in the mood.

I study him for a moment longer, then suggest something I think will break him out of his funk. "So when we get to Yshrem, what's the plan?" Talking war strategy with the men always makes him light up. If nothing else, it makes him talk, sometimes endlessly. Right now I'd be happy to let him fill my ears about troops and battle plans if it means he'll just talk to me. "Carry on as we have been? Or amass an army to take out your opponents? Do you think we'll need to fight our way there?"

He shrugs.

He *fucking* shrugs.

That's the only answer I get.

This is…not my Aron. Something's definitely wrong.

I pat his arm and move away, heading back inside. I turn and look at the man standing on the balcony, just in case he's messing with me, but Aron continues to stare out at the gray waters, seeing nothing.

And suddenly, I know what this is. I know exactly why he's like this…but I need proof.

Fear makes my heart thump loud in my chest. I hitch up my skirts and storm my way up the ramp. I walk slow at first, but as the path winds around the tall tower, I start running. By the time I reach the room of the webs, I'm at a full-blown sprint.

One of the Spidae is there, gazing up at the web. He looks the same as he always does—long white hair, long white robes—and I don't know if it's one I've met before or a different one. It doesn't matter. I rush toward the web. "Where's his strand?"

The Spidae doesn't ask for more details than that. He knows what I mean. He gives me a look that might have something like pity in it, and then strolls forward, gesturing at another section of the web. I follow him, moving in close. As I approach, each strand seems to take on its own individual life, and out of the cluster, I see the shining golden strand that has to be Aron's. I lean in, studying it, making note of where it crisscrosses with other threads, and continue to follow it into the weave.

There are three strands…or there should be. I see the one that is Aron—my Aron—intertwined with my own. I follow the others instead. Two of the strands have moved closer together, so close they were almost interwoven. Now, one hangs loose, broken free from the web itself.

"One of his Aspects is dead," I murmur, as if saying it aloud confirms it.

"Yes," the Spidae moves to my side. "Killed by another, it seems."

I stare at the two closely tangled threads. Hedonism and Apathy moving together. Now only one thread remains. I turn to look at the Spidae. "It's Apathy that died, isn't it? Someone killed his anchor?"

He inclines his head. "He is gone. Aron is re-absorbing him. His personality will be different for a few days."

I know that. I do. Didn't we go through this with Liar Aron? But my heart still hurts. I ache for the Aron that's gone—even though I know he has to go—and I'm a little afraid that only one Aron remains.

Hedonism.

"Motherfucker," I mutter.

"Aron has many flaws, but that is not one of them," the Spidae says in that cool voice of his. "Have you made your decision?"

I clench my fists, straightening. "What decision?"

Instead of answering me, he walks slowly behind the web, and my skin prickles. I know where he's going. Reluctantly, I follow, and I see the second web—the Earth web—and my strand, stretched taut across the two. Is it just me, or are the few threads that are pulled tight between the two webs—displaced people like myself—fewer in number than before? Or is it my imagination?

"Have you decided if you wish to return to your world or stay with Aron?"

"You know my answer." I thought it was obvious after the weeks that have passed. "You want me to say it aloud?"

He inclines his head in a nod.

Bastard. "I'm staying. I won't leave my Aron."

"Very well." He reaches out and pinches my thread, tearing it away from the Earth web. Something small and fragile feels as if it's tearing away inside me, too, and I choke on a gasp.

He just did that. He just fucking did *that*.

He didn't have to. He could have left it for however long it needed to be up and he fucking pulled me free. I stare at him in horror and then turn and leave the room, too furious to speak.

"You are angry, Faithful?" he calls after me. "Why?"

I don't answer. I storm down the hall, determined to never look at those bastards again. Forever will be too soon. I hate that as I head away, I know he's following me. I can hear his light footsteps on the spiderweb-covered ground. Is he following so he can twist the knife? Or is there more to this story?

If there's more, I don't want to hear. It's clear I'm not dealing with stable entities. He might think it's no big deal, but I can't stop seeing his hand twisting and plucking at my thread, tearing it away from the web.

Tearing it away from my past.

Now I have no choice but to go forward, and that's completely tied to Aron, who's currently full of apathy.

"Faith?" Yulenna appears in a doorway, startling me. "Is everything all right? I thought I heard..." Her voice dies and her eyes go wide as she sees the Spidae and shrinks back ever so slightly.

I immediately step in front of her, feeling protective. I turn and face the Spidae who followed me, a curious look on his normally blank face. "Can't you just fuck off, already?"

He just blinks at me. "You are angry. I wish to understand why."

"Because you're playing with us. We're not people to you. We're strings to be pulled and manipulated." I shake my head, unable to articulate just how unsettled and angry I am at his actions. I pinch the bridge of my nose. "You don't snip someone right in front of their eyes, okay?"

"Because you came in to see if Aron had been affected," he murmurs, and for a moment, I get that his robot brain is trying to understand why I'm upset. "You were not asking about your-self so you should not have been…tampered with?"

"All I'm saying is try to think like a real person, all right? We're not puppets. We're not strings. We're flesh and blood people and when we're having a bad day, maybe you don't fucking snip our strings in front of our eyes."

Yulenna quivers behind me and I realize I've raised my voice.

"I see." He nods slowly. "So I wait for…a good day to do such things?"

"Or not do it at all!"

"I must. It is my job."

I frown at him, thinking. He said there were three of them in this tower. I've been thinking of them as past, present and future, but what if I'm all wrong and they're hedonism and lies and arrogance? Apathy? He doesn't seem to strike me as any of those, just so bizarrely out of touch that he doesn't grasp how the mind works. "You're…you're not split like Aron is, are you?"

He inclines his head, his eerie pale eyes locked on mine. "I am not part of the Anticipation. This is how I have always been."

As we talk, another Spidae arrives, this one exactly the same as the other Aspect, but his eyes are pale gray and so colorless they look like ice. He stands next to his other-self and watches us, his head tilting to the side like a curious bird…or a spider.

I can feel Yulenna's fists in the back of my gown. She's not leaving, but she's clearly afraid. I don't back down from the two of them. I'm not afraid of them, strangely enough. Sure, they can snip my string, but there's a reason they're helping Aron—my Aron—and that makes me safe. Whatever it is that's going on in their strange minds, I think they want him to succeed.

I also wonder if that's why they push with so many weird questions.

So I lift my chin, staring at the newcomer. "Which one are you? Past, present or future?"

"Is that how we are designated, then?" He smiles, and the expression is more creepy than reassuring.

"What are you, then?"

"The Spidae," they answer at the same time.

"But you're supposed to be split? Like this?"

One spreads his hands in a gesture while the other answers. "The High Father cannot leave the fabric of space and time unattended. Whatever our flaws, they will remain with us for all time."

"Here, in our exile," chimes in the other.

I exhale a sharp breath. "You really need an anchor to keep your shit together, dude. Both of you."

"It is true," the original Spidae says. "We do not know—or care—about humankind because we interact with them so very little."

"But they are fascinating," his brother murmurs, his gaze on my furious expression.

I fight back a shudder. Is this how Aron would be if he had no anchor? "Yeah, well, when Aron's himself again, maybe we'll see if we can send someone back from Yshrem to come stay here with you. You need an anchor, you really do."

"Because we cannot keep behaving as we are?" the one asks, while the other tilts his head.

God, they are so creepy.

"Perhaps we should just pull a human from the other web. The web that sweet Faithful came from," the first Spidae says, and the look in his eyes grows sly. "They seem eager to serve the gods in all ways."

The breath explodes out of me. If they're baiting me, they found the right way to do it. "You fucking bastard, you wouldn't dare—"

"Faith." Yulenna's soft voice makes me go quiet. Her hands tug at my dress, like a child wanting attention. "Don't. Okay? There's no need to be upset. I'll do it."

At first, I don't understand what she means. "Do what?"

The two Spidae go completely still, and their attention focuses on Yulenna, not me. "An interesting thread," one murmurs.

"I see it now," says the other. "Very interesting."

Yulenna swallows hard, then lifts her chin. Her thick hair is pulled in a thick braid, and she's wearing a pale gown with a square fur collar that shows her cleavage and clings to her body in all the right ways. She's gorgeous, as usual. Her eyes are wide and frightened, but she smiles at me. "I will serve the gods."

I shake my head, grabbing her shoulders and pulling her away. "Wait, Yulenna, no. You don't have to do this."

"I know."

"You...you really want to serve them? An anchor has to go willingly." Who would willingly tie themselves to these two? As I look back at them, a third joins, identical to his brothers, this one with eyes so black they look like coals in his pale face. Did I think one was creepy? Three is a nightmare. "You want to stay here?" I hiss at her. "Really?"

She swallows hard. "Not really. I'm kind of scared, actually." But she gives me a brave smile. "But if you can learn a new world, so can I."

"Yulenna, no, this is different—"

One of the Spidae glides forward and touches Yulenna's fat, red-ribboned braid. He practically hovers over her, studying her with fascination. "You would serve us in all ways? The three of us?"

She nods.

"Time out," I call out, making a T with my hands. "No. Absolutely not. Yulenna, you're not a whore any longer, okay? You don't have to do anything like this."

Yulenna shakes her head, her eyes earnest even as the Spidae hovering over her toys with her braid. "I want to do this, Faith. Here, I have a purpose. I can serve the gods. Once we leave this tower, I'm just an unnecessary whore for a god who is in love with his anchor. I cannot fight in Aron's army. How long do you think he will keep me around?"

My throat goes dry. I take her hand in mine. "You're my friend. Aron would keep you as long as I want. You've been good to me, and to him."

She squeezes my hand, and I feel like crying, because I can tell her mind is already made up. "You have been my friend, too. Thank you for making me feel like your equal in all ways." Yulenna gives me a smile. "But now I must find my own path."

I swallow hard.

"I can see the guilt on your face," Yulenna teases. "Don't. I'm choosing this, just as you choose to be with Aron."

"If you're sure," I begin, but Yulenna pulls her hand from mine and turns to look at the Spidae. One extends his hand to her even as the other plays with her braid.

"I'm sure," she says, and I hate the tremble in her voice. But she's brave and strong as she takes the hand extended to her and walks away with the gods.

I watch her go, feeling helpless. Did I just give my friend up...?

I'm surprised when one of the Spidae – the one with blue eyes – turns back and approaches me. I back up a step as he heads in my direction, and there's a look on his face I can't decipher. He pauses in front of me, thinks, and then leans in.

"They won't check your pockets, you know."

"O-kay...thanks?" I pat my pockets, but they're empty. And before I can ask him what the hell he's talking about, he's gone.

CHAPTER 69

*T*his horrible day seems to last forever. Aron is distant and vague, gazing out at nothing and speaking to no one. He answers when I ask him questions, but his answers are always along the lines of "I don't care" or "It doesn't matter" so I stop asking. I just have to wait this out, I tell myself a hundred times as I try to stay busy.

Yulenna is gone as if she was never with us. I go to her room and her things have been removed, and sometimes I catch a hint of her voice, but she never materializes. I suspect that the Spidae are keeping her from us so she won't change her mind. They're hiding their new toy.

It falls to me to talk to Markos, Kerren and Solat. I tell them about Aron's apathy, and they listen with solemn expressions.

"So we no longer have the advantage," Markos says. "Now, each Aspect of Aron has killed another."

"Was that an advantage we had?" I joke lightly. "It doesn't feel like one."

"An advantage is an advantage." Markos shrugs. "But when Aron is himself, we will discuss plans."

I bite my lip and nod.

"What of Yulenna?" Solat asks. "Where has she gone this day?" He paces behind Markos and Kerren, his expression tense.

"That's problem number two," I say hesitantly. "She's decided to anchor for the Spidae. They've taken her away."

Solat goes pale. "She what?"

"It was her decision," I say quickly. "She spoke with them and decided. It has to be given freely—"

Solat slams out of the room. "Yulenna!" he bellows, storming down the hall.

I wince. I knew that would go badly, especially given that they were clearly friends-with-benefits or more. "It was her choice. I have to honor it."

Markos rubs his mouth, shocked. "This has been a day of surprises, none of them good."

"We need time," Kerren says, then corrects himself. "*Solat* will need time to understand."

"Aron's going to be out of it for the next few days if it's anything like when he took on Liar Aron's Aspect," I say, twisting my hands in my lap. For once, I'm not hungry. I just want to close my eyes and go to sleep. Maybe Aron's apathy is affecting me, too. "But once he's back to himself..."

"We should leave," Markos agrees. "To Yshrem."

"To our destiny," Kerren adds, and I flinch.

Funny how that word "destiny" keeps popping up and it sounds more awful every time I hear it.

IT TAKES two full days before Aron snaps out of his "apathy." Two days of wandering around the somehow lonelier tower, now that both Aron and Yulenna are gone. Well, the Aron I know is gone, and in his place is a stranger who stares at the walls and gives a shit about nothing.

I ignore him. I have to, or I'll snap. I pretend like he isn't there, and when he wanders from room to room in that listless way of his, I make sure to leave. I can't stand to see him like this. I know it's not him. I know it isn't. I just…can't have him look at me with that same bored, uncaring look that he gives the others.

It's quiet with Yulenna gone, too. There's no one to talk to, really. The men are busy. I see Markos packing up the men's supplies or sparring with Solat, who's turned into an angry, silent man and not the laughing tease he was before. I see Kerren praying over the marker for Vitar's grave, and I'm a terrible person because all I can think is that I'm glad there was no body, since the dead aren't staying dead right now.

I try to sew, but it's not fun without company. I should practice my staff-work like Aron showed me, but I don't have the heart. I can't concentrate. As companions go, I'm pretty useless, and it fills me with panic.

I don't have a way home. Not any longer. I'm here now, forever. It hits me by degrees. Sometimes I'll be fine with it, and sometimes I'll think of how distant Aron has been for the last few days and want to vomit over the choice I've made.

I love him. I just am utterly terrified for what the future holds, because it feels like we're barreling toward it.

And I can't stop thinking of the thread that the Spidae pinched off as if it were nothing. I see it every time I close my eyes. Are they going to pinch off the front of my thread like that when it's my time? When Aron has to ascend again? Or do they pinch Aron's thread with the same carelessness? The thought makes me sick.

I take to my bed, pulling the covers over my head and sinking into a fitful nap.

I wake up to a hot mouth on my neck, and a big body pressing mine into the mattress. Electricity—that delicious static that always builds between me and Aron—crackles in the air and I moan as he pulls my gown open, exposing my breasts.

"Faith," Aron murmurs. "Wake up."

I jerk awake with a gasp as I realize what's happening. Aron looms over me, his eyes troubled, but they're clearer than they were before. I grab his jaw and study his face, trying to see if any remnants of Apathy remain. "How are you feeling?"

"I am a god," he says. "Why would I not be fine?"

Well, that sounds like Aron, but I'm not entirely sure. Time to test the waters a bit more. "I've been thinking about getting kinky in the blankets. You finally down for some butt stuff?"

"That depends." He kisses my nipple and gives it a gentle tug with his teeth. "Are we talking your butt or mine?"

"Does it matter?"

"Not to me." He grins wickedly.

For a moment, the breath catches in my chest. The relief I feel immediately turns to ice. What if...what if something happened to Hedonism and that's why Aron wants to have sex? "I changed my mind," I say quickly. "No butt stuff. No anything. Can we just talk?"

Aron tilts his head. "Talk?"

"About anything but sex," I say desperately. "What about strategies? How are we going to get to Yshrem without an army? Is it safe? Or should we go back to Novoro?"

He snorts and reclines on the bed on his elbow, gazing down at me. "I will sooner walk all the way to Glistentide before I take an army of Novoran fops as my protectors. Do you know that their idea of a combat tourney involved capturing flags? Flags! Because they did not wish to hurt themselves." His lip curls in disgust. "If I am to acquire an army, it has to be the best one possible. You know this, Faith." And his hand goes possessively to my stomach. "And the best are most certainly not Novoro's pathetic troops."

That's arrogance and battle, all wrapped up into a pretty bow. He's not hedonism. I don't need to check the strings to know that, and I'm so relieved that I burst into tears.

"Shh," he murmurs, and pulls me against him. "I'm sorry. I haven't been myself for the last few days, have I?"

"Apathy," I manage to choke out. "Apathy is dead."

"I know." He strokes my hair, letting me weep against his chest. "There is only one left, which means we cannot stay any longer. He will move to meet us, and I would rather meet him with an army on the fields of Yshrem."

I nod, but all I can think about is my thread. How easily the Spidae plucked it from its moorings and snapped it. How it fell against the Aos world web so limply. How it's only tied to Aron now. "And once we beat him…what happens to us?" I whisper. "What happens to me when you win?"

"If you worry that I will send you away, the answer is 'never,'" Aron says. He holds me tighter. "You're not leaving my side. I won't let them part us."

It might not be his choice. I hug him close. "Just promise me that when you absorb the last guy and then re-ascend, you'll never forget me, all right? Even if we can't be together, I need you to always remember me. Promise it."

His hand clenches possessively in my hair. "You are not going anywhere, Faith. I have promised."

"All right," I whisper, but I'm not entirely sure I believe him.

He holds me close, but I don't want to leave it at that. I need him as much as he needs me, I think. Maybe more. I turn toward him and kiss his cheek, kiss the scar that crosses the left side of his face. I kiss his mouth, and when he kisses me in return, I push him onto his back. I straddle him, hiking up my skirts, because in this moment, there's nothing I want more than to feel him deep inside me. I *need* him to claim me and remind me why I do this. It's not just the sex. It's never been just the sex. It's everything Aron is, and how much I believe in him.

How we're good for each other in all the right ways.

Aron tilts me forward, pulling off his leggings, and then I ease down against his cock. I'm not yet wet enough to take him, so he snags a hand behind my neck and pulls me down for a harder kiss, his mouth fiercely claiming mine even as one hand grasps my breast and teases the nipple. He works it to a hard point with his thumb, rubbing back and forth as I rock against his cock. I want to take him deep, need the connection between us, and when he gives a little push, I sit back, letting gravity do what my body won't.

That's not enough for Aron, though. He growls my name, a single syllable of need. "Faith." One hand clamps on my hip and the other goes to my clit, and he rubs his thumb against it as I rock over him. Oh, fuck. That does it. I close my eyes, losing myself to pleasure as he rubs my clit and slowly I sink onto the hard, thick length of him.

I ride him, my hips working as I move over him. I need this. Need him. I've missed him, even though it's only been a few days since he was lost to me. It made me realize just how much I've come to crave him. Not just my body, but my heart.

Maybe even my soul.

"I love you," I tell him as our bodies work together, faster and harder. "Love you, Aron."

He doesn't say it back. I didn't think he would. But when I climax and collapse atop him and he flips me onto my back and uses me for his pleasure, he growls out something that sounds like "mine."

It's enough for now.

I'M NOT sad to leave the Tower of the Spidae.

Well, I am in a sense. I want to stay at Aron's side and do nothing but simply exist. I want to have those lazy, blissful days forever...but I know that won't happen. That's not in the cards for us. Aron has to defeat his other Aspect and I'll end up...who knows where. I'm not dwelling on semantics yet. But staying at the tower? That's a no-go. The feel of the place has changed since Aron had his apathy spell. Maybe it's the memory of the Spidae snapping my string right before my eyes. Maybe it's that, or maybe it's the Spidae telling us in a subtle way to leave now that they have Yulenna all to themselves. It feels a bit like we've fed her to the wolves, but when we pack our final supplies to leave, she's there to send us off with a smile and a wave.

And she looks...happy. Renewed. Like she has a purpose, even if it's just to be the servant of a trio of creepy spider gods. So, good for her, I guess. I certainly can't judge.

Kerren loads our supplies onto the cobweb raft (I recognize the material now after being surrounded by it for weeks) and poles across while the woales wade on through, gliding through the water with light bounces as their feet land and hit the shallow bottom. The lake is wide, but it's not deep in the slightest, and if I thought it was dead before, it's a tomb now.

I worry a little, though, thinking of Vitar. "It's safe," Markos reassures me from the woale ahead of mine, his grip on the harness as we swim-bounce-plow through the water. "Lord Aron killed everything in a single breath when we arrived and it's been safe to cross ever since."

"Oh, I haven't forgotten." I clutch at my woale's harness as it dips lower in the water, surging forward after it pushes off the bottom. It even swims like a damn hippo. I'm a little nervous to be riding by myself, but with five woales and five riders, it doesn't make sense to double up. I miss being able to hold onto Aron, though. He's decided it's safest if I ride in the middle, so he pulls up the rear while Markos and Kerren ride ahead.

Once we cross the lake, we change out of our wet, cold clothing, and remount again. I wrap my cloak tightly around my body and give the tower one last, final look before it disappears as we head into the mountains.

We're heading to Yshrem. To our destiny.

I've never been so damn scared in my life.

CHAPTER 70

ONE MONTH LATER

I wasn't expecting that the war would beat us to Yshrem.

We sit atop our mounts on the edge of a cliff and stare down at the plain below us. It stretches out for miles, and I almost expect to see more of the tiny villages along the roads that we've seen up until now. Instead, there's a massive, white stone keep with a huge crenellated retaining wall. It butts up against a wide river, and on the other side of the river is an army.

In between them is a war zone.

Trenches are dug all along the river's edge. A bridge that looks as if it used to cross to the other side is demolished in the middle. Spikes have been pushed into the ground to act as barriers and all over I see churned earth, scorched piles of ash that still smoke in the late morning sunlight, and in the distance, a field full of tents. Men crawl behind the barricades on the other side of the river, and even from here, I can see armor and spears. Flags flutter in the breeze, and as I watch, yet another rises behind a spiky barricade as if to taunt the cool-looking keep on the other side.

"What is this?" I ask, a little shocked. Part of me thought we'd show up to Yshrem—the capital city of the kingdom Yshrem which bears the same name—and maybe regroup a little before building an army. Clearly we've been beaten to the punch.

"It's a siege," Aron says, his gaze on the tableau below, eyes darting as he takes in the sight.

"But who's sieging Yshrem? They're the castle, right?" I raise my hand to my eyes, shielding the sunlight as I gaze at the massive fortress. On the far side of the wall, roads and fields lie spread and ordered in neat rows...but they're empty and I don't see crops growing. The last village we passed was completely empty and we didn't know why.

Now I guess we know—they've all hidden inside the keep.

"Adassia," Markos says, and Aron nods.

Over the last month, I've been given a crash course on Yshrem and Adassia history. They're neighboring kingdoms, both conquered by the Cyclopae—who are barbarian warriors—about twenty years ago. Yshrem is fully under Cyclopae control, as their queen married the cyclops king, but it seems Adassia is not as big a fan. They've rioted in the past and fought against cyclops control before.

"Right. I guess that makes sense that they wouldn't be happy." I scan the army, at the bright red banners that fly over every tent and rise over multiple parts of the scarred up battlefield. My heart stutters when I see a familiar axe symbol. "Aron, they're carrying your mark."

"I see that." His voice is flat. "That explains much."

"What does it explain? Spell it out for us slow people." Were they waiting for him? Did they know he was coming?

Have the Spidae betrayed us already? Is this all one big game?

"My last Aspect will be there, with Adassia." He gestures at the sea of tents. "Why else would they war against a much stronger kingdom? They must have something—or someone—on their side to tip the scales in their favor."

Hedonism Aron is there? I look at the sea of tents for signs that it's him, but all I see are Aron's symbol on flags, Aron's symbol painted onto hammered breastplates. He can't be wrong, though. The air feels charged, the troops a little too happy as they laugh behind their barricades. They're laying siege to a hella big castle, but they act like they're going to win. Even from here, I can tell there's no tension in them. It's like they've got this in the bag.

They would think that if they have the god of battles on their side.

You will meet your destiny in Yshrem.

Well fuck. They weren't exactly wrong about that. Our "destiny" has already amassed an army when my Aron refused one. I bite back my sigh. Sometimes I wish Aron was a *leeeetle* less Aspect of Arrogance and more the Aspect of Common Sense, but I guess that wouldn't make him who he is. Even so, staring down at the massive Adassian army that Hedonism Aron has manifested makes me think I'd feel better if we went back and got the Novoran army my Aron had been promised. "What do we do?" I ask, looking over at Aron as he gazes down the cliffs at the mess below. "What's our new plan?"

Kerren, Markos and Solat are silent. I know we're all waiting for Aron to decide. We can't take on an army on our own. There's no freaking way, and Hedonism Aron isn't going to shove his anchor out in front of us so we can take potshots at it just for funsies.

My skin prickles, and I feel more vulnerable now than ever. I hitch my hood a little higher over my head, as if that will somehow hide me from my inevitable fate.

"We go to Yshrem as planned," Aron says, nodding at the forbidding keep. "The Spidae will not steer us wrong."

I'm not so sure about that. I can't shake the feeling that we're all being manipulated.

Even so, I'll follow Aron's lead.

He dismounts from his woale, casting one last glance over the armies below before turning his attention to me. He comes to my side, offering his hand, and I take it and slide down off my mount, only to be pulled into his arms. Aron cups my face and pulls me to him in a fierce kiss, and I can practically feel the anticipation rolling off of him in waves.

He's excited that we're here. He's excited there's a war.

Of course he is. He's the god of battle. I have to keep reminding myself that. This is his bread and butter. This is what he loves. I'd probably feel the same about a new *Twilight* book or an entire box of Cadbury Creme Eggs magically showing up. But it scares me.

That army down there means we're nearing the end.

After a month of crossing the mountains and then the endless forest to get to Yshrem, you'd think I'd be prepared for this. I'm not, though. While I don't miss the cold of the mountains or trying to lead my woale through the forest for hours on end, I still enjoyed every day I spent with Aron and the others. It was "our" time, strangely enough. Sure, the travel was no fun, but the company was great. And every night, I got to curl up in Aron's arms and make love to him. Sometimes it would be slow and sweet lovemaking, and sometimes it would be rough and exciting, but it was always good. Between rounds of sex, we'd talk about everything and nothing. I've told him all about my life before—how I was just one of dozens of cubes in an insurance company call center. How I was a no one. He doesn't believe it, and I find that achingly sweet. In his eyes, I'm so important that he can't imagine anyone overlooking me.

Aron tells me all about his stories, too. About how once

upon a time, in the dawn of Aos's civilizations, Aron was a mortal. A butcher, of all things. He tells me of how his village was invaded by a neighboring war-tribe when many of the men were conscripted into serving their king, and so the village was left undefended save for Aron, who had been recovering from a broken hand and was left behind. He told me how he defended the village from soldier after soldier, slaughtering them with his butcher's cleaver and held off the enemy one handed long enough for the women and children in the village to flee to the hills.

He died in the fight, but the High Father was so taken with him that he raised him to the Aether and made him the god of battle. And storms, though I'm sure there's a connection there I don't know yet. Every day, I learn more about Aron, and it makes me sad that this man who has come so far is being punished by the High Father like this. There has to be a better way to set the gods back on the right path than this, though what it is, I don't know.

Not that I'm ungrateful. I'm just happy to be with Aron, to wake up in his arms and feel a little bit of contentment, however fleeting.

I feel all of that slipping away as Aron gazes back down at the field of battle below.

Aron wants to be down there. I can tell. He's recharged in a way I've never seen before at the sight of the battle preparing to happen below. It's early, but I can see troops gathering on the walls of the Yshrem keep and the Adassian soldiers are organizing, getting ready to move. It's sure to be a bloodbath, given that they'll be running up against stone walls protected by a river, but it also looks like no one cares.

For a moment, I want to take Aron by the hand and lead him away from this, from all of this. There's no time limit on how long it takes for Aron to kill his other Aspect. We can find a little cabin somewhere, hide out from the world, and just live together, taking each day as it comes. Hell, we can wait for old age to decide things. Maybe Hedonism Aron's anchor will go first—a likely scenario since he—or she—has got to be affected by his master's pleasure-loving slant. Maybe we just let fate sort things out.

But…that's not who my Aron his. He can't sit by and wait for life to happen. He has to make things happen. He has to go to battle because it's part of who he is. He's war. It's not just about winning and controlling which Aspect re-ascends to the Aether.

It's about Aron being a war god. I have to accept it, because I have to accept Aron as he is or not at all.

I understand it, even if it fills me with terror.

So I take Aron's hand and link his fingers in mine, and gaze out at the battlefields below. "He'll be hiding his anchor," I guess. "He's going to want him close enough that he can keep an eye on him, but far enough from battle that he won't get hurt. That means he's probably somewhere in one of those tents." I gesture at the sea of them in the distance.

"Or he's put him in armor and is hiding him in plain sight. It might be worthwhile to see if any of the soldiers remains behind when the others surge ahead." Markos moves to the other side of Aron, gazing down at the field.

I look over at my Aron. "What would you do?"

"I'm arrogance," he answers simply. "I won't think the same as he does. Did he pick his anchor because it was a soldier that volunteered? Is it a wench he wanted to bed? Or did he simply have no other options like I did?"

"Oooh, burn on me," I tease. "Just call me Last Resort Faith."

Aron flashes a playful smile in my direction. "I've come around to liking how things turned out, though it probably would have been wiser to pick someone who knew how to carry a sword."

And who he didn't want to stick his dick into constantly. I mean, I get it. For a god of battle, a wimpy girl like me is a bad call. I have no muscle strength, I can barely sit on a woale for a few hours without bitching about it, and I've never used a bladed weapon. I'm a poor choice. A sitting duck.

No one will ever care for Aron as much as me, though. No one. I'm the best woman for the job.

A horn sounds from down below, and the men line up. We watch atop the distant cliff as the men bellow out a cry, a narrow bridge is dropped over the river, and then they surge forward to attack the keep. Ladders are produced and just as quickly destroyed by the men crowding the ramparts. Trash—and hot oil—are thrown down on the enemy men, and on and on it goes. They're not getting a toehold in the slightest. It seems senseless to me.

Then, off to the side, a massive keep gate opens on the far end of the river. Men ride out on horses—the first horses I've seen since I arrived here—and carry spears. They're deeply tanned, with long, flowing hair, and scream war cries as they raise their spears into the air.

"The Cyclopae," Aron murmurs.

As I watch, a group of Adassian warriors split off and approach the Cyclopae riders, who surge across the water farther down the river and then regroup on the far side. One of the Adassians steps forward, flinging his cloak off and then brandishing an axe with a flourish. He stands on the ground before the others, and they surge around him, like waters parting. Avoiding him.

That'd be Hedonism Aron.

A brave man approaches, his horse circling, and then he zooms in for the attack. He's quickly cut down, and then newcomers approach. I swallow hard. He can't be killed. This isn't even fair to watch. I turn away, because I don't want to see more men fling themselves at certain death. "How do we get down to the keep?" I ask, trying to focus. "How do we get inside it?"

"There's no getting around that army," Kerren says. "We'd be giving ourselves a swift death if we approach."

"The cover of night will hide us if we want to get closer," Solat adds, his voice flat. "But the question is, if we get close, what do we do then?"

"I know the keep," Aron says. "The Cyclopae are dedicated to me. I have seen glimpses of this keep many, many times." He turns to me, a hint of a smile on his face. "And I know its secrets."

"You do?"

He nods. "I know that King Mathior had a secret passage built from his wife's private chambers leading down to the crypts so she can escape if things get too dangerous." He rubs his chin. "Mathior is one of my favorites. Very devoted. Amazing in battle."

I stare at my lover like he's grown two heads. "Crypts? Hell to the no."

"There is a passage hidden there," Aron says. "It's our best way to get you safely inside. I remember that they installed a passage behind a statue dedicated to me." He frowns. "Damned ugly statue, too."

"Hey, remember what happened the last time we hung around with a bunch of dead guys?" I say desperately. I hate this idea already. "The cemetery back in Katharn? Where everyone tried to come up and say hello?" I gesture at the smoking piles below. "Why do you think they're fucking burning their dead, Aron? Come on."

"It's the best way," he says stubbornly. "You can't stay out here in the open. I don't care if I have three loyal men or three thousand, you wouldn't be safe from my other Aspect."

"Where is the crypt, my lord?" Markos asks.

Aron points, past the river, where the trees cluster at the edge of the horizon. "That way. They trail under the earth near the castle."

I put my hands on my hips, because I hate this idea. "If you know about this crypt because the king is so super loyal, then your other Aspect knows about it, too."

Aron nods. "Truth. It's still the best idea." He arches one of those arrogant brows at me. "Unless you'd prefer to go through the front gate?"

I throw a hand up, gesturing at him. "You can. You're fucking invulnerable."

Aron blinks at me, and then a smile curves his mouth. "You're right." He moves toward me, puts his hands on my shoulders, and kisses me hard. "Clever, and right."

Dazed, I stare up at him. "W-what did I say?"

"When it grows dark, Markos and the others will take you to the crypts. They're sure to be guarded, but with a diversion, we can hopefully distract anyone there long enough for you to get in."

"Distraction?" I echo.

He grins at me, and I can practically see the battle-lust in his eyes. "I'm going to go through the gate, just as you say."

I look down at the clusterfuck below, then back at my Aron. My everything. "Aron, no. This is a really, *really* bad idea."

"It is the best idea," he says fiercely. "Do you not trust me?"

"Oh, I trust you. I just can't forget about that 'arrogance' thing."

Somewhere to the side, Solat stifles a snort of amusement.

Aron just grins at me. "I know. This is why I have you at my side. You see things differently than I do. And this is an excellent idea. I cannot be killed as long as you are safe, Faith." He cups my face in his big, gloved hands. "And the men will go with you. I will be the distraction. They will not know what to think when a second Aron of the Cleaver arrives. I will pull them away, and you will be able to sneak in to the keep."

I fight back a sigh. "Fine. I don't have to like this, but fine." Realistically, I know he can't get hurt. I know that. I do. I'm still utterly terrified though. If they see him, they'll know he has an anchor somewhere and they'll come after me.

What other choice do we have? I look down at the torn up battlefield, at the men that fling themselves at the stone walls even as others get mowed down by Hedonism Aron, and feel a hint of despair.

I don't see how we're going to get close enough.

CHAPTER 71

$\mathcal{W}$e remain a safe distance away from both city and battlefield as we wait for the sun to go down. Aron sits atop a rock and instead of practicing with the men, he holds me close and presses his mouth to my hair.

"I won't let anything happen to you, Faith. Trust in me."

I love that he's trying to comfort me in my obvious terror, but it doesn't make me feel better. The only thing that would actually make me feel better would be if we didn't do this at all. I know it's not an option, though, so I keep my thoughts to myself. Kerren, Solat, and Markos talk in low voices, sharpening their swords and adjusting their traveling armor. We let the woales go, setting them free, because one way or another, our path ends here.

I try not to panic at how *final* that feels.

Despite my wishing that they day would never end, the sun goes down and we get to our feet. "Faith," Aron murmurs as he presses a kiss to my palm one last time. "Take something for me, yes?"

"What?" I ask, curious.

He goes to his pack - now sitting in the grass - and pulls the long wooden staff from it. The staff he trained me to use. I bite back hysterical laughter. "You think I can bludgeon a zombie to death with this, then?"

"I just want to know you have a weapon you can use while you're gone," he says, and the look on his face is no longer easy or playful. "Markos, Solat and Kerren will protect you, have no fear with that. If they do not, I will make certain that they suffer eternally."

It's eerily quiet with that pronouncement. I glance over and see that the men are pale, their gazes averted. Markos's hand twitches over his pommel, as if he wants to pull his blade and protect me even now.

I step closer to Aron as I take the staff from him. "You should be nicer to them."

"A little fear will speed their footsteps," he murmurs to me. His gaze devours my face, and for a moment I think he won't let go of the staff. He finally releases it, though, and it's like he's releasing me, too. I can see the tension in his shoulders.

He hates this. He hates this so, so much. And that's the only reason I don't freak out. Because he's taking this as seriously as I am.

Aron turns to the others. "Take only what you can carry easily. I will not have you encumbered. Your only goal is to get Faith into that keep alive. Do you understand me?"

The men nod and as I watch, Solat drops his pack and picks through it one last time, discarding a few items. A metal buckler —a plate-sized shield meant to attach to the arm—is discarded, and I pick it up. "Can I take this?"

Solat frowns at me. "Of course, but why?"

I pull out the neck of my gown, shove the buckler down the front of my dress, and then tap my chest. The lip of it rests against my thick Novoran belt and it remains in place right over my heart and breasts. "Because I want armor, too."

His lips twist in a wry smile. "If they get that close to you, we're already doomed."

"Fair enough, but I like being safe."

"You should go," Aron says. "Before it gets too dark to see. I'll wait until the moon is higher in the sky before I head out."

I swallow hard and nod. I want to run to him and hold him tight in one last hug, but I also don't want to be a pain in the ass. "Be safe, okay?"

He gives me a swift nod, and I turn away, moving toward Markos and Kerren. There's a hard knot in my throat that I do my best to ignore, but I clutch the staff and head forward...to my destiny.

Man, just thinking that phrase makes me want to barf. I steel myself for the evening ahead. Please be safe, Aron—

A heavy hand lands on my shoulder.

I turn and Aron's hard mouth is on mine, his hand on the back of my neck as he gives me the hardest, most fiercely possessive kiss ever. His tongue slicks into my mouth, claiming me with every stroke and reminding me that I love the hell out of this big, arrogant bastard. I cling to the front of his tunic, our mouths molding, and when he finally breaks the kiss, I give him a dazed look.

"Remember that you belong to me," he says in a low voice. "And I do not give you permission to die."

It's the right thing to say. I laugh, because it's the most absurdly arrogant thing I've ever heard. "I love you," I whisper, and then move away before I fling myself at his feet, bawling like a baby. "Be safe."

"I will."

Arrogant right down to the end—no, right down to his *pores*, I amend.

This is not the fucking end.

WE'RE a lot farther away from the crypts than I anticipated. Aron told the others what to look for and the direction to head, and we hike silently down the cliffs and across hills, then cross the warm, gentle river far upstream. The light from a jillion fires is just barely in the distance, and if I squint hard, I can make out the castle's walls ahead. We're at least a football stadium away, maybe two. It seems like an impossible distance to cover.

Because there's enemy soldiers even here. They're freaking everywhere. We barely manage to duck behind some bushes as a few men on horses patrol past, and armor clanks somewhere in the distance. We squat behind the greenery, and Solat points up ahead. "That looks like a cemetery."

"It's the place Lord Aron said it would be," Markos nods. He turns to look at us. "Kerren and I will scout and try to clear the way. You stay here hidden. If we're not back by the time Aron begins his diversion, go on without us."

I bite my lip, nodding, and Solat fingers his sword. I watch as Markos heads in one direction and Kerren in the other, dark figures that stick to the shadows. Within the space of a breath, they disappear into the night, and I desperately hope they know what they're doing.

Minutes pass. I turn to look over at Solat. "This is some shit, huh?"

His eyes narrow at me. "We will keep you safe, Faith. Aron demands it."

There's a bitter note in his voice. It's been there ever since we left the tower, and I know it's because he's still carrying a torch for Yulenna. I don't blame him. She was sweet, friendly, and apparently liked to fuck. Of course he's half in love with her. But he needs to focus. I know he can't be happy that Yulenna paired off with a god (or three) and he's stuck here protecting me, the anchor of another god.

"Do we need to talk?" I ask. "Because you've been kind of pissypants since Yulenna left."

Solat glares at me in the darkness. "Does it matter?"

"I like to think it does." I clutch my staff across my legs, careful not to hit him with it. "Thing is, I'm not thrilled about her staying with them either, but she chose to do that. If she's not happy there, well, those are the guys that can fix it. They can pull her thread free and release her if she changes her mind. Those are about the only people in this world that can make that sort of change."

"She won't change her mind. She's happy there," he says, bitterness in his voice. "She is no longer a slave. Now she's important. It's all she ever wanted." His jaw clenches and he stares out into the night.

I pat his shoulder. "Then be happy for her and get the fuck over it, okay?"

He looks startled at my words. He nods, and then gets to his feet as Markos returns. Markos is sweating, his dark hair plastered to his skull. "Six men," he says in a low voice. "All armed."

"Even out here?" Solat makes a sound of frustration. "We are practically sitting in the fields and he still sends troops out?"

Markos shrugs as Kerren heads in our direction, another figure cloaked in darkness. "I counted them twice to be certain. The Adassian Aron knows about this. He is covering the area just in case."

Kerren nods as he approaches. "Six, but if we do not move soon, I worry there will be more. I overheard them speaking and one mentioned he would be returning to camp soon. If they are switching shifts, we don't know how many we could be facing.

I clutch my staff, terrified as I stand up. "But we have to wait for Aron, don't we? For his diversion?" I'm terrified for my guy, even though I know he's immortal, that I'm the one in danger.

But that crazy fool plans on walking right through the army to announce himself. "Shouldn't we wait—"

A horn blasts in the distance, three times.

Someone shouts.

Fuck.

"That's Aron," Markos says, grabbing my arm and hauling me forward. "Come. Let us waste no time."

I nod and let Markos pull me along, and then we're all running, trying to keep to the shadows in the darkness. There are a few trees nearby, and then a fence surrounding the cemetery that's seen better days. Two guards stand in front of the gates of the cemetery itself, and I get a sense of déjà vu, back when Aron and I crept through Katharn.

We huddle at the edge of the fence, someone's hand on my hip. Kerren's big, sweaty body is blocking me from seeing anything, but I can hear voices. There's confusion, and the jingle of armor.

Then, I see a torch bobbing as it heads toward the gates of the cemetery.

"What's going on?" an unfamiliar, strangely accented voice says.

"It's another god. He's come to attack the Lord of Storms."

"No!" another man laughs. "A showdown? Our lord will hand him his ass, wait and see."

"I'm going to go watch," one calls, breathless.

Yes, everyone go watch, I silently chant. *Go and see the spectacle.*

"Bad idea," says another. "If you leave your post, that's desertion."

The man groans, and then the guards shuffle their feet. In the distance, the horn blasts three more times, and my heart clenches for Aron, who's all alone in the middle of the battlefield...

And probably loving it, actually.

"They're not leaving," Kerren hisses. "What do we do?"

"We need more of a distraction," Solat says, and then surges forward. Markos tries to grab him, but Solat sneaks to a bush nearby, close to where the two soldiers stand at the gate. Just inside, I can see two more patrolling. They said there were six total. All of the guards look to be paying attention to the sea of torches in the distance, across the river, where Aron's saying hello to the enemy army. I'd give anything to see that sight myself, but first I need to save my own bacon.

Then, Solat throws a damn rock.

Markos shoots him an angry glare, and no one moves. One of the guards turns his head, frowning in our direction.

Solat throws another, a short distance away from his bush.

I can feel the tension vibrating off of Kerren. Off of Markos. I hold my breath, just in case I breathe too loud and someone hears it.

The guard say something in low voices, then one leaves the front gate and approaches Solat's hiding spot. One step. Two. I feel like I'm going to explode as he takes out his sword, heading toward the bush, ready to attack.

To my utter surprise, Markos leaps from his hiding place and latches onto the guard the moment he gets close enough. His knife flashes, and then there's a horrible gurgling noise. The guard falls to the ground, clutching at his throat and rolling in pain.

Oh shit. That's not like the movies at all. It's not a fast death. It's not swift and painless. The man keeps making sounds and writhing, and I freeze, petrified. I knew we were going to make a break for the crypt, but I didn't think about the fact that people were going to *die*.

I'm such a naïve idiot.

The other guard shouts, and then men are racing toward us, drawing their weapons.

Kerren grabs me by the arm and hauls me forward. "Come on. No time to waste."

Solat and Markos confront the soldiers, while Kerren shields me with his body and keeps me against the rails of the fence. His sword is out, but because it's dark, no one's noticed us yet.

"In the gates," he whispers to me.

I run forward, my staff clutched in my hands…right into a pair of guards.

They look startled to see me. "A woman?" one blurts out. "Here?"

"Surprise," I yell, adrenaline rushing through me, and swing my staff like I'm trying to hit a home run. I don't stop to think about what I'm doing, or if they're going to kill me. I just swing.

I was pretty good at softball back in high school, and I definitely remember what the crack of the bat felt like against the heft of the ball. My staff slams into the side of the guard's face and…it doesn't feel the same. It feels a thousand times worse, and it makes a wet, cracking sound even as his jaw moves in a weird direction and blood flies and teeth spray and I can't stop gasping as he stares at me, then staggers. He's not going down, so I hit him again.

And again.

When he crumples to the ground on the third hit, I suck in a deep breath—fuck, there's not enough air in the world right now—and try to focus. I just killed a man.

Later, Faith. Worry about that later.

Kerren struggles against two guards, parrying their blows as they push him back against a large stone grave-marker. I rush forward and swing for the closest guard's head, but I only hit him a glancing blow from behind.

He immediately pivots and his sword slices out at me, too fast for me to avoid.

CLANG.

It feels like a truck hits my stomach, and I fall backwards as if kicked. I gag on the sensation of vomit creeping up my throat. I smack my staff against the back of his knee and he goes down like a rock even as I crawl onto hands and knees. While he staggers, I slam my staff against the side of his head, crushing his ear and knocking him over. A second swing makes him go still, and then Kerren shoves his knife in the man's throat.

Markos and Solat jog up to us. One whistles, staring at the guards I mashed. "Damn, woman."

I tremble, squeezing my eyes shut. It's either that or vomit. I remind myself that it was them or me. Them or me. If they knew I was Aron's anchor, they would have killed me just to get to him.

I still bend over and puke on some poor person's headstone.

Markos gives my back a pat. "Hurry it along, Faith. More will be coming."

Right. Right. Never mind that I just murdered two soldiers that were doing their jobs. *This is war.* I chant that to myself as Solat takes my arm and the men half guide, half drag me along with them, heading for the crypts.

Once we're in the cemetery, I realize we never asked what the crypt itself looks like, but it soon becomes really obvious that we don't have to. There's one building in the midst of this place, with a statue of the god of the dead in front of it, skulls at his feet. Behind him rises a square building with columns, and absurdly, I think it looks a bit like a bank. It's got double doors and columns and...well, bank. A hysterical laugh bubbles out of me.

"Get inside," Solat hisses. "Hurry."

The double doors are chained and locked with a delicate padlock that looks extremely expensive, and that Markos breaks with two swings of his sword. Then, the doors swing open and we step inside...and down.

Stairs descend, and it's pitch black inside. The moment the doors close behind us, we're in utter darkness.

"Um...?" I say aloud. "Did we think to bring a light?"

"I'll get the sparker out," Kerren says, and then there's a rustling noise as he digs through his pack.

"Hurry. Hurry." Solat's voice is the essence of impatience. "The moment they find out we're in here, we're trapped like rats."

"Let's not mention rats," I whisper.

Something taps. A skittering, scratchy sort of noise. It's a noise I've heard before.

Ah, damn.

"What was that?" Markos asks.

"The dead. Can we hurry things along?" I ask. "Kerren? Please?"

The striker flares, and then Kerren lights a fat, ugly tallow candle shoved into a cup. He holds it up, and then hands it to me. "So we can keep our hands free," he says.

Good call. I want them to be doing the fighting, not me.

The scratching noise starts again.

"Did you say that was…the dead?" Markos asks, confused.

"They're coming back," I say, stepping forward in a far braver fashion than I feel. "The god of the dead isn't home to receive them any longer so they don't have anywhere to go." I shield the candle with my hand as I move forward.

Kerren mutters a prayer under his breath.

The crypt itself is long and cold and dusty. As I step down the stairs, I see niches carved into the walls, and each niche has a heavy coffin already in it. Cobwebs hang over everything, and as we pass by the first coffin, I notice there's a heavy rock atop the lid. It's not something that fell there by surprise—it's easily the size of a shield, and not just the one tucked into my shirt. It's enormous and would take several men to move it.

The coffin scratches, and Markos jumps, jostling me.

"Sorry," he says.

I look across and the coffin on my other side has a similar rock. As we step forward, I see each one has something to weigh the lid down. "We're safe," I promise them. "Someone's already been down here to do damage control. The dead can't get out."

"Safe," Solat snorts. "How do you kill something that's already dead?"

"Let's hope we don't have to find out, all right?" I say cheerfully and walk a little faster. "Look for a statue of Aron. An ugly one." I pause then add, "It might not be that ugly. That just might be his vanity talking."

Someone snorts.

We walk. And walk. I can't go too fast or the candle will blow out, but I really want to get out of this crypt, and it seems like it snakes along for forever. We pass row after row of coffins, some with dried flowers left in vases by the floor, others covered in such thick dust that they've been here for forever. The scratching dies down the farther in we go, but I'm hyper-aware that Aron's outside, getting pummeled just because he can't die. I don't want him hurt. As silly as it sounds, I worry about him. For all that he's arrogant as hell and a god, sometimes he's clueless. There's a lot of things they can do to a man without actually killing him…and then I shake those thoughts out of my head because I don't even want to consider it.

Then, the passage changes. It turns into a larger chamber, and at the far end is a statue of a man holding an axe, his head bowed. The entire thing is a little…stumpy and the expression on the man is downright constipated. I can't help but laugh, because this had to hurt poor Aron's huge ego. "All right, I think we've found our man."

"How do we get inside?" Kerren asks, curious.

"No freaking clue," I admit, and hand him the candle so I can run my hands along the wall itself, looking for a hinge mechanism of some kind. I run my fingers over the cracks, and I find a narrow, straight line between the large stone bricks that has to be our secret door, but no amount of pushing or pulling will open it. "Is there a lever somewhere?"

"Faith," Markos warns. "Hurry up."

"We can all look, you know," I snap back at him, studying the floor. Is there a panel we step on? I push on one tile experimentally but nothing moves.

He readies his sword, and Solat does, too. "Someone just came in," Markos whispers.

Then, I hear it, too. Voices. Distant, but definitely in the crypt. Fuck. We have to get out of here, and soon, because we're cornered. Frantic, I run my hands over the wall one more time, but when I find nothing, I turn to the statue. Maybe our answer is here. I run my hands all over the ugly dwarf-Aron made of stone, checking the mouth, the crotch, the hands, but it all seems to be entirely one piece. Even as I move, I hear footsteps approaching, the clank of armor, and then shouting.

"Come on, Aron," I whisper. "Help a girl out."

I jerk on the axe, hoping that it's the key I'm missing, but when it doesn't move, I glare at the statue itself, frustrated.

And stop. The eyepatch covering Aron's left eye looks strange. I run a fingernail under the patch itself and it flips up. Inside Aron's eye socket is a pupil, which shouldn't be there if he's missing an eye, right? I shove my finger inside and push it, and it clicks like a button.

Stone rumbles, and the wall slides open in a cloud of dust. A new, dark passage opens.

Fuck yes! "Let's go," I tell the others, flipping the eyepatch down and snatching the candle from Kerren. I lead the way, down a second narrow passage, and the men file in behind me. The stone scrapes behind us a second later, indicating that the secret door is closing once more. My candle blows out at the rush of air.

Then, all is silent.

"Did they see us?" I whisper into the darkness.

"I don't think so," Markos murmurs. "Where are we?"

"Hell if I know. No choice but to go forward, right?" I put a hand out and take a few steps into the dark. I don't hear the dead scratching, so I'm really, really hoping this is just a small antechamber and not crypts 2.0. Sure enough, my fingers brush over stone, and I'm touching a wall. "Here we go."

I run my hands up and down the stonework in the dark, and to my surprise, there's something protruding—a door handle? I turn it and the door swings outward. Light spills in.

CHAPTER 72

a group of women sit in the room in front of us. It's a library of some kind, the walls filled with books and scroll-nooks. Chairs are seated near a fireplace, and one woman sews on an embroidery pedestal while another holds a book in her lap. A third woman stands as we stumble inside. She's got a long, thick braid and wears a pale lavender dress that looks incredibly ornate and very expensive. There's a circlet on her brow. Her pregnant belly is rounded and in her arms is a child of no more than one or two years old.

Her eyes narrow at the sight of us. "Guards. Bar the secret passage and arrest these intruders."

"Hi," I say, waving. "So this is terribly awkward, but Aron told us to come here."

A man rushes out of the room and I can hear him bellowing for guards. Markos and Kerren pull closer to me, holding their swords, while Solat tries to shove me behind him to protect me.

Sweet thought, but no.

I shove him back and take a step forward. "We mean no harm, okay? We just had to get away from the Adassian army and Aron told us there was a secret passage in the crypts because the ugly statue was dedicated to him. I swear we're not here to hurt anyone."

The woman holds her baby closer to her chest and takes a step back as guards flood into the room. "If you mean Aron of the Cleaver sent you, then you must be working for the Adassians." She holds her baby's head protectively and steps behind one of the guards. "Take them to the dungeons. My husband will want to know how they managed to sneak in."

"Of course, Your Majesty," one man says, moving forward.

Markos raises his sword and I put my hand on his arm. We're not attacking anyone. "So this is awkward. I think you're talking about Aron of the Cleaver—Hedonism Aron, who's shacked up with the Adassians and is attacking you guys, right? That's not who I'm with. My Aron is the Aron of Arrogance. He's just outside, creating a diversion so we could get away. He's come here to join the Yshremi army."

The woman—the queen—pauses. "Your Aron?" She arches an eyebrow.

Aw shit. I might have just given myself away as his anchor. I ignore the flutter of panic in my chest. "I'm a devotee," I lie. "But I'm telling the truth—there's a second Aspect of Aron here, and he's fighting his way toward your gates even now. If you don't believe me, look outside."

The queen gives us a tight look. She hands her child to another one of her women, who scuttles out of the room with the baby, accompanied by a few guards. More file in to take their place, and the room feels stifling.

"Give us your weapons," she says in an imperious voice. "You're surrounded and there's no hope for your plot to work."

I gesture at Kerren and the others to do so. "There's no damn plot. We're here because my Aron wants to fight the other Aron and he said the Yshremi are faithful to him. I promise, just go look outside."

The queen exchanges a look with one of her guards. She

leans in close to him, whispering as others take our weapons away. I give up my quarterstaff and grimace as I pull the shield out of the front of my dress. Damn thing must have cut into my sides somewhat awful, because my skin hurts. I hear the word "husband" mentioned, and "front lines" and the queen's expression grows even more pinched. She seems to age in a matter of seconds. But she straightens, looks at me, and then flicks a hand, indicating she wishes to be followed. "Take the woman. We will see if this is truth or not."

"No," Kerren says, trying to push in front of me. "She stays with us—"

"It's okay," I say quickly, putting up my hand before he can get himself killed. Or me killed. "We have nothing to hide. It's fine. I promise."

"If Aron finds out," Markos begins, warning in his voice.

"Then we tell him it was necessary." I step forward, and I don't panic when two guards immediately grab my arms. "It's fine. This is all fine."

It's really not fine. I'm kind of freaking out, but if the queen can wear a serene expression, I can, too. I smile as if this is all totally going as planned and let the queen's guards drag me along as she sweeps out of the room.

"Faith!" I can hear Markos yelling as I'm taken into the keep itself. We move quickly, following behind the queen, and there are so many guards around me that I can't really see much about this particular castle, other than it's got a high stone ceiling in the rooms we cut through and banners cover each wall, most of them emblazoned with a red hand over an eye or a scroll.

We march up stairs, and my bruised front and sides ache with every step. That shield must have been a bad idea. I can just imagine the mark it left—then again, it saved my life...and Aron's. I'll take a few bruises.

The queen doesn't speak as we go up twisting stairs after twisting stairs. I'm panting by the time we get to the top, and then our small group steps outside into the night. The queen moves to the edge, her hands on the crenellated wall as she stares down at the gates just in front of the broken bridge.

I jerk against the arms holding me, and the guard glares at me. "I want to see, okay? I just want to see."

The queen glances over at me, then points. "Something's happening down there. Let her look her fill."

I practically run to the wall the moment their hands loosen on me and peer over the side, down at the scene below. The tower we're in is at the edge of one side of the city, and there's a cluster of close-packed houses below us that seem to go on for forever, right up until they butt up against the wall. We're high enough that I can see beyond the wall, and it looks like a swarm of ants on the far side of the river, surrounded by torches. The rickety temporary bridge is down, but no one's crossing it, and I fidget anxiously, looking for signs of my Aron.

Surely he didn't just hang out in the enemy camp just because?

Then, the crowd just in front of the bridge—the swarm of ants—erupts, and I can hear a man bellow. Lightning crashes and thunder booms overhead. It sounds angry, and I immediately brace myself for a surge of pain if Aron reaches for his powers. My head's fine, though...which means Aron's not angry.

He's having fun.

"That fucker," I breathe, unable to tear my gaze away. "He's going to get himself killed."

The anthill spills, and then they give space to a single man in the center, a man riddled with arrows, his clothing torn and bloody. He brandishes an axe—not sure where he got one—and then lets out another battle cry.

Men charge at him, and they lose. Every single time. Within moments, there's a pile of bodies in front of him, and he whirls the axe again.

The queen shoots me a look. "He's attacking the Adassian troops."

I nod. "He's creating a diversion so we could get here safely."

"Why does he want to come here?"

"Your army," I admit. "He was offered one in Novoro but he wasn't a fan. He said the Yshrem and the Cyclopae kick everyone's ass and so if he was going to have an army, he wanted the best army in the world. We didn't know the other Aron was here until today."

She stalks toward me, her eyes wide, and grabs my sleeve. The queen leans in, studying me. "You keep saying 'we.' Are you...his anchor?" Her voice lowers in a hush.

I swallow. If I say so, am I condemning myself?

Before I can answer, a look something like relief crosses her face. "You are. He sent you here for safety...because he's coming to our side?" Her hand clutches my arm tightly. "To join forces with our side? You're certain?"

"Well, he's sure not joining the other guys."

For a moment, the queen stares at me. Her shoulders sag, ever so slightly, and I catch a flash of relief in her eyes. "Thank the gods. We have a chance."

CHAPTER 73

$\mathcal{W}$e watch as the one-sided battle plays out for a while. Eventually, the men stop attacking Aron, and he spreads his arms wide, a taunt for them to continue. To take a chance. No one takes him up on it, though, and he throws the axe to the ground and then crosses the bridge into Castle Yshrem.

"They're opening the gates," the queen murmurs. "Come. My husband will be with them."

We head back into the keep and down the stairs, the queen utterly silent and the only sound the jingle of armor of the men who accompany us. When we arrive into a large hall, a cheer goes up, and for a moment, I think they're cheering the queen. But it's clear when we get inside that no one even knows she's there. The place is absolutely packed with men, some dressed in leather and fur, some dressed in armor of varying types. All of them are filthy and cheering.

They also completely block the doorway, so the queen can't enter.

She turns and looks at one of her men in frustration.

"Make way," he bellows, storming forward, only to have his

words drowned out by another cheer. The man shoves his way through the crowd, clearing a path for the queen, and once people realize she's approaching, they part for her.

I follow close behind, because Aron's somewhere around here. He—

He's there, right in front of me. I stop as I clear the wall of soldiers standing shoulder to shoulder, jostling each other. Aron's in the center of the room, standing next to a young-looking man with long black hair and an eyepatch. He wears a cloak of startling white fur and leather leggings, and grins at the queen when she approaches, offering her his hand. Is that the king? Not that I care.

All of my attention is on Aron, who's practically unrecognizable.

From head to toe, my Aron is covered in blood. His hair is plastered to his scalp, his clothing demolished and shredded, and his skin is a mucky, dark red. His eyes shine bright—green and brown—in his face, and as I watch, he pulls another arrow out of his arm. I can still see two more sticking from his side.

He looks like a damn mess.

I'm so relieved to see him I want to cry.

He grins at something the king says, and then I can't stop smiling as I approach. I'm so thankful he's here and whole, so happy.

The queen whispers something in her husband's ear and then he looks at me. Aron does, too.

And his pleasure fades away to rage.

"Why is she *bleeding?*"

Thunder booms overhead, and my head feels as if it was just struck by lightning.

I stagger, pressing my palm to my forehead. "Aron! Stop it! Control your temper!"

He immediately moves to my side, his hands on my gown. It's a pale green and my hem is muddy from all the running around. "I will control my temper when I see for myself that you aren't hurt."

I look down as his big hands move over my abdomen, and hiss when his fingers burn over my scrapes. Sure enough, I look down and there are two dark, wet spots, one on each side of my stomach. I'm confused until I remember the sword that tried to slice me in half. "Oh. I guess that guy's blade connected a little more than I thought."

"Blade?" Aron says quietly, and the thunder grows louder.

I grab his chin and force him to look me in the eye. "If you give me another nosebleed it's going to hurt you a hell of a lot more than these little scratches do."

He clenches his jaw, but I can hear the thunder ebbing. The room around us is utterly quiet, as if no one is sure what to think. "Tell me you're not wounded badly," he finally manages, straightening. His fingers twitch, as if he wants to haul my tunic off my body and check for himself right here, right now.

"I'm not hurt badly," I promise, and give him a light pat on the cheek. Truth be told, I've had so much adrenaline rushing through me I don't know if I'm hurt that bad or not. I'm pretty sure it's all right, though. I'd feel it if things were worse, wouldn't I? So I beam at Aron as if it's all good. "We made it in one piece, though, which is more than I can say for you." And I gesture at the arrows sticking out of his side.

Something rumbles in his chest that sounds like amusement. A hint of a smile flashes across his face and then Aron grabs me and hauls me against him. He kisses me fiercely, his teeth clashing with mine. It seems I'm not the only one feeling the charge of adrenaline. I kiss him back, my hand going to his neck...which is wet with blood.

I pull away, making a face. "You're filthy."

He just grins at me, looking like a crazy person. "It seems I need to clean up before I claim my anchor."

To say the least. But he keeps his arm locked around my hips as he turns back toward the king, and I scrub a sleeve over my face, only to find it smeared with gore. That crazy son of a bitch…I'm so glad to see him.

The king drops to a knee in front of Aron and makes the clenched-hand symbol over his chest in honor of the Lord of Storms. "We are at your disposal. Yshrem and Cyclopae are honored to serve. Anything you need from us, we will provide."

The queen hesitates, then tries to drop to a knee, clutching her rounded stomach.

"That's not necessary, right, Aron?" I poke him in the side gently.

He grunts at me.

I poke him again.

He shoots me a look, then offers his filthy, filthy hand to the queen. To her credit, she takes it with a gracious smile. "You and your anchor are welcome here. Our home is your home for as long as you like."

"What I would like," Aron says slowly, "is to take down my opponent across the river and give Yshrem victory."

Cheers fill the room. The Cyclopae king gets to his feet, and he's got that war-hungry, eager look that Aron gets in his eyes, too. "With you leading us, we are sure to prevail, Lord of Storms. And if we do not, it will be a glorious battle to the end!"

The men cheer.

I don't. Neither does the queen. We share a look, instead. The guys might be cool with dying on the battlefield, but the thought terrifies me.

"I'm tired and dirty," I say to Aron, forcing a smile to my face. "And you're filthy and I'm pretty sure you still have a crossbow bolt between your shoulders. Can we get somewhere we can clean up?"

"Oh, by the gods," the queen says, shaking her head. "Of course. Please, come with me. We will house you in the finest rooms Castle Yshrem has to offer. And baths for both of you."

"And food," I add, taking the hand she extends me. "Please."

"And food," she agrees. "Whatever you like."

I turn to look at Aron, strangely reluctant to leave his side again.

"Where are her guards?" Aron asks, frowning.

"I'm sure they're upstairs just hanging out where I left them," I say brightly, because I can feel the queen's hand clench against my fingers. "We sort of scared everyone when we dropped in. It's fine, Aron."

His eyes narrow.

"Fine," I say again. I let go of the queen's hand and move back to him. I take a hold of the front of his filthy, filthy tunic—or what's left of it—and tug him down closer to me. "I'll make sure they stay outside the room and guard it, okay? And I'll take a nice hot bath, and you'll take a nice hot bath, and then you'll come upstairs once you've finished talking war and you can make love to your anchor all night long, all right?"

"I am a god, Faith," he murmurs. "We do not love."

"Right. Sure."

But he kisses me fiercely, and the room fills with cheers from the soldiers I forgot were there, and it seems to me that for a god that doesn't love, he sure is affectionate.

OUR FIRST STOP upstairs is not a bath after all. I'm taken to a healer and the two gashes on my stomach—surface wounds, really—are cleaned and neatly stitched up while the queen's men retrieve Markos, Solat, and Kerren. Then, I'm brought down an opulent hall and the queen gestures at the room at the end. "These were my father's chambers when he was king. I couldn't bear to take them after I became queen, so they are used for visiting dignitaries. Will Aron mind if you're both in the same room?"

Her inquiry is so polite, so sweet.

"If you're asking if we're sleeping together, the answer is yes. One bed is cool."

She nods, and we continue into the room. She pushes open double doors and then I'm staring at an opulent chamber swathed with tapestries. A large, ornate wooden bed is in the center of the room, and by the fire in the fireplace, servants are pouring water into a large tub. I can smell fresh-baked bread and hot food, and my stomach growls.

"I know an anchor must eat to fuel her bond with her Aspect, so I've had the servants bring a large tray. If it's not enough, say the word and I'll make sure the cooks are ready to prepare you whatever you'd like." She moves to the center of the room and waves in a new servant, this one carrying a small trunk. "A few things for you. Combs. Scented oils. Fresh clothing."

"Thank you. This is all really great."

She turns and gives me a smile, ever the gracious hostess. "My name is Halla, and it would please me if the two of us could talk in the morning?" She gives me a searching look, and I get the impression that there's a lot going on behind that sweet exterior.

"Sure." I nod. "I'll be happy to talk."

"Excellent." She heads out in a sweep of lavender embroidered skirts, and then servants flee after her, everyone exiting the room at the same time. I'm left alone with Markos, Solat, and Kerren.

"Are you guys okay?" I ask. "You didn't get hurt, did you?"

"They stripped our armor and weapons from us and were just about to take us to the dungeons," Markos admits. "But we were not hurt, no."

Solat adds, "You should have seen the looks on their faces when they found out you were telling the truth. They couldn't bow and scrape quick enough for 'Lord Aron's guardsmen.'" He smirks and moves to the tray of food, picking up a wedge of cheese.

I head over to it and slap his hand. "That's mine."

He grins at me and eats it anyway. "Shall we sleep in the doorway and keep you guarded?"

I think about Aron, how happy he was to greet the king. How he let me leave with the queen, no questions asked. He trusts these people. Even so, it's been a hell of a journey to get here. "We'll ask for you guys to have an adjoining room," I decide. "One can stay on guard at the doorway while the others are relaxing. And ask for a tray from the kitchens," I say, slapping Solat's hand again when he reaches for another piece of cheese. "If you eat any more of that I'm going to throw you from the rafters."

"Never come between an anchor and her meal," he says with a wink, but he pulls back. Good.

I flick my hands at them. "I'm filthy, and Aron kissed me and transferred his filth to me. I'm going to bathe and then eat until he gets here. Are you guys okay to do your own thing?"

"We'll find a servant," Markos reassures me.

"A pretty one, hopefully," Solat adds.

"Glad to see you're back to being yourself." I eat a piece of cheese myself as they file out, and then Kerren points at the door, indicating he'll be just outside.

Then, the heavy doors are shut, and I'm all alone in the sumptuous room.

I spend the next hour in the tub, eating cheese and meat, drinking wine, and relaxing in the scorchingly hot water. It's so damn nice that I hate to get out, but I do when I tragically run out of wine. I get out of the tub, towel off, and then wrap myself in a fur-trimmed sleeping gown I find in the trunk. I crawl into the epic-looking bed and sigh with pleasure.

And fall asleep.

CHAPTER 74

I wake up in the middle of the night to a big, naked body spooning my backside and hiking up my nightgown.

Aron kisses my neck, his breath hot on my skin. "Should I let you sleep?"

I moan, reaching for him. "Not now that I'm all turned on."

He chuckles, the sound low and delicious. "Then my plan worked." He continues to kiss my neck, his mouth devouring with need as he rolls me onto my belly, and then hikes my hips into the air. "I need you, Faith. Are you wet for me?"

His hand slides between my thighs and he strokes my folds, teasing me. I moan as he pushes a finger into my pussy, working it back and forth. He's not giving me any time to think about things, his hands insistent. He must still be fired up from the battle earlier, because I can feel his enormous cock stabbing into my thigh as he presses his big body against my backside.

Arousal, quick and urgent, shoots through me, and when he pushes my nightgown up to my shoulders, leaving the majority of my body exposed, I get on my hands and knees, arching my backside even higher into the air like a cat in heat. I need him just as badly as he needs me. I want his touch. Need it. "Aron," I pant. "Claim me like you mean it."

"Oh, I always mean it, my Faith." His fingers glide over my folds, teasing my clit expertly. "Look at how wet your cunt is for me already. You like it when I take you, don't you?"

"If I didn't, you'd know about it," I manage, my fingers twisting in the blankets under my hands as he pets and strokes me. He's right, though, I'm so wet already that I can hear the slick noises my pussy's making as he touches me. Just his touch is enough to get me all worked up within seconds. I've never wanted anyone as badly as I've wanted this man. It's like there's some charged connection between us at a deeper level—he turns me on as I've never been turned on before.

He laughs, easing a second finger into my pussy and fucking me with it. "Always with a retort," Aron murmurs. "Never willing to admit that you need to be fucked, and fucked hard."

I moan, burying my face against the blankets. "*Aron.*"

"You do, don't you, though?" he says, determined to dirty-talk his way through my orgasm. "You need me to fuck this wet, juicy cunt. You need my thick cock deep inside you until you scream. You need my fingers on your breasts—"

"They haven't been on my breasts yet, have they?" I manage, panting.

"Is that what I'm doing wrong?" he teases in a sultry voice, and then his fingers slide out of my pussy and move to my breast, teasing it with a wet caress. "Now will you scream for me?"

"I'll scream if you don't get inside me in the next minute." I wiggle my backside, trying to entice him.

I get what I want—he pushes into me in the next moment, and my cheek skids across the blankets. I don't even care—it feels so amazing that my toes curl and I'm gasping as he thrusts into me again, so hard and deep that I swear I can feel him all the way to my belly. He holds onto my hips and uses my body—

I can't even keep a rhythm with him because he's so quick and fierce, and each thrust is so hard that it takes me by surprise. He's pumping into me with such power that there's a pleasure-pain edge to things, and I can't last longer than a few moments before I shatter into a million pieces, choking out his name as I come.

Then, he reaches between my thighs and toys with my clit until I come again.

By the time he finally comes, I feel wrung out. I curl up on the bed, utterly sated as he gets a towel and then washes us both off. Funny, that I wouldn't think of the god who just fucked my brains out as tender with aftercare, but he is. He washes my pussy clean of his release with gentle hands, then tosses the cloth aside. He tucks the blankets around us and pulls me close to him, his lips on my brow.

I start to drift off to sleep again when he speaks. "You'll be safe here with the queen."

"Mmm?" I manage. "I'm staying with the queen?"

"I told First Warrior Mathior that it is my command. No one is more guarded than the queen and her son. You'll be safest with them." He pauses thoughtfully, his hands brushing my hair off my brow. "He loves her."

"Good for him. She seems like a nice lady."

"They are very different," Aron muses. "The Cyclopae are not as civilized as the Yshremi, but he has wanted her ever since he was a small boy. The moment he became First Warrior, he took her as his bride. I remember him offering many times to me, determined to have his way. I liked his spirit." He presses his mouth to my brow again. "Which is why you will be safest with her. The entire kingdom would have to collapse before Mathior would let the enemy approach Halla."

I tuck myself closer to him. "So you're leaving me tomorrow? You can't go far—we're tethered, remember?" I frown at the memory of the intense pain I felt when in Citadel, all because I didn't realize that I couldn't step away from Aron's side.

"I'm not leaving," he corrects. "But every day, I will be on the front line of the battlefields."

I lift my head and look up at him, and he's smiling.

Men.

"So you're excited about war?"

He grins. "Of course."

I am decidedly less thrilled, but I console myself with the fact that he can't get hurt. I stroke a hand down his chest. "What's the goal?"

"What do you mean? The goal is to win."

"He can't die, though. And you can't die. So are you charging through to look for his anchor? Or what?"

"Mmm...eventually. I need to figure out his strategy first."

I suspect his strategy will be 'take out Aron's anchor,' since that's our strategy. "I'm afraid. What if he sends assassins?"

Aron hugs me closer. "You will be guarded at all times. Your food will be tasted, your wine, too. No one will get close enough."

I really, really hope that's not arrogance talking.

CHAPTER 75

The next morning, I wake up to the jingling sound of Aron putting on his belt. He's nearly completely dressed, his tunic a blazing white with a scarlet axe emblazoned on each shoulder. He's got a long, fur cape of pure white, and it contrasts with his long, dark hair and tanned skin.

I sit up in bed, watching as he dresses. "Should I wish you luck?"

"I need no luck," he says, and looks like an eager schoolboy for a moment. He's ready to get out there and kick some ass. "You'll stay here? Safe at the queen's side?"

"Yup. You won't do anything crazy like get yourself captured?"

He grins. "Never."

I hug my knees to my chest as he props a booted foot up on the side of the bed and adjusts it. "I just don't understand the point of battling the other guy, Aron. Help me understand. He's not going to let his anchor near the front lines, just like you're hiding me. He can't die. You can't die. What's the point?'

"If I overtake his encampment and break his army, I can search for his anchor. He cannot fight an entire army."

Can't he? I mean, I'm guessing that will be Hedonism Aron's strategy as well as ours. He's going to keep flinging men at the keep to try to break in. "You're sure this isn't just fighting because you like fighting?"

He moves to my side in the bed and cups my face. "I am a god of battle, Faith. This is part of who I am."

"You're also a god of storms, but no one's suggesting you do that," I mutter.

Aron laughs again and then leans down, kissing me fiercely. "Stay by the queen. I will return this evening, after I have broken his army."

I nod but say nothing else. This is war, and that's who he is.

I watch him go, and then my stomach growls, so I get out of bed and dress. There's a plate of food waiting for me, but I don't want to stay cooped up in my rooms. There's a big window in here, but all it is is a view to the wrong side of the city. From my bedroom, all I can see are the houses and streets that squeeze together, making up the cramped-looking medieval city of Yshrem. So I grab a handful of cheese and shove a roll into my mouth, and head out of my room.

Markos is there, waiting for me. He nods and falls into step behind me as I gnaw on my bread. "You guys treated ok?" I ask him.

"Like kings," he says with a wry twist of his mouth. "We will not be allowed to join the battle. Our task is to stay at your side."

"Aron told me I have to stay with the queen."

He gestures down the hall. "I have instructions to take you there, or for you to stay in your rooms. Aron doesn't want you wandering."

My mouth twists a little. I get it. I understand that safety is in having controlled spaces with limited access, but I don't like the thought of sitting on a silk cushion while he goes to war outside. I itch to do something. Anything. But what? I'm the one that's the target. "Let's go say hi to Her Majesty, then."

Markos leads me forward, his hand lightly at my arm, and I can't help but notice he's fully armored and brimming with weapons. So much for the keep being completely "safe." There are two armed men standing outside the queen's chambers and even more down the hall. Markos nods at all of them and as we approach, they open the doors and let us in to the queen's inner quarters.

It's the same library-study we busted into before. Like yesterday, there are chairs by the fireplace, and the queen sits in one while two ladies sit nearby, sewing. Like yesterday, she wears another lavender dress, but this one is practically crusted with embroidery, the sleeves long and dangling. She has her infant son in her lap, playing with him, and looks over at us when we enter.

"Don't let me interrupt," I say with an awkward smile, and look for somewhere to sit.

"You are an honored guest," Queen Halla says, getting to her feet heavily. One of the ladies gets to her feet and reaches for the child, but Halla shakes her head. She holds her baby close as she approaches me. "Did you sleep comfortably?"

I flush, because I'm pretty sure Aron and I were loud last night. Did they hear that? "It was great, thank you."

She turns to one of the maids. "Caitria, tell the kitchens we need a very large tray of food and more wine. Lord Aron's anchor will be hungry."

The girl curtsies, her head bowed, and then leaves the room, hands clasped.

"Please," the queen says, gesturing at her quarters. "Make yourself comfortable."

I smile at her and her baby. The little one has darker skin than Halla does, and his hair is jet black and shaved on one side of his head in the Cyclops tradition. He sucks his thumb as he looks over at me, and for a moment, his expression is purely that of his father. "Cute kid."

Her eyes flash with pleasure as she gazes at her son. "His name is Alistair, after my husband's father. If our second child is another boy, we will name him after my father." There's a look of pride on her face, and it's clear she loves her family. She looks over at me. "And you? We are of an age. Do you have children?"

"Me? Oh, god, no. I can barely muster the energy to run around after Aron." Her eyes widen in surprise at my words, and I hesitate. "Did Aron tell you that I'm not...local?"

"I knew from your accent," she admits. "You are from across the seas?"

"A bit farther out than that." I wince. How do I explain that I'm from Earth without weirding her out? "Like, way, way out."

Halla inclines her head. "Wherever you are from, I'm thankful that you and Aron came here. My home is your home."

I look around the room as a maid opens the door—and she's accompanied by Markos as she enters. As I watch, the girl sets the tray down and then takes a bite out of each of the foods. I'm startled, but I realize she's tasting everything. There are two jugs of wine, and she pours herself a cup from each, tastes them, curtsies and leaves.

The baby gets fussy, so the queen moves back to her chair and hands him a ball, murmuring at him as her ladies smile and try not to look too closely at me. I guess I don't match what they think Aron's companion should be. Their hair is worn in intricate, looping braids that crisscross over their heads and are decorated with bits of jewelry. Mine's loose and finger-combed. Their dresses are corseted and it looks like they're wearing a dress over another dress. I glance down and realize that the dark red dress I put on today that belts loosely at the waist is just the under-dress. I didn't realize it was a two piece. Whoops. At least I remembered shoes.

There's a large window in the room, and I gravitate toward it. From here, I can see the battlefield in the distance, the clash of men, and the sea of banners that move as if alive. A distant horn sounds, and I glance back at the queen. "How long have the Adassians been camped at your doorstep?"

"Ever since the Anticipation," she admits, settling her son on a thick rug at one of the women's feet and then moving to my side. "We think Lord Aron arrived from the Aether into Adassia directly, and that is why he chose them. For a time, my husband was quite upset. He and his people are very devoted to the Lord of Storms." She studies me. "Where are the two of you from?"

"He showed up in Aventine," I tell her. "I was a slave there. Someone caught me wandering where I shouldn't and decided I should be property. Then, I was taken to Aron's temple to be a cleaver bride, but I opted to be his anchor instead."

"Cleaver brides," she murmurs. "A barbaric practice. The Cyclopae prefer for their warriors to give of themselves, not slaves." She shakes her head. "Aventine is very far. Did you sail, then?"

"No. It was a lot of riding. A lot. We ran into one of Aron's other Aspects outside of Katharn, and I think Apathy died a month or so ago. It's only these two left." I gaze out the window at the clash of men, the swords and armor gleaming in the early morning sunlight. Aron's somewhere down there, eating this shit up.

"Then this is over soon," the queen says, and there's obvious relief in her voice.

I say nothing. Part of me wants it over soon, sure. Part of me is terrified at what happens "after." I can't stop thinking about what the Spidae said. I watch the field, but from here, I can only see movement, not individuals. "I don't suppose you have a tele-scope, do you?"

"A what?"

"Er, a spyglass?" I gesture at my eye. "With a long tube and a piece of glass at the end that enables you to see farther?"

Her brows furrow. "I can ask if the court wizards have such a device."

"It's okay." I shrug. "I just wanted to see what was going on down at the field."

She shudders. "I can't watch it. My husband is eager to be at Aron's side but…"

But Aron is immortal and her husband isn't. I get it. "So… Adassia had a god show up, huh? Did you hear of any other places that might have had one? Everyone's supposed to be down here for the Anticipation but we've only run into a few, and they weren't my favorites."

"All of the major city-states have been graced with a god," she admits, her expression carefully blank. "Or so the rumors go."

"Except you guys…until now?"

"No," the queen says after a moment. "We have a goddess here. Magra, Lady of Plenty, is here."

I gasp. "Really?" I'm shocked. I guess I thought I would "know" somehow if another god was lurking nearby. No one's said anything at all. Even now, Halla's expression is even, but I get the idea that she's a little uncomfortable. "I have a friend that was a priest of hers. He sent a scroll with me in case I met her. Can I…can I see her?"

Queen Halla's expression is the definition of neutral. "Are you sure you truly wish to? She is…not as Aron is. Her presence here is both blessing and burden."

"What do you mean?"

"Come. I will show you." She nods to her ladies. "Watch over Alistair for me, will you? We will return shortly."

Markos pushes away from the wall in a clank of armor, straightening. "My orders are to follow you at all times, my lady Faith."

Lady Faith? I want to correct him—or laugh—but I get that he's trying to be polite. To give me the reverence I'm due as Aron's anchor. Feels weird, though. "Come on, then."

We stop by my rooms to get the scroll from my bags, and

then I clutch it tight to my chest as Queen Halla leads me—and Markos, and about six additional guards—through the keep. My hands are sweaty as I hold it, because I think of Omos and how kind he was. He was the first polite person I met in this world. I want this to go well for him. I want her to look at the scroll and smile happily that such a devoted man is thinking of her. Just once, I want to have something go right. To bring good into this strange new world.

I'm surprised when we ascend one of the many towers in Castle Yshrem. The stairs seem to climb endlessly, and I wonder at a goddess that wants to hide away from everyone like this. She's a goddess of plenty, so that means feasts and food and things like that. Crops, harvests, good times. Pleasant things. "So far away from everyone?" I ask as we continue up another set of stairs.

Halla gives me a searching look. "Lady Magra has requested rooms here because of the noise in the lower chambers. She prefers to be left alone."

Oh. I think for a moment. She could be one of four Aspects —I don't think it's hedonism. But anyone else could fit with a little bit of fudging. We arrive at a plain wooden door, and Queen Halla knocks, then enters, casting another glance in my direction.

I follow her in…and I'm surprised.

CHAPTER 76

*I*t's dark inside. There's a sputtering candle in one corner, but the large windows are shut, the casement shutters closed. Very little light streams in. In the bed, a beautiful older woman with russet hair lies staring at the ceiling.

"My lady Magra," the queen says in a gentle voice. "An honored guest wished to meet you. Lord Aron of the Storms has arrived and brought his anchor with him. She has a message from one of your most loyal followers."

The woman in the bed makes a sound like a sigh.

I hesitate, not sure what else to do. The moment we walked in and I saw her in the rumpled bed, I knew what this was. It's not arrogance, it's not lies. It's apathy. No wonder Halla has been so wary. I thought hedonism would be the worst Aspect to visit given my experience with Tadekha, but clearly I see it's this one. Just being in her presence is depressing. I look around the room, and sitting in a chair in the dark is another woman, an older one, her face hollow, her expression tired. She has a blanket in her lap and looks nearly as worn down as the woman she's serving—because this has to be her anchor.

"Greetings," I say, inwardly wincing at my own too-cheery

tone. "It's wonderful to meet you, Lady Magra. I met a monk of yours a few months ago, a man by the name of Omos. Do you know him?"

She fixes her gaze on me, and her eyes are just...blank. Bored. "So?"

So?

"He was very excited at the thought of your arrival in this world," I lie. Didn't Omos say something like this would happen? He knew, somehow. He didn't want to meet her because he didn't want to see her like this. At the time I thought he was just being a little fearful. Now I think he was right. Even so, I've carried his message this far and I want to deliver it for his sake. He's my friend. "Omos sent along a message should I meet you in my journeys." I hold the scroll out, the precious scroll I've protected over miles and miles, because I owed it to Omos. I'm almost reluctant to hand it over.

Magra doesn't reach for it. She simply looks at it, then looks at me, and rolls over in bed and faces the wall.

The queen grimaces.

Oh. I clutch the scroll for a moment longer, wondering if I should hold onto it or leave it anyhow. I try to think of what Omos would want. Maybe...maybe this Aspect of Magra won't care enough to see it, but perhaps the next one will? I set it down on the table next to the bed. "I'm just gonna set it here, for whenever you feel like reading it." When there's no answer, I add, "He was a really good man, you know. One of the best I've ever met. I hope you'll see that..."

The goddess doesn't respond. She simply stares at the wall and I want to reach over and shake her. To tell her I know she's not sleeping because Aron doesn't sleep.

As I hesitate by the bed, the queen moves to the woman by the window. She takes the thin, veined hand in hers and leans by the woman. "Do you need anything?" Her voice is soft, gentle.

The old woman—the anchor—shakes her head. She closes her eyes. "Tired."

Queen Halla pats her hand and sets it down gently on the blanket once more, then straightens and nods at me, indicating we should leave. I follow her out, and I feel like I can't breathe until we shut the door behind us and head down the stairs.

"That...sucked," I eventually manage.

"It has been difficult," the queen admits. "We were overjoyed to be blessed as a kingdom, but we soon realized it was not as we expected. Her presence here has been both joy and pain. With her here, our stores never run dry. They are magically replenished every evening and it allows us to feed all of the people who have fled here seeking safety from the Adassians." She touches my arm. "But...she has drained three anchors already."

I swallow hard, thinking of the hollow cheeks of the woman in the room with her. "She's using her powers to replenish your stores."

"Yes. Once we realized what she was doing, we asked her to stop but...she simply doesn't care." Halla's lips purse. "Those that volunteer to serve as her anchor know it is a death sentence, but they do it out of love for her, and because she feeds the city."

That is indeed a hairy, awful situation. "So what do you do?"

"We are trapped right now," Halla admits, holding onto my arm as we go down the stairs. Her steps are slower, and she holds onto her belly, and then I feel guilty for making a pregnant woman waddle all over this enormous castle. "The sacrifice of a few loyal anchors allows thousands to be fed while Adassia lays siege. But..." Her voice trails off.

Yeah, I see what she means. Do they boot the goddess out of the city or do they let her keep draining anchors? If they force her to leave, will she be angry? If they withhold an anchor from her after she uses this one up, will she remember their cruelty once she ascends again?

It's a no-win situation.

We return to the queen's rooms, and I see a pair of men holding plans and discussing as they study the wall that hides the secret passage. I look at them curiously and Halla speaks. "We're bricking it up so the enemy cannot use the passage against us. It has been sealed on the other side, the statue destroyed."

"Ah." I look at the little boy, playing near the skirts of his nursemaid. "What if you have to leave in a hurry?"

"That is not the only hidden passage out of the keep," Halla admits with a tiny smile. "If we must run, there are many ways to go. But hopefully it will not be necessary now that Lord Aron fights on our side." Her hand grips mine. "And if we work together, perhaps we will be able to bring things to a close sooner rather than later. The men like war, but all I want is to be able to raise my family in peace."

I squeeze her fingers back, nervous at the intense look she gives me. She seems to think I know how to stop things? I can't even get Magra to take a message written exclusively for her.

This world has shown me time and time again that I don't matter. That I'm nothing in the scheme of things. I'm not the one brought here to bring forth change. It's Aron and all the others...isn't it?

You will meet your destiny on the plains of Yshrem.

Or was that a hint? Is there something else I should be doing?

I shake my head at Halla. "I wish I could do more. I'm just one person. I'm not super strong. I'm not super smart. I'm just an outsider who got caught up with Aron because no one else wanted his arrogant ass."

"You're brave," she tells me simply. "Sometimes that's all we need."

THE DAY IS long as hell. I pace Halla's rooms, trying to watch the battle going on below. Part of me wants to put on some armor and a helmet and join them, because then I'd at least be doing something, but I know the biggest thing I can do is stay safe so they have Aron at the front. So I eat, and pace, and play with baby Alistair. I chat with Halla. I stare at all of the books in the room that I can't read as Halla pages through an old tome.

"What's that about?" I ask at one point.

"It's a recording of the last Anticipation," she says. "Six hundred years ago." She gestures at one page with a delicate hand. "Recordings of sightings of gods, who fought alongside who, and for how long it went on."

"How long did it go on?"

"Ten years." She grimaces. "Let us pray that is not the case this time."

"Yeah," I say faintly. Ten years with Aron would be amazing. Not enough, but still amazing. I think of what the Spidae said, how I'm not getting out of this alive. It could be a lie. I feign idle curiosity. "Does it say what happened to the anchors of the gods that won? The last ones left standing?"

She shakes her head. "The anchors are rarely mentioned by name."

"Of course not," I say sarcastically. "Why would we be important, right?" Just to my Aron.

Only to my Aron.

The men return at dusk, dirty, sweaty, and covered in shallow wounds. The queen panics at the sight of her husband sporting a broken arrow out of one large shoulder. Aron's riddled with them, but he's also invulnerable. It's clear the king's in some pain, and the queen insists in him going to the healer. Another clerist offers to help Aron out, but he only wants me and a hot bath.

"How was it?" I ask as we go up the stairs to our room, Kerren following close behind.

The smile on Aron's face is pleased. "Glorious. It was an intense battle. Neither side gained much ground from the other. I am well pleased with the Cyclopae army."

"No ground gained?" I ask, dismayed. "None at all?"

"Patience, my Faith. Battle will decide all things."

I help him bathe and remove the arrows from his chest, neck and back. His wounds close up the moment the arrows are plucked free, and he's in good spirits as he bathes. He's practically fucking cheerful.

"Once you're off to bed, I'll rejoin the men," he says as he towels off, a hot look in his eyes. It's the look that promises some hot lovin', because post-battle Aron is clearly a randy Aron.

"Rejoin the men? Why?"

"They are burning the dead," he says. "I would give them an honorable send-off on their journey to the afterlife since they died in my name."

I bite my lip as Aron takes my hand and pulls me to bed. He drags me against him and cups my breast, teasing the nipple even as he kisses my neck. His touch feels good, amazing, really, but I can't stop thinking about his words. "How...how many men died?" I ask, trying to bite back a whimper when his mouth goes to my breast.

"A hundred, maybe more," he murmurs, then licks my nipple.

A hundred? In just one day? Just to run up against the brick wall that is the opposing army? "Aron, maybe there's another way—"

"I am the god of battle," he says, pushing me onto my back on the bed. His big hand goes to my pussy, and he strokes it with his fingers. Even though I want to talk more about war, he's far too good at distractions. "The men will spend eternity at my side. They will be rewarded. Now, let me touch my anchor."

And he lowers his mouth to my belly, completely distracting me.

We make love twice before Aron tenderly washes me and gives me a kiss. "Sleep," he murmurs, caressing my face. "I will wake you up when I return."

For more sex, most likely. I can't even be mad—I crave his touch like a junkie. But even after he leaves, I can't stop thinking about the battle.

A hundred men gone in one day. For nothing. I think of the pinched look that came over Halla's face as the king showed up with a wounded arm...and I'm starting to see why she's so worried. How many people will die to gain a few feet of ground across the river? That still doesn't get us Hedonism Aron's anchor. It just gets us a toehold closer.

There's got to be a better way.

CHAPTER 77

"You see what I mean," Halla says in a fretful voice the next day as we sit in her library. "I have tried to beg Mathior not to go out, not to fight such sense-less battles, but it is in their very nature. Everything they believe is that battle is glorious and honorable. To die fighting in Aron's name? To die for him? There is no greater glory. But...we are getting nowhere and every day, more men die." She shakes her head, her hands trembling as she turns another page of the book. "Every day, it is the same."

I pace near the window, rubbing my growling stomach. Halla has sent a maid to bring food, but this one's new and a little slow. She's taking her time biting all my cheese and tasting all the meat. We're probably getting the best stuff in the castle, so no wonder she's being pokey. I do my best not to glare at her, but staring out the window as men die is surprisingly hungry work. "What do we do?" I ask Halla for the millionth time today. "What if your husband refused to go out on the battlefield with Aron?"

Solat watches me pace as he leans against the wall. "Ask a

cyclops warrior not to go to war? Better luck asking the sun not to shine."

I scowl at him. "Not helping, buddy."

"He's right," Halla says. "He will never refuse Lord Aron. This is the greatest honor he can imagine. You don't know how it's rejuvenated him to fight alongside Aron. Having him here makes me have hope once more. I've been so worried." She pauses and closes the book in her lap. "So no, my Mathior would never agree to that."

The maid drops a piece of cheese on the floor.

"Dude, seriously," I say. "That's my lunch."

"Sorry, my lady." She bobs in a curtsy. "Almost done, I promise." And she picks up another one of the myriad cheeses and nibbles on it.

The cook should just send up an entire wheel of cheese so I can gnaw on it, instead of all these teeny tiny wedges that all have to be tasted. I bite back a sigh.

"Will Lord Aron consider a parlay with the enemy?" Halla asks. "To discuss terms?"

"Seeing as the whole goal is for them to kill each other? Highly doubt it." I clasp my hands behind my back and pace back and forth. "The goal here is for each one to murder the other's anchor so they can be the last one standing. There's no peaceful way about this—"

"What are you doing?" Solat's low, casual voice distracts me.

I turn to look at him, confused, but he's not watching me. He's staring at the maid, who's frozen in place as she hovers over the tray.

Halla and I exchange a look. "What's the problem?" I ask.

"I'm done, my lady," the maid says brightly, curstying again. "All safe." She turns and heads for the door, but Solat steps in front of it, blocking her.

The queen's guards bristle with attention, and everyone's staring at the maid.

She bows her head. "Please, I would like to go back to the kitchens now."

"You weren't eating Lady Faith's food," Solat says casually, arms crossed. "You were just pretending to."

"O-of course I was," the maid stammers. She looks at me and the queen. "I ate a bite out of everything, just like I was asked. You can look at the cheese."

I pick up a piece, which does have tooth-marks in it. "It's bitten—"

"I'm sure it is. But I also saw her spitting out each bite. That's very curious, isn't it?" He tilts his head, his handsome features growing hard as he stares at the maid. "You put the food in the front of your dress."

The woman looks shocked, her hand going to the front of her gown. "You just want to see down it. Is that what this is? Harassing a servant—"

This entire situation seems odd, but after all the time I've spent with Solat? I trust him. "I'll look if you're worried about a man seeing your boobs," I offer. "If he's wrong, I'm sure he'll apologize nicely." And I smile at her.

Her face goes pale as she looks at me. A second later, she turns and tries to race to the far end of the room, not that there's anywhere to go. She just wants to get *away*. As the men run after her, she races toward the window, as if she's going to fling herself out of it. Solat tackles her before the guards can, and then the sobbing girl is lifted to her feet even as bits of food spill to the ground around her.

"You were trying to kill Lady Faith, weren't you?" Solat snarls, and I've never seen him so angry.

"No!" she cries.

"Then eat this." He grabs a cake from the tray and holds it to her lips. "Go on. Take a bite out of it right now and swallow."

Her mouth trembles and she stares at him long and hard, but never moves toward the food.

My jaw drops. I stare, hoping that he's wrong, that she'll eat the damn thing and show him he's overreacting, but she just starts to cry.

"Did the Adassians send you?" He grabs her jaw, startling me with how rough he is. "Did they?"

"I am faithful to Lord Aron of the Cleaver," she cries, collapsing at his feet.

I can't believe it. Someone just tried to kill me and I wasn't even paying attention. I was freaking impatient because I was hungry. I knew my food was being tasted for such a thing but I didn't really think someone was going to *do* it. Numb, I watch the girl weep as two guards move forward and pick her up from the floor.

"I don't understand. How did they find out I'm here?" I ask, approaching the woman.

"Who else would sit with the queen?" She cringes back from me, trying to wrestle free from the guards. "I am faithful to Lord Aron!" she wails again when Solat leans in.

"So am I! What the hell?" My shout startles her and she stares at me with wide eyes. I thump a fist against my chest. "You think I'm not loyal to him? Bitch, I am the most loyal person there is!"

"It's not the same—"

I make a sound of frustration in my throat, turning away. I hate that she's right. It's *not* the same. Just because she's working for Aron of the Cleaver doesn't mean that it's my Aron. I rub my brow, frustrated. I'm hungry, I'm scared, and I feel really, really alone right now.

Nothing is safe. They're going to try to kill me. Everyone is.

Why wouldn't they? The gods command it. I can't fight against that.

And even if they don't succeed...I still have to die. I close my eyes, and I can still see the snap of my thread under the Spidae's fingers. They knew all along. Just as they knew that Hedonism

Aron would be meeting us here in Yshrem, they knew I was going to die.

It occurs to me that maybe the Spidae have known the outcome of things all along. They're guiding it in their own, warped little way. That my coming from the Earth web to this one "just because the veil between worlds was thin" is a crock of shit and it's another thing they've manipulated. How do I know they're not teasing and toying with outcomes just to guide things? How do I know they haven't been drawing me towards this ever since I got my fortune read? Even the cards back then had spiderwebs on the backs.

I know, suddenly, without a shadow of a doubt that this is their doing.

They want me here.

Which means they want my Aron to win.

Which means I'm going to die to ensure that happens.

A strange calm settles over me. I continue to pace even as the guards take the woman away. Solat remains at my side, a furious scowl on his handsome jaw, like he's personally offended that someone tried to get rid of me.

New guards arrive in the room and settle at the doors. Queen Halla gets to her feet, picks up her cup, and then tosses the contents into the fire. "Get my chamberlain," she says to one of the guards. "From now on, tasters will only be my ladies. The kitchens will be guarded. All food will be tasted, even that granted by the goddess—"

"And we won't tell any of this to Lord Aron," I add.

The queen turns to look at me in shock. "We cannot keep such a thing secret. The enemy knows—"

"—that a stranger's hanging out with the queen? It's not hard to put two and two together." I tap my hand against my thigh, trying to think. "They'll try again. If not poison, then something else. Arrows. Maybe someone will burn down the whole keep. I don't know. As long as they know I'm here, though, everyone's in danger. They'll take out the whole city just to get to me and you know I'm right."

Halla purses her lips. "I don't feel comfortable using torture—"

"No torture," I agree. "We just have to act before they try again. We have to get the upper hand. Somewhere over there is his anchor. Unless we have a way to poison their entire encampment and can live with murdering thousands, we need to figure out who his anchor is and take him or her out."

"But how?" Halla protests. "We have tried that before—"

"I'll go," Solat says, speaking up for the first time since the assassin left the room.

We both turn to look at him.

"What?" I sputter. "No. Absolutely not."

"It's a good idea," Solat continues. "I'm good at ingratiating myself. I'll get one of their uniforms from off the dead and start hunting around. I know what to look for, how an anchor is guarded." His gaze locks on me. "I'll find the information and we can mark the tent he or she is hiding in."

"You think we haven't tried?" Queen Halla asks imperiously.

"I know how Aron thinks. Two different Arons," he adds. "I know how they are different, but I also know the ways they are similar. I'll be able to spot the anchor."

And he looks at me for approval.

An infiltrator. Of course it's smart. Of course Solat knows how Aron thinks. He was with Liar Aron and then he was with my Aron. He knows what to look for, more than any Yshremi or Cyclopae warrior because he's ridden with Arons of different flavors for months now.

"It's dangerous," I admit to him.

"Does it matter?" He asks, all cockiness. "I never expected to get out of this alive. Did you?"

Queen Halla's hands fly to her mouth.

He's...not wrong, though. I think he's bluffing, because a

man with no future wouldn't have been so upset at Yulenna's choice. But if he wants to go, how can I stop him? Especially when I know if we sacrifice our lives, we'll be saving hundreds on both sides—maybe thousands?

The Adassians could have spies in the city right now. Who's to stop them from setting fire to the keep and burning us out while we sleep?

Great. Now I'm never going to eat or sleep again. I rub my aching stomach. "Solat, I don't know—"

"We won't tell Aron," he reiterates. "Kerren and Markos will cover for me. I'll sneak into the other camp and when I find the tent in that sea of tents where the anchor is hiding, I'll mark it."

"How?"

"With a symbol." He grins. "Maybe a spider."

"Solat…"

He moves forward and takes my hand in his, and for a moment I think he's going to kiss my knuckles, but all he does is raise my hand and bow over it like a courtly gentleman. "I know how to be ingratiating, Faith. Trust me to do this. Give me a few days and I'll find that anchor."

What other choice do we have?

MARKOS TASTES ALL my food for the rest of the day, and Kerren hovers over the cook down in the kitchens to make sure nothing is compromised.

When Aron returns that night, I'm filled with love for him—love and desperation. He's in his element with the war, the battles, pitting himself against an opponent. His eyes gleam with enthusiasm. Aron's never been handsomer to me. I don't care that he's a god of war, or a god of storms. I just care that he's mine.

And tonight, I'm feeling more than a little desperate. So I

tackle him the moment we're alone, and we make love three times straight before I collapse in the bed and he pulls me against his chest for snuggling.

"I think we are making headway, Faith," he murmurs, pressing kisses to my shoulder. "It's just a matter of time."

I hold his arm to my stomach and lean back against him. "I hope you're right."

CHAPTER 78

*T*hings fall into a pattern for days.

Solat disappears, as promised. I watch anxiously at the window as the armies clash at the walls and at the side-gate every morning, and neither side seems to be gaining or losing ground by the time both sides retreat to their respective territories. Every night, bodies are burned.

The next morning, the men wake up and do the same. They put on their armor, cheer when Aron gives a war cry, and fight gloriously at his side.

Both sides are fighting for the god of battle, Aron of the Cleaver. The strange irony of that doesn't escape me. No one's going to ever back down because why would they? Their god is on the front lines, eating this shit up. The queen cries as her husband goes out to war every morning, convinced this will be the last time she sees him. I can't imagine her terror. The only reason I'm calm is because I know Aron can't get killed. He's loving this, in his element with every swing of the gigantic double-bladed axe he now carries at all times. I want to be happy for him, but they haven't made progress into the enemy camp, and I worry how long this will go on.

Will both Arons keep flinging their armies at each other until they run out of men? What happens then? It's a sobering thought, and I think of poor Queen Halla, who clutches her infant son to her chest every day and frets over her husband.

As for me, I wait. I wait for Aron's army to take control of the Adassian territory. I wait for Solat to send word that he's found the other anchor. I wait for another assassin to appear. I wait for Aron to come back to me every night.

What else can I do?

I can't leave. I can't help.

All I can do is stare out the window and hope that there's a break on one side or another, or that Solat appears with the information we need...or that the Aron on the other side disappears because Solat's somehow assassinated the other anchor.

The only thing I can do is stand around and wait for something to change.

But days pass and there's nothing.

It's been maybe four days when everything breaks. The day starts as it always does. Aron wakes me up early for a fierce round of quick morning lovemaking before he puts on his armor and heads off to battle. I bathe and dress, then head into the queen's chambers accompanied by Kerren and several other Yshremi guards who now shadow my every move. The queen sits with her ladies, her face pinched with stress. She was so happy that my Aron arrived, but it's been days and we make no headway, and people just keep dying.

I sit down across from her and Kerren immediately starts tasting the food set out for me. "Morning," I say to Halla, rubbing my eyes.

"Good morn to you." Her voice is even, sweet. She's good at hiding how she feels in front of the guards. It's only after they settle to their places against the door that she lets some of her stress show. "Another day of this." She spreads her hands in her lap. "I want to pray to the gods to watch over my husband, but there is no one in the Aether to hear."

"Aron says they're gaining ground," I tell her. "I hope he's right."

"But will it be soon enough to save the lives of hundreds of good men?" She presses her fingers to her lips. "I'm sorry. I know you have as much control as I do on such things. I do have a small bit of good news for you on this day. My wizards have a spyglass for you." Her smile is faint.

"Oh? That's great. Where is it?" I'm itching to get a good look at the battle in the same way I'd pick at a scab. I know I shouldn't, but I can't help myself.

"We can visit them once you have eaten," she says, gesturing at the tray of food where Kerren even now stuffs his face, chewing as fast as he can. Tasting my food is a full-time job practically, because I eat so much. Poor Kerren.

I snag a fruit-stuffed tart that already has a large bite out of it and start eating. I know somewhere down in the kitchens, Markos is watching every bit of food that goes onto my plate. "Tell your cooks I appreciate the efforts. I've eaten better here than—"

There's an urgent knock at the door. Before anyone can answer, the knock comes again and then a soldier rushes in, a chest in his hands.

The queen goes white as a sheet. "What is it?"

Oh god. I stare at the soldier's grim face, wondering who's died. What terrible thing has happened...because I know this can't be good.

"Your Majesty." He bows his head and sets the trunk on the ground. "We found this left in the bushes by the side gate. It says it should be delivered to Lord Aron's anchor."

"Is it a trap? Has my wizards been consulted?" The queen's voice is sharp and I don't know if it's anger or relief.

"It carries no magic," he says and bows his head. "We looked inside to ascertain this before we brought it in and…it is a man's head, Your Majesty."

My stomach churns. Someone's sent me a head? Whose?

The answer comes before I even reach for the trunk. Oh god. I swallow hard and force myself to get to my feet and lift the lid. I open it just a crack, just enough to see Solat's sightless eyes staring up at me from his handsome face. There's blood crusting his hair, and…and I shut the lid again.

Solat.

I close my eyes and return to my seat, hands shaking. I can't even process this right now. *I'm so sorry,* I silently tell him. *I pray this wasn't in vain.* I pray all of this wasn't in vain. He deserved better than a brutal, lonely death. I'm not going to remember him like this, I decide. I'm going to remember him as the laughing, flirty man who loved to tell stories in Novoro. *I'll remember you, Solat. You and Vitar both,* I promise. "Please bury him," I say.

The guard hesitates. "The dead—we should burn him, my lady—"

"Then fucking burn him," I snap. "Just do it respectfully." I get up from my chair and start pacing, my entire body feeling like a live wire about to spark. This is all going horribly wrong. All of it.

Solat's dead. Captured by the enemy and they knew he was with me. I want to cry but I'm not sure I have the tears left inside me. I feel hollow.

The newcomer leaves with the trunk, his armor jingling. Kerren moves to my side when I stop in front of the window, and puts a kind hand on my shoulder. "Faith," he murmurs. "You cannot blame yourself. He knew the risks. He did it because he wanted to help."

None of us are getting out of this alive. And Solat grinned at me like it was no big deal.

But it is a big deal. I look at Kerren, his kind face, and I wish I could save him. I wish I could save all of them, the men throwing themselves into battle at the gates, determined to push the Adassian army back by meters, as if that will make a difference somehow. As if that's worth dying for.

I swallow hard and nod, forcing a smile to my face. "Thanks, Kerren."

"Come," the queen says, getting to her feet. She puts a hand to her rounded belly. "My son is staying with his nurse this morning. Let us go and see my court wizards and take a look at this spyglass they have made. If nothing else, it will be a distraction."

We leave the room and our contingent of guards flank us from all sides. I half expect the queen to head to the dungeons or some deep bowels in the castle inhabited by monsters, but instead, we cross over to the far side of the keep, down a well-lit hall lined with chairs. I can see maps on the walls of a room that we pass - a war room, no doubt - and then we enter another chamber that opens up into a large, book-lined study with a kitchen-like alcove. There are bottles and books on every surface, and two men in tiny, wire-rimmed glasses look up as we enter. Immediately, I'm reminded of Omos's monastery and a surge of homesickness wells up inside me. Strange how I'm homesick for that and not Earth.

"We are here to see the spyglass," the queen says politely, folding her hands in front of her belly.

One of the wizards bows. He doesn't look to be older than me, and the beard on his jaw is scruff more than anything else. "Of course, your majesty. We found the details of it in an old book. A curious invention, long forgotten." With a swish of long, lavender robes, he moves to a table across the room and starts to pick through a clutter of objects. The other wizard continues to work at a table full of bottles, pouring one murky looking liquid into a flask and frowning at it.

"Here we are," the wizard announces, and holds out two leathery-seeming telescopes. "We took the liberty of making two based off of the plans, so both the queen and her guest might amuse themselves without having to share."

Amuse ourselves? He thinks this is a fucking game? "This isn't for a party game, Harry Potter," I retort. "People are dying." I take one of the spyglasses and examine it. There's a thick, warped piece of glass at each end but it looks about right. "Cool the misogyny for a hot minute, please."

"I did not wish to offend," he stammers, handing the queen the other. "Shall I show you how it works?"

Oh dear lord. I bite back a sharp retort. "We're good, thanks."

"I...realize there is a war going on, my lady," he says, inclining his head. "I did not mean to insult. If you both like, I can show you what else we are working on? The ancient tomes have provided fascinating information, and we are working on something I am confident the enemy does not have."

"What is it?" Queen Halla asks, curious.

I toy with the telescope in my hands, impatient. I want to find a window and start looking for the spider symbol Solat promised he'd use as a signal. Maybe he was able to do it in time.

"The ancients called it Godsfire," the wizard says, his eyes alight with excitement. "It is a liquid that burns through everything it touches, destroying with a few drops. The ancients would carry it in globes and throw them at the enemy army, turning them to char in a matter of moments."

Her eyes go wide. I stop examining my telescope and look over at him.

"You made this?" I ask. "This grenade?"

He nods, all pride. "We've tested it in small ways, but a vial of it can burn down an entire tent. A full batch could destroy all of the Adassian army." The wizard holds one vial up, and I can see the dark red liquid churning inside.

"Then make us enough to destroy their army," the queen says.

"It...is not that simple. We have worked for months just to produce this much." And he shows us the vial. "It's small enough to fit in a pocket, but quite destructive."

A pocket.

Of course.

And suddenly, I know what I need to do.

CHAPTER 79

"*K*eep looking,"

"I see nothing," the queen says at my side. "I've scanned the entire camp twice, and still I see nothing."

We stand atop the tallest parapet, spyglasses in hand as we watch the enemy camp. With the spyglass, we can see right into the depths of the distant enemy camp, and the symbols they have written all over their tents.

Nothing like a spider, though, and it's frustrating.

I know you did it, Solat. I know he succeeded. Isn't this what the Spidae have been hinting at all along? Everything is coming to this moment, and they've pushed and pulled and manipulated us along the way for this to happen.

They won't check your pockets, you know.

At the time, I didn't know what that meant. Now, it's all too clear. I'm both excited and filled with terror.

"I see no spider marking," Halla says, peering through her spyglass. "Are you certain?"

"It'll be there," I promise the queen. "We just have to keep looking."

We've been staring through them for an hour, studying the

tents from afar. It's tempting to watch the battle instead, to watch Aron—either one—hack and slash his way through the men. But after seeing a few close-ups of heads being chopped and necks sliced open, I focused on the tents instead.

To a one, the tents are muddy and dirty, and the Adassians are fond of writing on them. Halla says they're blessings or invocations, an old Adassian tradition to cover a dwelling with such to keep out bad spirits. That's fine and all, but it makes it difficult to look for one symbol amongst all of it. It's literally looking for a needle in a haystack.

But it has to be there. I don't think the Spidae would have us come this far just for it all to collapse in the last minute. Then again, who knows what the Spidae are thinking? I stare through my spyglass, watching soldiers as they move between tents. There's a huge, pitched battle at Castle Yshrem's walls, but the Adassian camp is filled with people anyhow. There are soldiers guarding tents, wounded men, and women of all kinds. There's also a fair amount of wine barrels, livestock, and the biggest, splashiest looking tent in the center of all of it.

The Aspect is hedonism, after all.

It would be obvious to have his anchor there, in the fanciest of tents, but there's no marking on it at all. If his anchor's in camp, he or she is likely being hidden away for such a reason.

The queen sucks in a breath.

"What?" I ask, immediately scanning the battle to find Aron. My heart pounds in terror, and I find him easily enough—the flash of the great battle-axe ever moving as he works his way through the tide of men. He's covered in blood, his stark white tunic soaked, and he's muddy up to his thighs, but he looks beautiful.

He smiles at his opponent, and I ache for him. Our time is almost up.

"I think I've found it," the queen says, grabbing my arm.

"Look. The tent with the fat man in front of it. Center of camp. It has two flags atop it—one for Aron and one for Anali."

The goddess of healing. "So it's a medical tent."

"Or they want us to think that," she agrees. "There is also a weapon rack out front."

I raise my spyglass to my eye and scan the sea of tents, trying to find the exact one she's speaking of. "You're sure?"

"There are people going in and out, certainly, but none of them look wounded. I thought that very curious and started paying attention to the writing on the tent itself, and then I saw it."

I find Anali's flag, and then a weapon rack. Sure enough, there's a guard out front of the innocuous-seeming tent with a fat belly and a scruffy chin. He scratches at his stomach absently and looks around, holding a spear. As I stare, the tent flap opens and a very healthy-looking man leaves, a new equally healthy one walking in. Curious. I scan the writing on the tent, though it's all squiggly jibberish to me...and my entire body tenses when I see a spider casually drawn between two triangular symbols near the bottom of the tent.

"That's it," I murmur. I make note of the tent, memorizing where it's at in the busy camp. Like Halla said, it's near the center, but a good distance away from the obvious tent of Lord Aron.

Getting there? It's doable.

I lower the spyglass and turn to the queen and Kerren. "That's got to be it." Markos enters the room with a tray of food just as I speak, and I wave him over. "We need to act."

"Shall we share the news with Lord Aron, my lady Faith?" Kerren asks, a hint of a frown on his face.

"Or send an assassin?" Markos adds, coming to my side.

I shake my head, because I know what has to happen.

They won't check your pockets, you know.

"It's the encampment for Aron of the Cleaver," I say to them,

"But it's also the encampment for Hedonism Aron. There's a lot of women there. Whores. I can go. I'll wear something slutty and I don't know, flash my tits if anyone asks questions."

Immediately, Markos and Kerren protest. "You cannot risk yourself," Kerren says.

"Everyone's risking themselves," I say, gesturing at the battle. "Except I can stop all of this. If we can get to that tent, get to his anchor before he gets to me, we can *win*. No more pointless killing. No more scratching and scraping to gain a foot on the battlefield at the cost of a hundred lives a day. The right Aron will win and this will all be over." The more I talk, the more right this feels. "The wizards have Godsfire, right? I can take a vial with me, hide it in a pocket, and pretend I'm there for some booty action. I get in, I use the Godsfire, boom. Problem solved."

"How will you get there?" The queen asks.

"They haven't finished bricking the wall over the secret passage that leads to the crypts," I point out. "I can go that way and then enter their camp after it's dark."

Halla arches a brow. "And how do you plan on leaving the camp once you have done this?"

"Does it matter at that point?" I ask. "I'll figure something out. If we cut off the head of the snake, the rest will follow."

"Aron won't allow this," Markos says with a shake of his head. "He's far too protective of you."

"Which is why we have to do this now," I say. "Before he returns tonight and finds out that Solat's dead." My voice wobbles a little, but I put my spyglass away and head for the door. I'll be sad about Solat later, when all this is over. "We have to do this now because if the other Aron finds out that we know where his anchor is, he'll move him. Her. Whoever. And we can't keep hiding everything from Aron. He's going to find out about the assassin they sent, and Solat's death, and then all hell will break loose."

"But to go in alone?" Halla frets.

"Not alone," Markos says, and Kerren nods.

"No, guys," I begin. I don't want anyone else dying because of me.

Markos shakes his head. "You go with us or not at all."

I look at their determined faces. "If we're doing this...then let's do it before I think about it too hard and freak out." I nod at them. "I'll get changed."

"I'll meet you in my study with the wizards," Halla says. "And with the Godsfire."

A SHORT TIME LATER, Markos, Kerren and I emerge from the far side of the crypt and into the graveyard. Markos and Kerren both wear Adassian cloaks over their armor and I'm dressed like a camp ho. We took one of my low-cut, Novoran gowns and threw a corset over it, which practically shoves my tits in the world's face. The skirt is cut all the way up to my thighs, and the queen assures me that I look sufficiently tartish.

I guess I'm going out of this world like I came into it—called a tart. Heh.

I know I'm not making it back out alive. I know I'm not returning to this castle. I know I'm never going to see my handsome, arrogant, wonderful Aron ever again. I want to grieve for it, but there's no time. I've known this all along somewhere deep inside, and I think the Spidae were trying to prepare me for this.

I'm here to meet my destiny.

"Be safe," Halla told me as she gave me the vial of Godsfire. I tucked it into a pocket in my cloak and pulled the fabric tight around me.

We make it out of the crypt without seeing another soul, replace the doors, and creep out of the graveyard. The moment we get to the entrance of the graveyard, though, we run into two other Adassian soldiers. We've been rushing so quickly I didn't even think about this being guarded.

Then, Markos grabs my ass.

I squeak in surprise, jumping. My boobs nearly fall out of my corset.

"Next time, let's just do it in a tent, eh?" Markos says, manhandling me in front of the guards. "You're a hot piece but it's a long fuckin' walk."

I feel totally obvious as Kerren grabs my waist and plants a sloppy kiss on my cheek, getting into the groove of our playacting. "I'll do it in the graveyard if she likes," he says. "Wherever she wants, as long as she does that thing with her tongue."

The guards just roll their eyes. "Stay out of this area," one tells us, pointing. "Back across the river to your commander."

"Fuckin' hedonism," the other mutters as we walk past. "Can't nobody keep it in their damned pants."

And just like that, we walk past them and toward the distant river. I let out a breath slowly, and eventually Markos takes his hand off my ass.

"Sorry, Faith," he murmurs.

"No, it's cool. Good thinking." Heck, he was quicker on his feet than I was. Of course hedonism is affecting all of the camp. I remember how Tadekha's citadel affected me, how I practically humped Aron every chance I got.

Man, good times.

Even so, we can use this. Maybe it won't be as hard to get into the Adassian camp as I thought.

We wade across and skirt wide around the battlefield. Even now, I can hear the distant clash of weapons, of men screaming, of people dying. As it fades away, we approach the camp itself, the cluster of hundreds of tents, and it's like walking into another world.

From afar, I didn't notice the empty wine casks everywhere. Or that men are sleeping wherever they fell, nursing hangovers in the middle of the day even as others die out on the battlefield. As we approach, I can hear a woman crying out in what is clearly sex, and there's a tent with tits drawn on it which must be a brothel of some kind. Even though there's a battle going on, there's still tons of soldiers, and as we move between the cluster of tents, people start to watch us. My skin prickles uncomfortably.

"Do you know where you're going, Faith?" Kerren asks, voice low. His expression is calm but his gaze is darting everywhere.

"I do." I'm nervous as shit, but I remember the tent. Two flags. Weapon rack.

"Be ready to run there if we get caught," he says. "Don't stop for anything. Just run."

I nod.

"You should—"

"What's this?" a man says as he approaches us. He scowls in our direction. "What regiment are you in?"

Markos gestures at me. "Brought a tart for Lord Aron to enjoy."

The man's eyes narrow as he looks at me, and I stick my boobs out and do my best to look enticing. He studies Markos and Kerren, and then frowns. "Who's your commander?"

Kerren and Markos immediately close ranks, standing so close that the man can't see me. "It's Lord Aron, of course. Who else would we be commanded by?"

"Don't play dumb with me. Have you partaken of nose spices?" When the men pause, he continues. "Are you drunk? Wounded? Because you do not look like any of the above to me, and while Lord Aron expects his soldiers to enjoy serving him, he also expects healthy men to be on the field at dawn. The whores are for nighttime."

"Apologies, sir." Kerren shifts his weight and gives me a shove.

Fuck. Now?

I glance around and duck my head, scooting away even as I hear the man continue to upbraid Kerren and Markos.

"For the last time, who is your commander?"

I wince, hating that I'm running away when they're getting in trouble. I feel like I'm abandoning them, but I have to do this. I have to. I move quickly between tents, keeping my head down. I'm fifty feet away—maybe more—when I hear a man shout and a scuffle breaks out.

Please don't die, Markos. Please don't die, Kerren, I silently chant. I won't be able to stand it if everyone dies because of me. I'm so close. I'm approaching the center of the camp, and as men rouse themselves to move toward the fight, I discreetly head in the opposite direction.

"Hey," an unfamiliar voice calls. "Hey, you. Tart. Stop."

I pause, looking around. I think I see the tent in the distanc—

A man with a thick beard and bushy gray hair grabs my arm. He eyeballs me. "Who are you, sweet?"

CHAPTER 80

*U*gh. Trapped.

I play with a lock of my hair and try to look as vapid as possible. "Hey, sugar. I'm looking for the whore tent but all these tents look the same." I manage to choke out a high pitched giggle. "You know where it is?"

He squints at me. "You new?"

I nod eagerly. "I'm to serve Lord Aron tonight."

"Sure you are." He reaches forward and puts his hands on me. Stunned, I wait in silence…and realize he's patting me down, looking for weapons. "Not just any tart can show up here, you know. You have to be invited."

"Oh, I was invited," I reassure him, doing my best not to kick him in the balls when he feels my ass and then moves down my thighs. "I don't have any blades."

Just the vial of Godsfire in my pocket, that's all.

"I'll be the judge of that." He turns me around roughly and then continues to pat me down, and I try to act like it's normal. Like it's what I expected to happen and I'm not out of my mind with terror right now.

I squeak in surprise when he grabs my tits, and shove them off. "Unless you're Lord Aron, that'll cost you some coin."

He barks a laugh and then slaps me on the ass. "Maybe I'll see you later then, tart. Whore tent's that way." He gives me a little shove in that direction and then leaves.

Oh thank fuck. I fight back the dizzying relief that threatens to choke me, blinking hard, and then continue on toward an entirely different tent.

The one with the spider.

I'm shocked I'm able to get there without being stopped again, but I make it. There are men in the front, so I carefully circle around the back. Here, it's sludgy and muddy, but one end of the tent is loose, the stake losing purchase in the muck. I glance around, then get down on hands and knees, crawling underneath the side on my belly. I'm covered in mud from chin to toe, but I didn't come this far just to get stopped now.

I have the Godsfire and I have my purpose. It's now or never.

When I come in on the other side, I'm hidden behind a bunch of trunks. I get to my feet as quietly as I can and peer out from behind them. The inside of the tent is pretty nice. There's a bunch of trunks, but there's also a large assortment of food on a table, a mirror, and a loom for weaving. A woman sits on the edge of a cot, a book in her hands. She's rather average looking, with brown hair and a young face. I kind of thought Hedonism Aron would pick someone more like Yulenna, but this is just a girl. Just an ordinary woman a few years younger than me, who can apparently read.

As I watch, she gets to her feet and moves to a trunk across the room, setting her book down and rummaging through the trunk. She pulls out a pouch and leans over it, and then I hear her snort deep.

Nose spices. She's getting high. That works for me, though. Now's my chance. I can't wait any longer.

I close my eyes, think of my beloved Aron's face. I think of the arrogant jerk and when he first held his hand out to me. Tadekha's Citadel. Picking glass out of his back. Curling in bed with him. Touching him. Loving him. How he smiled down at me this morning as I lay in bed and I felt so protected and loved and...happy.

I'm doing this because I want that Aron to live on forever.

I open my eyes, ready to move out, when the tent opens. The flap rustles and a big man walks in, scanning the room. Outside, I hear the distant crackle of thunder. "Where are you, Naeri?"

The girl rubs her nose, sniffing again. "Here."

The man steps forward, and as he moves out of the sunlight and into the interior of the tent, I bite down on my lip to keep from shouting in surprise. It's Aron.

Sort of.

If I didn't see the mismatched eyes, I wouldn't have recognized him. This Aron is covered in glittering armor that's been encrusted with gems. A long cloak sweeps over his shoulder, and it's encrusted with embroidery and trimmed with thick fur. Everything about him is gaudy, from the jeweled beads braided into his hair to the pierced ring in his nose and the trio of gold chains that stretches over his cheek. He doesn't wear simple clothing like my Aron.

As I stare from my hiding space, he snatches the bag from his anchor and lifts it to his nose. "Did you finish the nose spices again?"

She quivers. "I'm sorry. I just needed a little." Her voice turns whining.

"You didn't leave any for me." He flings the bag at her, smacking her on the cheek. "Where's my wine? And my sweets?"

"Here," she says eagerly, scrambling to the nearest table. "Shall I feed you?"

"I want you to eat them," he says, petting her hair. His hand goes to his belt and as I watch, he unfastens what has to be the most jewel-encrusted codpiece ever. I'd laugh at this guy if it wasn't Aron's face underneath all that crap.

The anchor – Naeri – shoves a few sweets into her mouth, chewing loudly, and then tilts her face up to his. Aron – Skank Aron – leans down and covers her mouth, slicking his tongue against hers even as she eats.

Okay, gross. I get that he doesn't need to eat, but damn, that's nasty.

"Now wine," he tells her, and she grabs a goblet and starts to slurp it down, her gaze locked on his as he pets her cheek. His hand keeps moving over his waist, and then his armor jingles as his pants go down.

Oh shit. I do not want to see this.

I drop down to the floor, squeezing my eyes shut. I hate that being near this is affecting me, just like it was in Tadekha's palace. I recognize how it feels. There's an intense, needy yearning deep in my belly that's growing by the moment. I don't want to be turned on by this. I don't. But my body's responding anyhow. I can feel my pussy flooding with heat even as they make loud, sloppy noises on the other side of the wall of crates.

"Take me in your mouth," he tells her, and I flinch.

He's hedonism. Of course he's going to want her to blow him. I hate that she's doing it, though, and for a moment, I hate him too. I hate all of this, and it makes me want to throw the vial of Godsfire at both of them. Thing is, my Aron is impossibly fast and strong. I don't know if I can take him out, even if he is distracted. I have to wait…and endure.

It's the longest five minutes of my life. It might be less. It might be more. I have no way of knowing, only that the smacks and moans and groans seem to go on for far too long. Aron's armor jingles faster and faster, and then he gives a low groan that breaks my heart, because I've heard that groan before. That's his orgasm groan.

I dig my fingernails into my palms so hard that I draw blood.

I don't know if I want to shove my hand down my pants or burst into tears. Both sound good right about now.

The girl gives a throaty giggle, and I hear the light slap of skin. "That's for finishing off my nose spices," Aron murmurs. "You'd better find me more before I return from the battlefield."

"I will," she promises breathlessly.

"Good. Today will be a glorious day." His armor jingles again, and when I dare to peek over, I see he's putting his codpiece back on with her help as she kneels in front of him. "We'll break them today. I can feel it. And tonight, we celebrate."

Naeri giggles again, gazing up at him with a sly look. "We celebrate every night, my lord of storms."

He grunts, taps her cheek with a jewel-crusted glove, and then heads for the entrance to the tent, the beads in his hair swaying. He pauses before he leaves. "Find those red-haired twins and tell them to be in our tent tonight."

"Of course," she says breathlessly, and then he's gone.

I want to vomit. So much vomit. I stare with hatred as the girl moves to the table and drinks more wine, then saunters back to the trunk and digs through it. She pulls out a new pouch from behind something, and as she turns her back to me, I hear her sniff deeply again.

Bitch is holding out on him.

I hate her. He's not even my Aron and I hate her.

It's now or never. I kick off my muddy shoes and move, barefooted, over the thick rug on the ground. I creep up behind the woman as she rummages through the trunk, the vial clutched in my hand.

She's twenty feet away from me.

Then ten.

All I have to do is cross the distance between us, break the vial over her head, and run like the wind.

I can do this.

Five feet.

The woman tenses in her crouch, then whips around and looks at me, her eyes wide. I stand over her in my wench clothing, the vial clutched in my hand, and she stares up at me in shock. She looks so young, no more than eighteen or nineteen.

Her lower lip wobbles. "Please don't kill me."

Oh fuck. Every time I played this scenario in my head, the anchor never had a face. Staring down at this girl as she begs me to live? I hesitate. "I—"

She surges forward and in the next moment, plunges a knife into my belly.

I stagger. Pain rockets through me, overwhelming in its awfulness. Somewhere outside, I hear a distant unearthly scream as thunder crashes overhead. That would be Aron. Blood fills my mouth, and I clutch the dagger in my stomach even as the girl gets to her feet.

The look on her face is no longer helpless. It's feral and cunning. My fingers curl around the cool handle of the metal knife and I realize the mirror off to the side let her know my every movement. I was so focused on getting to her, so distracted from Hedonism's visit that I didn't pay attention to it.

Fucking dumb, Faith.

The woman grins and approaches me as blood dribbles down my chin. She reaches for the knife, her hand covering mine. "Fuck you, cunt." Her voice is low and cold.

I lift my hand—the one with the fragile vial—and smash it against the side of her face.

"That's tart to you," I choke out.

Flames erupt. It's like she explodes into flame, and her shrieks fill the tent even as I stagger backward and collapse on the rug. She screams, high pitched and wailing, as she pours water on her face and the flames lick across her clothing and ignite. The smell of burned hair fills the room and people rush in.

They take one look at her, burning like a pillar, and me

collapsed on the ground with a knife in my gut, blood pouring from my mouth—

And they run.

Blackness creeps in and out of my vision. Pain makes it hard to concentrate.

The girl's still screaming, but it ebbs back and forth. Or maybe I'm the one screaming. It's hard to tell.

Time passes.

I think.

Spots dance in front of my vision. My hand hurts. I squint to look at it, and even that's difficult. My palm faces the ceiling of the tent, and I see that it's entirely blackened, the last of the flames licking the charred remains of where the Godsfire touched me.

I lost a hand. Oh well.

My belly feels cold. I can't even feel the knife in my gut. Not anymore. I can't feel the pain, either. Everything just feels... really cold. And distant. I try to move my good hand, but it's like trying to communicate with a block of ice. It doesn't respond.

I fade in and out again. Right now, it's not a question of which of us is going to die. We're both going to die—the only question is which anchor will outlast the other in her death-throes. Will I bleed out before she burns to death? Who knows.

Who...cares. It suddenly seems to matter very little.

My heart throbs slowly. Painfully. My gut does, too. Belly wounds are bullshit.

I want to vomit, but I don't have the energy. Oh god, every-thing hurts. I moan, and I can feel sweat on my skin. This is a horrible way to die. I think of the man with his throat cut. I think of the woman, burning alive under Godsfire. I think of poor Vitar. And Solat.

Fuck, there are no good ways to die, it seems. Just a lot of awful.

The woman. I turn my head, trying to look around the tent.

One of the rugs is on fire, I notice belatedly, and her charred, unmoving corpse is atop it. She's not screaming anymore. She's utterly silent. The Godsfire keeps going, though, and as I watch, the bed lights up, the silks zooming with fire and crackling like they're covered in gasoline.

Huh.

Won't be long now, at least. If the gut wound doesn't take me out, the fire will.

I close my eyes and think of Aron, and I'm...content.

I did it. I saved him.

I hope he remembers how much I love his arrogant ass.

Because I do.

I shouldn't. There's nothing normal about the guy, nothing humble, or easygoing. He thinks the world belongs to him, he's bloodthirsty, and he can be a jerk. But he's also protective and tender and good to me and I'm going to miss waking up in his arms and seeing that smile of his. I can't imagine a day without him, without his laugh, his arrogance, his self-assurance.

That's what I'll miss the most about this place. It's not that I'm dying in a strange land. It's that I'm dying after I just found the man who makes me want to live.

To me, he's always been more than a god. He's Aron. My Aron.

And he's going to win.

I clutch my burning, wounded stomach and I'm strangely at peace.

CHAPTER 81

"*FAITH.*"

The heart-rending bellow of my name jars me from my peaceful sleep. I wake up and moan with pain, at the agony in my hand and the ice in my gut. Why am I not dead yet?

Someone grabs the front of my dress and hauls me in their arms.

"Faith," a familiar voice pants, and then a big hand strokes my hair back from my face. "No, Faith. You can't die on me now. I won't allow it."

Aron. My Aron.

I'm no longer mad at him because of Hedonism Aron's actions. It's all okay. He's so upset at me dying that I know he loves me and only me. I smile. Or try to. It feels like my face won't behave. "Hey…there."

"Faith," he growls, clutching me close against him in a way that hurts really bad, but I don't mind. I just like that he's holding me. He's covered in blood and soot, and his mismatched eyes stare down at me with a wild expression. "You are not doing this. You are not. I will not allow it—"

"I was always going to die, Aron," I manage. Man, it's hard to talk. My lungs feel heavy, and my tongue slow. "Knew it. Spidae...knew it, too." My vision grows fuzzy and I struggle to focus on his face, because he's so beautiful, so perfect. Even if he's the god of war, he's just...lovely. I smile. "Had to make sure you were the last."

Fuck that other Aron and his anchor.

"We're getting you out of here," he says, and the big, wonderful hand strokes my hair again. "You will live. I command it."

I cry out as he touches the knife in my belly and everything hurts. "Don't," I manage, panting. "Hurts too much."

I expect him to ignore me, to ignore it. Instead, his cool fingers touch my face again. "Very well." He sounds...defeated.

That terrifies me. "Aron...dead? Bad Aron?"

"Dead," he says. "Rest, Faith. I have you." His voice is so tender, and he presses a kiss to my brow that makes me so, so happy. Oh, I love his kiss.

I saved him. I'm smiling inside, even if my lips are slow to respond. The ice in my belly feels like it's creeping up my neck, so I watch Aron closely. I want to get one last good look at him before everything fades out. Already the black is creeping around my vision. It won't be long now. I'll die, and he'll return to his fortress in the Aether, to rule as the just, firm, newly compassionate god of storms that he is. Maybe a little arrogant, but that's ok. It's just part of his charm.

"You...won't forget me, will you?" The black fades a little more and all I can see is his mouth. His pretty, pretty mouth.

"Never forget you," he rasps, and I barely feel him brush his lips over mine again. "Never, Faith. I love you."

I know he's saying that to me because he wants to make me feel better, but in this last moment, he needs to realize I'm okay with everything. It's good. He doesn't have to pretend. I love him enough for both of us. "Gods don't love," I remind him. "It's...okay."

And I'm smiling as I die.

CHAPTER 82

*D*eath is...strange.

I thought there would be a light. You know, a go-towards-the-light sort of light. Instead, everything's just kind of gray. Foggy, and gray. I sit on a stone bench, and even though there are others around me, I feel alone.

Rudderless. Like I said, strange.

I sit with my hands on my knees, trying to figure out how much time has passed. The wound in my stomach is gone and nothing hurts, but I'm positive I'm dead. Others pass by me, stranger after stranger, men and women, and they wander past with the same bewildered look on their faces that echoes how I feel. Muted, and confused. Like emotions are very, very distant things that belong to others.

I can see through the other people, too, so that's how I know we're all dead. We're gray, and we're spirits, and if that's not a big honking clue, I don't know what is.

I think of Aron, my Aron, and find myself smiling. He's probably mad at me right now, if he remembers me. I have no regrets, though. I'd do it a hundred times again, because I love him and that's what you to do help those you love. Even now, the sad ache of losing him is distant. This must be what death does. It makes you not care about…anything.

"Faith?" A hollow voice calls out my name. It sounds vaguely familiar.

I get to my feet, looking around at the sea of drifting, non-corporeal strangers. One steps forward, wearing armor and carrying a sword.

It's Vitar. "Oh wow, hi."

He smiles at me, and I go to hug him—and our arms pass through one another. Figures. "I am sad to see you here."

"It was inevitable. I'm sorry you got eaten by a giant lake-worm." I want to touch him, to squeeze his hand, but my fingers just pass through him. Another person steps forward and it's Solat. "Hello friend. I'm so sorry."

"It is all right," Solat says, and it is. Nothing much seems to matter here in the afterlife.

"Where are we?" I ask, curious as more people shuffle in.

"This is where the dead go when there is no body for us to be attached to any longer. We are between all webs. Between life, death, everything." Solat shrugs. "So we wait."

"Wait?" I echo.

"Wait for the god of death to return to his throne."

I nod. "Can I wait with you guys?"

"Of course."

We sit together in the gray, and it occurs to me that if I have no body to inhabit, I must have been burned, like all the others. I wonder if we stopped the war in Yshrem. I wonder if we saved lives. I guess it doesn't matter one way or another. Death isn't so bad. It's just kind of…blah.

Time passes. It's not so lonely with Solat and Vitar here. We talk some, but mostly we're content to just sit in the fog and wait together. Eventually, a distant light flares, like a firework rising into the sky.

"What's that?" I ask, pointing.

"One of the gods is re-ascending to the Aether," Solat says. "Beautiful, isn't it?"

I nod, thinking of Aron. "Was Aron's star beautiful?"

"It was perfect."

That makes me happy.

IT'S hard to know just how long I sit with my friends. The gray is...endless. There's no hunger, no need to eat or sleep, nothing to break up the endless time. I feel no boredom, no nothing. I'm just...waiting.

Then one day—or many days—later, a large man stalks through the sea of gray spirits that wander in the fog. He wears a long, black cloak, a heavy hood, and seems to be heading straight for us.

"Should we run?" I ask Vitar and Solat, but I can't bring myself to care, not that much. Death does that to a person. I get no answer, and look around. They're gone.

In fact, everyone's gone.

Well, I guess that's my answer.

I get to my ghost-feet, but the man is already standing in front of me. He lowers his hood.

This must be the god of death. His skin is deathly pale, his hair black as night. His brows are black slashes and his nose is big and would be overwhelming if it weren't for the cloud of thick, loose waves that somehow break up the harshness of his features, and the softer line of his mouth. He's missing an eye.

A green one.

"I know who you are," I say, surprised. That surprise zings through me. It's the first real, honest emotion I've felt since I died, and it feels...good. "You're Rhagos, aren't you? God of the Dead? Original owner of Aron's left eye?"

He reaches up and touches my chin, and his hand doesn't

pass through me. Huh. He tilts my face up and studies it. "So this is Faithful." His voice is deep and smooth, like rich chocolate.

"Nooo, this is *Faith*." I point at my face.

"I was curious to see what made you so different from the others, but I see it now. You're not afraid of us, are you?" He considers me. "You're not worried about offending the gods."

I shrug. "You're not my gods."

"Just so." He smiles and offers me his hand. "At any rate, you belong to me."

I hesitate. "That's nice of you, but I'm pretty sure I belong to Aron."

His smile broadens, as if my answer amuses him. "That bond was severed in death, Faithful. You are dead, thus you belong to me. Come. I have things to show you."

I move to his side, but I avoid taking his hand, and that makes him smile wider. I cross my arms over my chest and when he starts to walk away, I walk faster to keep up. "Can my friends come?"

"No, they remain in the Field of the Forgotten until their god retrieves them. Their hearts are dedicated to another."

For a moment, I wonder if I should stay with Vitar and Solat, but I have too many questions for this Rhagos guy. So I jog after him as he heads through the fog. "So, you're back on your throne? Which Aspect won? Which Rhagos are you?"

He just looks at me. "Does it matter?"

"I guess not? But for the High Father to make such a big deal out of splitting your personalities, it seems weird to me that it'd all be forgotten the moment you return home. Like, my Aron? I'm pretty sure I can't imagine him without arrogance. It's part of who he is, you know? And that arrogance isn't bad, not really. It just has to be tempered. He's a good guy." I try not to stare at the scar over Rhagos's missing eye. "Well, sometimes he's a good guy."

"Mm. You talk a lot. I'm not used to the dead having so much to say."

"Because they're afraid of you?"

He nods. "Because of the places I can send them for eternal torment if they antagonize me."

Is that a threat? "I guess it's a good thing I've never heard of those places or I'd be shitting in my pants about now." The fog parts, and a massive, ominous-looking palace rises from the middle of nowhere. It's all black stone and darkness atop a rocky cliff, and overhead, the stars twinkle in the sky like thousands of pinpricks. I'm not entirely surprised to see a drawbridge drop down, and we step inside to more red and black gothic-looking decor. "Nice place."

"I'm glad you approve, as you will be remaining here until the negotiations are over." There's a dark amusement in his voice.

"Negotiations?" I ask, curious.

But Rhagos ignores me. He waves a hand and a door at the end of the hall opens, and we head into a throne room. I don't know if I'm supposed to keep following him or what, but I do. Inside the room is a large, uncomfortable-looking granite throne on a dais, a bajillion skulls lining the walls, and fire-lit sconces to provide more ominous lighting.

And between two pillars? There's an enormous spiderweb that makes the pit of my stomach drop as Rhagos approaches it.

Not this shit again.

To my surprise, he waves a hand in the air and the web shimmers and a picture begins to form in the center. That's... unexpected. "What is that?"

"It is my connection to the Aether, since I must spend my time here in the realm of the dead. It allows me to communicate with the other gods."

"You can see the other gods?" I clutch his arm, full of longing. "Oh my god, can I see Aron? Please?"

He shrugs me off. There's a look of shock on his hard face. "You dare to touch me?"

Like I care? I'm dead. What's he going to do to me, condemn me to a thousand years without Aron? There's nothing he can do that I'm not already prepared for. "I just...please, can I see him? I died and I don't know if he ascended back to his home. I want to know if he's still the same guy and if everything's okay—"

Rhagos stares at me with that one green eye, his expression cold.

"Please," I ask again, clasping my hands together. "I won't ask for anything ever again."

"Somehow I doubt that," he says drily. "You truly love him? Aron of the Cleaver? Lord of Storms? Butcher god of battle?"

I frown. "Everyone has flaws."

He barks a laugh. "Flaws? Is that what we call them?"

"Look. He might not be your favorite person, but he's been good to me. If he's a little battle hungry, he's just a guy devoted to his work. There's nothing wrong with that. I love him. I even love his arrogance. I just...I need to know he's okay."

"He is a god. Why wouldn't he be 'okay'?" Rhagos gives me an imperious look.

I'm starting to think arrogance might have won out in Rhagos, too. "Please."

The god of death studies me for a long moment. Then, with an impatient flick of his hand, he gestures at the web and the shimmering gives a subtle shift. A second later, I see mismatched eyes under dark brows, and scars. I ache at the sight of him, all of my body full of yearning. My Aron. He's so handsome.

The web "zooms" out and Aron's moving, fighting as he swings his mighty axe, surrounded by men. It's an enormous battlefield, full of swarming, fighting people and as I watch, Aron raises his axe and lets out another battle-cry.

I press my hands to my mouth, horrified. "We didn't stop the war?"

"Oh, you stopped the war." The god's voice is full of irony. "He started another."

"*What?*"

Rhagos gives me another one of those fascinated looks, studying my face. "Aron ascended the moment you died. He was rather furious, because it seems he was unaware you had to die in order for him to return. He is laying siege to the Underworld."

I clutch my throat, shocked. "Why?"

"You have to ask? It is because you are here and he refuses to let you go."

Oh. Warmth floods through me. He said he wouldn't forget me. It's all I wanted. Now, I have a new want. A new yearning. I want to be with him. I don't care if I have to spend my afterlife surrounded by a bunch of bloodthirsty warriors. As long as I'm with Aron, it'll be the happiest forever-until-eternity. I turn to look at Rhagos, pleading in my eyes.

He simply studies me, like I'm something he can't quite figure out. "I'm told he approached the High Father and demanded your return. That he shouted so angrily that storms flooded the mortal world for a month straight. Magra was quite displeased at his little tantrum."

Aron's fighting to get me back?

He approached the High Father?

I feel so warm and fuzzy. "God, I love that man."

"Yes, you have said so."

I send another pleading look to Rhagos. "Will you let me go to him? Please? I can make him stop."

"Do you think I care? Let him fight. The dead are dead." Rhagos shrugs. "He knows I will give you back, but only under very specific conditions." He nods at my direction, and the web goes dark, the picture of Aron fading. "Take her away. There is time yet."

Take me away? I look around, but suddenly invisible hands are on my arms, tugging me forward, and then I'm dragged out of Rhagos's throne room and down a hall. I'm led deeper into the palace of the lord of the dead by his unseen servants, and then a door opens. The room I'm led into is opulent and lush—I'm guessing so Aron won't be pissed that I'm being mistreated—but the doors shut behind me and click, and then I'm locked in.

I look around my new prison, but even this can't stop the giddy rush in my heart.

Aron's coming for me.

He's storming the underworld. For me.

CHAPTER 83

S o I wait.

Impatiently.

It seems that whatever weird "between" I existed in is no longer the case—my hands are solid, my mind is sharp, and my stomach is hungry. Plates of food are offered up to me, appearing like magic in my room, and for a while I think I shouldn't eat them. I remember stories of Persephone in the underworld and how she couldn't leave after she ate one shitty pomegranate. This isn't pomegranates, either. It's fresh fruit, sure, but it's also Yshremi sweetcakes and thick slabs of amazing looking cheese. It's roasted meats and breads, bowls of nuts, and it all smells so heavenly—and I'm so hungry—that my hunger strike lasts all of a day.

I mean, I'm already dead. Isn't "being stuck in the under-world for the rest of my days" kind of a default at this point? So I eat. And I sleep in the big, fluffy bed. I bathe in the tub that shows up full of hot, steaming water, and I try not to think if the invisible servants are watching me scrub my girly parts. I wear fresh clothes, and I wait for Aron.

My Aron.

I'm bursting with love, and I can't wait to touch him again. To hold him, to hear his sexy voice. I want to hear him laugh. I want to breathe in his scent. I want to bask in his presence.

He didn't forget about me.

I'm just an anchor, a mortal, but he *remembered* me. I matter to him. That makes me so happy. My Aron wants me back at his side so much that he's coming to the underworld to claim me. I can't stop grinning.

One morning—at least, I assume it's morning, since time is impossible to tell in the underworld—a trunk of clothing is delivered with the food. The hint seems pretty obvious to me, so I get dressed in the somber black gown trimmed with red. It's better than the gray shift I was wearing, though I'm still not a fan of the color scheme. I take a few bites of food, and then an invisible hand touches my arm.

"What is it?" I ask.

I'm tugged at, indicating I should follow.

I get to my feet, take one last bite of food, and then brush my hands off. "Okay, but this better be good. Breakfast is sacred."

The doors to my room open as I stand, and to my surprise, I'm staring right at the man I love.

Aron of the Cleaver.

Lord of Storms.

Butcher god of battle.

He walks in, his axe sheathed on his back, and he wears studded armor that's covered in blood, and thick, heavy boots. His hair is pulled back in its war-braid and he's wearing an eyepatch.

He looks so fucking good.

I let out a squeal of happiness as his gaze locks onto me, and before he can say a thing, I launch myself into his arms.

Aron catches me. Of course he does. He's amazing. He grabs me and holds my hips even as I fling my arms around his neck and my legs around his hips. His mouth crushes mine in the hardest, most delicious kiss ever, and lightning crackles between us.

I moan against his mouth. "Fuck, I missed you."

"Faith," he murmurs, biting gently at my lower lip. "I do not know whether I should throw you down on the bed and take you, or if I should put you over my knee and spank you."

"Who says we can't do both?" I ask him, breathless. I pepper his face with kisses. "Oh my god, Aron. I can't believe it's you. I've missed you so much."

"Faith." He kisses me back, equally as frantic. "Don't you ever, *ever* do that again."

"Do what?"

"Sacrifice yourself."

"Spoiler, I'm already dead." I nip at his jaw. God, I am so horny already. He growls low and I lift my head. "Wait. Am I dead? Did you make a deal with Rhagos?" I stare up at his face, at the eyepatch where a bright green eye used to be.

"Is it not obvious?" He gestures at the patch.

"Oh, Aron," I say softly, caressing his cheek. I reach up and peek under the eyepatch, but he doesn't push my hands away. Where his eye used to be is just a long, flat scar. It's not grisly or gross, it's just gone as if it was never there. He's still handsome —maybe even more so like this—but I ache for his loss. "Are you sure?"

He grabs my chin between thumb and forefinger. "Faith. If you are asking me if one stolen eye is worth your life, then you are the most foolish mortal I have ever met."

I bite my lip. "But I'm already dead, Aron. It had to happen. The Spidae told me."

"I know," he says grimly. "The moment I returned to the Keep of Storms, I immediately went to the Spidae and demanded that they work you into the web again. They said it had to happen. That anchors are the final sacrifice before one re-ascends." His mouth curls with irritation even as he cups the back of my head and studies my face. "So I went to the High Father instead."

I'm breathless at how much he's done for me. Me. "You did?"

"I did. I told him that casting us out in an Anticipation every few centuries is a mistake. That we would retain our humanity far more if we were given an anchor constantly instead of just when we misbehave. That all of the gods have a companion at all times to keep us in touch with our human side."

I gasp, clenching at the collar of his armor. "Does this mean—"

"You are my anchor. For now and forever." His gaze is intently focused on my mouth, and he leans in and brushes his lips over mine with the softest of kisses. "As long as you are willing to serve as my anchor, you will be at my side for all time."

"What does that mean, serve as your anchor?" I rub my thumb against his neck, over where his pulse beats, hard and fast. Everything about him is hard and fast, and lordy, I love it.

"You give me perspective," Aron says. "You tell me when I fuck up. You tell me when I am too ruthless. You are my humanity when I threaten to lose mine."

"And what do I get out of this?"

"My love. Eternally." With one arm locked around my waist, he takes the hand I have at his collar and presses his mouth to my palm. "You said a god cannot love, but you're wrong. Ever since you left me, I have been hollow. I am not whole unless you're at my side, Faith. Be with me? Forever?" He hesitates. "You'll have to remain with me in the Keep of Storms on my personal plane, but if you like, we can also visit my temples and—"

"Yes," I say quickly. "Yes to all of it. We can live in the sewers of Katharn if it means we're together."

Laughter rumbles up out of him. "We don't have to go that far. But you accept?"

"Of course. I love you, Aron. I have *always* loved you." I smile at him, at his beloved, wonderful face that even the eyepatch doesn't mar. He's just my big sexy pirate now. "I would do anything for you. That's why I did what I did—I needed to make sure you were the last man standing. Does this mean we get our bond back?"

"All you have to do is take my hand," he says, and offers it to me, palm up.

I slap my hand in his so fast that our palms smack. Lightning crackles.

The world flashes around us. Air swirls, and there's a boom of thunder, and I swear it's like riding a cyclone. I squeeze my eyes shut and hold onto Aron, his arms tight around me. My clothing whips around my body as I hold onto him, and I'm not entirely surprised to see that it looks like we're standing in the middle of a hurricane, the wind so thick and fast and crackling with electricity that it makes my hair stand on end.

"This is how you travel?" I shout into the wind, clinging to his thick neck.

I feel his laughter rumble through my body and he presses his mouth to my skin even as we surge and the tornado seems to move faster. I hide my eyes against him, holding tight.

Then, slowly, the wind dies.

"You can look up," Aron murmurs.

I do, and we're no longer in the underworld. We're in a new place, and I see green, grassy fields framed by distant mountains. There's a large, stone fortress at the foot of the mountains, and over it, lightning seems to crackle on a constant basis. Above us, the deep purple clouds dance with light and swirl like they're in a snow globe. It's terrifying, but also beautiful. "Where are we?"

"This is my home, the Plane of Storms. Here, my faithful make war and then feast with me when the day is done." He strokes my hair and gives me a hungry look. "I am not a god of peace, or a god of kindness, Faith. I worry you won't like being here with me."

I give him an incredulous look. "I've known who you are the entire time, Aron. You can be a god of battle. You can be the god of storms. You can be the god of dirty brown assholes, remember? You just have to be my man." I lift one shoulder in a casual shrug. "Besides, my schedule's a little empty at the moment."

"I will treat you like the goddess you are," he promises me.

"Am I a goddess, then?"

"You are my anchor and immortal because your life is tethered to mine. In that sense, yes. You will still need to eat and drink and sleep like a mortal, I'm afraid." His gaze roams over me, and for a moment, there's a fierce possessiveness in his eye. "But you will never be hurt ever again. *Ever.*"

"I'm down with that." I pat his chest. "Can we go home now?"

"Of course." He lifts a hand to the air, and the tornado whirls around us once more, and we ride it toward the castle.

CHAPTER 84

The Keep of Storms is very much a man cave. There are weapons everywhere, a thick, heavy throne that sits atop a dais made entirely of shields, and long, long tables full of food and drink, waiting for the warriors that clash outside. There are weapon racks all along the walls and more weapons hang from the stonework. And...that's about it. Well, there's a web in one corner between two pillars, but I half expected that after seeing Rhagos's throne room. Still, it's not the most comfortable of locations unless you're a fan of swords, swords, and more swords.

Oh, and axes.

I'm clearly going to have to set up a girl-cave of some kind. Something with some books—once I learn how to read the languages of this world—and a few soft places to sit. Music. A bath. Something. It's doable, though. Aron's a god. He'll figure it out.

I sigh happily at Aron as he looks at me. "Take me to bed?"

My big, brawny man pauses. "I...have no bed. A god does not sleep."

"But you'll fix that for me soon enough, right? You'll get a bed for your anchor?" I give his chest a pat.

"I will get anything for my anchor," he vows, a smile on his lips as he gazes down at me. "She just has to ask."

"I'll give you a honey-do list soon enough." I lay my head against his shoulder. "For now, it's just enough to be here with you." I stroke his chest, despite the armor. I can hardly believe that I get to be here with him, after everything that's happened. It doesn't seem real. For the first time since we've been together, no one's trying to kill us. No one's plotting to attack. It's just...us.

Aron carries me over to his throne like a bride over the threshold. "For now, this will have to do. I'll get you your own chair soon enough but right now I'm not letting you out of my sight."

"What, you can't wave a hand and magic up a chair?" I tease. "This fucking godhood thing is a sham!"

He sits down in his throne and settles me in his lap, my legs over the opposite arm of the chair. "That would be Tadekha, and she has yet to return. But tomorrow, I promise I will create a war in Glistentide so I can demand tribute in the form of fine goods for my anchor."

It's on the tip of my tongue to tell him not to go to war, but this is who he is. I'm not going to suddenly change him to the god of peace. I like Aron just as he is, flaws and all. "Just make it like, a trade war or something. Something benign. I'm tired of all the death."

Aron throws his head back and laughs. "Very well. A trade war." He chuckles and then cups my face, gazing down at me. "Never leave me again, Faith. I nearly went mad with grief when I realized what you did."

"I had to. The Spidae had hinted at things and they all sort of lined up. I realize they were angling for us to win." I stroke his chest, content. "Maybe they saw the anchor thing coming up? In the future? And this was the best way to do it—to dick over the two of us."

The lord of storms grunts in agreement. "If I never see them again, it will be too soon." His hand slides down to my breast, and he teases the nipple through the slinky fabric of my black gown. "Also, I don't like that you're wearing Rhagos's colors. It reminds me of what I had to go through to get you back. From now on, I only want you in my colors, red and gray."

"I can do that." Hell, I can do any and all of it. I don't care. I'm just...ecstatic to be with him. "I saw Solat and Vitar in the underworld. No, it wasn't really the underworld. It was the place between, where the faithful wait to be retrieved."

Aron nods. "I will get them and the other faithful tomorrow. You will go with me."

Not a request, but a command. My bossy, arrogant Aron. I fucking love this man. I brush my fingers over his eyepatch. "You gave up your eye for me?"

"It wasn't mine to begin with. An easy concession. I lost mine to the dragon One-Tooth many millennia ago. Remember?"

I remember. "It still makes me unhappy—"

"As does the fact that you went behind my back to try to fix things on your own," Aron says in a deadly voice.

"If you want to be fair, I didn't 'try' to fix things," I point out. "I did fix them. You're welcome."

His single eye gleams, his expression hard. "I still think you need punishment."

I sputter at the word "punishment," but then he shifts his weight and I can feel the hard length of his erection pushing against my hip. Ah. That kind of punishment. I'm wet just thinking about it, and I squirm in his lap. "What are you going to do?"

Aron considers me, then reaches for the shoulder of my dress. He grabs a handful and rips it off, exposing my breast. "I don't like how Rhagos looked at you," my god murmurs. "He was very intrigued by you, you know. He had no idea a female of your world would be so…"

"Independent? Strong willed?"

"Mouthy." Aron runs the pad of his thumb over my nipple. "He thought to keep you for his own. I'm tempted to go to war with him, too, for daring to even look at you."

I moan, shifting in my seat as he teases me. "I don't want to belong to anyone but you."

"Even if I punish you?"

"What, a spanking?" When his eye gleams with interest, I rise to the challenge. "You want to spank me? Fine, then." I get up, shuck the rest of the black dress off, and then bend over in front of his throne, deliberately teasing him. "Spank away."

I love that he growls low in his throat, that he snatches me from around the hips and drags me backward. He's gentle even as he pushes me over one arm of the chair, and then my bare butt is in his lap and I'm bent in half.

One big hand settles over my ass, and I suck in a breath to feel the heat of his palm resting on my skin. I'm so turned on right now.

"No," he says, caressing my buttocks. "Striking you is never the answer, my sweet anchor. You require a different kind of punishment."

He spreads my thighs apart, then pushes two fingers into my pussy.

I moan, jerking in response at the sensation. Oh god, I hadn't expected that, or how good it'd feel. "Aron," I pant, clutching at his throne. "Oh god, please—"

"Yes, I do think I am your god now," he says in that same low, sexy voice, even as he thrusts deep into me with his fingers once more. His thumb skims along my wet folds and rubs against my clit, and I cry out. "You are my anchor, tethered to me for all time, and I am your lord of storms. Nothing will ever separate us again, Faith."

His finger shifts inside me, and then he's rubbing my g-spot. I choke out his name, wheeze, curse, and basically lose all control until I come, hard. Then, I just laugh and laugh even as the orgasm rolls through me and my legs feel like rubber bands stretched too tight, because that was amazing and perfect.

I've missed this man so badly, with every aching fiber of my being. I feel incredibly lucky that I get to have this time with him, to be in his lap, in his keep, celebrating his return. I want to cry with how perfect it feels. A hot tear slips down my cheek, then a second one, and then I'm sobbing because I thought I'd lost him for good. I'm overwhelmed.

"Shh, Faith. I have you. I'm here." He pulls me off of the arm of the throne and back into his lap. His hands are on my face, stroking my arms, caressing me anywhere and everywhere. "Nothing will ever separate us again."

"I missed you," I sob against his mouth between kisses. "I missed you so much."

"You were brave," he tells me. "You did what you felt you had to in order to save me. I'm both humbled and terrified at the way your mind works." When I let out a watery laugh, he kisses me again. "And I love you. I didn't think gods could feel such things, but what I feel for you…there is no better term. You are everything to me. Everything I could ever want, everything I need."

"I love you, too," I whisper, caressing his dear face. "I love you so much."

He simply holds me close, lightly kissing my mouth with gentle nips. I love that this big, fearsome man—this god—can be tender with me and fierce to the rest of the world. How I love him. I kiss him again, and then the kiss becomes something deeper, more erotic, and I moan with a new need.

"Can we make love on this throne?" I ask him, breathless.

"On this throne," he agrees. "Or on the floor. Or on the tables. Anywhere and everywhere my anchor desires."

I give him a sly look. "Can I wear the eyepatch?"

He laughs, head thrown back, and then hands it to me.

The only thing sexier than the lord of storms when he's driving deep inside me? Is when he's smiling in my direction and devouring me with his gaze.

That's how I know I'm home.

EPILOGUE

$\mathcal{I}$ run my fingers over the threads of the web, waiting for the picture to change. The threads shift, forming pictures and eventually outline Yulenna's face. She's standing in her personal chambers at the tower, surrounded by spiderwebs. Her smile is bright as she waves at me.

"Hey!" I say in greeting. "About time!"

"Sorry," she says with a small laugh. "I was, ah, distracted."

"Ew, gross, don't tell me any more." I pretend to plug my ears. "I'm still scarred from your last story."

Her laughter peals through the hall, and I grin back at her. Yulenna's so ridiculously happy, it's obvious even from long-distance. Serving the Spidae suits her admirably, and her skin practically glows with pleasure. She doesn't mind that they're weird since apparently they spoil the hell out of her and end up doting on her as much as she dotes on them. Being an anchor to them has been good for her, and good for them, though she is overly fond of sharing sex stories that I'd rather not hear.

I still find the Spidae creepy, after all. I don't want to hear about her pleasuring all three of them at once. Again. I'm still trying to scrub the image of that from the last time she told me about it.

Still, it's nice to have a buddy to chat with. I liked being friends with Yulenna before, and now that we're both anchors serving gods, we catch up regularly through the web and chitchat about daily life...among other things.

"So?" I ask, practically dancing in place. "Did you check?"

"On the woman for Markos?" She nods. "Her thread is strong and not currently entwined with anyone else's. Are you sure you can maneuver the two of them together? Or should I get my masters involved?"

I wave a hand. "I can handle it. I'll make Aron go to war with someone or other. She's Cyclopae, right? She's bound to love war."

"True. Well, let me know if you need me to have their threads tweaked." Her eyes gleam with anticipation.

"Let's not make it too obvious just yet," I say. "If Markos knows we're matchmaking from the Aether he's bound to get stubborn." Both Yulenna and I have decided that Kerren and Markos are our projects. They're both great guys and honorable, and it's time they met some equally awesome women. We've been eyeing a really fierce, badass Cyclopae chick for Markos, but I think Kerren needs someone sweeter, because he's shy. A warrior woman would eat him alive.

Then again, maybe that's what Kerren needs. We'll figure it out.

"That wasn't why I was calling, though," I say, even as I make a mental note to put a bug in my Aron's ear about setting up some skirmishes on the Yshremi border that will allow a Holy Warrior of the Cleaver to hang out with a lady barbarian. "I was going to ask about the other thing."

"Calling?" She tilts her head, curious.

"Uh, web-calling?" I gesture at the magic spiderweb that we

communicate through. The gods are able to see each other from afar through the webs, and I have enough control after hours of practice to snoop on some mortal places. "It's a telephone sort of thing. Long story."

"I see. From your old home?"

I nod. Funny, I haven't thought to look and see if I can view the Earth web. It's another part of my life that's dead to me, in a sense. I don't need Chicago, or pizza, or cars. That belonged to another Faith, another life. There, I was Faith Gordon, phone jockey at an insurance company.

Here, I'm Faith, eternal anchor and loyal companion to Aron of the Cleaver, Lord of Storms and the Butcher God of Battle. I know which one I'd rather be.

Yulenna's dark eyes gleam and her mouth curls up in a smile. "I think you already know the answer to that."

"Oh god. Do I?" I clutch my stomach. "I'm so nervous. You're sure?"

"The threads don't lie," she tells me in a singsong. "You'll see."

I nod absently, even as thunder crashes outside. "Oh, that'll be Aron. Can I call you back later?"

She chuckles. "Yes, do this 'calling' thing later. You know where I am." And she waves from within the web and then fades out.

I turn away from the web and smooth my hands over my hair and then down my dress. It's new, just like most of the stuff in my private chambers in the Keep of Storms. As promised, my Aron waged a (teeny tiny) war on Glistentide and accepted the spoils of offering. Now I have a ton of pretty dresses, urns full of incense and fine fabrics, and the best damn palatial bed I have ever seen. I have chairs and vases and books I can't read and a harp that I have no idea how to play, but I was thrilled with all of it and made sure Aron blessed Glistentide appropriately as a thank you.

I picked something a little flashy today to get Aron's attention. Not that it's hard to get his attention, but I love it when he gives me one of those long, heated looks that tells me his mind is nowhere near the battlefield. The dress I'm wearing is a long, shimmery pink that fades to blue at the skirt, with a deep, deep embroidered neckline that shows off my impressive rack.

The massive double doors of the Keep of Storms open and men pour in, wearing armor and speaking in loud voices. They laugh and jostle each other, full of enthusiasm even though not a few moments ago they were fighting each other on the field of battle. That's all they do here in Aron's slice of the heavens—battles after battles after battles, then they come and feast. I smile at them as they surge in like a wave, and each one makes Aron's symbol in my direction. Some even move their hand up slightly with a second thump over the heart, a new gesture people have started to do for me specifically. Aron says that I'm not worshipped—not yet—but he wouldn't be surprised if I started receiving prayers in the next millennia or two asking for him to intercede.

I scan the faces of the men—and women—as they crowd the feast tables that magically replenish themselves and begin to eat. Solat's here, and Vitar, and I wink at them as they pass by. Solat's following a female warrior from Old Suuol with a look of interest that tells me he hasn't changed, even dead.

I'm about to ask where my Aron is when thunder crashes overhead again and I roll my eyes, even as I smile. Dramatic entrance incoming. I clasp my hands, waiting beside my throne and pretending I'm about to sit down in my smaller chair next to his. It's a game we play—I move to sit, and Aron grabs me before I can and pulls me into his lap. It doesn't matter how fast I am, my ass never gets in that chair.

Even now, I barely put my hands on the arm of my throne and then a massive gust of wind and a crackle of lightning sweeps up against me, rustling my skirts. A big arm locks around my waist and then I'm hauled into Aron's lap as he sits on his throne.

"My love," he growls, his throat full of thunder and pleasure at the sight of me. He's become fiercer and more magical as he adjusts to his return in the Aether. Today, wind makes his hair constantly blow—even inside—and lightning sparks his eye. The other day he wore a crown of pure lightning in bed.

Fucking sexiest thing I've ever seen.

He nips at my neck, sending sizzles of pleasure through my body. "Did you miss me this day?"

"Nope," I tell him.

Aron throws his head back and laughs, because he knows I'm lying.

I just grin and smooth his long hair back from his face, caressing his jaw even as I do. I'm getting used to the eyepatch and I have to admit, it does good things for my lady parts. "How was your day, dear?" I ask, teasing.

He gives me a pleased look, one hand gripping me high on my thigh. "Eventful. Prayers are coming in from Rastana. They are on the verge of civil war. I shall have to evaluate which side deserves my blessing." He takes my hand and pulls my knuckles toward his mouth, pressing a kiss there. "You will help me?"

I squirm with pleasure. Aron doesn't have to include me in his "job." He's the God of Battle, after all, but he likes to get my thoughts on things, and I love that he respects me enough to listen. "Of course."

"After dinner," he amends. "You must be hungry. Shall I feed you?" His eyes gleam with intensity.

"Maybe later." I pat his chest. We both know that feeding me usually turns into some hardcore sex. The man gets wildly aroused when I eat a piece of fruit, and well, I do too. "We need to talk about something important."

He turns my hand over and presses a kiss to the inside of my wrist, his tongue flicking against my skin. "More important than me feasting between your thighs?"

Unf. This man makes me crazy with lust. He's good at distracting me, and it makes me super hot that he's this affectionate in front of the Faithful—his army of soldiers who've earned their place at his side. There is nothing I'd like more than to drag him to our private chambers, jerk his pants off, and suck on his length until he's pulling my hair. I'm all aroused but I really did want to talk to Aron about important things. "We have a...I don't know if you'll call it a problem," I begin, a little worried.

He looks up from raining kisses on the inside of my arm. "Problem?" He frowns, and his other hand tightens around my waist. "You did not eat yesterday, either," he says, remembering. "What ails you?"

Thunder crashes overhead, different from the booms that normally accompany Aron. This is rage—and fear. He's worried about me. The others quiet in their seats at the table, the massive hall going silent as all eyes turn to us.

Awkward.

I pretend to pick a piece of lint off of Aron's battle-tunic. "It might be nothing..."

"Woman," he growls.

"Has a name," I remind him.

"Faith." His eyes flash brighter than any lightning and he grips my wrist tightly. "Tell me what is wrong. Has someone bothered you? Do I need to destroy them?"

"You romantic," I tease.

He doesn't laugh.

I bite my lip. "I'm not trying to scare you. I'm just..."

Aron's jaw clenches and he pulls me tight against his chest. He leans in close, his breath mingling with mine. "There is nothing to be afraid of, my Faith," he murmurs. "You know I will cross the Aether to keep you at my side. If I must invade the

Underworld once more—"

Oh gosh, now he's getting super worked up. I pat his chest, trying to calm him down. "Nothing as bad as that. No need to go to war. I just..." I try to think of a delicate way to put it because I'm not entirely sure what he's going to think. Or if he'll even like the idea at all. My stomach clenches and not for the first time in the last few days, I feel sick. Really, really sick.

What if Aron hates this?

"I'm pregnant," I blurt.

He stares at me. "With a baby."

I slap his chest. "No, with a fucking roasted chicken. Yes, with a baby!"

Aron's big hand goes to my stomach. He presses lightly against it. "Here?" His voice is low, smooth, impossible to read.

"Do I need to give you an anatomy lesson, big guy?" I half tease, but I'm quietly freaking out. Aron's a god of battle and thunder. He likes destroying things and going to war. How's he going to handle a baby? "It seems that because I'm still mortal-ish, I'm in the weave. Yulenna saw a new thread coming from mine and I've been sick the last few days and my boobs inflated and—"

Aron's hand goes to my breast and he cups it thoughtfully. "They do seem larger."

I slap his hand away, conscious of all the Faithful staring. "Aron," I whisper. "You haven't told me if you're happy or not."

"I never thought," he murmurs, and then caresses my stomach again. "Truly?"

"Truly." I watch his face, anxious.

"And...it will not harm you to give birth to my child? To a god?" He looks worried for a moment. "I will not have you in pain, Faith—"

I shake my head, cutting him off. I realize his reluctance is fear—fear of losing me again. Sometimes when I sleep, Aron comes in from the endless battles and just holds me for hours on end because he's terrified of losing me again. I love that. And I love him. "I'll be fine. We'll talk with the god of family if we have to. You said he was back, right?"

"Gental? Yes." His gaze flicks over my face and then he cups my neck. "This is...you're certain, Faith?" When I nod, his face splits into a boyish grin. "A child."

"Or a roasted chicken. You guess which one."

He laughs again, the sound booming and not unlike the thunder that constantly rolls across the plane of Storms. He gets to his feet, me in his arms, and tilts his head back, shouting to the heavens, "I am to have a son!"

"Or a daughter," I chime in as the keep erupts in cheers.

His eyes really light up, then, and I can tell he fucking loves that idea. "A daughter of battle."

"Or whatever he or she wants to be," I tell him primly.

Aron laughs, the sound so full of joy that it makes all my worry disappear. He's not a man that can hide his emotions, and it's clear he is utterly thrilled. "A child," he roars again as the Faithful thump their mugs on the table in appreciation. "Our child!"

More thumping.

He looks at me, his eye alight with fierce pleasure, and then turns on his foot and storms away from his throne.

I cling to his neck as he carries me down the hall. "Where are we going?"

My gorgeous Aron grins down at me. "I am going to worship my anchor's body, because she has given me the greatest of gifts this day."

For a man that's pure arrogance, he sometimes knows just the thing to say. I lean against his chest and sigh happily, knowing that I'm going to have hours of sweet pussy-licking to look forward to. If there's one thing Aron loves, it's to go down on me, and I am all too happy to receive. "I suppose if I must appease my lord's hungers," I say, pretending to be long-suffering and patient. "Then I must."

"Your lord is utterly ravenous for his beautiful, mouthy anchor," he says, kicking open the door to my rooms. "And one good mouth deserves another."

So it does. So it does.

AUTHOR'S NOTE

Hello there!

It feels very, very weird to have this book out in the world.

I've been sitting on it for so long and not mentioning it to anyone that it's almost become a THING. Like, now that you have read it, we have to enter into a super secret pact to never share what we have learned. Except...I hope you love it and tell all your friends about it, because that's how books succeed, right?

So I'm just going to have to get over it. ;)

The reason why I feel weird about this book is that it's been several years in the making. If you've followed me along at all, you know I like to publish on a monthly schedule. Sometimes I run behind, and then I'm scrambling to catch up. There's never a ton of 'boredom' time because I'm always moving onto the next project. However, two (maybe three?) years ago I got into my head that I wanted to write a fantasy romance. A big, fat, filthy one with all of the tropes that I love. I wanted to give it enough time to be as long as it needed to be. I didn't want to rush the story. I loved the idea of it being slow burn but still sexy as hell. I loved the idea of a portal fantasy.

There was ZERO time in the schedule to do this, and why would I take away from Ice Planet Barbarians or Fireblood Dragons or anything else, right? So I backburnered it for a while. Then, I made a file and said, Ruby, you can work on this, but ONLY a little every day after you're done with your regular work. So I did. I started in February 2017. I worked on it a little bit at a time, and it was my secret play project when I needed a break, or the thing to look forward to at the end of a long writing session.

And I told no one about it. Well, I told Kati about it, because I tell Kati everything. :) And I told a few readers about it or left hints that I was working on something on my downtime, but I didn't say what or when, because if I mention I'm working on something...people want to know when it will come out. And since this was a side project, I had NO idea. So I worked on it here and there when I could, and it became my secret, my precioussss.

Cue January 2019. Still not done. My husband took me aside and said I needed to work ahead if I ever wanted to get this book done. I knew he was right. So I did. Ever since January, I've been pulling double shifts and long, long writing days to try and make time in my schedule to finish this book. I finally carved out about a month of nose-to-the-grindstone writing...

And here we are!

Faith and Aron have their happy ever after, but there's still a million stories in the book that I didn't get to tell. There wouldn't be enough time in my day to go over how Yulenna first felt when she was taken by the Spidae, or if Markos ever gets a badass Cyclopae lady, or if Rhagos gets himself an anchor of his own...or what the blood glacier is. #feelsbadman

Those are stories for another day. :) Hopefully I can wedge more of them in my schedule at some point.

(Speaking of stories, if you want Mathior and Halla's story, they're in The King's Spinster Bride which I wrote a while back!)

I hope you enjoyed this. I hope it made you laugh, made you cry (maybe a little?) and made you turn the pages faster. More than anything else, I hope you're entertained!

I would love for you to leave a review. Tell me what you thought! <3

Ruby